Marching With Caesar®
Fraternitas

By R.W. Peake

Also by R.W Peake

Marching with Caesar®- Birth of the 10th

Marching with Caesar-Conquest of Gaul

Marching with Caesar-Civil War

Marching with Caesar-Antony and Cleopatra, Parts I & II

Marching With Caesar-Rise of Augustus

Marching With Caesar-Last Campaign

Marching With Caesar-Rebellion

Marching With Caesar-A New Era

Marching With Caesar-Pax Romana

Caesar Triumphant

Critical praise for the Marching with Caesar series:

Marching With Caesar-Antony and Cleopatra: Part I-Antony

"Peake has become a master of depicting Roman military life and action, and in this latest novel he proves adept at evoking the subtleties of his characters, often with an understated humour and surprising pathos. Very highly recommended."

Marching With Caesar-Civil War

"Fans of the author will be delighted that Peake's writing has gone from strength to strength in this, the second volume...Peake manages to portray Pullus and all his fellow soldiers with a marvelous feeling of reality quite apart from the star historical name... There's history here, and character, and action enough for three novels, and all of it can be enjoyed even if readers haven't seen the first volume yet. Very highly recommended."

~The Historical Novel Society

"The hinge of history pivoted on the career of Julius Caesar, as Rome's Republic became an Empire, but the muscle to swing that gateway came from soldiers like Titus Pullus. What an amazing story from a student now become the master of historical fiction at its best."

~Professor Frank Holt, University of Houston

Marching with Caesar Fraternitas by R.W. Peake

For
Henry Richard Peake

Marching with Caesar
Fraternitas

Foreword

For as long as I can remember, I've been fascinated by all things martial. The original focus of my passion was the American Civil War, and believe it or not, my goal is to one day tell the story of a descendant of Titus Pullus carrying a musket. As far as which side, let's just say you'll have to wait and see. The first "adult" book I ever read came as a result of my membership in the Military Book Club, and I got Basil Liddell-Hart's "Strategy," along with Jomini's "Art of War" as part of my "free trial offer." As I recall, I was around ten, but in the spirit of full disclosure, I can't honestly say I did more than read the captions of the pictures, and perhaps some of the text.

But equally fascinating to me is, from *where* exactly, did my passion come from? Certainly not from my family; at least, the side with which I was most familiar, my mother's side. I don't have any intention on explaining why this was the case, because it's not germane. What is, in fact, the important part of my story is that, from a variety of circumstances, I knew next to nothing about my father, or his family. Why I didn't know my father is fairly straightforward. He died, in uniform, on April 1st, 1959; my birth came three weeks later. However, it wasn't until I was twenty that, not only did I learn more about where I came from, but I saw for the first time, a picture of my father. And when I did, something just....clicked, if only because I was staring at anyone who's seen both me and his picture will acknowledge is a carbon copy.

Suddenly, I was aware that, while I had never felt this way with my mom's side of the family, I *belonged* somewhere. I want to stress, my disconnect with my mom's side of the family has nothing to do with who they are or how I was treated; like most families, they are for the most part good, hard-working people, with no more or no less of the black sheep that pepper any family tree. Except that I was the black sheep, but not by virtue of my actions, nor by the way I was treated by other members of my family. I just never felt any real sense of connection, yet as I learned more about my father and his kin, the more things just made sense.

Why am I bringing this up? Because *Marching With Caesar®-Fraternitas* is about brotherhood....and so much more. It's about the power of blood, and how, despite all the "advances" of our modern world, there is something primal and instinctive that guides us all, whether we recognize it or not. Two thousand years ago would have made this reality even more immediate.

This has been the hardest book title for me to conjure up, because in many ways, it's unlike any book of the series. And, speaking frankly, I completely understand the inherent risk I am running in not giving readers more of the Pullus family where they're wading in blood and gore. However, one of my primary goals in this quest to tell a story that began so many years ago was to be authentic in the telling of it, and that I would come as close as I could to the spirit of Titus, both in the original and now in his grandson. Consequently, once I thought about it, I realized that, if I was writing a record of my life for whomever carried my name to follow, it was highly unlikely I would leave out such a formative and powerful period as this, a time where, as far as the history books say, not much was going on during the "Pax Romana."

After all, what makes up our lives? Is it only the victories we've won in our professional careers, the opponents we vanquished in our respective arenas? Or would we talk about the other successes, and failures, that make up the bulk of a person's life? How realistic is it to read a story where the protagonist essentially skips over what you're (hopefully) about to read in the pages of *Fraternitas*?

"Yeah, I fell in love; yeah, my brother's actions impacted me; yeah, my boss' ambition got all of us in trouble, but that's not worth mentioning. Let's just skip to the part where I thrust my sword into another man's body."

I don't believe (and I feel cautiously confident you'll agree) that this would be the case. Victory, and defeat, takes many forms, and even in the times in which Titus Porcinianus Pullus lived, not all of these successes and failures occurred on a battlefield, facing a man with a sword in his hand. Hence, we have this continuation of Titus Porcinianus Pullus' story, *Fraternitas*.

And of the word itself, essentially it means "brotherhood" or "the state of being a brother", but as I suspect you'll agree, there is *much* more involved in that word. It's about the power of our common blood, and the hold it has over us all. It's about "fraternity brothers," but in a deeper sense of the word than what covers the world of keggers and initiation pranks.

Going back to my own story, it doesn't take Dr. Phil to figure out that, growing up the way I did, without any tangible connection to the man who gave me life, has exerted a powerful influence on my life. But, thanks to the Internet, I've been able at last to fill in some of the missing pieces of my particular puzzle, and in doing so, I suppose in some small way I'm answering the call of my blood.

In its simplest form, the two people who created me, and by extension created Titus Pullus, can be divided into two camps. My mother's side of the family is, without exception, from what we in the United States call "The North," and going back now to about eight or nine generations, none of them served in uniform.

My father's side of the family is another story, one that's almost diametrically opposite of my mother's, where I am the only Southern-born member of the family. But more specifically, the Southern branch of my family has fought in every war in which this country has fought, and with the same uniformity, every member of my father's family originates in the South, as I do. And, as I have discovered, this tradition goes back even farther, to the English Civil War, where one of my ancestors was given a knighthood for refusing the oath of allegiance to Oliver Cromwell.

My conclusion is this: It's the power of blood that set me on a path that found me here, after doing my part to serve my country, and I'm now writing stories of fighting men.

And, if I had to sum up what *Fraternitas* is about, it's the almost mystical hold our heritage and those microscopic strands of DNA have on each of us, whether we want to acknowledge it or not. Titus Porcinianus Pullus does what he does, suffers what he suffers, and achieves what he achieves, powered by the ichor flowing through his veins that serve as the driving force behind who he is and what he does. It is, after all, the power of blood.

As always, I need to thank my always ready, always faithful team; my editor, Beth Lynne, for encouraging me to take this path, to my artist Marina Shipova, who manages to capture my almost-manic attempts to describe the visual part of the story that graces this cover. And to Stu MacPherson, who managed to carve out time to read this part of the story, despite the lack of, as he calls them "the stabby stabby bits."

But, ultimately, *Fraternitas* is to Henry Richard Peake, and all those of his line who came before him, and me. Scots-Irish to the core, inhabiting the hills and valleys of the area around North Carolina and Tennessee, in the Asheville area, they answered the call of their country, and as far as I know, they never asked *why* they were serving; they just did it. It's what those of us who share the same blood do, after all.

Semper Fidelis,

R.W. Peake
June 26, 2015

Chapter 1

I remember reading in my Avus' account, about how some moments seem to last for days, while years can pass by in what one is sure is a blink of the eye. Such was the case after the year of the Consulships of Gaius Marcius Censorinus and Gaius Asinius Gallus, which by any definition was an eventful year for the men of the 8th Legion. The fact that if one asked the average citizen of Rome of any class their likely answer about the state of affairs in Pannonia, they would have probably uttered the words, "All is quiet in Pannonia" does not necessarily make it so. As I have come to learn, the difference between what my fellow citizens are told about matters along the frontiers of this Empire, and the reality, are often stark. And in the aforementioned year, not only did we have a revolt by two tribes, the Colapiani and the Varciani, we lost Publius Canidius, our Primus Pilus. Even more than one might expect, the turmoil from the series of events that culminated with the appointment of Gaius Sempronius Atticus as Primus Pilus was substantial, and rippled outward from the event itself, impacting many lives. However, once matters settled down and I became more comfortable in my role as Sergeant of the First Section, First Century of the First Cohort, the life of a Legion in garrison quickly settled into a routine. A routine that, seemingly overnight, meant I awoke one morning and three years had passed. This is not to say there were not notable events during that time, just that they were more of a personal nature than anything that would have been recorded in the annals, or even in the Legion diary. Although, being fair, the enlistment of my younger brother Sextus into the Legion was worthy of an entry being made. However, while it rated little more than a single line entry in the diary, in my personal life, it created quite a stir.

It began when, on Sextus' seventeenth birthday, almost eighteen months after his arrival back into my life, I, standing in as *paterfamilias* in place of my father, informed him that while he would be enlisting as we had planned, it would not be into the Fourth Cohort as he expected, and it would not be for another year. In retrospect, I recognize that I shoulder much of the responsibility for the acrimony and bitter feelings stemming from my announcement because I had known this for quite some time. In fact, this was something I was aware of within a few heartbeats after I learned from Sextus, and Diocles, of his intention to enlist. Now I can clearly see why I should have spoken up earlier; if not then, I had eighteen months where I spent several watches a week with my little brother, teaching him in the same manner in which my father had taught me. This is not to say my father had not done the same for Sextus, but as I had learned from Diocles, and Sextus finally admitted, grudgingly, my brother had not been as studious in his pursuit of martial skills as I had been. Nor, as it became apparent, did he have the same level of dedication, or enthusiasm, to attain those skills which are, frankly, indispensable to a Legionary with any ambition to ascend the ladder of promotion. Nevertheless, the day I told him he would not be enlisting that year, or entering the Fourth Cohort, was one I would like to forget.

"What??? But why?"

Yet one more error in my actions that day was that I had told him this just a few heartbeats after he had entered the main room of Diocles' apartment, where he had his own room. Our long-time friend – I can never think of him as a servant, let alone a slave, despite the fact that this was his status when he became connected to our family – had just presented my brother with the gift from the Greek and his family. Compounding my error was the fact that the rest of Diocles' family was present as part of the celebration of this day. Specifically, the presence of one member in particular meant my announcement to him that he would not be entering the Fourth Cohort was practically a guarantee that there would be a conflict, and it would be spectacular in nature. The fact that it was Birgit, Diocles' wife, made matters, if not more complicated, certainly more interesting. By this time, not even a blind man could have missed the signs that Sextus was hopelessly smitten by Birgit, although I am positive that his passion was unrequited, because equally as obvious was the fact that Birgit only had eyes for Diocles. Granted, I will be the first to admit that, at least from appearances, the idea that a beautiful young woman like

Birgit who was, and still is a true beauty, could be so hopelessly in love with a Greek in his sixties who was actually shorter than she was, even if he still had all of his hair and at least some of his teeth, was hard to fathom. Until, that is, you knew Diocles. But, as anyone who has been alive for a substantial number of years can tell you, there is no logic to what the heart wants, and this is especially true when one is young. Consequently, my choice to tell Sextus of my decision in this environment guaranteed the worst possible result. Nevertheless, I was determined to be the calm one, so when I answered my brother, I tried to keep my tone level and matter of fact.

"Because they're a first line Cohort," I explained to him. "And, Sextus, you're not ready to be in a Cohort in the first line. And you're not ready to enlist yet, either."

This was my next mistake, although at least with this one, I understood I had erred the instant I opened my mouth; the fact that it was true only made matters worse.

"Why do you say that?" My younger brother's face had turned a deep shade of red, and his tone was bellicose, prompting me to think, If only you'd shown this kind of passion at the stakes. "I'm farther ahead than just about every other *tiro* who enlists," he pointed out.

"That," I was forced to admit, "is true. But, Sextus," I decided to try a different approach, using reason, even though I was sure it would be futile, "you know who you are, who *we* are. And anyone who bears the name Pullus is going to be expected to be better than any other *tiro*."

"And you're saying I'm not?" he retorted, drawing himself up to his full height, which it must be said was only a couple inches shorter than mine.

Sighing, I paused as I tried to think of a diplomatic way to express my concerns; as usual, I ended up just telling him bluntly, "Yes, that's what I'm saying, Sextus." Before he could say anything in protest, I held up my hand and allowed, "I'm not saying that you wouldn't be ahead of the other *tiros*. What I'm saying is that you're not good enough....for a Pullus."

I do not believe if I had slapped him that he would have looked more stricken than he did then, and for a brief moment, I felt horrible. But, I reminded myself, your eyes aren't deceiving you; you've seen him and sparred with him. Still, despite understanding it was the right decision, I did not feel good.

"I'm going to write to Tata," he suddenly announced. "I'll tell him how hard I've been working, and how far I've come. Something that even *you*," he pointed an accusing finger at me, "have admitted."

"You have," I agreed, wondering why I was the one sounding defensive, "from where you started. But, Sextus," I had to make an effort to remain patient, "you should have been farther along when you got here than you were."

"That's not true." He was shouting now. "I came here because of the other…problems!"

"And those other problems are why Tata couldn't make you stick to your training," I shot right back.

Now I was getting angry as I thought about my father, missing his leg and standing at the stakes our Avus had set up in his villa at Arelate, waiting for Sextus to come for his daily lesson. I do not remember when or how it happened, but my brother and I were now standing nose to nose; what it also told me was how truly angry my brother was.

"I'm writing Tata," he said again.

I believe it was the sight of his lip sticking out that finally ignited my ire, yet while I did not physically strike Sextus, I knew how to hurt my younger brother without leaving a mark on him.

"You can," I snapped, "but I already did! And he fully supports my decision! In fact," there was no need for me to add this, other than the fact that I was truly irate, "he told me that if I decide to hold you back for even another year after this one, he'd support my decision!"

Sextus' mouth dropped open, although he did not say anything. It was the sight of his eyes filling with tears that made my anger disappear as quickly as it had come. Suddenly, he spun about, and, without a word, fled into his room, slamming the door, leaving me and Diocles' family standing there. The children, all four of them, were standing there wide-eyed, while the youngest, Scribonia, burst into tears, making me feel horrible as I realized this was the first time they had seen the man they called Uncle Titus truly angry. Suddenly, I felt terribly embarrassed, but apologizing, despite my growing maturity, was still something I did not do well; being honest, I am not much better at it now, in my thirties.

"So," Diocles broke the silence, "that was enjoyable."

As I am sure he hoped, this made me laugh despite myself, while Birgit and the children began giggling. Despite my best effort to stifle my laughter, I could not help it.

"This isn't helping," I scolded Diocles, shooting my eyes to Sextus' door.

"You should talk," he snorted. Turning serious, he asked me, "So, what's this all about?"

"Weren't you listening?" I replied, hoping that he would be satisfied.

But Diocles had known me since the day I was born; he had seen me grow up, and when I turned ten, he became my tutor. And this day, he was not fooled in the slightest. However, as usual, he knew that by not saying anything and just waiting me out, I would finally divulge my real reasons.

"Fine," I finally relented, grumbling as I did it. "You win." I paused as I tried to frame my thoughts. Finally, I just blurted out, "As long as Corvinus is Pilus Prior, Sextus isn't going to be in the Fourth Cohort. And," I added firmly, "he's not ready for any Cohort, not right now."

As I knew he would, Diocles reacted with equal measures of both surprise and bewilderment, gasping, "But why? I mean," he amended, "about the Fourth? I understand about the delay, but surely after another year, he'll be ready for the Fourth."

That was the question, wasn't it? I thought bitterly. How had I come to view Gnaeus Corvinus, my first Pilus Prior and my father's best friend, in such a negative light? Before I explained, I took a seat at their table and asked Birgit for a cup of wine, unwatered, from which I drank deeply before I began.

"Do you remember me telling you about everything that happened two years ago?" I asked him.

"I'm old, but I'm not decrepit just yet," he commented dryly. "So, yes, I remember. About Urso, yes?"

"Yes," I had to laugh at his words, although my mirth did not last long, "about Urso. But," I drew an extra breath, "there was more to it than that. I found out something about Corvinus' involvement in what Urso was doing that…" My voice trailed off as I struggled to find the proper words. Finally, I settled with, "…bothered me."

Diocles did not respond immediately, sitting back in his chair, seemingly more interested in what was in his own cup than what I had said.

Finally, he broke the silence, asking, "And was it that he started out as partners with Urso in running their off-the-books…business?"

Frankly, I was too stunned to respond, at least immediately. How had he known that? I wondered.

"And," I managed to articulate that thought aloud, "how did you know that?"

Diocles shrugged, but I could not help notice that he seemed careful to keep his gaze on his cup as he replied, "Because your father told me about it when he found out."

I must confess this revelation struck me hard; it was beyond my imagination that the man I knew my father to be could have knowledge of such matters and still remain friends with Corvinus.

"What do you mean, 'when he found out'?" I challenged Diocles. "Surely you're not saying he knew what they were up to!"

Once more, there was a long, and for me at least, extremely uncomfortable silence as Diocles seemed to ponder the question and whether or not he should answer.

Finally, he answered, "Your father did know. At least," he held up a hand to stop my protest, "he found out about it at some point. Relatively early."

"How can that be?" I demanded.

I am not blind to the irony of the moment; just a short time before, I had told my younger brother something that had rocked his view of our father. Now here I was, reacting exactly the same way because Diocles had told me something that did not fit into my own mental picture of him.

"Because your father saw things as they were, not as he wanted them to be," Diocles said. "And neither Corvinus nor Urso, for that matter, were unique. It's been a game played by Centurions on their men for…" He finished with a shrug.

"That doesn't make it right," I argued.

"No," he acknowledged, "it doesn't. And I'm not saying your father liked it. But he also realized that there wasn't much he could do about it."

I pondered this for a moment, but it did not mollify me in the slightest. When all was said and done, at that moment, I was still a ranker, and I viewed our officers as being paragons of virtue and honor; at least, I believed this was how they should behave. Even now, while I am certainly no longer so naïve, I cannot deny there is a part of me that still wants this to be true. What I have come to accept, albeit grudgingly, is that at this point in my life and given my current station, I can only control my own actions, and right now, that of my Optio. When I take command of a Cohort is another story, however.

"But he let it happen," I grumbled.

Now I could see I was trying Diocles' patience, his lips thinning down in an expression I knew all too well.

"Your father didn't let it happen," he snapped, "because it would have happened no matter what he did!" Suddenly, he leaned forward and stabbed a finger at me and continued, "And what does that really have to do with anything?" As quickly as his anger came, it seemed to disappear, and he slumped back into his chair. "The question you should be asking is if you think Gnaeus Corvinus and the Fourth is the best spot to put your brother so he has a chance to survive his first battle."

When put the way Diocles did, the question was no longer quite so clear, and inwardly I cursed the Greek for always providing the truth, no matter how awkward.

Despite myself, I was forced to consider the question, but while Diocles' point did remove one obstacle, it had nothing to do with the other.

"No," I finally relented. "You're right. If I wanted to put Sextus in a spot where he'd be looked after by someone, the First of the Fourth would be the spot. But," I shook my head, "there's more to it than that."

Thankfully, Diocles either took pity on me or he had just worked it out for himself, so he relieved me of the burden of articulating what, if I am pressed to admit, was the real cause for my decision.

"You don't think Sextus is ready for a first line Cohort," he said.

"No," I answered grimly but without hesitation. "I don't think he is."

"It's true that he's been a bit…lax in his training," Diocles admitted, "but…"

He got no further.

"Stop it," I pointed a finger at him, feeling a resurgence of the anger I felt whenever I considered this subject. "Stop making excuses for him, Diocles. You," I heard the bitterness I felt in my voice as I continued, "and my parents have been making excuses for him ever since he was a child!" I shook my head, feeling as if I was truly all alone in this. "But he's not ready."

Rather than argue, Diocles surprised me by nodding his head in agreement. However, I was not prepared for what he said next.

"You're right," he admitted. "And I know you are. But," he looked at me levelly, "remember that I'm older than you. And my history with your family goes back to…"

He did not finish, nor did he need to, but I was unprepared for the sudden glinting in his eye as he thought back to earlier days. Understanding him, I reached out and put my hand on his arm as, for a moment, we shared the memory of my Avus, the great Titus Pullus of legend, the greatest man who ever marched under the standard of a Legion of Rome.

Once he regained his composure, Diocles said, "What I'm thinking back to is how your Avus worried about your father."

Cutting him off, I was sure I knew the story; I was wrong.

"I know that," I interrupted, "but this isn't just about worrying about Sextus the way Avus worried about Tata. I understand it's going to be part of my life from here on."

"I'm not talking about that," Diocles retorted. "You read your Avus' story, didn't you?"

"Of course." I was nettled, to say the least. "I've read it twice."

"Obviously not." He was no less adamant. "Or you'd remember how hopeless your Avus thought your father was when he came to us from the 14th."

Much to my chagrin, I suddenly realized I had, in fact, forgotten about that. Once Diocles brought it up, I did recall reading about Titus Pullus' initial despair that his nephew would be able to survive his first battle. But it was my Avus' best friend, and not lost on me, my father's first Pilus Prior who had insisted that young Gaius Porcinus, as he was known then, would give a better accounting of himself than Titus Pullus believed. However, as I was discovering, when I was actually the one who had to make the determination about my brother's fitness to hold a sword, it was not nearly as simple.

"I do remember that," I finally allowed, if unwillingly. "But this is Sextus we're talking about." Suddenly inspired, I pointed out, "And if I remember correctly, Tata actually was willing to work quite hard at it, wasn't he?"

I saw that I had scored a major victory with Diocles, his face shadowing as he admitted, "Yes, yes he was. And he did work very, very hard."

"Well," I was not about to relent now, "Sextus isn't as willing. I have to drag him out to the stakes just to get him to train."

Nothing was said between us for several heartbeats, but finally, Diocles signaled his acquiescence, if not his complete agreement, asking, "So where do you want to put him?"

"The Seventh," I answered instantly.

In some ways, I understood it was not quite fair; I had given this a lot of thought, while Diocles was just dealing with this now.

"Why the Seventh?" he asked.

"Because Tiburtinus is the Hastatus Prior," I told him. "And I trust him."

"Gnaeus Tiburtinus?" he asked, squinting as he tried to place the name. "Wasn't he your…?"

Before he could finish, I supplied the answer for him. "He was my Optio when I joined the First. But then he got promoted to the Ninth. He got bumped up to the Seventh when a slot opened up there."

"Opened up?" His eyebrow raised, yet although I flushed a bit, neither could I deny his jibe, understanding he knew our system as well as anyone. "You mean he saved enough money?"

"Maybe." I could not help my defensive tone, but I was not about to be swayed in my belief that Tiburtinus was truly worthy of his promotion. "But I'd be happy to move to the Seventh if I could!"

The Greek stared at me for a moment, except I could return his gaze because I was being completely sincere.

Seeming to sense this, he grunted as he sat back, asking in a light tone that did not fool me, "And is Tiburtinus willing to take Sextus on?"

"Yes," I assured him. "And honestly," I leaned forward in an attempt to impress on Diocles I was being truthful, "I think that Sextus would be happier in the Seventh than the Fourth. You know the second line Cohorts are the ones who're sent out for independent duty more than us. That should make him feel..."

"Like he's not worthless?" Diocles supplied for me, and although I winced at the blunt way he put it, neither could I deny the truth of his words.

"Exactly," I confirmed. "He'll get the chance to march around the province, and maybe get blooded in a way that's not like what I had to face in Germania."

"This isn't going to make him happy," Diocles commented. "I know he's dreamed of at least matching your record."

"He can dream all he wants," I replied harshly, "but he hasn't put in the same amount of work that I have. And," I jabbed my finger at Diocles, "you know that's the truth."

Like I had been a few moments before, Diocles was in a position where he could not deny the truth of my words.

"I suppose," he finally allowed, "that you're right."

"I am," I assured him. "And I'm doing what's best for Sextus."

I believe that is the truth to this day, no matter how things transpired.

Once Sextus realized I was deadly serious about holding him back for another year, he accepted his fate and even I was forced to admit that he became more dedicated with his training. The delay had a hidden benefit; I was able to convince him over the course of that extra year that he was better served in the Seventh than in the Fourth. I could tell one reason this appealed to him was the idea that his climb up into the First Cohort, which he made no secret was his ultimate desire, would be more spectacular than mine was.

"When I go from a second line Cohort all the way to the First," he had boasted one day, "you're going to be known as Sextus Pullus' brother!" We were at the stakes this day, and I will always remember his grin as he crowed, "They'll say 'There goes the brother of Sextus Pullus! What was his name again?'"

As I am sure he hoped, this made me laugh and, at least temporarily, forget how he was still sloppy on his recovery after he made a third position thrust. Being honest, I was more relieved that the struggle between us concerning his enlistment delay did not last the entire year, despite the fact that, unlike the Legions in other armies, in Pannonia the "plumping up" process of taking on new *tiros* occurred twice a year instead of the normal one time. Once the first training period passed, I believe even Sextus recognized he was better served to wait until the next autumn, instead of being thrust into a Century in the middle of the campaign season.

The other major event in my life was the fact that I became involved in my first semi-permanent liaison with a woman in town. I say "woman"; she was all of seventeen when we met, the daughter of an equestrian. Giulia Tullia was the only daughter of Lucius Julius Livinius and the fact that I was able to approach her at all was based in one simple point; Livinius had been a resident of Siscia for many years, moving there to pursue his interests in a shipping company, although he branched out fairly quickly. Consequently, my last name was not only well known to him, my father's status as Quartus Pilus Prior, and I suspect being an heir of Titus Pullus, particularly of his name, did not hurt my chances. I spied Giulia at the market one day as she was perusing the wares of various merchants, with an escort of course. Accompanying her was an old crone named Plotina; at least I thought of her as ancient, although she was probably in her late forties. As I would come to learn, Plotina had been Giulia's nurse since she was born and was devoted to her young mistress, fiercely so, and she would prove to be an even tougher obstacle to navigate than Livinius, or Giulia's mother Tullia. The main reason for that is, putting it in its simplest terms, she saw right through me, understanding me and my motivations much better than probably even I did. I wish I could say that her fears were groundless, but they were not, because from the moment I saw Giulia, I confess I had one goal in mind, at least in the beginning. She was the most beautiful girl I had ever seen to that point, even more so than Birgit, and the sight of her had frozen me in my tracks as I watched her haggling over a bolt of cloth with one of the merchants. Her style of dress and, more importantly, the quality, announced her status as belonging to a family of some means, and with her hair being partially covered with a veil, announced to the world she was an unmarried maiden. Still, while she dressed conservatively, I thought I saw a hint of daring in how she allowed the veil to only partially cover her hair, and although she wore an otherwise normal *stola*, it was cut in such a way that it accentuated her figure rather than hid it. Her hair was a deep black, but was naturally curly, hanging in ringlets that framed her face that, to my eyes at least, was a perfect oval shape.

On this day in the market, I found myself completely paralyzed; until, that is, she concluded her business and turned to leave the forum. Quickly determining her direction, I hurried around the edge of the stalls to put myself in a perfect position for an ambush, while my mind worked rapidly, trying to come up with the perfect array of words that would captivate her interest. I desperately wanted to impress her, certainly, but the truth is that my self-assurance was such that I was confident that just my very size and the way my tunic was stretched so tightly across my body would obviate the need for words. The sleeves of my Legionary tunic were similarly tight because of my upper arms, but although I was self-conscious of my horribly scarred arm, which was fading very slowly and was still mostly pink, I also considered it to be a secret ally. All of the other women with whom I had dallied in the intervening time since I suffered this wound had cooed and fawned over my arm, telling me how brave I must have been and how this was as much a mark of my courage as any *phalarae* or *torq*. However, it was the scar on my cheekbone that I was the proudest of back then, thinking it lent me an air of mystery, hinting at exploits I would be too modest to mention. Unless I was asked, of course. As I was about to learn, my conviction that my scars would stand me in good stead with this young maiden was based on a faulty premise, that the whores who service a Legion and utter such flatteries to young Gregarii like I was then about how attractive they found my scars, and the idea that a daughter of an equestrian would feel the same way. Making matters worse, the instant I pivoted from behind the stall to stand in the path of this maiden and her escort, the witty, seemingly offhand remark that I had been sure would capture her interest fled my mind as rapidly as barbarians routed from the field. In retrospect, I believe it was being close enough to notice that, in striking contrast to her black hair, her eyes were a color of blue I was sure I had never seen before, which rendered me mute. Consequently, instead of saying anything, I stood there like a huge lump of meat, with my mouth hanging open.

The old crone glared at me and, while I was completely flummoxed, I did notice how she stepped in front of my quarry, partially blocking my view. Only because I was so tall was I able to keep my gaze on the girl, my eyes riveted on her face. While she had suddenly looked down at the ground in the modest way our maidens are supposed to behave, I was sure I had seen the flicker of a smile before she looked away.

"What do you want?"

The old crone asked the question, scowling at me with a distrust and disapproval that informed me I was hardly the first young man to act in such a bold manner.

I opened my mouth to respond, which was when I discovered my wits had completely deserted me, and while I know the pause was only a few heartbeats, it felt like a week had passed before I finally thought of anything to say.

Even now as I write this, I am wincing, because I blurted out, "I'm Titus Pullus." Then, I thought to add, "Actually, Titus Porcinianus Pullus," as if that explained everything.

If the crone was pretending like she had never heard of me, her talents were wasted because she should have been on stage.

"Is that supposed to mean something?" she asked. "You're standing in our way, young man. Now, step aside."

Suddenly, I was on the verge of panic; this was not going at all like I had seen it in my mind, and it was in desperation that I said, "I…I just wanted to know your mistress' name!"

"Why?" the crone replied suspiciously. "Surely you don't think she'd have anything to do with the likes of you!"

"But I'm Titus Porcinianus Pullus," I protested before I could stop myself.

This had turned into a nightmare of the worst kind.

"Yes, you mentioned that before," the crone retorted, and adding to my mortification, I heard the girl giggle from behind the crone's back.

"I'm a Sergeant in the First Section of the First Century of the First Cohort of the 8th Legion," I pointed out, as if this distinction would immediately clear matters up; surely she would know what a signal honor that was, especially for someone as young as I was.

"Congratulations." The crone refused to be impressed. "Now please step aside. You don't want me to call the town watch, do you? That," she pointed a bony finger at me, "would get you in trouble with your Legion, wouldn't it?"

Understanding that I had been soundly defeated, I do not really remember what I said; I do recall stepping aside to allow them to pass. I was in utter despair, sure that I had ruined any chance I ever had of knowing this beauty. Then, seemingly out of nowhere, I was saved by an unlikely, but wonderful rescuer.

The girl, still trailing the crone, who had just passed by me, glaring her disapproval at me, was still looking down at the ground. Until, that is, the last moment when just before they rounded the corner to the street leading away from the forum, she suddenly looked back over her shoulder at me. Naturally, I could not tear my eyes away from her, so I was rewarded with a smile that showed even, white teeth.

I was also close enough to see the flash of what I think might have been mischief in her eyes as she said, "My name is Giulia Tullia Livinius, Titus Pullus, and I know who you are."

I walked back to camp; at least, I believe I did, although I cannot say with any certainty that my feet ever touched the ground once along the way.

"How do I get a girl's attention?"

It was bad enough I was asking this of anyone; the fact that it was my little brother Sextus made matters even more mortifying. However, as I had learned to the detriment of my coin purse, while Sextus was younger than me, in one area, he was vastly more experienced than I was; twice since he had arrived in Siscia, I had been forced to assuage the outrage of the father of two different maidens because Sextus had gotten them pregnant. The fact that my brother had two bastard children alive never seemed to bother him, nor did he ever show any real interest in finding out, yet what could not be denied was that as skilled as I might have been on the battlefield, when it came to the war that some claim love to be, our roles were reversed. Being honest, Sextus had not been my first choice; I had gone to my close comrade and best friend Titus Domitius first, but he had proven to be as hopeless about matters as I was. Consequently, I found myself seated across a table from my younger brother in a *taverna* near his apartment. Because he shared the living space, I had no desire for Diocles, or worse, Birgit and the children to hear me confess to my complete ineptitude in impressing the fairer sex, at least in a way that did not involve holding up a coin purse and jingling it.

Now, Sextus was staring at me, open-mouthed, finally managing, "What? How? Why?"

"If you're going to just ask that, I might as well go ask the next man I run into," I grumbled.

He shook his head in a manner that suggested he was trying to clear it of troubling or useless thoughts.

Finally, he answered, "No, Titus. I'm sorry. It's just that…you surprised me. That's all."

"What? That I have no idea how to make a woman like me?" I knew how defensive I sounded, but I could not stop myself. "Well, I'm sorry, but I've been too busy learning how to stay alive in battle. There hasn't been time for anything else."

"It's not that," he countered, then looked away as an expression I had never seen on his face crept across it. "It's just that you've never asked my help before. For anything."

This was when I realized that he was pleased, but also embarrassed, I guess, at this admission. Frankly, I did not feel much differently; at least as far as the embarrassed part.

"Well," I replied gruffly, "I'm asking now." I could not stop a grin from breaking out. "Besides, I know you're the expert in things like this." I produced my coin purse. "This is a lot lighter because of it."

As I had hoped, this made him laugh, yet also reminded him that, when all was said and done, he did owe me a debt of sorts for making sure he was not gelded, or even worse, married and therefore ineligible to enlist.

"Fair enough." He chuckled, then he surprised me by saying, "Besides, how could I refuse this first chance to help out my big brother? This," he sat back expansively, giving me that damnable grin of his that always seemed to get him out of trouble, "is the best day of my life!"

"Gods," I groaned, "I hope not." Shaking my head, I sighed and decided to get on with it. "So, tell me what to do."

"First," he leaned forward, peering at me intently, "I need to know who it is you're interested in."

"No, you don't," I retorted. Truthfully, I was somewhat worried that once Sextus learned the identity of my interest, he would steal her for himself.

"Yes, you do," he insisted. "Because who she is depends on who she is, if you take my meaning. And," he added meaningfully, "who she's not."

Inwardly, I cursed, but I relented and told him. I do not have any idea why I was surprised that he knew exactly who was I talking about when I said her name, yet I was. He whistled softly, shaking his head.

"I'll say this for you," he finally spoke, "you certainly aim high." He grinned at me then, and added, "And I compliment you on your taste."

Suddenly, his face clouded, and he bit his lip in a manner I knew all too well, and I braced myself for whatever problem had occurred to him.

"Titus," he spoke slowly, "are you planning on winning this girl so you can marry her?"

I started in surprise.

"Gods no," I exclaimed, then reminded him of what most of us under the standard use as the pretext for avoiding a state that we sought to avoid at all costs. "Besides, you know a ranker can't be married!"

"Avus was," Sextus replied, "and so are Tata and Mama."

I stared at him in disbelief.

"Avus, yes," I agreed. "But surely you know that Tata and Mama aren't married in the eyes of Rome!"

He stared at me, equally incredulous, even if for completely different reasons.

"Of course they are," he argued. "Everyone knows them as husband and wife!"

This was the moment I realized how sheltered my brother had been, although my next immediate thought was actually for my sisters; in many ways, the reality of the situation between my mother and father and whether their union was legally recognized had more of an impact on them. Fortunately, I learned fairly quickly that my father had taken steps after he was out of the Legion to ratify our parents' marriage so it was legally binding. In reality, Sextus was technically correct at the time we had our conversation, although I did not know it; where he was mistaken was in how this was a relatively recent development. In the eyes of Rome, while my siblings and I were Roman citizens through our father, in other ways, we would be considered bastards by certain segments of Roman society. The idea that Giulia's parents might view me in this light occurred to me during this conversation. Deciding not to pursue the matter of our parents' marital status, I steered Sextus back to the topic at hand.

"Besides, what does it matter whether I plan on marrying her or not?" I asked Sextus.

"It only matters as far as how you approach her," he replied, then paused for a moment. "Because, Titus, this isn't a girl you're going to have a tumble with just because you're...you."

"I know that," I snapped. "That's why I'm asking you!"

"There's really only one way you can do this," he told me. "And that means you're going to have to lie to her."

"About what?" I asked warily.

"About the fact that you have no intention of marrying her," he replied instantly. "You need to give her...no," he suddenly shook his head as he changed his mind, "...you need to convince her father that you're doing this for the right reasons."

I considered this for a moment.

Then, I shrugged and said, "I can do that."

Of all the moments in my life where I have had cause to regret my actions, this was one where, despite the fact that it had nothing to do with my professional life, I caused a massive amount of damage. My only excuse, as flimsy as it is, was that I was still young and callow, and if truth be known, in many ways was just as immature as my brother Sextus. After all, he was the only one who cautioned me that my actions could have such drastic consequences. All I saw in the moment, however, was another kind of conquest to make, and I approached it with the same level of single-minded focus and determination that I had used to my advantage under the standard.

My brother Sextus Scribonius entered the rolls of the 8th Legion as a *tirone* the week after we held this conversation, joining the Fifth Century of the Seventh Cohort, under Gnaeus Tiburtinus, his Hastatus Prior, almost exactly one year later than Sextus had originally planned. Despite my best intentions, I found myself escorting Sextus to the Seventh's area, where he would join four other *tiros* for this Century of about fifteen total for the Cohort. They would be replacing men who had either been shifted up into slots in other Centuries or Cohorts, or in at least two cases of which I was aware because Tiburtinus had confided in me, men had deserted. This, unfortunately, is a simple but undeniable issue that I do not believe my Avus had to face, at least as much, because back when the recruiting parties traveled the country, times were very different. As the original Titus Pullus understood, for a man of his lowly status, enlisting in the Legion was an opportunity to better himself, and his record speaks for itself. During his time under the standard, Legions were recruited in their entirety, and they marched for the term of their enlistments without having those men who fell, were invalided out, or deserted replaced. Consequently, when his 10th Equestris lined up for the battle of Pharsalus, under the command of Divus Julius, the Legion was less than half strength. Our wise Augustus saw the problem, and as part of his reorganization and reforms, commanded that losses suffered by a Legion are replaced fairly quickly, so that at any given moment, a Legion is as near to full strength as possible. This is not to say it has worked perfectly; there have been times where those men assigned to a recruiting party have returned, if not empty handed, then well below their expected quota. And, if I am being honest, the quality of the *probatio* these men have returned with is not the best, and that is being kind. More often than not, at least two or three of any given complement of potential replacements are half-wits or have some physical defect that precludes them from marching under the standard. At the time, I was not aware that, although this is an endemic problem for all of the Legions throughout our Republic, it is particularly bad here in Pannonia. Part of the reason is due to the fact that, although it was settled by Rome some time before, it is still considered the frontier, meaning that the pool of Roman citizens is lower than elsewhere. That, in my opinion, is the lesser of the challenges confronting the Legions stationed in Pannonia. I believe the nature of the tribes who inhabit this province are the real cause for the difficulties. While it had been three years since the last major revolt, mainly by the Colapiani, then the Varciani, rarely a month went by without some sort of hostile contact from one of the tribes. The most common occurrence was when a Century was out on a routine march through the area, showing the natives that Rome was still here and in control. As any veteran of Pannonia will tell you, the tribes who inhabit this province are unparalleled experts in using the rugged terrain and thick patches of forest to their advantage, employing hit and run tactics that have proven to be maddeningly frustrating to combat. One moment, a Century will be marching along, their boots stamping out the rhythm of the march, while men are chattering about all manner of things, sometimes arguments that have been taking place over a period of days, while other conversations recount past exploits, usually of a carnal nature. Then, without any warning, the normal sounds of the march are obliterated in an explosion of noise that is almost always accompanied by a flurry of missiles, usually javelins, but sometimes arrows or even rocks. Only occasionally would our previously unseen attackers then rush from their hiding spots to engage in the kind of combat in which we Romans excel; that is also the explanation why the natives seldom do this. Most of the time, these attacks do little damage; unless, of course, you are one of the unlucky men felled by a well-aimed missile. However, this is also a reason why the recruiting parties, which we had heard in other areas only went out once a year, in

Pannonia was a twice-yearly exercise. The only thing I could guarantee in the case of one *tirone* was that he would not be one of those who skulked away in the night; otherwise, I still had reservations about Sextus' commitment to this path he had chosen for himself. The reason was that just a few months before this day, a rumor had surfaced that Augustus was seriously considering lengthening the term from sixteen to twenty years; this turned out not to be false as much as premature. Frankly, there was a period of several days where neither Diocles nor I had much confidence that Sextus would actually enlist. Even to me, as dedicated as I am to my career, just hearing the length of term gave me pause; there just seems to be something different between the numbers sixteen and twenty, over and above four years. However, I cannot say I was not a bit surprised when, after a couple of tense days, my brother announced he was still enlisting.

When I delivered Sextus to the office of my former Optio, Gnaeus Tiburtinus was actually in the outer room of his quarters that serves as the Century office.

"Hastatus Prior Tiburtinus," I offered him a salute, not only because it was required but due to the fact that I respected the man tremendously, "I'm bringing you some fresh meat." I glanced over at Sextus, who looked nervous, understandably so, although I still gave him a grin that I cannot say was not without some grim humor at the ordeal awaiting him.

Tiburtinus returned my salute, except he was not smiling, although this was not unusual. Slowly, he walked around Sextus, inspecting him up and down.

"Well," he finally allowed, "he doesn't have as much meat on his bones as you do. But," for the first time I saw the glimmer of a smile cross his face, "he *looks* smarter than you at least."

"Oh," I laughed, "he is. He's the clever one in the family." Glancing over at Sextus, I could not stop myself from adding, "Just don't let him loose out in town too often or you're going to have to be making trips to pay off angry fathers."

Tiburtinus snorted, which was his laugh, and he replied, "Ah. We have a real Eros on our hands, neh? Well," he had made a complete revolution and was facing my brother, "we'll just have to make sure he's too tired to lift a finger, let alone anything else."

I laughed, probably more heartily than the jibe deserved, but just the look on my brother's face added to my mirth. Done with his inspection, Tiburtinus suddenly gestured to me to follow him outside, ordering Sextus to remain inside. The wink I gave Sextus was not meant to make him feel better, and I was happy to see it was successful. I bet you're wondering what I'm going to tell your new Centurion, I thought with some amusement.

"So," as was his habit, Tiburtinus jumped right into matters, "what do I need to know about young Pullus?"

Suppressing my natural tendency to be flippant, I gave his question the serious consideration it deserved. Truthfully, I had been wrestling with this question long before it came from Tiburtinus' lips, understanding he would ask this question of any new *tiro*, but especially with my brother.

The silence drew out, and I sensed his impatience, before I finally said, "He's…good with his sword," I began. "Not great, but good. His shield work?" I shrugged and sighed. "That's another story."

As we stood there, I recognized that I was experiencing a previously unknown emotion, one where I not only felt guilty, but torn as far as my loyalty. To whom, after all, did I owe more? My flesh and blood, or my Legion? It was a distinctly peculiar and quite unpleasant feeling, but if Tiburtinus sensed my awkwardness, he gave no sign, for which I was thankful.

"What part of his shield work needs the most...help?"

"His recovery after a punch," I answered instantly. "When he pulls it back, he tends to drop it."

"That's not good," Tiburtinus grunted, then gave me a piercing look. "But I'm assuming you've been working with him." When I nodded, he asked, "So why weren't you able to break his bad habits?"

That was a question I had been asking myself quite a bit; unfortunately, I could not provide a good answer.

"Because," I finally ventured, "he's my brother, I suppose. Oh, trust me, I've bashed him. A lot." This caused him to give a small smile. "But he's stubborn."

"Really?" He raised an eyebrow in mock surprise. "I wonder where he got that from?"

"I have no idea," I replied innocently. "Certainly not from me."

I had planned on laying the blame at my mother's feet, except I could not keep a straight face after that, and we shared a laugh at my blatant lie.

"As long as he doesn't get into the habit of wandering off by himself to wage his own private battle," Tiburtinus said, "then we can fix all the other problems."

"I don't think that's going to be an issue." I chuckled. Turning sober, I suddenly felt an awkwardness akin to when I faced Giulia as I continued, "But I can't think of a better spot for him than where he is." Swallowing, I made sure to look down into the Centurion's eyes and finished, "Look after him, will you, Tiburtinus? He's...he's really important to my parents and the rest of the family."

"No more important than any other man in my Century." Tiburtinus' tone was harsh and unyielding, as it should have been at my request of special treatment for my brother. Then he softened a fraction. "But he is a Pullus, so I'll keep an eye out for him."

I saluted him, but when Tiburtinus offered to let me watch him swear in Sextus and the others who were now assembled in the Century street, I demurred. As far as I was concerned, from that point on, Sextus Porcinianus Pullus was just another "slab of fresh meat that needed to be tenderized" as my first Optio Aulus Galens liked to say. Consequently, I left the area without looking back.

While Sextus was suffering and being tenderized, I continued my quest to win fair Giulia, employing the tactics my brother had assured me would work, despite my misgivings.

"How can ignoring her make her interested?" I had asked, but he had just grinned at me.

"Trust me," he insisted. "Just do what I told you, and watch what happens."

And I did. Now, I did not truly ignore her; in fact, I planned out my days as assiduously as if this had been a campaign to subdue a barbarian tribe. It took some shuffling of my schedule, which means it cost me some money, paid to my Optio Asinius, but this is a long-standing practice going back for decades, if not centuries. And I am fairly confident that, because of our relationship, Asinius actually charged me less than other men, although I would have paid any amount. Nevertheless, it allowed me the flexibility to essentially spy on Giulia as I tried to learn her habits and routine. Fairly quickly, I determined that every afternoon she went walking about the market stalls with her crone as escort; I even found out the escort's name. Finally, the day came when I felt ready to begin carrying out my plan. Naturally, I was even more nervous this day than I had been during my first awkward attempt, as part of me still refused to credit that my little brother could have been correct.

Still, this time, when I saw the pair at the far corner of the forum, I knew they followed a regular route as they wended their way through the stalls. Positioning myself, I waited until I caught a glimpse of the pair in between the shops, then turned the corner so we were approaching each other.

Since I am hard to miss, I saw the crone's eyes turn to focus on me, then her mouth turn down, and I am fairly certain she was prepared to dismiss me, except before she had the chance, I simply stopped, bowing slightly and said, "*Salve*, Mistress Giulia," then turning to the crone, I actually bowed a bit more deeply, saying, "Madame Plotina. I hope both of you are enjoying the day."

Then, before either of them could speak, I walked past them as if I was headed somewhere very important. Not, however, without glancing out of the corner of my eye over at Giulia. Whatever reservations I had about following Sextus' advice vanished in that instant, because there was no missing the look of irritated surprise on her lovely face.

"Why are you avoiding Mistress Giulia?"

To my recollection, it was three weeks to the day from our last encounter. However, it was also after, again going by Sextus' plan, I had skipped my almost daily trip to Siscia for a week. And on the first day I resumed, I was confronted by a visibly angry Plotina. Now, this was not exactly what Sextus had predicted; he had assured me that it would be Giulia herself who was standing in front of me with crossed arms and blocking my way in the manner in which this old woman was doing.

Thinking quickly, I did my best to affect a look of surprise as I answered Plotina. "Why? Because you told me I wasn't good enough for your mistress and told me not to bother talking to her!"

Suddenly, the crone did not look quite as sure of herself in her indignation.

"Yes, er, well," she fumbled. "That was before…"

"Before," I prompted her gently, "you knew who I was? That I'm not just some Gregarius?"

She had the grace to look embarrassed as she admitted, "Yes, Master Titus."

"And now?" I asked, but I was certainly not prepared for her answer.

"Now," she said, "I've been commanded to invite you to the villa of my master, Lucius Julius Livinius, tomorrow at the beginning of the third watch."

Before I could answer, I became aware of a sudden spate of sweat running down my back and chest, and I remember hoping it did not soak through the front of my tunic. This was a completely unexpected development, and I cannot deny there was a part of my mind warning me that, given my true intentions, I should find some way to decline this invitation. It would be a simple matter, I knew; I could plead duties, although this was a time when being a Legion in garrison means more free time than normal. Nevertheless, I was acutely aware I had inadvertently been given an opportunity to extricate myself from a potentially bad situation.

"I'd be honored," I found myself saying. "Please tell your master I am looking forward to it."

Standing outside the gate inset in the wall surrounding the villa of Lucius Julius Livinius, I allowed Diocles to fiddle with the drape of the toga I was wearing as I tried my best to avoid squirming and undoing his work. That he was even present was only after a long and sometimes acrimonious debate between the two of us had taken place.

"You're a freedman now," I had argued. "That means you don't have to…"

"I don't have to do anything I don't want to," he cut me off, speaking calmly.

I suspect he did so precisely because he knew how much it irritated me that whenever I got agitated, he always remained placid.

"And," he continued, "I think I should go along with you, if nothing else to make sure Lucius Livinius remembers that he's not dealing with just some grimy ranker."

"What you mean," I retorted, "is you don't want me making a fool of myself."

"That too." He grinned at me. "Your parents wouldn't be happy to hear you're giving the family a bad name."

Even in the moment, I felt a sudden stab of guilt, and once more, a part of me urged myself to stop matters right then before it was too late. Naturally, as with most young men, what little thinking I did when it came to the fairer sex was with the wrong head, so I ignored my own warning. Now I was standing there, waiting for Diocles to finish, then once he did, I rapped on the wooden door. I had to rap once more before the tiny hatch that slaves use to identify callers was opened, and I instantly recognized the wrinkled eye of Plotina peering out.

The door was quickly opened, and I was suddenly faced with a sight to which I was unaccustomed; Plotina trying to smile at me as she bowed and said, "*Ave*, Master Pullus! Welcome to my master's home!" Then she peered over at Diocles, her supercilious manner instantly changing as she mistakenly assumed that Diocles was a fellow slave. "I see you've brought your…."

"I've brought Diocles, a freedman who's served my family since long before I was born," I cut her off, and I imagine the fact that it was with unfeigned ire that I added, "And you'll treat him as if he and I were brothers. Or," I confess I had to grin at him, "father and son."

"Of course, Master." Plotina returned to that normal state of the slave confronted by someone higher up the ladder than they are, which is basically everyone, bowing her apology. "And I ask for forgiveness from Master…"

"Diocles," he told her, but his tone was much gentler than mine had been, and he reached out to take her hands in his as he said quietly, "and please don't call me Master. I was a slave just like you, but I was lucky enough to be given my freedom by Master Titus' grandfather."

Strangely moved by his actions, I felt a lump form in my throat, especially when I saw the old woman's reaction as tears formed in her eyes.

Then she completely surprised me when she asked, in a tremulous voice, "His grandfather? You mean…" Her voice trailed off, but while I was mystified, Diocles instantly understood.

"Yes," he answered her. "Camp Prefect Pullus was my master."

"You know," she turned her head to address both of us, "I saw him once, when he was leading the army back to Siscia from campaign." Her eyes took on a faraway look as she thought back to when she had been young, like I was then, and she fell silent for a moment.

"Was it the campaign to Thrace?" Diocles asked, doing so before I could.

But while we each assumed she was referring to the last campaign in which he participated, we were both surprised when she shook her head.

"No," she replied, "it was the one led by the grandson of the Triumvir Marcus Crassus."

"Ah." Diocles nodded his head, then turned to me to add, superfluously in my opinion, "That was his first campaign as Camp Prefect, before you were born."

"I'm aware of our history." My tone was sour.

Meanwhile, Plotina was clearly swept away by the memory as she continued, unmindful of my irritation, "Oh, I remember that day! Your grandfather was riding alongside the young Crassus, but he was such a large man." Suddenly, she turned to examine me closely, giving me the feeling that she was actually seeing me for the first time. "Although you might actually be broader across the shoulders. Still," she shook her head, "he was quite a sight, I assure you! Crassus was a handsome, dashing young man, there's no doubt about that. But I can tell you one thing," for the first time since I had known her, the old woman gave me a grin that, despite the missing teeth, gave me a flash of Plotina as a young woman, "the women of the town barely gave Master Crassus a glance! Oh no," she sighed, and the way she did it suddenly made me a little uncomfortable, although Plotina seemed not to notice as she stared off into space. "We only had eyes for your grandfather, and I'd never seen a specimen like Titus Pullus, I can tell you that!"

"Why, Plotina," Diocles laughed, putting a hand on her arm as if they had been friends for decades, "were you one of those women?"

"Maybe," she grinned again, in a somewhat sheepish manner, but then the smile faded as she added, "but anyone with eyes could see your grandfather wasn't interested in anything we had to offer." Shaking her head sadly, when she turned to look at Diocles, I was astonished to see the Greek's eyes glinting with tears as she finished, "As handsome as he was, I also thought he looked like the most melancholy man I'd ever seen."

While I know she did not intend to, I was unhappy with Plotina because here I was, about to meet the father of the girl I wanted to bed, and I was on the verge of tears myself.

Neither of the two older people noticed, lost in the reverie of years gone by as Diocles said sadly, "That campaign was barely a month after his wife Miriam died." That was when he seemed to remember I was there, and he turned to me to explain, "Your Avus was never the same after she died, you know. He never really got over that."

Although I did not actually know in the sense I had been alive to witness it, I had certainly heard my parents, and Diocles, make reference to the event as I was growing up, always in the context of how it changed my Avus. Although I had a better idea about the depths of his despair after reading his account, frankly, his grief was the kind of thing that a young man as I was then could not fathom. At least, until I experienced something similar myself, but that was still in my future.

Seeming to sense my discomfort, Diocles wiped his eyes, then cleared his throat and said, "Yes, well. Enough of reliving old times." Turning to Plotina, he gestured in the direction of the villa and said quietly, "Plotina, if you would be so kind to escort young Master Pullus here, perhaps you and I can spend some time reminiscing."

She turned to comply, except I intervened, saying firmly, "No. Diocles is coming with me."

Suddenly, she looked uncomfortable; truthfully, so did Diocles, who protested, "Titus, that's not necessary!"

"Yes," I remained firm, "it is." I grinned at him and added, "Remember why you came in the first place. You're here to stop me from making a fool of myself, and you can't do that in the kitchen."

As I had hoped, this made both of them chuckle, and we followed the old woman as she led us to the *triclinium*, where Lucius Livinius waited to determine what kind of scoundrel I was.

Honestly, I cannot say who was more surprised at how smoothly and well my interview, for that is what it was, went with Giulia's father. This is especially true because, as I discovered when I entered, with Diocles trailing behind me, the subject of all the excitement was actually present. I immediately became thankful on Diocles' insistence that I actually wear a toga for the occasion, because unlike a tunic, sweat does not show through the snowy white folds. The beads of perspiration that began popping out on my forehead were another matter, but fortunately, it was cool enough inside the villa that rivulets of fluid never began coursing down my face.

"*Ave*, Titus Porcinianus Pullus." Livinius was a portly man, with a bald pate surrounded by a fringe of hair that he grew longer on one side to pull over his head, but his grip was firm, if a bit moist, as we clasped arms. "Welcome to my home, humble as it may be!"

"The honor is mine, sir," I replied, while a corner of my mind tried to remember whether it was in my Avus' account or something I had heard elsewhere about Divus Julius doing the same sort of thing to cover his bald spot. "And thank you so much for this invitation."

"Well," he boomed; as I was to learn, Lucius Livinius had a set of lungs on him that a Centurion might envy. "I had no choice. All this one," he gestured with a meaty hand in the direction of Giulia, "has been doing is chattering about this young version of Mars himself she's seen in the market! This was the only way to keep her quiet!"

"Tata!" Giulia gasped, but I was absurdly pleased to see I was not alone in my nervousness as her face turned a deep red. "That's not true! I said no such thing!"

Despite her protest, what I instantly discerned, and later had confirmed, was that this kind of bantering teasing was their common method of communication, and it became clear that Lucius Livinius loved his daughter very much. Which, I freely admit, should have been enough to dissuade me from my quest.

"Well," the words came tumbling out of my mouth, "I can assure you that the number of times she's mentioned me is nothing compared to how often she's been in my thoughts!"

"That's not true." Giulia, who was still seated on a couch at the far end of the room, had turned to face me directly, except she was not smiling as she continued. "You barely paid me any attention every time we met! You said more words to Plotina in one conversation than you've said to me in all the times we've seen each other!"

Thank you, Sextus, I remember thinking quite clearly.

"That's only because whenever I saw you, I couldn't think of anything to say," I told her, acutely aware that her father was following this exchange with keen interest. "Your beauty does that to me." Although the words felt awkward in my mouth, I saw her father suddenly start beaming. "I forget whatever's in my head to say to you." Most importantly, Giulia suddenly broke her gaze and stared down at the mosaic at her feet, but while a slow flush returned to her face, this time, it was from the neck up and, as inexperienced as I was, I understood I had said the right thing.

"She is a beauty, isn't she?" Livinius had turned to regard Giulia with a fond smile, which only increased the discomfort of my honorable side.

"Yes, she is," Diocles agreed, and while I do not know if it was his intent, it seemed to break the spell in the room.

Suddenly, Livinius turned back to me, but while he was smiling, his eyes were sending a different message.

"Well, now that we all agree about my daughter's radiant beauty, it's time for her to retire so the men can discuss matters."

"But, Tata," Giulia protested, yet while her reaction was somewhat unusual, in that a daughter of a Roman family is expected to obey her *paterfamilias* instantly, and certainly without any protest, I also saw that Livinius treated his daughter more indulgently. "Titus just got here, and…"

"And you've seen enough of him for one day," Livinius informed her, but while to my ear his tone remained the same, Giulia clearly understood that he was, in fact, serious.

"Yes, Tata," she mumbled, but despite the fact that she was clearly unhappy, she obeyed, moving across the room to stand in front of me. Dropping into the kind of curtsy I had only seen once or twice in my life, she extended her hand while looking demurely down at the floor. "I am happy to see you again, Titus."

Somehow, I knew to take her hand and kiss it, and it was the first time I had any physical contact with Giulia Livinius. When I close my eyes, I can still remember the warmth of the back of her hand against my lips, and more powerfully, her scent, an intoxicating combination of fragrances that my unsophisticated nose had no ability to identify, other than to say it was the most wonderful thing I had ever smelled in my life. Fortunately, she managed to depart quickly enough so I could not mar the moment in some way, although I could not seem to tear my eyes away from her as she and Plotina, who had been standing unobtrusively in the corner, left the room. With some trepidation, I turned to face Lucius Livinius who, only then, offered me a seat on a couch sitting across from me. To my surprise, however, he did not address me first, but Diocles.

"Well, Diocles, my Greek friend," he boomed, smiling over at my tutor. "How long has it been?"

"I'm afraid to try and count up the years," Diocles replied while I looked on in surprise.

"You two know each other?" I asked, I suppose both of them.

"We're acquainted," Livinius replied. "Surely you remember when Siscia wasn't as big as it is now, young man. You grew up here, after all."

"I did," I agreed, then added, "although we moved away for a few years when I was ten."

"Yes." Livinius' face turned, if not grave, then serious. "After your father's unfortunate…" Suddenly, he did not seem to know how to characterize what had befallen my father.

I sensed Diocles glancing over at me, but I supplied the missing word. "Accident, sir. It's true that he was in battle, but he actually broke his leg in a fall during the fight."

"Ah." Livinius nodded his head. "You know, we never heard exactly what happened, just that your father had been badly hurt."

"He lost his leg," I said, then instantly realized he would know that already.

Fortunately, Livinius did not point that out, asking instead, "And how is your father now?"

I assured him he was fine, although I did not go into any details that would give Livinius the hint that, in fact, my family was probably better off financially than his was. Thanks, I reminded myself, to Diocles.

"And your mother? How is the lovely Iras?"

That was when I was truly surprised; I had not been aware the merchant had known my mother, and I asked him how they were acquainted.

"Actually," he admitted, "I've only met her once or twice. But she was good friends with my wife Tullia Livinia, and she'd flay me if I forgot to ask about her." He gave me a grin then, and added, "But you'll find out what that's like, neh? Answering to the woman of the house?"

At this mention of his wife's name, the memory of the whole sordid affair between her and the Legate that resulted in the bankrupting of Urso leapt to my mind, and I was worried I would somehow blurt out that I knew all about it. My throat suddenly seized up, and I was sure my hesitation would be noticed, but it must not have been as long as I thought.

"Yes, sir…I suppose so," was all I managed, although he misunderstood my hesitation.

"Oh, you will," he assured me, slapping me on the back, but as he did so, he winked at Diocles, the other married man in the room.

Who I was somewhat put out to see laughed right along with Livinius. I had not confided in Diocles that my interest in Giulia was strictly of a carnal nature; at least, that was how it had started. This, as I was rapidly discovering, was turning into something else altogether. As if reading my thoughts, right after refreshments had been served by another slave, Livinius' manner suddenly changed, the smile disappearing as he examined me over the lip of his wine cup.

"So, young Pullus," he began, "what are your intentions towards my daughter?"

In yet another sign, which I ignored, that this was a stupendously bad idea, I realized that, while I had been expecting his question ever since I received his invitation, I did not know how to answer. Even over the multiple watches I had prior to this day, where I could have come up with and rehearsed a reply that would lower Livinius' guard while not tying myself down by an open declaration that I intended to marry Giulia, I had not done so.

"My intentions…" I cleared my throat, stalling for time. "Yes, well, sir. My intentions…"

"You said that already," he pointed out, although I thought I saw a slight twinkle of mischief in his eye as he said this.

And, as he probably intended, flustered me even more.

"Yes, sir. Sorry, sir," I stammered, "but it's just that…I…I haven't really thought about it."

What? Thankfully, this scream at myself was within the confines of my skull. That is the worst thing you can say!

"Haven't thought about it?" His eyebrow lifted, but I was completely unprepared for what came out of his mouth next. "I'd be surprised if you had! And, I admire your honesty, young Pullus!" He leaned forward in my direction, giving me a smile and the kind of wink men share, "It's mostly womenfolk who worry about that, neh?" Then, his smile vanished. "But while I understand, we're also talking about my daughter. My *only* daughter. And I love her dearly. So, what I need to know is…" He paused for a moment. "…is marrying my daughter something you would consider?"

During the time between the invitation and this meeting, my mind had run through all the various directions this conversation could take. This was one I had not even contemplated. Out of the corner of my eye, I saw Diocles suddenly shift in his seat, leaning forward and becoming more intently focused on our exchange.

"Well," I began, "as you said, sir, I haven't given it much thought. But," I suddenly had an inspiration, "as you undoubtedly know, we rankers can't get legally married."

"No, you can't," he agreed, then he added something. "But once you're promoted to Optio, you can ask for a dispensation, can't you? From the Princeps?"

Now that some time has passed and I have become if not wiser at least more worldly, I can only imagine how it must sound to non-citizens, or even Roman citizens who have no experience with the army, that the marriage of a lowly Optio could only happen with the personal permission of our supreme leader. Considering there are sixty per Legion, with twenty-eight Legions, I suppose that in and of itself it is not a huge task. However, considering that our divine Augustus is also responsible for almost every detail of not just the military, but the administration of our very government, this is another matter altogether.

"Yes, I can," I answered Livinius, not liking where matters seemed to be headed.

"And, given your family connections and the history of the Pullus line," he went on, "combined with your own record. About which," he pointed a finger at me, "I've made inquiries and your own achievements are quite impressive, I can assure you! Well, I'd say that your prospects for promotion and advancement are quite bright!"

Am I interpreting this correctly? I wondered. Is he actually the one who wants this match?

"That," I finally said, "is very flattering, Lucius Livinius. I mean," I hastened to add, "that you'd do such honor to me and my family."

"Nonsense." He waved a hand. "I know I don't have to tell you that your grandfather is a legend here in Siscia! And," he gave me another smile, "that he was elevated to the Equestrian order by Augustus himself. I know this," he accompanied this with a wink, "because I had my lawyer in Rome consult the annals. So we're in the same class!" Shaking his head, he finished, "No, it would be an auspicious match, for both of our families!" Leaning back, he beamed at me and asked, "So? What do you say?"

What do I say? I thought. I say how in Hades did I get myself into this? And how do I get out of it? If I were perhaps even three years older, at twenty-five, I might have been able to put my desire in a compartment that was locked away and that allowed me to view matters dispassionately. But right then, it was not possible; indeed, my desire for Giulia had actually strengthened in some ways.

"I say," I finally said, "I'd like some time to think about it."

"Oh?" He suddenly started scowling. "What's there to think about?"

Deciding to actually tell the truth, at least partly, I replied, "It's just that I'm still new to this, and I don't have any experience in matters where there are so many factors to consider. My parents," I pointed out, "were married because it was a love match. And I suppose I've seen enough arranged matches where both people are miserable…"

"But Giulia is a perfectly wonderful girl," Livinius interjected, and now he was scowling, "and you'd be lucky to have her!"

"I know that!" I assured him. "After all, it's why I'm here!" Suddenly, I had an inspiration, "But I know you want her to be happy! What if she doesn't like me?"

He did not reply immediately, looking at me warily, as if he was trying to find some sign that would hint at whatever flaw in my character would be what made his daughter unhappy.

"So," he finally broke the silence, "what did you have in mind?"

"Only that we be allowed to get to know each other," I answered instantly. "That way you can be sure that it's not only a good match between our families, it's the kind of match like my parents have. And," I added belatedly, "like you and your wife have."

"Ha!" he barked, clearly amused, although I was sure I detected an underlying note of bitterness there. "You've never seen us together! But," he allowed, "I suppose you're right. I know I spoiled her, but more than anything, I want Giulia to be happy." He thrust a finger in my face and added, "But if you break her heart, young Pullus! And, you should know you'll always be chaperoned. You may come from a good family," he smiled grimly, "but I was young once too."

And, with that, I was one step closer to my goal; the fact that I had just become aware of a number of complications seemed to be of minor importance.

"How," I asked Diocles on our way back to his apartment, where I would doff my toga and it would be put back away, "does he know you?"

"We did…some business together," Diocles admitted. "Only," he added hastily, "a couple of times. But," his face turned grim, "somehow, he either has learned or figured out for himself that your family is…"

"Rich," I supplied, quietly amused at this reluctance to utter the word from the man partially responsible for making it happen. "We're rich."

"I know that," he snapped irritably. "But what I don't know is how he's aware."

"Maybe," I suggested, "he's got eyes and ears. Maybe he's just got common sense, and knows that someone like Avus who managed to get all the way to Camp Prefect would be rich."

"Maybe," Diocles agreed, but I saw it was not wholeheartedly. "Still, I'm worried about that. But," he suddenly turned his attention back to me, "that's not the biggest problem."

"What's the biggest?" I asked.

Only after I thought about it did I understand why my mind did not immediately recognize the threat like Diocles had; he was missing one crucial piece of information that only I had, and that was about my true intentions.

"Really?" He regarded me with a raised eyebrow. "You really don't see what the problem is?"

That instant was the first time I had thought about it, although I will say it came to me immediately.

"Our status," I sighed.

"Yes, your status," he snapped. "Sooner or later, Livinius is going to find out that only your Avus was elevated to the Equestrian order and that it doesn't extend to his heirs."

Even as callous as I was about this matter, the mention of this slight, and injustice, done to my family aroused my ire, as it always did.

"Well," I answered bitterly, "maybe if Augustus didn't hate Avus so much because he's…."

Before I could finish my thought, my Greek friend reached out and, I believe deliberately, grabbed my left forearm, which, even three years later, was still more sensitive to pain than it had been before I was wounded.

"Don't. Ever. Say. That. Again." He said it softly, but there was no mistaking the real anger and fear in his voice.

"I know, I know," I assured him before rubbing my arm as I glared at him. "You didn't have to grab that arm."

"Apparently," his tone was tart, "I did. Because you clearly lost your mind for an instant."

Before I could snarl at him, I reminded myself why he was so adamant, and that he was only showing the same level of devotion and loyalty to my family that had made him the giant that he is, or was, now that he has joined my Avus.

"What," I knew him well enough to know his sudden switch of subject was no accident, "are your intentions with this girl, Titus?"

And there it was, laid out in the open, the question to which only I knew the answer.

"My intention," I answered him, albeit slowly, "is to find out if I even like Giulia."

It did not surprise me when he snorted and shot back, "Anyone with eyes can see you like her. At least," he amended, "you *lust* for her. But," he came to a stop, staring up at me intently, "that's not the same thing as someone you want to spend the rest of your life with, is it?"

"No," I admitted. The silence went on for several heartbeats. I finally shrugged and said, "Honestly, I haven't really thought about it."

"Ah," he said quietly. "So, she's a challenge, is that it?"

I actually turned to face him, intending to deny this, but looking at him, I could not force myself to utter the lie, at least completely.

"Maybe," I admitted, albeit grudgingly. "But," I felt this was important, "I *do* like her! At least, I think I do."

"Well," he commented dryly, "that's good."

Thus began my courtship of Giulia, although just the thought of the word sent shivers up my spine. This period also marks one of the most confusing times of my life, one that I still do not know exactly how I feel about all that transpired. Although, I suppose, there is enough of an honorable man in me that one of the few clearly identifiable emotions is a sense of shame at my behavior. I suppose it began the very next day when I met with Giulia, and of course Plotina, in the forum, and we did nothing more than walk about the market, talking.

"Have you always been the biggest? Among your friends and family, I mean?" she asked at some point.

"Yes," I replied proudly.

"So," her face was serious, "that means you've always had things easier than everyone else."

"Why would you think that?" I asked, more shocked than hurt at that moment.

"Because of the way you carry yourself," she answered instantly. "The first time I laid eyes on you, I could see you're someone who's used to being the best at everything and who gets his way most of the time."

"Why do I feel," I mumbled, "that you're not saying this as a compliment?"

"Because it's not meant to be," Giulia said seriously. She must have seen something in my face because she hurriedly added, "But I don't mean it as an insult, Titus. Truly, I don't. It's just an...observation."

There was a brief silence between us, then I found myself saying ruefully, "Well, it's a good one." Sighing, I realized that although I did not really want to do so, I could not keep from looking down at her as I added, "But you're right. In a lot of ways, I have had it easier than most people, I suppose." Shrugging, I could only say, "It didn't have anything to do with my size, but I guess I have used it to my advantage."

"As you should." The sudden intensity in her voice caught me by surprise. "Tata says that men who are successful are that way because they make the most of whatever gifts the gods gave them to the best of their abilities."

"That," I admitted, impressed not just with the wisdom of Lucius Livinius, but with his daughter, "is very true. And your father's a wise man."

"Yes, he is," she agreed.

She surprised me again, though, when she suddenly pointed down at the scar on my arm and said, "But I don't believe that everything's come so easily. That scar is proof."

I looked down as she touched it lightly, her finger tracing along the jagged outline, while I was sure that whatever awesome power is contained in Jupiter's thunderbolt was somehow being channeled through this girl's hand.

"How did it happen?" she asked me softly.

Suddenly, I was reluctant to tell her as I realized how she was a far cry from the whores in town who, in their own way, were every bit as tough and hardened as the men they serviced.

"I don't remember," I finally answered, but she laughed at that.

"Liar," she teased me. "I don't believe that you could ever forget something like that."

"You're right," I acknowledged, then I paused in our walking to look down at her, and I said, "But it's not something someone like you should be hearing about. It's too…ugly."

"Why?" Her face flashed a sudden burst of irritation. "Because I'm a woman?"

"That," I admitted, then hesitated and added, "and I don't want to spend my time with you thinking about anything ugly. Or talking about it."

She did not say anything for a long while, then she nodded thoughtfully.

"I can understand that," she said. Then her expression changed as she continued, "Titus, I want you to promise me something."

"If I can," I replied cautiously, but she was not going to be denied.

"That's not good enough." She shook her head adamantly. "I want you to promise me!"

"I can hardly make a promise about something I don't know anything about!" I protested.

"Then there's not much point in continuing to see each other." Her voice was very quiet, yet I could see she was serious.

Here's my chance! I remember thinking. If only we had not been looking into each other's eyes at the moment; if only I had not noticed the tiny flecks of what I still believe were pure gold interspersed within the icy blue depths of her eyes. If I was not close enough to breathe in the scent that I had first experienced when I kissed her hand, I told myself, this would be the perfect chance to stop this before the inevitable catastrophe occurred.

"Then," my voice did not sound like my own to me, although Giulia reacted in such a way I knew it was, "I promise." I found myself grinning at her. "Now, what did I just promise you?"

"That you'll never lie to me," she replied instantly.

I have never been stabbed in the heart with a sword or javelin, but I cannot imagine it would hurt any more than the pain I felt at that moment.

"Giulia," I tried to frame a response to what I now understood was a promise I could not keep, "there are some things that I can't," I shook my head, amending myself, "I *won't* talk to you about. I won't lie to you, that I promise. But there are some things you can't ask."

We stood there, still looking at each other, and I clearly saw Giulia did not like my words; my tone probably did not help because she had crossed her arms as she glared up at me. I also noticed that her nostrils flared slightly, which I actually found quite endearing. Finally, our impasse was only broken because Plotina cleared her throat in an obvious attempt to break the spell between us, which worked.

"Fine," Giulia fumed, actually stamping one tiny foot on the ground. Then, she surprised me by laughing, and the sound of it was so pleasing to my ears that I experienced a shiver of delight. "I suppose I'm just used to getting my own way too."

"Which is why," I joined her laughter as I added without thinking, "we're such a good match!"

This stilled her laughter, and mine died along with hers as her face took on an intense expression as she peered into my eyes once more. This time, however, I had the distinct feeling she was trying to plumb the depths of my soul, looking for a sign of falsehood or deception. Which, I am very ashamed to say, I was able to hide from her.

"Maybe," she finally said softly, "we are."

Plotina had clearly determined we had spent enough time in each other's company because she brusquely inserted herself between us to sweep Giulia away. I stood there watching them leave, and just before they turned the corner onto the street that led to her home, Giulia looked over her shoulder and blew me a kiss, although I did not return the gesture, mainly because I was still in a stupor of sorts.

"I," I remember saying this aloud, "am in trouble."

One thing that every man under the standard learns very quickly is that the business of the Legions do not take our personal lives into account. While Pannonia was quiet – in fact, we were in the middle of what would be the longest peaceful stretch in the short history of the province – that did not mean we were allowed to idle our days away. Aside from the normal construction projects, repairs and renovations on existing structures, and our weapons training, for which I was responsible in the First Century, but not the entire Cohort as my Avus was, something that niggled at me, we were still required to march. Most of the time, these occasions occurred at regular intervals; for example, one Century a week from among the Cohorts would be sent out into the province, except the range was limited by the order that the Century only be gone overnight. Once a month, a Cohort was sent out from Siscia, meaning the 8th; while the 15th sortied from their new base to the far northern edge of the province in Sirmium, while from Poetovio it was the 13th; and from the far eastern side of the province, the 11th would march from their primitive base located a few miles west of where the Danuvius turns to the south. These excursions lasted a minimum of two weeks, as each Cohort would make what was in essence a tour of the part of the province for which their Legion was responsible. However, just to keep the natives guessing somewhat, the interval between each Cohort being sent out was varied, so that sometimes there would be a two-week period of time; other times, as one Cohort marched back, another was marching out, and sometimes, there was only a week in between. In this way, our Legate, who had replaced the man who so disastrously and ineptly handled the uprising of Draxo and the Colapiani, did what he could to keep the natives from taking advantage of our routine. We were sent out in this manner throughout the year, which meant that in a given period, each Cohort would go marching out of the gates of their camp three, and sometimes four times a year. Unless, of course, the native tribes started making mischief. Or, as I learned, one was in the First Cohort, and your Primus Pilus is not only politically connected but considers himself an active player in the great, and often bloody game that are politics in Rome. Consequently, just a little more than a week after my first formal meeting with Giulia, Asinius entered our hut to announce that we were heading out for a two-week foray.

"But we did one two months ago!"

I cannot recall which of my comrades uttered this, but I wholeheartedly agreed with the sentiment, even if it was for purely selfish reasons. Things between Giulia and me had been progressing quite nicely, although not as rapidly as I would have liked; I suspect that this is a characteristic shared by every human on this planet who urinates from a standing position. Perhaps I can be forgiven my reluctance to do my duty for Rome when the fact that, just the day before this announcement, Giulia and I had managed to steal some time to kiss while Plotina had become absorbed in a conversation with one of the vendors in the forum, thereby allowing us to slip away. Although, as Giulia whispered to me, this was no accident; the revelation that it was, in truth, Giulia's idea was only slightly more satisfying than the realization that I had managed to win Plotina over to my cause. Now, here I was being ripped away from the arms of the woman I, if not loved, at least desired, and I was unhappy about it, to put it mildly.

"It doesn't matter," Asinius had snapped at the unremembered complainant. "We're going out again, day after tomorrow! So there's an inspection after morning formation tomorrow! And Pullus," he called to me, "you know how the Primus Pilus likes us to look."

I did, very well, unfortunately. Although I had not experienced it personally, there were enough men left who recalled with a great deal of bitterness the thankfully short tenure of Quintus Barbatus, the other Primus Pilus who had come from the ranks of the Praetorian

Guard. From what I gathered, Atticus had even higher standards for our appearance than Barbatus. Which, as I well knew, meant there would be no going into town that night for any of us. And, as Sergeant of the First Section, any discrepancy between what our Primus Pilus expected, and what he found during inspection would be held against not only the offending party, but their Sergeant. It was a lesson I had been forced to learn the hard way, fortunately very early on in the relationship between the First Section and our then-new Primus Pilus. Although there had been some hard feelings between a couple of my comrades and me when, after a repeated failure to meet Atticus' standards, I had been warned by Asinius that my tenure as Sergeant was in jeopardy, the bumps and bruises I had inflicted were sufficiently in the past. Nevertheless, I split my time between taking care of my own gear and prowling about the hut, checking on those of my comrades I had learned needed to be supervised more closely. At times like this, I forced myself to remember how much worse it would have been if the composition of the section were still as it had been when I first joined. But Appius Asinius had proven to be an extremely shrewd judge of character in replacing the missing men in the section that is the first rank of the Legion, and consequently, the most visible. While men of the lower sections sometimes escaped with a cursory examination, or were even skipped altogether if the inspecting officer was in a hurry, we men of the First Section, First Century, First Cohort could be assured that we would be minutely examined. And when the man inspecting us was our Primus Pilus, who seemed determined to match, if not surpass the standard set by the Praetorian Guard, it meant certain tasks were done more than once before I was satisfied. Despite the fact that those comrades who had replaced the likes of our former Sergeants Philo and Caecina, along with one of their toadies Mela, were superior in most ways, this did not mean they did not present me with a challenge. My nemesis in the section, the man who seemed determined to do things his own way, and in his own time, was a man named Tiberius Balbinus. Although it was true he had actually been in the Century longer than I had, he had been moved from the Tenth Section to the First after distinguishing himself in what turned out to be Urso's last battle. The fact that I had been decorated for my own actions that night, and had even been given the spoils taken from the Colapiani chieftain Draxo's body, did not seem to impress him in the slightest, nor did the fact that the reason I had been awarded the spoils was because I had slain Draxo myself. Granted, he was no longer as recalcitrant and obstinate as he had been when he first moved into our hut and I was a new Sergeant; I had finally dispensed bathhouse justice one night that almost landed me in trouble because I had gotten a bit carried away and he had actually been forced onto the sick and injured list. Still, as I looked down at the sloppy coat of varnish he had applied to his leather harness, I was not a bit surprised.

"Really, Balbinus?" I sighed.

"What?" His tone, at least when addressing me, was a particularly irritating mix of belligerence and defensiveness that sounded, to my ears at least, like a petulant whine. "What's the matter with it?"

"You know what the matter is! That's never going to pass inspection and you know it!"

That it was, in fact, Domitius who said this still did not make an impression, something I knew full well would be the case.

"I can't help it if the Primus Pilus expects us to shine and look as pretty as those Praetorians he came from!"

"Just do it over," I ordered him, my tone short.

This conversation, or some variation of it, had been repeated at least once or twice a month for the previous three years, but I counted my blessings that I did not actually have to beat him anymore. He would whine and complain, muttering under his breath about the injustice of it all, then he would actually do it. It was in this manner we passed the night; meanwhile, even as I performed my own tasks, I tried not to think of a pair of blue eyes and red, full lips.

In something of a surprise, the Primus Pilus was apparently pleased enough with what he saw during his inspection the next day that we were given liberty of the town, although only until midnight. Consequently, I wasted no time, hurrying out of the camp into Siscia. Of course, I was far from alone; the road leading the short distance between our gates and the town wall was filled with at least three quarters of the Legion. Domitius, Asinius, and I were walking together, but while Asinius was headed to the *taverna* he favored, where he would meet up with some of our old friends from the Fourth, Domitius' mission was similar to mine, if quite a bit more advanced. In everything but name, my friend had a wife, the daughter of a retired Legionary with whom I had grown up, at least until I moved to Arelate at ten. Her name was Petrilla, and when I had learned she was the one who my friend had been interested in, although he had quite smartly kept quiet about it, I was very happy for the both of them. Petrilla was about the same age as my sister Valeria, just short of twenty years old, and they had been childhood playmates, running the streets of Siscia together. Not that she was doing any running now, but not just because a young woman does not do such things; she was expecting their first child. Still, while I was happy for Domitius, who shared my *praenomen* Titus in honor of Domitius' grandfather's best friend, the first and greatest Titus Pullus, I cannot say that when I looked at the pair of them together the thought crossed my mind that I wanted the same for myself. At least, so I thought; the actual truth was that by this point, I was no longer sure what I wanted, or even what I thought about anything having to do with my personal life. I suppose this was in large part why I felt more comfortable keeping my attention on my professional world and all that it entailed, because whenever I thought about Giulia and the unspoken but insistent expectation that we would one day join permanently, the predominant feeling I experienced was utter confusion.

"So, what are you going to do about Giulia?"

Inwardly, I cursed my friend; I am convinced he is part mind reader because he always seems to be able to divine in which direction my thoughts are going. I thought briefly about pretending I did not understand what he was asking, but I realized I could not.

Instead, I sighed and said simply, "I don't know."

I felt him regarding me as we trudged down the road. As was his habit, he never went into town without some sort of gift for Petrilla. They were never big; sometimes, it would be a handful of flowers plucked from the roadside, or perhaps an apple that he was sure was the most wonderful tasting thing and he wanted to share it with her. Frankly, it made me a bit nauseous seeing him mooning about like this. Lately, however, while he still brought gifts, they were of a different nature. That day, he was carrying a tiny carved Legionary, made by one of the other men who had skill in such things.

"For the baby," he had explained, seeing my raised eyebrow.

He considered my answer for a moment, then said quietly, "Well, you need to decide."

"I know," I shot back, a bit crossly, I must admit. "You don't need to remind me."

"Apparently, I do," he countered. "Because you've been giving me the same answer for days now."

This was something, I knew full well, I could not argue. Just like the last few times I had gone into town, I had risen that day, resolved to break things off before matters got even more serious, for both of us. Yet every time I saw her, my determination was swept away like a twig in a torrent.

"At least," I broke the silence again, "we're going to be gone for a couple weeks. So I don't have to decide tonight."

I saw him shake his head, although he did not say anything. Reaching the gate, we split up; the apartment he had secured for Petrilla was in the part of town that people of Giulia's class avoided at all costs.

"Titus," he called to me, but I only turned around reluctantly, sure I knew what he was going to say. I was wrong, because he only said, "You're probably right to wait. Telling her, I mean."

"Thanks." I was more bemused than anything. I waved and turned back around.

Navigating my way through the town, it always struck me how much Siscia had changed, even in the relatively short period of time I had been back. The town was becoming much more Romanized in the style of buildings, and I do not mean the private residences belonging to Roman citizens. The forum is now ringed with temples, along with the various offices of the civil government, and while I had not seen Rome yet, from what I had heard, Siscia was similar in style, if not scale. Because we had not arranged a meeting, I went straight to the house of Lucius Livinius and not to the market. When I rapped on the gate, it took longer than normal, but then when the hatch opened, it was not Plotina looking out at me. Still, this was not unusual either.

"*Salve,* Soter," I said to the slave who, as far as I could tell, was Plotina's male counterpart, if not in role than in relative age.

"Master Pullus." His tone was flat, which was normal, except he made no move to open the gate, which was not.

"I realize I didn't send word ahead," I told him, thinking this was the problem. "And please give my apologies to Lucius Livinius for disturbing him so late in the day. I just wanted to have a word with Giulia…"

"She's not receiving visitors," he cut me off, and while there was not much to see through the hatch, I had the sense he was feeling uncomfortable.

"Ah, well," I fumbled. "Then, could you please tell her I came by, and could I give you a message to give her?"

Soter did not answer, and now I saw it was not my imagination, because the one eye I was able to see started shifting about.

"Well, er, Master Pullus," a part of me took note that he sounded as awkward as I had a moment before, "you see, the thing is, the Mistress is not accepting messages either."

I was so surprised I could not seem to move, but there was a little, tiny voice in the back of my head that seemed to be shouting for joy. Unfortunately, the rest of me overwhelmed that voice, and I tried to think of something to say.

"I see," I finally got out. "Well, may I ask if she's not receiving messages from everyone? Or," I swallowed hard, "from me in particular?"

The pause seemed to last a hundred heartbeats before Soter finally mumbled, "Only you, Master. I'm sorry."

"Oh."

I did not say anything more, spinning quickly about to begin moving away from the gate, trying to keep my shoulders back and my gait steady, although I felt like staggering; it felt like I had been punched in the stomach. You should be happy about this, the rational part of me said. True, you didn't bed her, but it's probably for the best you didn't. There was nothing but trouble ahead of you.

"Then why don't I feel happy?" I surprised myself with the sound of my own voice.

I had gone about fifty paces, approaching the intersection where I would turn and go back to camp, and had just crossed the street to head in that direction.

"Titus! Titus!"

At first, I was certain that my mind was tormenting me with the memory of her voice calling my name.

"Titus! Wait! Please!"

I turned around slowly because, honestly, I was afraid to believe my ears, but it was, in fact, Giulia, running down the street toward me. While she had grabbed a shawl to drape over her head in the proper manner, she ran so rapidly that it had blown off, so that her black hair streamed behind her as she approached, moving with a light, lithe grace that took my breath away. But she did not run into my arms, as a part of me hoped; thankfully, I had not extended them to sweep her into an embrace. Instead, she came to a stop a few paces away, slightly breathless. Her back was to her house, although I could easily look over her head to see Plotina and Soter come bustling out of the gate.

"Why don't you want to see me?" I just blurted it out, and even I could hear the hurt in my voice, making me wince, on the inside at least.

"Because Tata told me we couldn't talk. Not until..." She paused, suddenly biting her lower lip, which I had learned was a sign that she was fretting about something.

"Until what?" I asked her, then thought of something. "Oh, he's probably heard we're leaving tomorrow."

"You are?" She was clearly surprised. "I didn't know that."

"That's why I came to see you," I told her quietly. "To let you know."

I think she must have followed my eyes then, because she glanced over her shoulder and saw that her servants were within twenty paces, causing her to turn around quickly.

"It's not about you leaving." Her words came out in a rush. "It's because Tata said he'd learned something that he needs to investigate to see if it's true."

"About what?" I asked, but I was sure I knew the answer; at least my stomach seemed sure, judging by the knot in it.

"I don't know," she replied. "I was hoping maybe you did."

I shook my head and lied, "Nothing I can think of."

"You promise?" she asked me. "You promise that you don't have any idea what it could be?"

Plotina and Soter, huffing and puffing, had slowed like Giulia had, but while I expected Plotina at least to look, if not angry, then at least irritated, instead, she seemed, if anything, sad.

"Mistress…" she began, but Giulia held up a hand, silencing her.

"I know," her tone was sharp, "but it's not fair, what Tata is doing! I should at least be able to talk to him!"

"But that's not what your father…"

"I said," Giulia snapped, and even though it was approaching dark, I saw that dilation of her nostrils, and even with everything that was happening, I had to suppress a grin, "I know."

Suddenly, without any warning, which is why I suppose she did it, she crossed the few steps between us, and before I had any conscious thought about what to do, we were kissing. Except that, while we had done so before, this was the kind of kiss that made me feel like I had burst into flame, while my head began spinning.

"MISTRESS!" Plotina gasped loudly, but when Plotina grabbed Giulia by the arm, neither of us resisted, our lips parting as she was pulled away by the older woman.

"I…I'll try and find out what Tata is worried about," she told me. "But you need to promise me something else."

Plotina, now with Soter's help, was pulling her by the arms and, while she was clearly reluctant, Giulia was moving with them back to her villa as she looked over her shoulder at me.

"What is it?" I called to her, trying to maintain what was left of my composure, cursing the fact that this last view of her was marred by the shimmering of my own tears. "What do you want me to promise you?"

"That you'll come back in one piece!"

This made me laugh; it was the first time in my life that I laughed and cried at the same time.

"I will!"

It was really all I could think to say.

Before I returned to camp, I stopped at Diocles' apartment, where his family had just sat down for their evening meal, but although Birgit did her best to shove food down my throat, for once, I was not hungry.

"Something's happened," I told Diocles, then explained what little I knew based on the things Giulia had told me.

He listened with a grave expression, then sat silently for a moment.

"I think," he finally said, "what we were worried about has come to pass."

Despite knowing this was his likely answer, I suppose I had still held out a hope that he might have been able to offer some encouragement of some sort.

"So what do I do?"

He shrugged and replied, "I don't think there's a whole lot you can do. At least," he added, obviously seeing my distress, "until you know for sure. While it's the most likely explanation, there could be another reason." Eyeing me shrewdly, he asked, "Titus, why are you so upset? Surely it can't be just because you're probably not going to be able to bed this girl."

That, I confess, nettled me.

"Who said I'm upset about that?" I shot back. "Maybe it's because I'm worried that once Lucius Livinius finds out I'm not an equestrian like my Avus, he'll be sure to make that known."

"What do you care about that?" Diocles scoffed. "You're a Gregarius in the ranks, Titus! That pretty much lets the world know you're a Head Counter! How many equestrians would start out in the ranks?"

"I'm not a Gregarius; I'm a Sergeant, thank you very much," I grumbled, although his point was taken. Sighing, I could only shake my head as I confessed, "Honestly, I don't really know why I'm so upset about it. I mean," to my recollection, this was the first time I articulated what the rational part of my mind knew to be true, "I know that if I continued seeing her, it would just end badly, for one of us. Or," I admitted, "both of us."

"I know why," my former tutor replied, and I had a hint of what was coming by what I perceived as the smug tone to his voice as he sat back and finished with just a little too much satisfaction. "You're in love with Giulia. That's all."

"That's all?" I echoed, but I shook my head stubbornly. "I can't be in love!"

"And," he asked quietly, "why not?"

"Because," I answered, or at least started to, except nothing more came out. Finally, I shrugged and said, "Just because I said."

As I feared, Diocles' reaction was to laugh as he raised his cup and gave me a salute.

"Welcome to the Land of the Lost, Titus! I'm afraid you'll never be the same again!"

In that, he was more correct than even my wise Greek knew.

Although I know that I marched out of camp the next morning, I really cannot comment on any aspect of the first day because I do not remember it. So occupied with other thoughts was I that when we were ordered to halt by the Primus Pilus, then the orders were given to begin making a marching camp, I looked around in dull surprise, wondering how we had gotten to this spot. Our stopping point was along the northern bank of the Oeneus (Una) River, which is south of Siscia, and such was my state of mind, it was not until I saw the river that I even remembered where we were marching this time. Although, at this moment, we were in the territory of the Oseriates tribe, one of the smaller tribes in Pannonia, once we crossed the river the next morning, we would be entering the lands of the Maezaei. The Oseriates are not numerous in people, and their wealth is also minuscule when compared to the Maezaei, whose source of wealth came from the extensive iron mines that riddled the steep hills of their lands; consequently, they were not much threat to us, meaning we had the standard guard that night. While the Maezaei territory is not as rugged and wild as that strip of land where the Legions often found themselves, trying to root out one rebelling tribe after another, nevertheless, none of us looked forward to traversing through their holdings. And, as we were about to learn, there was a specific reason we found ourselves marching earlier than was normal, given the rotation of Cohorts. We were seated by the fire as usual that night, although honestly, I was only partly listening to the conversation, my attention only brought back to the present when Asinius stopped by our fire.

Squatting down, he began idly drawing in the dirt with one of the sticks next to our fire, and this unusual hesitation from our normally straightforward Optio was enough to draw my attention, then he finally said, "We're marching for Splonum."

As I am sure he expected, this elicited a groan from all of us, and my voice was one of them.

"Why?" Avitus asked our Optio.

Shrugging, Asinius answered, "It appears that the Maezaei have been shorting their quota of iron again."

Once more, there was a chorus of curses, and again, I joined in. Being who we were in the First meant we were all veterans, not only in battle but in the workings of this province that, from our perspective at least, had to be the most troublesome in the Republic. And, as Asinius had said, this was not the first time one of the tribes had done something like this and, frankly, while not particularly warlike, the Maezaei were one of the most egregious offenders in their attempts to thwart our officials charged with ensuring that all of the various metals contained in the hills of their territory went where they were supposed to go. Which, of course, is to Rome. However, one of the most common complaints we would hear whenever we were out in the province was how miserly our officials were when paying for the various goods produced. Being fair, we heard this from more than the Maezaei, and about more than metal; to hear the natives tell it, this extended to anything and everything they produced. In the case of the Maezaei, however, the fact that it was iron was a matter of more strategic importance to us than if it had been leather, or wood, for example. And the chieftain of the Maezaei, a man named Admetos had earned a reputation for being one of the most persistent in his attempts to cheat Rome out of our due. However, while Admetos' behavior was not a surprise; that we were returning less than two months after his last chastisement was.

"Old Admetos," opined Sido, "is getting greedier as he gets older."

"Any idea who he's been selling our allotment to this time?"

I believe it was Domitius who asked this, and this was the other prong of the problem, so to speak. As bad as it was that he was trying to cheat Rome, what we had learned was he had been selling what was rightfully ours to tribes and peoples not exactly friendly with us.

"The Primus Pilus told me it was the Roxolani and the Getae," Asinius said grimly. "And there's been talk that one or both of those tribes seem to be preparing themselves to make some mischief. Now," he shrugged, "it's just as likely that they're going to start killing each other. Or they're going to go after the Scythians. You know how it is with these barbarians. But," he spat onto the ground, "we need to stop it, whoever that iron is going to."

His message delivered, he rose and left our fire, leaving us cursing the perfidy of all barbarians.

We crossed the Oeneus first thing the next morning, then followed along its southern bank, heading in a southwesterly direction, mainly because it provides the only relatively level ground on which to march. Once we reached the junction of the first river with the Valdasus (Sana) River, we began following that, which meant we almost doubled back on our previous track. I suppose, on a map, the kind of armchair general like our previous Legate had been would have chastised Atticus for not heading directly south to cut across to the Valdasus. However, the presence of the heavily wooded ridge that thrust itself along an east/west axis, between the two rivers meant that our Primus Pilus was making the correct, and really only decision. Not that we were in any mood to thank him for this kindness; we were still unhappy about our destination, although listening, and participating in the kind of grumbling this engendered helped the miles pass under our boots. It was still early spring, so there were clumps of snow in the shaded spots, and in the mornings, we could see our breath, but by midday, it would warm up to the point we could put our *sagum* away. In many respects, it was a fine day to be out in the countryside, and normally, I would have reveled in the feeling of marching with my friends and comrades, enjoying the simple pleasures, like the way the sun glinted off our eagle, sending rays of what looked like molten gold out in all directions, or the buzzing sound as men talked, laughed, joked and sang the miles away. Not this march, however; instead, my thoughts were wholly consumed by the memory of a kiss that had set me afire. The problem, though, was not the physical aspect of those flames; I was well acquainted with the feeling of physical lust. It was how I *felt,* not in my loins but in my head, that was the issue. It was at moments like this one I wished Domitius actually marched next to me, but in our marching formation, he was in the middle of the second rank that composed our section. I briefly considered broaching the subject with Avitus, but quickly realized that he and I were of a like mind when it came to the idea of attachments, preferring them to be of a definite and finite duration. At least, that was how I *had* felt. Consequently, I remained silent, and it must be said, morose.

What makes Splonum the kind of place we did not like to visit is that there is only one approach to it, at least from the north, following the Valdasus south along the narrow valley floor. There is a spot where there is a natural choke point, where the distance across is less than a half mile between hills that tower some four hundred feet above the river. On the western slope, about a hundred feet above the floor and built where there is a sheer rock face directly below it, is a small fort. Although it can hold no more than a hundred men, the reality is that it does not need to; if those hundred men have missiles, or even rocks, they can rain death and destruction down on our heads. Once past that, the valley does open up, although at its widest, I do not believe it is more than three miles across from east to west, while it is about twice that distance from north to south. However, as menacing as the fort is, and was that day, it was Admetos' stronghold that truly gave us the most concern. Several times the size of the small fort, it was perched in a similar manner, except that it was on the top of a hill overlooking a very narrow valley, branching off the main one, and leading east. What we knew was that it was up that road where the Maezaei iron mines were located, which meant anyone who wanted access to the mines had to pass under Admetos' stronghold. From the floor of the finger valley up to the outer rampart of the stronghold was perhaps two hundred fifty paces, measured as if one was walking up the slope. While this would be long for a bow shot and completely out of range for javelins, the elevation of the stronghold and the angle of the slope actually put anyone traversing the narrow road well within the range of arrows, if fired from above. And although whenever we first subdued the Maezaei, their artillery pieces had been confiscated, I know I was not alone in my belief that the wily old chieftain had replaced them with new ones he had hidden away somewhere. The final challenge facing us was that the only way up to the stronghold was by following a winding road located on the opposite, or southern side of the stronghold from the road leading to the mines. Working in our favor was one simple, yet extremely important fact, which was that by this point, almost twenty years after Augustus first pacified the province, the tribes of Pannonia had each gotten a taste of Roman retribution, brought down upon their heads when they had forgotten who was in control of their collective fates. Nevertheless, it is one thing to consider this and rely on it for protection when one is sitting in your section hut; marching under the fort as the stronghold came into view as we followed the slight curve was a different matter altogether.

When we were in view of the first small fort, but still out of missile range, we were halted by the Primus Pilus. Our *Cornicen,* Varo, sounded the notes summoning the other Centurions of the Cohort, while Atticus and Asinius walked backward a short distance. The conference was very brief; why this was so became apparent when Atticus returned. Although he still insisted on wearing his hair longer than had been the fashion with the rest of the Army of Pannonia, I admit I was somewhat disgruntled that, over the previous three years, some men had begun copying his style, rather than his adapting to our practice. In other ways, however, Atticus had become more accustomed to life on the frontier, and the most notable change was his language. When he had first arrived, it did not take us long to notice how bland his talk was, without any of the verbal seasoning added to the stew of his language that was, and is, such an integral part of communication between men of the Legions. We came to the collective conclusion that vulgarity was not allowed in the Praetorian Guard; fortunately, it was one of the first bad habits our Primus Pilus picked up from us.

"All right," he began, "it's time to tell you bastards what's happening." He paused a breath, then said, "Legate Sabinus has ordered that we bring Admetos with us back to Siscia." There was a ripple of comment about this, except it was about to get worse. "To stand trial."

"Pluto's cock," I swore, but under my breath, although my comrades around me were no less disposed to curse this news.

At least now, I thought with a bit of bitterness, I know why he didn't tell us until just this moment.

"The Maezaei aren't going to like that much," I heard Avitus mutter, but while there was no way Atticus heard him, when he continued, "I know that the Maezaei aren't going to be very happy about this," neither of us could help snickering.

"Pullus, I'm glad you and Avitus think this is funny," Atticus snapped, and I felt my face start to burn. "Especially since you're going to be with me when we break the news."

The probability that he had planned this all along did not make me feel any better, nor, I could tell, Avitus, as we glanced at each other, both of us silently blaming the other. I suppose Atticus was satisfied he had ruined our day sufficiently, because he returned his attention back to the Century.

"We're going to show them we're here and mean business, so I want shield covers off. Also," he pointed to the side of the road opposite the river, "ground your packs here. Tenth Section, you're gear guard!"

"Lucky bastards," someone behind me murmured, but I was determined I would not give the Primus Pilus any more chances to chew on my already tender rear parts.

"We're going to be coming back this way, so that's why I'm sending the Sixth up to occupy that fort. But," he warned us, "we're not going to make a show of it. The rest of us are going to march by, while the Sixth peels off and climbs up there and makes sure none of these barbarian *cunni* are in a position to make any mischief when we leave."

This made sense; it was at times like this where I imagined the difference between Atticus and the dead Barbatus was most evident, despite them both being Praetorians. It was a tiny thing, perhaps, but could prove to be the difference between returning to Siscia whole, or carrying casualties with us. Now that we understood why we were there, we hurried to comply with our orders, moving off the road to drop our *furcae*, then stripping off our shield covers. There was an air of suppressed excitement, but although it was nowhere near the level we experienced before we actually went into battle, one difference I noticed was there was more anxious nervousness than normal, the cause of which I am sure came from the element of the unknown. Whereas before a fight we knew what to expect, although we had all witnessed or been part of encounters with the natives where passions had flared up into some sort of violence, never before had we been dispatched to arrest a chieftain to bring back for trial. The Legate – this man I have no fear of naming, Gaius Calvisius Sabinus – was only about thirty, it is true, but he was not made of the same material as our previous Legate, and I mean that as a compliment. However, I will also admit this was his most drastic and aggressive action by far. Still, we did not hesitate in carrying out his orders, quickly forming back up on the road. Seeing that the other Centuries had done as we had, he ordered Varo to sound the call to advance, and we resumed marching toward Splonum.

Splonum, at least then, was still a barbarian town, although there was a section where those Roman inhabitants, mostly merchants and men involved with the iron ore business in some way, lived and worked. However, somewhat to our surprise, their behavior at our appearance was more aligned with the barbarians than that of Roman citizens. After thinking about it some, I recognized we should not have expected them to welcome us with open arms. After all, they would be left behind after we came and left. And, somehow, not only the Roman contingent but the Maezaei seemed to understand our purpose for being there. I find it hard to credit that they knew the specifics, yet they did seem to recognize that our appearance was not part of the regular routine where Rome reminded the natives that it was, in fact, us in charge of the province. While it was not stemming from the same reasons, when we marched into Splonum, I was struck by the similarities between this day and one where I had accompanied Urso into Topulcava. On that occasion, however, we had been operating off the books, as we say, as part of our former Primus Pilus' scheme that, at the time, I knew very little about. The fact that we were here for purely official reasons certainly did not seem to matter to the barbarians who immediately started gathering in the center of the town. Since we could not turn around to gawk, I had to listen for signs that might give me a hint of the Sixth's progress, but while I heard some shouting, it was impossible to discern the meaning. Like the rest of the First Cohort, we had to count on the Primus Hastatus Posterior, my former Optio Aulus Galens, and the men of the Sixth to secure the small fort. It is a hard, hard lesson for a man under the standard to learn, yet I believe it is crucial to an individual's success to pick up how to put away those things over which he has no control, tucking them into a corner of his mind instead of worrying about something outside his power to change. Being brutally honest, while I had gotten better at it, on this day, it was still a struggle, and in some ways, it was a benefit that the Maezaei villagers began congregating so quickly, because I had little time to dwell on the success of the Sixth. While Atticus sounded the halt, by prearrangement it became clear this was just meant for our Century; the Second continued on past us, moving in the direction of the narrow finger valley that led to the mines, while the Third moved past us, still heading south, to the opposite end of the town from which we entered. The Fourth marched to a spot directly opposite us, but on the far side of the common area, while the Fifth did essentially the same thing, but positioning themselves on the western edge of the common. Because the town was actually nestled in a loop of the river, the Fifth had it to their back, meaning an attack from the rear by any Maezaei warriors would come with plenty of warning. Certainly, I was still uneasy, but the way Atticus had positioned us did much to calm me, and I believe my comrades felt the same way. Regardless of that, I reminded myself, this is the easy part.

"First Section, come with me!"

As we obeyed, Atticus beckoned to Asinius, who trotted up, but I could not hear what was said, although I saw the Optio nod his head. However, trying to judge from his facial expressions what was taking place I knew from long experience was a fruitless exercise, so I barely gave either of them a glance. Instead, I studied the faces surrounding us, finding some comfort in the fact that, while the villagers were looking on coldly, they did not seem disposed to open violence. Nevertheless, I also understood how quickly this could change, so I did not relax my guard at all as Atticus beckoned us to follow him. We began walking in the direction of where the road that led up to the stronghold began, but before we had gone a hundred paces, a man wearing the colors of his tribe came hurrying from that general direction. He was accompanied by a half-dozen other men who were clearly warriors; judging from their manner and dress, these men were part of the Maezaei king's royal guard. Still, I could not fault the man's demeanor as he gave a clear signal to the guards to halt while he continued a few paces farther on, lifting his hand with his palm out in the kind of salute we all recognized as a signal of peaceful intentions. At least, I thought grimly, to begin with.

"Centurion!" His accent was thick, but he spoke Latin clearly. "To what do we owe the honor of this…visit?"

"Who are you?" our Primus Pilus asked bluntly, although if the man took offense, he gave no sign.

"My name is Dodonis." He bowed as he said this. "I am privileged enough to be the chief councilor to our great king Admetos, son of Rando, ruler of the mighty Maezaei and…"

"Yes, yes," Atticus cut him off testily. "I know. There's no need to list all his titles and honors. Where is he?"

Now there was no mistaking the outrage on the face of the king's councilor who, to my eyes at least, looked as oily and soft as any of the pampered patricians who fawned about Augustus, at least as I imagined them to be since I had never seen them personally. Soft he may have been, but he glared at our Primus Pilus, refusing to answer.

Seeing that he was not going to get a response, Atticus snapped, "Fine." Then, turning to us, he beckoned and said curtly, "Follow me. We're going to see if we can find him." He barked to Asinius, telling him, "Keep the rest of the Century down here, but if you hear me blowing the whistle, you better come like Cerberus is about gnaw on your balls!"

Ironically enough, this was one time where I found myself in complete and utter agreement with my Primus Pilus; honestly, I would have preferred to be accompanied by the entire Century.

However, as I understood, this would have made matters worse. Knowing this and feeling secure, on the other hand, were two very different matters altogether. Ascending the road, I am sure I was no different from the rest of the men of the First Section, trying to keep one eye on the stronghold above us while maintaining a straight line of march. The road leading to the stronghold was wide enough for a wagon, with just a bit of room left over, although there were no wagons on it at the moment. Who was present, however, was much more troubling. Lining both sides of the road, starting about halfway up it to the stronghold, were what I assumed were the rest of Admetos' royal guard who had come out of the fortress to arrange themselves thusly. But, in accordance with the laws governing Pannonia, none of these men were armed, or at least they were not openly displaying them. Nor were they adorned in their full armor, at least as far as we could tell, although it was possible they had donned some sort of protection underneath their tunics. Between their hostile gazes and how many of them seemingly happened to have suddenly decided to go for a walk, judging by how many of them were holding walking staffs, my heart was beating even faster than the climb required. As we did in such situations, the First Section was following behind the Primus Pilus in a column that was four abreast and four deep, and since he was leading us, it was impossible to have a hint of what he was thinking at this sullen, resentful reception. I will say his stride never faltered, nor did he deign to turn his head in either direction, clearly ignoring the implied threat. That, I supposed, would be our problem, and our job to handle should matters degenerate.

Although the predominant sound came from our boots on the hard packed road surface, since I was on the outside and closest, once we reached the first of the warriors, I clearly heard the muttered curses, although they were mostly in the barbarian tongue. Frankly, I stopped listening after a few moments, yet while I tried to emulate Atticus by keeping my gaze straight ahead, I am afraid I was not as successful as he was. The road reversed on itself four times as it climbed the hill, but even so, the grade was still fairly steep, so that we were all puffing by the time we reached the top. There, a flat space had been carved out of the side of the hill to accommodate the stronghold, along with room left over for what I imagine was an assembly ground outside the heavy twin doors. The walls of the structure were not that high, perhaps twelve feet, but there was clearly a parapet because there were even more men standing above us on the walls. Despite these men being empty handed also, I held no illusions, nor I am sure did any of the others, that each of them did not have a weapon of some sort close to hand, just out of view. The man Dodonis, who had started out walking backward as he tried in vain to stop Atticus but had given up and was walking alongside the Primus Pilus, paused outside the gates of the stronghold, one of which was opened.

"I will let our king know that you request an audience with him," Dodonis, despite his soft appearance, was actually puffing less than the rest of us.

His words prompted a harsh snort from Atticus as the Primus Pilus turned and pointed at the Maezaei with his *vitus*.

"I'm not requesting anything." His tone was hard and unyielding. "Your chief Admetos' presence is required. I'm to deliver a message! Now," the *vitus* moved to point to the stronghold, "go get him. And be quick about it!"

The low chorus of conversation that had surrounded us grew instantly into what sounded to my ears like a growling outrage, prompting me to wonder how many of these barbarians around us spoke our tongue. The recipient of this treatment was clearly as angered by our Primus Pilus' words and tone, but he managed to contain his anger, giving a stiff bow before turning about and walking on stiff legs into the stronghold.

"Deliver a message?" I heard Manius Catulus say from directly behind me, his normal spot in our formation fifth down from me, putting him directly behind me at the moment. "Why did he say that? We're not here to deliver a...."

"Quiet, idiot," the man to his left, who happened to be Balbinus, hissed. "He just said that to keep these *cunni* calm for as long as possible."

"Oh," Catulus muttered sheepishly.

While we waited, I noticed that although the men who had been lining the road stayed where they were, a small crowd was gathering, and their appearance puzzled me. The composition of this growing group was not uniformly male, but it was not until I saw a couple faces I had recognized earlier when we first arrived before I understood these people had followed us up the road. We were not waiting long; perhaps the span of two hundred heartbeats, yet in that short period, very quickly, there were at least two hundred people surrounding us on the level ground outside the walls of the fortress. It made me wonder how Asinius, standing with the rest of the Century, had allowed them to follow us up the road, although the answer to that was unimportant in the moment. Naturally, the addition of more people meant the noise level rose, as the villagers surrounding us speculated on the meaning of what was taking place, which only increased our anxiety. Finally, an older man emerged from the stronghold, followed by Dodonis, who was clearly deferring to the first. In age, I estimated him to be in his fifties, and what hair he had left was an iron gray that, in color at least, reminded me of the Colapiani chieftain Draxo. That, however, was where the similarity ended. While Draxo had been large, one of the few men who matched my size, Admetos was slightly built, walking with a minor stoop. And, while his clothing was of good quality, his cloak almost swallowed him whole, adding to his air of frailty. Atop his head he wore what I assumed was a bronze circlet, but it was very worn and tarnished, although I thought I saw the glint of some sort of gemstones embedded in it. Like his guard, he wore no armor; all in all, he was a completely unremarkable man, with a sallow complexion that belied a life spent indoors, at least recently. Maybe, I remember thinking, he was different when he was younger. But he was old then, and looked feeble to my eyes. The idea that this might have been exactly the impression he wanted to convey did not occur to me until later. He approached Atticus, and I saw that he at least made an effort to draw himself erect so that I could see he was actually a couple of inches taller than our Primus Pilus. Yet even with this height advantage, to anyone with eyes it was clear to see who was the man with the power and who was not.

"Are you Admetos?" Atticus asked peremptorily.

Admetos did not reply, verbally at least, but inclined his head.

"Our king does not understand Latin well enough to feel comfortable speaking it," Dodonis explained.

"Then you can interpret this for him," Atticus replied. Reaching down, he withdrew a scroll he had been carrying under his *baltea* and unrolled it. Reading from it, he spoke in loud, ringing tones, "By the authority vested in the Legate of the province of Pannonia, Gaius Calvisius Sabinus, given such authority by our divine Princeps, Gaius Octavianus Caesar Augustus, and the Senate and People of Rome, I, Gaius Sempronius Atticus, Primus Pilus of the 8th Legion, have been ordered to take into custody the Maezaei known as Admetos..."

If he got any further, I could not hear it, as those few who understood our tongue instantly relayed the essence of the order being read by Atticus to the others, who were understandably enraged. As reasonable as their reaction might have been, it nevertheless did not bode well, yet despite the sudden roaring of the crowd, Atticus turned and beckoned to us.

Forced to bellow over the crowd, he ordered, "Front rank! Come forward and take the prisoner into custody!"

"We're fucked," I heard Avitus say, but he stepped forward without hesitation as I did, and the four of us – Avitus, Sido, Bovinus, and I – surrounded Admetos who, if I am any judge, looked bewildered by what was happening.

"You cannot do this!" Dodonis shouted, over and over.

"We can, and we will." Atticus, I must say, looked completely unflustered by the rapidly growing commotion. "He's being brought back to Siscia to stand trial."

"For what?" Dodonis screeched, although he had to pause between outbursts to apprise his king in his native tongue of what was going on.

"For theft and fraud," Atticus informed him. "Your *king*," this time, he pointed his *vitus* directly in Admetos' face, "has been cheating us on your shipments of iron ore! And he's been selling what he's supposed to be giving to us to enemies of Rome!"

"That is not true!" Dodonis shouted, and this time, he actually began hopping up and down. "He has done no such thing!"

"Then," Atticus gave an elaborate shrug, "he's got nothing to worry about. He can clear his name at the trial."

As this exchange was taking place, most of which I gleaned from reading the lips of the two parties, the villagers had begun closing in their circle around us. I cannot say with any exactness, but it was about then I was suddenly transported, at least in my mind, back to an eerily similar scene, when I had briefly been under the control of Urso for his off-the-books business. That time, we had been taking young Colapiani back to Siscia with us as part of the arrangement between Draxo and Urso, one part of the payment by the Colapiani for the old armor and helmets Urso had been selling to them. While it was true that in Topulcava we had been taking more than one man away with us, I suspected that the identity of this lone tribesman outweighed the collective value of a bunch of raw barbarian youths, at least to these people around us. They now understood we intended to take their leader with us, but in a manner similar to the way I had seen Urso cow a clearly enraged Draxo, who was a much more formidable figure than this Dodonis or Admetos combined, Atticus addressed Dodonis. I could not hear what was said, but I can guess; essentially, our Primus Pilus informed this Maezaei of what awaited him and his fellow tribesmen if we were not allowed to conduct our duties. I did see Atticus point, first back from where we had come, which was now blocked, then at us. Actually, he pointed directly at me, which I did not like at all. Whatever he said was what seemed to make the most impression as, first Dodonis, followed by Admetos once Dodonis translated, turned their gazes at me, then slumped in a clear sign of defeat. I saw Admetos close his eyes, then take a deep breath before raising his hands in a gesture for silence. Much to my surprise, the crowd fell silent, or relatively so, more quickly than I would have thought given how worked up they had become. I suppose they wanted to hear from their king what was happening, but the sudden drop in noise was dramatic, and at least for me, much welcomed. Despite my time in the province, I had still only picked up a smattering of the native languages; making matters more difficult was that each tribe speaks a different dialect, with different inflections and even words. From what I could gather, however, Admetos was doing his best to assure his people that this was a huge misunderstanding, and matters would be resolved peacefully. At least, that was what I thought he was saying; it was not until later that I learned that the word I had translated as "misunderstanding," while it meant that with most tribes, with the Maezaei, it actually meant "injustice." Also, the old chieftain demonstrated a level of cunning in the way the language of his body posture seemed to communicate to us Romans who could not understand his spoken words that he was trying to placate his people, but as we were about to learn, those gestures did not align with what he was saying at all. Fortunately, as I learned later, the other four of us who were slightly separated from the rest of the section, all saw and interpreted the reaction of the surrounding Maezaei correctly, and just in time.

"Shields up!" Atticus snapped over his shoulder in the eyeblink before the relative quiet was shattered by the explosion of outrage as Admetos finished what turned out to be a plea for protection from his people.

If it had been only verbal, while it would have been unsettling, it was nothing we could not handle, but we were instantly surrounded by the people who had previously been giving us space by standing in an invisible ring that, by no coincidence, was just beyond the reach of our swords. This buffer evaporated, but while those nearest us were mostly the civilian villagers, and at this moment were content to shake their fists, because of my height I could look over their heads to see that a line of men were shoving their way through the crowd. Just before they pushed their way to the first line enveloping us, I glanced over my shoulder at Admetos who, I must say, no longer looked quite as frail as he had a moment before. Our eyes met, and the hatred and malice that glittered in his eyes was a look with which any of us who had served in Pannonia were intimately familiar. In the confusion of the moment, Dodonis had been shoved aside by the irate villagers, but he came elbowing his way through the surrounding crowd now, panting more from this effort than he had exerted ascending the road, his face red and shining from perspiration.

"You," the only overt action Atticus had taken was to take a single step backward, closer to us, and I had to marvel at his calm as he pointed his *vitus* again at the councilor, "better explain to your king what's going to happen if he doesn't call this rabble off!"

As one might expect, Dodonis looked like the unhappiest man in Splonum at the moment, as well he might have been.

"He is my king," he pleaded with Atticus. "I cannot command him to do anything!"

"Fine," Atticus snapped, but I was completely unprepared for what he did next.

Wheeling about, putting his back to the crowd, an extremely courageous or foolhardy move, probably an equal mixture of both, he pointed his *vitus* once more.

Except this time, he was pointing at me, yet as he did so, he looked over his shoulder at Dodonis, making what he said difficult to hear over the noise, but I managed to make him out as he said, "I told you who that is, didn't I?" I saw Dodonis' head bob up and down; I had not thought it possible, but he was clearly even unhappier, and I understood why as Atticus continued, "If he could slay Draxo of the Colapiani, what do you think he'll do to your king?" Whipping his head about, his gaze pierced me and I felt my bowels lurch as my Primus Pilus ordered, "Pullus! Go stand behind that *cunnus*! But *don't* draw your sword until I give the command!"

My mouth was too dry to utter the expected reply that tells our superior that we not only heard and understood our orders, but would obey them, and I saw his eyes narrow as I complied with his command. That's perfect, I thought miserably, he's going to chew me to ribbons if we get out of this alive. Nevertheless, I felt my body moving, yet as I did so, Atticus did as well, except when he did, it was to move into the spot I vacated so the overall integrity of our small formation was still intact. Now, if looking from above, it was Admetos and I surrounded on four sides by my comrades and Primus Pilus. I must admit I did take some grim satisfaction that, suddenly, Admetos did not look quite so smug as I stepped past him, and while I was careful not to touch him, I could see he was trembling. Meanwhile, from his new spot, Atticus continued his harangue of Dodonis.

"If you don't get this bunch to step aside," he warned Dodonis, "I'm going to have my Sergeant here rip your chieftain's head off with his bare hands."

That was why he didn't want me drawing my sword, I realized, but on the heels of that came the thought: Am I actually strong enough to do what he says? It was a decidedly peculiar feeling, and I found my eyes looking down to the chieftain's neck, while I felt my hands beginning to flex as at least a part of me considered how to go about this task. Granted, his neck was scrawny, but my instinct was that he would prove to be similar to what happened when an old mule went lame and we were forced to consume it; the meat was tough and stringy, and difficult to chew, or tear apart. Somehow, I felt it was probable that ripping Admetos' head off would prove to be a similar experience.

"If you do that, Centurion," Dodonis' words were at odds with his tone, which was clearly pleading, "I cannot hold these people from descending on you!"

"And then, we'll die," Atticus agreed, but his tone was as matter of fact as it was grim. "And you know what happens then. None of these people," this time he did not raise his *vitus*, but indicated the crowd with his head, "will survive." He paused for a moment, then said something else that, while it proved to be the clinching argument, it also sent a shiver through my body, as I am certain it did to the others. "Do you remember what happened to the Varciani after the Primus Pilus who came before me fell? Surely you've heard about it."

When Atticus uttered the name of the tribe upon whom we had exacted such a terrible vengeance after Urso was slain, Admetos' body went rigid, and I noticed there was a sudden sheen of sweat on his neck. Well, well, I thought with cruel humor, you may not understand much, but you heard him bring up the Varciani, and I'll wager you know what he's talking about.

One more time, I saw Dodonis' body announce our victory, his head dropping as he closed his eyes and replied just loudly enough to be heard over the still-shouting crowd, "Yes, Centurion. All of Pannonia knows you Romans butchered the Varciani."

"Then you know that unless you get these people in hand," Atticus' tone remained as harsh as before, "the same fate is going to befall your tribe as well. Now," this time he did point back at the crowd, "get this mob under control. Or," he picked up the bone whistle on the lanyard around his neck, "I blow this, and my men will know we're under attack up here."

As proof of his seriousness, Atticus placed the whistle between his lips, and that action seemed to be exactly what both Dodonis and Admetos needed, because suddenly, it was the old chief speaking.

Thrusting his arms up into the air again, this time it took longer to get the crowd under control, but finally, they became quiet enough so he could be heard. Given my mangling of his speech before, I actually only listened for a couple words, and one in particular, and when he uttered the name of the Varciani, I instantly looked past him to the mob. Their first reaction seemed to be one of shock, but while their residual anger returned, there was also a palpable fear on their collective faces as, presumably, Admetos explained the fate that awaited them should they not allow us to leave. What I can say is that, although I took some comfort in the idea that everything Atticus had described to Dodonis would happen, the fact that it would only happen because we were dead certainly dampened that feeling. Nevertheless, despite their anger and obvious reluctance, very slowly at first, the crowd started to shuffle back away from us. I glanced over my shoulder and saw that the people behind us were doing the same. The relief at the reappearance of the other members of the section, still standing in their spot, was so overwhelming my legs started shaking.

With Dodonis preceding us, our progress back down the road was slow, and every step was fraught with a tension I had never experienced before. The only thing I can liken it to is if one were going to try and cross a frozen lake where it is not clear whether the ice is thick enough, so that each step is tentative as one shifts their weight, waiting for the cracking sound that gives a warning that you are about to plunge into the icy water. Since those presumed royal guards lower on the road had been out of earshot, they had to be informed by Dodonis that we were indeed leading their king away to an uncertain fate. Twice, Admetos was required to assure his guards that Dodonis was telling the truth. Only then did the men step aside – grudgingly, it is true – but move from our path they did. Their hostility was almost palpable as we marched by, even from where I was, still behind Admetos, my hand on his shoulder at Atticus' order. Which, speaking bluntly, I thought was a mistake. Growing up in these parts, I believed, and still do, that I had a better idea about the peculiar customs and practices of these wild people, and I knew that touching someone they considered royalty without their permission was a grave insult and offense. Fortunately for all concerned, my fear that there would be some sort of backlash proved unfounded, and we managed to reach the valley floor safely. Still, our troubles were far from over. Once we were reunited with the rest of the Cohort, and Atticus had Varo sound the reassembly, we were facing north, back in the direction from which we had come, when Dodonis approached Atticus.

"Surely you are not going to just take our king away unaccompanied?"

For the first time, I saw our Primus Pilus exhibit some uncertainty, but he shook his head and replied, "Our orders are to escort your king back to Siscia. They didn't say anything about bringing his concubines and slaves."

I suppose, given his role, it should not have surprised me that this was one insult too many for a courtier like Dodonis to bear, because for the first time, he displayed a sense of anger and indignation that approached that of his fellow tribespeople a short time before.

"That," he snapped, apparently forgetting to whom he was talking, "is unacceptable!"

What was not surprising in the least was Atticus' reaction.

"I don't give a fart in a *testudo* whether you think it's acceptable or not!" he snapped right back. "My orders are..."

"Your orders are to escort our king back for a *trial*," Dodonis cut him off, and although I was certainly not on his side, I must admit my respect for this barbarian went up a notch. Not, however, that it meant much. "And you Romans make a great deal of noise about the superiority of your legal system. And," I saw Atticus opening his mouth, but Dodonis held up a hand and I had to stifle a grin at the look of shock on Atticus' face as I wondered when was the last time someone had cut him off, "one of the principles of your system is that the accused is entitled to a defense."

"Which will be provided for him," Atticus began, but again, Dodonis interrupted him.

"A *Roman* will defend him?" Dodonis shook his head adamantly. "That is not justice! Our king is entitled to at least have one of his advisors with him as he faces these charges. Which," I suppose he felt compelled to add this, "are completely untrue."

I cannot say what was in my Primus Pilus' mind, but from outward appearances, he seemed to share my respect for this Maezaei despite not wanting to do so.

"That," he finally said grudgingly, "makes sense." His smile was not comforting, nor was it meant to be as he pointed at Dodonis. "So you need to go gather some things for you and your king, and be quick about it. Since you'll be the one going."

If Atticus hoped to surprise Dodonis, he clearly did not, because the councilor merely bowed his head in acknowledgement, then turned to inform Admetos of what had just happened. Except, much to our surprise, Admetos did not seem to be happy with this at all, which prompted a brief but intense discussion between the two before, once more, Dodonis bowed to his king.

Turning to face Atticus, Dodonis said, "There is one other…complication."

"By the gods, what now?" Atticus groaned.

"Are you expecting the king to walk?" Dodonis asked.

"Of course," Atticus replied, but this was too much for my self-control, and before I could stop myself, I cleared my throat, loudly.

Atticus clearly understood this to be a signal, and he whirled about to glower at me.

"What is it, Pullus?" he snapped.

While I did want to say something, I did not want to say it out in front of either Dodonis or Admetos, and it took him a moment to realize that. With a curse, he relented, walking over to me, then dragging me several feet away.

"What?" he repeated.

"Two things," I whispered. "First is that it's considered a huge insult for a king to walk anywhere. Unless he chooses to."

"Then he better fucking well choose to," he snapped. "Because there's no way I'm letting him sit on a horse."

This was the reply I had expected, which was why I had a second point to make.

Indicating the chieftain with my head, I asked him quietly, "How fast do you think we're going to be able to move if he's forced to walk?"

This, I could see, scored a blow, and he sucked in a breath as he recognized what I was saying.

"That," he allowed, "is a good point." Nevertheless, he shook his head stubbornly as he repeated, "But I'm not letting him sit on a horse. That would give him ideas." A shadow of a smile flitted across his features as he stepped back and made a show of looking me up and down. "Maybe I should have you carry him. You're strong enough."

Now, this was not at all what I had in mind, so I hurried on to explain my idea. As I did, the shadow of a smile turned into a real one, and he actually laughed.

"That," he slapped me on the shoulder, "is an excellent suggestion, Pullus!"

Turning away from me, he called to Dodonis, "I think we have a solution!"

About a third of a watch later, we were fully formed back up, although this time, it was not the First Century leading back the way from where we had come. Instead, we had the rearguard, but while we were followed for a short distance by Maezaei, mostly members of the royal guard who watched sullenly as we marched away, we were unmolested. Not, it must be admitted, without one last drama, when both Dodonis and Admetos came close to refusing the mounts we had offered. Being fair, I could understand their sudden reluctance; there is no way for any man to look dignified astride one of the Legion mules. And when those mules are tethered together and their leads are held not by their riders but by a Legionary, their humiliation at the very idea was such that they balked. Nevertheless, when we marched away, it was with them astride their mounts. It was not a complete victory for us; by the time all was said and done, there were no less than a half-dozen Maezaei aboard their own mules, which created another set of problems. When the load normally carried by a section mule has to be distributed to other animals, when it is one or two animals, it is not a real hardship. With a half-dozen, however, matters become more complicated, at least for the animals, and before we stopped for the day, we had two more animals go lame. Which, of course, further hampered our progress. Normally, this is an inconvenience, but I bring it up because I believe it was a contributing factor to what happened. Because of our slower movement, we made camp well short of the spot we had stopped on our way to Splonum, which meant instead of two days, our return march would take three. From the perspective of my comrades, I know this was hardly a consideration; after all, when we had marched out of Siscia, we had expected to be out of camp for two weeks. I, on the other hand, did not share this view; for me, an extra day was a tragedy, although it was only partially because of this fever for Giulia that was consuming me. Never far from my mind was what I had learned just before we left, and my fear was that whatever it was her father had learned that had led to his decision to stop Giulia from seeing me would come to light while I was gone. Looking back at matters now, I understand that even if I had been present, it would have been unlikely to change anything, but in the moment, I was sure that if I had the opportunity to react immediately, I would be able to answer any challenge.

Sitting around the fire that night, my mind was far away until I was jerked back to the present when Avitus spoke up, saying, "I thought Pullus was going to drop a load of *cac* when the Primus Pilus told him to go stand behind that old bastard."

"I was not," I protested. "I just didn't know how I was going to rip his head off with my bare hands!"

"Bah." Domitius laughed. "That'd mean you thought you might not be strong enough! And we all know that's not even possible."

Not surprisingly, this made the others laugh, but honestly, I did not mind the diversion away from my more troubling thoughts.

"I didn't say I wasn't strong enough," I shot back. "I've just never actually ripped someone's head off, so I was trying to figure out how to do it!"

Naturally, this led to a lively debate on exactly how one would go about such a task, yet when I asked for volunteers to try the various methods suggested, for some reason, I had no takers.

"If you're so sure I couldn't do that," I aimed this at Balbinus, who had been the most vociferous in expressing his doubt, "then why should you be so afraid to let me try?"

Still, he refused to rise to the bait, and the rest of the evening passed with relatively high spirits, and my other woes were forgotten, albeit temporarily. We retired for the night with the Third Century standing guard, at half strength, which to those unfamiliar with the composition of the First Cohorts of Legions might appear to have contributed to the events of later that night. However, it must be remembered that, since every Century of the First Cohort is twice the size of a normal Century, half strength means the equivalent of a full Century on guard. And, while our camps are laid out in the exact same manner no matter what size of force it encloses, it means it is a matter of scale. Instead of the *praetorium* tent that is used by a Legate, in its place is the tent of the Primus Pilus, and the forum in front of the tent is correspondingly smaller. While this certainly helps matters in the construction of our camps, as we learned that night, it also means that our enemies know exactly where to go when they mean to strike us in a surprise attack. Or, in this case, attempt to rescue their king.

The regularity of the layout of our Cohort camp also meant that it was me and my comrades who were the closest to Atticus' tent when, towards the end of the third night watch, about a full watch before dawn, when people are at their deepest level of sleep, a party of seven Maezaei somehow managed to slip into the camp. Only after the fact was it learned how this was accomplished; the body of a Gregarius, his throat slit, was found in the ditch outside his part of the wall. And, as much as it pains me to say it, if it had not been because a Gregarius in the Fifth Century was suffering from a bout of dysentery that sent him staggering to the latrine who happened to see a series of dark shapes crossing the forum in the direction of the Primus Pilus' tent, they might very well have succeeded. If not in freeing their king, perhaps in slaying or wounding Crito, the Legion's chief slave and clerk who slept in the outer portion of the Primus Pilus' quarters, along with Atticus' body slave and maybe the Primus Pilus himself. Not that they would have found Admetos or Dodonis;

they and the rest of the Maezaei party were actually being held under guard in the tent of the Primus Pilus Posterior, Aulus Macerinus.

"Intruders! Intruders! In the forum!"

By this point, my fifth year under the standard, while I was not nearly as heavy a sleeper as I had been when I joined, by the time I roused myself, the other seven occupants of my tent were already up and scrambling outside. I grabbed my harness, but I did not even bother with my armor, and all I can say in my defense is that I was only a couple paces behind the rest of my comrades. The Gregarius' alarm had, as one might expect, roused the camp, so there was a clamor of shouting accompanying the flurry of activity that was only dimly illuminated by the torches that are placed at regular intervals. Just outside the entrance to the Primus Pilus' tent, I saw several darkened figures; these warriors had rubbed charcoal over every inch of exposed skin, while wearing dark clothes as well. Even as we ran in their direction, I heard a shout from inside Atticus' tent, and another dark figure suddenly emerged from inside. It took a moment for my eye to take in the scene and make sense of what it was seeing, that the man emerging from the tent was, in fact, staggering backward several paces before he collapsed on the ground. Although I do not remember doing so, I obviously dropped my harness after I unsheathed my sword, but I lengthened my stride to first catch, then outstrip my comrades racing towards our Primus Pilus' tent. It is only after moments like this where I think back on my actions and I can view matters more objectively, I recognize this one was another occasion where my overwhelming desire for glory and to perform deeds in which my Avus and father could take pride took over. That it was my grandfather's Gallic-forged sword that Sextus and Diocles had brought with them three years before, and this was the first chance I had to use it for its true purpose in slaying the enemies of Rome only played a role in my subconscious. In the moment, all I saw were foes who had managed to penetrate our defenses, and that was enough of a blow to my pride in both a personal and collective sense that I almost elbowed my friends aside in my haste to reach our adversaries. I do not want to give the impression that it was just the First Section coming; from every direction around the forum, other men of the First Cohort came running, all of them as intent on slaying these intruders as I was. It was only because of my longer legs that enabled me to be the first, at least from our side of the forum, to reach them as the dark warriors of the Maezaei, without any order I heard, suddenly arranged themselves in a rough approximation of an *orbis,* each of them facing outward. As was usual, they were not as uniformly armed as we were; the only weapon missing were their war spears, but I assumed at the time this was due to the difficulty posed by trying to sneak about with a spear catching on things. The other commonality among them was that none of them carried shields, although a few of us had thought to snatch our own up; I was not one of them, nor was the rest of my section. I selected the nearest warrior who held his sword out in front of him, waving it about in an attempt to confuse his foe, yet I barely paused as I came charging in at him. Despite my seeming eagerness, however, there was a method to my attack; even in the dim light, I had seen he was waving the longer, Gallic-style sword with the more rounded tip – a slashing rather than a stabbing weapon. Consequently, I knew that my best tactic was to get inside the arc of the warrior's defensive circle, and this I did quite easily. This is not to say he did not attempt to stop me, but he was slow; no doubt, the dim lighting did not help his cause, so that when he swung his sword, I was already inside the most dangerous part of his attempt to decapitate me. And, being honest, this man was quite strong, because while I deflected his blade with my own, even as mine struck his less than two feet from the hilt of his sword, my arm was jerked violently back and down from the force of his blow. However, although I was not holding my shield, in an automatic reaction my left arm thrust out, except instead of the boss of my shield, it was my fist that struck him in the face, the blow sneaking inside his own blade. Despite the fact that after my wounding at The Quarry, my left arm has never been exactly the same, in a punch launched from my shoulder where my arm is within the plane of my body and thus supported, the power behind it is almost unchanged. Consequently, my foe staggered backward as my fist connected with his face, yet he was no novice, making another swing with his blade as he recoiled that forced me to imitate him and dodge backward, thereby buying him another few heartbeats. Unfortunately for him, that was the length of his reprieve, because before he could fully recover, I was already stepping forward and keeping up the pressure on him. He did manage to parry my first thrust, but the second I launched came too quickly after the first for him to bring his longer, more cumbersome blade to bear. The point of my sword struck him just under his breastbone, but while there was some resistance, I knew just from the feel that this warrior was not wearing mail; after it was over, we discovered that every man was wearing a *cuirass* of boiled leather, which is better than nothing, but not by much.

With my first opponent falling backward, I was already pivoting to fall on another Maezaei, who by this time, had his hands full trying to fend off the attack from Publius Appuleius, who was easy to identify despite the dim lighting just from the way in which he wielded his sword. Appuleius was an ardent follower of gladiatorial games, and in my role as weapons instructor, I had noticed he had a tendency towards what I would characterize as a more flamboyant style, where his slashes began from a point farther outside his body than the way we are trained. However, in this instance, this worked to Appuleius' advantage because his opponent reacted too quickly, overcommitting because of the wider angle, thereby allowing my comrade's blade to come flashing in behind his foe's parry, and that quickly, another enemy was down before I could offer any assistance. Again, without hesitating, I took advantage of this gap in the ring of iron that our intruders had attempted to construct, crossing the few paces across the middle where, without a pause, I plunged my blade into the back of a Maezaei on the opposite side of their makeshift defenses. Before I could wet my blade any more, however, the fight was over, with the last three defenders suddenly throwing down their blades and dropping to their knees.

"Hold! Don't kill them!"

My arm had been pulled back so the point of my blade was near my ear and about to plunge down into the mouth of one of those who had surrendered; nevertheless, I obeyed, stepping back as Primus Pilus Atticus came striding out from his tent, stepping over the prone body of the man who, as we discovered, had been slain not by Atticus but by Crito. Our clerk had been sleeping in the corner of the outer office, but had leapt up from his pallet and, using his dagger, had plunged it into the neck of the first warrior who entered. Atticus ordered the three survivors bound, whereupon I and the others nearby were ordered to drag them over to the tent of Macerinus. Naturally, by this point, he was up and about, standing outside his tent where Admetos and Dodonis were being held; only then did we learn the other captives were being kept in a separate tent. Those two Maezaei were obviously still in that state of confusion that is common to someone who has just been roused from sleep, but we were hardly sympathetic to their plight. I, for one, do not like having my sleep disturbed, and I knew from experience that now that I had been roused, especially to the level of frantic activity and madness that is required in order to kill another man, I would not be going back to sleep this night. Judging from their expressions, my comrades felt much the same way, so we were hardly a receptive audience for the scene that played out before us.

"Ask your king," Atticus demanded of Dodonis who, I must say, actually looked harder and more capable without his robes and whatever preparations he made to appear the courtier, "if he knew these men were coming."

"Of course he did not," Dodonis replied instantly; the point of a sword applied to his posterior by one of my comrades prompted him to turn and actually ask Admetos.

Who, it must be said, appeared in striking contrast to his councilor, with his gray hair awry and still blinking away the remnants of sleep. If anything, he looked completely bewildered, yet I was sufficiently wary of the man, as I could see my comrades were as well, reminding myself that this not only could be an affectation but in all likelihood was nothing more than a ploy by the old king.

Despite our suspicions, the Maezaei chieftain shook his head in what I supposed he hoped would be a clear repudiation of the actions of his subjects. His tone was shaky, but there was a quick exchange between the pair, and all I will say is that Admetos never seemed to waver in his denial.

Turning to Atticus, Dodonis announced, "My king denies knowing anything about this rescue attempt. He swears upon our gods Genusus and Zeau that he did not know these men would make this attempt."

"Well," Atticus' tone was mocking, "as long as he swears on his gods, then I know he's telling the truth!"

Suddenly, he spun about and pointed to one of the captives.

"Pullus," he ordered, "bring that *cunnus* here!"

Why me? I groaned, but I contained it within myself and did as he ordered. Grabbing the man by the arm, I recognized this might have been the reason Atticus chose me, because I was strong enough to drag the man despite his obvious reluctance. Like the others, every inch of exposed skin was blackened, although the exertions of the previous moments had caused his sweat to wash the charcoal away in rivulets that showed up as tracks down his face. Honestly, at the time, I had no clue that Atticus had chosen this man at anything but random; I instantly learned that even if he did, it was a remarkably lucky guess, just from the reaction of the elderly king. Almost in one motion, I dragged him forward and pushed down the man onto his knees in front of Admetos, whereupon the king reacted in the exact same manner, and I did not need more light to see the stricken expression on his face as he fell.

"Noooooooooo," the Maezaei king wailed, holding his hands out in supplication, first to Atticus, then towards the kneeling warrior, whose head was bowed as he refused to look up.

My confusion was cleared up, ironically enough, by Dodonis who gasped, "Euneas? Is it you?"

The kneeling man did not answer verbally, but his head raised in response.

"This," Dodonis whirled around to face Atticus, "is Euneas! He's the son of Admetos! Please, Centurion!" I admit I was a bit surprised when the councilor also dropped to his knees to join his king and, presumably, the king's heir. "Please, spare him! He is Admetos' only son! He's the crown prince of the Maezaei!"

"He should have kept that in mind when he came sneaking into our camp." Atticus' reply was harsh.

It must be noted that this exchange happened before the body of our sentry was discovered; if it had been after that, I am sure events following this would have been quite different.

"He was showing his loyalty to his father by trying to rescue him," Dodonis countered, the desperation in his voice clear to hear.

I will admit that our Primus Pilus' reaction surprised me, suddenly rubbing his chin in thought in a sign that Dodonis' words had struck some sort of chord within the Primus Pilus.

"That," Atticus' tone was grudging, "is understandable. But," he pointed a finger down at the Maezaei councilor, "that doesn't change the fact that he and these other…" his mouth twisted in contempt, "*savages* came skulking into this camp like thieves!"

Since in this account I am writing I have sworn to be as truthful as possible, I must confess that my first thought at Atticus' words were, if not disloyal, at least more sympathetic to the Maezaei cause than I would have liked known. What did you expect them to do? I wondered silently. Going further, though, my next thought was that we would have attempted something similar if it had been our Legate, or even Atticus. Some things, however, are better left unsaid; unwritten, on the other hand, is another matter when one is trying to be as honest as possible. Unaware that one of his men was at least sympathetic, Atticus stood there, glaring down at the kneeling prisoners, his words hanging in the air. Even as he did so, the other two men who had surrendered had been dragged to a spot just behind the prince, who I will say stared up defiantly at the Primus Pilus as he considered what to do.

"But," Atticus finally broke the silence, "if we execute this one, and that one," he jerked a thumb at Admetos, "is found guilty at trial, then that will mean there will be some sort of power struggle with these *cunni*, and we all know what that means, that we'll be back here."

He paused for an instant, but as he opened his mouth to continue, there was a cry from outside the ring of flickering light of the forum. We all turned in the direction from where the cry had come, but it took me a moment to make out that two men were approaching, carrying something between them. Puffing from the effort, the two Gregarii, who I recognized as Third Century men once they came into the light, laid their burden down with a gentleness that was at odds with everything else going on.

"Primus Pilus," one of them gasped, still trying to catch his breath, "these...these *cock sucking savages* killed Columella here! We found his body down in the ditch! His throat's been cut."

Even as the Gregarius was informing all of us, my eyes took in the sight of one of our own, the armor on his chest black and gleaming in the poor light, while what looked like a gruesome extra smile glistened just below his chin. His eyes were open, I could see, and I wondered what was the last thing he actually saw, if he had at least gotten a glimpse of the man who slew him. Atticus whirled about, his face hard and unyielding, his mouth turned down in suppressed fury, except he did not point to the kneeling prince.

Instead, he pointed to one of the two men just behind him and ordered, "Pullus! Kill them! Both of them!"

Why me? This was the first thought; the second was that although it was not in the way in which I would have chosen, as part of this first occasion to blood the Gallic sword once wielded by the original Titus Pullus, avenging the death of a comrade was not such a bad way in which to do it. And I did exactly as my Primus Pilus ordered, except just before I was about to plunge the point of my blade down into the crevice of the first Maezaei's shoulder, right between the collarbone and shoulder blade, he stopped me.

"Kill them the way Columella was," he ordered, his mouth set in a smile that had nothing pleasant about it.

The only surprise to me was that neither Admetos nor Dodonis uttered a word of protest; the only resistance came, unsurprisingly, from the two condemned men. Not that either of them were successful. With that task done, we were dismissed back to our tents, while one more prisoner was added to the list, the only survivor of the ill-fated attempt by the Maezaei to rescue their king.

On our return to Siscia, I barely paid attention to the words of Atticus, who praised our conduct and performance on this mission to Splonum. Frankly, I should have; it was a rare event when our former Praetorian offered anything resembling approval, yet I offer the fact that when my name was mentioned by our Primus Pilus as he singled me out for my actions, I barely noticed, proof of my distraction. In fact, I only became aware when, after we were dismissed, I was suddenly assaulted by some of my comrades who surrounded me and pounded me on the back.

My bemusement did not go unnoticed by my closest friend, and Domitius demanded, "What's wrong with you? Usually, you'd be strutting around like a peacock because the Primus Pilus mentioned you."

I admit I felt slightly ashamed, and more than a little embarrassed; all I could think to say was, "I've got…other things on my mind."

It is a sign of how well Titus Domitius knew me, and how much of a friend he was, because he instantly understood, offering, "We've got the rest of the day off. Let's go into town and find out what's happening."

"But you've got your own woman troubles," I protested, but he waved me off.

"Petrilla's pregnant," he countered, "not dying. Besides," he grinned at me, "as long as you don't tell her she wasn't my first stop, I certainly won't!"

I found it impossible to say anything in reply; instead, I just squeezed his shoulder in mute thanks, and together, we left camp and headed to Siscia.

Rather than head directly to the house of Livinius, I thought it wise to stop at Diocles' apartment; I am thankful that I did, although I was not happy about what I heard there.

"Apparently," Diocles' tone was suitably grim as we sat at his table, "Lucius Livinius learned about Augustus' refusal to allow your father and his heirs to claim equestrian status."

While not unexpected, it was a bitter blow nonetheless.

"Any ideas how he heard?" I asked the Greek.

"No," he admitted, then hesitated before continuing, "I have my suspicions, but nothing definite."

I regarded him, sensing that there was something he was not divulging, so when he did not seem disposed to continue, I pressed, "And? What are your suspicions?"

Now he looked distinctly uncomfortable, and he seemed determined to avoid meeting my gaze, something that was so rare I could probably count the times on one hand.

"Diocles," I tried to remain calm, "what don't I know?"

"What you don't know," he replied, "is what I don't know either. I told you I don't know anything definite, just that I've heard some…things."

It is probably no surprise that I was becoming impatient, and I am afraid I snapped at him. "Just come out with it! Enough of this tiptoeing around!"

He glared at me, yet his tone did not match his expression as he told me, "Apparently, your brother's training has gone fairly well."

I was completely unprepared for this; what could this possibly have to do with what we were discussing?

"I heard the same thing." I tried to be patient. "But I don't see…"

"Well, a few days ago, Tiburtinus allowed the *tiros* in his Century to go out into town." He paused as if trying to see if I had caught on; at least my stomach was clearly beginning to because it started hurting.

"And?" I am afraid my tone, while quiet, was one with which Diocles had sufficient experience to know that there was a seething volcano of rage just beneath my seemingly calm exterior. "What happened?"

Sighing, Diocles went on, "Well, supposedly, your brother got quite drunk. And," he hurried on, undoubtedly seeing I was at the end of the tether that kept my anger in check, "he made some…statements. Statements that may have been…unfortunate."

I put my head into my hands, sure that I was about to vomit.

"What," I asked, "did he say exactly?"

"I don't know with any certainty," Diocles admitted, then before I could thump him, he added, "but it had to do with the fact that the Pullus family didn't need to be in the equestrian order because between him and you, your deeds would be so great that not even Augustus could keep you from being elevated."

Sitting back, I sat there, stunned.

"And, obviously Livinius heard about this, and started making inquiries," I said dully.

"That," the Greek admitted, "is my guess. Although," he pointed out, "the truth is that right now, he may be only acting on what your brother said, and actually hasn't had it confirmed."

From where I sat, this was an awfully thin reed for me to cling to in the torrent of events that threatened to sweep me away.

"Titus," Diocles' tone turned almost gentle. "Is it really so bad if he finds out? It's not like you're in love with this girl. You just want to bed her, neh?"

"That," I sighed, "was before."

"Before?" For a moment, he seemed confused, asking, "What do you mean 'before'?"

I did not answer – verbally, at least – I just looked at him steadily for a moment. His face cleared, and he sat back in his own chair, regarding his cup.

"Ah," he said softly. "I see. So I was right. You *are* in love with Giulia."

The trepidation I was feeling as I made my way to the villa of Livinius was so overwhelming that I stopped no less than three different times, arguing with myself about whether or not I should actually confront whatever was awaiting me there, or wait and see what happened. That passivity, unfortunately, was not then, nor is it now part of my makeup, although I will say that when I approached the gate to the villa, there was a part of me screaming to turn around. I did not; instead, I rapped on the door, then waited for entrance. Soter opened the hatch, and I saw the deep seams around his eye as he peered out. I remember thinking it would have been better had I been able to see his entire expression.

"*Salve,* Master Pullus." Even under the best circumstances, the old man's voice had a quaver to it, which was another difficulty in determining his frame of mind. "I am afraid that Master Livinius' orders have not changed. You are not allowed to see Mistress..."

"I'm not here to see her," I cut him off. "I'm here to see Lucius Livinius."

"Oh." Soter was clearly surprised, but he asked me to wait, closing the hatch and disappearing.

I was beginning to think that either Soter had forgotten, or more likely, Livinius did not want to have to deal with a probably embarrassing and uncomfortable scene. Just when I was about to turn and leave, I heard footsteps on the other side of the wall, then the door inset into the gate opened.

"Master Livinius will receive you in the *triclinium*," Soter announced, but did not wait to see if I followed.

Naturally, I did, suddenly thinking what a bad idea this was and wondering how Livinius would take it when I threw up on his shoes. Nevertheless, I followed the slave into the villa. I did not really expect Giulia to be present, but I still experienced a stab of disappointment when I entered the room and it was just her father. My initial impression, judging from his facial expression at least, was that he would have preferred to be on the sand of the arena with a blade in his hand facing some giant Gallic gladiator. Oddly enough, his appearance actually made me feel a bit better.

"*Salve*, Titus Porcinianus Pullus," Livinius said formally, yet despite his clear discomfort, he offered his arm. "It's a pleasure to see you again." I think the ridiculousness of his words hit him, because he hurriedly added, "Although I'm not happy with the circumstances of our meeting."

Seeing an opening, I took it, asking him even as we were still clasping arms, "And what circumstances may those be, sir?"

The older man grimaced, then turned to Soter and whispered something to him, prompting the old slave to disappear.

"I'll explain, but frankly, I don't think this is a conversation we should be having with dry throats. I sent Soter for wine. Some of my *best* wine," he emphasized.

"Oh my," I tried to sound nonchalant and even forced a chuckle, "that sounds rather ominous."

"It is," he replied heavily, then waved me to a couch, directly across from him.

The same couch, I remembered with some bitterness, he asked me to sit on when he asked me to court his daughter. But that was before, and I actually thought about remaining standing, feeling the need to be in a superior position, so to speak. Fortunately, I quickly dismissed it, taking the offered seat; I was determined to maintain my composure and, contrary to my normal practice, not destroy a bridge that I was being thwarted in crossing. Maybe I'm finally growing up, I told myself.

"Pullus," Livinius began, "I want to start by telling you that I have nothing but the utmost respect. For you, and your family."

He paused then, so I felt compelled to thank him, which seemed to make him feel worse as he waved a dismissive hand.

"No need to thank me, young man. In fact, I should be thanking you, and your father and grandfather, for helping to make this province a place where a man like me could have a fresh start and make something of himself." Pausing again, he seemed to be considering something, and when he spoke, I understood his hesitation. "There's something I think you should know, Pullus. About me."

Before he could continue, Soter had returned, carrying two cups and a pitcher, so the next few moments were absorbed in the pouring and taking a sip. Honestly, it was actually a very good vintage, even if I hardly noticed it.

Clearing his throat, Livinius resumed, "I wasn't always what you see me as today, Pullus."

Not really understanding, I replied, "Time changes all of us, I suppose."

"That's not what I mean." He shook his head. "I'm talking about more than my appearance. I'm talking about all…" He waved a hand at the villa in an all-encompassing gesture. "…of this. The villa. The money to buy the villa. What I'm saying," his tone turned intense and he leaned forward, putting his elbows on his knees to draw closer to me, "is that when I was young, about your age, you and I had more in common than you might think. I was poor, you see, but more than that, I was…" He closed his eyes, and I had the impression that there was an invisible man trying to drag the words from him. "…I was a man of the Head Count, not equestrian."

I sat back, stunned, although I do not know why. A number of things flashed through my mind, the sum total of the few times we had spoken and my inner sense that he was, in fact, not a man who came from a long line of equestrians and been born into his wealth. Again, I am not sure why I had this belief, but his words confirmed something I realized I had surmised some time before.

Clearly expecting me to say something, all I could manage was, "Ah. I…see."

The smile he gave me was not unkind, and he replied, "No, I don't think you do, young man." Sighing, he paused again, then said, "Titus, may I call you by your *praenomen*?" When I indicated that he could, he continued, "Titus, I need to ask you a question, but I want to ask your forgiveness in advance, because it will be an…unpleasant one."

"You want to know if what you heard about my family is true." I am not sure why, but I decided to take pity on him, or perhaps, both of us.

He did seem relieved, nodding his head and saying, "Yes, that's exactly what I want to ask you. Because I…heard something the other day that disturbed me. Naturally, I thought it was a mistake, but then I made some further inquiries with some men I know who work for the civil administration here. And, what they told me is that there had been some…difficulties regarding your family?"

"That," I commented, my tone dry, "is certainly one way to put it." Taking my own breath, I plunged ahead. "But, yes. While I don't know exactly what you heard, what I can tell you is that although my Av..." I bit the inside of my lip, cursing myself for this lapse of using my childhood name for Titus Pullus, especially in front of Livinius, "…grandfather's name is in the rolls as being elevated to the Order of Equestrians by Augustus himself, after he died we were informed that his status would not transfer to my father. Or any of us, his children," I added, probably superfluously.

He did not reply immediately, just sat there considering what I had said.

Finally, he asked, "Might I ask about the specifics of this situation?"

"You can," I knew my tone was cold, but he was banishing me from Giulia's presence, so I was not feeling charitable, "but that doesn't mean I'll tell you."

Somewhat surprisingly, he did not actually appear angry or offended, simply nodding his head. Although I cannot say for sure, now I suspect that Livinius might have known me better than I would have assumed, because when he did not object in any way, I actually felt compelled to fill the silence. It is something I have noticed about myself; I am extremely uncomfortable when I am with others and nothing is being said. Being in formations and the like, of course, is the exception.

"In all honesty," I began, choosing my words carefully, "neither my father nor I have ever been given any details. Other than the fact that Augustus claimed that some 'new information' had come to light, but only after my grandfather's death. And based on that information, not only were we not allowed to claim equestrian status, a large portion of the money that's a qualification for elevation was confiscated. Honestly," I finished ruefully, "before that, I thought having enough money was the *only* qualification." I could not stop a bitter laugh from escaping my lips. "But we certainly learned differently."

"That," Livinius broke the awkward silence, "is a terrible injustice. And," suddenly, his face twisted into a sneer that matched my own resentment, "make no mistake. It's *always* about the money with the upper classes." He became animated, adding, "I could tell you stories, young man! There are things I know about our so-called *betters* that would curl your hair!"

"It's not long enough to curl." My reply was only said offhandedly, but this made him laugh.

Meanwhile, my thoughts were running back to more than three years before, and I experienced an instant of grim amusement as I thought about how Livinius would react if he knew I was aware of the scandal regarding his wife and the previous Legate. And for a bare moment, I considered bringing it up, but the truth is that I actually liked Lucius Livinius a great deal, and even as he was barring me from any contact with Giulia, I still had no wish to offend him.

"That's true," he acknowledged, lifting his cup in the general direction of my head. "Nevertheless, you have not only my sympathy, you have my understanding that in all likelihood whatever the supposed cause was probably had nothing to do with the real reason. And," he added, "that the real reason is probably nothing more substantial than your grandfather having given the Princeps offense at some point in the past." As is always the case when the name of the divine Augustus is invoked in anything but a positive or reverential manner, he dropped his voice to close to a whisper. "Our Imperator never forgets a slight, even when it's unintentional."

I do not know if he was trying to make me feel better, but if so, he was not succeeding. And what came next was even worse.

After a pause, Livinius said, "Be that as it may," I congratulated myself on not being lulled by his sympathetic words, "unfortunately, it doesn't change the fact that you aren't in our order. And as *paterfamilias,* it's my duty to arrange the best match for Giulia." He hesitated for a moment, then added something that actually was the most painful part of our conversation. "No matter what her own heart wants."

I have been told by more than one of my comrades in the Legions that I have an extensive vocabulary for a man of my station; not once has this remark been rendered as a compliment. Nevertheless, I cannot find the words that would do justice to the swirling assault of emotions that gripped me in that moment. She loves me? I do remember this bursting through all the others, and the sudden joy at the thought made me physically dizzy. However, it was a short-lived feeling, because that same part of my mind that remains detached and aloof that kept, and keeps me alive in battle did not allow this thought to take root, sweeping it away with the brutal tide of cold-eyed logic. That's meaningless, the voice said to me. You heard her father, and you know that if it was Tata in the same position with Livia, he'd do the exact same thing. All he's doing is what he thinks is best for his family.

This was what prompted me to surprise myself when I finally answered, "I…I understand, sir. I do." Taking a deep breath as the reality settled in on me, I felt compelled to add, "I don't like it. Not one bit. But…"

I did not say anything more because I could not.

"Titus, if you did, it would actually make me feel better about this decision, because I'd know that you're not the right man for my daughter, no matter what your station." Leaning back, he took a deep draught from his cup, and I followed his lead and did the same. Wiping his mouth with the back of his hand, he continued, "And I want you to know that this pains me. Not," he added hastily, probably seeing my expression, "as much as it does you. Or Giulia, for that matter."

"How is she?" I hated myself for asking, but I could not help it. "I mean, have you told her?"

"Yes, I told her," he sighed. "And she's not taking it well." He gave a quiet laugh that sounded like it contained as much sorrow as humor. "Actually, that's putting it quite mildly. She told me she hates me."

Despite myself, I was moved by the sudden glinting in his eyes, which caused me to lean forward and give him an awkward pat.

"No, she doesn't," I tried to assure him. "She's just…upset. As am I." Realizing that there was nothing more to be said, I lifted my cup in a mock salute and made no attempt to hide my bitterness as I toasted, "To the Princeps and all that he does for us in the name of Rome."

I was not altogether surprised when Lucius Livinius decided not to join in.

Chapter 2

My return to camp gave me the time for my anger to build, which was an unfortunate thing for my brother. Consequently, I did not bother stopping at my own hut, heading instead to the area belonging to the Seventh Cohort. Stopping at the building containing the Century office and Tiburtinus' quarters, I was informed that my former Optio was, in fact, in his office, filling out ration requests and the daily report. In a moment, I was standing in front of his desk, but he made me wait as he finished what he was doing, which I expected.

"I hate these fucking things," he grunted, then returned my salute as he sat back and eyed me. "Coming to check on your brother, Pullus?"

"Something like that," I agreed grimly. "Where is he?"

"He and the rest are out at the stakes, I imagine," he informed me. "Esquilinus is out there with them. I'll be joining them as soon as I'm done."

Esquilinus was Tiburtinus' Optio; frankly, I did not think much of the man, at least at that point. I suppose something in my demeanor, or perhaps in my tone seemed to catch Tiburtinus' attention, and I was reminded how well this man knew me.

"I was going to ask if you wanted to join me and watch." He frowned. "But something tells me that might not be a good idea."

"I just need to talk to him," I tried to make it sound casual, as if it was a routine matter.

Tiburtinus was clearly not convinced, and shook his head, saying, "I'm not buying that. What is it, Pullus? What do you need to talk to him about that can't wait until after duty time?"

"It's a...family matter," I told him. "Just something I need to tell him." Suddenly, I had an inspiration. "Some news from Arelate, from my father."

"Well, if it's something like that, it can definitely wait."

Realizing he had outmaneuvered me, I inwardly cursed, but I said aloud, "It's just that I learned something that's...important to my family, and he's the only one who can supply the answer because he's the only one who would know."

Tiburtinus did not say anything for several moments, just studying me, making me feel acutely uncomfortable. Which was nothing unusual when I was in front of him, going back to when I first arrived in the First Section and he intervened with Philo, who had gotten it into his head to try and give me a beating as an introduction.

Finally, he shrugged, and said, "All right. Let me finish this, and we'll walk out together."

It was as we were walking out of the camp to the training ground when I learned that, although Tiburtinus may not have known the details, he understood me better than I would have liked.

"You know," he said this in a conversational tone, "if you lay a hand on *Tirone* Pullus, that I'll have to report it. And," he turned to look at me, "you'll be flogged."

I opened my mouth to deny I had anything violent in mind, but nothing came out.

Sighing, instead, I asked, "How did you know?"

He gave his barking laugh and pointed up at my face. "Because you're one of the easiest men to read I've ever seen, Pullus. The instant you walked into the office, I could see you had murder in your eye."

"I wouldn't murder him," I protested. Then, after thinking about it, I mumbled, "At least, I don't think I would."

We walked on in silence for a bit, then he asked me quietly, "You want to tell me what he did?"

I must admit I was sorely tempted to unburden myself, and in that moment, I realized that not stopping by the hut to at least tell Domitius what had transpired had been a mistake. Now it was like there was a part of my insides acting as a dam, but one under extreme pressure as my rage kept building, threatening to come bursting through to sweep everything before it away. In that instant, I realized Gnaeus Tiburtinus was actually acting in my best interests, as a true friend would, keeping me from doing something I would regret the rest of my life. Nevertheless, I still did not feel comfortable in informing Tiburtinus of the specifics of all that had taken place.

Instead, I settled for, "I found out my brother said something when he was out in town last week that he shouldn't have. And it's caused not just my family but me personally some problems."

"Ah," he said softly, then shook his head. "I knew it was a mistake letting them out into town."

Glancing over, while I was still absorbed in my own problems, his words compelled me to ask, "Why? What happened?"

He grimaced, and explained, "Well, the good news is that it wasn't just your brother who acted like an idiot." This made me chuckle, and he shot me a half-amused, half-irritated look. "I'm glad you think it's funny. But I actually had to stripe two of the stupid bastards." Seeing my sudden look of alarm, he assured me, "No, your brother wasn't one of them. Although," his tone was dry as he glanced at me again, "I have a feeling that he's going to wish he had been."

Just before we approached the men of Tiburtinus' Century, he reached out and grabbed my bad arm; I knew this was no accident because he not only made sure to put his hand around the scar tissue of my forearm, he gave it a squeeze.

"Pullus, remember what I said," he reminded me softly. "Don't do anything both of us will regret."

While I did not at the time, now I appreciate Tiburtinus' admonition because he used the only thing that he knew would be enough to dissuade me from hurting Sextus to a degree where it could not be ignored by the army, my career. Swallowing hard, nevertheless, I nodded my understanding.

"*Tirone* Sextus Pullus! Attend to your Centurion!" Tiburtinus bellowed.

I had already spied my brother; like me, he towered over the others and I saw the startled, and somewhat worried, look on his face. As you should be, I thought with grim humor, just not because of

Tiburtinus. He came trotting over, but while I knew he saw me, I could not fault his demeanor as he kept his attention on his Centurion.

Coming to *intente*, he snapped, "*Tirone* Pullus, reporting as ordered, sir!" while rendering a salute with which I could find no error.

Neither did Tiburtinus, because he returned it, then said simply, "Your brother needs to talk to you. Once he's done, go back to work. You're still sloppy on your recoveries." He shook his head in mock sadness, adding, "I don't know who trained you, but they should be scourged." Before he left us, he glanced over at me and said softly, "Remember."

I watched his retreating back, wondering if his mention of scourging was another hidden warning. Waiting until he was out of earshot, I turned back to Sextus, who was standing there uncertainly.

"You know why I'm here?" I asked him quietly.

"No," he shook his head, then gave me a grin that had always worked in the past, "but I'm sure it's just to check on me and make sure I'm being tucked in at night."

Under other circumstances, it would have worked; instead, it only made me angrier, and I felt the sudden uncoiling sensation in my stomach. Careful, Titus, I thought.

"No," I replied coldly, "that's not why. I'm here because of something you did."

Now he looked confused, and he shook his head as he said, "What did I do?"

"You remember going out into town last week?"

The fact that he grinned at the memory only made matters worse, and laughing did not help either. "Actually, not much! I haven't been that drunk in…"

"I don't want to fucking hear about what a great time you had!" I snapped, then despite myself, I found my finger poking him in his chest. "I want to hear about what you fucking said!"

Confusion returned to his face as he asked plaintively, "What I said? How should I remember?"

"You *should* remember," I heard my voice rising in volume and I tried to rein in my fury, "because what you said ruined my chances with Giulia Livinius!"

"How by Pluto's balls could something I said cause you problems with her?" he asked, and I believe his bewilderment was genuine.

Forcing myself to be patient, I asked him, "Do you remember saying something about our family?"

"No," he replied instantly, which told me he was lying. "I don't remember anything like that!"

I was just able to keep my mouth shut, instead staring down at him, which meant it was not long before the shuffling of his feet began, and as always, his ears betrayed him.

"I mean," he mumbled, "I don't remember exactly what I said."

"Really?" I did not contain my sarcasm. "Because those," I pointed at his ears, which I knew would infuriate him, "are telling a different story. Like always."

Apparently, Sextus decided a change in tactics was in order because he became defiant.

"So?" he shot back. "So what if I did say something? I didn't say anything that wasn't the truth! And you," now it was his turn to point fingers, because just like with me, my brother knew the thing that was guaranteed to ignite my own ire, and this is something that I cannot abide, "know it!"

At that moment, I was actually proud of myself because I did not actually hit him then.

"What do you think our father would say to that?" I asked him quietly.

If I had not seen it with my own eyes, I would not have thought it possible that his ears could become even brighter.

"He," he admitted grudgingly, "wouldn't like it."

My laugh held no humor in it as I agreed, "No, no, he wouldn't. And," I pressed, "what do you think he'd do about it?"

Sextus did not reply, verbally anyway, lapsing back into a shrugging, sullen silence as he studied his feet.

"And now," I continued, "Lucius Livinius heard about it, and he did some checking and found out it was true. He just told me I can't see Giulia anymore."

Honestly, I do not know whether or not I would have managed to restrain myself no matter what Sextus said, but when his response was to laugh and joke, "So? There's plenty of other women out there to fuck, Titus. Just throw your net back out there, and you'll see…"

My next memory is of an unseen force slamming into me, knocking me to the ground with such power that it drove the wind from my lungs, as thousands of stars burst into being when my head slammed into the hard-packed earth.

"*What the fuck do you think you're doing, Sergeant?*"

Thrust into my vision were a pair of Legionary boots, and I rolled over on my back to see Gnaeus Tiburtinus standing there, his face a mask of fury, his *vitus* thrusting down into my chest, hard.

"What? I…What?" I remember mumbling this, but I was only gradually becoming aware of what was going on around me, and I noticed another prone body at the edge of my vision, with Tiburtinus' Optio crouching next to it. "I...I don't know. Sir." I did remember to add this.

"Get on your feet," Tiburtinus snarled, "and stand at *intente* when addressing a superior officer!"

It took two tries before I managed to climb to my feet, except the training ground kept tilting and I was beginning to notice a throbbing pain on the side of my head. Regardless, I managed to assume at least a semblance of the position, as weaving and unsteady as it may have been. Suddenly, Tiburtinus' face thrust into my vision, hovering just inches from my face, his lips pulled back into a sneer.

"What the fuck did I tell you, Pullus?"

The fact that he was not yelling this actually got my attention more than the words themselves, and I felt the first shiver of fear ripple up my body.

"Not to do anything stupid," I said, partly sighing, partly groaning, although only partially from the physical pain that was building.

Not that this would be anything compared to the flogging that was in my future, I thought dismally. I wish I could say that the idea I might have killed my brother was part of my consideration in that moment, but it was not. Even now, I do not know what that says about who I am as a man.

"And yet, here we are," he hissed in frustration. "Now I have to write you up for striking a Gregarius!"

"That's not true, sir."

It took a moment for my mind to register that a new voice had spoken, but Tiburtinus was no less surprised. Both of us turned to see Sextus standing, weaving like I was, and with the assistance of an arm on the shoulder of Esquilinus, but standing nonetheless.

"What do you mean, Pullus?" Tiburtinus snapped.

"I mean, I'm the one who struck Sergeant Pullus, sir. He just defended himself."

"Sextus," I gasped. "You…"

"*Tacete!*"

Tiburtinus really did not need to bellow this as loudly as he did considering his proximity, although it did have one salutary effect, the last of the cobwebs in my head blown away by his verbal blast.

"What are you saying, *Tirone*?" Tiburtinus' tone became formal. "Are you telling me you struck a superior officer?"

As angry as I had been with my brother – and make no mistake, if Tiburtinus had not stopped me, I very well might have beaten my brother to death – I could not allow this to happen.

"Shut up, Sextus!" I yelled at him. "Don't answer…"

For the second time, I hit the ground, although this time, I was acutely aware not only from where the blow had come, but where it landed as Tiburtinus thrust his *vitus* right into the pit of my stomach. Gasping for air, I looked up at Sextus and since I was unable to speak, I could only shake my head in mute appeal. My brother was as much a child of the Legions as I was, meaning that despite his status as a new *Tirone*, he knew the penalty for striking a superior is, always, death. Yet, he stood there looking defiantly at his Centurion, although I could see his legs shaking.

"*Tirone*," Tiburtinus' tone was almost gentle, "do you know the penalty for striking a superior?"

"Yes, Hastatus Prior, I do," Sextus answered, and if his voice broke, he nevertheless said it strongly.

Tiburtinus heaved a sigh that displayed the kind of discomfort and regret that comes from being forced to pronounce a decision on a capital offense, saying, "And because it was out here on the training ground, in front of the gods and everyone else, my hands are tied."

"Hastatus Prior," Esquilinus suddenly spoke up, "may I speak?"

"Go ahead, Optio," Tiburtinus said wearily.

"I was actually watching everything," Esquilinus continued, "and I think it's just a misunderstanding."

"Misunderstanding?" Tiburtinus asked warily, as he should have been.

I had climbed back to my feet, and I felt a flare of hope as I stared at the Optio.

My opinion of him was about to change quite drastically as he explained, "What I saw was *Tiro* Pullus showing his brother some of the techniques we've been working on today. But like all *tiros*," he laughed, and if it was forced, I chose to ignore it, as I hoped Tiburtinus would, "he's still a fucking clumsy bastard. And the Sergeant here," he nodded towards me, "just demonstrated to his brother what the *tiro* did wrong. Granted, it was a bit…excessive," Esquilinus acknowledged, "but it was just part of our training, sir. Nothing more than that."

I held my breath, as I am sure Sextus did as well, both of us staring at the man who would ultimately decide whether to accept this fiction. For his part, Tiburtinus rubbed his jaw with his free hand, looking at Sextus, whose lower face was covered in blood from the nose I had broken, while one eye was rapidly swelling shut, then over to me. And, if anything, the look he gave Sextus was kinder than the one he directed at me, as it should have been.

Finally, he asked Esquilinus, "Are you willing to put that in the diary so we can send Pullus here to the hospital without too many questions being asked?"

"Yes, sir," Esquilinus did not hesitate.

Sighing, Tiburtinus nodded his head and said simply, "Very well. Esquilinus, you take young Pullus here to the hospital. I'll," his glance at me was as cold as I had ever seen, "take care of the rest of this mess."

Esquilinus took Sextus by the arm as my brother had pulled the collar of his tunic up to partially cover his face, but before they left, I reached out for him.

"Sextus," I called to him, "I'm…sorry."

"So am I." His tone was muffled, yet I felt as if a boulder had been lifted from my soul; not that I felt particularly good about myself – just better than I had an instant before.

I watched him wobble back to camp, dreading turning around and facing my old Optio. But when I did, I was not prepared for what came next.

"Get the fuck out of my face," Tiburtinus said coldly. "And if I ever see you over in my area again, I don't care how fucking big and strong you are, I'll beat you into bloody meat. You're restricted from the Seventh's area until further notice."

He did not wait for a reply; not that I could have said anything to change his mind. Walking away from me, he did not glance back, yelling instead at his Century to quit fucking about and get back to work.

Nothing ever came of my striking my brother, at least in an official sense. I returned to my hut, but my intention of talking to Domitius had been quashed by what happened on the training ground. It was not for a lack of trying on his part, yet no matter how he phrased his questions, I did not answer. At least, not in any detail that would satisfy him. It was not until the next day before I felt sufficiently recovered from my shame, and while there was still a residue of anger left, it was not focused on Sextus as much as it was the situation in general. Our society is so rigid, with a man's class supposedly set for all of his days under the sun, and it is no crime for me to say that this hierarchy is most strictly enforced by those at the top of our society. And men like the first Titus Pullus, who are not satisfied with the status into which they are born through no fault of their own but are willing to perform the deeds and do the work that is necessary to prove their worth, are not viewed as welcome additions to the class to which they aspire, but as threats. Of all the things I have learned, both with my own personal situation, what I observed with my father, and from reading the story of my Avus' life, this is the ultimate reality of what it means to be a Roman who may be born with ambition to improve himself. And, although I try to emulate my father, who has accepted the injustice of this with an attitude that would do honor to the most ardent practitioner of the school of philosophy that is called

Stoic, I am afraid that, in reality, I am more like the original Titus Pullus. The injustice of my situation and that of my family ensures that, as I was coming to learn, there is always a fire smoldering in my soul, waiting to ignite into open flame, inflicting my anger on those I view as either actively obstructing my family's ascension, or representing those who would do so. Now, as I write this at the age of thirty-three, one thing I have learned is that always carrying this emotion is wearing, feeling as if I am always bearing a burden on my soul that, if I am not careful, can explode into full view and into a form of action that communicates my resentment. Which, as I have learned full well, can threaten to either damage or destroy all that I have worked for these many years. I am acutely aware that, if the circumstances are right, I could easily act in such a rash and impulsive manner that, while it might give me satisfaction in the moment, it would prove catastrophic to not only me, but to my entire family. This is especially true because ours is not a forgiving society, especially when it involves a man of my class.

After I explained all that had transpired, first with Livinius, then with Sextus, Domitius sat on my bunk, considering matters.

"Titus," he finally broke the silence, "I'm going to ask you a question." He paused as if to gauge how receptive I was, but I had learned to trust him implicitly, so I nodded for him to continue. "Even if you did marry Giulia, and lived a long and happy life, with many children, when you get to the end and look back on your life, who will have been part of that life the longest?"

"My family," I answered, "but I mean my…first family. My parents, and my brothers and sisters."

"Exactly." He nodded. "And Titus, you need to face the truth. Livinius isn't going to change his mind about you marrying Giulia. So the idea of you and her spending a life together isn't happening."

"I know," I sighed, and I truly did.

That did not mean I was able to stomach it, which I pointed out to him.

"I know," he echoed me, then gave me a sad smile, "but that doesn't change anything, does it?"

"No," I admitted. "No, it doesn't." Thinking for a moment, I said, "That means I have to forgive Sextus and his big mouth, doesn't it?"

However, Domitius surprised me with his answer. "That's up to you. I understand why you're angry, and Titus," he hesitated for an instant, so I waved at him to continue, "about your brother…"

His voice trailed off and he was clearly reluctant to keep talking.

"What about him?" I prompted him, although I had a deep suspicion I knew what he was going to say.

"It's just that," he fumbled for the right words, which of course made me impatient, "he's not like you."

"I know that," I assured him.

"Do you?" he asked me, his tone quiet as he regarded me steadily. "Do you really?"

Suddenly, I was not sure we were talking about the same aspect of Sextus.

"What do you mean?"

"I mean…" He seemed to be feeling his way along; only now can I appreciate his caution. "…he doesn't have the same fire in him that you do, Titus. Anyone with eyes can see that."

"That's because I'm the firstborn," I argued. "And that's about me, not him."

"That's true," he granted, "but it's more than that. Remember, Titus, I've been around Sextus enough to see the difference. He just doesn't take anything we do seriously, and he behaves as if just because of who he is and whose blood runs in his veins, he doesn't need to put in the work."

Of all the things said about Sextus Porcinianus Pullus, at the end of it all, Titus Domitius' words that day summed matters up better than anyone else.

Completely unmindful of my own personal drama, the trial of Admetos the Maezaei began, although I do not believe matters turned out the way either the Legate Sabinus, or Admetos, for that matter, expected. Honestly, I was barely paying attention, so absorbed was I in my own miseries, yet as distracted as I was, even I took notice of the series of events that occurred from the outset of the Maezaei chieftain's trial. The first was the appearance of a party that was identified as the Romans who lived and worked in Splonum, coming to attend the trial. Actually, this was not that unusual; oftentimes, those involved in legal matters, on either side, choose to attend the proceedings. What Sabinus found shocking, however, was that these men, all Roman citizens, came to support Admetos, not to denounce him or provide testimony against him. I believe this episode illustrates what those who spend all their time in Rome have a hard time understanding. From the perspective of our Legate, these men were being disloyal to Rome; looking at it from the other side, the plain truth was that Legates come and go, while these men stay behind, living, working, and yes, in some cases, marrying into the tribes whose lands we had conquered. Even putting on my Roman *toga*, so to speak, I would have been hard pressed to condemn these men for doing what was in their best interests; because of my own situation, I confess I took some satisfaction in seeing a member of our nobility embarrassed, even if it was at the hands of one of their counterparts in the barbarian tribes. I suppose it should be to Sabinus' credit that, once he was thwarted, he simply did not declare the old barbarian guilty and have his head taken off. Fairly quickly, we learned that his forbearance was not done out of justice for its own sake, because when Admetos was allowed to return to Splonum, it was without one member of the party.

While I cannot say with any certainty, my assumption at the time was that our Primus Pilus actually improved Sabinus' situation concerning Admetos by not killing the man's son when we captured him. Whatever the reasoning was, the result was the same; the crown prince was now a hostage to Rome. Ultimately, he was actually already on his way to Rome the day after the trial concluded. I caught a glimpse of Admetos, Dodonis, and the others of their party as they were escorted out of the gates, and I was struck by the thought that at least this time they were not consigned to mules. They were accompanied by a *turmae* of cavalry, quantities of which we never had enough of in the province. Even with this happy outcome, at least from the viewpoint of Admetos and the Maezaei, I was not optimistic that we would not be marching again, heading back to Splonum at some point in the near future.

Diocles himself came into the camp looking for me one day, near the end of our official duties. He found me easily enough; his ability to come and go as he pleased in the camp at Siscia was based on the fact that, as legendary as my Avus is, his man Diocles is just as much of one with the silent, invisible faces that support the Legions, and without whom we would not be a shade of what we are. When Titus Pullus assumed the post of Camp Prefect, in the early days of the reforms of the Legions made by the divine Augustus, which even then, in my fifth year, were still ongoing, Diocles was his right hand. Since Pharsalus, this slightly built, rather meek-looking little Greek had been part of some of the most famous, and brutal, campaigns in the history of Rome. Consequently, his presence in camp was a surprise only in the sense that he was coming to see me, and not one of his old friends like Lysander, the Fourth Cohort clerk.

"Can you come to the apartment after you're off duty?" he asked me.

"I suppose," I said, but since I had not planned on doing so, I was moved to ask him why.

"You'll find out when you get there," he assured me, and while there was something in his demeanor that made me uneasy, I agreed I would come as soon as I was able.

Which I did, although it would not be accurate to say I actually met Diocles in his apartment; in fact, I ran into him, Birgit, and his entire family, all four children, just after they had descended the steps. Whereas before I had been mildly puzzled, now I was completely confused.

"I thought I was meeting you up there." I pointed in the direction of his rooms.

"I never said you were meeting me," he answered evasively. "I just asked you to come to the apartment."

"But why?"

In answer, he simply pointed up the stairs, but it was the children who were giggling and whispering to each other, making sure that Uncle Titus was aware they had a secret he did not know that was the most befuddling. Nevertheless, I did as he had directed, climbing the stairs with a thudding heart. Being frank, I honestly had no idea what to expect, yet what I found was so far out of anything I could imagine that I am sure I made quite a sight, standing there with my mouth open, weaving like a drunken sot.

She had worn a cloak with a hood, but while she still had the cloak on, her head was uncovered so that I saw those locks of curly hair; however, it was her eyes that I most remember from that moment.

"Why," her voice was shaking, except what I thought was fear I quickly learned was something else entirely, "didn't you fight for me?" Her chin lifted slightly, and while her eyes were shining, it was the dilation of her nostrils that told me she was truly angry. "Why, Titus? Why did you let Tata scare you off so easily?" This was bad enough, but then one side of her mouth lifted in disdain as she scoffed, "I thought you were a brave man! A hero of Rome! So, why…" This was when her voice broke, along with her composure, and mine.

She did not finish, at least not right away, because her mouth was covered by mine after we rushed into each other's arms.

What followed was the most wonderful, confusing, and considering how matters ended, the most heartbreaking two months of my life. Despite my sacred vow to be as forthcoming and honest as it is possible to be, following the example of my Avus, I simply cannot bring myself to divulge any details of my love affair with Giulia Livinius. It is not, however, because I am a prudish man; the reason is twofold, although it mainly stems from my ardent desire to avoid bringing any shame onto Giulia herself. I know she acted as she did out of love for me, and was willing to risk everything that is important to a woman of Rome – her honor, her integrity, and most importantly, her chastity – throwing it all away for my sake. However, while this is the main explanation for my reluctance, if I am to be honest, at least as much as I am willing to be, the second reason is more powerful. After everything else, it is simply still too painful a subject for me to dwell upon, and the fact that it still ranks as such, even after the other losses I have suffered, should be instructive in itself. This is not to say I have no fond memories that I do not relive, although every time I do, despite my best attempts to avoid it, I find my thoughts sliding down into the abyss of those other memories that followed. However, in order to do justice to this account I am leaving behind, I will do my best to recall those golden moments, when anything was possible and for, at least a short time, the fact that my family birthright as equestrians had been denied me did not matter.

Of that first meeting, all I will say is that Giulia and I took possession of the other's heart and soul in the most fundamental and simple way. I cannot say that, after our first few moments together in Diocles' apartment, I was surprised that she was willing; what did was the fact that, when I led her into what had been Sextus' bedroom, where she only briefly hesitated, the room itself had been transformed. Despite my relative naivety in such matters, I was at least able to see how my brother's room had been transformed. Granted, the bed was still there, but on it was a much more elaborate and better quality blanket than I had seen before, and there were what seemed to be an inordinately large number of pillows. That, however, was only part of it; the room itself was lit with a number of small lamps, while the windows were shuttered tightly. Capping it all off, there was a lingering scent of such sweetness that it competed with that worn by Giulia herself, but only for a moment.

"Birgit," I breathed, and out of the corner of my eye, I saw Giulia nod.

"She…she…understood." Giulia's tone was as soft as mine.

I knew I should be the one taking the lead here, if only because I was more experienced in such matters, at least the physical aspect. Yet, I confess I was as nervous and uncertain as she looked, so instead of just plunging into things, so to speak, I led her to the edge of the bed and sat down, patting the spot next to me. That, at least, was how we started out.

"What about your father?" I asked her as we lay together for the first time after I made her my woman.

While I expected some defiant remark, instead, Giulia sighed; the feeling of her soft breath on my chest as her head was nestled in the crook of my shoulder is another one of my most treasured memories.

"I…I don't know," she replied honestly. "I mean," she shifted so her chin was on my chest so I could look into her eyes, "I know he likes you, Titus. In fact, he more than likes you. The only reason I could even forgive him was because I saw how upset he was after he learned about…" Her voice trailed off, and in that instant, I made the decision that, if only for her own sake, one of us had to be honest about our situation.

"About the fact that I'm not an Equestrian," I finished for her.

While she was obviously reluctant to do so, she finally nodded.

"Yes," she agreed, "that. But, Titus, I don't care about that! I truly don't!" Suddenly, she sat up, but in a move that both surprised and aroused me at the same time, she did not draw the sheet lying atop us to cover her nakedness. "If you never became an Equestrian, I wouldn't care!" she declared, and I did not then, nor do I doubt now her sincerity.

"Well, you should." I was determined to maintain some level of practicality; if I didn't, I reasoned to myself, what hope would either of us have?

"I don't," she replied fiercely, and this was when I noticed that, along with the flared nostrils, she had a defiant tilt of her chin when she was upset. "And even if you chose to stay in the Legions for the rest of your life, and I had to live like the camp wives, I'd do it!"

This actually startled, and quite frankly, disturbed me; just the thought of someone like Giulia forced to live the life of a Legion wife was too much to bear.

Which was what prompted me to say, "Well, there is some good news on that front. Not," I hurriedly added, "that it makes any difference. But," I hesitated, although it was not because I did not trust Giulia, "even though my family isn't actually *in* the Equestrian order, that doesn't mean you'd have to live like a camp wife."

"Why?" I could see she was genuinely puzzled, and I suppose it prompted her to ask, "Are you already about to be promoted? To – what is it called?"

"Optio," I supplied and, frankly, I was a bit put out she did not know the next rank up my ladder immediately, "but no, I'm not eligible for promotion yet." I was struck by an idea, and I asked her, partly to tease her, "But what if I'm one of those men who've risen as high as he's going to go? I mean, there's only sixty Optios in a Legion," I pointed out. "That means that most men don't actually get promoted."

"Then," she replied immediately, with no hesitation, "it's off and forget what I said." My mouth dropped open in shock in the instant before I saw the smile in her eyes. "I'd never marry a man without ambition!"

As I am sure she hoped, this made me burst out into laughter, which she joined in, and soon we were consumed in mirth, giddy with the moment and all that it meant. Which meant, naturally, that what I was about to inform her about concerning my family and our fortune was postponed for a time.

"What was the good news?" she asked me, except this time, while I was still lying on the bed, I was watching her dress. "You said there was good news about me being a camp wife."

"Oh, that." I yawned, although it was feigned. Deciding to torment her a bit in repayment for her jibe, I said, "Actually, I forgot what I was going to say."

"Liar." She laughed at me as she bent down to slip her shoes back on, whereupon they disappeared under her *stola*.

I believe it was her simple action while preparing to leave that prompted me to be truthful.

"Let me put it like this," I said carefully. "My family's in the Head Count, it's true. But, the truth is that as much as Augustus knows," I could not keep my mouth from feeling like I had tasted something bitter, "about my Avus, he didn't know nearly as much as he thought."

"Your Avus?" she asked, puzzled.

This was when I realized that, unlike with everyone else, I had used the name I called Titus Pullus from childhood without being careful to call him my grandfather.

"Titus Pullus," I said quietly, and I was absurdly pleased when she smiled at me.

"I like that you call him your Avus. I only saw him once, when I was very little, and Mama and Tata took me to watch the army return to Siscia. All I remember was being afraid of him. He was so…fierce looking! And he was so…huge! Like you!" The way she said this makes me believe this was the first time she actually made the connection, and my heart felt like it burst when I saw the pride in this association hit her. "I hadn't realized I'm in love with the grandson of a legend!"

If she's trying to stoke my ego, I suddenly thought with some wry amusement, too bad Domitius isn't here to assure her it's not necessary.

"Yes," I said awkwardly, but it was because she had just openly declared her love for me. "Well, Titus Pullus…Avus," I grinned, "made a lot of money when he marched for Divus Julius. But Diocles," I continued, "the man whose apartment this is…"

"I know Diocles," she interrupted. "I met him last week."

This was completely unexpected, and I felt a frown on my face, thinking that he had been meddling by going to seek out Giulia.

"You mean," I tried not to sound cross, but I could not help it, "he came looking for you? He…"

"No," she cut me off, shaking her head firmly, "he did no such thing! It was the other way around! I came looking for him. Or," she amended, "I came looking for you."

"Oh." It was all I could think to say, although I was mollified. "That's different. Anyway," I was determined to get through this once and for all, "while he started out as my Avus' slave, as you can see, he's no such thing anymore. And it was because of him and the way he managed my Avus' money that, even after Augustus confiscated three hundred thousand sesterces," I was cautiously happy that she gasped at the sum, "and supposedly left us with just one hundred thousand, we had…more."

"More? How much more?"

That, in fact, was a good question. For my own safety, my father had never allowed me to sit in on discussions where actual figures were discussed. However, as a child and teenager, I was a bit of a snoop, and I suppose I still am. But more than once, I had listened outside the door as my parents discussed such things with Diocles, before he and Birgit moved back to Siscia.

"I'm not exactly sure," I admitted, "but I know it's somewhere around…a million sesterces." I finished this mumbling.

I do not believe she could have looked any more shocked if I had slapped her.

"A *million* sesterces??" she gasped, and actually sat down heavily on the edge of the bed again as she tried to fathom this amount. I knew she was surprised, but I was not when the sudden joy suffused her face as she turned to me and said excitedly, "Titus! Don't you know what this means?"

"Apparently not," I said cautiously.

"Titus, a million sesterces will buy a seat in the Senate!" Seeing my face, she hurried on, "I'm not suggesting that you actually do that, but if my father knows how much money your family actually has, he's not going to give a rotten fig that you can't be an Equestrian! All we have to do is tell Tata that…."

"We can't do that," This prompted me to stand up myself, completely naked, and her face suddenly suffused with color, except it was not from embarrassment but desire, and it was only with a huge effort that we did not find ourselves back in bed. I did find it difficult to keep my mind on what I was saying, yet somehow I managed, "We can't do that," I repeated, adding, "my love." That made her blush again, although I was insistent as I explained, "Because if we do that, it won't be long before Augustus hears that his knowledge about my family's affairs wasn't accurate. And," I warned, "while you may not know as well as I do, but you've been alive long enough to know that the Princeps isn't one to make the same mistake twice."

Giulia stood silently for a moment, then closed her eyes and sighed, "You're right. I should have thought of that."

"There's no reason for you to think that way," I assured her. "But," I stepped closer to her to put my hands on her shoulders, "please don't breathe a word of what I just told you to anyone."

"I won't," she vowed, and judging from the fact that nothing ever happened to my family, at least in this regard, she never did.

I pulled on my tunic to walk her to the door, where we kissed again and, laughing, pushed ourselves away from each other as our bodies responded in the way they do.

"I'm already late as it is," she said, which did more to dampen my ardor than anything she could have done.

At least, almost.

"What will Plotina say?" I asked her, suddenly concerned, late as it might have been. "Will she tell your father?"

I was not prepared for her reply.

"Plotina," she smiled at me, kissing me on the cheek, "already knows. She helped this happen."

"I wonder," it came out without thinking, "if I just gave Plotina fifty denarii, your father would notice?"

The sound of her laughter rang in my ears as she left my arms.

With the aid of not only Plotina, but Diocles and Birgit, Giulia and I managed to see each other two or three times a week, although only one of those days was of sufficient duration to satisfy either one of us. My brother's bedroom became our own little world, and much to at least my surprise, of all the moments I treasure the most, those of a carnal nature come second to those where we just talked. Now, I must admit that at least part of my appreciation stems from the fact that these moments came after our lovemaking; while I might have loved them as much if that was all they were, just conversations, I know myself well enough to doubt that. The only thing I can say in my defense is that I do not believe any man is different in this regard. Still, it was in the quiet moments where we got to know each other, which prompted me to match Giulia's declaration of love she had given that first time, just a few days later. As much as I appreciated and loved her beauty and her physical essence, I found I adored her sharp mind and, perhaps more than anything, her sense of humor. She had an extremely sharp tongue, and as I found out, somewhat to my mortification, was very observant, not just about the physical habits of others, but their behavior. For example, she quickly saw how much pride I took in my physical size and prowess, and one afternoon, I was subjected to her performance as Titus Porcinianus Pullus which, despite my discomfort, had me doubled over in tears, laughing as hard as I have ever laughed, before or since. And yet, despite seeing me in a way that was less than flattering, she loved me nonetheless, and it was a love I returned. What had started out as a quest to bed a young maiden, for no other reason than I viewed it as a challenge, became something else entirely. I still vividly remember the day when this realization hit me, and ironically enough, it was not in her presence.

It was during the evening meal in camp as I sat with my comrades, Domitius by my side, when just as I was about to take a drink from my cup of watered wine, I was struck by it. Apparently, I froze, my cup hovering in front of my lips long enough that Domitius noticed.

"Titus, what is it?" He laughed. "Did you forget we've got guard duty tonight?"

Startled out of whatever place I was in, I turned and looked at him, the words coming slowly as, for the first time, I articulated the truth that, "I'm in love with Giulia."

This prompted him to laugh even harder, and he slapped me on the back.

"Really? I never would have guessed it," he hooted, his tone so mocking I could not have missed it no matter how much I might have wanted.

"You knew?" I asked, somewhat mystified, so sure was I that I had kept my feelings hidden.

But, before he could reply, Avitus, who sat across from me, spoke up.

"We all know," he assured me, grinning at me through a mouthful of porridge. "We've known for a long time!"

"But," I protested, "that's not how it was supposed to happen!"

If I did not see their reaction with my own eyes, I would have never believed that my comrades laughed harder than I had ever seen before.

"It never is," Domitius shouted in what I thought was unseemly delight. "You look like I did when I realized I loved Petrilla!" He shook his head and said more softly but still loud enough to hear over the shouts and hoots of laughter from my comrades, "Welcome to Hades, Titus! Welcome to Hades!"

Finally giving in, I joined in the laughter, despite it being aimed at me yet knowing it came from a good place as my comrades welcomed me to the brotherhood of those damned to have fallen in love.

In the outside world, the seasons advanced as they always did, and the business of the Legions continued apace. It was during my time of complete distraction that my brother Sextus was deemed to have completed the four months of training all *Tirones* supposedly undergo. I say "supposedly" because, in my case, this was not the case. However, while I did receive only a month of training, my fellow *Tirones* and I found ourselves on campaign at the end of that month, one that saw us all blooded. With Pannonia in the relatively peaceful state it was, here in the year of the Consulship of Lucius Cornelius Sulla and Augustus himself, his twelfth, my brother and his fellow *Tirones* were able to fulfill their entire four-month phase of training without interruption. While I knew in a very vague sense that the day was approaching, it was not until one morning formation when I noticed that the Seventh Cohort was actually missing that it occurred to me that it was about that time.

"Where's the Seventh?" I asked Asinius after we were dismissed.

"It's their turn," he replied.

There was no need for him to expand on this, and I groaned in dismay.

"So they're out in the field?" Sighing, I confided, "I forgot to talk to Sextus before they went out."

Asinius eyed me, but while he sounded sympathetic, he did point out, "That's not surprising. You've been walking around here with your head in the clouds. Or more likely," as always, his face was serious, "up your ass." He shrugged. "Anyway, it's not like there's anything going on."

"All's quiet in Pannonia," I agreed, using what had become the trite and often ironic term that our Legates sent to Rome.

This, as I was about to discover, was not exactly accurate. Two weeks and two days after they marched out of Siscia, the Seventh Cohort returned, but they did so with three of their own whose remains were contained in urns, and more than a dozen men bearing some sort of wounds. This kind of thing becomes common knowledge so quickly that before the Seventh was arranged in formation on the forum while their Pilus Prior gave his report to the *Praetorium*, the rest of us knew there had been at least one incident. I may not have been the first man to hurry to the forum, but I was among them, free to do so because we had ended our day shortly before. Standing on the edge of the forum, I watched as the rest of what is for the most part a ritual that is conducted a certain way, before the Septimus Pilus Prior bellowed the command for the Centurions of the other Centuries to take command and finish the process of returning home. Some Centurions allowed their men to fall out on the forum and make their own way back to their huts; this was usually only done with veteran Centuries, meaning that Tiburtinus did the same. Released from the iron discipline of the Legion, men instantly began chattering and moving in the direction of their area, competing with each other on how drunk they planned on getting, and how many whores they planned on engaging for their traditional night out in town after a march. And when a Cohort loses men, even in other Centuries, there is an added element to the debauchery, almost a frantic aspect as men simultaneously salute their fallen comrades in their own way and, more than anything else, in my opinion, revel in still being alive. As always, Sextus was easy to spot because of his height, and I instantly saw that, while he was in a small knot of men I assumed to be in his section, he did not seem to be engaged in the conversation. Drawing closer, I instantly saw he was distracted, withdrawn into himself, which I suppose is a family trait at certain moments, and it was that look of preoccupation that actually kept me from approaching him immediately. He had not noticed me, so taking a different route, I hurried to Tiburtinus' quarters, deciding to risk his wrath for showing up in his area, catching up with him just as he reached them. Seeing me coming, he stopped, wearily removing his helmet and wiping his face with his neckerchief as he waited for me to approach.

"I suppose," he spoke first, returning my salute, "you're here for a report on your brother."

"Yes, sir." I nodded, wondering why I had a knot in my stomach.

I suppose that feeling was prompted by what I had seen in Sextus' demeanor because I had a suspicion I knew its cause.

"We were lucky," he began, then stopped himself, "No, really, we were more than lucky. Your brother actually spotted something when he was part of the advance section. We were in Latobici territory, and we were approaching a spot that Arrianus had picked out as a likely spot for ambush. We were the lead Century that day, and just like the Pilus Prior thought, a bunch of the *cunni* were waiting. Except one of them obviously did something that caught your brother's eye."

Sextus Arrianus was the Septimus Pilus Prior, and was young for a Pilus Prior, even in the lower Cohorts, but he had earned a reputation for being a formidable fighter and good leader of men. There were some in the Legion for whom wagering on the prospects for promotion among our Centurions was akin to a business, who had tapped him as one likely to at least rise to the First Cohort, if not the entire Legion.

Tiburtinus continued with a chuckle, "I can see he's your brother, though."

"He's certainly tall," I agreed; I must laugh at myself how grudgingly I ceded even that, but to my surprise, and a moment later, irritation, Tiburtinus shook his head.

"That's not what I'm talking about." He eyed me with an ironically amused glint in his eye. "I'm talking about how fucking stubborn he is, and how convinced he is that he's right."

I must have given him a sour look; whatever it was, it made him laugh outright, which was a rare event in itself.

"That's exactly how he looked," he pointed at my face, "when Crispus told him he was imagining things. But your brother not only didn't listen, he actually stopped and wouldn't go another step." Shaking his head in amusement at the memory, he continued, "They almost got into a fistfight because Crispus was so sure that your brother was overreacting and seeing *numeni* in the trees." As quickly as it came, his good humor vanished, and he turned sober. "And it's a good thing he did. The sight of the advance guard stopping obviously spooked the bastards, because they came swarming out of the fucking bushes and launched a couple volleys of javelins."

He paused, forcing me to ask, "And?"

"And what?" His tone was innocent, but again, I saw his expression and realized he was toying with me again. "Oh, how did your brother do?" He considered, then said, "Well, aside from the fact that he went charging after those *cunni* without being ordered to and could have gotten himself killed, he actually did quite well. And," he added, "it's not like he was alone."

I believe he added this when he saw the look on my face, but frankly, this did not make me feel better. For the first time, I got a bare sense of what it must have been like for Tiburtinus to control me and my eagerness to prove my prowess.

As if reading my thoughts, he gave me a light punch in the shoulder and asked, "Does that sound familiar?"

"Maybe," I agreed grudgingly. "But that was different."

The instant I said it, even I could not keep a straight face at the irony, and we shared a quiet laugh.

"So," I returned to the topic at hand, "did he get his sword wet at least?"

"Yes, he did," he told me, then a shadow crossed his face that gave me an instant of warning that there was more, "but it wasn't without cost. He caught up to a pair of warriors, and he got himself in a bit of trouble. You know how it is," he shrugged, "with new *tiros*. They're all…"

"…balls and no brains," I finished for him.

This was Tiburtinus' favorite phrase when describing most *Tirones*, and I knew that if Sextus was anything like I had been, it applied doubly for the Pullus boys than for most others.

"Exactly," he confirmed. "But he managed to get out of it himself. He doesn't see it that way," once more his face changed, returning to its normal sober, even grim countenance, "especially because of what happened."

Again, another chill went through me, because as familiar as I was with Gnaeus Tiburtinus, I was able to interpret the subtler signs of his emotions as shown through what, to most, appeared to be the same, expressionless face.

"What did happen?"

Shrugging, he continued, "He's sure that he caused what happened to Crispus. Both Lucanus and I, Pluto's cock, the other men in the section," he emphasized, "tried to convince him that what happened was on Crispus' books, not his."

Spurius Lucanus was Sextus' Sergeant, a hard man in the mold of Tiburtinus himself, but I was impatient to hear exactly what had happened, not who was involved in trying to make my brother feel better.

"So?" I demanded. "Why's that? Why was it on Crispus?"

"According to the others," Tiburtinus explained, "Pullus had clearly ended one of the *cunni*, and the other one was falling as Crispus caught up. Your brother had already turned to give chase to another of the bastards as Crispus approached the second one." He shrugged and said simply, "Crispus assumed that the man was dead, and he wasn't, not quite. Crispus paid for it."

There was a silence as I considered what Tiburtinus had told me, not needing any more information about what had occurred. Our days are filled with all sorts of bits of what might seem to be random information, but are, in reality, important things to know, gleaned through hard-won experience by men more veteran than we are. And one of those pieces concern the importance of making sure a dead enemy is actually truly dead. Every veteran has either heard, or seen firsthand what happens when a mistake is made; it sounded like Crispus was one of those who did, and now Sextus was punishing himself.

"But Sextus blames himself," I muttered as half-question, half-statement.

Tiburtinus only nodded in reply, and I had to sigh as I shook my head.

"Can I go talk to him?" I asked Tiburtinus, somewhat proud of myself for actually acting in the proper manner.

"If you think it'll do any good," he replied. "My experience is that men have to work through things like this on their own. But," he jerked his head in the general direction of Sextus' hut, "it wouldn't hurt to try." Thanking him, I turned to go, but he called out, "Just don't take too long. He's got other duties."

I had to smile at this; sympathy is a precious commodity in the Legions, and Tiburtinus had just expended his quota, probably for the month. Such are the Legions.

My talk with Sextus, as so many of them had, did not go at all as I planned. Perhaps the only thing I did correctly was to pull him out of his hut and away from his other comrades. From the instant he saw my face, his reluctance was clear to see, which unfortunately did not put me in a good frame of mind; as I think about it now, I can see that this attempt to act as big brother was doomed to failure from the beginning.

It began awkwardly with the two of us standing facing each other, both of us eyeing the other, before Sextus blurted out, "Well? What is it? I've got a lot to do."

"I just wanted to come and see how you were doing," I could hear the defensive tone in my voice.

"How I'm doing?" His eyebrow raised as he eyed me skeptically. "Why? I mean, why now? I haven't seen you in weeks. What's so special about now?"

"I know about that," I admitted, "and I'm...sorry. I've just been..."

"Busy," he cut me off. "Yes, I know. I've heard all about how...busy you've been!"

Although I was not sure what to expect, Sextus being angry with me was the farthest from my mind, and in some way, this helped matters from ending even worse than they did for the simple reason I was more shocked than anything.

"Sextus, I said I was sorry." I held out my hands. "Besides, I just thought it would be better if I stayed away for a while, because..."

"Because you broke my nose?" He folded his arms. "Is that why? Or was there some other reason?"

"No," I acknowledged, "that was the main reason."

"Oh," he countered sarcastically. "Really? You mean it's not because you've been busy with that girl? What was her name again?"

"Giulia." I felt the first stirring of anger. "Her name is Giulia."

"Yes, her." He waved a dismissive hand.

That, unfortunately, was too much, and before either of us could blink, I had a fistful of his tunic, pulling him close so our faces were mere inches apart. Oh, he struggled, but while to everyone else, Sextus was deceptively strong, as I had learned almost since we could walk, when I chose to, I could handle him the way our sister Miriam treated one of her rag dolls. Which was what I did, shaking him several times with such force his head snapped back and forth.

"If you don't show her some respect," I snarled, although my tone was still at a conversational level in order not to attract undue attention, "I'll make what I did to you on the training ground look like a pat on your ass!"

He struggled mightily, pushing against me first, then he launched a wild swing at my head, but I saw it coming and simply jerked out of the way. Still, it was sufficient to cool my ire enough that I suddenly released him, doing it in such a way that he staggered backward a step. For a matter of several heartbeats, we stood glaring at each other, then I forced myself to calm down.

"I came," I said between breaths, "to make sure you were all right because I heard you saw some action. I…I was worried."

That seemed to startle him, although I did not, nor do I now know why. Frankly, he did not seem to comprehend this; at least, it did not seem so to me.

"Oh," he finally spoke, then looked down at the street, kicking at a paving stone. Finally, he shrugged and said, "I'm fine."

"I heard you were more than fine," I replied, which seemed to please him. "Tiburtinus told me that you were the one of your section who sniffed out that ambush and refused to go along with the rest of them. He told me you were responsible for saving some lives. That," I pointed out, "is something to be proud of, Sextus."

"It didn't save Crispus." He blurted this out with such vehemence that even someone who did not know my brother would have recognized this caused him pain. "I didn't…"

"No," I cut him off emphatically, but this time when I reached for him, it was to put a hand on my brother's shoulder. "Sextus, what happened to Crispus is *not* your fault! That mistake belongs to him, and…"

"Well, he's the one paying for it, isn't he?" His face twisted into a bitter grimace, and I saw his eyes start to shine.

"That's true," I agreed with him, but I am ashamed to say that in the moment I was more worried we would be seen while my brother was crying out where everyone could see. "But, Sextus, how many times have Tiburtinus and Lucanus reminded you *tiros*…?"

Again, he interjected, saying hotly, "I'm not a *tiro* anymore! Which you'd know if you'd been there for the ceremony!"

This was when I realized what this was about; his feelings were still raw from the fact that I had neglected to come to see him and his fellow recruits officially recognized as *Miles Gregarii*, and I admit I felt badly. The fact that the ceremony happened to coincide with one of my times with Giulia meant I did not feel as badly as I probably should have. Nevertheless, I was not so insensitive to ignore his feelings, and I did try to assuage them.

"Sextus," I tried to infuse as much sincerity in my tone as I could without being obviously false, "I am truly sorry I missed that. I know it's a big moment, and I should have been there. But," I felt compelled to point out, "that's not what we're talking about now. We're talking about the fact that you feel guilty when you have no reason to. Besides, I also heard you were blooded too, neh? And two men at the same time? That's impressive!"

Suddenly, he broke out into a laugh, shoving me as he said, "Oh, please! How many times have I heard you boast about how many men you killed your first time in battle?"

"Well," I could not help grinning, "what can I say? I *am* the older brother, after all. Nothing you do will ever be as good as me!"

"Says you," he retorted. "Just wait and see!"

We bickered back and forth like this for the next few moments, and I was happy to see that when we parted, things between us were right again, and he seemed to have accepted that he was blameless when it came to the first death of a comrade he would experience. It is just too bad that both of those were temporary conditions.

If I learned anything from reading about the life of Titus Pullus, it is that, ultimately, whatever joys the gods give us mortals, they can take them away just as quickly. When measured against the years I have lived even now, the actual length of time where I was deliriously happy is so brief that sometimes I wonder if it was actually real. This is especially true when I actually sat down and calculated the total number of watches Giulia and I spent together, and watches are the proper term of measurement. Not even days, certainly not weeks, but watches, spread over eight short weeks, including one wonderful night when, with Plotina's help, Giulia and I were together when her parents went to visit her mother's ailing sister in Poetovio. After dark, Plotina smuggled my love out of her villa, Giulia wearing the cloak she had donned for her first visit to Diocles' apartment, but while

Giulia thought it was all a great adventure, I was, frankly, quite out of my mind from nervousness at her being discovered. Nevertheless, once she was there, my fears were quickly forgotten, and for that, I owe a debt of gratitude to Diocles, Birgit, and the children, who insisted that Giulia sit down and share the evening meal. Oh, it was awkward at first, but fairly quickly, there was conversation and laughter as first Diocles regaled her with a number of tales of my misdeeds when I was young, then the children, very shyly at first but growing increasingly bolder, started peppering Giulia with questions. The fare that night was more extravagant than normal, telling me that Birgit was also invested in what I was beginning to suspect was a conspiracy to see me tied to Giulia; I could not have been happier about that. Only one topic was never discussed, at least openly, and that was the huge, jagged rock of our problem that, while submerged, was still lurking there just under the surface and waiting to rip out the bottom of the vessel containing Giulia's, and now my, hopes.

The only time matters became a bit tense was when Gisela, Diocles and Birgit's oldest daughter, asked her timidly, "Are you going to be our aunt?"

Not surprisingly, this stopped all other talk, and the room became silent, uncomfortably so, at least for me. But when I tried to give Giulia a subtle shake of my head, while she clearly saw me, I knew her answer when her chin tilted in response, creating in me a unique feeling of happiness, pride in her defiance, overlaid with a strong sense of anxiety and unease.

"If," she told Gisela, "I'm lucky and the gods are good to us, yes, Gisela. I would like that very much."

This clearly pleased Gisela, who was not quite ten at the time. At least so I thought; keeping track of birthdays and ages has never been a strength of mine. Glancing over at Alexandros and Titus, the former now almost twelve, and the latter six, I saw they were grinning as well, which only added to that mix of feelings I described earlier, each of them strengthened in equal proportions. It was the expression on Diocles' face, however, that was most unsettling, although I was thankful Giulia was facing away from him as he looked on with a sadness that told me more than any words. I remember this moment as one where, albeit briefly, I was pulled out of my temporary madness, recognizing that my Greek's face reflected the reality and hopelessness of the situation in which Giulia and I found ourselves. Unfortunately, my return to sanity was short-lived, at least right then. Nevertheless, that one night, however brief it was, where Giulia and I were able to pretend that this evening was simply a taste of what our future together would be like for the rest of our lives, is a bittersweet memory that, despite my best efforts, my mind returns to quite often. Especially since, as it turned out, this would be our last time together.

One reason the night spent with Giulia was so special was due to the fact that two days after this, the first line Cohorts of the 8th were sent out into the province. Unlike the last time, when we were informed only when we arrived at Splonum the reason for our foray, this was an expedition planned well in advance and actually occurs every year after the campaigning season is officially over. Something Rome learned early on when subjugating then colonizing new provinces, dating back to the time of Divus Julius, an occupying army that settles in for the winter without rousing itself to remind the natives they are still ruled by Rome is practically begging for all manner of trouble. Consequently, this sortie out into the countryside, conducted around the month of December, was also one of the most hated of our duties, simply for the hardships involved in living under the canvas during the winter. It is at times like this, especially when I looked around at some of my comrades, that it was emphasized to me how fortunate I was in the sense of having enough money to purchase items that made life in the field easier. Specifically, I had augmented my winter gear with a *sagum* lined with fur, along with several Gregarii's tunics, dyed the proper shade of red, but made of two thicknesses of wool instead of one. Finally, I had also invested in something that, as trivial as it may sound in some ways, actually gave me more problems in the form of scrutiny and suspicion than any other article of clothing. Whereas before, like all of my comrades who had invested in their own comfort and protection with fur-lined socks, of which we wore on both feet and hands, at least when we were on the march or when we were performing duties where they did not hamper our abilities, I had gone one step farther and had a pair of fur-lined gloves made. As one might expect, gloves of any sort are expensive; lining them with fur even more so, except in having a pair of my own, to some of the men around me I was exhibiting thoughts and ideas above my station.

"Where did you get enough money for those?"

That it was Balbinus who asked this was not much of a surprise, but I confess I had not anticipated it would be a pair of gloves that ignited his suspicion.

"Is that any of your business?" I replied coldly.

Naturally, he did not like this, but neither could he argue with me about it, at least, openly. What he could do, however, was exactly what he did, which was to begin a whispering campaign with the rest of the Century, although I did not learn of this immediately. I am lucky in the sense that, within my own section, none of my comrades of the First seemed interested in his insinuations aside from Publius Appuleius, but not only was he a close comrade with Balbinus and was obligated by custom to support the holder of his will, anyone with eyes could see his participation was a case of feeling obligated to do so and that his heart was not in it. But, as I quickly learned, outside of my section, the view of me was decidedly mixed, and as much as it pains me to say it, those who liked me and those who loathed me were evenly divided. Going further, as I was about to learn, very few of my comrades in the First Century viewed me in a neutral light; it seemed that I was either loved or hated in almost equal proportion. And for those who held the latter view, those gloves turned out to be all the fuel for their particular fires they needed.

"He thinks he's better than us," was how it was put most often. "Just because of who he's related to, he thinks that puts him above the rest of us."

This is something of an amalgam of what men were actually saying, yet this was the essence of the sentiment being expressed. And I can see now I did not help matters at all, reacting in a way whereby I inadvertently gave them fodder that fed their beliefs about me. All I can say in my defense is that, not only was I still young – I was approaching my twenty-third birthday – I was also distracted by my personal affairs in the form of Giulia. The result was that instead of trying to show men they were wrong about me, I went out of my way to emphasize our difference, except it was not along class lines, but in my superior strength and skill. Whereas before, taking a lesson from my Avus' account, where he earned the enmity of many of his comrades because of his almost obsessive need to prove he was the better man in any form of contest, at least as they related to his job as a Legionary, I had always held back a bit against men I faced. The only exceptions to that, of course, were against Gaius Maxentius in my first year, and Aulus Bestia when I transferred to the First of the First. However, besides those two occasions, I had always made sure I was careful not to overwhelm my opponent, especially when I was acting in my role as instructor for the First Century. As my Avus had said, while neither of us had anything to do with our respective size and the natural strength that came from it, we would have been foolish not to use those gifts. The difference between us had been in our application of those favors, yet when the whispers about me started, I took out my frustrations on my comrades, both as a way to keep from exploding in anger, but also to demonstrate that their belief that I thought I was superior was not just my opinion, but was a demonstrable fact. And the only person who was surprised I was, in fact, making matters worse instead of quelling the talk was me; that it was Titus Domitius who was the only man who would tell me this to my face is not just a mark of his courage, but in how far gone I was in my own rage. This, however, only came later, after our foray into the province. Also, it is with some sincerity that I claim I was distracted, because the night before our departure, when I went to Diocles' apartment, I had received a cryptic message, written in a feminine hand I knew was neither Giulia's or Plotina's, informing me that Giulia would not be able to meet me that evening. As much as I tried, I could not put this missive in a positive light; try as I might, I could not recall seeing or hearing about another female slave who might have been part of our conspiracy to be together. Regardless of the true meaning, it would have to wait for our return to Siscia.

While it was cold, after the winter of three years before, all of us were inured to the elements, at least as much as a man can be. And, frankly, I fared much better than the others, thanks in no small part to those gloves that had already begun causing such problems with the others. The four Cohorts of the 8th marched east, our first stop at a spot about seventeen miles east of the town, a village belonging to the Sisciani, for whom, of course, Siscia got its name. The name of the village has escaped me; as any man stationed in Pannonia will tell you, more often than not these places have no real name, but instead were described by their location. In this case, the village was situated at the base of a hill, next to a large stream that originated somewhere up the slope that ultimately fed into the Savus. More importantly, at least as far as we were concerned, the Sisciani were actually one of the tribes friendliest to Rome; I believe their proximity and constant contact with us helped. When a man's belly is full, as is his wineskin, and when he can travel without fear of being preyed upon by a roving band from tribes hostile to them, it tends to make whatever resistance they might have to Roman rule a bit problematic. When all is said and done, it is hard for most men to keep the flames of resentment burning brightly when they see that their wives and children are fed, sheltered, and safe. Granted, in exchange, they must give Rome a portion of their earnings, whether it be in the form of coin or goods, and they have to abide by our laws. That, at least from the viewpoint of Rome, and one in which I share, is a small price to pay for all that Rome provides. And, while I would not put the reception we received at the same level as the one whenever we returned to Siscia, it was at least nice to see the faces lining the road into the village were not hostile, or even sullen in any way. The bitter cold was, at least somewhat, assuaged by the reception we received, particularly from the young women of the village as, inevitably, some of them managed to attract the attention of one of the men marching in the ranks. Stopping for the night, I will say that, although the camp we made was the normal one for whenever we were out on campaign, the duty Century was a bit lax in enforcing traffic to and from the camp, if one takes my meaning. Subsequently, when we left the next morning, the relatively small tail that is almost always part of a Legion on the march had added perhaps twenty to their numbers, which led to inevitable squabbles as men vied for the affections of these new additions.

All of this I barely noticed, as I was completely absorbed in my own problems. The fact that I was warmer than my comrades only mattered, or was noticed by, them; I barely registered the muttered comments and looks that communicated the feelings of men like

Balbinus. Despite my self-absorption, throughout it all, Titus Domitius proved to be a true friend. Although we did not march together, whenever we stopped for a rest break and when we halted for the day, he would be by my side, and while I can admit now that at the time I found his constant chatter somewhat grating, even then, I was more thankful for it than I could ever express to him, understanding even then he was trying to keep me from wallowing in misery, despite my determination to do that very thing. Every day I spent away from Giulia I was convinced was a torture that no other man in the history of the world could possibly understand; the fact that I could not have been more wrong was one reason I believe Domitius was as intent as he was on turning my attention away from my own desolation. Who else but another man, especially a young one, could understand the depths of despair and longing that suffuse a soul in love?

Our Primus Pilus had other things on his mind beside a lovesick Sergeant in his Century, and from our first stop, we continued east. In doing so, the farther away from Siscia we got, the chillier the reception from the natives. Once we left Sisciani territory, we passed into the lands of the Breuci, one of the larger tribes, larger even than the Maezaei. They had been one of the last tribes to submit to Rome, back when Augustus had led the campaign against them. Not surprisingly, their greeting was in direct contrast to that of the Sisciani; my comrades made many jokes about the fact that we were unlikely to gain any more adherents to the tail already following us. Regardless, I do not believe any of us had the slightest idea or suspicion that the Breuci would express their displeasure in the way they did. Making camp in the middle of a wide valley where a Breuci village was situated just south of the complex of hills that marks the boundary between the Jasi and Breuci lands, because of the light in which the Breuci still viewed Rome, our Primus Pilus, rather than acting in a manner that I would have expected from the late Publius Canidius, he had us make camp some three miles from the main Breuci town rather than adjacent to it. His decision brought about much second-guessing and speculation by those of us in the ranks who had been exposed to the style and attitude of the late Urso.

"He'd have never camped so far away," was how Avitus put it. "We'd have been set up right next to that fucking town, just daring those *cunni* to try something like what they did."

What he was referring to was what had taken place during the night we were camped near the Breuci town. At some point, a small party of warriors slipped into the ramshackle collection of homemade hovels and shelters in which those women, and some men, who had decided to follow along, used to keep out the cold. The intruders were nothing if not careful in their targeting; only those women who were not obviously Roman were slaughtered, along with the handful of men who were native to Pannonia. In the case of the latter, most of these men were either servants of Centurions who were not on the Legion rolls, serving as extra body slaves, although there were also a handful of the merchants who always travel with us in the hopes there is an opportunity to buy plunder we may take. About a watch before dawn, a series of shrill screams woke the men of the Centuries whose tents were nearest to the Porta Decumana, where the smaller camp is always located a short distance away. The duty Centurion alerted Atticus, who was sufficiently alarmed to rouse the rest of us. As quickly as one more Century was up and armed, Atticus ordered the guard Century out through the Porta Decumana, sending them out to determine the cause for the disturbance. By the time they returned to the forum, the remainder of our force was already arrayed and waiting; yawning, and grumbling, but still ready for whatever came next. Thanks to our spot, we were close enough to see the Centurion of the returning men stride up to report to Atticus, who was standing just a couple paces away, and even in the dim light, I could see how shaken the man was.

"Primus Pilus, by the time we got there, there wasn't anything we could do," he informed Atticus.

"Do about what?" Atticus asked, which I, for one, thought was a perfectly reasonable question.

But the Centurion – I recognized him as the Secundus Princeps Prior – did not seem to know how to answer, hesitating as he tried to frame his response, finally coming up with, "W-what those Breuci bastards did!"

Except he stopped there, but either Atticus was feeling patient, or more likely, he was still shaking the sleep from his mind, because he simply asked, "And what was that?"

"They slaughtered the camp followers!" the Centurion exclaimed. "But not all of them! Just the women who joined us yesterday!"

This seemed to wake Atticus up.

"Pluto's thorny cock!" he exclaimed bitterly, then began rubbing the back of his neck. "This," the way he spoke seemed as if he was talking more to himself, "is bad."

"Really?" I heard someone behind me mutter. "You think so?"

The inside of my cheek started bleeding as I bit down hard to keep from laughing outright.

"How many?" Atticus asked the Centurion; frankly, I was just happy I had managed to keep myself from drawing his attention.

The Princeps Prior considered, then answered, "We didn't take an exact count, but I'd guess at least twenty dead. A couple of them were still alive, but I doubt they'll see another sunrise."

"Fuck me," Atticus groaned. "Why? What did they hope to accomplish?"

Since it was a question, the Princeps Prior actually seemed to consider this, but before he could reply, Atticus waved him to silence.

"Never mind," he said wearily. Turning to address the rest of us, he bellowed, "The Cohorts are dismissed! Return to your tents! We'll sort this out in the morning!"

That, I remember thinking, will be easier said than done.

Rather than resume the march the next morning, we were ordered instead to the forum, where we were given our orders. They were simple, as far as they went; the three full Cohorts and five Centuries of the First were to surround the town, while we would accompany Atticus into the center of it to confront the village headman. It was impossible for me not to shudder as I thought back to when we had marched into Topulcava. I reminded myself this was a different matter altogether; we were there officially, for one thing. And we were not coming with the purpose of seizing any of the inhabitants like we had with the Colapiani, or the Maezaei, for that matter. But what made me feel better, if I am being honest, was the fact that instead of just fifty of us who were part of Urso's off-the-books business at Topulcava, or just the First Cohort with the Maezaei, I was accompanied this time by four full Cohorts. Nevertheless, I could see I was not the only one feeling nerves as we marched out of the camp. A third of a watch later, we approached the village at the foot of the hills, but when we were still several hundred paces away, Atticus ordered the halt for our Century, whereupon we waited as the rest of our force spread out. Once in position, each of the *Corniceni* from every Century blasted the sound that signaled their readiness.

"Century!" Atticus bellowed. "Forward...march!"

Our heavy footsteps announced our entrance, where the sound of the horns had alerted the Breuci of our presence, causing the people of the village to come streaming out of their low huts to line the single, muddy street that led directly the headman's hall. Emerging from it was a man, about the age of Admetos of the Maezaei, except that was where the resemblance ended. I cannot say he reminded me of Draxo, exactly, but I believe the best way to describe him is by saying that, just by his appearance and the way he carried himself, this man was closer to Draxo than Admetos. However, the other thing I noticed was what seemed to me to be a look of resignation on his face, which made me wonder if he had either ordered his men to slaughter the Pannonian women in the followers' camp, or what I believed more likely, he had learned of it before our arrival. Whatever the case, he strode out to meet us, or Atticus to be precise, who was marching a few paces ahead of us. Judging by the demeanor of the quickly gathering crowd, it was not lost on them we had not marched in column, but in our open, fighting formation, meaning that, with a series of blasts on his whistle, we could make a few quick adjustments and form all manner of formations, depending on the situation. I just hoped we would not need any of them.

"Are you the headman of this village? Or do you have a higher rank among the Breuci?" Atticus asked brusquely, although it instantly became apparent that the older man neither understood nor spoke our tongue, because he turned and looked questioningly to a man just a few years older than me, standing slightly behind him.

There was a brief exchange before the younger man presumably answered, "This is Zeno."

Instantly, Atticus' manner changed; if anything, becoming more wary, as he should have. Zeno of the Breuci had been one of the last sub-chiefs to submit to Rome, and he was regarded with open suspicion by most of us who were veterans in the province. While it was true he had not been actively rebellious against Rome since their uprising was crushed, there had been persistent rumors that Zeno had not given up the struggle, but was continuing it by indirect means. Specifically, he was supposedly using the wealth of the Breuci to persuade other tribes to make our lives miserable. If this was true, I had to admit he was doing a good job of it. I would not have been a bit surprised, for example, to learn that Admetos had been selling our shipments of iron ore to others at the behest of Zeno.

"Zeno," Atticus repeated the name, making it sound like a curse, which unsurprisingly did not seem to settle well with either the older chief or his interpreter. "I've heard about you." Suddenly, he turned his attention to the younger man, asking bluntly, "And who are you?"

Again, I was not surprised to see the flush of color on the younger man's face, although his voice was steady and even as he replied, "My name is Zagreus." He paused as if he was considering something, and it became clear why when he added, "I am Zeno's son."

The lack of reaction on the part of our Primus Pilus told me he had at least suspected this, but Atticus was not finished with the younger man yet, asking him, "And which son are you?"

Now the man Zagreus hesitated again, but he finally replied, "I am his firstborn son."

"Which means you're his heir, correct?"

"Yes," Zagreus' reaction was a mixture of reluctance and puzzlement, "Centurion. That is correct."

An unfamiliar expression came over Atticus' features as he took this in, then seemingly dropped the subject, proceeding instead to describe the cause for our entrance into the village. Once he did so, Zagreus relayed the information to his father, and despite my earlier impression, if he was playing at being surprised, he did a good job of it. However, now that the words were in a tongue all could understand, the crowd, which had been silent and sullen, suddenly began buzzing with talk, and out of the edge of my vision, I could see my comrades to my left begin looking about for signs of trouble. The old man started speaking rapidly, yet while my understanding of their language was limited, I could pick out enough words to know he was denying not only any responsibility, but knowledge of the event itself. Then, just before Zagreus started the process of repeating his father's words, from over our shoulder, in the direction of the hills, came the blast of a *cornu.* This had two effects; one was that we instantly became alert, while it reminded the villagers we were far from alone. Very quickly, the *cornu* from the other Centuries sounded, making a ring of noise that surrounded the village, and I saw Zeno close his eyes in what I took to be despair at this announcement that Rome had come to their village. Only then did Zagreus finish his father's denial, which did not impress Atticus in the slightest. Turning, he beckoned to Asinius from his spot in the rear, and our Optio came trotting up, whereupon they withdrew out of both our earshot and that of the villagers, but only after some of our men stepped out of the formation and pushed the Breuci away to create a buffer. Despite my best effort, I could not hear anything they said, then Atticus spun about and returned to Zeno and his son, still standing in front of us. Again, a quiet exchange between the trio I could not hear, then I saw Zeno shake his head emphatically, while Zagreus did not seem any less perturbed, waving his hand in a motion like he was trying to shoo us away.

Without any warning, Atticus turned and pointed to Avitus and me, snapping, "You two! Come take custody of this man!"

Again? I groaned, but I was moving as I did so.

"Which one, sir?" Avitus asked, but we were both surprised when Atticus pointed to Zagreus.

At first, it did not seem the crowd understood what was happening, but then once I grabbed him by one arm and Avitus the other, there was an explosion of noise as the people surrounding us started protesting.

"You better tell them what will happen if they try and stop us." I leaned down and said this in the younger man's ear. "We've got your village surrounded."

I saw Zagreus' mouth turn down in a bitter grimace, then he gave a nod. Saying something to his father, Zeno nodded as well, although no less reluctantly than Zagreus. The young man raised his hands in the air, which made Avitus and me jerk in surprise, except it was only to quiet the crowd, which he managed to do somehow. It was not instantly, but it happened quickly enough it surprised me, nor was it truly very quiet. Fortunately, he spoke loudly enough to be heard; once he was done, there was an angry mutter rippling around the throng, but none of them tried to stop us. Still not completely sure what was going on, nonetheless, we spun about and marched out of the village, going the same way we had come, except this time, there was a Breuci in the middle of our formation.

We learned more from Asinius after we returned to camp, and while I cannot say I agreed with the logic behind Atticus' choice of Zagreus, I could only admire the cunning turn of mind displayed by our Primus Pilus. However, it also reminded me where he had come from, where this way of thinking is practically a requirement if a man wants to not just survive, but thrive and advance.

"The Primus Pilus took the youngster for a couple reasons," Asinius explained to us when he stopped by our tent. "First, he thinks it's unlikely that the old man was responsible for what happened."

This I agreed with, at least judging from the chieftain's reaction, and I saw the others agreed with me, although I, for one, was not prepared for what else Asinius had to say.

"No," the Optio went on, "he thinks that it's Zagreus who's behind what happened."

"Why?" Domitius asked, beating the rest of us.

"Because the Primus Pilus believes that the young wolf is getting impatient waiting for the old one to leave the pack and die," he said, but as I studied his face, as usual, it was impossible for me to tell how Asinius felt about this, and I knew if I could not, knowing him better than the others, I was sure the others were as unsure as I was. Going on, he informed us, "He thinks that Zagreus orchestrated the attack, knowing we'd be forced to respond, and that the most likely suspect would be his father." Shrugging, he added, "And even if it's not true, we still have a powerful lever to use on the old man."

"So what's next?" Sido asked.

"The Primus Pilus has sent a messenger to Zeno, giving him until sunset tonight to surrender the men responsible for the attack, or we execute his son."

We sat, considering this, and I forced myself to try and think in the same way a member of our upper class would, where everything they do is carefully considered as part of an overall strategy that is part of their goal of achieving their political aims.

"What if," I ventured, "Zeno doesn't lift a finger? What if he thinks we're bluffing?"

"Do you think the Primus Pilus is bluffing?" Asinius asked me quietly.

"No," I admitted, "but that doesn't mean anything. It's what Zeno thinks that's important."

"Well, as it happens," Asinius favored me with a small smile, "I thought the same thing, and asked him about it." Shrugging, he continued, "And our Primus Pilus has thought of that possibility, and the way he sees it, either way, we gain something."

"How so?" Avitus was the one who asked and, frankly, I was happy he did so first.

"Because," Asinius replied, "if Zeno doesn't think we're bluffing, he's going to give us whoever's responsible. But, if he does, we execute his son. And," he added meaningfully, "the one who they both admitted was his heir. Which means it's highly likely that this will create all manner of problems for Zeno of the Breuci. You know that these barbarians' nobility are just like ours, always maneuvering and scheming to seize control. The Primus Pilus believes that if we execute Zagreus, we won't have to worry about the Breuci making any mischief for us for months. He's confident that Zeno will be more concerned protecting his line's claim to their kingship than exacting vengeance on Rome for killing his son."

This was quite a bit for us to chew on, and he left us in a thoughtful mood, whereupon we passed the time arguing the merits of Atticus' gambit back and forth. Despite my misgivings, I silently saluted the Primus Pilus, although at the same time, I felt a sense of distaste as I thought about where he had learned how to think in this manner.

I have often wondered how Atticus truly felt when, shortly before sundown, the *bucina* sounded the call that a party was approaching the gates. No orders were given for those of us not on duty, but it appeared as if our entire complement surrounded the small forum to watch as more than two dozen Breuci warriors, all of them wearing as close to the same clothing as barbarian tribes can achieve, while being similarly uniform in their height and demeanor, marched in a double column, with eight other men between them, each of these men with their hands bound and linked together by a length of rope looped around their necks. Leading them was Zeno, the only man who was mounted, which was slightly unusual for a tribe of Pannonia, although I understood it was done for the sake of appearances and strategically, since it gave the older chieftain the high ground, in a manner of speaking. The prisoners were understandably subdued, but were evenly divided between those who kept their eyes on the ground and those who stared at us defiantly. One of the prisoners even spat on the ground, eliciting a low growl from those of us watching, but Atticus, while not saying a word, simply raised his *vitus* in a silent signal that stopped the sound immediately. It was not lost on any of us that by doing so, we were demonstrating one of the most important distinctions between the Legions of Rome and warriors of the barbarian tribes; our discipline and instant obedience to orders is unparalleled, and is why I, and all of my comrades with whom I ever talked about this, do not believe we will ever be defeated in any meaningful way. When Rome desires it, we conquer and subdue all those who stand before us, and make no mistake, at this moment in a forum of a small camp in Pannonia, we understood very well we were giving these barbarians a reminder of that fact, if only by our sudden silence. The men escorting the prisoners, who I am certain were members of Zeno's household guard, were more disciplined in their mien than the prisoners, yet they clearly were not happy about this particular mission. Awaiting them was both Atticus, and Zagreus who, despite looking unhappy, was none the worse for his short period of captivity, while his presence there was not only proof to his father he still lived, but to interpret the coming exchange. Since the forum was not the normal size, nor had we actually been called into a formation, it allowed us to edge closer, enabling us to hear Zeno begin speaking, although he still sat astride his horse.

"I'm surprised the Primus Pilus lets him sit up there like that," Domitius murmured to me, but while I agreed, Atticus did not seem perturbed in the slightest.

Once the older man was finished, Zagreus said, "My father has brought you those men responsible for the attack on your followers' camp. He turns them over to you for...*Roman* justice to be done," I suppose he could not help endowing the name of their conquerors with such bitterness, but as understandable as it may have been, it still did not go well with us.

"Fucking bastard," I heard someone mutter; I believe it was Aelianus. "If he'd kept his *cunni* in hand, he wouldn't be here now in front of us!"

"You're just angry because one of those bitches who got their throat cut was one of your new tasty bits," his close comrade Norbanus mocked him, prompting a reply from Aelianus.

"That's not the only reason," he protested, then grumbled, "All right, it's most of the reason. I hadn't even learned how to pronounce her name!" He turned and gave us a leer. "We were too busy for conversation!"

"There will be more where she came from," Cocles said encouragingly.

"Not from this fucking village," Aelianus replied sourly.

That, as we all knew, was completely true. Any woman who attached herself to us from this village, after what we were about to do to these prisoners, would never be able to return here. Probably not surprisingly, while this would be a topic of conversation later, at the moment, our attention was more on what was taking place in front of us.

"Tell your father that he did the right thing," Atticus instructed Zagreus, "the *only* thing he could have done that wouldn't have been...bad for him and his people." Suddenly, he chuckled with a heavy-handed, grim humor and added, "Of course, it would have been even worse for you."

Zagreus' mouth twisted, which I thought might have been more of an ugly smile than grimace, but he made no reply to Atticus, turning instead to his father and, presumably, relayed the Primus Pilus' words. Zeno's face looked like it was carved from stone, yet I was close enough to see how white his knuckles were as he gripped the reins of his horse which, as they tend to do, felt the tension of his rider and was beginning to twitch nervously and paw at the ground. The chieftain said nothing, but then he gave a slow, grave nod, and still without saying anything, turned his horse, and maneuvered past the condemned men and their guards. Then, before he reached the edge of the forum, Zeno turned and looked over his shoulder, back where Atticus and Zagreus were standing.

"Zagreus," he called his son's name, then issued what sounded like a command.

The son glanced over at Atticus, who only gave a curt nod, releasing the crown prince from captivity, and I cannot say I blamed the younger man a bit for his haste in leaving our camp. Our men gathered at the edge of the forum gave way before the bulk of Zeno's mount, but while none of them were smiling, neither were they taunting the chieftain and his son. I would argue this was due to my belief that since we were all veterans of this province, and knowing how proud tribes like the Breuci were, we had a grudging respect for a man like Zeno, who was willing to make the hard choices for the greater good of his people. Zagreus stopped to summon the royal guard, who immediately turned about and followed their leaders. The condemned men, who had been forced to their knees by their own tribesmen, none of whom showed any of them the slightest sign of sympathy, were the only Breuci remaining. Of the eight condemned men, four seemed to be resigned to their fate, and two of these men were clearly determined to show their contempt for us as they glared around at the faces surrounding them, as if daring us to approach them. The remaining two, on the other hand, were weeping, although one of them was doing so quietly, the tears running down his face as he stared at the ground, while the other one was crying with great, hiccupping sobs; frankly, it turned my stomach. Little did I know that my stomach was feeling better at this moment than it would be for some time to come.

"Sergeant Pullus!"

I am not sure which is more uncomfortable; knowing your Primus Pilus is calling you at a moment like this, or there are a couple thousand men surrounding you, their eyes on you.

Still, I do not believe I hesitated when I hurried to stop in front of Atticus, coming to *intente* and snapping a salute; at least not very much. The expression on the Primus Pilus' face was difficult for me to decipher, but I certainly was not prepared for what was coming.

"May I see your sword?" he asked politely, making it sound as if it was a simple request.

"My…sword, sir?" I asked uncertainly.

"Yes." His tone was pleasant, at least as pleasant as a Primus Pilus can be when addressing a subordinate, I supposed. "I've heard so much about it, but I just realized I've never actually seen it before."

Why now? I wondered, but I was drawing my blade and handing it, hilt-first of course, to him even as the thought ran through my mind. He accepted the blade, and I do not believe his appreciation was feigned as he examined it closely. Just as he was about to run his thumb along the blade, I opened my mouth to warn him, then thought better of it; I suppose it was my way of exacting revenge of a sort. He gave a small yelp as the edge bit into his thumb, yet he did not seem to be angered.

"That," he said admiringly, and for that instant, we were as close as we had ever been, two men who appreciated a weapon such as this, "is one of the finest blades I've ever seen. And," he added, "it's almost as famous as your grandfather was."

"It is, sir," I agreed.

"It must be hard," Atticus replied suddenly. ", knowing that you're the man carrying Titus Pullus' sword." He caught himself and chuckled. "I mean, the original Titus Pullus."

"Yes, sir, it is." Despite being a bit offended at what I saw as his implication that such a distinction needed to be made, or that I was unaware of the difference, I still was honest as I said, "I think about it quite a bit, actually."

"As you should," he agreed. Then, he looked up at me with a smile on his face I could not understand, although I was about to when he continued, "And I can't think of a better weapon, or a way to administer Rome's justice on those bastards over there."

At first, I misunderstood, because I was in the process of sheathing my blade. Thinking he meant to use it himself, I stopped and withdrew it again, offering it back to him, except he shook his head.

"No." His tone was quiet. "I've decided you're going to be the one. After all," he held out his thumb, which was bloody, "you know that once a blade has gotten a taste of blood, it can't be returned to its sheath until that thirst has been slaked."

Now, I knew this was something we often said, but this was when we were sitting around the fire; frankly, I had never really thought of it in a literal sense. Yet, I instantly saw the Primus Pilus was serious. Saluting, I turned about, determined not to hesitate because I was sure he was testing me in some way. Or, more ominously, wanted to put me in a position where, if I did balk, he would have something to hold over me. And, dear reader, despite the fact that Urso was now dead a few years, the feelings that ran through me whenever I thought of that period of time were still quite strong, and in some ways still are to this day. Consequently, I strode strongly over to the first of the kneeling men. The fact that he was one of those who were defiant made what I had to do much easier, but the sound of his head thudding onto the ground quickly removed all signs of insolent anger from the rest. Nevertheless, it did not stop me from performing my duty. By the time I reached the last man, the one who had been crying so loudly, he had lost control of his bodily functions, and it was with my lip curled in disgust that I finished him. Even in the moment, I was aware my Gallic sword had maintained its edge so that the last man's head parted as easily from his shoulders as that of the first. The one small grace was when Atticus ordered others to thrust the heads of the dead men down onto javelins shoved into the dirt, in a row in front of his tent, which was how we left them the next morning when we broke camp.

From this camp, we continued east, swinging slightly north, skirting the lands of the Scordisci, although this was less about avoiding contact with this tribe than the large stretch of marshy ground along the Ulca River that the locals call the Hiulca Palus. The Ulca, which feeds into the Danuvius, and which some of the older men still referred to as the Ister, is the southern boundary of one of the smaller Pannonian tribes called the Andizetes, whose territory consists of the strip of land wedged between the Ulca, the Dravus to the north, and the Danuvius to the east. Despite their size, they have also been troublesome in direct opposition to their size, and this recalcitrance is aided by the lands in which they live. Because this was considered more of the domain of the 15th Legion, we did not venture often into this part of Pannonia, which is at the far eastern edge of the province. On the other side of the Danuvius is Dacia, which is even wilder than Pannonia, except it was accepted as an article of faith that, despite their location in Pannonia, the Andizetes had more in common with the Iazyges, whose lands are on the other side of the Danuvius, and who had been steadily migrating from their original homes in Scythia. This was also during the time when the dynasty begun by the Dacian king Burebista back in the early days of my Avus was starting to disintegrate, meaning there was a great deal of fluidity to where people were settling. Even without our intervention, there were small wars over territory all along the great border of the Danuvius, both here in the south, and farther north.

What makes the Andizetes particularly troublesome is that they are as difficult to pin down as a column of smoke. Depending on the direction from which pressure came, they could melt away into that horrible marsh of the Hiulca Palus to the south, or using their small fleet of boats, row east across the Danuvius; naturally, they did not send the boats back, meaning that anyone unlucky enough to pursue them either had to have their own fleet or build one. Making matters even more difficult was due to the ground along the west bank of the Danuvius which, while better than the Hiulca, was still a nightmare of small tributaries, with what appears to the eye to be small islets and patches of solid ground, but once across the waterway surrounding them turns out to be anything but solid. I would liken it to those boggy parts of the Black Forest, although the only saving grace was that the trees are not so thick that the sun never shines through. Nevertheless, the foliage is dense enough whereby the Andizetes can simply vanish into the glades and glens of their land. I say this now with all the knowledge that comes from hindsight; frankly, before we experienced it for ourselves, we were dismissive of the 15th's claims. The only thing that saved us was the fact that it was the dead of winter, although that made it only marginally less miserable. Despite there being a layer of ice over the rivulets and smaller streams that were solid enough to walk across, while the boggy stretches had a similar crust, it was not thick enough to keep us from plunging through. And it is no exaggeration when I say that, because of my weight, even those places where the bulk of literally lesser men was supported, I invariably went sinking down to almost my knees. If there is anything more unpleasant than being covered in stinking mud, it is being covered in freezing, stinking mud.

However, none of this would have been known to us if the Andizetes had actually been where they were supposed to be, yet as we discovered immediately after we forded the Ulca at a spot about five miles west of the Danuvius, and approached the first Andizetes village, they had vanished. This village, as I recall, was called Kopava or something like that, was moderately sized but was heavily fortified, at least for a barbarian village, with a solid wall made of a double layer of logs, with dirt in between the two layers. As anyone with experience in such matters can tell you, barriers of this nature are some of the most difficult to breach; unlike rock, wood is more flexible, while the dirt layer absorbs the shock from attempts to breach it with a ram. Even undermining it is problematic, although we were lucky in the sense we did not have to worry about that, if only because every gate into the village was left wide open. There was even still some smoke curling from a couple of chimneys, yet when we entered those houses, it was simply a case of smoldering embers. Everything portable had been taken, although to the disgruntlement of all of us, the Primus Pilus specifically forbade us from sacking the town and performing a thorough search.

"They're just gone; they haven't done anything wrong," Asinius explained to us.

"If they didn't do anything wrong, they wouldn't be gone," argued Metellus, and I had to admit that this made sense to me, but Asinius was not swayed by the logic.

"It doesn't matter," he countered. "And the Primus Pilus says any man caught inside one of these houses is going to be striped."

This was something we knew was no idle threat. Although Asinius' dire prediction about Atticus, when he first arrived to take command of the 8th, that the new Primus Pilus was a proponent of using the lash had not come to complete fruition, he certainly did not hesitate to use it. Therefore, when our Optio repeated Atticus' orders, they were not taken lightly. Now, this is not to say there were not men who were still willing to risk the punishment, convinced there were some treasures to be unearthed, usually from under the hearth, but as far as I know, none of those brave or foolish souls were rewarded in their risk. Thankfully, at least for them, none of them were caught either. Perhaps a third of a watch after we entered the village, we left it behind, mostly unmolested, while sections were sent out as scouts to try and find a trail. The condition of the ground made it difficult, but that was just the beginning of the difficulty; as they normally did, the Andizetes split into smaller groups, and appeared to be heading in the general direction of the Danuvius. Once this was determined, it was not long afterward we were split up into our own smaller groups composed of three Centuries apiece for the Second through Fourth Cohort, while the First, because of our larger size, was split into three groups. Arraying us along a roughly north/south axis, the *cornu* sounded the call to advance, then we headed east in the direction of the Danuvius. If the others were bothered by the absence of any orders from our Primus Pilus about what it was we were supposed to do should we find them, I consoled myself with the idea that at least he was with our Century, so we would be the first to know. However, it was less than two hundred paces from the edge of the eastern wall when we ran into our first barrier, a stream that was iced over. Fortunately, it bore everyone's weight, although this was where the good fortune ended, at least for me.

Not long after that, as we were sweeping east, our boots crunching the frozen vegetation and creating quite a racket, I took another step on ground that looked no different from what we had just traversed. Except this time, it held just for an instant before I shifted my weight, then my right foot plunged through as I went up to mid-calf. It was a struggle to withdraw my foot, but my fur-lined socks did help insulate me, at least at first. However, once this happened several times to both legs, not even those helped to keep out the cold.

Making matters, if not worse, at least more frustrating was the fact that there was no sighting of any barbarians, while the closer we got to the river, the harder and slower the going became. Finally, perhaps a watch before it got dark, a clearly unhappy Primus Pilus sounded the command to halt, immediately followed by the order for all Centurions to converge on his position. The idea our officers would be forced to slog their way from wherever their Centuries were in our long line actually cheered us considerably. My personal pleasure was muted by the loss of sensation in my feet, not to mention the stench from the mud, which was only slightly lessened by the cold. I consoled myself with the thought that because of my gloves, I was not forced to constantly blow on or clap my hands together to keep some feeling in them like everyone around me. Judging from the dirty looks my comrades gave me, they were not happy this was the case. Fortunately, the conference was not long, whereupon we found ourselves retracing our steps, except that once we arrived back at the village, instead of skirting it to find a spot to build our camp, the Primus Pilus marched us directly back into the center of it. We quickly learned why.

"We're going to be sleeping under a roof tonight, boys," he announced to us, which, as might be expected, was met with cheers. "If these barbarians want to spend the night out in the elements, that's up to them. We're going to be comfortable!"

The only issue was that there were not enough houses; actually, I should say there were not enough beds. Still, lying on a dirt floor, surrounded by wooden walls and roof, even if the roof is thatched, is still superior to a night under canvas. Naturally, there was some arguing about who got the relatively few beds available, and I was not ashamed in the slightest that I used my rank as section Sergeant to justify taking the one pallet in the house assigned to us. Although it was certainly not the headman's hall, which I will say the Primus Pilus shared with the other Pili Priores, including Corvinus, being in the First of the First does have some advantages; our accommodations being an example. Naturally, there was no stove, just a fire pit in the center of the house, but once the fire was going, it was quite comfortable. Somewhat unusually, instead of doing it myself, I handed my muddy boots to our section slave, Boraxes, to clean off, while I peeled off my filthy socks and stuffed them into the bottom of my pack, pulling out one of the two clean pair I had left. While we were cooking our meal, Asinius showed up, explaining our presence in a village that our Primus Pilus had ordered us not to molest just a couple watches before.

"The Primus Pilus doesn't want to be wandering around in that muck any more than you do," he explained, "so he decided that the best way to get them to come back is if they find out we're making ourselves at home." He scanned our faces, then grinned and asked, "So? What have you light-fingered bastards found so far?"

There were some guilty looks exchanged, mine among them, then seeing he was not there to censure us, it was Domitius who answered with a smile of his own. "Well, we *might* have stumbled across a thing or two. Down there," he pointed into the fire pit, "or maybe even up in the rafters." He indicated the roof.

"Good." Our Optio laughed, then turned completely serious, finishing, "As long as you *cunni* cut me in."

Before we could reply, he turned on his heel and left the hut, making us wonder if he was serious or not. Which, I am sure, was his intent.

The next morning, not long after the *Bucinator* announced the official start of the day, the call sounded again, using the signal that alerted us that one of the guards on the wall had spotted movement. The common area could barely fit us, so we assembled quickly to march out of the village and align ourselves in a way that not only allowed us to be ready for whatever came, but sent a message of preparedness to anyone with eyes. Fortunately, there was no need; in fact, the headman of Kopava actually seemed a bit embarrassed, yet while his Latin was atrocious, between a makeshift system of translation involving a handful of villagers and Romans, we soon learned why.

"They thought we were a tribe from across the Danuvius," was what we were told. "When they raid here, they usually cross about twenty miles south of here, then approach from the same direction we did. When one of their children who was minding the herd saw us marching, he ran and told everyone it was them, not Romans."

Personally, I thought it was a bit suspicious, but I had no voice, nor did it really matter. It was not long into the conversation that Asinius appeared from his spot, and his expression was troubled. Surreptitiously signaling the Primus Pilus, who backed away from the small knot of villagers, our Optio pointed something out I had not noticed before.

"There aren't many men of warrior age in this bunch," he told Atticus quietly.

Judging just from his reaction, Atticus had not noticed for himself, nor can I say I did either, or any of us, for that matter. But once Asinius alerted him to this, I could tell it made an impression. Turning abruptly back to face the headman, Atticus' tone was harsh as he demanded an explanation. Instantly, there was a babble of noise as not only the headman but those around him, who I assumed were some sort of council, began either offering an explanation, or protesting innocence. Very quickly, it became obvious that, even if they were not attempting to dupe us, our chances of learning the truth was minimal, and finally, with a wave of disgust, Atticus stomped away. Conducting a quick meeting with the other Centurions, we marched out of Kopava immediately thereafter, heading northwest as if we were continuing on our way, following the main road that roughly parallels the Danuvius. However, once we were about two miles away, we were halted, then new orders issued to turn back east, heading in the direction of the river.

"Again?" I groaned aloud, which prompted a thump on the back of my head from Asinius.

Although Optios no longer carry the *vitus*, they have come up with other measures to enforce discipline; in the case of Asinius, he used the handle of a turf cutter, cutting it down so that it was about two feet long, which he suspended from his *baltea*. Even with a helmet on, I had a headache for a good part of the day, which did not help my mood any as we returned to the same stinking muddy ground over which we had traversed the day before. During the night, a light layer of snow had fallen, but it was not sufficient, nor was it cold enough to keep a repeat from the previous day occurring all over again. Soon, I was occupied in my misery, realizing I was down to my last clean pair of fur-lined socks. Once more, we were aligned in a long line, except this time, we were along an east-west orientation, marching south back in the direction of the village. From the viewpoint of the rankers, it became apparent our Primus Pilus was determined to at least locate where the men of warrior age of this Andizetes village were skulking about. What we would do once we found them, or what they would do in response, was a different question entirely. It did not seem likely they would be eager to fight us; from the size of the village, I doubted they could field more than three hundred spears, which just the First Cohort outnumbered. Unfortunately, not long after this thought crossed my mind, it was followed by another; if it's just them out there. If they had vanished, with the goal of merging with bands from other villages, then that was a whole other kettle of porridge. Somehow, I managed to restrain myself from bringing this up with Avitus, or Domitius, for that matter, when we took our rest break.

Then, about midday, one of the sections ranging ahead of our line of Centuries and attached to a Century just out of earshot to the east in the direction of the river, sounded the alarm, which was relayed by *cornu* call down the line to us. Immediately, the Primus Pilus had the entire First Cohort execute a wheel maneuver, but whereas most of the time the First Century is the pivot point, this time, it was the Sixth. What this meant in a practical sense was that our Century had the farthest to travel as, like a door swinging shut, our line moved into a position where any attempt to escape to the south by whoever had been spotted was cut off. And, being the farthest man of the entire Cohort meant I had the farthest to go, across the same kind of soggy ground, and while I was aware that my long legs helped cover the distance, I cannot say I was especially thankful. Nevertheless, we got into position, then the order was given for us to move east, while the other Cohorts continued driving south. Because of the terrain, while there was enough space to our south, which was the First's right flank, for whoever it was to move past us, there was little chance of them doing so undetected. It was in this way that slowly but inexorably, and using the Danuvius as a boundary, we closed our net. Although the river was not iced over, there were floating chunks of the stuff drifting with the current, making any attempt to cross in some sort of boat or on a raft difficult and dangerous. Frankly, though, this was my secret hope, that these itinerant warriors would have a means of escape. My reasoning was simple; if there were warriors who chose to stand and fight, our chances of moving on and thereby returning to Siscia would be severely compromised, and I was determined to get back to find out what was happening with Giulia. And, despite the fact that I did not make any sacrifices to make this so, perhaps they were watching and took pity on me, because essentially, that was what happened.

The anchor of our force, which was the Second Cohort, was the nearest to the river, and consequently in a perfect position to watch the previously missing warriors paddling across the wide river in what we were told was a motley variety of watercraft. Apparently, one small boat capsized because it was overloaded, but if any men made it back to our shore, we never found them. Once we learned that our quarry had escaped, there was some talk of returning to the village to exact some sort of punishment, but nothing ever came of that. Later, I heard that it was my old Pilus Prior Corvinus, who was nearing the end of his time in the Legions, who convinced the Primus Pilus that doing something of this nature would create more problems than it solved. And I must say, despite my ambivalence towards a man I once looked up to with a respect close to that with which I view my father, I knew he was absolutely correct in his assessment. It might take many years, but having spent as much time here in Pannonia as he and, frankly I, had, Corvinus understood better than most Romans exactly the kind of complications that would arise should we punish the Andizetes. Therefore, instead of returning to the village, we marched to the nearest patch of level and solid ground, then made camp, and none of us were disappointed we had not gotten into some sort of fight with the natives. On top of that, I felt particularly hopeful because it had been cold enough that the fact that my last pair of fur-lined socks had survived intact was important.

The next day, we reached the Dravus, marking the northernmost point of our planned foray into the province, whereupon we turned west, heading back to Siscia once we reached the river. Before the end of the day, we reached the largest village of the Andizetes, where the Colonia Aelia Mursa is now located. Even back then, there was a wooden bridge over the Dravus, which from the viewpoint of any of us who had been in Pannonia for any length of time, was perhaps the greatest accomplishment of the Pannonian tribes, at least in an engineering sense. Because of its locale, Mursi, as it was known then, was a thriving center of trade, meaning that the chances of the occupants clearing out at our approach was not only impractical, it was impossible. The town is located on the south side of the Dravus, but because it is a trading center, the town is situated so that the bridge across the Dravus is in the center of the town. While there were men on the walls, the construction being identical to that of Kopava but higher, the gates were open as we approached, and they stayed that way. The common area of Mursi is also larger, so that we all fit into it, in formation. And, as always, everything else stopped with our presence, the townspeople suddenly finding a reason to stop what they had been doing to watch our arrival. What I always found amusing was how the adults almost uniformly made at least an attempt to appear uninterested, pretending instead to chat with someone as they eyed us marching past. The children, however, made no pretense of finding us fascinating, and the smaller ones jumped about us. One boy, bolder than his friends, who it must be said were clearly the instigators, approached our Century. This is not unusual; while we do not march with the Eagle when it is not the full Legion, anyone with eyes can pick out the First Cohort because of its size, and the First Century because we are always on the end. Although we were at *intente*, I watched the boy as he sidled up to us; actually, he inched up to me and Titius, our *Signifer,* who had replaced Flaccus after our battle with Draxo. Like me, Titius was completely immobile, his face straight ahead, but I am sure that, just like me, he was eyeing the youngster. The boy appeared to be about ten, his friends around the same age, some a bit younger, others a bit older. With dark hair and a filthy tunic, frankly, he did not look that much different from the children of the Legions running around Siscia, or I imagine as I did at that age, other than my size. He continuously glanced back over his shoulder at his friends, who were clearly encouraging him as he inched closer to us. Stopping directly across from me but about ten paces away, despite keeping my eyes straight ahead, I could not miss him, and evidently, he was counting on this, because suddenly, he began capering and dancing about, waving his arms wildly while making faces in an attempt to attract my attention. Specifically, he was trying to get me to break my *intente*, smile, or otherwise forget my discipline for a moment. Naturally, Avitus saw him as well, as did Titius and the men immediately behind us, and their muted snickers made keeping my composure difficult. Made bolder by our lack of reaction, the boy drew a bit closer, still spinning about, waving his hands and sticking his tongue out. Suddenly, once I judged him close enough I unleashed a low, guttural growl, much like a wolf would make, which made him yelp in fright as he turned and scrambled back to his friends, who doubled over in laughter.

"You're not a nice man, Pullus," Avitus muttered, but with a chuckle.

"No," I was no less amused, "I'm not."

While we were distracting ourselves, the Primus Pilus was conferring with the Andizetes elders, a half-dozen men clad in their tribal colors, all of whom clustered around Atticus. Unlike the last exchange at Kopava, none of these men seemed agitated or furtive in their demeanor, although I was aware how little this actually meant. Still, Atticus was apparently satisfied as well, because we were in Mursi no more than a third of a watch before we marched out of the common area, exiting the town from the opposite side we entered. From Mursi, we could have headed slightly southwest, using the road that would take us right back through Breuci lands and Zeno's town. It was the shortest way back to Siscia, but very quickly, I determined I was the only one among us who wanted to take that route.

"If we go marching past them just a few days after we lopped off some of their heads, it's practically an invitation for them to attack us again," Asinius commented when it became apparent, at least to me, that we would not be taking this route.

Instead, we took what was the right hand fork in the road, which paralleled the Dravus, following it as it moved northwest. I was acutely aware that by taking this route, every step we took to the west closer to Siscia was accompanied by a step north away from it. Thinking about this only compounded my misery, and I was not good company the rest of that day. Matters were made worse when, without my knowledge, Domitius, Avitus, and Metellus colluded with the rest of the section to spread the word about that we were following this route all the way up to Jasa, the village of the Jasi where the springs that are renowned throughout the region for their medicinal qualities are located. Although the road we were traveling on was in better condition than most in the province, it had yet to be completely Romanized, meaning that thirty miles a day was not possible. By supposedly taking this route, we would be going almost all the way to Poetovio, adding several days to this tour of the province. I can laugh about it now; they fooled me completely, casually mentioning it around the fire the first night outside of Mursi, claiming they had heard it straight from Asinius. At the time, however, I did not find it amusing in the slightest, especially since they continued this ruse until we came to the spot where there was another intersecting road, two days from Mursi, which heads almost directly south. When we took that road, I glared at Avitus, who tried to look innocent but within a dozen paces broke into laughter, and he was quickly joined by the others.

"You should see your face!" Domitius exclaimed from his spot in our second rank.

"It looks better than yours is going to," I replied pleasantly, but he was either not fooled or was not cowed, probably both.

However, the fact that we were taking what was at this point in the march the most direct route back to Siscia did more to repair my mood than anything anyone could have said or done. Fairly quickly, once I realized where we were, I compared our position to the mental map all veterans carry of their region, and I understood what Atticus was doing. By following the Dravus as far as we had before turning south, we were bypassing the Breuci. Where our original intent was concerned, we had accomplished our goal, but as we would discover we had missed something important. I am not saying this in any judgment of our Primus Pilus, or any of the other officers, for that matter; perhaps if we had lingered in Mursi for longer than we had, one of the Centurions or Optios might have noticed what turned out to be the key clue that all was not well. However, Mursi, being much larger than Kopava, was big enough that the fact that there was a segment of their town population conspicuously absent was missed by all of us. Only afterward, as we discussed matters among ourselves, did we realize that there had been a dearth of men of warrior age in Mursi, and although there is no way to prove it, I now suspect that the antics of the child to distract our attention was not a random event. This became especially clear after we talked with men in the other Cohorts at the far end of the formation, and while it was not in the form of capering children, their attention was sufficiently distracted as well, the difference being that our comrades had been diverted by the breasts and nether parts of a number of village maidens. It is because of this I do not believe any of these actions were random, but whatever the case or cause, the result was that not one man of the four Cohorts of the 8th Legion noticed the absence of the Andizetes warriors from the towns we visited.

Marching into Siscia as late in the day as we did meant I had to wait to go into town the next day; not surprisingly, the time seemed to drag on before, finally, at the end of our second day, I was allowed into Siscia, along with the other men of our Century. As usual, Domitius and I walked into town together, but we were both preoccupied with our own thoughts; Petrilla's time was growing near, while of course, my thoughts and fears were focused on what awaited me at the villa of Lucius Livinius. As I was about to discover, nothing could have prepared me.

In retrospect, I should have stopped at Diocles' apartment first so that he could have warned me that neither he nor Birgit had heard from Giulia since my departure. Although I cannot imagine he would have dissuaded me, I suspect he might have prepared me, since I was about to learn of Giulia's disappearance. More accurately, I think Birgit understood matters better than Diocles and certainly better than me. At the very least, I might have been made aware of the possibility of what I was about to learn. With my heart in my mouth, I approached Livinius' villa, and it took me some time to work up my courage to rap on the door. After all, I understood that as far as Lucius Livinius was concerned, my courtship of Giulia had ceased with his command, so that my appearance at his door would be unexpected. This time, I did not have to wait long, except the eye looking out at me was not Plotina's, but that of her male counterpart, Soter.

Before I could open my mouth, he whispered harshly, "You're not welcome here, Master Titus! Please go! Now!"

I was somewhat prepared to be rebuffed, just not by a slave, so I stood there, refusing to move. Even with the limited view I was offered by the grate on the door, I saw his visible eye rolling as he appeared to look over his shoulder. Whatever he saw apparently caused him to change his approach.

"Please, Master Titus," the volume of his voice did not raise appreciably, yet I could hear there was more than anger there, "I beg you! Leave, now! Before…"

"Soter!" A voice came from somewhere deeper in the villa, but although I had prepared myself for the inevitability of facing Lucius Livinius, I was taken by complete surprise when I heard a woman's voice. "Who are you talking to?"

"Nobody, Madame." Soter turned his head to reply. "I mean," he added hastily, "nobody you need to worry about!"

"I'll be the judge of that," the unseen woman said with the kind of tone that informed me who she was before I laid eyes on her, or she on me.

Suddenly, Soter's eye vanished as he was shoved aside, none too gently judging by how quickly it happened, but I was totally unprepared for the eye that thrust itself into view. Aside from the fine web of wrinkles, I was looking into the eye of Giulia herself.

"You!" the voice hissed, although the eye disappeared instantly.

Unfortunately, it was just so she could open the inset door, and suddenly, before I could compose myself, I was confronted with Tullia, Giulia's mother. Despite the circumstances, I heard someone gasp, and I am sure it was from my own lips as, for the first time, I laid eyes on Giulia Livinius as she would appear when she was older. The resemblance was unmistakable, even with the fact that the expression on the older woman's face was one I had never seen on Giulia. What also suddenly made sense was why the Legate had found her so desirable, although I suppose considering how hopelessly in love I was with the younger version of herself, this was to be expected.

"How *dare* you," she hissed, her fury radiating from her in such waves that, even as I towered over her, I felt myself moving back a step. "How dare you," she repeated, "show your face here? HERE? Of all the places? You come here, to the home of the family you've dishonored?"

"Dishonored?" I asked, still bewildered. "Madame, I assure you, I don't..."

"Oh, stop," she spat the words. "Don't pretend you don't know what I'm talking about! You have *ruined* my daughter's reputation!" She raised an accusing finger at me, which was shaking with her fury. "Don't deny it!"

"But, I still…" I must confess this was the moment when I suddenly understood our trysts had been discovered; I still was far from informed, however.

"She admitted everything!" she cut me off. "*Everything,*" she emphasized, which I admit caused a sudden flush to rise up my neck as I thought, Gods I hope not! "And now she's gone! And you'll never see her again!"

"Madame," I tried to remain calm, "I assure you that, despite whatever may have…happened," I could think of no other way to put it, "I have every intention of marrying your daughter. I…I *love* her!"

Sitting here now, scribbling away, all I can say in my defense is at that moment, I actually believed this would make a difference to Tullia. However, I was about to learn differently.

"Oh," she sneered, "you *love* her. Well," her smile was not really a smile, just a sign of her lacerating mockery, "that's different! As long as you love her, then her marrying some…some…*Head Counter* is perfectly fine!"

I confess I made mistakes, except I was not the only one to do so that day, and before I had a conscious thought, I had crossed the little space separating us as I glared down at her.

"My family," I did not yell, although this was no accident, and my voice was as cold as I could make it, "are the ones who made it possible for you to have all *this*." I waved a contemptuous hand around over her shoulder. "And your husband was more than happy to have me in your family, just because of who my father and Avus are! Do not say another word about my family, Madame."

For the first time, she looked uncertain, yet at the same time, she was a mother defending her child, which as I first learned that day gives even the meekest among us courage. And, as I would discover, Tullia was anything but meek under the best of circumstances.

"Your family," she had taken a deep breath, "is not to blame. Your father and grandfather were honorable men. But *you*," that damned finger not only started pointing, now that I was close enough, she began poking it into my chest, "are *not* honorable! You have ruined our daughter! She will never, ever be able to regain her honor! Not now, not once she became..." Then she seemed to catch herself, but it was too late.

Once more, I staggered backward, staring at her as everything became clear.

"What?" My voice was not my own, strangled and barely audible. "What are you saying? Are you telling me...?"

"I am telling you nothing," she snapped, regaining her own composure. "All you need to know is that you will never lay eyes on Giulia again! And if you show up here, I will have you *flogged!*" An expression came over her then, one of such harshness and cruelty that in that instant, I realized her resemblance to Giulia was superficial, and my recognition was confirmed as she finished, "Just like I had her slave whipped! Oh, yes," evidently, she saw how she had shaken me, because Tullia went on relentlessly, her mouth, the one I had thought so beautiful just moments before because it reminded me of Giulia, twisting into a mask of such bitter hatred that I confess I was suddenly scared for my love, "I made sure *she'll* never betray her mistress, her *real* mistress again!" Suddenly, she beckoned to me as she stepped inside the wall of her villa. "Come, let me show you!"

Despite every fiber of my being screaming at me not to do so, I followed her, and only then did I notice Soter, who was staring at me with a look I had never seen on his face before; it was one of anguish, yet also endowed with a hostility that I could only understand when I looked at the object to which Tullia pointed. It was nothing more than a post in the ground; it is quite commonly found in the courtyards of villas of the size and quality of the one belonging to Lucius Livinius. In fact, there is one even now in the courtyard of the villa in Arelate where my parents still live. Most of the time, it is used to tie the reins of the mounts of any visitors who arrive on horseback, but while I was aware it served another use, it was not until I actually looked at the post that its second purpose was revealed in a way I could not deny. About midway up the post, there are usually affixed at least two iron rings, but while I had always seen them, I never gave much notice to the ring at the top of the post; at least until that moment, when Tullia pointed it out to me. Actually, my eye was not drawn to the ring itself, but the dark stains that made the pole look as if it had been dipped in some substance, but it was the sight of the gobbets of what had to be flesh, given the swarm of flies that went buzzing away at our approach, scattered around the base of the pole in a rough semicircle that informed me.

"What," I could not suppress my shock and dismay, "did you do to Plotina?"

"What? You're suddenly asking after the wellbeing of a *slave*?" she sneered. "You certainly didn't care about what would happen to her when her treachery was discovered! Why are you so concerned now?"

Personally, I believed this to be an exceedingly stupid question, yet somehow, I managed to curb my natural tendency towards the cutting remark, stilling it before it left my lips, at least for the moment.

Instead, I asked, "How long before she recovers?"

Tullia opened her mouth to say something, but I got my reply in the form of a shuddering sob from behind me, and I whirled to see Soter standing there, his eyes fixed on the post like me.

"Oh," my attention was yanked back to Tullia, who, to my eyes, was growing uglier with every passing heartbeat, "I'm afraid there's no possibility of that happening! But," her lips pulled back in what I suppose was a smile, "I'm sure you and she can console each other when you're both in Hades!"

This was too much; once more, I cannot remember doing so, but suddenly, I was standing just inches from her, towering over Giulia's mother, and I confess that the fear I saw in her eyes was the most gratified I had felt to that point as she cowered before me, I suppose at the sight of my fist, drawn back to my ear.

"And who's going to send me there?" I asked her quietly, then instead of hitting her, pointed first to the scar on my cheek, then down to my arm. "You have eyes in your head, don't you? Surely you can see men have tried. A *lot* of men," I emphasized, "but here I stand."

"Yes," for the first time she seemed less angry than distraught, "there you stand, Titus Pullus! You stand here, in my home, in *Giulia's* home, but she's not here! And she can never come back here! And it is all your fault!"

"Maybe if you hadn't been so busy fucking that Legate behind your husband's back, you'd have a better relationship with your daughter," I snarled, rewarded by her face turning as white as a politician's *toga* on election day. "And then maybe she would have felt like she could come to you for your support! Your daughter," it was a struggle to maintain even a semblance of control, yet somehow I managed, "deserves a better mother than the one she got. But," this time, I was the one jabbing my finger in her face as she recoiled in fear, "she's not the whore here! We love each other and want to be together the rest of our lives! What was your excuse for cuckolding a good man like Lucius Livinius?"

I finished this with a sneer, and I admit I took great satisfaction in seeing her stagger back a step before landing, hard, on her rear end, right in the middle of the pile of gore that had once been Plotina. After that, there was nothing more to say, so I did not try. Turning about, I tried to walk steadily, despite how difficult it was to do so, refusing to look in Soter's direction as I passed by him. Opening the small door, I exited out onto the street, my only thought to get to Diocles' apartment, simply because it was the nearest refuge where I could sit and think about all that I had learned.

Turning in that direction, I had gone only a dozen steps or so when I heard, "Pullus! Pullus!" I ignored the call, then, "Titus! Please!"

Only then did I turn, reaching down to check that my dagger was not stuck in its sheath as Lucius Livinius approached. I suppose I was not subtle because he slowed down, his manner wary, then he held out both arms to show he was unarmed.

"I just want to talk to you, Titus."

"What about?" I blurted out, unable to stop myself once more. "Your wife already told me…"

"Tullia is…distraught," Livinius interjected, but his tone was careful. "And rightly so. However, that doesn't mean I agree with how she's handled matters." I did not reply, and his face hardened as he continued, "Be that as it may, you did bring shame to my family, Titus. And," he added grimly, "I've borne enough shameful acts by the women in my family already."

"I...I know," I admitted, although I felt compelled to add, "but that wasn't my intent. And it wasn't hers either! I wanted to marry her!"

"I know," he sighed, and there was a heaviness to it that actually brought me closer to tears than anything else that had happened to that point. "But you can't, and you know why."

"I know your reason," I shot back, "but that doesn't mean I agree with it!"

"Nor did I expect you to," his agreement surprised me, except then his face grew colder as he finished, "but I did expect you to respect my wishes!"

"I did," I protested, but quickly realized the absurdity of this, so I added, "at least, I intended to. But then, Giulia…"

I refused to say any more; I was not going to lay any blame at her feet. When all was said and done, I could have refused her when she showed up at Diocles' apartment; even as the thought ran through my mind, I dismissed it as impossible, although I still did not speak.

"Yes," Livinius' voice grew softer, "I know. She confessed that she's the one who came to your freedman's apartment. And Plotina confirmed that when she was being…questioned," he finished awkwardly, looking down at the ground and away from me.

"You mean when you tortured her," I cannot say why, but although I barely knew the woman and she was a slave, what had happened to her bothered me greatly.

Livinius' head shot back up at my accusation and he said, "I didn't! I didn't lay a hand on Plotina, nor did I order anyone to…punish her!"

"Then who did?" I demanded, the answer not even occurring to me.

Closing his eyes, he shook his head and replied sadly, "That was Tullia."

"You mean your wife ordered one of the other slaves to whip her to death?" I gasped.

"No." The words seemed to be dragged from him. "I'm saying that Tullia is the one who actually…"

He could not seem to finish the statement, but although I understood why, I was determined that he at least acknowledge it.

"She's the one who flogged that woman to death." There was no warmth in my tone, nor sympathy. "And you just stood by and watched it."

This clearly angered him, and he retorted, "I did no such thing! I was gone when it happened! I was escorting Giulia to her aunt's in…" He caught himself then, just barely, and finished weakly, "…where her aunt lives. When I returned, everything had already happened."

"Does Giulia know?" I asked, suddenly concerned for her welfare given her condition.

"By the gods, no," he assured me. "And I don't plan on telling her anytime soon."

"What are you going to do about your wife? Especially after what she…did before?" It was the only way I could think to phrase it.

"What can I do?" he replied plaintively. "Tullia has always been…high-strung. And she was mortified when she learned about Giulia. As far as that other…incident?"

He did not finish, just giving me a helpless shrug that told me that, despite all that I had seen of his wife in the moments before, he was still hopelessly in love with the woman. And for that, I forced myself to recognize, he's no different than I am.

Still, I felt compelled to ask him, "You're clearly taking it better than she is. Why are you even talking to me, and why don't you have a sword in your hand?"

His laugh was bitter, but he just waved a hand at me and said, "Because you'd kill me without raising a sweat. As to why," he shrugged, then looked me in the eyes, and said sadly, "because I remember what it is to be young and in love. I also remember what it felt like when Tullia's parents tried to stop us from seeing each other."

This was something I had never heard before, yet despite my curiosity, I said nothing, understanding that if I was patient, more would be forthcoming.

"You see," he explained, "as I once told you, we had something in common. But while that was true, it was only partially so. What I didn't mention is that Tullia's family is from the equestrian class, and were when we fell in love. Her father came after me once with a stave." He chuckled at the memory, although I failed to see the humor in that thought as I glanced around for something similar close to his hand. "And banished me from his sight. So," he shrugged, "one night, Tullia stole away out of her villa, met me, and we went to the temple of Hercules and paid the priest to say the words. Then," he gave me a grin, "we consummated our union before we returned to her parents to inform them."

If this was an attempt to make me feel better, it did not work, and I felt compelled to point it out to him. "That's exactly the same situation we're in!" I exclaimed. "But you forbade us from marrying? Even after what you just told me?"

"It's not the same, Titus," Livinius' humor vanished, and he pointed a finger at me, "because I didn't get Tullia pregnant until after we were married! But," he allowed, "I admit there are similarities. Which is what makes this so difficult."

"And is why you're even talking to me." I thought I had kept this within the confines of my skull, but I obviously said it aloud, because he only nodded in reply.

"But, Titus," his tone changed again, and the warning in it was clear, "just because I understand doesn't mean I would forgive you if you make any attempt to find Giulia. She's never coming back to Siscia, even after the child is born."

"And what about the child?" I asked, feeling very strange as I did so. "Don't I have some say in this? It's just as much mine as it is hers!"

"You lost any right to that child by your actions."

Despite the harsh tone, I saw the glint of tears in his eyes, which stilled the words in me that I was about to utter. While I do not know if they would have made any difference in what was to come, I have no way of knowing, because they stayed inside me. We parted then, and I avoided that part of Siscia for quite a long time, yet even as I walked away, I had to fight the urge to turn and warn him of the possible fate of a woman who carries the child of a Titus Pullus. My Avus had killed his mother when he was born; his child had killed Miriam, and while both he and I survived, and in my case, my mother did as well, it was still something that haunted me. And continues to this day.

"So you found out?" Diocles asked me after I burst through his door, staggered to his table, and fell into it.

The question made me look at him sharply, asking, "Yes. But how did you know?"

"Because I told him this was the most likely reason for Giulia to disappear." Birgit had appeared from their bedroom, having just put the children to bed.

If anyone would know, I realized, it would be another woman, which cooled my anger as quickly as it had come.

"So," I tried to sound matter of fact, although I clearly heard the plaintive note in my voice, "what can I do?"

The pair exchanged a glance, reminding me of my own parents, who seemed able to communicate with each other just with a look, and I did see Birgit give a slight nod, so it was Diocles who said, "Titus," he paused as he sighed, then continued sadly, "I'm afraid there's nothing you can do."

Naturally, this did not set well with me, especially then; even now, being told I am helpless is a practical guarantee to force me to do whatever I can to disprove the statement. Yet, for whatever reason, that night, I just sat there dumbly, still trying to cope with all I had learned.

"But," I finally managed a weak protest, "I'm the father!"

"Yes," he agreed, "you are. But," he put his hand on my arm, squeezing it gently, and the fact that he did this when he was trying to impress a point on me was not lost on me, "you know that you have no legal standing here. Giulia's father did not enter into a marriage contract," he began enumerating the obstacles on his fingers, another habit of his that I did not care for very much, "so your union isn't recognized. And," another finger joined the first, "even if it was by the priests, it wouldn't be by the army. And," he paused again, but that third finger came out nevertheless, "Giulia, and you, disobeyed the *paterfamilias* of her family."

I thought this last point was unfair, and I protested, "But the two of you helped us! So you," I pointed first at him, then Birgit, "and you bear some responsibility!"

"Yes, we do," Diocles agreed, and I saw Birgit open her mouth, presumably to argue the point, but he stopped her words in her throat with just a look, reminding me that, despite his outward appearance, Diocles was very much the *paterfamilias* of his own family. "And it was a mistake," he went on. "But," he glanced back at Birgit, and this time, gave her a fond smile. "let's just say that the both of us have a…weakness for couples who love each other. Still," he shook his head, "we shouldn't have."

We sat there silently for some time, then I realized it was time to return to camp, and I got up to leave.

"Titus," Diocles had stood as well, and moved around the table to reach up to clasp my shoulder, "I don't expect you to forget Giulia. But please don't try and go against the wishes of Livinius and his wife. Down that road is nothing but trouble, and it will make things worse. For both of you," he warned me.

And, in one of the rare instances, I did as he suggested, and did not try to find Giulia's whereabouts.

Chapter 3

Winter came and went, followed by another spring. I never saw Tullia, although I caught glimpses of Lucius Livinius from time to time, but every time I did, I turned and went in the opposite direction. The only real notes of any interest were that we lost our Legate, who returned to Rome to be named Consul, along with Lucius Passienus Rufus, and we learned why the Andizetes warriors had vanished from sight. They had crossed the Danuvius, launching a foray into the lands of the Iazyges, waging war against people who had been their enemies long before Rome ever arrived. And the type of warfare was that of barbarian tribes in this part of our world; bands of warriors roving about the countryside, falling on the farms and villages of their tribal enemy, hitting fast but not lingering in one spot. Being completely honest, I can say I was not alone in being thankful that the Andizetes were wreaking their havoc on the other side of the Danuvius, because it meant it was not our problem. We still conducted the regular forays into the province, yet for most of that next year, there was little excitement, at least of the type that makes the Legion diary. Unfortunately, as far as Sextus was concerned, his year was very eventful; by extension, of course, so was mine.

While I cannot blame Sextus for keeping his troubles hidden from me, I can for getting into them in the first place. However, I know now, as I did back then also, that I share a portion of the responsibility for allowing matters to escalate to the height they did before I intervened. My only real defense was that, although I thought I had moved past Giulia's disappearance, at least a part of my mind was clearly occupied thinking and worrying about where she was and how she was faring. Actually, this is only partially true; being around

Titus Domitius, Petrilla, and their new baby daughter, who he had named Domitilla, never failed to send my thoughts down a path that, as hard as I tried, I could not keep it from treading. It was not just the idea I had a child somewhere; never far from my mind is the part of the Pullus family history, where by our entry into the world, we claim the life of the very person who gave it to us. Once I became fully grown and developed, I had been told by more than one person that, while it appeared I was a shade shorter than my Avus, I was at least as broad if not broader across the chest. It was something I never believed, at least until Diocles and his family came back to Siscia, because he brought with him a couple of my Avus' old Legion tunics. When I put one on, it was so tight across my chest it restricted my movement; however, there was another difference in the fit of the tunic on me, because it hung a couple inches lower than it should have. So while I am shorter, I am also broader than my Avus, and it tortured me to think what that might mean for Giulia if she bore a son. What I can say is that it is in this one way whereby I do not like being compared to my Avus, and hearing such remarks, especially during those days, was exceedingly painful. Ultimately, I offer this only as an explanation for why I did not pay as close attention as I should have to my younger brother.

Once he became a full-fledged Gregarii, and he had been blooded, Sextus went through a period that I believe all of us under the standard must experience. I would call it the Swaggering Soldier period, whereby once we have completed training, then lived through our first battle, our confidence in ourselves is probably at its highest. Consequently, when coupled with Sextus' lineage and all the expectations that come with it, he quickly became quite the sight in town. At least, so I was told by men in his Century. And, even more alarmingly, he was beginning to get a reputation as a bit of a brawler. I say it is alarming, but that is now; back then, frankly, I was happy to hear it, because I had feared there was a softness in Sextus that other men would sniff out the way wolves smell the drop of blood shed by a wounded animal. Thinking about it now, I suppose this was what happened in some ways, despite his love of a good fight, although it was not so much being too soft as it was in being too confident in himself and his abilities. Even so, I think that if the trouble he found himself in had been due to some sort of physical altercation, matters would have been entirely different. But it was something else, as an old bad habit of my brother's resurfaced.

As so often happened with my brother, the first I heard of anything was from someone other than he; the fact that it was Diocles meant it was serious. The winter had been extremely hard on our old tutor; he had developed a cough that continued to linger well into spring, and his energy was clearly sapped by it. Nevertheless, his mind was still as sharp as ever, and his loyalty to our family was as unwavering as always. Some years before, although I do not know exactly when, he had formally taken the Pullus name, which is not at all unusual for a freedman to do. However, he had taken the extra step of having the name change legally registered with the *Praetorium* in Siscia, and I am not exaggerating when I say that our entire family was as honored that he did so as he was in doing it.

"There's been some talk in the forum," was how he began.

As usual, we were seated at the table, and because it was past dark, the children were being readied for bed by Birgit.

I did not pick up on his sober demeanor at first, causing me to joke, "What? People are talking in the forum now? What's the world coming to?"

When he did not laugh, or even smile, I felt the first stirring of unease, causing me to shift in my seat as I regarded him warily. I had long since learned to be patient with Diocles; whatever it was he thought it important to tell me would come out without my prodding him.

"It's not so much as there's talking, it's who's doing it," he finally said. "And," he finished grimly, "who it's about."

For once, I was at least partially caught up; somehow, I knew the subject would be Sextus, and I immediately began to wonder whose father I would have to visit this time.

"What did he do now?" I groaned. "Or should I ask, 'who' he did now?"

Despite the gravity, this elicited a chuckle from the Greek, except it had a bitter edge to it that I could not mistake.

"If only," he said grimly, "it was that simple." Shaking his head, he frowned down at his cup and hesitated before plunging on. "No, this is a lot more serious, I'm afraid. And it concerns Servius Labienus."

He paused again, and I could tell by his intent gaze that he was expecting a reaction from me, but immediately after he mentioned the name, I was completely lost. Despite my obvious bewilderment, he remained quiet, and I quickly understood why; it would take me time to associate this man's given name with the one by which he was most widely known. His patience was rewarded as, from somewhere in the recesses of my mind, the piece required to finish this puzzle fell into place.

"Wait." I heard the gasp wrenched from my lips. "You don't mean Pulcher, do you?"

I suppose I was holding out a faint hope I had made the wrong association, but that flickered out in the amount of time it took Diocles to give a grim nod.

"The one and the same," he confirmed.

"And what," it felt like I had to drag the question out, probably because I knew the likelihood of hearing an answer I did not want, "was he saying about Sextus?"

Again, the Greek paused, and I saw the knot of his throat bob up and down before he answered, "That Pulcher isn't...pleased with your brother. At all."

When Rome conquers a new province, especially one as wild as Pannonia, it takes a special kind of man to be one of the first to settle it. I believe that one of the reasons Legionaries were once given lands in these provinces as part of their retirement bonus was because it takes rough men who are dangerous in their own right to not only lay claim to a patch of territory that had belonged to someone else in the very recent past, but to keep it. Those settlements that spring up, usually in the shadow of a Legion camp, attract a similar kind of man, one for whom the niceties and rules that one must abide by in Rome are either more laxly enforced, or just plain nonexistent in a town like Siscia. While this was no longer as true with the town, which was almost thirty years old by this time, at least the Roman version, in the early days when I was born, Siscia was about as lawless a place as one could find in the Republic. In short, it was a perfect spot for men like Servius Labienus, although by the time Sextus ran afoul of him, he was most commonly known by the name I had uttered to Diocles: Pulcher.

As with so many things in the Roman world, this *cognomen* was not awarded because it was true, but was, in fact, the opposite, the kind of cruel, barbed jest aimed at a man that he then adopts for himself, wearing it proudly, in open defiance and contempt for those who awarded it to him. Labienus was anything but handsome; oh, I suppose he might have been once, but once a man's nose is sliced off his face, it is hard to consider him comely in appearance. Over the years, I have seen cases where a maiming, disfiguring wound does something to a man who had been heretofore perfectly normal, his inner character changing to match the ugliness of his altered countenance. Such men are made this way by the constant taunts and torment from those around him, as ours is a society that views any disfigurement, especially in the face, as a sign of the gods' punishment. These poor souls finally start matching the ugliness without from within, but it is done as a defensive measure. That, however, I do not believe is what accounted for Pulcher's malignancy; from everything I saw, and had heard, he was an ugly man in every way long before his nose and face parted company. Supposedly, he had once been a slave of none other than Titus Labienus, the man who had betrayed the trust of Divus Julius, for whom he performed brilliantly during the Gallic campaign, but then joining instead with Pompey Magnus when the two great men broke. Labienus had become Caesar's most implacable enemy, and if my Avus' account is to be believed, he was the one most loathed by those who stayed loyal to Caesar. I suppose his origins are possible, although he had to have been very young. But whether he came about the Labienus name honestly or not, he absolutely earned the comparisons to his supposed master's cruelty and barbarity.

Pulcher had been one of the first civilians to Siscia; as far as any of us knew, he had never served under the standard. This lack, however, did not make him any less dangerous, because the one thing both his enemies and those who claimed him as friend, few as they were, said about him was that he could fight. Not standing in the ranks, or even in the sands of the arena; no, where Pulcher made his reputation was in the back alleys and grimy *tavernae* that cater exclusively to the lowest sorts of our society. Which, of course, means that these places are one of the favorite spots for Legionaries. It is understandable; after all, we are all members of the same class, the lowest class of citizen, and for most of the men under the standard, places like those first run, then owned by Pulcher would be more familiar to them because it is where their fathers went, as did their fathers before them. It is where most of the men of the Legions had their first drink of something stronger than water, and first sampled the pleasures of the flesh; if not within the establishment itself, then around the corner in the alley.

The story was that Pulcher had arrived in Siscia in the employ of another man whose name is long forgotten, working as muscle for him. At a later point – some say it was two years, others three, and even others saying four or more – the original proprietor of what was one of the four *tavernae* then in Siscia suddenly went missing. According to Pulcher, who by that point had become the original owner's strong right hand, the man had received urgent news about his beloved father, back in Umbria, or maybe it was Latium. Whatever the case, the owner's face was never seen in Siscia again, although Pulcher continued running the place, taking care of it as if it was his own, which was what he would tell everyone who asked about his employer. Over the years, the account of this became more fully developed; a cynical man might say the story was embellished quite a bit, so even then, sitting there with Diocles in his apartment, it was impossible to separate fact from fiction. Whatever the cause, once the proper interval had passed whereby the original owner could be pronounced dead, Pulcher was cleaning out the office of his former employer, which he also made sure to mention he had been leaving completely undisturbed so that in the event the owner came back, he would have no cause for suspicion or complaint about Pulcher's loyalty. This was when, much to Pulcher's professed surprised, he came across a copy of what turned out to be the owner's will, and was how he learned that his former employer, recognizing the steadfast devotion and fidelity Pulcher had shown him, had decreed that his former bodyguard should inherit all of the man's worldly possessions. That, as it would turn out, was just the start. Again, depending on who one believed, within a year, or perhaps two, or maybe three, Pulcher had expanded his holdings to the point where he either owned or controlled three of the four original *tavernae*, along with two brothels, and only the gods know what else. In the case of the former owners, at least two of them suddenly developed serious issues with their health, selling to Pulcher at what I can only assume was a price dictated by him and not them. However, these were not his real sources of income; they were just the means to an end that gave him the ability to exercise his true passion, gambling. Although, it must be noted, that Pulcher never gambled; at least, he never did so when there was a chance he would not win. Until, that is, he met my brother Sextus.

"I don't know any more details than that," Diocles informed me. "I just happened to overhear him talking about someone who thought they were smarter than he was." That, I had to admit, sounded a bit like Sextus. "I hadn't heard a name mentioned yet, and honestly, it's just a matter of luck that I wasn't out of hearing when he said your family name, because I was just walking by."

Whether it was luck, or just another moment where one of the gods who view my family as one of their pets decided to favor us on a whim remained to be seen.

"Naturally, I suddenly became interested in some potions and elixirs so I could linger," Diocles continued, "but all I heard was that somehow your brother angered Pulcher. I assume it has to do with gambling of some sort."

"No doubt," I agreed dryly.

After all, it was why he had suddenly showed up in Siscia now almost four years before, at the age of fifteen. In Arelate, he had used our familial connection to the *ludus* we secretly owned, getting inside information from Maximus Vulso, the *lanista* who, ironically enough, had actually been my first tutor in the skill of arms. By all accounts, Sextus had been quite successful; that was the problem, and in doing so, he incurred the wrath not only of some unsavory elements of the type who tend to express their displeasure in painful ways, but of my father as well, albeit for different reasons. His activities were exactly the opposite of the sort of thing our father wanted us involved in, because it drew undue attention to our family. Hence, Sextus' arrival in Siscia; now it appeared he had gotten into a similar sort of trouble.

"Titus," Diocles' tone altered just enough that it caused me to look up from my cup, "there's something else, but I'll only tell you if you give me your word you won't lose your head."

That sounded ominous, but once I gave him my word, I must admit that, while I was as angry as he had feared I would be, it was also with a fair amount of heavy humor, because he knew me so well.

"Your name came up," he began, "but it wasn't Pulcher who mentioned you. It was one of his cronies who gave what sounded like a warning to Pulcher. And," he paused, and despite the subject, I saw the ghost of a smile as he finished, "he didn't sound very worried about you. But," the Greek warned, "he knows who you are."

I sat there for a moment, pretending to consider what I had been told, but really it was to give my temper time to cool down.

Finally, I said, "I need to talk to Sextus."

There was no time to arrange a meeting with my brother that evening, so the next day, I made sure that I sent our section slave early in the day to the Seventh's area to give a message to Sextus. Frankly, while I did not think Tiburtinus was still angry for something that had happened months before, I was unwilling to risk it, and he had never formally lifted my ban from his area, despite allowing me to visit with Sextus after he had been blooded. Once our duties were concluded, I made my way to Diocles' apartment, arriving before my brother. I did not mind; it gave me time to play with my *de facto* nieces and nephews. The oldest, Alexandros, was just becoming interesting to talk to, and I know Diocles was as relieved as Birgit that he was clearly on the way to outgrowing his father. He was an interesting mix, with the bronze skin of his father, but with blue eyes and hair that was a very light brown. Extremely active, Alexandros was also quick-witted and his father had been his tutor like he had been mine. One thing I quickly learned with him, however, was that while he exhibited an interest and enthusiasm for what I did, his mother did not share in it, and despite her quiet demeanor, Birgit was no less a fierce protector of her children than my own mother Iras. That evening, as we were waiting, Alexandros had gone to his room and returned with the cut-down *rudis* I had given him on his previous name day, demanding that I show him the proper form. Sitting where I was, Birgit was several feet away, just at the edge of my vision, but I did not need to turn and look, feeling her glaring at me as I glanced over at Diocles who gave a rueful smile.

"You're on your own," he said quietly.

Tousling his hair, I winked at Alexandros, saying loudly, "Now's not the time for that, Alex. Go put it back in your room." But as he turned away, I whispered, "I'll show you later."

"Promise?" he asked me, but although I had viewed this as a lighthearted matter, I took notice of his earnest expression, realizing this was actually something he was taking extremely seriously.

Knowing that I was risking Birgit's wrath, I nonetheless offered him my arm as I would have to another man with whom I was concluding an agreement or making a promise to, gravely swearing I would do that very thing. His beaming smile as he trotted away partially helped buffet the storm that was brewing over my shoulder, and I took a deep breath before I spun about on the bench so I was facing Birgit. If her looks were any indication, I needed to go work my forms myself because an attack appeared imminent.

"What?" I asked her, trying to sound as innocent as I could.

My demeanor was not helped by the sight of Diocles' head dropping, as he suddenly found something interesting in his cup.

"You know what!" she snapped, and I saw she was not amused at all.

"He's just curious! It can't hurt him to at least know how to hold a sword properly."

"Yes it can! He can get hurt very easily! And," she pointed dramatically down to my scarred left arm, "you know that better than anyone!"

"She has you there," Diocles interjected mildly.

Now it was my turn to glare at him, and in all likelihood, I was about to make things worse by making some acerbic comment about husbands being the rulers of their homes. Thankfully, the sound of footsteps ascending the stairs stopped me. There was a sharp rap on the door, but as was his habit, this was just the precursor to Sextus entering. Yet, when he did and entered the apartment, I was not alone in gasping aloud at the sight of him.

"Who did it?"

While I want to be as honest and forthcoming as I can be in my account, I will not belabor that question, other than to say I asked it no less than five times. Once more, my battered and bruised brother shook his head stubbornly, prompting me to mutter a curse as I sat back in frustration.

Diocles, as was his habit, did not waste his time posing questions that were clearly fruitless, asking instead, "*Why* did it happen?"

And, as I should have recognized, this was the first crack in my younger brother's mulish silence. If anything, he looked worse than he had after our confrontation over Giulia, and he was also clearly favoring his left leg.

Forced to answer Diocles' question, I saw the emotions warring for control of my younger brother's face, and oddly enough, I was not without sympathy, at least as far as the beating went. I had been set upon myself, by Gaius Maxentius, with the aid and abetment of one of my former comrades Manius Tubero, and while I did not think then, nor do I believe now that Sextus was endowed with quite as much hubris about his fighting ability that seemed to be part of me, enduring a beating scars a man on the inside as well as the outside. It was the cause that was different, I reminded myself, and like Diocles, I waited for my brother's answer. Sextus was hard to make out; I suppose having a jaw as swollen as it was, along with the two missing teeth, made matters difficult.

"I had a…disagreement," he mumbled.

"Yes, well, thank you for that information," I snapped, my already thin patience fraying even more. "But what was the disagreement about?"

Once more, I thought he would not answer, and I felt my right hand unconsciously form into a fist, then he answered, "I won some money gambling. And the…man I was gambling against accused me of cheating."

"Were you?"

I saw Diocles' mouth thin in disapproval at my bluntness, but my brother replied immediately, "No!" There was a pause, and he amended, "Well, not exactly."

"What does that mean?"

Now Diocles was looking concerned, and I admit I took some satisfaction in his sudden unease.

"It means," Sextus sighed, and as he did so, he winced, telling me he at least had bruised ribs, "that I pay attention more than most men, and I saw something…interesting." Shrugging, he tried to sound as if it was not of great import. "So I made some money off it." He said nothing more, instead choosing to take a deep swallow from the cup of wine he held.

"That's not good enough." While my left hand is now naturally curled into a fist because of the wound I suffered at The Quarry, my right was starting to join its twin again. "And stop wasting our time! Tell us what's going on."

"What's going on is that I'm smarter than that *cunnus* Pulcher, but he can't stand being beaten."

This confirmed what Diocles had heard, although I did not say anything about this, at least right then. Instead, I stared at him steadily until he was forced to continue, reminding me that I was not the only one uncomfortable with silence.

"I noticed something at Mercury's Feast." This was the name of one of the *tavernae* where gambling was the main pursuit; accompanied by vast quantities of bad wine, of course. And by no coincidence, this establishment belonged to Pulcher. "He has men on his payroll who pretend they're just as drunk as everyone else, and then they goad others into a game with them."

To that point, he was not telling either of us anything new; I suspect these tricks were used even before my Avus marched.

"I remembered seeing the same man in the *taverna* from more than a week before."

"So you saw a drunk who loves Bacchus and dice?" I snorted derisively. "Well done, I suppose."

Ignoring me, Sextus turned to address Diocles instead. "But what I remembered was that he was saying almost exactly the same thing, in almost exactly the same way he did the first time I saw him. Like he was...."

He paused, and Diocles supplied, "An actor?"

My brother nodded, albeit carefully. "So that's when I started really paying attention."

As we sat and listened, I must admit I was torn between a sense of admiration for my brother and his cleverness, and disgust that he was essentially cheating, even if it was another cheater. The essence of his explanation was that, as he observed, the man he now knew was working for Pulcher, once he had hooked his fish, would proceed to lose several throws in a row. Not, as Sextus explained, without an occasional win, but salting them in just enough so the man's victim would not become suspicious. And, of course, more wine was flowing. Finally, when Pulcher's man was nearly broke and down to his literally last few *sesterces* or *denarii*, some sort of ruckus would develop. And over the course of days as Sextus sat there in a quiet corner, he noticed that the source of the disturbance was inevitably behind the man who thought he was having a night blessed by Fortuna. In any *taverna*, and particularly in a town like Siscia, men are well advised to pay attention to all that is going on around them. Naturally, when a brawl erupts somewhere behind a man, it would take a rare one not to at least glance over their shoulder. Which was all Pulcher's man needed to switch out the dice, which he was rattling around in the cup. As Sextus explained it, making that noise was actually important to the scheme, because the intended victim would hear the sound of the bones continuously rattling in the cup, even as his eyes were turned away. In a subtle but important way, his ears would assure him that there was nothing amiss.

"Once that happens," Sextus explains, "that's when I show up. And no matter how drunk Pulcher's man appears to be, I'm even worse off." When he grinned, the broken stubs of two of his upper teeth, the two behind the pointed fang we all have meant I did not return his smile. "And I make a lot of noise about how I've been touched by the gods and I have the sight, and I know what the next throw will be. Of course," he added, "I don't say this until I've heard what Pulcher's man is calling. So if it's Venus he's calling, which is the hardest to get, that's what I bet."

Again, this is not unusual; most dice games have multiple bettors at any time, although only one is actually throwing the dice. However, I still did not see how Sextus was using this to his advantage.

"I offer odds," was his explanation. "I tell them I'm so confident that the dice are going to come up Venus or whatever he called, if I lose, I'll pay them double the bet."

"That's easy to say," Diocles replied cautiously, "but surely the kind of men who frequent Mercury's Feast aren't going to believe you, just on your say-so."

"No, they don't." Sextus produced his coin purse from under his *baltea*, and I suppose the bulging of my eyes was commensurate with his purse, which he held up, jingling it. "But once they see this, they do!"

"Where did you get that much money?" I gasped.

"From Pulcher's men. I've only done this a few times, so…"

"It looks like you've done it one too many times." I pointed at his face, and even around the bruises, I saw him flush.

"That still doesn't explain how it works," Diocles interposed.

"Yes, well," Sextus returned to his explanation, "it actually does. Pulcher's man has got the fixed dice that he knows are going to go his way. But he also knows he only has three, or at most four throws to wipe out the fish before he becomes suspicious. Also, remember, he's pretending he's desperate, so he's going to bet all he has left. Now," despite himself, I could see Sextus was warming up to the subject, clearly pleased with himself, "it's not like he can switch the dice back and let Fortuna determine the roll. And he knows that unless he goes ahead and throws his money down, the fish will get suspicious that he's suddenly playing it safely when just before he was practically begging for the chance to win his money back."

"Which," I felt compelled to point out, "is what any normal man would do when a stranger shows up and tries to change the odds of the bet."

I must say I felt rather proud of myself for throwing out this objection.

"That's true," Sextus granted, except any flush of victory I might have felt at scoring this point was quickly washed away, "for men who are sober. And," he added, "as I said, I watched, and Pulcher's man only drank wine from his amphora, not from the fish's, so I'm almost positive that there was just enough wine in the water so it at least smelled and looked right."

"All right," I grumbled, "I see what you're saying."

"So," Sextus picked up, "he has no choice but to throw, and it'll come up Venus. But just before he does, I make another boast, about how I'm so confident that I'll even split the proceeds of the bet with the fish should I win. That way," he shrugged, "he won't lose anything."

"Which he wasn't going to win in the first place." This came from Diocles, and whether it was his tone or the words themselves, it caused my brother to shift uncomfortably.

"Yes, but Pulcher's man can't let on that I know I'm onto his game. Besides, by the time I'm done, the fish is so confident he's now willing to risk everything because he's so sure he's going to double his money either way. All I do is keep talking, delaying the throw and building up the pot by what I say, because now more men are joining in."

Judging from his expression, I suspected that Diocles was as torn as I was; admiring my brother's cunning while at the same time being troubled by it.

"So what happens then?" I sighed, although I was sure I knew how it all ended.

I was wrong, as I was about to learn; Sextus had one more surprise in store for us.

"Pulcher's man throws the dice, they come up what he called," Sextus explained.

"And Pulcher's man wins, but only part of the pot, not all of it," Diocles interjected quietly, and again, I saw Sextus flush.

"That's true," he granted, but even with his jaw so swollen, I recognized the set of it as he continued, "And I just repeat it for however long Pulcher's man continues to throw. The first time, it took the bastard three throws before he figured out he wasn't going to win anywhere near what he thought. Now they usually just stop after the first throw. But that's what he deserves! It's true he doesn't get everything in the pot, but he doesn't lose! Everyone wins!"

"Except the poor bastard who got gulled," I replied angrily, but this was when I learned Sextus' surprise, because he shook his head.

"Not true," he countered calmly. "Naturally, I get out of there as quickly as possible, but I found a spot where I can see the entrance and not be spotted myself. When I see the fish leave, I follow him, and once it's safe, I approach him, and give him back however much he lost. I mean," he added, "he doesn't walk away any richer, but he at least breaks even."

That clearly startled Diocles as much as it did me, and we exchanged a look that mirrored our shared confusion.

"And why would you do that?" The Greek beat me to the question.

Now my brother's expression changed, except as always, I glanced at his ears, which started glowing in the lamplight like they had a light from within.

"Because I don't think what Pulcher's doing is right," he finally mumbled. "And I decided that someone should teach him a lesson. So," his lower jaw, which had returned to its more normal position right underneath his upper one, jutted out again, "I cheated the cheater."

If anyone knows how to properly describe the mix of emotions I was feeling at that moment, they are worthy of praise. Almost despite myself, I felt a sense of pride that when all was said and done, Sextus' dirty deeds had been performed from nobler motives. Nevertheless, I could not ignore the larger, more practical and pressing issue that his actions had laid at our doorstep. And just by a glance over at Diocles, I could see he was no less bemused by the situation.

"Sextus," I finally found myself saying, "I'm not even sure where to begin."

"I do," Diocles interjected, and he leaned forward to pin my brother with an intense gaze. As he did so, his face was more illuminated and I could see that, along with the worry, our Greek was angry. "Sextus, what you did was foolish, irresponsible, and dangerous!"

"Says you," Sextus shot back, and just as Diocles had leant forward, he now sat back and crossed his arms, indicating the bulging coin purse he had laid on the table with a gesture of his head. "From where I'm sitting, I'm not the one who's the fool!"

Diocles did not respond, verbally at least; instead, he simply pointed at my brother's battered features, causing the one ear I could see to increase its luminosity even more. Despite the grave circumstances, I had to suppress a chuckle at the unbidden thought that came to mind that, should the light at the great lighthouse in Alexandria ever be extinguished, all we had to do was drag my brother up to the top of it and embarrass him, and ships at sea would see his beacon from many miles away. Somehow, I managed to tuck this thought away and shove the smile off my lips.

"If you're not the fool," I asked for both Diocles and myself, "how do you explain that?"

"I...got careless," my brother admitted, yet he still was not ready to give in, "but it won't happen again! I swear on the black stone that they'll never catch me by surprise again!"

"That," I commented dryly, "is actually one oath I know you'll keep, because you're not ever doing this again."

"Says who?" Sextus flared, turning his head to face me, clearly challenging me. "You're not the *paterfamilias*! And you may outrank me, but you're not in my Century, so you can't stop me! I'm a grown man!" I was a bit surprised at how worked up Sextus was getting, and even though he winced as he did so, he stood up and pivoted to challenge me. "I've killed, just like you! I'm not a boy anymore, Titus! You," he thrust a finger at me; I suppose only brothers know the best way to provoke a sibling, "don't have any say in what I do!"

Oddly enough, while I was angry, there was a sudden sadness so powerful that I realized with some horror I was close to tears. Somehow, in that moment, I realized this was about so much more than a beating that had been inflicted on my brother Sextus, that for whatever reasons I could only guess at, this outburst and defiance was a burden that lay at my feet, not his. Perhaps I am performing what philosophers call a rationalization of the moment, yet even with everything that transpired, I still feel this way.

"Sextus," Diocles broke in, his tone gentle, "you know that we're worried, don't you? That's why we're talking to you about this?"

This seemed to settle Sextus a bit, and he dropped back onto his seat as he answered, "I know you are."

Perhaps it was my imagination, but I thought I heard an emphasis on one word that sent a message to both of us that my brother believed only one of us was sincere.

"And," Diocles continued, pointing again, "despite your words, your face tells a different story. Now," his voice turned grim, "we need to talk about how we're going to handle this moving forward."

"We're going to handle it by him not going anywhere near any spot that Pulcher owns or has an interest in," I interrupted, but this time, when Sextus glared at me, I returned it with equal vehemence.

As usual, it was Diocles stuck in the middle between us, trying to steer a middle course, so I did not begrudge the sigh he heaved; especially when he said, "Sextus, your brother is right."

"I knew you'd take his side," Sextus shot back. "You always have! Ever since we were little! When you look at him, all you see is our Avus, not who *he* is!"

Even if he had not pointed his finger again, I am not sure I could have contained myself, but it was a convenient target, and I reached out and grabbed the lone digit, twisting it until he yelped in pain.

"Would you stop whining about things that don't have anything to do with what we're talking about?" I muttered this through gritted teeth.

"Would you *both* just stop it????"

Birgit had appeared from somewhere; I could see by Sextus' expression I was not alone in forgetting all about her, and she was clearly enraged. As she pointed down to her husband, every word felt like a nail being driven through my skull.

"Can't you see what it does to him to see you like this? Can't you see how much he loves the both of you, and only wants the best for both of you? And this is how you behave? What would Master Titus think if he could see the two of you this way? What would your parents say?"

As powerful an effect as her words had on us, when I glanced over at Diocles and saw the tears streaming down his face, in that moment, I was sure I had never felt as ashamed of myself before.

"I…I…" I knew what I wanted to say, yet somehow at that instant, I could not form the words, so all I managed was a weak, "I'm sorry, Diocles. And," I turned to his wife as I released my brother's finger from my grip, "Birgit. You're…right." I suddenly felt as if I was about to collapse from the weight that I always felt, and still do, the responsibility that comes from being not only firstborn but being so intent on not only upholding but adding to the history and legend of the man whose name I bear. Only now that I have gotten older can I dare to commit to this account how crushing this burden can be at times, although I believe I have learned to cope with it better.

Impulsively, I reached out for Diocles; as did my brother, at the exact same moment, and I believe this simple gesture did more to repair the rift and to smother the growing fire between us. Oh, it was awkward, at least physically so, trying to lean across the table to embrace Diocles, who had begun sobbing openly.

"I just miss him still," I barely heard him say; between his sobs and being smothered between Sextus, Birgit, and me. "It's just that he'd know what to do right now."

I confess hearing this from Diocles shocked me, because not once, not ever had I ever heard him express any doubt about what course the Pullus family should take.

"Yes," Sextus' voice was similarly muffled as he agreed, "he would. He'd just go and kill all of them."

As quickly as we had been crying, we were all roaring with laughter, and while the tears continued flowing, they tasted so much sweeter.

Finally, we settled back down, and Diocles wiped his eyes, still chuckling as he said, "That is exactly what he'd do," he agreed. "But I don't think that's a good idea in this case."

Unfortunately, for both Sextus and me, the seed had been planted, although I resolved to keep any sign of its taking root hidden inside me from the others.

Turning back to Sextus, Diocles admonished him, "Sextus, do you at least understand why Pulcher had you beaten?"

"Yes," he mumbled. "He doesn't like being outsmarted."

I was about to open my mouth to counter that, sure this was not the answer for which Diocles was looking. From my viewpoint, it was about the money, but Diocles surprised me by nodding his head.

"Absolutely correct," the Greek replied, but he must have seen my expression, because he turned to explain, "A man like Pulcher has more money than he knows what to do with, Titus. And at this point, it's about keeping that money. If word gets out that his men are vulnerable to being outsmarted; at least," he amended, "without repercussions, he's going to have a nightmare on his hands. Every sharp operator," he indicated my brother, "like this one will descend on his establishments, sure that there's easy money to be found."

While I understood the logic, I still was not convinced, although my mind had started to move more along the same path.

"It's also a blow to his pride," I pointed out. "And a man like Pulcher has to rule by fear."

"That's true too," Sextus agreed. "So, why didn't he kill me?"

Diocles pointed at me, answering quietly, "Because despite what I heard him saying in the forum about not caring who you are, he's many things, but stupid isn't one of them."

I tensed, prepared for Sextus to offer some argument to this, except he surprised me by nodding and saying, "I thought as much. After I got knocked down, one of them was about to kick me in the head, but one of the others stopped him and said, 'Remember who he is. We don't want that kind of trouble'…" He shrugged. "…or something like that."

Since this was the first time the subject had veered in this direction, I was not about to let it wander off, and I pounced.

"How many were there?"

Sextus thought for a moment, then answered, "Three. At least, I think, although I could have sworn I heard someone else's voice besides the three *cunni* who did this." He pointed to himself.

"And," I knew I was treading on dangerous ground, "you said they caught you by surprise. How did that happen?"

Suddenly looking away, Sextus mumbled a reply, and he had to be prompted to repeat, "I was following a girl." Diocles and I exchanged a glance, and I suspect our thoughts were identical; my little brother and women were an expensive combination. "She lured me into an alley." He shrugged, then finished, "Then before I could get out of there, they'd blocked both ends."

"Where exactly did this happen?" I asked him.

He went on to describe the intersection, several blocks away from Siscia's forum, and I was not surprised to hear it; if viewed from above, the alley was strategically located roughly equidistant from three of Pulcher's establishments, one of them this Mercury's Feast, and was adjacent to another, although I did not remember the name at the time. Sitting there, listening to Sextus talk, the shifting sensation began in my stomach that always signals the coming of my rage, except this time, I did not try to quell it. What I did do, however, was to…nudge the beast in a slightly different direction, because I recognized that in order to do what I planned, I could not give in to this fit of madness that was passed to me by my Avus. As we sat there, outwardly I was still calm and unchanged, although I was focusing the power I knew would be available to me once I gave in to it in exactly the same manner as I had done only once before, with Gaius Caecina, my former Sergeant.

Although I had procured an overnight pass from Asinius, Sextus had to return back to camp, which was a good thing from my viewpoint. However, despite his protests, I insisted I would accompany him back.

"They've made their point," he protested, "and they're not going to do something again. Not so soon. Especially since I haven't gone back and taken them again."

"And which you're not going to do again," I countered, but while he opened his mouth to argue once more, instead, he snapped it shut abruptly.

"All right," he mumbled, and I glanced over at Diocles in some surprise; this was when I saw Birgit, standing just behind her husband, arms folded with the residue of her warning glare at Sextus still on her face.

Ah, I thought; of course. Frankly, it was something both Diocles and I should have thought of earlier, that the only one in that apartment who could control my brother was the woman he had loved for years. Telling Diocles I would be back, we departed the apartment, yet despite Sextus' protests, I took a slightly different route than normal back to the camp.

"What did Tiburtinus say about that?" I pointed to my brother's face.

"What do you think?" Even with his swelling, I saw him make a face.

"Probably that you deserved it." I laughed. "But what did he say when you reported for the list because of non-duty injuries?"

"Nothing," Sextus replied, which I found hard to believe; he cleared up my confusion when he added, "because I didn't put myself on the list."

"What?" I came to a stop, then grabbed his arm to bring him to a halt as well. "You mean not even a *medicus* has looked at you?"

"No. At least, not officially."

This eased my fears somewhat; my greatest concern were not his teeth or his face. Bruises heal, and broken off teeth become less sensitive, but I was worried by how gingerly I had seen him perform twisting movements, which might mean he was bleeding inside.

"Did he check your ribs?"

"Yes." He made another face. "It hurt like Dis, but he doesn't think I actually broke my ribs."

"Well, you didn't," I said without thinking. "They did."

"Thanks," we resumed walking as he gave a hoarse chuckle, "for reminding me about that. At least it's not because I'm so clumsy I trip over my own feet!"

"That only happened once," I shot back, again without any thought, picking up what had been our longest running argument, going back to the only day Sextus had bested me at a physical contest.

"Once was enough," he taunted, yet when I glanced over at him, even in the darkness I could see him grin as he finished with what had become another tradition. "The greatest day of my life."

"And the worst of mine," I finished, laughing despite myself.

Reaching the camp, I stopped at the gate, watching to make sure he appeared to be heading to the Seventh's area. Once he was out of sight, I turned and returned to Siscia, but not to the apartment; I had a stop to make first.

"I need your help."

It was unfortunate that Titus Domitius answered the door to Petrilla's apartment holding his daughter, who was several months old by then. The fact that Petrilla was standing behind him, staring at me with a look of fear, did not help.

"This isn't army business, Petrilla," I tried to assure her. "We're not marching."

This, as I quickly learned, did not help matters, because she scowled at me.

"What are you up to, Titus?" she asked me sharply.

"Nothing," I lied, but while Domitius knew Petrilla better, I had known her longer; we had grown up together in Siscia, before I moved away to Arelate.

"You forget I know you," she snorted, which was nothing but the truth, "and I know how you always seem to find trouble."

"No I don't," I protested. Then, before I could stop myself, I added, "I can't help it if it finds me."

Completely forgotten for the moment, the object of my quest spoke up, long accustomed to Petrilla and me bickering back and forth.

"What do you need, Titus?"

"I just need you to take a look at something for me," I decided on the spot that a half-truth would serve better than an outright lie. "That's all."

"Look at what?" Petrilla interrupted.

"I just want a second opinion on something," I hoped this would be enough to appease her.

Thankfully, Domitius turned and handed Petrilla their daughter.

"How long do you need me? Will I be coming back here?"

"You better be coming back here!" Now Petrilla was becoming shrill, which was something I remembered quite well from when we were children. "Titus Pullus! Where are you taking my husband?"

"Petrilla…" Domitius cut me off, and while his tone was quiet and I could not see the look on his face when he glanced back at her, it seemed to be enough.

"Well," she finally mumbled, "just be careful."

Assuring her that he would do so, I thought of adding my own promise, then decided to let that dog stay asleep, and we departed. Once we were away from his apartment, which was actually located in the same part of town where most of Pulcher's businesses were, I explained.

"Sextus got in trouble with Pulcher," I started, ignoring his sudden intake of breath at this, "and I need to go straighten it out."

"Then I need to go back and get my dagger at least." He made to return to his apartment, but I stopped him, fighting the sudden lump in my throat at this show of loyalty by the man who had become, and still is, my best friend.

"No," I shook my head firmly, "you're not going to be involved in any of that. I just need you to go find him for me."

"And then what?" he argued. "I suppose you're just going to wade in there and…what?"

"You let me worry about that," I said.

"If you think I'd let you go after Pulcher by yourself, you're mad." While he was not speaking loudly, I recognized the tone.

The last time I had heard this determination in his voice was a cold night when we were on outpost duty and we had gotten cut off by the Colapiani, led by Draxo. The pair of us had spent a great deal of that night running for our lives, yet I am not ashamed to say that if it had not been for his presence, I would not have lived through the night. Nor, do I believe, would he; when I looked at it this way, I recognized I should not have been surprised at his insistence that night either. Unfortunately, knowing this was undoubtedly true meant I had to revise my plan, because Domitius had not been far wrong. However, I was not going to charge in blind; this was why I had Domitius with me, except once I was in, neither was I just going to be indiscriminately trying to kill any man who appeared as if he might be on Pulcher's payroll. However, while my friend's presence complicated matters, it also gave me another idea.

"All right," I finally agreed, but I clasped his shoulder and tried one last time. "But, Titus, you don't have to…"

"Would you shut up?" he grumbled. "Stop wasting your breath. But," he warned me, "I need to know what you have in mind."

"What I *had* in mind," I retorted, "probably won't work now. But," I suddenly turned and began walking, back in the direction of Diocles' apartment, "I have an idea."

When we got to the apartment, Birgit and the children were nowhere to be seen, presumably in bed, leaving Diocles sitting at the table. Perhaps it was the way the lamps had started guttering, but when I entered, I was stopped short, suddenly seeing Diocles as if he was a corpse. He had always been thin, but the lingering cough had clearly melted away what little fat remained on his frame, and with the shadows cast by the lamps, he looked so frail, so old, and so tired. Still, his eyes were alert and burning with what I am sure was a combination of concern and curiosity at the sight of Domitius with me.

"I need to get something," was all I said, but when I went into the bedroom that was designated for the use of the Pullus brothers, then returned carrying two swords, he did not look surprised.

"I thought so," he sighed. "Titus," even his voice betrayed a weariness I could not imagine, "what do you think you're going to do? Just march in wherever Pulcher is at and slaughter everyone?"

"No," I answered instantly, which I could tell surprised him. "These are only a precaution, a…" I tried to think of the correct word, settling on "…a warning for others not to interfere."

"Interfere," Diocles asked warily, "with what?"

"Yes, Titus," Domitius turned and regarded me, "what *is* the plan?"

"You should have asked me before you agreed." I laughed, except he remained serious. "But you're right. No, I don't plan on cutting Pulcher down. It's something both you and Sextus talked about that gave me the idea. I'm going to use Pulcher's pride against him."

"Against him?" Diocles frowned, his expression wary. "And how are you going to do that?"

Once I finished explaining, the Greek sat back, looking at me thoughtfully.

"That," I could see the words came grudgingly, "actually might work. But," he shook his finger at me, "there's only one flaw."

"Which is?" I asked him, yet while I cannot say I would have changed my approach, I had long since learned ignoring Diocles was never a good idea.

"What if you're wrong? About being able to beat him?"

"That," I promised him, "isn't going to happen."

The sigh he gave again seemed to sum up the many years this man had spent seeing someone bearing my name ignoring his good advice, and I was moved to assure him I had one extra roll of the dice in my cup, although I did not because I had no idea how I would explain it.

Pulcher was not in Mercury's Feast, which was the first place Domitius looked. He was, however, in the second, a spot almost identical to Mercury's Feast except that, instead of gambling being the focus, whores were. This was the place I had envisioned, exactly where Sextus had been lured into the alley. It was not a brothel; this was a step below, the kind of place where the actual transaction took place just outside in the alley next to which the spot is conveniently located. The only limit to the debauchery was more one of space than any other consideration; the alley was narrow enough that the positions were limited. Not that it mattered, judging from the moans and counterfeit cries of passion of both customer and proprietor, and while I waited, I occupied myself with trying to count the number of couples crammed into the alley. Between the dark lighting and the frequency of couples coming and going, I quickly gave up. I saw Domitius emerge from a small knot of men gathered at the entrance to this second location, heading in my direction, and even with just the torches above the doorway, I could see the energy radiating from him.

"I found him," he told me.

Immediately, I broke out into a sweat, although I believe this was the only outward sign of nerves I showed, and I did not bother wiping my palms; if all went according to plan, I would not need them to be dry.

"All right," I remember muttering, "let's not waste any more time."

Of all the plans, schemes, plots, and ideas I had dreamed up to that point in my life, what I can say is this one was the simplest in its execution, and I suppose it was, if not the first time, close to one where I actually used the knowledge of myself and applied what I knew was a weakness of mine to a foe, because he possessed the same characteristic. A man like Pulcher did not achieve what he had without a set of skills with which I could identify, and possessed on my own. I had only seen him from a distance a few times, and while he was not as tall, he was very broad and his arms were probably a bit larger than mine. However, as I suppose most men of my profession do, whenever I look at another man, I have come to realize I do so from the aspect of sizing him up as a potential adversary. What I remembered from one of my brief examinations was that despite his bulk, when a barrel being rolled up into a wagon suddenly went off the plank, Pulcher had leapt out of the way with a grace that was at odds with his previously lumbering gait. In fact, he moved like an experienced fighter would. To this, I added an aspect that, while I was unwilling to say it aloud, or acknowledge even it to myself then, was another trait I knew I shared with Pulcher, and combined it with something I had learned from my Avus' account that he dictated to Diocles and finished not long before he died. In fact, it was within the first few lines, about how no matter how much a man ages, the one thing that stays eternally youthful is his desire and pride. Pulcher had built something up because of his ambition and ruthlessness that even now, in the later years of his life, he wanted to protect and I was counting on that.

I walked into the *taverna*, reminded of the name then by the sign, Pan's Grotto; after a time, the names of the places in which Legionaries spend their idle time run together. Almost immediately, I had second thoughts because there were more men from the Legion there than I would have thought on a night in between market days. Taking a moment just inside the doorway, after a moment, I determined that while there were more men under the standard than I would have liked, none of them carried a *vitus*, nor had a white stripe on the shoulder of their tunic.

"I'm right behind you," Domitius whispered, and although I knew he was, it was still good to hear it.

We had both donned our cloaks, although I shed mine as I entered from the small vestibule into the *taverna* proper, handing it to Domitius, who used both of our cloaks to cover the swords. As always happened, once I fully entered the premises, I could feel all eyes on me; like most such places, the ceiling of this one was perhaps a foot over my head, the presence of which I made a mental note, reminding myself this would restrict my movement more than it would Pulcher. Looking toward the far end of the *taverna* in the direction Domitius had indicated, I need never have laid eyes on Pulcher before this moment; I would have recognized him for what he was immediately. Seated at the end of the farthest table, nearest to the bar and the fireplace, but naturally in a position where he could see the door and anyone who entered, acting in much the way a king of a barbarian tribe would, Pulcher had not noticed me straight away. My assumption was the breast of one of his whores, which he was holding in one hand, was occupying his attention. But before I went more than another couple steps, I saw a man sitting next to him, his eye picking up my movement, turn and alert Pulcher. There were two men on each side of Pulcher, although all but one of them were similarly occupied as Pulcher, with a woman on their laps. The people at the other tables closer to me became aware of a change in the *taverna*; at least, so I suppose, because I was keeping my attention on the men at the end of the table. All the noise; the raucous laughter of both men and women, the buzzing of conversation as men swapped lies with each other slowly died down as even those completely absorbed in their debauching took notice of the change. Meanwhile, my eyes never left Pulcher, and even in the dim lighting, seeing a man without a nose is a disconcerting sight. The other times I had seen him, he had a false nose strapped to his face, although I never got close enough to see what it was made of to determine if the tale it was made of gold were true. Apparently, within the confines of this place, he felt comfortable going without it; the whore on his lap certainly did not seem to mind, but I imagine he owned her. Judging from the way he shoved her roughly off his lap as our eyes met, she was not one of his favorites, or perhaps this was just the way he treated all women. Whatever the truth, by the time I had maneuvered between the tables to stop a few paces away from his, the *taverna* had become as quiet as it probably ever had been, and I made sure to stand at such an angle where Pulcher could not suddenly shove the table at me with a leg, a trick I had seen played more than once.

"*Salve*, Titus Pullus, and welcome to Pan's Grotto." Pulcher's voice was booming, although he was somewhat hard to understand because both his upper and lower front teeth were gone. "What brings you here to my humble place of business?"

"You know why." I had to concentrate on keeping my tone as cold and flat, but I managed to do it.

"Do I?" He raised one eyebrow as he glanced about at the men around him, who were grinning. "Now why would you think that?"

I was determined not to let Pulcher control what was happening, or drag matters out, which was what prompted me to snap, "Do you really want to play a delaying game, Pulcher? You know why I'm here." I forced a harsh laugh that sounded false even to me, but I did it anyway, "You weren't enough of a man to beat my brother yourself, and it took four of…" I pointed at the men around him, who had suddenly stopped grinning, "…these gutless *cunni* to do it! You're nothing but a fucking coward, Pulcher, and I'm going to kill you with my bare hands."

This certainly broke the spell of silence as all four of his men jumped to their feet, each of them shouting curses as they discarded their women in much the same way Pulcher had a moment before. At the same time, the occupants at the other tables jumped up, except they were scrambling to get out of the way, and my detached observer noticed they seemed to do so in such a way that spoke of practice in doing so.

"Titus!"

I turned just in time, yet even so, I barely caught the scabbarded sword he tossed. Nevertheless, I managed to do so, even drawing it from its sheath in one motion as if we had planned it, while at the same time, I heard the scraping sound of his own blade as he drew it. Suddenly, Pulcher's men did not seem quite so eager, instead standing around him motionlessly while glancing at him with uncertain expressions. Domitius appeared at the edge of my vision to my left, but just far enough to the side to give us both room to work. I must say that only Pulcher seemed unworried by the naked sword in my hand.

In fact, he pointed down to it and said in a voice loudly enough for everyone to hear, "But you're here with a sword in your hand, when you can see I'm unarmed? And *I'm* the coward? How can you make good on what you just boasted if your hand's full with a sword?"

I cannot say if he realized it, but he was saying exactly what I had expected. The confirmation also served to allow the twin of what I think of as my beast of rage to rouse itself, and I felt the familiar but subtly different tension that always started deep down within my gut. The best way I can describe it, and I suppose this is why I think of it as an actual beast, is it feels like it has been curled up in a ball, sound asleep, then on being roused uncoils itself and begins to stretch its limbs, readying itself to be unleashed.

Just the feeling of this shifting gave me the confidence to make a show of sheathing my sword, while giving Pulcher a smile that was more a baring of my teeth as I said, "This is just a precaution from those *cunni* from interfering with our business. Now, if I have your word as a…." I actually could not think of a proper term. "…whatever it is you call yourself – pimp, cheat, liar, thief, fucking coward who has others do his bidding – " with every epithet, his face turned darker, his lips twisting with rage, "that your men won't interfere, I'll give you my word as a Pullus that I won't need to draw this blade again to kill you."

"You're going to wish you'd never come in here, soldier boy," he sneered. I suppose he sensed I was expecting some answer because he added, "And I don't need any of my boys to tear you apart!"

"We're about to find out," I replied, actually feeling the calmest since I had walked in. Setting the sword down on a table, I turned to Titus, who still kept his sword out, telling him, "Keep an eye on the others, will you?"

"Of course," Domitius' tone was cheerful, "but is it wrong for me to wish one of them would make a move? I haven't killed a man in months!"

I did not even have to pretend to laugh at this; Domitius was always liable to say something in tense moments that I found funny, and this was one of them. At Pulcher's command, his men dragged the tables away from that end of the *taverna*, arranging them in a line to serve as an artificial barrier in roughly the middle of the *taverna*, before moving to a spot on the opposite side of the tables. Like those patrons who had scrambled out of the way, the manner in which his men performed this task told me it had been done before, although this was noticed only by my detached observer. Now that Pulcher had accepted my challenge, I kept my attention on him and him alone; this might give an indication of how much I trusted Titus Domitius to watch my back. Pulcher was carrying a dagger, but he drew it and tossed it to one of his men, who were standing just on the other side of the line of tables. The quiet was gone as if it had never been, and I would liken the atmosphere in the *taverna* as being akin to that of the arena during a gladiatorial game, which I suppose is appropriate. I allowed Pulcher to make his preparations, mainly because I did not want to leave any doubt about who would be the victor at the end of this, with his supporters making the excuse that I had not allowed him to properly prepare. At the same time, my intention was to prolong this fight as long as I could; in short, I planned on torturing Servius Labienus, and punish him for what he had done to my brother. I was not unaware of the risk in not trying to finish Pulcher quickly, and I admit there was a part of me that was concerned his men might be able to overwhelm Domitius by sheer force of numbers, but that was only if two or three of them were willing to sacrifice themselves for their boss. And that, I felt fairly confident, they would not be willing to do. Pulcher was stretching his arms, shaking his legs, and I got the sense he was trying to delay the coming battle. It's almost, I suddenly thought, like he's waiting for something!

"Titus!" I shouted, not taking my eyes off of Pulcher. "Has anyone left?"

"Not that I've seen," he called out, and he laughed again as he added, "From the way this bunch looks, it seems Pulcher may not be as well-liked as he thought! They look ready for blood!"

Partially because of the close confines, his voice was almost drowned out by the roaring agreement of the small crowd, which I suppose Pulcher took as a good time to begin, because with a roar of his own, he leapt across the short space between us.

I would guess I knew within twenty or thirty heartbeats that defeating Pulcher would not be as difficult as I feared. He was strong, certainly, and he was skilled in this kind of fighting, but he was an old man whose stamina was a fraction of mine. When he rushed at me, I made no attempt to dodge, nor did I block his first blow, which landed flush on my left cheek, causing the old sword scar there to split open, and I felt the warmth of my own blood start running down my cheek. Certainly if I had to do it again, I would not have absorbed this blow, but not because it was the wrong thing to do. Putting it simply, now that I am older, I am no longer as resilient as I was when I was young. And, although his punch did snap my head back, the rest of my body did not move as I saw the sudden flare of worry show above the gaping hole in the middle of Pulcher's face.

"My little sister hits harder," I sneered before I went on the offensive myself.

Rather than retaliating by trying to strike his face, neither did I aim my first blows at his gut; instead, I pounded his arms, launching one punch after another in a flurry of movement that kept him on the defensive. Although his face was partially hidden by his arms, I could tell by his reaction that while he was surprised, he was also pleased, which was how I wanted him to feel. Yes, Pulcher knew me, but only by reputation; I seriously doubted he had ever asked more than a couple of cursory questions about my size and supposed strength. Judging from his reaction, he had no idea that I did not just carry the name, size, and strength of my Avus, but he had imparted to me an overwhelming desire to crush my opponent and leave no doubt in either their mind, if they lived, or the minds of those who witnessed it, who was the victor and who the vanquished. And, although it pains me to acknowledge this, from somewhere other than my Avus, as I learned with Gaius Caecina, there is a streak of cruelty in my makeup, where it is not just victory I desire so strongly, but to inflict real, terrible pain on my foe. The original Titus Pullus was a hard man, with a mean streak in him, yet as I have come to learn and been forced to recognize in myself, there is a difference between meanness and cruelty. And it was this twin of my rage, this cruelty, that was now unleashed on Pulcher. While it is similar in nature, in the sense I seem to move more quickly than my opponent, to a point where I can anticipate their movement and react more quickly than they can, where it differs is that there is a level of calculation and awareness of what is going on around me that accompanies what I was feeling at this moment with Pulcher. Those moments in battle in which I found my comrades and myself in such danger I was forced to call on what, in my family at least, has been called my divine fit, not only is there this physical, tangible change that takes place, more importantly, all concern for not only my safety but my very life vanishes. In that moment, I sincerely do not care about not only what happens to me, but what is taking place around me; I lose myself and the awareness of the larger situation. This was not the case here, and I stopped as if I needed to take a breath, inviting Pulcher to seize the initiative. I cannot lie; it was extremely satisfying watching his sneering smile disappear when he threw his first punch, or at least attempted to do so. There was no missing the look of alarm crossing his marred face when the blow he had intended to land with such devastating force was so altered by the beating his arms had absorbed that I knocked his incoming fist aside with contemptuous ease.

"You thought you were smarter than my brother, but he proved you wrong." I said this loudly enough so all could hear. "And you thought you were stronger than me." As I finished, I rushed at him, catching him by surprise, positioning my body so our right legs were more or less aligned, then swinging my right leg slightly left and thrusting it out behind his own legs, all while grabbing his throat with my right hand. Pulling my right leg backward while shoving my right hand forward, I executed what is one of the most devastatingly effective attacks that is the hardest to defend, which I had learned from Maximus Vulso. Pulcher's arms flailed wildly as his body crashed down, hard, onto the wooden floor, the force made even greater by my own weight driving downward. As Vulso had taught me, if I had locked my elbow while closing my fist wrapped around his windpipe, the fight would have been over. In retrospect, this was what I should have done; instead, I released my grip on his throat, then stiffened my first two fingers, intent on driving them into one of his eyes. He managed to bring his left arm across his face, but in doing so, gave me another target. Spreading his left hand out as widely as possible to provide the widest coverage to protect his eyes, by doing so, I was able to grab his smallest finger, snapping it with as much effort as it takes me to wrench the leg of a chicken from a roasted bird. Even as this happened, he had been aiming a wild swing at my head with his right fist, except the sudden pain obviously caused him to abandon this attack, as he howled with pain so loudly that, frankly, the most damage he inflicted was to my ears. I rose from my kneeling position, then backed away, allowing him to scramble to his feet, and I did not need more light to see his little finger sticking out at a right angle from his left hand, rendering it useless. All signs of his sneering disdain and confidence had vanished, and his demeanor reminded me of a trapped animal, which he was in many ways.

"What's the matter, Pulcher?" This time when I laughed, I did not need to pretend. "You don't look so good."

"Come closer, and you'll find out just how good I am," he growled, except it sounded hollow, and I saw his eyes darting about.

I probably should have paid closer attention to exactly where he was looking, yet in my defense, I was suddenly distracted by a sound originating from outside the *taverna*. It was the shrill, piping whistle used by members of the town watch.

"Provosts!"

Someone shouted this, and behind me, I heard the sudden noise of hobnail soles slamming onto the wooden floor as all the men under the standard fled. In military towns like Siscia, while there is a town watch that is separate from the Legions, with every shift, there is at least one man, usually two who are attached to the contingent of provosts who are permanently attached to the *praetorium*, not to a specific Legion. They are the bane of most rankers' existence, at least for those whom the pursuit of all manners of vice is of utmost importance.

"Titus," Domitius' voice called out a warning.

"I know, I heard," I snapped.

As I pieced events together later, the only conclusion that makes any sense is that, although I did not believe I had done so, I must have taken my gaze away from Pulcher for a heartbeat as I turned my attention to Domitius' warning. Also, in the heat of the moment, while I had seen Pulcher was slowly sliding across my front to my right, I had assumed he was trying to position himself for a lunge at me; however, he was not. With a speed I can admit surprised me, even given my heightened sense of time, which I believe was born of a desperation as Servius Labienus recognized I was clearly his superior in this fight, instead of throwing himself at me, he lunged for the sword I had completely forgotten was lying on top of a table. Thankfully, my reflexes did not fail me, because somehow, I instantly divined I would be unable to stop him from reaching the sword, so instead of attempting to cut him off, I moved in the opposite direction, thereby putting a couple more paces distance between us. And thankfully, since Domitius had turned to warn me of the approach of the provosts, he saw what was happening and understood what he needed to do in the time it takes to blink one's eyes.

"Titus! Catch!"

Once more, a sword came towards me, and somehow, Domitius launched the sword in such a way that it seemed to aim itself for my hand in the same instant I was thrusting it out. In all truth, I seriously doubt if we tried this maneuver a hundred times, we would have been able to come close to performing it as perfectly as we did in that *taverna*, at least no more than four or five. Fortunately, at least for me, we only needed to be perfect once, so that one moment, I was standing there empty-handed, the next, I was grasping the hilt of a sword, fingers over thumb in the Vinician grip and the blade was already moving in a sweeping first position thrust. Before Pulcher had really begun his own attempt, the point of my blade punched into his body, entering it at the precise spot for which I aimed, right under his breastbone. As had happened to me so many times, what was one of the last breaths expelled from the lungs of Servius Labienus blasted me, our faces inches apart as I stared into his eyes, trying to make sure it was my face burned into his mind here in the last moment of his life. I will say he did not scream, although I believe this might have been due more to the fact that the force of my thrust drove the breath from his lungs than any fortitude on his part. And, as usually happened, my hand and wrist suddenly became wet and sticky, especially after I locked my elbow against my body while I grabbed

Pulcher by the back of his neck, pressing my forehead against his so that my eyes were still boring into his as, using my hips, I twisted my body to the side, ripping the blade across his midsection. Ironically enough, this seemed to give him a last burst of energy because he let out a shrill scream, one which caused me to let out my own bellow of triumph, even as the hairs on the back of my neck suddenly came to *intente.* No matter how many times a man hears another's death cry, it is a chilling sound, if only because you wonder if you would do the same if circumstances were reversed. Except circumstances were not reversed, and I continued staring into Pulcher's eyes as he dropped to his knees, while I felt the hot viscera of his insides falling onto my arm.

"This is for Sextus, you cocksucker."

At least, I believe this was what I said, yet even as those words were leaving my mouth, from behind me came another warning cry.

"Titus! What the *fuck* did you do?"

Whirling about, for the first time, I staggered as if I had been struck, except this was not caused by Pulcher, who lay dead at my feet.

"Sextus???"

The timespan of the next two hundred heartbeats or so are hopelessly muddled in my mind, therefore I cannot attest to the veracity in terms of any kind of timeline of events that happened so rapidly that, for all I know, the reality is that what I thought was two hundred was perhaps fifty heartbeats of time. Staring across the rapidly emptying *taverna*, I saw Sextus standing there, next to Domitius.

"What the fuck are you doing here?" I believe I managed.

"Because I knew you'd do something stupid," he shot back, crossing the short distance between us. Poking his finger in my chest, he shouted, "Just like you did!"

"The provosts are almost here!" Domitius warned, which at least snapped me out of my stupor.

"Titus," I called to him, pointing to my brother, "take him and go! There has to be a back way out of here."

My brother refused to move, shaking his head with that same damn stubbornness as he said, "I'm not going anywhere! But you," he jabbed me with his finger again, "are!" Before I could respond, he turned to Domitius, and of the three of us, my brother was the calmest, insisting, "You need to get Titus out of here. If you're the friend you say you are, you need to go. NOW!"

Domitius did not respond immediately, at least to Sextus. Instead, he wheeled about and pointed his sword at what appeared to be the only one of Pulcher's men left in the *taverna*, which looked as if a sudden storm had blown through, knocking over tables and chairs, leaving puddles of wine that in the guttering light were an almost perfect match to the pool of blood that was slowly expanding under Pulcher's body, whose eyes were staring dully up at me over the gaping hole of his non-existent nose.

"Is there another way out of here?" Domitius demanded of the cowering man who, just a few moments before, had been full of belligerent swagger.

He did not answer at first, but then Domitius took a threatening step towards him, the sword still outstretched, causing him to yelp in fear. However, he also pointed in the general direction of the hearth and bar.

"Behind the bar, there's a hidden door," the coward shouted, adding, "Please! Don't kill me!"

My mind was still trying to catch up as Sextus snatched the sword from my grasp, then before I could react, knelt down and thrust his right hand directly into the gaping gash in Pulcher's midsection, covering his hand in the gore and offal of whatever it was Pulcher had ingested for what turned out to be his last meal. Straightening up, my brother turned to look at me directly in the eyes.

"Titus, this is my mess, not yours. You need to get out of here now. Before the provosts get here."

"But," I shook my head, "Sextus, you're going to be…"

"Flogged," he finished what I could not, yet whatever quaver there was in his voice, I chose to ignore, "but I'm just a Gregarius. Barely more than a *Tirone*. But you," there was a sudden intensity to his voice I had never heard from him before, "you're made for this. And this is your career. Me?" he shrugged, but I noticed this was the first time he refused to look me in the eyes, "this is just what I'm doing for now. I figured out really quickly that this wasn't for me."

Despite the urgency of the moment and every instinct that was screaming at me to flee, I could not stop myself from asking, "When did you figure that out?"

"About a month after I joined."

He said this in such a way I could not help laughing; neither could he. Only Domitius kept his composure enough to hear the slapping of hobnailed soles outside.

"Titus!" he shouted. "We need to go! Now!"

And to my everlasting shame, I did, leaving my brother to face the consequences of my actions.

The fact that Servius Labienus was a civilian, and because when all was said and done, none of his supposedly loyal men were willing to step forward and give any information that could have gotten Sextus executed, worked in my brother's favor. From the viewpoint of Rome, meaning the divine Augustus, when weighed and measured, a Legionary, even a Gregarius, is more valuable than a Head Counter. If Pulcher had been an equestrian, I shudder to think what might have happened. Nevertheless, my brother was punished for what was thought of by the army and those who were not there as the killing of Servius Labienus.

"Titus, you're doing the right thing," Domitius kept trying to assure me as we hurried away from Pan's Grotto. "And your brother's right, at least in this. It was his mess to begin with." When I did not answer, he added hopefully, "Maybe this will be what he needs to wake up, Titus."

"What?" I finally burst out, the bitter anger and regret becoming too much. "That he's going to be flogged, at the very least? Or," I turned to stare down at my friend, "executed?"

Domitius did not answer me, at least immediately.

Then, he said quietly, "I doubt it'll come to that, Titus. But if it does?" He paused for an instant, then shrugged and added, "Your family has enough money to buy anyone off, even Augustus."

As odd as it might sound, this actually made me feel better because I knew he was speaking the truth of it. But that was only part of my anguish; I was struggling with the shame of running out and leaving my brother behind, and it is one I still grapple with to this day. Nevertheless, I did not turn around and go back. Instead, Domitius and I agreed we would return to camp, despite the fact that we both had passes for the night, but before we returned to our area, we went to the bathhouse so I could clean all of Pulcher's blood and gore off me, while he kept lookout for anyone on guard duty. Together, we slipped into our hut, thankful that the rest of our comrades were already asleep, whereupon I threw myself down on my bunk, sure I would not get any sleep that night. Consequently, when the *bucina* sounded the call to begin the next day, I almost jumped out of my own skin, so startled by the sound was I, telling me I had indeed fallen asleep. It was not more than a sixth part of a watch after this, as we were about to consume our morning meal, when there were two sharp raps on the door, announcing that Asinius was about to enter. Jumping up from our bench, despite the fact that I was expecting something like this to happen, the sight of both our Optio and the Optio of the Fifth of the Seventh, Esquilinus, made my heart leap into my throat. Their expressions did not help my state of mind.

"Pullus," Asinius called out, except I was already moving, and I saw he did not miss this, his eyes narrowing as I approached, but he only jerked his head and said, "We need to talk. Outside."

Because I had to cross the hut, the pair were standing there waiting for me, but the instant Asinius returned my salute, he pounced.

"You obviously know why we're here."

"No, sir," I lied, then pointed to Esquilinus, "except it must have to do with my brother since Optio Esquilinus is with you. Is he all right?"

Asinius did not reply immediately, instead exchanging a glance with his counterpart, who gave him a minute shrug.

"No," he answered, then amended, "at least not exactly." It took a huge effort on my part, but I kept my expression as close to puzzled concern as I could; I was not sanguine about fooling Asinius, yet he seemed to believe what his eyes saw was sincere. "But he is in trouble."

"What kind of trouble?"

"What do you know about his dealings with Servius Labienus?" This came from Esquilinus.

"Servius Labienus?" I echoed, still trying to look confused.

"Pulcher," Esquilinus supplied.

"Pulcher?" I had decided to play the Stupid Legionary part to the hilt. "What about him?" Hardening my expression, I went on, "Did he attack my brother again?"

"So you know about what happened?" Esquilinus asked, but it was Asinius' eyes I felt boring into me, making it hard for me to maintain both my attention and my composure.

"Yes, sir," I answered him, thankful I at least did not have to feign my anger, "I knew about it. But why would Sextus be in trouble for being attacked by that…Pulcher?"

It was the best epithet with which I could come up.

"Because Pulcher's dead," Esquilinus answered.

Acutely aware that at least Asinius was still suspicious, I attempted to give the best performance of my life, forcing my face to slowly change expression, starting with confusion, then dawning recognition.

"What are you telling me?" My gaze went back and forth between the two Optios. "You think Sextus is responsible?"

"There's not much question of that," Asinius replied, but it was Esquilinus who picked up the rest. "He was caught by the provosts at Pan's Grotto…"

"So?" I cut him off. "Just because he was at one of Pulcher's places doesn't mean he's responsible. Pulcher owns a lot of the spots around Siscia!"

"No, his presence there by itself isn't proof of anything," Asinius agreed, "but the fact that Pulcher's body was at his feet, and he had a bloody sword in his hand is…" He spread his hands as he shrugged, but he did not need to continue.

When I opened my mouth to reply, I honestly could not think of anything at first, then finally settled on, "What does Sextus say about what happened?"

"Oh," Esquilinus answered, "he admitted killing Pulcher, but insists it was a situation of mutual combat. And," when Esquilinus glanced over at Asinius, I wondered why, "the provosts did say there was a sword in Pulcher's hand."

"So that should be a case of self-defense," I argued.

"Yes," Esquilinus admitted, except it was Asinius who finished with, "and no, Pullus."

Turning to look at my Optio, he looked at me levelly as he took over and continued, "While it seems that at the very least Pulcher was attempting to shove a sword into your brother's guts, it's not that simple. First," he extended a finger, "if your brother took a sword into town, you know that's against regulations. And," his voice turned hard, "you know the punishment for that."

I did; the least he could expect was a flogging.

When I did not say anything in reply, he continued, "Second," another finger joined the first, "why was your brother there in the first place, if not to exact revenge on Pulcher?" It was the third finger that was the most damning, and dangerous. "Third, he said that he walked into that spot alone, with nobody to watch his back. And that," now there was no mistaking that Asinius was directing this at me, "doesn't make a fucking bit of sense." Folding his arms, he kept looking at me with that steady gaze of his and simply asked, "So what really happened?"

Over the course of my time under the standard, I have either aided someone else, or performed myself, a number of acts that brought harm, and worse, to men who, at least by virtue of the uniform they wore, were on the same side as I was. Starting with Gaius Maxentius, then with Gaius Caecina and Appius Mela, there have been Romans who were my enemies, and who I destroyed, either by crippling or killing. Yet, nothing I did to them brings as much pain, and shame, as the knowledge that I allowed my brother Sextus to be punished for my actions. Once my questioning by the two Optios was done, where I continued to stick to my story, I was finally allowed to visit my brother, who had been confined to his section hut.

"Sextus," I told him once his comrades gave us the privacy of the hut, "you don't have to go through with this! Let me tell them the truth."

"No." He shook his head; the sight of his jaw sticking out in a manner I had seen since I could remember was more eloquent than anything he could have said. "I made this mess, Titus! I'm not letting you get flogged for something I caused!"

"You didn't!" I shot right back. "At least," I amended, "you didn't kill Pulcher. I did." Reaching out, I grasped his shoulder, and I am not ashamed to say I was pleading with him, "Please, Sextus. Don't take the blame for something I did!"

"You only did it because I fucked up! You were only protecting me," he retorted. "No," he repeated, shaking his head again, "I made this mess, I need to pay the price."

"Do you know what that price is going to be?" I admit my tone turned harsh, yet there was a surge of desperation that came roaring up from deep within me, recognizing the mulish cast to my brother's jaw. "Have they told you what the punishment's going to be yet?"

"No," he admitted reluctantly, except he shook his head again, making me want to slap him. "But it doesn't matter!"

"Well, I know," I shot back, because Esquilinus had informed me it had already been decided. "Do you want to hear?"

For an instant, I thought I had reached Sextus, because suddenly, he looked like my little brother again, and I abruptly reached out and put my arm around his shoulders.

"Yes," he finally managed.

"They want to flog you, Sextus." The words seemed to catch in my throat.

I was not prepared for him to look relieved, yet he let out a huge breath and, shakily it is true, still laughed and asked, "Is that all? Thank the gods!"

Instantly, I realized he did not understand, so I tightened my grip around his shoulders as I told him quietly, "Sextus, they're going to scourge you."

I felt his body stiffen under my arm, and his face went so white I was compelled to add hurriedly, "Only five lashes will be with the scourge. They're going to give you fifteen, but only the last five will be with the scourge."

"Well," although he laughed again, this time, I could hear the edge of hysteria there, "as long as it's only five!"

"That's why it's not going to happen," I told him firmly. "At least, not to you."

I rose then, and as the gods as my witness, I was determined to go and tell Tiburtinus the whole story. It was why I moved quickly, standing up from Sextus' bunk to begin moving towards the door, not even looking back. Which, as I quickly learned, was a mistake. Suddenly, a huge blow from behind not only sent me off my feet and lurching forward, but drove the wind from me as I hit the wooden floor of the hut, barely able to get my arms out in front of me in time. When I felt the weight of Sextus' body on me, even through my shock, I distinctly remember the thought that this was the first time my little brother had knocked me off my feet without me being off balance because of my own clumsiness to help him.

"You're not going to do anything!" His mouth was pressed against my ear, which meant he did not need to speak as loudly as he did; I would have yelped in pain just from that if there had been any air in my lungs.

I struggled to push myself up, but Sextus, despite being lighter than me by thirty pounds at least, was still from the same stock as Titus Pullus, meaning he possessed more strength than other men his size. It was an odd, and a distinctly unpleasant feeling, I will admit, being pinned to the floor by my younger brother.

"Titus, I'm not letting you ruin your career." He at least lowered his voice, yet there was an urgency to his tone that got me to stop struggling, at least for the moment. "I've already told you I don't plan to stay past my first enlistment. But you! You were born for this, Titus, and we both know it! You're the one who's going to follow in Avus' and Tata's footsteps and bring more glory to our family name! Not me! I know that! So please," if only he had not started pleading with me, "let me do this! Not just for you, but for the family!"

I cannot say how long we lay there, with my brother on top of me, both of us panting from the exertion and the emotions of the moment. Finally, I felt my head nod; only then did he relinquish his hold on me. Then, helping me to my feet, we stood there for a moment, looking at each other, and I am not ashamed to say I could barely see him through my tears.

"Are you sure?" I finally managed, only slightly appeased by seeing he was no less affected, crying just as much as I was.

"Yes." Even through the tears, I saw he did not hesitate. "Absolutely. This is for the best. For you; for the family." Choking back something that was half-laugh, half-sob, he added, "It's not so good for me, but..."

I hugged my brother then, and we stood for several moments; I do not think either of us wanted to let go.

Because of the audience for whom I am writing this account, and my hope that they are also following the path created for the Pullus line, my desire is that they understand when I say the day I stood witness to the punishment meted out to Miles Gregarius Sextus Porcinianus Pullus was one of the most agonizing...and proudest of my life, and they do not find it ringing falsely. My presence was also another source of contention; only if my brother was being executed would the entire Legion have been paraded to witness it. However, this was one thing in which I would not be denied, although in this case, I did not use bribery but the threat of a horrific beating that by rights should have gotten me strapped on the punishment frame next to Sextus. Fortunately, despite my earlier misgivings about Tiburtinus' Optio, Esquilinus absorbed the threat with surprising equanimity, and judging from what happened, or actually what did not afterward, he never spoke to Tiburtinus about my threat. Regardless of how it happened, when the day came for the Fifth Century of the Seventh Cohort to stand in the spot right off the forum where the punishment frame is located, and I was standing there alongside Tiburtinus and Esquilinus, there was a part of me that was sorry I had been so insistent. Regardless, as I told myself then and still believe now, this was the least I deserved for allowing Sextus to be punished for something I had done. The man from the special detail who is permanently assigned to the *Praetorium* and is responsible for both punishments of Legionaries and torturing of our enemies was standing there, stripped to the waist despite the cold. Not surprisingly, the fact that his musculature matched mine, despite being almost a foot shorter than me, did not bring me comfort. I could not take my eyes off of him; more specifically, my gaze was fixed on the lash, although not the one in his hand at the moment. As I had been informed, the first ten lashes would be administered with the normal whip, which consists of several pieces of leather attached to a handle, then is braided for about four feet of its length, before the nine strips are separated. From that point forward, each strip becomes slightly thinner, so that the ends are about half the width of the fingernail on my smallest finger. The very ends are cut on a bias rather than straight across, which dig small furrows into the back of the man being punished. However, while those are painful, comparing it to what would be coming after the first ten lashes would be like comparing a whisper to a scream. Consequently, once the charge and punishment was read by Tiburtinus, his voice loud but completely devoid of emotion, and Esquilinus offered my brother the leather-wrapped round dowel to bite down on and he refused, I could not stop myself from doing something completely unusual in events like this. Striding the few paces distance, I approached Sextus from the opposite side from where Esquilinus was standing, with my brother's body in between us, his arms stretched out and securely tied to the edges of the frame. Stripped to the waist like his punisher, his pristine back showed starkly white when compared to the darkened frame, and I tried to ignore the even darker stains that showed in splotches around the part covered by Sextus' body.

"What do you think you're doing?" I demanded of my brother.

I would not have thought it possible, but his face was even paler than his back, and this sight alone threatened my composure even more, yet despite his obvious fear, Sextus' voice was strong when he answered me, "I don't need it."

"The fuck you don't," I retorted. Pointing in the general direction of where the man who was waiting to execute the sentence, I pressed, "Sextus, nobody is going to think less of you if you use the gag, because that bastard is one of the strongest men in their detail!"

He did at least try and shrug, except he was too tightly secured to do so, although he still resisted. "All the more reason I'm not going to use it." For the first time, he turned his head to look me directly in the eye, and while he spoke quietly, I am sure Esquilinus heard as well when he said, "I'm going to show the boys what a Pullus is made of. Although," the fact that he even attempted to laugh brought tears to my eyes as, like always, my brother made a joke, "I didn't plan on it being quite so literally. But, Titus, you understand that, don't you?"

No! I wanted to cry out, except that would have been a lie, so instead, I only nodded my head, which was all I could manage. I patted him on the shoulder, then Esquilinus stepped away in a signal to me, and I did the same. Together, we walked back to the Century, and as we did, I saw there was not one face among his comrades that could have been described as pleased at seeing Sextus being punished. That, I forced myself to acknowledge, would not have been the case with me; Balbinus would have been unable to contain himself if I had been strapped to that frame. When we reached Tiburtinus, he waited long enough for us to turn about before he gave a nod to the punisher, who had been loosening up his arm by swinging it in easy circles. Even from where we stood, we could hear the slight whistling sound the leather strips made as they cut through the air, and my stomach clenched at the thought that this was just while he was warming up. Finally, he turned to face my brother's bared back, his left foot forward and the lash dangling from his waist level, pausing for an instant. Then in one motion that, as horrible as it was, a part of me had to admire for the fluidity and awful grace displayed by a man who was clearly skilled at his craft, the lash made a perfect arcing circle, stopped only when the lashes cut into my brother's back with a wet, slapping sound that made me even sicker. Naturally, my brother reacted, his body stiffening as his head shot up and back from both the impact and the pain, yet while his mouth opened, no sound came from him. Across his back had sprouted nine narrow welts, arrayed diagonally, while the end of each one had a small, bloody hole. That, I thought with a grim horror, is as good as his back is ever going to look again.

"One!"

Ironically enough, it was the sound of Tiburtinus' voice that made me jump slightly; I suppose because I had expected this reaction when the first blow landed on Sextus' back, I was able to stop myself then, while this caught me by surprise. If either the Centurion or his Optio noticed this, they made no sign, and I made sure I kept my gaze straight ahead. The lash arced again, the sound repeated, and Sextus' body jerked again…but he still made no sound.

"Two!"

On and on it went as I watched my brother's back slowly transform from a clean piece of skin into a series of red, bloody lines. By the third or fourth lash, there was no way for the lashes not to cut across those furrows already carved into my brother's flesh, creating a gruesome pattern, but still my brother made no sound, and with every blow that counted down to the final five, my own tension increased. As I stood there, trying to be as impassive as the other two men next to me, inwardly, I was fervently offering up prayers to every god I could think of to give my brother the strength to at least achieve his own form of victory by not making a sound. And, by the time the tenth and final blow landed, Sextus still had not, except the worst was yet to come.

The punisher paused to switch from the regular lash, dropping it on the ground while withdrawing the scourge from his belt. Nominally identical to the regular lash, at least in its configuration and the number of strands, where it differs is with the pieces of deliberately jagged metal tied into each strand. Also, those bits of metal are not arrayed evenly; instead, one is tied at the very end of one strand, another an inch from the end, and yet another perhaps two or three inches. As all *tiros* learn, usually from gleeful veterans who try their best to scare their new comrades, this is done to evenly spread the devastating damage.

"After all, if they all landed next to each other in the same spot, it'd only take two or three times before there wasn't anything left but bones! Then a man couldn't lift a shield or a sword and he might as well be executed!"

As I recall, it had been Servius Metellus who had been happy to relay this piece of information to me, just a few days after I joined the First Century, Fourth Cohort, now almost six years past. Recalling his words in this moment was bad enough, yet I found my eyes could not stay away from the lash while I tried not to think about why those nine pieces of metal did not reflect any light in the dull way iron does. However, despite my best attempt, there seemed to be a part of me determined to torment myself as it practically shouted the reason the bits were black was from all the flesh and blood from its previous victims. As this struggle was taking place within me, the punisher was now grasping the scourge, but then, before he could apply the first blow, something unusual happened.

"Wait!" Tiburtinus called out, then turned to Esquilinus, holding his hand out as he ordered the Optio, "Give me the gag!" Taking it, he indicated me with his head and said abruptly, "Pullus! Come with me."

Nothing was said between us as we walked over to Sextus, which was a good thing because my jaws were clenched so tightly I could not have done more than mumble. Sextus' back was crisscrossed with welts, and enough blood had been drawn that there were trails of his ichor traveling down his back in several single lines. At first, I thought he might have been unconscious because he was not moving; then he obviously heard our approach and turned his head to look over his shoulder at us. His face was completely wet from the tears, while his lips were pressed so tightly together they were almost white, but despite my own vision being blurred, I saw that damned jaw of his was still set.

"Pullus," Tiburtinus said quietly, "you're almost done. But," he thrust the gag out, and continued softly, "the worst is about to come. You really should take this."

Sextus actually opened his mouth, and for an instant, I felt a surge of relief.

However, it was only to say, "No, sir. I don't need it."

Sighing, Tiburtinus turned to me, one eyebrow lifted in a silent command that I understood meant, "You try talking some sense into this stubborn bastard."

Except I did not; instead, I pointed to the lower part of his face and said, "Sir, I've grown up with that look. You're wasting your breath with this one. He's not going to change his mind."

Tiburtinus' face darkened, which I had long since learned was a sign of a storm brewing, then he took a deep breath, except instead of speaking, he actually chuckled harshly, and said, "You're right; I should have known better and I do recognize that look." He turned to face me, a grim smile as he added, "But not from him."

"It runs in the family." Sextus' voice was weak, but clearly understandable. He shook his head again, and said, "I'm sorry to waste your time, sir. But I don't need it."

Answering with a curt nod, Tiburtinus spun about, while I lingered for an instant.

"I'll be fine, Titus," Sextus assured me, then jerked his head in a silent command for me to leave as well.

I opened my mouth, but nothing came out, so I followed Tiburtinus.

As bizarre as it may sound, on this day, I had never before been prouder of my brother. Going further, I was humbled by his display of courage, and it must be said, quiet defiance, because he was good to his word and did not cry out. Only when he was taken down from the frame did a groan escape his lips, although he was unconscious when it happened, and it was barely audible more than a few paces away. He was lowered, face down, onto the stretcher brought by the two *medici* summoned from the hospital, but whether they handled him as gently as they did because of their nature, or the fact that I was standing there, both hands curled into fists as I watched, made no difference to me, then or now.

"Pullus, you should…" Esquilinus began, but I cut him off.

"I'm going with him to the hospital," I told him, and again, for whatever the reason, the Optio did not try and stop me.

As we covered the short distance, I tried to keep from looking at Sextus' back, but even from the corner of my eye, I saw the dull white of bone poking through the savaged, bloody mess that was my brother's back. I had seen other men scourged, of course, just never this closely, nor had it been someone I cared about, let alone loved as I did my brother. I can clearly recall in this moment thinking back to when, not long after I had joined the Legion, I was on my first campaign, under Nero Claudius Drusus. One night, I had the guard duty outside the *praetorium*, and Drusus himself stopped to talk to me. It is not as noteworthy as it might sound, at least as far as why he deigned to stop and talk to a lowly Gregarius. First, he was well known for his approachability by men of all ranks, but more importantly, he knew me already; at least, as much as a Legate in command of an army can know someone who was barely more than a *Tirone*. He had decorated me a few weeks before when, completely by happenstance, I had managed to slay a man named Vergorix, a sub-chieftain of the Chatti. Consequently, just before he entered the headquarters tent the night I was on guard duty, he had spied me and stopped to talk. During our admittedly brief conversation, he had asked me a question that, even now, I believe is the first time I was ever asked.

"Do you love your brother?"

Truthfully, up to that moment, I had never given it any thought, but his question forced me to consider it, and I realized, not without some surprise that, in fact, I did. This conversation was what was in my mind as I walked beside the stretcher bearing Sextus' torn body to the hospital.

My brother survived the scourging, and while it took some time, he got back on his feet and was able to perform his duties. I cannot say with any certainty, but my suspicion is that the hundred *sesterces* I paid to the physician, along with the fifty I paid to the *medici* who cared for him, might have helped him recover without any major issues. Nevertheless, like many men who have been scourged, my brother found previously simple tasks were made more difficult, particularly the wielding of his shield, because the scourge had done the most damage to the muscles on the left side of his body. However, this was one area where I felt uniquely qualified to help Sextus compensate for this new challenge, since I had faced a similar one, albeit for different reasons. Nevertheless, because of my wounds that had ravaged my left forearm a few years before, when we had been ambushed at a place we called The Quarry, I had been forced to work harder than I ever had prior to that time, learning to compensate for the damage done to the muscles of my forearm. Oddly enough, whereas before I had always had trouble getting Sextus motivated for training in the almost three years he spent in Siscia before he enlisted, for the first time, he displayed a level of determination and desire that had been missing before. Still, for about three months after his flogging, Sextus suffered more now than at any time previously in his life, yet I never heard him utter one word of complaint. As I reflect on matters now, I believe this period of time cemented our love and regard for each other in a way that had heretofore been missing from our relationship. In the past, I had always viewed Sextus with an indulgent irritation, the little brother who was more of a nuisance than anything, and not a man in his own right. The watches we spent outside the camp at the stakes, long after the sun went down, changed all that. And, of all the many regrets of my life, the one that haunts me the most is that I never told Sextus how proud I was of him, and how much I respected him as he worked to return to a level of performance that would not bring shame to the Pullus name.

When Sextus was released from the hospital and returned to his Century, although he was exempted from training, at his insistence, I met him after duty at the stakes, giving me my first indication that something had changed in my brother. He was still too weak to lift a real shield, let alone one of the heavier training shields, so instead, we worked on simple movements, and while I cannot say it was as painful for me as it was for him, it was distressing nonetheless to watch him.

Just before we were done, he turned to me, his face gleaming with sweat from the effort and pain, and I still remember the look of intensity he wore when he said, "Titus, I have to ask you something."

As I usually did, I was about to make some sort of joke, except the expression on his face was such that I just nodded.

"Have you written to Tata?" he asked me. "I mean, since…?"

"No," I replied; truthfully, I had been struggling with this very question even before Sextus was actually flogged.

"Please, Titus," he begged, "don't tell him about…about this." For the first time since the day he was punished, I saw his eyes suddenly brim with unshed tears, and his voice broke as he continued, "I just don't want him to be ashamed of me."

Any idea I might have had of relating my brother's punishment back to my parents ended right then, and even to this day, I have never brought it up with my father, even after everything else that occurred.

However, that was in the future; in this moment, looking into Sextus' eyes, I swore to him, "He'll never hear it from me."

And I kept my word, which would end up causing me some difficulty much, much sooner than I expected.

It was somewhere in the aftermath of Sextus' flogging that another event occurred that, in some ways, was more painful for me than what transpired with my brother. Actually, this is also a moment it is impossible for me to say with any certainty exactly when it occurred, at least in a calendar sense; I believe this is how a man's mind acts to protect itself. What I do vividly remember are the circumstances, because it fell to Sextus to relay the information to me that, ultimately, shattered a part of not just my world, but who I am as a man. We were meeting for an evening meal at Diocles' apartment, and what I do vividly recall is seeing my brother standing at the base of the stairs, which was something unusual and giving me the sense he was waiting for me, which he was. However, it was his expression as I approached that caused my step to falter, although I still was not thinking anywhere along the lines of where our conversation was about to lead.

As usually happened between us, I greeted my brother by joking, "By Dis, Sextus! You look grim! What is it? Did your favorite whore get married or something?"

The fact that he did not respond with his own cutting remark gave me an instant's warning, yet I still was not prepared for what I was about to learn.

"Titus," he said quietly, "I have something I need to tell you, and I wanted to do it out here."

"What is it?" I recall the sudden stab of alarm I felt, my first thought being he had received word from home. "Is it Mama? Or," I swallowed hard, "Tata?"

"No." He shook his head, yet I was not relieved because his expression was still so grave, but when I involuntarily glanced up at the apartment, he shook his head again, assuring me, "No, Diocles and his family are fine. It's…something I learned today, when I was in the forum."

This threw me, and I tried to think of how something he heard in the forum of Siscia could possibly be of such import he was standing there looking like he was about to battle with Cerberus.

"Then what is it?" I am afraid I snapped at him. "Why are you looking like that?"

"It's about," I saw the knot in his throat bob as he swallowed, then said, "Giulia, Titus."

I do not blame my brother for causing my reaction, because my first thought was, she's come back! And, for the span of a heartbeat or two, my mind took flight as I thought about the implications that went spinning out from my mind, before I could do anything to rein my hopes in, knowing just by my brother's demeanor this was futile. She had the baby, I thought! And now she's back, in defiance of her parents, and we'll live together as man and wife! In that fragile stretch of time that probably numbered no more than two or three heartbeats, I experienced an intense rush of hope and happiness, swept along by a fantasy that, only now do I recognize had been buried deeply within me somewhere, waiting to be released for a moment such as this. As hard as it may be to believe, during a span of two or three heartbeats, I lived a lifetime, a reality where Giulia and I loved, laughed and grew old together, as her father, who I had seen loved his daughter very much, had swallowed his pride and given us his blessing, a world where this child was just the first of many, all of them strong, healthy young sons and daughters who would carry on the legacy started by Titus Pullus, a poor boy from Baetica who had accomplished so much.

"Giulia's dead, Titus." Sextus' voice was choked with what I suppose is whatever emotion is evoked when someone is giving dreadful news to a loved one.

My initial reaction was, frankly, none at all, and I heard a voice that sounded like my own but which I was sure did not belong to me mumble, "What? What did you say?"

"I said," Sextus reached out then to grab my upper arm, and as I learned, even in moments of extreme grief there is still a part of me who seems detached from what is happening, because I distinctly recall being thankful he did not grab me around my scar, as Sextus repeated, "that Giulia's dead, Titus."

"But…how?" I shook my head, more to dislodge the horrible word "dead" my brother had just uttered, twice. "And how could you know?"

"I was in the forum," my brother explained, "and I was approached by a man. I didn't recognize him. But he knew who I was, because he asked me if I was your brother." Sextus hesitated, but when I looked into his eyes, he suddenly closed his own, and went on, "He told me he belonged to the house of Lucius Livinius, and he had a message for you." What I remember is shaking my head again, trying in vain to stop Sextus from delivering news I had no desire to hear, and what I will say is that his face was wet with tears as he continued, "He said he wanted you to know that Giulia died, in childbirth."

It took every bit of my composure to remain standing, but I still did not recognize my own voice as I asked him, "And the babe?"

Sextus did not reply, at least verbally, shaking his head with a sorrow that conveyed the grief he felt at being the bearer of such horrible news. We stood there for only the gods know how long as I stared off into space, thinking dully about how, if this was a sign from the gods that I was indeed following in the footsteps of the first Titus Pullus, I no longer wanted the burden. Somehow, I managed to tell my brother to inform Diocles and Birgit my regrets that I would be unable to attend the meal, but honestly, this is the last I remember of the night, although I assume I wandered the streets of Siscia. Still, when the morning call to awaken sounded, I rolled out of my bunk, immediately losing myself in the routine of a day in the life of a Legion in garrison. Sextus and I never talked about that day, while I immediately buried the grief deep inside so that only those who knew me well, like my brother, and Titus Domitius, sensed anything was amiss. Yet, despite Domitius' best attempts to engage me, trying to get me to discuss, and more importantly acknowledge the loss I had suffered, I steadfastly refused. In fact, this account marks the first moment where I have ever openly spoken about the day I learned that the woman I loved died bearing my child, thereby tying me indelibly to Titus Pullus in a bond of blood and loss of the most profound way.

The winter passed, and our Legate left Pannonia to take the Consulship, along with Lucius Passienus Rufus, and, at least at the beginning, it seemed as if it would be a normal one, where we marched out of Siscia and grumbled about being away from town, while the Pannonian tribes grumbled about our presence but did nothing else. And, at least as far as the Pannonians behaving themselves, for the most part, they did exactly that, confining themselves to the usual small displays of defiance, while we had learned which of those to ignore and which to punish. But it was in March where my world, and that of my brother, was turned upside down. My first indication was when Crito came to find me; as I recall, we were at the stakes when he suddenly appeared, puffing.

"You need to come with me," he told me, only after speaking quietly to Asinius, but while I had not heard what the clerk told him, I had seen him suddenly stiffen, which naturally put me on my guard.

However, while Asinius gave me leave to go with Crito, I was acutely aware how the Optio refused to look in my direction, nor would our clerk answer my repeated questions. It should not be a surprise this increased my anxiety with every step, yet despite my best attempt to prepare myself for any possibility, when we arrived at the Legion office and I saw who was standing there waiting for me, I came to a sudden stop, my body suddenly seeming to freeze up so I was still standing several paces away from the open door, where someone awaited me.

"Alex?" I remember asking, forgetting to use the proper name of Diocles' oldest child. "What is it?"

The boy, now fourteen, did not say anything, but honestly, there was no need; looking into his eyes, I got my answer. Suddenly, without another word being spoken, it felt as if my strength completely evaporated, and I collapsed onto my knees. All I remember from this horrible moment is feeling sure that the world had suddenly turned upside down and I was in danger of sliding off into an abyss. In that instant, I was forced to confront a reality I had always known would present itself one day, and yet I realized I had not truly believed would ever happen. Somehow, I had convinced myself that, while my Avus had succumbed to the claim mortality places on all of us, somehow, his most trusted servant and his second-longest friend would escape death's surly bonds. The boy, whose hair was as black as his father's had been, although very curly, stood there, and a part of me noticed that he was the one not weeping; only over the next few watches did I come to understand he was still in shock.

"Can you come with me?" he asked, his voice quavering, although it could as easily have been because his voice was changing.

I looked at Crito, except he was unable to speak, reminding me once more that Diocles was as well known among the clerks of the Army of Pannonia as my Avus had been with the men under the standard. Instead, he simply proffered a small scroll that was my pass out of camp, which I took, reluctantly, but I took nonetheless. Turning, I put my arm around Alexandros' shoulders; his head was still just about mid-chest to me.

"Let's go," I told him, and together, we walked out of the camp.

I cannot even imagine how odd a sight we made, but I know I was oblivious to the eyes of others as Diocles' oldest son and I walked into town, where Birgit was standing there at the door, no doubt alerted by the sound of our footsteps ascending the stairs. During our entire walk to Siscia, I had been unable to say anything, and I was no less bereft of words when I saw her, with puffy eyes and a face marred by tears so that its normally perfect oval shape was distorted. Nevertheless, she stood erectly, with her chin lifted, and I understood the display she was showing to the world was more for her children than anyone else.

"Birgit, I…" It was all I could get out before we fell into each other's arms, and I finally allowed myself to weep openly and unashamedly.

Only the gods could say how much time we spent before I was able to compose myself enough to ask, "What happened?"

"Nothing," she replied, which confused me at first, but she explained, "I mean, he didn't suffer a fit or anything. We went to sleep last night, and when I rolled over in the morning to wake him…."

Her shoulders began heaving again as she put her face in her hands, and I do not know why, but this act finally made me aware of the children. Gently guiding her into the apartment, I saw them sitting there, smaller copies of their mother, at least in their grief, while Alexandros was doing his utmost to take on the mantle of *paterfamilias*. Seeing this, I felt compelled to address him once I had settled his mother on the chair she normally occupied at the table;

when, that is, she was not up and about in the kitchen, bringing her family their meal.

Crouching down, I looked the boy in the eyes, and I suspect the pain and anguish I saw in them mirrored my own.

I placed both hands on his shoulders as I spoke to him gently, "I know you're hurting, Alex. You know why?" He shook his head mutely, and I supplied the answer. "Because I am. This hurts us, both of us. It hurts your mother, and your brother and sisters. And the next few days are going to be hard." Suddenly, I felt a lump forming in my throat that was so powerful it caused me to amend my statement by adding, "No, Alex. The next few *years* are going to be harder without your father in them. You know I've known him all my life, don't you?" Again, he nodded solemnly, and my heart threatened to rend itself as I recognized his attempt at maintaining his composure, when I was sure all he wanted to do was go find someplace quiet and private, and pour out his grief, alone. I knew this because it was what I wanted to do, yet I forced myself to continue. "So, it's up to you and me to make sure we don't disappoint him, neh? We have to set the example for the others, don't we?"

"Y-yes, Uncle Titus," he mumbled, but the shining in his eyes belied his brave words.

Unable to continue, at least with Alex, I turned back to Birgit and the other children, going to each of them, kneeling down and hugging each of them in turn. I hugged Gisela next, who was in that awkward age between girl and woman, then young Titus who, although he bore the name, was not built in the same way as I and the man for whom he was named. Finally, I pulled Scribonia, the youngest at seven, onto my lap as I sat down at the table, then took a deep breath.

"We need to send word to my parents," I told Birgit, but she surprised me.

"I've already done it," she told me, then added, "At least, I've started it. I sent Belarus, the neighbor downstairs to see Silva. He came back just before you got here and told me that Silva was leaving immediately."

This should not have surprised me; Decimus Silva was a trusted friend with ties to both my Avus and my father; he had made the trip to Arelate once before in my time of need when I required money to achieve my goals of ensuring Asinius stayed my Optio, and I retained my rank of section Sergeant.

"Can I…go see him?" I asked Birgit, and she nodded.

Walking into the bedroom, I was relieved beyond words that Birgit had already lovingly cleaned Diocles' body. One of the bigger shocks I ever received once I was around death for the first time is the smell of *cac* and piss that is almost inevitable with the deceased, no matter how they may die. In battle, this competes with the odor of blood, vomit, and the stench of evisceration, but there is another one that men claim they can smell as well, and that is of decay. I have heard more than one Legionary claim that the smell begins almost as soon as the newly made corpse hits the ground, and I cannot adequately express how relieved I was that none of this was present in the room holding Diocles. His hair had been brushed with the same love and care shown to the rest of his appearance, and his arms were folded across his chest. I had to fight the urge to reach out to shake him awake as my eyes insisted that Birgit had been mistaken, that he was just in a deep, deep slumber. Which, of course, was exactly what he was doing, and then and now I cannot think of any man who deserved eternal peace more, next to my Avus. It was this thought that brought me to sit down heavily on the edge of the bed, and I reached out to put my warm hand on top of the Greek's now-cold ones, as he disappeared in the shimmer of the tears that resumed again.

"I hope you and Avus find each other," I remember saying, or sobbing, "in Elysium." Despite the circumstances, I found myself laughing as another thought occurred to me, "Although you and Avus could never agree on where either of you would end up."

It was something I had not thought of in many years before that point, yet as I sat there, I recalled with a bittersweet fondness the constant bickering back and forth between Titus Pullus and Diocles about their respective beliefs.

"How can any man whose body is stuck in the ground expect to be able to climb to the heavens?" my Avus would start the argument that would last throughout the evening and continue long after I was put to bed; I know this because I usually crept out of the bed I shared with my siblings to go listen at the door, unknown to either of them or my parents. At least, so I believed at the time; I was disabused of that notion shortly before I left for Siscia by my mother.

"Because it's not his body; it's his *pneumos* that's released with a man's last breath," Diocles would sigh.

"So you Greeks say," Avus would snort derisively, "but everyone knows the only way for a man's *numen* to be released is for the body to be burned away. You can't," he would add gleefully, "release your spirit with a breath! How would you keep it in if you could do that?" He would always laugh as he made the same joke. "If that were true, I'd just punch you in the stomach and knock the wind out of you, and you'd drop dead at my feet!"

Just as he always roared with laughter at this, so Diocles always responded the same way as well, saying patiently, "It doesn't work like that, and you know it. You're just trying to be difficult. Although," this was always his Parthian shot, "it's one of the few things you don't have to try at! That's the one thing that comes naturally!"

The echoes of those moments sounded in my mind's ear as I sat there with my hand resting on his, and I mourned the loss of yet another giant whose shadow crossed my life. And in some ways, the fact that his physical size was such a mismatch compared to the impact he had on not just me, or my Avus, but the entire Pullus family, I believe is worthy of its own story. And, as I was about to learn, Diocles gave our family one last chance to be together, reunited not just in grief but in body.

"He what?"

"He wants to be interred in Arelate, next to your Avus' tomb," Birgit repeated quietly.

I had returned to the main room, resuming my seat, and I tried to absorb what I had just heard. Once I got over my initial surprise, I admit I felt a bit chagrined that this was my reaction; where else would Diocles be laid to rest? As soon as this was settled in my mind, I began to think of the practical problems involved in such an endeavor. It was early in the year to be traveling, although ironically enough, this worked in our favor, for the unpleasant but simple reason that the body would not decay as quickly as long as the temperatures remained stable. Every morning would see any buckets of water left outside frozen with a fairly thick skin of ice, although if the sun was out, by the afternoon, we would shed our cloaks. Additionally, there were still blocks of river ice available, but that was only one challenge. However, this was another time where being one of the wealthier members of the Head Count made matters much easier. Finally, the time of year was sufficiently early to allow both Sextus and me to procure leave, provided we were willing to pay for the privilege, which we were. Although Primus Pilus Atticus had not followed in the footsteps of Urso when it came to the multitude of schemes he ran outside the Legion, within it, he had established quite a thriving business. Essentially, anything and everything that was not tied directly to our training and duties in the primary business of the Legion was negotiable, and could either be avoided, delayed, or modified in some way, as long as a ranker was willing to pay the costs associated. And, as one might expect, asking for a leave lasting six weeks, for two men, was an expensive proposition. The fact that the request came from two rankers with the name of Pullus meant that, ultimately, it cost even more. As I had suspected for some time, Atticus had obviously either deduced or been informed that we possessed, or at least had access to a level of wealth beyond our visible means. Ultimately, a pass, for the two of us, signed by the Primus Pilus and endorsed by the broad striper cost us a full year's pay for one Gregarius. And, because of my distraction, I made matters more difficult for us both in the future when I did not hesitate, either in agreeing on the amount, or the length of time it took me to hand over the bag of coin into our greedy Primus Pilus' hands. Although, to be accurate, I handed the money to Crito, who had been pressed into service as our Primus Pilus' chief accountant.

I will say I was somewhat mollified at Crito's clear discomfort, as he whispered, "I'm sorry about the Primus Pilus' price, Pullus. If it were up to me, you wouldn't have to pay a brass *obol*, just because of who it is you're taking with you."

It was just another of the small ways I was reminded that Diocles had friends and admirers on his own account.

"You know," Crito continued as he handed me the two scrolls for Sextus and me, "I worked with Diocles early in my career."

This surprised me, prompting me to ask, "You mean you weren't always clerking for the Legion?"

He shook his head, telling me, "No, when I started I was one of the junior clerks in the *Praetorium*. This was when Marcus Crassus was Legate." Smiling at the memory, he continued, "Oh, I was as green as spring grass! And there was another clerk there." His mouth twisted. "Piraxis. And oh, how he lorded it over the rest of us! We hated him. But then, your grandfather arrived! And he brought Diocles with him. You know," his eyes, just beginning to show the rheumy quality that comes from watches spent squinting at cramped writing under poor light, turned to look at me directly, "Diocles' name was already something of a legend to us."

While I knew this in a general sense, I learned the specifics in this conversation.

"Oh, some of it was the reflected glory that came from your grandfather," he allowed, "but I mean in his own right. While your grandfather was with the 10th under Antonius, remember that Diocles was with him too! Which means he was in Parthia himself! And at Actium!"

"Don't forget Pharsalus," I pointed out, "and Thapsus. And Alexandria."

Crito's face showed his confusion, asking, "Alexandria?" His face cleared and he added, "Oh, yes! You mean when the 10th went with Augustus at the end of the war."

"No," I corrected him, "I'm talking about before that. With Divus Julius." I could not help grinning as I added, "You know, when Cleopatra somehow found herself pregnant with Caesar's child." Even as the words left my mouth, I could not help thinking about that now-dead son, named Caesarion, but I instantly shoved him out of my mind, knowing nothing good could come if his name was mentioned now.

Crito did not say anything for a moment, clearly trying to understand my reference to Alexandria, and he finally said, "But the 10th wasn't with Divus Julius in Alexandria. They had refused to go with him, as I recall. It was the…"

"The 28th, and two Cohorts of the 6th," I supplied for him, proud that I was able to do so. "And my grandfather was made the Primus Pilus of the 6th because the 10th mutinied. All except my grandfather." Even as I was saying this, I felt a queer sensation and, frankly, I was happy that Titus Domitius was nowhere nearby.

Especially when Crito's expression cleared and he nodded his head as he replied, "Ah, yes! Now I remember! That's right! It was at Pharsalus and, as I recall, your grandfather was quite…emphatic in his show of loyalty to Divus Julius. It was…wait, don't tell me…yes, it was his close comrade that he threatened to strike down with his sword, when your grandfather refused to join the rest of the Legion! Do I have that right?"

I had already begun to wish I had not brought it up, but I was forced to acknowledge that, in essence, Crito was correct.

However, before it could go any farther, I pointed out, "And it was at Pharsalus where my grandfather grabbed Diocles out of the prisoners from Pompey's camp."

"And they were both better for it," Crito answered, and I thought this was as fitting a conclusion to this conversation as one could expect.

While I was busy handling the pecuniary arrangements for our leave, Sextus had been out in town, hiring a wagon to carry Diocles' body, along with horses for us. However, when we met at the apartment, this was when I learned that my brother had not hired two horses, but four.

"Four?" I asked him. "We won't be traveling faster than the wagon, so we won't need to switch out mounts."

"I know that," Sextus replied calmly, but then his eyes went over to Alex, then back to me.

"Ah," I said softly, and actually, I was impressed at my brother's foresight, although I was still confused. "But I still don't understand the fourth."

"You will," he said, and there was a smugness to his tone I immediately distrusted.

However, while it was a surprise, it was a pleasant one. We had just sat down to the evening meal, the last one we would eat before our departure, when there was a knock on the door. When I glanced at Birgit, I saw she did not look surprised, while Sextus just grinned at me.

"Go answer the door," he urged, and I hope I can be excused for my suspiciousness as I rose and did so.

Since I had no idea who to expect, I do not believe my surprise would have been any greater at the sight before my eyes.

"I heard," Quintus Gallus said, leaning against the doorway, "you needed a bodyguard."

With the addition of Quintus Gallus to our company, despite the differences in the identities of the children, I was struck by such a strong feeling of living an event from my past that when we assembled in the pre-dawn morning, I was forced to stop for a moment to collect myself. Sitting down on the stairs, I stared down at the street where the wagon was already loaded with Diocles' body, while Sextus and Alex sat their horses, and Gallus' mount tied to the back of the wagon. In that moment, what came to my mind was a sudden, irrational hope that when we arrived in Arelate, there would be a large, gray stallion waiting for me. Sextus, seeing me suddenly stopping and collapsing on the steps, rode his horse over to me, a chestnut mare with a white blaze on her face that reminded me of Thunder, the horse belonging to Diocles who was probably the most misnamed horse I have ever seen.

Sextus looked across at me, our heads roughly aligned, and he said softly, "I know. Me too."

This was all he said; it was all he needed to say, and my brother and I shared the moment before I forced myself upright, then descended the steps. Naturally, the largest horse was reserved for me, but while it might have been an accident, I suspect that when Sextus chose our mounts, he made sure that the horse I would ride was not gray. Although it was a stallion, it was of a color similar to the mare Sextus was riding, except instead of a blaze, it had four white stockings, but sitting astride him was almost as emotional an experience as descending the stairs, as I realized how long it had been since I had last sat in a saddle. Consequently, I forced myself to nudge my mount past where Gallus was sitting on the wagon, Birgit seated next to him, exactly as my mother had done some fifteen years before, when we left the only home I had ever known. I led the way, and our small procession rolled through the streets of Siscia just as the sun was coming up. I could hear the muted chatter of the three children in the back of the wagon as we left the town. However, instead of taking the road that leads directly westward, we turned in the direction of the camp, which Birgit noticed immediately.

"Why are we going in this direction?" she asked.

Sextus and I glanced at each other, and I nodded my silent permission for him to be the one to tell her what little we were willing to divulge.

"You'll see," was all he would say, even after the children became aware something unexpected was taking place, so quickly there was a chorus of insistent voices demanding to know what awaited us.

Their answer came, as I knew it would, when we rounded the slight bend in the road that is less than a half mile to the camp, the visibility now aided by the sun, which allowed us to see the dark cluster of people gathered outside the walls of the camp.

"What…what is this?" Birgit asked.

"It's the clerks, the *medici,* and I suppose some of the older Legion slaves," I answered her. Her mouth dropped open in surprise, while I added, "It was Crito's idea. And Lysander," I amended, because in all honesty, it had been his idea, but Crito, by virtue of his status as the chief clerk of the 8th, was able to make it happen.

And what was happening was the equivalent, in its own smaller way, of the time we had borne Nero Claudius Drusus after he died back to Mogontiacum. These simple men had asked for the opportunity to offer their own salute to Diocles, and had arrayed themselves a short distance from the gate, lining either side of the road. Turning my mount, I trotted over to Alexandros, who was doing his best to appear impassive as he rode alongside his mother on the opposite side of the wagon.

"You need to be in front," I told him, which clearly startled him.

"Why?"

"Because you're the man of your family now," I replied, "and that's where your father would want you to be, leading him and the rest of the family."

He looked uncomfortable, but he did as I bid him, moving in front of the wagon, and we rolled past the assembly. Nothing was said; the only sounds were made by the hooves of the horses and the rattling of the wagon over the paving stones. This did not detract from the moment, however; in fact, it seemed to add to the solemnity of it as we rode past the upturned faces of so many men who, if I am being honest, most of my fellow rankers, and I, ignored. Unless, of course, they failed in some way, then they incurred our wrath, but as I have mentioned, it is on their shoulders where the true burden that comes from maintaining a Legion of Rome rests. And once, as the older men like Crito and Lysander knew, the man lying in the bed of the wagon, his body contained in a box and packed with ice, had performed exactly the same task. Over the years, I have often wondered how much of my Avus' rise in the ranks was owed to Diocles; I have no doubt, nor do my parents or my Avus, for that matter, that our wealth would have been a fraction of what it was and still is if it had not been for his shrewd and wise management. Yet, especially after I read my Avus' account, I realized how integral a role his Greek, who started as nothing more than a body slave who knew how to perform certain duties but had become one of Titus Pullus' longest and most trusted friends, played in my Avus' rise to the post of Camp Prefect. One of the original Camp Prefects when the previously informal post was made official in the first of Augustus' reforms, it must be said. Some of the men standing there, I knew, had been present when Titus Pullus and Diocles had first assumed the post here in Siscia, where I and four of the children borne by my mother were born, at least those who lived past infancy; there were three other children whose names my parents, nor the surviving children mention. The faces in the crowd were familiar to me, if not all of their names, but I say with some shame that, in this moment, I realized that, if Diocles was still alive, he would have known and recognized each and every one of them. While they did not speak, at least loudly enough for me to make out what they were saying, many of them reached out, some of them up to touch Birgit's hand, which she had extended outward, while others just brushed the sides of the wagon as it rolled by. With the exception of Alex, Sextus and I rode behind the wagon, and the impromptu processional finished quickly. We left those former contemporaries of Diocles behind, and just before we reached the bend in the road, I glanced over my shoulder to see them still standing there, watching us carry his body away.

Our progress was predictably slow, but the one blessing was that the weather held, in every sense of the word. Despite it being cold, it was usually clear, even at night, which kept the temperature blessedly low. Sextus and I had discussed at length what we would do should the weather turn too warm to keep Diocles' body frozen; I could easily envision the effect a decaying body would have on the children, which would be made even more dramatic by the knowledge it was their father, and it occupied most of my waking moments worrying about it. We had briefly discussed going to Birgit to discuss our concerns, then decided against it. To anyone who did not know her, she appeared to be bearing up extremely well, particularly for a woman originally from Gaul; indeed, she could have been mistaken for a woman from one of the finest families of Rome if one were to judge only by her composure and resolve. Sextus and I, however, knew her well, and we both agreed that what she was showing the world was an extremely thin and fragile shield that would instantly crack at something as horrible as the proof of death that comes from the stench of decay. Thankfully, this never became an issue, and as had happened with me and my siblings, despite the pall hanging over the party, all the new sights and experiences quickly captured the attention of Diocles' children. Both Sextus and I spent part of the day riding with Alex, regaling him with tales of his father's deeds and all that he had seen and done with my Avus. Fairly quickly into the journey, however, Sextus had started volunteering to spell Gallus driving the wagon, reminding me of my brother's unrequited love for Birgit. Honestly, I did not think much of it at the time; my only excuse is that I was preoccupied.

Day by day, we rolled towards Arelate, and I have to believe that the gods were smiling on our party. Not only did the weather hold;

only once did we have to acquire new river ice for Diocles' body, but there was no excitement in the form of bandits or rebelling tribes, something that disappointed Alex enormously, no matter how many times I tried to gently steer him away from hoping something exciting would happen.

Finally, one day, I had heard enough, and I am afraid I lost my temper when I snapped at him, "Boy, you don't have any fucking idea what you're talking about! You need to wish that the exact opposite thing happens, not that we have to fight for our lives!"

I abruptly jerked my horse's head around, instantly regretting my action, having forgotten how angry it made me when I saw other riders do this to their mounts, and I muttered an apology to the horse as I trotted back to where Sextus was plodding along, next to the wagon, which had become his favored spot whenever he was not driving it.

"That looked like it went well," he commented dryly, but I was in no mood.

"You need to shut your mouth," I growled. "The boy wants something to happen that he doesn't know anything about!"

"You mean like someone else I know?" He laughed, then added, "All because they wanted to use the new sword Tata had made for them?"

Suddenly, I found it hard to stay angry, but I grumbled something about people who knew too much for their own good. Then Sextus kicked his horse and trotted up to where Alex was riding, shoulders hunched, making me feel even worse, but while I pretended not to listen, I heard Sextus talking to Alex.

"Alex," he began, "do you know why Uncle Titus got so angry?"

The boy did not verbally reply, but I saw him shake his head, his hunched shoulders making me feel even worse.

"It's because of something that happened a long time ago, when your uncle was younger than you are now, and I was even smaller. Do you know what I'm talking about?"

Another shake, which prompted my brother to tell Alex the entire story of the first time he and I had made this trip, although, being fair, it was on our way back when the trouble happened. Just as I had a few years before, for the first time, I heard another version of a tale that is part of Pullus family lore, when my family, Birgit, and Diocles had been traveling back to Siscia and we had been attacked by rebelling Latobici. When I had read the letter my father sent along with Diocles and Sextus when they had come to Siscia, it was the first time I was ever given a glimpse into what it had been like for my father, who was waiting for us in Siscia, back when he was still Quartus Pilus Prior, and still whole. Now, I was listening as Sextus added another dimension of the story, of what it had been like for the youngest children, particularly he and Valeria, since Miriam was still at my mother's breast and had no recollection. With Alex listening raptly, Sextus described how terrifying it had been, bouncing around in the back of a wagon, the animals whipped mercilessly by Simeon, our Armenian slave who cared for Ocelus, as they bolted for the scant safety of a farmhouse that had been abandoned by fleeing settlers. That part, at least, I had been present to see, albeit from outside the wagon, on the back of Ocelus. But when Sextus went on to describe the day and night spent waiting, not knowing if I had escaped the Latobici pursuing me, gave me a fresh perspective on the event. As Sextus continued his tale to Alex, I glanced over at Gallus, who at first did not seem to be paying attention. Then, when Sextus mentioned how relieved he and my sister were when Gallus and Diocles came bursting into the farmhouse, where Simeon held the marauding warriors off with his bow, resurrecting his skill as one of the famed horse archers of the East, I saw the old bodyguard's expression change. And when Sextus mentioned how it had been through the sacrifice of our other bodyguard hired by my father, the one-armed Tiberius Libo, who drew the attention of enough Latobici to allow me to slip past on Ocelus, I saw the glint in Gallus' eyes that told me he was indeed paying attention. Only after Sextus finished did I feel right in trotting up alongside the pair, on the other side of Alex, who did not say anything at first.

However, I saw him shooting me a sidelong glance, but I believe we covered another mile before he broke the silence, asking me, "Is all that true? Or is Uncle Sextus telling stories again?"

Despite the gravity of the moment, I had to laugh, although while Sextus muttered a protest, it was only half-hearted, and he did so with his own grin on his face.

But then I answered him, "Yes, it's true, Alex. I was listening, and every word is true. This time," I added, leaning away as Sextus reached across Alex and tried to hit me.

This made the boy laugh, but then he became serious again, and turned to look at me directly.

"You weren't scared, though? Were you?" Before I could reply, he said, "Because I know nothing scares you! You're the biggest, strongest man in the Roman army!"

"And who told you that?" Sextus asked him, except he was looking at me, and I felt a flush creeping up my neck.

"He did." I did not have to see Alex to know he was pointing in my direction, which elicited a howl of outrage from my brother.

"And you accuse *me* of telling stories?" he demanded, and honestly, I was not sure if he was jesting or not.

Still, given the subject, I decided to be as honest as I could be with Alex, so my expression and tone was serious when I answered his question. "Alex, listen to me now, because this is important." I leaned toward the boy so I could be sure he saw my face, and said, "I was as scared as I had ever been in my life that day, and particularly that night. And you know what?" I continued before he could answer with his own question. "It still ranks as one of the scariest times of my life. Even now that I've seen battle and been wounded." I nodded down to the horrible scar on my left arm; when he was younger, Alex would run his fingers over it, wearing a look of what I suppose was awed wonder, and probably a little desire. If, at least, he was anything like me at his age. "Any man who tells you he's not scared; at least," I added hastily, "when he's being serious, or," I grinned down at him, "not trying to impress his nephew, is not only lying, he's dangerous to be around on the slight chance he's telling the truth. It's the fear in us that actually allows us to do things like I did that day."

"But," Alex objected, and there was no missing the plaintive tone, "how? I mean, how can you do something brave if you're scared?"

"That," Sextus interjected quietly, "is the *only* time a man can truly show courage, when he's scared."

Alex glanced up at me, but I nodded in confirmation, adding, "Uncle Sextus is speaking the truth, Alex."

"So," Alex asked, "how do you do it?"

I considered for a moment, then as happened so often, the first Titus Pullus came to my rescue, as he had before.

"I remember," I told him, "something my Avus used to say to me, when I was about young Titus' age," referring to Alex's own younger brother, "and some boys had ganged up on me. I wanted to get even with them, mainly so they would leave me alone, but I was afraid, and he asked me," I did my best to imitate his gravelly voice, although at that time, I had not done enough bellowing to do more than a shadow of his, "do you control your fear, or does your fear control you?" I paused for a moment to let Alex absorb this, and he was nodding thoughtfully, yet I still added, "And if you're like me, or most men, the thought of being controlled by anything, or anyone, that you don't choose to serve, that idea is unacceptable to any truly free man. And of all the masters we can serve, fear is the cruelest. If," I pointed at my own chest, "we let it take control of us, we'll be its slave forever."

"I'm not going to be anyone's slave!" Alex cried fiercely, then he added something that caused Sextus and me to exchange a troubled glance. "And anyone who'd rather live as a slave than die free doesn't deserve to live freely anyway!"

Despite myself, I glanced over my shoulder at Birgit, whose face was noticeably paler; if anything, she looked as if someone had just slapped her. I suppose, in a way, this was exactly what happened.

Because of the subject of our talk with Alex, once we stopped for the night, I felt compelled to draw Birgit aside.

"You know he didn't mean it," I told her, not having to preface my comment, since her expression told me it was still on her mind.

"Yes," she sighed, "he does." Birgit was a Gaul; as I recall, of the Anatilli tribe, and while her Latin was perfect, she still carried the accent of her upbringing.

"But why?"

Frankly, I was mystified about why the son of parents who had both been slaves would hold such an attitude; I received my answer in the way she hesitated before she spoke.

"Because neither Diocles nor I have ever told him that his parents were ever slaves," she replied, and there was no missing the bitterness in her tone, reminding me that, no matter how things might turn out, nobody I have ever met looks back with much fondness on their time spent as a slave.

I did not really know how to respond to that, so I decided to change the subject, slightly.

"And why didn't you tell him about what happened when we were on the way back to Siscia?"

This question apparently took her more thought, because several heartbeats of time went by before she finally looked up at me with an odd expression. Normally, Birgit was an open, almost always cheerful woman, and I do not want to give the impression I was unaware of her beauty, because I was not. Even then, when she was in her thirtieth year or thereabouts, she was extremely attractive, with hair the color of spun gold, although it was hidden by the mourning veil she wore, and even in the black *stola*, a man could not miss the curves of her body. Yet, somehow, I had been able to resist her allure in a way that Sextus had been unable to do, although I am sure much of that had to do with the fact that he lived under Diocles' roof for almost two years before he enlisted. Now, she stood looking up at me, and I had the distinct feeling she was deciding something before she answered.

"Because," she finally answered, "I didn't want him to get ideas in his head."

"Ideas?" I admit I was puzzled, but only for a matter of a couple heartbeats. "Ah," I nodded my head, "I think I know why."

It was quite an unusual feeling, I must say, knowing that Alex had not been told of an episode that figured so prominently in the lives of not just his parents, but the family of which, even if it was not by blood, he was an integral part. And this was exactly how I view all of them, as members of my family, meaning that I would kill, and die if need be, for each and every one of them. Now, if I was understanding Birgit correctly, I was being told she feared that if her son heard of my exploits, he would take it into his head to emulate them in some way. And, I was forced to admit to myself, considering how much Alex had been pestering me, her fears were likely well founded. Nevertheless, I cannot say I liked it much.

"Are you angry with me?" Birgit asked me once it became clear I was not going to say anything else.

"No," I sighed, but then added, "and yes, I suppose." I shook my head, telling her, "Honestly, I don't know. I mean, I understand why you'd think that way." I glanced down at her. "You know my mother, after all, and you know she didn't want either of us following our father."

"That's not true," Birgit interjected, surprising me a great deal. "At least, about your father." She paused for a moment, then said, "No, it wasn't your father she worried about you trying to follow."

"Avus," I breathed as she nodded in confirmation.

"And," she pointed to my arm, then reached up and touched the scar along my cheek as she said lightly, "she wasn't wrong, was she?"

I did have to laugh at that, although at the same time, I was trying to ignore the sudden feelings that suddenly burst into life at her touch, except their arousal was not due to any desire for Birgit, but because it reminded me of Giulia. At least, that was what I told myself in the moment.

"No," I admitted, "she wasn't. But," I turned back to the subject, "about Alex, and not telling him things you think will make him want to be like his uncles."

Although I had not indirectly called Alex my nephew with any forethought, I saw it pleased her that I referred to him in this way.

"The more you try to hide it from him, or try and steer him away, the more likely he's going to go down the path you don't want him going down," I told her.

"I know, I know." She seemed near tears, and I was regretting bringing it up. "But, Titus, I don't know what to do! I've seen all the pain and loss that your family has endured…"

"It's not all pain and loss," I cut her off by pointing out, "remember. Think about where we're going! The villa in Arelate, and all that comes with it."

"That's true," she granted, yet she did not seem swayed, which she confirmed when she added, "but remember this as well. While it's true I wasn't with your Avus that long, I saw enough to know that he was one of the saddest men I've ever met." If only her eyes had not filled with tears at the memory, I could have maintained my own composure. "Yes, he achieved all that he desired, and he accomplished his goals. And," she allowed, "he was also a great man in the ways that counted. But," she looked up at me with brimming eyes, "at what cost?"

And this, as I know from reading his story, is nothing but the truth; a brutal, uncomfortable one, it must be said. Still, as Birgit reminded me that evening, nothing great is achieved without cost, and I have often wondered if my Avus had been given the chance to do it all over again, if he would have done anything differently. That, dear reader, will be the first question I ask him when we meet again.

My original plan was to send Sextus ahead when we were within a day's ride of Arelate, but he balked, which should not have surprised me. Of all of us, he had been the least excited at the idea of returning to our family home, which I understood. Consequently, I sent Gallus ahead instead of Sextus, although in my mind, this was just a case of delaying the inevitable, although I could not fault my brother for being apprehensive. Rolling into the town, our entire party was excited, and I include myself. It had been seven years since I had last seen Arelate, and I was interested to see the improvements made since I had been away. The forum had two new temples, although I did not ride over to see to which gods they were dedicated, and the theater was finally finished. I made a mental note to go look at it, along with stopping at the *ludus* to see Vulso. Pulling up to the walled villa two blocks from the forum, we saw the gates were already open, and Gallus was standing there, waiting for us, but it was who stood next to him that caused my heart to suddenly start pounding, except this time, it was not from fear but happiness. Without thinking about it, I slid off my horse, crossed the few paces in perhaps a heartbeat of time, sweeping my mother into my arms and lifting her off the ground, something I had been doing since I was strong enough to do so.

"Titus!" She was laughing and crying. "Put me down! I'm too heavy!"

"Nonsense!" I scoffed. "Tata would never let you get that fat!"

"I don't know about that," my father said, grinning broadly. "I've always wanted a plump little woman to keep me warm at night!"

I turned to my father; he had gone grayer, which was not surprising, and there were a few more wrinkles and one less tooth, but otherwise, he was unchanged. I offered my arm, as a Roman man should, which he ignored, sweeping me into an embrace, whereupon we began competing about who could hug the hardest. While I had prepared myself, or believed I had, to be emotional at the sight of my mother, suddenly, I was swept away by a flood of feelings that, when I thought about it later, I was sure was triggered by the familiar scent of my father, and before I knew it, I was sobbing, almost uncontrollably. As, I must say, was Gaius Porcinianus Pullus, my mother Iras, and at some point, the entire family, blood and otherwise as we huddled together in the gateway. Then came the moment I knew I had been dreading for the entire journey, as I suspect Birgit had as well.

"Where's your husband?" my mother asked her, then leaning around the small group, peered in the direction of the wagon, looking for him.

"He's…" Birgit started, then could go no farther, then Sextus stepped in, and finished, "…in the wagon, Mama."

"Oh no! Is he ill?"

Before we could stop her, my mother darted towards the wagon; while she did not hear Birgit's stifled sob, my father did and, out of the corner of my eye, I saw him stiffen suddenly, but I was already hurrying to catch up with my mother. However, she was always damnably quick and nimble on her feet, so she made it to the back before I could stop her.

"Diocles?" she called out as she pulled back the flap. "What's the matter, old man? Have you gotten lazy in your old age?"

Writing the words even now makes me wince, because I know how badly my mother felt when the truth was revealed by the sight of the box resting in the back. I was only vaguely aware of the bond my mother and Diocles shared, but what I learned was that it was rooted in more than the fact that they were both once property of Titus Pullus, who had freed both of them in his will, even though it had been years since my mother had lived under his roof, and even longer since Diocles had been treated as property, if he ever had been. Theirs was a deeper bond of shared love and regard for Miriam, the woman who I still believe was my Avus' true and deepest love, although I know he loved Gisela and his children, who died in a plague in Brundisium. As I approached my mother, I was at least in time to catch her as she collapsed backward, stopping her from hitting the ground. However, I could not stop her wail of grief and loss, and I held her tightly as she began sobbing again. Because of where we were just behind the wagon, I could not see the others, but I heard them as they all began crying again, the children's temporary happiness and excitement of an adventure washed away by tears, brought on by this reminder of the cause of the adventure in the first place. This was our homecoming to Arelate.

"I still can't believe it," my father said that night after the sobbing children had been put to bed, along with my youngest siblings.

Valeria was missing; she had married two years before, to the son of the wealthiest merchant in Arelate, and an equestrian at that, but she came the next day. Miriam was now the oldest child at home, but there were still three children under the Pullus family roof; Gaius, a sturdy boy of eight, and Septimus, who was toddling about, almost three and would be the last Pullus child borne by my mother. There had been other babes born, but two had been stillborn, and another died less than a year old; we never spoke of those departed souls. At least, my parents never did within my hearing, although I suspect that, in their private moments, it came up at one time or another. In fact, baby Septimus' name was something of a private joke in the family, because by rights, his name should have been Octavian, but no member of the Pullus family will ever use that name, I am quite sure, although I have no intention of explaining why this is the case. Despite birthing eleven children, although my mother's waist and hips were wider and thicker, she was still small and slim, and I have often wondered how she managed to pump out as many children as she did, particularly as large as I was, and not only survive but have six of those children live to adulthood, whereas Giulia and Miriam, and it must be noted, my Avus' mother all died bearing the progeny of the Pullus line. This is where the gods show their cruelty and capriciousness when it comes to mortals, I believe, and I still recall reading my Avus' words about meeting the gods with a sword in his hand. However, it was not until all that happened with Giulia took place, and I learned her fate, before I truly understood how he felt. Sitting at the table that night, my mother's eyes were puffy and swollen, as were Birgit's again, and they were leaning against each other, clearly seeking the support and solace that comes with physical contact. Sextus and I were seated side by side, across from my father, each of us with a cup of unwatered wine, and I tried to provide my father some comfort, because I could clearly see he was as shaken and grieving as my mother.

"He died in his sleep," I offered, "and he didn't suffer."

"No, but we are," Birgit cut in bitterly.

"Yes," my father reached across my mother to place his hand on Birgit's and said gently, "we are. We all are."

"Do you remember," Sextus suddenly spoke up, "the time he caught us loosening the legs of that stool of his?"

Before I could either stop myself or admonish Sextus for bringing up such a subject, I burst out laughing.

"He chased us around the villa for what seemed like a watch." I shook my head at the memory of one of the few times we had infuriated the man who was our tutor to the point he not only wanted to thrash us, but was moved to actually do it.

I was heartened to see that Birgit and my parents were smiling, even through the tears, and this started a round of stories, provided by each of us, as the Pullus family paid tribute to the man who was almost as much of a giant in our lives as the one he served.

Suddenly, my father stood up, grabbing his crutch, saying only, "Hold on with the stories. I'll be right back."

Sextus and I exchanged a bemused glance, but when I looked over at my mother, she seemed no less mystified. I sat there listening to the sound of the wooden crutch tapping against the tiled floor as my father left the large *triclinium* that, while spacious and with vibrantly painted frescoes that made it seem as if we were actually seated outside in the country, was distinctly more Head Count in furnishing than the class for which this villa was originally designed.

Oh, we had a formal *triclinium* where there were four upholstered couches, but my parents rarely used it and, as children, we were never allowed in it. Which, of course, meant we could not resist sneaking into it, even as we wondered why we had done so once we did since it held nothing of interest to any of us. Instead, this room, next to the kitchen, had a long table and two long benches, although there were also four chairs to handle unexpected visitors who were treated more as family than guests; whenever the entire family was present, my father sat in one of the chairs at one end, and my mother sat at the opposite end. This villa, where I had spent seven years before enlisting and I still think of as home, was large enough that the sound of my father's crutch disappeared, yet fairly quickly, it was replaced by a racket of young voices and little feet, drowning out the tapping sound of my father's return. Trailing behind him were all of the children, rubbing their eyes from being awakened, or in the case of Alex and the other three of Diocles' children, wiping away the tears with which they had cried themselves to sleep.

"*Bona Dea*, what do you think you're doing?" my mother demanded, but my father was unworried.

"I want them to hear all the stories we're telling," he explained. "I want them to know what a great man Diocles was. And still is," he added as he sat down. Then, he glared at Sextus and me, adding, "So these stories need to be...appropriate. Do you hear me?"

This was how the rest of the night passed, until we heard the cry of the cock out in the courtyard, announcing the coming of day, as we honored the memory and exploits of Diocles. Very quickly, everyone got into the spirit of the moment, and there was as much laughter as there were tears, where we seemed to naturally fall into a pattern where one of us would recount something humorous, then another of us would add something that recalled our Greek's wisdom and courage. I believe the most poignant moment came when my father spoke of what was his first campaign, one that to this day is the most famous, or perhaps notorious campaign in the history of the Roman army, Marcus Antonius' failed foray against the Parthians. One of my most vivid memories is how quiet it became as my father spoke of an event that we children had never heard him talk about more than in passing; later, I asked my mother, and she informed me they had only spoken of Parthia once, back when we were living in Siscia. While she did not go into detail, one thing that sticks with me is the context in which my father spoke had to do with the affair with Quintus Barbatus and all that was going on during that period. But on this night, with the children given seats on the benches, while Sextus and I took the remaining chairs, my father did not just speak, he told a story so vivid that I saw the children shivering as he talked about the awful cold. However, what Gaius Porcinianus Pullus relayed that night was not about battles, but how vital was the role Diocles played in helping not just my Avus, but a young Gregarius on his first campaign who had had dreams of glory, following in his uncle's footsteps, literally and figuratively speaking, survive a grueling ordeal. He told us all how tirelessly Diocles worked, behind the scenes, scavenging up every scrap of firewood, every morsel of food, both of which were in such scarce supply that those profiteers who are an unfortunate reality of army life and had managed to hoard precious rations were charging fifty *sesterces* for a quart of wheat. As we sat there, raptly listening, I could see my father was present, but not; he had gone back to a place I know he had sworn he would never visit again, even in his mind, yet he did so now to honor the memory of Diocles.

He finished by saying simply, "Your father not only saved my life and that of my father, but the entire 10th Legion owes him a debt that we can never repay." Turning his gaze on Diocles' children in particular, he added, "Just because a man doesn't carry a sword, that doesn't mean he's not brave, or a hero. And your father was both. But he was also very, very wise, and he was the most loyal man I've ever met. If you grow up to be half the man your father was, you'll still be a man worthy of respect."

The funeral of Diocles took place on the second full day after our arrival in Arelate, and it was attended by a relatively small number of non-family members, which was understandable. He was known in Arelate, but my Avus had been dead more than ten years, meaning that those very few men who had marched under the standard of the 10th were almost all dead. Sextus Scribonius, my Avus' best and longest friend as well as my father's first Pilus Prior, had also died two years before, in Alexandria, where he had relocated in the aftermath of my Avus' Tribunal, along with the wife of his brother and the great love of his life, who chose to flee Rome with him and live in self-imposed exile for the rest of their days. And because of his relatively lowly social status as a freedman, none of the leading men of the city deigned to show up. However, there were a half-dozen old men, clearly veterans because of their scars and their weathered, battered features, who came in a small group. The priest we had hired was familiar with the Greek rituals, but even knowing what to expect, it was strange watching his shrouded corpse lowered into a hole in the ground, even taking into account this is how Pannonian tribes do it, although their nobility have elaborate tombs that are above ground. My father, Sextus, and I had already visited the stone carver whose monuments are most prevalent along the roads leading into Arelate; he was the man who had created the marker for Titus Pullus, and according to his wishes, Diocles was interred immediately next to the large engraved marker for my Avus. As befitted his status, it was one of the largest markers, while my family had purchased the strips on either side of it, extending perhaps fifty paces. At that moment, it was alone, waiting for the rest of us to come join him, and Diocles was the first to do so. Once the final rituals were performed, we returned to the villa, and again, I did not pay much attention to the fact that Sextus was next to Birgit, nor did I think much when she leaned her head on his shoulder as he comforted her. My mother, on the other hand, did take notice.

"Nothing good is going to come of that," she muttered, and since this statement broke the silence, I looked down at her in surprise as we walked back into Arelate.

"Come of what?" I asked; being absorbed in thoughts of my own, I was lost.

We were walking side by side, but because we were matching the pace of my father, who had refused to ride despite his infirmity, we had fallen behind the rest of the funeral party. My mother did not point, at least with her finger, instead just nodded her head to where Sextus and Birgit were walking close together.

I have to say I was relieved that my father was as mystified as I was, and he was the one who said, "What are you talking about? He's comforting Birgit! She just buried her husband!"

In the *duumvirate* that are my parents, it is my mother who tends to view the world through a more cynical light; I suppose it comes from her upbringing as a slave in the court of the Ptolemies, along with being a half-sister of the dead Cleopatra VII, through their father Ptolemy, the result of a union between the Egyptian monarch and my maternal grandmother, who was a slave herself. My father likes to see the good in people, and tends to give others the benefit of the doubt, and I could tell he was hard-pressed to see anything remotely problematic with what his eyes were seeing.

"And do you know how long he's loved her?" my mother scoffed.

"I know that," my father granted, "but Sextus falls in love whenever a woman looks his way."

That elicited a laugh from me, but a scowl from my mother, who shot me a look I realized I had not seen in some time, yet was still powerful enough to stop my mirth in my throat.

"And who's the one woman he's loved the whole time?" she argued, and then she did point at Birgit.

What disturbed me was my sense that her anger was not directed at my brother, but at Birgit, prompting me to say, "Mama, why does it sound like you're saying it's Birgit's fault? Because I promise you, I've been around them for the last few years, and she's *never* given him any encouragement!"

She looked up at me with an expression I could not easily identify as she sighed and said, "I know that. But it's true, she did just lose her husband. And she's going to be vulnerable." As she said this, her face became troubled, and she glanced over at my father and finished, "I just don't want Sextus taking advantage of that."

It was my turn to peek over at my father, waiting for him to dismiss my mother's fears, except I saw he was of the same mind, which was ultimately more often the case than not. Still, neither of my parents brought the matter up with Sextus, at least in my hearing. And I knew that, whatever thoughts were running through my brother's head, a large part of his mind was occupied on matters other than Birgit. And as both Sextus and I learned, there is very little that could be hidden from either of my parents.

"So, when did it happen? And why?"

In retrospect, I know now it was no accident that none of the rest of the family was present, although at the time, I believed my mother's suggestion, which we all knew was an order uttered with the same authority her husband carried when he was Quartus Pilus Prior, that the entire family go to the forum on the first market day, was done for the purpose of giving the grieving family something else to occupy their attention. With, as I noted uneasily, the exception of Sextus, my father, and me.

"No, you boys stay here," she told us firmly when Sextus commented about how he was looking forward to getting out of the villa. "Your father never goes to the market, and you need to stay here with him."

Nevertheless, we were outside but still within the confines of the villa. I had risen that morning, our third full day, and realized I felt…odd, I suppose. It only took a few heartbeats for me to realize the cause, which was how we found ourselves standing together in front of the scarred stakes my Avus had ordered placed in a corner of the large courtyard. As Diocles had told us on more than one occasion, my Avus had spent a third of a watch, including the last day of his life, working on his forms, a practice his son and grandsons had adopted as their own. Although, it must be said, my father had stopped doing so and Sextus had never been particularly diligent. I suppose my own adherence to what is still a ritual for me was strengthened by the feeling that, as his namesake, it fell upon my shoulders to uphold the practice in a way in which my Avus could find no fault. And since I had been unable to do so on the journey, once I was home, it was not long before I felt that itch. However, the one slightly unusual aspect was that, unlike times in the past, Sextus had not only not resisted my command to rouse himself and join me, he had not hesitated or complained. Much, at least; I will say I had the strong impression that what grumbling he did was more out of habit than real resistance. Regardless, we were both standing in front of a stake, and as my practice, I was stripped to the waist, while my brother still wore his tunic, which was now darkened with sweat. My father's questions had caught both of us by surprise, and I instantly understood this was his intent; in fact, he had managed to come up on us without either of us seeing him, not an inconsequential feat for a man on a crutch.

"When did what happen?" I echoed him, giving him a false smile as I waved my *rudis*, "When did I become the best you've ever seen?" I gave an elaborate shrug and said, "Oh, I imagine after my first campaign. You know, when I killed..."

"Yes, I recall you telling me all about how you slew, what was his name, Vergorix?" my father said dryly, cutting off my attempt, as futile as I knew it was, to divert him away from his true purpose. "At least thirty times. But," he turned to look directly at my brother, "that's not what I'm talking about. And I suspect you both know that. So," he repeated, "what happened?"

Being brutally honest, I was sure I had done all I was willing to in order to protect Sextus from my father's examination; nevertheless, I still felt guilty when my brother glanced my way and I only gave him a helpless shrug. His lips thinned down, the sign I had angered him, although he could not afford to pay me more than a passing look.

"I'm not sure what you're talking about," Sextus replied carefully, but my father was clearly in no mood for his prevarication.

"The fuck you don't," he snorted, and it was the use of the oath that told both of us he was in no mood for my brother's delaying tactics. Pointing at my brother, he indicated the large sweat stain on the front of his tunic and said, "This is the first time I've ever seen you not like your brother when you're working the stakes." Sextus opened his mouth, except my father made a chopping motion with his hand that we both knew very well as he continued, "But that's not the only thing I've noticed. You haven't been to the bath once since you've been home. And before you left home, I couldn't drag you out of it." Shaking his head, he finished, "So we can either play this stupid game, or you can be honest and tell me why you were flogged."

This observation about Sextus avoiding the bath, I knew, was nothing but the truth; one of the many luxuries of my Avus' villa to which we all quickly became accustomed was that there is a small bath, housed in its own structure a few paces away from the back of the villa. It has everything but the *apodytarium* and *frigidarium*, but the *caldarium* and *tepidarium* are large enough that the whole family could fit at one time, although we never did. And my father, in his ongoing attempt to maintain a low profile in Arelate, had decreed that the fires needed for both the steam and tepid water only be lit once a day and not be kept going at all times, which would require a slave whose only duties would be to attend the fire.

Despite my resolution to let my brother defend himself to our father, before I had any conscious thought, the words came out. "It's true that Sextus was flogged, but it's completely my fault, Father." The fact that I did not use the normal method of addressing him was calculated, and his head turned as he looked at me sharply, his brows coming down together in a look I had dreaded ever since I could remember. "I did something out in town, but Sextus took the blame for it so my career wouldn't be ruined. I'm the one you should be angry at, not Sextus."

My father rarely showed his fury in the sort of way that my Avus, or I did, for that matter. Even more rare, however, was catching him at a loss for words, or him being unable to react quickly to a sudden change in circumstances. This, however, was exactly what I accomplished as he stared at me, a range of emotions flashing across his face.

"That's not true, Tata," Sextus broke the sudden silence.

My father's attention returned to Sextus, but when I opened my mouth to argue, my brother looked at me and shook his head.

"No, Titus," he said softly, "no. I'm not going to let you do that again. Once was too much." Turning to my father, my brother tilted his head in a way that both my father and I understood was the sign Sextus had made up his mind. "You're right, Tata. I was flogged."

Suddenly, he dropped his *rudis* to shrug out of his tunic; then, he turned around. The sound of my father's gasp caused me to look over at him. However, while the tears that had begun rolling down his cheeks did not surprise me all that much, I mistook the cause, thinking they were from a combination of anger and embarrassment that one of his sons had managed to run afoul of the army.

"Oh, my boy," his voice was choked with emotion as he hopped forward, reaching out with his free hand to gently touch the horrible scars, still pink, causing my brother to flinch as my father sobbed, "what did they do to you?"

Not surprisingly, this caused my brother's own composure to crack, except he was not the only one, and before I thought about it, I crossed to my brother and father as we poured out all the feelings of grief and loss that, as Roman men, we are expected to keep inside us, tightly stoppered. In that moment, I was only dimly aware of it, but now I recognize that while this moment was ostensibly about the signs of my brother's shame, it was as much the residual of our shared loss, as we were all adjusting to life without Diocles.

Once we regained our composure, we retired to the table, whereupon my brother told my father the entire story. Not, I must say, without a bit of prodding, at least about the cause of the troubles with Servius Labienus, and despite the somber reason, I saw the ghost of a grim smile flicker across my father's face as he listened to Sextus explain how he arrived at the method to fleece Pulcher.

Once Sextus was finished, my father glanced over at me with a raised eyebrow, but when I nodded my head, this apparently prompted him to grunt, "Well, you always were too clever for your own good. And," he added grimly, "Pulcher wouldn't have been my first choice to go after. Still," he allowed grudgingly, "I remember all the trouble he caused my boys, so I suppose you removing him helped the Legion in the long run."

"Exactly!" Sextus was never one to pass up such an opportunity to make us laugh. "And that's why I did it! It was for the Legion!"

My father glared at him as I tried to suppress my own laugh, but then he could not quell his own, and just as we shared in the tears not long before this, now we joined each other in laughter. Then my father's smile disappeared as he turned to glare at me.

"Now," his voice turned stern, "let's talk about your stupidity."

Sitting the way we were, I could not miss Sextus' look of relief, and I made a mental note to find a way to punish him for that.

"It was stupid," I admitted, but I felt compelled to point out, "I just didn't think that..."

"Stop right there," my father cut me off. "Because you just summed it up perfectly. Anything you were going to say after that doesn't matter." Jabbing his finger at me, he said harshly, "And that's always been your problem. He," my father jerked a thumb over his shoulder at my brother, "thinks too much, and for the wrong reasons. And you don't think at all! You're all balls, no brain!"

There was a sudden rustling feeling in my gut as my anger started to rouse itself, but I was determined to keep my composure, if only to prove to my father I could keep my head; I certainly did not want to prove his point.

"That's…true," I said carefully, "but would you at least hear me out?"

"No," he replied instantly, then seemed to reconsider, although he was clearly reluctant about changing his mind. "All right. Go ahead."

"Believe it or not, I actually did put a lot of thought into this," I began, choosing to ignore his snort of clear disbelief. Deciding on the fly to change my tactic, I asked him, "So, do you think that Pulcher would have been satisfied at giving Sextus a beating and leave it at that?"

I admit it was a nice feeling to see his sudden change in expression, and after a moment, he allowed, "No, probably not."

"That," I agreed, "was my thinking. Oh, it would have sufficed at first. But then he'd have seen Sextus out and about in town, and then men would talk about how Sextus had not only succeeded in cheating Pulcher, but lived to tell the tale. 'After all,' they'd say, 'bruises and cuts heal. Why not take a beating if it means making that much money?' And we both know that the amount of money doesn't matter, because it would grow with every telling, until the story was that Sextus had taken Pulcher's entire fortune." I paused then, watching my father, and I saw he was impressed despite himself. Perhaps not convinced, not yet at least, but it was no longer a foregone conclusion that I was an idiot. "So," I shrugged, "I decided I needed to move quickly to keep that from happening, because if I were Pulcher, I'd have done it before he healed. Because it took four of them to give him a beating as it was, so I'd make sure he wasn't at his best when I tried to finish him off."

"Is that true?" my father turned to Sextus. "There were four of them?"

Sextus nodded, and we could both see my father was impressed yet again.

"He may be a lot of things," I said, "but soft isn't one of them." I grinned over at him as I added, "And I should know. I'm the one who made him tough! If he could survive a beating from me, he can survive anything."

As I hoped, this made both of them laugh, lightening the mood considerably.

"Look who's talking," Sextus retorted, then turned to my father to explain, "I didn't see anything but the end of it, but I heard from Domitius that Titus was beating Pulcher without breaking a sweat. That's why Pulcher got desperate, and" he added forcefully, "stupid enough to try and take Titus with a sword."

My father looked at me, yet while I saw he was proud, he also looked thoughtful, and he said, "You've always been good with a sword. Maybe," he allowed, "close to being as good as your Avus. But," he admonished, "you need to learn from his example that not every problem can be solved with a sword."

"I know," I protested, and although now I do not know why I thought so at the time, I felt it was a good idea to point out, "and I wasn't going to kill him with a sword! I planned on beating him to death! He forced me to!"

My father did not say anything, just looked at me for a long instant before finally shaking his head. Now I understand why; I had completely missed his point that not every problem can be solved by killing the source. This was something I still had to learn; in many ways, I still do.

With the honoring of Diocles done, my brother and I took the opportunity to enjoy our time in Arelate. It had taken us twenty-two days to make it there, but we had already made arrangements that on the way back, depending on our progress, Sextus and I would press ahead on horseback so we could arrive back in Siscia within the allotted time, leaving Gallus to accompany Birgit and the children. By our best calculations, that gave us a bit less than two weeks to spend in Arelate itself, and both of us were determined to make the most of it. However, as I quickly discovered, Sextus and I had very different ideas about what this meant, as once more, trouble seemed to find him out in the streets of Arelate in the same way it seemed to find me within the ranks. Perhaps this is just our respective fates, although in my brother's defense, it was not because of his actions when we had returned to Arelate, but the reason that had forced him to leave in the first place. Ultimately, it was because of another pair of brothers who were the cause of cutting our visit short. Sextus and I had grown up with Quintus and Decimus Poplicola, but in circumstances, and character, we could not have been more different; their father Aulus was a renowned backstreet operator, running a small *collegia* modeled after one of the gangs of the Aventine in Rome, from where he came. However, both Sextus and I had been friendly with Quintus and Decimus, although as I was always aware, there is a difference between being amicable and being true friends; my time in the Legions had taken this understanding to a much deeper level. It was a lesson Sextus had learned as well once he joined, which makes what happened that much more ironic, because he was actually trying to avoid falling back into bad habits. What this meant in a practical sense was that when he was spied on the street by Quintus and Decimus, he was not overtly rude, and, in fact, they retired to a *taverna*, although Sextus made sure it was not one of his old haunts, whereupon they shared a cup of wine, but that was all. When Sextus came back that evening, about a week into our visit, I could tell he was agitated, although he managed to hide it from my parents. It was not until we were alone in the room we shared that I learned the particulars.

"I ran into the Poplicola boys today." He yawned as he said this, either forgetting or being unaware that I had long since recognized this as his ploy to bring up a potentially awkward or contentious subjects while seeming casual about it.

I was lying on my bed, although the lamps were still lit because we were both reading, and I have often wondered what role the scroll my brother had chosen from the family library played in what was to come.

On the subject of the scroll, it was when we were about a week away from Arelate that I mentioned to him, "You know, while we're home, you need to read Avus' scrolls."

Sextus surprised me when he replied instantly, “I know. I’ve been thinking about that quite a bit, actually.” He looked over at me and asked, “How long did it take you to get through them?”

I thought for a moment and replied, “A little more than a week.”

“Bah! I bet I can beat that.” He grinned. “I bet I can read it in less than a week! Want to bet on it?”

“And how would I know you read them all?” I pointed out.

I admit it was his crestfallen expression that made me laugh.

“Oh,” he said, “I didn’t think about that.” Then he brightened and suggested, “We have to do something to pass the time on the way back, right?” I agreed with a nod. “So you can test me! Ask me anything about what I’ve read, and I’ll bet you I can answer everything!”

It was a bit cruel of me I know, taking this bet, because I knew just how extensive and how many scrolls a life like the first Titus Pullus’ would take to fill. However, I will say that once he began the challenge, he realized two things; first, there was no way he would be able to read it all in less than a week, and second, that I had been…exaggerating about the length of time it took me.

“I should have known you were lying,” he grumbled when I finally revealed the truth to him. “Here I’ve been staying up nights trying to beat you!”

“I know.” I laughed, then could not resist adding, “But I just liked watching you work so hard to finally try and beat me at something. But,” I admitted, still grinning, “your studies have been cutting into my sleeping time as well.”

I had to duck the swing he aimed at me.

The night of his meeting with the Poplicolas, even before he brought it up, I could observe out of the corner of my eye he was restless and having a hard time concentrating, but while in the past this had been Sextus’ normal behavior whenever we were supposed to be studying some subject Diocles had laid out for us, I will say he had been quite the opposite with Avus’ account.

“And?” I asked him, putting down my own scroll. “How did that go?”

There was a pause as he frowned down at his lap, then he finally answered, “Not…well.”

Even in the moment, I knew I should not, yet I still heaved a sigh that caused him to look over at me angrily as I pressed him, "And what does that mean?"

"It means," he admitted, "that they wanted me to spend the evening with them doing our usual things, and when I refused," he shrugged, although the way he was concentrating on his lap told me more than his words, "they didn't take it well."

"Just because you didn't go out carousing and whoring with them?" I made no attempt to hide the doubt in my tone. "That sounds like a bit of an overreaction."

I was about to press him, then decided to give my brother the opportunity to expand on this topic without any prompting from me, which seemed to take him by surprise. My silence resulted in him breaking his gaze from his lap to look at me suspiciously.

"Why aren't you hounding me like you usually do?" he scowled at me.

Honestly, I was about to give him a flippant reply; suddenly, I recognized this was actually a question that was important to him.

"Because," I spoke slowly as my mouth tried to catch up to my mind, "I know you've changed, I suppose. And I know that if you're worried, you have a good reason."

Although it was not my intent, he looked startled and, frankly, more discomposed than he had a moment before.

"Well," he said finally, "I suppose I am; worried, I mean." He paused for a moment, then plunged on, "Because they wanted more than just to go out for the night."

Despite my suspicions that I knew why, I still asked him to expand.

"It seems that there's been a bit of a falling out between the Poplicola boys and their Tata, and they've decided they either want prove to him they're fit to take over the business or to branch out on their own. So," he returned his attention back to his lap, frowning down at it as he finished, "they want me to help them."

"Help them how?" I was lost.

"By convincing the…person I was working with at the *ludus* to start back up with the thing we had going when I was here."

"You mean Vulso," I was puzzled why he did not seem willing to name the man who had been supplying Sextus with all the inside information he had used to wager on the outcome of the bouts, but I was about to be surprised, at least at first, although it quickly turned to shock.

"No, it wasn't Vulso," he answered. "It was never Vulso…"

"That's not true," I cut him off, shaking my head as I recalled the conversation we had when Sextus had first appeared in Siscia. "You said it was Vulso that you were getting the information from!"

"Not true," he replied calmly, then pointed at me. "*You* said it was Vulso. I just didn't correct you."

"But you nodded when I said his name! That's the same thing as saying it's him," I grumbled, yet even as I said it, I realized it did not really matter. "So, who is it?"

Now he hesitated for such a long time I thought he was not going to answer me, then finally, he supplied the name.

"Gundorix," Sextus said, while I gasped in shock.

Gundorix had been a gladiator, like most *lanistae*, a Gaul from the Arverni as I recall, and he had been Vulso's assistant for about ten years by this point. Even before I left for Siscia, I was a frequent visitor to the *ludus*, because as unlikely as it may seem, Vulso and I had become good friends. Naturally, I had known Gundorix, who, like most former gladiators, was a walking mass of scars crisscrossing his chest, and he was missing an ear, while the other one was a gnarled knot of scar tissue. He was an expert with swords, both the curved Thracian style and the Spanish, yet like any man who has survived the number of bouts required for freedom and retirement, it was his utter ruthlessness and brutality that distinguished him. Now, while to an outside observer I could have been describing Vulso just as easily, as I had learned when I was a ten-year-old boy, there was also a streak of kindness in the *lanista's* makeup, as well as an earthy sense of humor that I enjoyed immensely. I was aware that Gundorix viewed himself as the man who would step into Vulso's *caligae*, yet despite the fact that my family made sure to avoid any activity or association with the *ludus* when it came to the daily operation of it, I had major reservations about Gundorix, and I knew my father did as well.

"So it was Gundorix who was passing you the information," I mused, except Sextus cleared his throat in a way that alerted me, and when I glanced over, I saw he looked distinctly uncomfortable.

"Not exactly," he mumbled. "It was more than just that. He…made arrangements."

"Arrangements?" I echoed, completely lost, at least at first. Somewhere deep inside my gut, the answer started creeping up, making me suddenly worried I might vomit. "You don't mean he did something that got one of those poor bastards killed?"

"I didn't know that was what would happen!" he replied, his tone desperate. "I swear on the black stone, Titus! And, at first, it didn't get any of them killed! He'd always stop the bout after blood was drawn!" His face turned paler as he continued, "But then when Peristo was killed, that's when I stopped! And," he looked over at me with an expression of such intensity I realized this was about convincing himself as much as me, "that's when I came to Siscia!"

"Does Tata know?" I asked him. "About Peristo?"

The lump in his throat bobbed up and down as he swallowed, then shrugged. "I'm not sure. But I think so."

Sighing, I sat back against the wall and considered for several moments. Peristo had been one of the younger slaves brought in before I left, and had shown promise in the sand. I had heard Vulso mention him as one of the up and coming champions of the arena in Arelate; in fact, I had rarely heard Vulso sound so enthusiastic about the prospects of one of the stable of gladiators in our *ludus*.

It was more out of curiosity that led me to ask Sextus, "How did Gundorix do it?"

"He drugged their food. At least, I think," he answered, clearly reluctant. "The truth is, I never asked. He just assured me that we'd never get caught." When he looked back at me, there was no mistaking the bitterness as he added, "He said he wanted the money to buy his freedom." Shaking his head, Sextus finished sadly, "But it wasn't until after I came to Siscia and thought about it, I realized what he was really trying to do."

"Force Vulso out," I answered for him, to which he nodded.

As plans went, I suppose it was not a bad one. *Lanistae* are judged by one rule and one only; how often their gladiators win against competing *ludii*. By drugging selected contestants, Gundorix was not only betting against our *ludus*, albeit in secret and through my brother, he was casting Vulso in a poor light. While I did not expect Gundorix to ever admit it, I felt fairly certain arranging Peristo's defeat, and death, was no accident.

"But I left before Gundorix could arrange more bouts that put Vulso in a bad light," Sextus added. "Which is why he's still the *lanista*."

"That explains why you left Arelate," I pointed out, "but where do the Poplicola brothers come in?" I was struck by a horrible thought. "Wait," I gasped, "please tell me they don't know about Gundorix."

"No," Sextus answered emphatically. "In fact, that's part of the reason why they approached me. They want me to tell them how I had it arranged, and introduce me to Gundorix. Although," he added, "they don't know it's Gundorix."

"Who do they think you were working with?"

"Vulso," he answered with a straight face, but I burst out laughing, and he joined in.

Soon we were both doubled over, and I gasped, "Wait. You're telling me they think that you were working with Vulso to put himself out of a job?"

It took some time for our mirth to subside, but somewhere in there, Sextus summed up matters perfectly.

"Now you understand why Tata Poplicola isn't keen on handing over the reins to his sons. They're not particularly sharp daggers, are they?"

No, I agreed, they were not. Nevertheless, we still had a problem on our hands that needed to be rectified. We spent at least another full watch discussing what to do about it, at least in a way that did not endanger the family.

"I knew it!"

Maximus Vulso spat in the dirt as he muttered a curse, his bulging arms crossed across his chest as he listened to what we had told him. We had sent one of our slaves, a youngster from Cantabria my parents had acquired just a couple years before, whose name was unpronounceable, so they called him Chickpea, to the *ludus*, where Vulso's quarters were located, to arrange a meeting outside of town. Sextus and I had announced we were going for a ride in the country, but while Sextus had never been an enthusiastic rider, our parents did not seem unduly interested, and now we were standing outside the roadside *taverna* we had named for our meeting. We told Vulso everything; I had insisted on it, and I admit there was an uncomfortable moment when Vulso glared at Sextus, but when the one-eyed *lanista* growled and unconsciously, or so I hoped, took a step towards my brother, I restrained him with a hand that was none too gentle, shaking my head.

"He didn't know that Gundorix was going to arrange for Peristo to die," I told him firmly.

"I know," Vulso allowed, although he was still clearly unhappy, and he turned to Sextus, "Remember, I was there. I saw your face, and I know you weren't expecting it to turn out as it did." Vulso surprised me then because he was clearly saddened as he shook his head, adding, "He was a good boy, Peristo. And he was going to be a *great* man in the sand!" He spat into the dirt again. "Fucking Gundorix. I've known for some time he's been after my job. And I always had my suspicions about what happened with Peristo. But he'd prepared the boy for every bout before this one, and honestly, I suppose I just couldn't believe the *cunnus* would be so much of a savage that he'd go to those lengths. Fucking Germans," he summed up bitterly, reminding me that Gundorix was, in fact, not Arverni. Then he returned his attention to me. "So? What are you going to do about it?"

"Me?" I asked him, although I saw he was not fooled in the slightest.

"Remember, I've known you since you were a boy," he pointed out. "And just like I was there with Peristo, I was there for Spartacus. Remember?" With this, he actually physically pointed at me; I suspect he did so simply because he knew how much it annoyed me, and I was already irritated at being reminded of the first man I had ever killed. Either ignoring or not caring how I was taking this, Vulso pressed on, "And you wouldn't have brought me out here if you didn't have something in mind."

Vulso was correct, I was forced to admit, and I told him as much.

"So, what is it?" he asked, clearly curious.

"Actually, the less you know, the better and easier it will go," I told him.

"Then why did you drag me out here?" he complained. "If you aren't going to tell me what you're up to, why bother?"

"We didn't say you shouldn't know *anything*," Sextus interjected, "just not *everything*. You're going to have a role to play."

"Oh, I know that," he replied instantly, and the smile that crossed his battered face contained nothing pleasant in it. "You want me to kill Gundorix."

"No!" I said sharply; I had been sure this would be his reaction. "In fact, that's the first and most important thing you need to hear from us. And," I made my voice harsh, "you need to obey us in this. If anything happens to Gundorix before we want it to happen, you're going to have to answer for it."

"But what if something happens to him before whatever it is you have planned takes place?" he protested, but I was having none of it.

"He's survived this long, so all you need to know is that if he somehow winds up dead before this, I'm going to be looking at you as being responsible. And," I added quietly, "I'm not going to be happy, Vulso. Do you understand what I'm saying?"

A series of emotions warred for control of his face, but I suspected he understood I was not making idle threats; by the time I left to enlist, Vulso had seen what I was capable of, both with a sword and my bare hands. And, as I knew and was counting on, he was no longer a young man; I was also his employer, or one of them, at least.

"Yes," he muttered. Then, sighing, he asked, "What else do I need to know? Or," he added caustically, "you're willing to tell me about my own life and career?"

"Only that you're going to be seeing the Poplicolas around the *ludus*," I told him, and as I expected, this did not please him.

"Those two?" he groaned, and I could not really blame him for his reaction. I saw Sextus redden out of the corner of my eye, which was just as understandable, since he had been the one to bring them around in the first place. "Why them?"

"Because, hopefully, we'll take care of two problems at the same time," I answered.

This, at least, was the plan, and I spent the next few moments apprising Vulso of his role that, although small, was crucial to success.

Perhaps I can be excused for gloating about hatching what, for me at least, was a scheme that, once I explained it, even Sextus had to admit was fiendishly clever. The part I was particularly proud of was that, should all work as planned, not only would neither of us dirty our hands, but we would be gone by the time all came to fruition. Being fair, Sextus' example with his scheme with Pulcher served as my inspiration, where he cheated those who were doing the same to others. We would use the avarice and desire of both the Poplicola brothers and Gundorix, yet in such a way that they would be at cross purposes, although if all went as I hoped, this would not become apparent until the proper, and last, moment. Whereupon, it was my fervent desire and, thanks to our machinations, the Poplicola *paterfamilias* would lose a great deal of money, for which he would blame Gundorix. And as dangerous as Gundorix was in his own right, Poplicola was no less so, even if it was by virtue of the amount of muscle he could hire to exact vengeance. As I had pointed out to my father, albeit about Pulcher, men like Poplicola would not, could not allow themselves to be made to look foolish, even over and above the loss of money. There was still much that could go wrong, but as we had talked about it, the conclusion that Sextus and I came to was that, even if our plan failed, the worst outcome would be that Vulso would have to come up with another way to thwart Gundorix's designs.

Nevertheless, we did take one step to ensure he would be able to do so, by telling our father what had transpired; at least, some of it. Naturally, we left out a couple of things, yet judging from the way my father took the news, I suspect he knew more than either Sextus or I would have liked. Our concern, at least mine, was that after rebuffing their attempt, the Poplicola brothers would become suspicious about Sextus' seeming change of heart, but I should have had more faith in my brother and his ability to lie. His acquiescence did not come without cost, in the form of a vicious hangover, except for once, I did not torment Sextus' sore head or sour stomach; frankly, he looked so miserable that even if I had been disposed to act on it, he was so pitiful I probably would not have had the heart to perform any of my normal tricks. Otherwise, we both spent as much time with our family as we could, and I know we all understood that it could be another few years before we were all together again. Valeria had come home, along with her husband, Appius Minucius Clustuminus, who, despite his three names, was a pleasant fellow, although I found him rather dull. He was managing his family's business, which is certainly honorable, although it makes it difficult to find much common ground when one's war stories are literal, and the other's are about how an unscrupulous competitor tried to steal a long-time customer. At least, this is what I remember of one of our conversations. However, Clustuminus was also an avid follower of the games, meaning that when we approached him with a task that was both simple and played to his interest, he was happy to help. Although Valeria, who seemed to be enjoying married life immensely, was positively beaming and enthusiastically extolled her husband's virtuous nature as the reason for joining our cause, I suppose I am cynical, because I suspected he was just happy to be seen favorably by his wife's family. The night before they departed to return back to Massillia, where they still live, my mother decreed we would have a dinner with every family member present; she did not need to verbalize that this included Birgit and the children.

Diocles' Titus and my next-youngest brother Gaius had become fast friends, while Scribonia and Septimus, being the babies of the family, were more or less stuck with each other, which neither of them seemed to be happy about. Only Alex seemed to be the odd man out; he was the only child who was too old to fit in easily with his younger siblings and *de facto* cousins, which I had noticed earlier and prompted me to spend time with him. The fact that my way of doing so was out in the courtyard at the stakes was quickly stopped by Birgit, and I can still recall the expression of horror on her face the first time she saw young Alex, crouched into the first position, scowling fiercely at the stake while I corrected his stance, although I did it much more gently than had ever been done with me, or how I did with the men of my Century in my role as weapons instructor.

The fastest I have ever seen a woman move was back when I was child, and the woman had been my mother, when she leapt from the wagon she was sitting on the day I chose to wear the sword my father had had made for me to take it away. Until, at least, this day in Arelate, when I saw Birgit move, if not faster, at least as quickly, crossing the courtyard to yank the *rudis* from Alex's hand in much the same way my mother had to me. She was so agitated, she had lapsed back into her native tongue, of which I know just enough to understand she was not praising my technique as an instructor. However, while this was not her intent, she actually helped me a great deal, because I was still determined to spend at least part of the day with Alex, helping him cope with all the changes that had come into his world, since I believed, and still do, that of all the people in his life, his Uncle Titus understood what he was going through better than anyone. As a result, I resumed something I had been avoiding to that point, going on a daily ride, on the big chestnut stallion, while Alex rode the horse Sextus had chosen for him. It had been a very conscious decision by me to view riding as nothing more than a means of transportation, and not about the joy of riding a horse for its own sake. Even so, the first two or three days out of Siscia had been difficult for me because I would forget myself for a moment and realize I was enjoying myself, except then, when I glanced down, the sight of the chestnut head bobbing up and down instead of the smoke gray of Ocelus was still painful. It was thanks to my desire to spend time with Alex that I think overpowered the feeling of loss I still felt whenever I was around horses, especially those who reminded me of the gray stallion, and for the first time in years, I actually began enjoying the feeling of controlled power that comes sitting astride a horse. Alex and I had gone for a ride earlier this day and I had actually toyed with the idea of turning the ride into an adventure for the boy, staying out until after dark, although while he would have escaped blame for missing the banquet my mother had planned, I would not have been so lucky. And, frankly, I am glad I did not, because this night was the best we spent in Arelate, and one I remember with great fondness even now. Having our entire family together was already an occasion, yet somehow, the conversation turned to the subject of not just Diocles, but my Avus. Except that, despite my fears that mentioning them would dampen the mood, for reasons I cannot explain yet know without a doubt was the case, it was almost as if both of them were there. And, perhaps they were, watching over us across that invisible barrier separating this world from the one that follows. Whatever the cause, although there were tears, most of them were from laughter, especially once my father joined Sextus and me in getting gloriously drunk. This was enough of a rare occasion to make it notable; the fact that my mother and Birgit dallied with Bacchus as well is a good part of the reason I remember it with such pleasure. That night, as I watched my mother, Birgit, and Valeria giggling like a bunch of girls doing wash at the fountain, even as I realized through my own wine-induced fog that it was at us, was such an unusual and pleasing sight, it did not offend me at all. Sextus had all of us doubled over in laughter as well; yet, as with the women, the fact that his funniest stories were aimed at me was inconsequential, because I was just enjoying seeing the people I loved most in the world happy, especially after there had been so many tears. There is much of that night I can only vaguely recall, but there was one thought that has stayed with me even now, and that was how sure I am Diocles would have been pleased at the sight of the Pullus family, all of us the happiest we had been in some time.

"Will I ever be a Roman citizen?"

Alex and I had gone for what was to be our last ride, at least one that was done for leisure and not to make our way back to Siscia. I cannot say I was altogether surprised by his question, but that did not make it any less uncomfortable.

I briefly considered either evading the question or lying outright; instead, I answered honestly, "I don't know, Alex. I know there's been talk about Augustus adding more citizens to the rolls. But," I felt compelled to add, "I've heard that talk most of my life. And there are powerful men in the Senate who are against it. Not," I finished hastily, "that it means that much. Their resistance, I mean. If Augustus decides to do it, then it will happen."

He did not reply immediately, looking down at his horse's head thoughtfully, which was his habit. Alex was a thoughtful kind of lad, wise beyond his years and rarely spontaneously burst out with anything, at least not until he had mulled it over in his mind. While I was curious where the question had come from, I also had a deep suspicion I knew why he was asking, which he confirmed.

"So if Augustus doesn't decree that by the time I'm seventeen, I'll have to go into the auxiliaries, won't I?"

I did my best to avoid cursing, or groaning, for that matter, aloud, and I chuckle now at the memory of how I suddenly looked back over my shoulder, although we were well outside the walls of Arelate and far away from his mother.

"Alex," I began carefully, "I'm very proud of you for wanting to be under the standard like your Uncle Sextus and me, but," I took a breath, "I don't think it would make your mother very happy."

"I know that," he admitted, and when he looked up at me, I could see how troubled he truly was by his eyes; the set of his jaw, however, told a different story, which he confirmed when he went on, "but once I'm old enough, it won't be her decision. And it's not just you and Uncle Sextus under the standard," he pointed out, "but your Avus and your father." He hesitated for a moment, then added, "And after hearing about how brave my Tata was, even though he wasn't in the Legion…"

"Stop right there," I cut him off because although I knew what he meant, I also felt it important to make a point to him. "You're wrong, Alex. No, your Tata didn't carry a sword and shield, but he was *very much* in the Legion. And don't ever forget that."

Honestly, as soon as it came out of my mouth, I realized I had made a fatal blunder, and Alex was a clever boy.

"So that means it's almost my duty to follow in his footsteps, and yours and Uncle Sextus'!" he declared, a scowl coming over his boyish face that I recognized as his look of determination I had last seen at the stakes on the day Birgit had interceded.

I did not answer him immediately, trying to think of something to say that would not make matters worse.

"That," I admitted finally, "is certainly one way to look at it. But there's more to it than that."

I was determined to at least make an attempt, however half-hearted it might have been, to warn him about the path he seemed determined to follow. Not, however, about the dangers all men of the

Legions face, because no amount of words would ever adequately do so, but about what I was seeing written across his face, in the set of his jaw, even in the way he had suddenly chosen to sit up straight. Because what I saw there was me, at that age, and what I had come to realize as I got older was the enormous amount of pressure I had put on myself to not only avoid bringing shame to my family, but to add to the legacy first started by the man for whom I am named. This awareness had begun to creep up on me after my second campaign as I realized I had not done myself any favors by setting my goals so high, and as I rode next to Alex that day, looking down at the boy, I also forced myself to acknowledge that desire was only part of what was needed to thrive in the Legions. Alex was a strong boy for his size, yet the brutal truth was that I could see he was not going to be anywhere near my size in either height or breadth. By my reckoning, he would be at the little end of a formation, and I worried that because of his exposure to us Pullus men, his own dreams and expectations were unrealistic. Regardless of this reality, at the same time, I also understood that they were his dreams, not mine, and I resolved then that, should Alex persist in his determination to join the army, either as an auxiliary or a Legionary, I would do what I could to help him, no matter how infuriated Birgit got.

"Like what?" Alex's question jerked me from where my mind had taken me back to the conversation.

"Like," I spoke slowly, "…a lot of things. Too many things to talk about now."

Then, before he could argue or ask anything more, I pointed to the top of the hill that the road climbed, and challenged him to a race. As I hoped, that quelled this little uprising, for the moment.

My father had spent quite a bit of time alone with both Sextus and me, although separately, listening to his sons unburden themselves about some of the things we had done and seen. With me, and I assume with Sextus, he had just sat and listened as I talked of those things I could not impart by letter, particularly about the campaign, now five years before, against the Colapiani. And I told him everything, leaving nothing out, including my crippling of Maxentius, and my killing of Caecina and Mela. I explained my reasons for my actions, and while I saw him lift an eyebrow, or heard him suck in a breath, he simply sat and listened to me. The last topic we discussed was one I had thought long and hard about bringing up, and I was not even sure I would until it came out of my mouth. Even at the time, I understood my reluctance; I was afraid of the answer I would get from him.

"Did you know about Corvinus and Urso's business together?" I finally blurted out, only after draining a cup of unwatered wine.

When he did not answer immediately, my heart began racing; although he was calm, at least outwardly, his lined face turned to look at me steadily for what seemed like a third of a watch at least.

Finally, he asked quietly, "Would it matter if I said yes?"

"Matter?" I considered for a moment, and a part of me wanted to shout that of course it mattered! Gaius Porcinus, at least the Gaius Porcinus I knew, would never have allowed his Centurions to abuse their rankers like that! That would be especially true once he took the Pullus name and was following in the *caligae* of Titus Pullus himself! Yet, what I said was, "No, not really."

"Then why did you ask?" my father replied, and I was made uneasy by his expression. He was not angry…yet. "If it didn't matter, why bring it up?"

"I was just…curious," I managed, yet even I heard how weak it sounded.

"Curious!" my father understandably scoffed, then shook his head, "No, Titus. I know you better than that! You asked me for a reason. And that reason is that you find it hard to believe that your father would have allowed that kind of thing in his Cohort."

"Not hard," I countered, although I spoke quietly, "impossible. I found, and find it impossible to believe."

"Titus," my father's voice suddenly sounded hoarse, "you've always expected too much. Of me. Of your mother. And," he pointed at me, "more than anyone, of yourself. You built me up in your mind to be this…this," he struggled for the right word, finally coming up with "*model* of virtue who never did anything wrong." Sighing, he said, "And I'm just a man, Titus. Just like your Avus. Just like you."

Instead of replying, I stayed silent for the simple reason I could not think of anything to say, and I suppose it was what prompted him to continue.

"But to answer your question, yes, I was aware of it."

Despite suspecting this to be the case, I still felt like I had been punched in the pit of my stomach; little did I know that I was destined to feel worse.

"Do you remember when I was promoted to be Quartus Pilus Prior?" he asked suddenly.

The fact that I did is due more to my Avus' account than any true recall of it; my memories of those days in Siscia were of my Avus leading me by the hand to feed Ocelus his daily apple, and playing with the boys of my age who were the sons of Centurions. Nevertheless, I was at least aware of the circumstances, and I said as much.

"Well, then you know that I passed over several men for that post," he went on, and I nodded again.

My father's promotion had been, if not the last, one of the last official acts of Titus Pullus in the role of Camp Prefect, and it was the result of a deal made with the man who was the Primus Pilus of the 8th, Aulus Honorius Macrinus, in exchange for my Avus ensuring that Macrinus took over as Camp Prefect when Titus Pullus retired.

Continuing on, my father explained, "So I didn't have any choice in the Centurions assigned to the Cohort. They just came with the job. Which included Urso and Corvinus."

Suddenly, I had a vague memory.

"I remember," I broke in. "I remember you and Mama talking about how your second in command thought the post should have gone to him, and how he was trying to undermine you. That," I sat back as the realization hit me, "was Urso, wasn't it?"

"The one and the same," my father confirmed. "But he was just one of five, and another of those five was Corvinus." He paused to sip from his cup, and I did not miss the faraway expression in his eyes, recognizing he was no longer fully sitting with me, but back in time as well. "And when I took over, they were already in business. At least," he allowed, "they were already in business with their Centuries." He turned to gaze at me, his expression giving nothing away as he said, "Which I put a stop to, as soon as I was able." Then, he shrugged and added, "Which is when they decided to branch out, into town, running protection for some merchants. At least, as I recall."

I considered this for a moment, then I posed a question.

"Why didn't you turn them in to the Legate? Or at least make them stop altogether?"

My father laughed then, but it held no humor, and he pointed down at where one of his legs should have been, saying bitterly, "You see what happened when I ran afoul of Barbatus. What do you think a man like Urso would have done?" He shook his head. "And I had, and have a family. Who would have looked after you, your brothers, and sisters, and your mother if I had backed him into a corner?"

Oh, it was a very, very bitter draught my father was pouring down my throat, yet as much as I hated the thought, I forced myself to admit he had done the right, no, really the only thing he could have done.

Heedless of my thoughts, he continued, "Honestly, my major concern was that they stopped squeezing their own men. And, I will say that when I actually took a good look at the diary, Corvinus wasn't the worst offender of the two, not by far. But I did stop that, Titus."

There was a catch in my father's voice then that caught my attention, and I looked up from my wine cup at him, hearing what I was sure was as close to a pleading tone as my father is capable of making, asking me to believe what he was saying was true.

"Yes," I agreed, "you did. And I would have done the same." I could not help but chuckle as I added, "And maybe I'll have to face the same situation someday."

"Speaking of that," my father seemed relieved at the chance to change the subject, "how do things stand with your promotion to Optio?"

"I'm third on the list to be promoted," I was happy to tell him, although that was where the good news ended, or at least so I believed. "But considering there's not any fighting going on, nobody's dying, so there's no empty slots to fill."

"Inconsiderate bastards," my father commented dryly, gently mocking my bout of self-pity. "Don't they know who they're holding up from climbing the ladder?"

As I am sure he hoped, I could not avoid laughing at that. Shortly after this, I took my leave to go to my room and read. Although overall I felt better hearing from my father's own mouth what had transpired all those years ago, it did not take long for a deeply troubling thought to enter my mind, destined to never really leave it, and honestly, it is the dominant thought now whenever I think about it. I could not help wondering if, by my father's insistence that Urso and Corvinus shut down their scheme on their Centuries, he had unwittingly pushed Urso to look for other ways to fund his ambitions. And if so, what role did my father play in setting off the series of events whereby a Primus Pilus of a Legion was selling Roman armor to Pannonian tribes that ended up being used to protect men we were trying to kill? And even more troubling, were trying to kill us first? Was Gaius Porcinianus Pullus the man who had set things into motion that found me in a Varciani town, watching Urso be killed by Draxo? These are questions I still ask myself, although when they pop into my mind, I try to banish them back from where they came.

Leaving Arelate was not nearly as difficult as I thought it would be, and I am somewhat ashamed to admit that part of that feeling stemmed from my desire to get away from the town now that the plot against Gundorix was advancing. It was crucial for both Sextus and me to be nowhere in the vicinity when what we hoped would happen did, but I also had a nagging worry at the idea we were leaving Arelate and my parents behind, along with Gaius and Septimus, to face whatever possible consequences there might be. Although I was not excessively concerned, I did ask Gallus to stay in Arelate to keep an eye on the villa and my family, but when I tried to pay him extra, he refused it.

"I haven't eaten this well since, well, since I don't know when," he confessed, patting his belly with a grin. "Every time your mother sees me, she's trying to feed me. And I'm not about to refuse her!"

Both Sextus and I had to laugh at this, especially since I believe he knew as well as I did that we were as much to blame for that as anyone. Keeping us fed was an endless chore for Iras Porcinianus Pullus, and while we could have easily afforded it, she had always refused having more than one kitchen servant like Birgit's mother, insisting on preparing our meals herself. It was a habit my father had long since given up trying to change; I suppose it came from being a slave herself, so the idea of someone else doing what she saw as her work was something she could not bear. Consequently, we did not have nearly the complement of slaves and servants one would normally associate with a villa the size of ours, and the last slave owned by my Avus, then my parents, had been Simeon, the Armenian horse master who had cared for Ocelus. While it was true he and I had gotten off to a rocky start – I viewed him as a rival for the big gray's affections – his skill handling not just Ocelus but all horses, and his obvious love for his charge, which I somewhat grudgingly recognized Ocelus returned, we had ended up becoming very close. But when Ocelus died, my father had manumitted the Armenian, and offered to pay his way back to Armenia where, as far as I know, he still might be living. Birgit's mother Glenora was still there, but there were only three other servants and just the slave Chickpea, so Gallus staying behind put my mind at ease.

Finally, the day we had chosen to return came, and we all began the day at the family altar, making sacrifices and offerings, while my father intoned a prayer wishing us a safe and uneventful trip back to Siscia. Once more, we had to endure a vale of tears, except this time, everyone was crying, including little Titus and his new best friend Gaius; even Septimus and Scribonia were, if not sad, suitably somber to be rid of each other. Just as I did when I arrived, I swept my mother off the ground, except this time, she was not laughing when I did so, and while I tried to do so, I am afraid I was not very successful. Finally, we were allowed to begin our journey back to Siscia, and it was as we were making our way out of Arelate that I suddenly realized I had never gotten to the new theater. If the gods were kind, I remember thinking, I will be back to see it.

Traveling across the Republic, particularly the distance we had to traverse, is certainly much safer than it was when I was a child. Even so, it is not without dangers, as we learned, although when compared to what both Sextus and I had faced under the standard, the incident we experienced was inconsequential, especially because none of us were hurt. Nevertheless, as the *de facto* commander of our small expedition, I bear the responsibility for what happened. It was the fifth day of our journey, and we, actually I, had made the decision to push on through Luca, because it would have ended our day earlier than I liked. Perhaps nine miles beyond Luca is a small settlement; I did not nor do I now know its name, but what I remembered from passing through was that there was a small inn situated on the banks of a river. Turning from the Via Aurelia, which continues south and heading on the road east past Luca, there is a heavily wooded low ridge situated on a north/south axis that is a little more than two miles from the settlement, and it was just as we reached the base of this ridge when I decided to press ahead and go to the inn to make sure there were rooms available. Moving at the trot, as I ascended the ridge, I realized it was steeper than I had remembered, although part of this was from the fact that we had come from the opposite direction, but between the grade and a series of outcroppings, the normally straight Roman road had to curve more than usual. Even as my horse began laboring slightly, I was observing this as a good spot for an ambush, although at this particular moment, it was more an idle thought than any real recognition of danger.

Over the years, I have discovered that it is not unusual for a military man to take in his surroundings with an eye that sees things differently than civilians. Where a farmer might see the stream running through his land as a blessing, a man of the Legions views it as either an obstacle or a possible means of defense; where the shepherd sees the small depression in the hill as a good spot to graze, a man of the Legions sees a possible method of concealment that can either be a blessing or a danger. I bring this up to explain why I did not immediately turn about and rejoin Sextus and the wagon, because frankly, I was simply allowing my mind to run freely. As I topped the ridge, the trees were still too thick for me to see down to the bottom, or even catch more than a glimpse farther out, where the small cluster of buildings, of which the inn was a part, were located. Even with the foliage, though, I could see my shadow lengthening in front of me, so after pausing for the span of perhaps fifty heartbeats to allow my mount to catch its breath, I kicked it back into a trot as we started to descend. Then, I hit the bottom of the slope, and I could just make out the shapes of the buildings, nestled at the base of the slope of the system of hills and ridges that dominate the northern reaches of Etruria. From where I was at, it was perhaps a tenth part of a watch to reach the inn if I continued at the trot, yet I only went perhaps a hundred more paces before stopping on the road. I cannot easily explain why; my guess is that my observation of the ground and its suitability for some sort of ambush had stuck in my mind, but although I turned around, I still did not immediately retrace my steps. Instead, I sat on the horse, looking back up the road, at least as far as I could before it disappeared from view because of the trees. There was a breeze that rustled the leaves, making it difficult to hear anything else, but after several heartbeats' time, I decided there was nothing to hear. Even now, I cannot say exactly for what I was listening, yet the lack of any kind of noise over and above that made by the gods of nature actually made me more unsettled. So, before I could talk myself out of it, I kicked the flanks of my mount, who responded willingly enough, despite the fact that we were climbing back up a road we had just descended. I was about halfway back up when, perhaps because of a stray breeze or some trick of the wind, I heard the first sound that was not part of the normal background, something that sounded like a shout. Whatever it was, once I heard it, I did not hesitate, slapping the chestnut on its rump with my hand, something I had not done with it to that point, and it reacted instantly with a huge forward leap that took us to a gallop within a matter of heartbeats. Bounding up the slope in a fraction of the time it had taken us to descend it, the roaring of the wind in my ears made it almost impossible to hear anything else, but my recollection is that I heard at least one more cry in a clearly female voice. This was what prompted me to do something I normally would not, cresting a hill in a dangerous moment without stopping, or at least slowing near the top so I could peek over it to get an idea of what lay on the other side. Because of that decision, I only had the barest fraction of time to take in the scene before me, understand what was taking place, then do something about it, so I cannot recall the exact sequence of everything that happened.

The wagon was stopped, perhaps a hundred paces from the crest of the hill, while Birgit was standing up in her spot on the seat, next to Alex, who had been given the job of driving the wagon, and was also standing. Fortunately, I was able to spot the reason why immediately; two men were standing next to the oxen, each one holding the bridle of a beast, while three more men were spread out, two on Birgit's side. This was bad enough, but they were all armed with a motley variety of weapons, although it was the man with the spear I saw as the most immediate threat because he was jabbing it up at Alex. The boy was holding the man at bay, barely, with wild swings of the goad he had been using to prod the oxen when they balked, while Birgit was kicking furiously at one of the two men who had reached out to grab her by the ankle. By the time my mind caught up to what my eyes were seeing, I had already turned my horse directly at the man with the spear, thankful that the beast did not hesitate at this obstacle in its path. Only at the last instant did the spearman become aware of the threat posed by me and my horse, so he was just turning and I got the briefest glimpse of an upturned face framed by greasy black hair, then felt the shuddering impact communicated up through my horse' body as it slammed into him. While we were not at a full gallop, it was close to it, so I was past him quickly, just catching a glimpse of him caroming into the side of the wagon with terrific force before bouncing off and hitting the ground, hard. My horse's momentum took me past the wagon, and this was when I saw Sextus perhaps fifty paces behind it and on the other side, understanding why he had not been next to the wagon. He and his horse were surrounded by at least four men that I counted in the brief glance, but the longest weapon any of them had was what was clearly a Spanish sword, just like the one Sextus had in his hand, which he was slashing down at first one attacker, then another. Unfortunately, Sextus had never been the horsemen I am, so he was having a hard time keeping the horse underneath him as he spun it back and forth in an attempt to keep his adversaries off balance.

I was torn; while I knew that the spearman was the most dangerous of the first three, at least as far as his choice of weapon, and I was fairly certain he was down and probably out, there were still two trying to grab Birgit, who was still shrieking at the top of her lungs. However, I could easily tell she was not calling for help, but instead was hurling curses in her own tongue at the pair of men, who I assumed, correctly as it turned out, were bandits. Therefore, instead of turning the horse back around, I let it continue in the same direction it had been heading, intent on helping Sextus. This time, though, one of the bandits surrounding him obviously spied the movement, because he danced backward a couple of steps from where he had been trying to get under Sextus' mount's belly, choosing instead to turn and face me. As he did so, he risked a quick glance over his shoulder, and while I heard him snap something to the other three, I could not make out what it was; I assumed it was either an order to them to keep my brother occupied, or his assurance that he would take care of me. Then, he crouched into a posture that caused me to draw frantically on the reins, but I instantly understood our momentum was too great, so instead, I laid the reins across the chestnut's neck while pressing hard into his left flank with my knee. To my great relief, the horse obeyed instantly, sheering away from the swordsman, who still made a lunge for us, although it came up short. Making sure I allowed the horse to continue traveling more than fifteen or twenty paces distance, I glanced over my shoulder and saw the swordsman seemed to be hesitating, clearly torn between coming after me or returning his attention to my brother, and only then did I slide out of the saddle. It may seem strange I did so, but once this bandit had assumed a stance that is only taught in the Legions, I knew he was prepared to meet my rush on horseback and had at least been trained in how to defend against cavalry; this was a man I would have to face on the ground, especially since I was not armed with a *spatha*.

Both Sextus and I had been wearing our swords, thankfully, although honestly, it was not nearly as much because of moments like this one, but the fact that it clearly marked us as men of the Legions, and being such gave us some extra benefits when traveling. Regardless of why, I still threw up a prayer of thanks as, before I had taken more than two paces after my feet hit the ground, my Gallic blade was in my hand. Just before I closed the final distance to come within sword range, I saw over the swordsman's shoulder the flash of Sextus' own sword, a blur of motion as it slashed down across the face of one of his attackers, who went staggering backward, away from my brother, screaming as he did so. Since my own foe's back was to this, the stricken man's sudden shout of pain did not seem to distract the man…much, except I saw the barest flicker of movement as his eyes moved in what I am sure was an unconscious reaction to what had just happened behind him. Whatever the reason, I took the opportunity to take two giant leaping steps forward, instantly closing the distance between us as I then made a lunging thrust with a loud bellow of my own. I did not get a truly good look at him in that moment, but I saw enough to see how sunken his cheeks were, how sallow his complexion, although it was his eyes that seemed to be made of gold, which a part of my mind realized was because of the jaundice that afflicted him. His lips were pulled back into a snarl as he managed to parry my lunge, revealing a row of nothing but blackened stumps along his lower jaw, while the upper jaw was the same except for one lone brown tooth, right in the middle of his mouth. When he parried, the sound of our blades clashing together was louder than I remembered hearing before in other fights; only later did I realize it was because there was not a battle raging around me. I recovered from the lunge, or at least pretended to, although he was able to dodge the slashing blow I aimed at him, leaning backward but not losing his balance.

"You're going to have to do better than that, boy," he sneered, "if you think you're going to get the best of me!"

So I did as he demanded. Instead of using one of the positions taught to us by the Legions, I fell back on a trick the old *lanista* Vulso had shown me. It is a move that can only be done in the arena, for a couple of reasons; the first is that it requires more room than a Legionary standing in his rank would have. The other is that any Centurion worth his salt who caught a *tiro* trying something like I was about to attempt would thrash him thoroughly with the *vitus*. Nevertheless, without any conscious thought, at least in that instant, the part of a man's mind that remains aloof in moments like this clearly understood I had to dispatch this *cunnus* quickly. I could not count on Birgit or Alex to hold the pair of men off for very long, especially if one of the pair holding the oxen still were to join the others, and this was even more true if the man I had run down had recovered his wits as well. Also, despite my concentration on my foe, the detached part of my mind used the upper part of my vision to see, just over the swordsman's shoulder, that my brother was not faring well, almost being unhorsed when he once more kicked his mount in the opposite direction. Therefore, I made a very hard feint to my right, not with my blade but with my body, taking a step with my right leg that opened my stance and seeming to plant my weight on it as I dragged my left foot back under my body. To my foe, my intentions were clear; I was trying to get around the arc of his sword for the purpose of my own attack from the side, and just as I hoped, he responded with a move of his own. Yet even as he was doing so, I was already moving again, except this time, it was to spin quickly on my left foot, made possible because despite appearances I had kept almost all of my weight on it. Performing a maneuver like this, where one spins about on one foot, means that for a fraction of a heartbeat, one's back is turned to their foe. If my opponent had not reacted to my feint, this account would not be written, because I would be dead at the hands of a toothless, filthy veteran and likely deserter dressed in rags. And I cannot honestly say that I knew when I started my move he had truly fallen for my feint; I merely assumed he did, and clearly, the gods were content to make it so. In essence, while my body, and most importantly, my sword were swinging in one direction, his body and sword arm were taking him in the opposite one, moving his blade away from a position where it could do any good, across his body to parry a thrust that would never come.

During my spin, I extended my sword arm straight out in front of me while using the mass of my body to create the speed and momentum to bring the sword around. From above, if one were to just watch the tip of my sword, it would have described an almost perfect circle, although if successful, it would be stopped from doing so by the man's body. Actually, in this case, his head, to be precise, because despite being fooled, this dirty bandit had clearly been quite skilled with a sword, meaning that he still managed to react, sweeping his own blade back across his body in a desperate attempt to knock my own astray. He was partially successful because I had been aiming at his neck; instead, my Gallic-forged sword clashed against his one more time and was deflected up just enough that I sliced right through his skull, about mid-forehead. The shuddering impact as the iron of my sword sliced through bone was tremendous, yet between the momentum of my much heavier body, along with my strength and the Vinician grip that kept my thumb protected from the tremendous force against it when blade met bone all meant that I sent the top half of his skull flying up in the air in a vivid spray of red and pinkish gray. Despite this, the bandit actually stood for perhaps a heartbeat, and his face, which I saw clearly just before it was covered by his own gore, bore a puzzled expression. Then he collapsed, except I was already moving, barely pausing as I stepped over the man's body, so that before the nearest man facing Sextus could heed the shouted warning of one of the other two who were looking in my general direction, I ran my sword through the base of his skull, feeling the grating resistance once more, although it was not as much as the first bandit. Whatever fight was left in the two men facing Sextus instantly deserted them, because almost as if they had practiced it, they both wheeled in perfect unison and began sprinting for the trees on the side of the road nearest to them.

Sextus turned his horse as if to pursue them, but I shouted at him, "Sextus! Go help Birgit!"

I pointed with my sword and he obeyed instantly, while I seemed to notice for the first time the blood and gore still dripping from it. There was another series of shouts, in male voices, and I caught just a glimpse of one bandit, also running as if Cerberus was after him, heading in the same general direction as the other two, but at that moment, I assumed I was just not at the right angle to see the other bandit who had been attempting to subdue Birgit. However, I was able to see the man who had been holding the ox on my side follow the lead of the other fleeing men, the only difference being he made for the trees on my side of the wagon. I briefly considered following him, then thought better of it. Only then did I glance back towards the wagon on the side where the spear-carrying bandit had been trying to skewer Alex. Because of the angle, I could not see if he was safe, understanding there was still at least one man unaccounted for, but when I shouted the boy's name, he answered, assuring me that he was fine. As he did so, I saw that the man I had run down with my horse was still prone, but he was moving. In fact, he was crawling, not in any stealthy manner, but in the way a wounded animal will try to drag itself off into the brush to either lick its wounds and recover, or die. This animal, I thought to myself, isn't going to be licking his wounds, so I strode over to him, my sword still out and ready to use. He did not seem to notice me, at least at first, and was using his hands to grab the dirt, then drag himself a foot or so, panting from the effort. For some reason, I stopped a few feet away, just to watch him, and I realized why; there was something about his movement that seemed odd, and it took me a moment to determine what it was. He was not using his legs at all, nor were they moving about; he was clearly paralyzed, either from the collision with my horse, or more likely from being hurled against the wagon. Once I thought about it, I recalled seeing him slam against the wheel specifically, his body hitting the wheel just above his waist, breaking his back. And I did not feel one flicker of pity, nor did I feel the need to put him out of his misery; instead, without actually deciding to do so, I found myself standing there, watching him, then moving a pace or two to close the tiny distance he was making between us. Standing as I was at his feet, he had not looked back once, so intent on getting away, his gaze was on the beckoning trees, although I did not really understand what he thought he was doing. At most, he would be postponing his death for a day, perhaps two, although I supposed it was possible someone would find him and take pity on him. Even then, our world is a cruel place, and any person, no matter where he is from or what class he is born into, who cannot contribute anything will quickly be discarded and left to fend for themselves. Someone who was so gravely injured they were paralyzed would be facing a non-existent future, and what little time they had left would be filled with suffering. As I watched, I was struck by another, more unpleasant thought, a reminder more accurately, of another time I had walked next to a man trying to crawl away and escape. I suppose this was what prompted me to stop what I was doing, and I took a couple more steps so that he sensed the movement out of the corner of his eye. He let out a gasp; at least, I believe he did, or it could have been me, because both of us were clearly equally surprised and disturbed.

"You…you're just a boy," I heard myself say.

"P-please, sir," his voice was hoarse, yet it was also deeper than I had expected, which oddly made me feel better. "Have mercy on me! We…we…just...we…"

"You just wanted to rob that wagon," I supplied the answer, and my tone was cold, but I was still moved to ask, "How old are you, boy?"

Suddenly, his eyes darted wildly, and I realized he was trying desperately to think through the fear and pain in order to determine what answer would be most likely to spare his life.

"Twelve," he finally answered, except it was the wrong thing to say, because I knew he was lying.

"You've got an awful deep voice for being twelve," I commented. "Care to try again?"

"No, sir…I mean, yes, sir," he stammered. "It's just that…I don't know, exactly. How old I am, I mean," he added helpfully.

Sighing, I hated to admit that what he was telling me was possibly, in fact, probably the truth. I have met more men and women than I can count who are not exactly sure about their age. However, this is more normally the case with the barbarian tribes; we Romans are very diligent in our record keeping, even we Head Counters. Before I could open my mouth to say anything, I heard the crunching sound of footsteps, and I glanced up to see Alex approaching from the prone youth's other side. He had a scratch on one cheek and the shoulder of his tunic was torn, yet otherwise seemed unharmed. Alex, on the other hand, did not even seem to notice I was standing there, his eyes only on the bandit.

"This is the one who tried to poke you with a spear," I said, although I am not sure why I did so.

"I know," he mumbled, and the youth's head whipped around to stare up at Alex.

"P-please, young Master," the youth said, "I was just telling your father that I'm only twelve. Or maybe, thirteen!"

"You tried to kill me," Alex replied in an eerily calm voice. "We didn't do anything to you! But you tried to kill us!" I could see he was coming out of his stupor, of the kind that is common to every man, and perhaps woman, after their first time either witnessing or partaking in some sort of violent act.

"Alex," I kept my tone quiet, as I often did with Ocelus when something had frightened him, "it's all right. You go back to the wagon and help your mother calm your brother and sisters down." I was struck by a pang of guilt as I realized something. "How is she? Is she all right?"

He nodded, and I exhaled the breath I had been holding.

"She's with Uncle Sextus. He's comforting her."

I believe it was in the way he said it that ignited a flicker of concern, but we had more pressing matters.

"Well, go back to the wagon anyway." I still spoke softly, except I used a tone I hoped would inform him this was not a request. "I'll take care of him."

"You mean you're going to kill him."

The way the boy said it was so matter of fact it caught me completely off guard; it also sent our lone captive into a paroxysm of terror, and he began clawing at the dirt again, frantically trying to drag himself away.

"Nooo," he moaned, clearly out of his mind with fear, and I shot a furious glance at Alex. "Please, sir! Please! Mercy! I beg you! Nooo!"

"Alex," this time I did not speak softly, "go to the other side of the wagon. Now."

For the barest moment, I thought he would not obey because he remained there, looking directly up into my eyes, although he did not say anything. I was about to cross over to him and take him by the arm and drag him to the wagon when, still without a word, he turned about and walked stiffly away.

Turning back to the grim business, I easily caught back up with the youth, where I squatted next to him and said, "You know that even if I don't do it, you're going to die."

This unleashed a fresh set of moans, except this time, he also shook his head violently, as if by the very vigor of his denial, he could somehow change his fate.

"This is what happens when you choose a life of banditry, boy," I pointed out.

That was when he surprised me, if only because it stopped his moaning, and when he twisted his head to look at me, for the first time, I saw anger along with the fear.

"I didn't choose to be a bandit," he snapped. "I didn't get to choose anything in my life."

I admit I was suddenly intrigued, and I asked, "How's that?"

"My Tata was a bandit, and so are my brothers. At least," he amended, "the ones that are still alive."

"You say your father *was* a bandit?"

I did not think it was because he had made enough from his banditry to buy a roadside inn, or even retire, and I was proven right.

"He's dead," he replied bitterly. "He's the one who made me do the same thing he did. And my brothers," he added.

"But if he's dead now," I pointed out, "that means you didn't have to do it any more if you didn't want to."

"And do what?" The youth shook his head, and I could see the light was already dimming from his eyes as the toll of his injuries were exacting their price. "This is all I know."

"Do you have any words you want to say?"

The youth swallowed hard, and now the tears were steadily flowing, but the earlier hysteria had fled, replaced by what I believe was, if not his acceptance, his resignation to his fate.

He shook his head and said in a whisper, "My father didn't believe the gods care about people like us. So he never let us say any words or make any sacrifices." Somehow, he managed a weak laugh, then finished, "I don't even know all their names."

Your father, I thought grimly, sounds like a real heartless bastard, and I, for one, am glad he's dead. Taking a deep breath, I straddled the boy, whose whole upper body was shaking violently, and using the skill I had learned during my first campaign, I sent him to the afterlife.

With the youth disposed of, I walked over and retrieved my horse, stopping only long enough to squat down next to the corpse of the sword-wielding bandit, using his filthy, torn and greasy tunic to wipe my sword clean. Then I did a quick search of the body, not to loot it as we do in battle, but looking for something specific. As I had expected, I found no identity disk that is handed to every man in the Legions who completes a full enlistment. While this was not definitive proof that he was a deserter – I had heard of men who lost their disks, either by accident or by gambling it away – I felt, and still feel, confident this man had been a deserter. Swinging back up into the saddle, I guided my horse, for whom my regard and affection had grown when he proved stalwart at a time when I needed him, towards the wagon. When I swung him around to the opposite side of the wagon, Sextus was dismounted, while Birgit was out of the wagon and on the ground. It was not that they were still in an embrace; it was the way they seemed to leap away from each other at my presence that sounded an alarm in my head, although I could not really form an articulate thought why it bothered me. Fortunately for all of us, my attention was quickly drawn to the sight of a prone body lying on its back in a spot that led me to conclude this was the formerly missing bandit who had been holding the ox on the other side of the wagon. Once more I slid off my horse; when I approached what I expected to be a corpse, and the man suddenly jerked one arm, I am afraid I let out a quite undignified yelp, even as I was hopping backwards. Behind me, Sextus burst out laughing, and I could even hear Birgit giggling, so I am afraid I was not particularly happy when I looked over my shoulder to glare at the pair of them, who were now standing ludicrously far apart, at least considering how close together they had been just a matter of heartbeats before.

"Why isn't he dead?" I asked Sextus sourly, but my brother was clearly unconcerned.

"I hit him with the flat of my sword," he replied, as if that was all the explanation needed.

"And why would you do that?"

Sextus opened his mouth to answer, except nothing came out, until he finally admitted with a shrug, "I don't know, exactly. I suppose I thought we'd take him prisoner. Maybe," his tone turned hopeful as he suggested, "there's a reward for him at that place we're stopping."

That made me laugh, just not in a particularly kind way, and I saw Sextus redden as I mocked him in front of Birgit.

"A reward? For him?" I kicked the man none too gently with the toe of one boot, and he responded with a low moan, although his eyes remained closed. "Did you get a good look at him? How much do you think we might get?" I teased. "A brass *obol*? Or maybe," I snapped my fingers, "even two!"

"All right, all right," my brother grumbled. "I get the point." He turned serious and dropped his voice, I assume so the children would not hear. "So who's going to do it?"

"You are," I retorted. "You should have finished him when you had the chance, so you might as well do it now."

"No!"

This startled me, not that there was a protest as much as who it came from, and Sextus, Birgit, and I looked over to see Alex emerging from the back of the wagon, where we could hear the other children still babbling from the excitement and fear of the moment.

"Alex," Birgit turned to him, her tone that of a mother informing a child of an unpleasant reality, "this is not your business."

"Why?" he demanded as he walked to join where we were standing, then pointed down at the man. "Why shouldn't I have some say in this? I'm the *paterfamilias*!" he declared, and his tone was so emphatic that Sextus and I exchanged glances of wry amusement, and I am sure his mind and mine were moving along similar paths. "It was my family they attacked! So it's my job to protect the family!"

Suddenly, I was not quite as amused, and I saw Birgit's expression turn uneasy as well, and she was the one who asked the boy, "What does that mean, Alex? You did your part," she pointed out, "and you were very brave! Wasn't he, Titus? Sextus?" She turned towards us and I saw the beseeching look in her eyes, and I realized she understood where Alex was heading.

"Very brave," I answered, Sextus echoing me at almost the same time. "In fact," I added, "the reason why I went past the wagon is that I saw Alex was doing such a good job of keeping those *cun*...bandits away from the wagon." I felt a sudden mischievous urge, and I grinned as I nodded at my brother. "Really, the only one who was in any trouble was little brother here! That's why I went and saved him first."

"Saved me?" Sextus' mouth dropped open. "You didn't save me! I was doing just fine without your help!"

"You were," I agreed, yet only did so to catch him off guard as I added, "doing a good job. Of not falling off your horse. Of handling those…bandits?" I gave him an elaborate shrug.

"Oh, go piss on your boots," he shot back, which for reasons I never learned, was one of his favorite epithets.

Turning my attention back to the more immediate problem, I asked Alex, "So what is it that you're saying, Alex?" As I suspected, he suddenly seemed unsure, and I decided that, as harsh as it was, I needed to press the advantage. "As you said, you're the *paterfamilias*, and you're correct that, by custom and rights, you have the responsibility for ending this threat to your family." I drew my sword back out, which caused Birgit to gasp in shock, except when she took a step to interpose, I gave her a look that, even as I did so, I understood risked changing the nature of our relationship forever because I had never used that expression with her before. Nevertheless, it stopped her, and her already pale face went a shade whiter. Seeing that she did not seem disposed to argue, I turned back to Alex, brandishing my newly cleaned sword as I did so.

"If you want to be the *paterfamilias* of your family," I told him sternly, "then you need to be willing to do everything that's required of you." I pointed to the last bandit, who was just seeming to come back to consciousness, and said, "Which means making sure nobody who attacked you ever does it again."

With that, I offered him the sword, hilt first. As I believed he would, Alex was suddenly not nearly as certain as he had been just a moment before, although he did tentatively reach out to grasp the hilt. Then, with his hand just a couple inches away, he dropped it, along with his eyes, suddenly interested in staring down at the ground and not up at me.

Nodding my head, I did not say anything; I had no desire to humiliate the boy. I just wanted to impress upon him the gravity of the action he had seemed determined to take. I cannot adequately express how thankful I was that he demurred because I had no desire to fight with Birgit who, despite remaining silent, looked ready to pounce if Alex had, in fact, grasped the sword hilt.

Having determined the boy was not going to pursue matters, I gently guided him towards his mother, indicating with my head that she should take him around the back of the wagon, out of sight of what I was about to do. This, however, Alex was not willing to do, and he refused to budge.

"I should at least be here to watch," he declared with a solemnity that was not only beyond his years, but told me he was not just intent on satisfying his boyish curiosity about what it is like to see someone die.

When I opened my mouth to argue, nothing came out because of that recognition, so instead, I merely nodded. What surprised me was Birgit's reaction, or lack of it, because she did not offer any resistance; instead, she leaned down and whispered something in the boy's ear, to which he gave a grave nod, although he did not say anything. Sextus was standing next to the man, whose head was beginning to move back and forth, the sign that he was about to regain consciousness, so I needed no urging from my brother to stride over to where he was standing. Pausing only long enough to kneel down, the act of drawing the blade of my sword across the bandit's throat must have served to yank him from his unconsciousness, if only for a matter of heartbeats, as his eyes opened wide and he stared wildly at me, his hands going to his throat as he tried to say something that only came out as a gurgle. Then, it was done; within a hundred heartbeats of that, Birgit and Alex were back on the wagon, Sextus and I were mounted, and we resumed our progress. We would not reach the inn before dark, so I was not confident there would be rooms available, yet that could not be helped because I was not willing to forge ahead again. If we were forced to, Sextus and I could sleep under the wagon, while Birgit and the children could make do within it. Fortunately, there was no need; there were more than two rooms available, but that was all we took, although sleep was long in coming, for all of us, I am fairly certain.

It was not until we had crossed the border from Venetia into the corner of Rhaetia our route took us through when we heard the first bit of news from Pannonia; Siscia, specifically.

"There's an outbreak of bloody flux," we overheard one of the other travelers say one night, when we were perhaps eight days away from Siscia.

We would make it with four days to spare, provided nothing untoward happened again. But as we all sat there listening, Sextus and I paying the most attention, what we were hearing made it sound as if perhaps tarrying a bit might be a good idea.

The speaker was a portly man with threadbare clothing and a well-traveled air about him; I had not been paying attention when he told the man seated across from him what his business was, but my guess was he was some sort of wagon driver.

"How bad is it?" the man opposite from him, a sharp-faced man, perhaps thirty years of age, who might have been called handsome except he had one crossed eye, asked of the first one. "How many dead?"

"Don't know for sure." The first man was hard to understand because he was speaking between mouthfuls of the stew served at this inn; according to the innkeeper, the meat in the stew was rabbit, but Sextus and I glanced at each other after our first bite, and our minds were thinking along the same lines as Sextus whispered, "I don't remember seeing any dogs around here, did you?"

Oblivious to our presence, the first one continued in between smacking his lips. "But it started in town, then hit the army."

My brother and I exchanged a look at that as well because this was somewhat unusual. Whenever an outbreak of some sort of disease hits, it unfortunately usually starts with the Legions, then moves to whichever the nearest town may be. Not, I thought, that it matters.

"I heard someone in town say there were at least two hundred dead," the man said, still either oblivious to or ignoring the fact that we were now openly listening to his words. "But I don't know if that's just in town, or just in the army, or both combined." He paused to take in another spoon of the greasy stew and concluded, "I'm just glad I only passed through."

While he continued talking, we quickly determined he had little more to say that interested us; his sharp-faced dining companion, however, was another story.

When the first man paused to drink deeply from his cup, the second man offered his own bit, saying, "When I left Rome, the talk there was that Tiberius is finally coming back to the city."

"What?" This clearly surprised the first traveler, as it did us as well. "When did you hear that?"

"The morning I left," the second man said, "but that was a week ago." I was seated so I could see him out of the corner of my eye, and I saw him shrug. "For all I know, he could already be back in Rome."

The first man did not answer immediately, and I suspect he was turning this piece of news over in his mind because his voice dropped in volume as he asked, "Is it with the Princeps' blessing? Or," I did not miss the anxiety in his tone, "is Tiberius coming back on his own? To...?"

His voice trailed off, but I easily understood his reluctance. One of the most common things said about the divine Augustus is that when a sparrow dies and falls to the stones of the Forum, Augustus knows before it hits. And as I knew from bitter experience, albeit secondhand, at least at this point, he had ears everywhere; I would learn more about this, but that happened later.

"I wouldn't know about that" The sharp-faced man's tone had become guarded, and I could almost sense the sudden arrival of suspicion, hanging so heavily in our little corner of the inn, I imagined it falling about my shoulders like a sodden cloak. The man from Rome continued, "But I'm sure everything's perfectly fine between them."

"And may blessed Concordia keep it that way," the first man replied fervently. "The gods know we don't need another civil war."

"I'm sure it won't come to that," the thin-faced man said mildly, yet while he spoke softly, he did so with an air of assurance, as if he possessed some other information that made him so confident I was moved to turn my head and take him in, examining him for the first time in any detail.

He must have sensed it, because he turned and our eyes met; at least mine met one of his since the other seemed to be examining his nose, yet instead of appearing either offended or nervous about a giant Roman wearing a soldier's tunic with a sword on his *baltea*, he gave me a smile, and lifted the cup he had been holding in what I assumed was some sort of greeting. Which I returned with a nod before turning back to my own company, even as a feeling of disquiet suddenly bloomed inside me, although I could not say why. During my admittedly brief visual examination of the second diner, I instantly saw that he was, at the very least, of the equestrian order, at least judging by the quality of his clothes. Still, this was not unusual; rich men have to travel as well, and when one is outside of a town of any size, one cannot be choosy about accommodations. It was true it was slightly unusual to see a man who claimed the city for which our Republic is known as his home so far away from it, but not nearly as much as it had been the first time I had made this trip more than ten years before. Whatever it was that bothered me, I could not put my finger on it, so I dismissed the man from my mind, jumping back into the conversation at our own table, where Sextus and Alex were arguing about whether candied plums or honey cakes were sweeter; at least that is what I recall. If by some miracle I could have been informed of the role this cross-eyed stranger would go on to play in my life, I am certain I would have gotten up and run him through right then and taken my chances on the consequences. However, the gods had other plans for the two of us.

On the subject of my brother and Birgit, although they both outwardly behaved in a perfectly proper manner, a blind man could have seen there was something brewing between them, and what had been a vague unease on my part had grown into a healthy concern. As far as the children, from what I observed, all but Alex were oblivious to what was going on between their mother and the man they thought of as their uncle, and I only caught Alex eyeing them once or twice when Sextus had offered some joke or observation about our surroundings that made Birgit laugh. I cannot say the boy seemed displeased, although neither can I say he was beaming from ear to ear, but that was, and is not his nature. Now, however, when we departed the inn the next morning, I had another matter to consider and decide on the best course, so to speak.

"Do you think we should stop short of Siscia for a couple of days, and wait to hear anything?" Sextus asked me, and it was a fair question, one that I was asking myself even then.

I am sorry to say I was not in the best state of mind to appreciate what was a valid question, yet despite my resolve to avoid saying anything about what was dominating my thoughts, as usual, my mouth refused to obey what my mind told it, prompting me to retort, "Why? So you can spend more time with Birgit?"

As always happened, it was my brother's ears that announced I had scored a telling blow, but he was just as much a Pullus as I, meaning he was not going to let that go unchallenged.

"Why do you care?" he shot back furiously. "I'm just helping take her mind off…"

I turned and looked directly at him as I cut him off, saying, "I know exactly what you're doing." Sighing, I felt compelled to add as I turned back away, "I just hope you do too."

He surprised me by not answering immediately, which compelled me to glance over at him again, and he was wearing an expression on his face I could not remember seeing before, or at least seldom enough I could not identify its meaning.

"I…I hope so too," he finally said softly, then shook his head as he looked over at me with a sad smile. "But I've loved her for as long as I can remember, Titus."

"I know." For some reason, I felt compelled to reach out and touch his shoulder, assuring him, "And I know you don't want to hurt her. But it's not just her I'm worried about."

"I know," he answered miserably. "The children will probably hate me."

"Them, too," I agreed, then added, "But I wasn't talking about them. I was talking about you."

This clearly surprised him; it also made him silent for some time before he finally spoke again.

"You never did answer my question."

"What question?" I kept a straight face, but he was not fooled.

"You know," he insisted. "Stop playing with me."

"Why? It's so much fun watching your ears catch fire." I laughed, then before this could degenerate into one of our usual sessions of bickering, I answered the question. "I think," I told him, "we should keep going, but keep our ears open. When we get to Emona day after tomorrow, we should hear more there."

Somewhat to my surprise, Sextus agreed readily enough, although as normally happened, before too much time had passed, he slowed his horse to drop beside the wagon, whereupon he picked up wherever his conversation with Birgit had left off, leaving me to worry on my own.

Once we reached Emona, we ended up staying just an extra day; we could have continued on but chose not to, although it was no longer because of fear of the outbreak in Siscia. We had learned from a dispatch rider bound for Rome, who we hailed on the road, that the bout of bloody flux had run its course. In fact, this was the dispatch the rider was carrying from the Legate; we only prevailed on him to stop by virtue of our clearly seen status as men of the Legions.

"How bad was it?" Sextus asked him, but he only shrugged and said he did not know with any certainty.

Seeing that he was either unable or unwilling to divulge this information, we bade him on his way. Subsequently, our stay of an extra day in Emona was as much about resting the livestock and horses as for any other reason. Since we had stayed in Emona on the way to Arelate, the children had quickly explored all the town had to offer, which was not much compared even to Siscia; after Arelate, it was downright dreary. Both legs of our journey had been blessed to that point by the weather gods; this blessing ended the last night in Emona, when both Sextus and I were awakened by a clap of thunder, followed by the drumming sound of a hard rain falling on the tiled roof of the inn.

"Maybe it'll blow through in the night," my brother suggested hopefully.

"Maybe," I agreed, although I was doubtful; the truth was I had been waiting for some stretch of bad weather, because it just did not seem likely that our entire journey to Arelate and back would escape it.

And while our brush with the bandits had been all the children talked about for the next three or four days, as happens with children, soon enough, their attention was on other things. Only Alex seemed to be suffering the lingering effects of what had happened, but I understood why. The other children had been huddled in the bed of the wagon, their view of everything blocked by the high wooden sides and canvas top. Diocles' eldest, on the other hand, had not only been forced into the fight, as short as it had been, but had chosen to stand witness to my dispatch of the last bandit. For reasons only he knew, however, he had not spoken to either Sextus or me about what had happened, which, being frank, I had expected him to do. I cannot say he was more withdrawn; at least from me. Unfortunately, the same cannot be said about his relationship with Sextus, so that by the time we reached Emona, it was impossible not to notice how the boy was avoiding my brother. Which, as one might imagine, takes quite a bit of effort to accomplish in a party of eight people, not even mentioning the increased tension that results when a boy who has just lost his father and views himself as *paterfamilias* sees his new position under assault by a sudden and unexpected suitor for his mother's affections. The fact that it was a man Alex had looked up to and always thought of as an uncle only made matters worse. And if I am being honest, even as harsh as it may sound, I lay partial blame on Birgit's shoulders, because while she did not act flagrantly in any way as far as showing Sextus the interest he had in her was mutual, she did nothing to stop it. A decade after this event, as I write this, I have enough experience of my own to understand why Birgit behaved as she did; it was true she was newly widowed, but she was still young, no older than thirty, and she was still a beautiful woman. Childbearing and all that comes with it had not been as hard a burden on her as it is with many women, and I suspect that, despite her clear love for Diocles, being wanted again, especially by a man like Sextus who had yearned for her ever since he first took notice of the differences between a man and a woman, was just as confusing yet exciting for her as it was for Sextus. Although I cannot really say my brother was all that confused about what he wanted, and Alex was not blind, to any of it.

The rain that came our last night in Emona was still coming down when we woke, and would continue for the next three days. Naturally, it made our progress even slower than any of us would have liked, meaning that now I was beginning to fret about the likelihood of being forced to leave Birgit and the children behind as

Sextus and I pressed on to Siscia to return within our granted leave time. It is true that, like most such things, we could escape punishment for our tardiness easily enough, as long as we were willing to contribute even more to Primus Pilus Atticus' purse, which neither Sextus nor I were eager to do, if only because of the admonishment we had received from our father. Whereas before Diocles and his family had returned to Siscia, my father had followed Titus Pullus' practice of letting our Greek handle all the financial matters, for which the entire Pullus family, hopefully for several generations, are thankful, this was no longer the case. Now, my father had taken over control of the family's fortune, and while he will never admit it, my strong belief is that his interest in our pecuniary situation can be ascribed to the loss of his leg, which combined with his need to feel useful again. What this meant to us Pullus boys was that Gaius Porcinianus Pullus had expressed his displeasure at what he called our profligate spending. Although he, very grudgingly as far as I am concerned, acknowledged that my expenditure of some seven thousand sesterces I had spent to retain not only my rank of Sergeant, but Asinius' spot as Optio, had been justified, he was not as forgiving with some of my other decisions.

"Fur-lined gloves?" he had asked incredulously, when we had retired to what we all still think of as my Avus' study for this discussion, held shortly before we left. "You had fur-lined gloves made? What were you thinking?

"I was thinking," I protested, "that I want to keep my hands warm, and still hold on to my sword and shield!" I freely admit I was more than a bit nettled by his criticism, which compelled me to point out, "Tata, you know as well as I do that trying to hold on to either when you're using a pair of socks isn't easy!"

"No," he granted, "it's not." Just for an instant, I thought I had scored a victory; just for an instant. "But who ever said life under the standard is supposed to be easy? I raised you," he chose to point his finger at me, "and your brother to be harder than a man who needs gloves." Before I could respond, he amended, "All right, maybe not your brother as much," which caused me to chuckle. "But *you*," the finger resumed its jabbing motion at me, and I was sure he remembered how much I hated that, which was probably why he was doing it, "you're the namesake of Titus Pullus! What do you think your Avus would say if he knew you were wearing fur-lined gloves?"

"I think," I rejoined mildly, "he'd slap his forehead and wonder why he didn't think to do that."

As I had hoped, this made my father laugh, although it was more of a snort that was only part surrender. Unfortunately, at least for me, my attempt to get him off the subject was for naught.

"It's not just the expense," he told me. "It's the kind of thing that get men talking…and wondering where you get the money from."

As much as I hated to admit it, I could not argue, since this was precisely what had happened with the gloves.

"Titus, you and your brother have to be more careful about how much money you're spending and what you spend it on. Because it's not like the days of your Avus, or even mine, at least in the beginning," he explained. "You're not on campaign every year like we were, at least when I started, so you don't have the same opportunities we did for loot."

"You think I don't know that?" I grumbled. "But that's not our fault!"

"No, it's not," he agreed. "But it doesn't matter. All men will care about is watching you and your brother out in town, carousing and spending freely. Or having gloves made."

As I found out once we left, Sextus had received much the same lecture, if not a bit sterner, at least to hear him tell it.

"At least you can say you're spending money on things that help you on campaign," he offered when we were comparing the severity of our respective tongue-lashings. "According to him, all I've been spending money on is wine and whores!"

"That *is* all you've spent your money on," I reminded him, which made him grin.

"Oh, that's right." He laughed. "I forgot!"

"That's what happens when you guzzle that cheap swill they serve in the places you go to in town," I shot back, completely unsympathetic and still thinking I was the winner in the contest of who was more roughly handled by our *paterfamilias*.

That was how it always seemed with us; everything became a competition, no matter what it was, and I was always determined to come out the victor. From what I have observed and heard from other men with brothers, this seems to be the case most of the time.

The second full day of rain coincided with our party reaching a section of the road that had yet to be Romanized, at least in the sense that it was paved and crowned so that the roadbed drained in all but the most torrential downpour. Subsequently, the wagon got stuck no less than four times, requiring Sextus and me to dismount, getting filthy as we struggled to get the wagon out of the hole in which it had bogged down. Normally, once would have been enough, except the entire road appeared much like a river, albeit one that ran in a straight line, making it nearly impossible to spot holes. After the first time, when we thought that Alex's inexperience would be a hindrance in avoiding hitting a deep rut in the road that had been made by wagons preceding ours, Sextus took over the driving of it, while Alex joined Birgit and his siblings inside, definitely warmer and relatively dryer, although the canvas top had started to soak through. Within a sixth part of a watch after Sextus took over the reins, the wagon bogged down again, for which he blamed me since I rode ahead of the wagon. Naturally, I did not see it that way, and I am afraid that Birgit and the children were forced to endure listening to even more of our quarreling as we heaved and shoved the wagon out of its current mire. The only bright spot, at least as I saw it, was when the wagon suddenly lurched free, causing my brother to land face first into the muck; for some reason, he did not find it as amusing. Nevertheless, it was the fourth occasion when, much to our pleased surprise, help arrived from a very welcome, if unexpected, source.

"What are you two idiots doing?"

As it happened, both Sextus and I had our shoulders against the back of the wagon, me on one side and him on the other, while Alex had been pressed back into service again as the driver. When I wheeled about, part of me cursed myself for missing the sound of an approaching horse, even if the rain was that loud. Fortunately, not only was it not a threat, the sight of a grinning Quintus Gallus, even snug and dry under his waterproofed *sagum*, was a welcome one.

"What are you doing here?" I gasped.

"Watching you two make fools of yourselves." He laughed. Gesturing to the wagon, he heaved a sigh that I could even hear over the patter of the rain as he swung out of the saddle and said, "I suppose I have to show you boys how to do everything."

With the extra muscle, the wagon was quickly extricated, and we were all back at our respective posts.

Not until we were a bit down the road did I turn and ask Gallus, "So? Why are you here?"

The old bodyguard grinned at me through the several streams of water that cascaded off his hood down in front of his face from the downpour.

"Well," he began, "I actually have a letter from your father, but," he glanced up at the sky, and continued, "this probably isn't the best time to read it. As far as how I got here?" He shrugged and explained, "Because you and this mob in the wagon are slower than honey on a freezing day."

This was something I certainly could not argue; instead, I asked, "Just give me the short version. If you're here, I'm assuming that matters with Gundorix went….?"

I did not finish the question, although I did not need to, as Gallus confirmed, "They went about as well as any of us could have hoped."

"Really?" It might sound strange, but I was skeptical, because I had never expressed what my desired outcome of all the machinations would be.

"He's dead," he said, proving me wrong. "That's what you wanted, isn't it?"

"Pretty much," I admitted.

"But there's more." Gallus' words were delivered with that kind of smug tone when one man knows something the other does not. "Poplicola's dead too."

This was unexpected, although I thought it might have been a possibility, especially since I had misunderstood him, sure I heard "the" before the name and "are" after it; I blame the rain. When the Poplicola brothers, thinking they had been cheated by Gundorix, confronted him, I was aware that any confrontation would be violent. Therefore, I did not think it out of the realm of possibility that during the clash, the former gladiator who, it should be remembered, had gone undefeated in the arena, would be able to kill both of the brothers, even if one of them managed to mortally wound him, as it seemed clear had happened.

"How did their father take it?" I asked him. "Is he liable to make trouble?"

My answer came in the form of no answer, at least at first. When he did not reply immediately, I glanced over at him to see him looking back at me, an expression I could not easily identify on his face.

"Didn't you hear me?" he finally asked.

"Yes," I replied, "you said the Poplicolas are dead."

"No," he shook his head, sending drops of water shooting off in different directions than the downpour, "that's not what I said. I said Poplicola, as in the old man, is dead."

This was not only unexpected, it took me a moment to try and comprehend his words, except I quickly realized I could not.

"Wait." This time, it was my head shaking and sending the spray in every direction from my own hood. "That doesn't make sense. How could he be dead?"

"Because," he responded dryly, the only dry thing in that conversation, "his sons killed him."

I stared at him; part of me did not believe him, yet the rational part of me knew, and most importantly, trusted Gallus, and understood he would not say something that was not true.

"But…how?"

"If you'd shut up," Gallus said equably, "I'd tell you."

For someone like me and Sextus, who not only love but respect their father, hearing Gallus describe the chain of events that, admittedly, I had started when I first conceived my plan, was both hard to understand and horrible at the same time. As I mentioned earlier, while Vulso's actual role was small, it was crucial, and it was based on a piece of information Sextus had supplied when he told me how Gundorix had been able to manipulate bouts like the one that had seen Peristo slain. It had not required any dark magic, or sacrifices to the gods who control the evil arts; ultimately, it had come down to Gundorix using some sort of concoction that had dulled the wits and reflexes of certain gladiators. The task I set for Vulso was to discover the method of delivery by Gundorix, then to figure out a way to switch out Gundorix's elixir for one of his own making. Obviously, he had been successful, because the gladiator who Gundorix had assured the Poplicola brothers would lose his match not only won, but according to Gallus, slew his opponent. The Poplicola brothers, in their bid to show their father he was wrong in his assessment of their abilities, had apparently put every *sestertius* they could scrape together on the match. Most crucially, they borrowed money to place their bet, sure they would be in for a huge payoff. Instead, they were wiped out, and consequently, were forced to go to Tata Poplicola on bended knee to beg for the funds to pay off their debts. From what Gallus put together in the aftermath of all that happened, the Poplicola *paterfamilias* went into, in my opinion, a justifiably towering rage at his two sons, not just because of the scope of the loss, but because of to whom the Poplicola brothers owed part of the money. In order to keep their wagering secret from their father, they had approached the elder Poplicola's most hated rival, a man who had been vying with Poplicola for control of all of the illegal or illicit activities in Arelate and the surrounding countryside for years. Forced to approach this man he hated, Poplicola beggared himself to pay the man off; at least, this was the word on the back streets of Arelate. Even worse, from what Gallus had gleaned, was that Poplicola's rival had forced the *paterfamilias* to meet him in the forum of the town, where his shame could be viewed by anyone who happened to be there at the moment. While Gallus did not go into more detail, I was willing to wager my own large sum that the witnesses to this humiliation were not a random collection of citizens who just happened to be in the forum at the right time, but had been specifically invited by Poplicola's rival so they could bear witness to what had to be a supremely satisfying moment. At least, this is what I would have done. Understandably, the senior Poplicola was unhappy with these developments, and I am certain his sons wasted no time in laying the blame at the feet of Gundorix, who ended up being found dead, with not only his throat slit, but his hands and tongue missing, and his genitals stuffed in his mouth. This alone would have been enough to make me breathe easier, especially because Gallus insisted the Pullus name had never been uttered in any way related to the events that had transpired.

However, there was one final surprise, and I must say if not necessarily pleasant, then it was at least fortunate for my family.

"Apparently," Gallus told me, "the brothers weren't happy about being forced to listen their Tata drone on and on about how stupid they were and how they weren't worth an amphora of his piss."

This was something I could easily understand; I certainly had grown tired of seeing my father's finger shaking in my face as he chastised me for things like fur-lined leather gloves. However, it would have never even occurred to me to take the steps the brothers had with their own father.

"One night," Gallus went on, "from what I heard, the wine had been flowing in that *taverna* of theirs." He seemed to fumble for the name, so I supplied it.

"Den of the Faun."

"Yes, that's it." He nodded, then thought to add, "I always thought it was a stupid name. Who wants to drink and fuck whores around some fauns anyway?"

"Gallus," I interrupted, "you were saying…"

"Ah, right." He did look a bit embarrassed at his rambling. "Well, as I was saying, the wine had been flowing, right enough. But then their Tata shows up, and when he sees them drinking and debauching like nothing had ever happened, well," he gave a laugh, "I'm sure you can imagine he didn't take it well. 'What are you lazy, good-for-nothing wastes of flesh doing?' he said. 'It's bad enough you ruined me, now you want to drink away what little bit we have left!'" He glanced over, as if to make sure I was still paying attention, and seeing I was, he continued, "From what those who were there said, it wasn't as much what the old man was saying as the fact that he was bellowing this at the top of his lungs, not just to the brothers, but in front of all their friends. So," he finished with a shrug, "they jumped up and carved him into little, bloody bits."

He stopped then, but I was sure he was just pausing to take a breath, or perhaps give me a chance to absorb this, except he remained silent.

"And?" I finally demanded. "What happened to them?"

"Oh." He looked startled, as if it had not occurred to him that I would be interested in hearing what happened to the two brothers who murdered their father, all because of a scheme I had set into motion. "Yes, well, they were arrested, and they're going on trial for patricide."

"Do you know when the trial is?" I asked him, but he shook his head.

Then I could see Gallus was done; he had told me everything he knew, and it was more than enough. We rode alongside each other in silence, and I know I for one was lost in thought. While my primary goal had been to rid Vulso, and my family, of Gundorix, while I thought it was likely that at least one, if not both of the Poplicola boys would come out on the losing end in the attempt to get revenge on Gundorix, which I had been sure they would do, my assumption had been it would be at the hands of the former gladiator. While I cannot say I cared all that much for the elder Poplicola, neither did I have anything against him, and honestly, if the brothers had emerged unscathed from any possible conflict with Gundorix, I felt confident that, at the least, they would be more cautious about who they approached to try and enlist in their own schemes and plots. Having said that, neither can I say I would be losing any sleep over what had happened to the family Poplicola; of one thing I was sure, and that was men who slay their own father are not long for this world once they commit the crime. Still, one cannot cook hen eggs without cracking the shell, so by the next morning, I had put it out of my mind. Frankly, I had other things to think about.

Chapter 4

"You made it with a day to spare. That's...good."

Those were the words from the mouth of my Primus Pilus, yet he did not seem all that happy Sextus and I had returned in time. I suppose he had been looking forward to the money he could have squeezed out of us. This was something else I could not dwell on because I was more worried about why I was standing in front of him in the first place. It is highly unusual for a Primus Pilus of a Legion to bother with the comings and goings of rankers, even when they are in his Century like I was; the only way I would have understood my presence being demanded by Atticus was in the event I returned late, except I had not, nor was my brother summoned to this meeting, which at least told me it was unrelated to our leave taking. In short, I was confused, which in turn meant I was extremely wary. And Atticus, who I could tell saw my unease, seemed in no hurry to inform me of the reason, choosing instead to ask me about our trip and what Arelate was like, since he had never been there. However, while I was forthcoming, it was only to a point, since I saw no need to apprise him of our troubles, small as they were, on the road, nor that we had been involved in an affair that ended up with at least two men already dead and two more, in the form of the Poplicola brothers, in all likelihood soon to follow. I was becoming increasingly tense, as Atticus seemed determined to rattle on about all manner of unimportant things, then finally, he got to the point of my summons, although it was indirectly.

"So you heard about the bloody flux that swept through camp?" he asked me.

Even if I had not heard about it on the road, we had arrived the afternoon before, meaning I had more than enough time for my comrades to supply all the details. Honestly, I was just relieved that none of my section had been claimed by the flux, even if two had come down with it but had survived. When I assured him I had, he did not respond right away, instead choosing to eye me, as if he was measuring up a side of beef and deciding how much meat could be cut from the bones.

Finally, he went on, "As it happens, you're actually in a bit of luck because of that flux." I did not take his meaning, yet he obviously did not believe me, because his laugh was not kind as he mocked, "Oh, come now, Pullus! Surely you're joking! I know how ambitious you are, so I don't doubt you know that the flux claimed men in both the Centurionate and the Optionate. Which means," he paused again, and I suspected he was deliberately tormenting me now that I had a hint of where this was going, "you're no longer third on the list for Optio."

The last word has still hanging in the air when my heart started beating furiously, worrying me that he would be able to see my tunic hopping about like I had trapped a small animal underneath it that was trying to escape.

"Sir?" The word felt strange, but I was determined to tread carefully, hence my speech was slower than normal. "What exactly does that mean? Am I at the top of the list now? Or second?"

"If you were, do you think we'd be having this conversation?" he asked evenly. "No, you're technically eligible for promotion as of this moment."

I did not miss his use of a word that told me he was, in fact, dangling a big, fat piece of bait above me, waiting to see how high I was willing to jump. If only, I thought bitterly, Tata hadn't just lectured me about not spending money, because I was now at least sure why I was standing in front of my Primus Pilus.

I almost blurted out, "How much?" Instead, I managed, "Sir, it sounds like there's more to this than me just being eligible for promotion. Do you have some sort of…reservations about my promotion?"

It is difficult to adequately convey how wonderful it made me feel to see the look of first surprise, then discomfiture cross the face of my Primus Pilus, and I hope I can be excused for feeling a bit smug. Oh, how I wished it could have lasted longer.

"Reservations?" Atticus repeated, and I am sure he was trying to delay answering, then he went on, "No, not exactly. You are certainly qualified for promotion, and the truth is you're going to be promoted because we need to fill the empty slots for Optios." Shaking his head, he seemed to regain his equilibrium, at least if the smile he gave me was any indication. "No, it's not about you being promoted. It's about where to put you. Because," I could tell he was trying to sound casual, but he was not fooling me, "we have two possibilities about where I can send you. And if it were me, I'd say one possibility was more…attractive than the other."

Ah, I thought, now I understand; he's trying to see how much I'd be willing to pay for a slot in the more "attractive" Century and Cohort.

"May I ask what my choices are?" I asked him.

He surprised me when he shook his head, and replied, "No, there's no need for that. After all," the smile returned, "if you're as devoted to the Legion as I've always believed, what does it matter?"

"It matters," I answered, careful to remain pleasant, "because it will tell me how much…devotion I'll need." Thinking this might have been too blatant, I thought to add, "Either way I can assure you that I'll do my utmost to show you that you've made the right decision, Primus Pilus. But," I shrugged, "it's hard to make an informed decision without all the information."

Atticus considered this, or at least seemed to, yet whether it was a pose or not, he relented.

"Very well," he said finally, "I can see your point." Pausing for an instant, he supplied my choices. "The Sixth of the First."

Apparently, he wanted to allow this to sink in because, again, he did not say anything for several heartbeats as he carefully studied my reaction. Which, I must confess, was difficult for me to suppress, and once more, I was sure my own body would betray me, particularly since I could see at the bottom of my vision that my tunic was now clearly fluttering. I am thankful, however, because Atticus remained silent long enough to allow me to understand that, as good and tempting as this spot was, it meant the alternative he offered would be as bad as this one was good.

Consequently, I was at least somewhat prepared when he supplied the other, saying, "The First of the Ninth."

Despite the fact that I was partially prepared, I freely admit that this was even worse than I expected, although my suspicion was it would be the Ninth Cohort. That I would be under the direct command of the Nones Pilus Prior, without the buffer of another Centurion from one of the subordinate Centuries, was about the worst possible spot I could have drawn. Therefore, it was a struggle for me to maintain at least the outward appearance of impassivity, but I did not have much confidence I was fooling Atticus in the slightest.

Finally, I managed to say, "As you say, Primus Pilus, it poses an…interesting dilemma." Up to this moment, I had been behaving in the normal manner of a ranker when in front of his Primus Pilus, looking at a spot above him, except now I looked him directly in the eye and asked him quietly, "How much for the Sixth of the First?"

As I hoped, this seemed to rattle Atticus, and he looked distinctly uncomfortable, despite the fact that we were alone; Crito was in the outer office and Atticus' body slaves were similarly missing.

"Well," he cleared his throat, "yes, well, that depends on you. Doesn't it?" This seemed to help him restore his confidence, and the smile returned as he asked, "How much are you willing to pay for the post?" Now that he had his feet back under him, Atticus gave an exaggerated shrug as he turned and began pacing behind his desk, pretending to be thinking. "If it were me," he mused aloud; personally, I thought the rubbing of his chin was overdoing it, "I'd be willing to pay….whatever it took. Say…eight thousand *sesterces*?"

I thought I had prepared myself, but I was wrong, and I was unable to contain the gasp that burst from my lips.

"Eight *thousand*?" I shook my head. "I'm sorry, Primus Pilus, I can't pay that much."

"Can't?" Atticus echoed, looking at me with a raised eyebrow. "Or won't? Because," the change in tone of his voice was subtle but unmistakable, "that's not what my information indicates. And I remember," he pointed out, "how quickly you were able to come up with the money, not just for your own post but for Asinius as well.

Who," I am not sure why he added this, "I must admit has turned out to be the best Optio I've ever had. But," he waved a dismissive hand, "that's beside the point. So," the Primus Pilus was clearly back on the offensive, "do you wish to reconsider that answer?"

"No, sir," I answered, albeit through gritted teeth. "I'm afraid your information is wrong. I had to borrow that money in the first place. And," I lied, "I'm still paying off the debt."

"Really?" Atticus sounded surprised, but the leaden feeling in my stomach gave the lie to it, which he confirmed. "That's surprising, since I made some inquiries in Siscia. And," he named the plutocrat with whom my family did business, "assured me that you had managed to pay off that substantial loan very quickly. So quickly," he chuckled, "the man seemed quite put out that he wasn't able to squeeze even more money from you since you paid it off within the agreed amount of time."

"He told you that?" I gasped. I am afraid my composure was shattered. "He's not supposed to divulge anything about any of his clients!"

"No, he's not," Atticus agreed. "But I'm your Primus Pilus, and I was concerned you had gotten yourself into trouble of some sort. You understand, this was before I'd gotten to know you," he added helpfully, "and you were very young to be handling that much money. I was just making sure your ambition didn't put you in a bad position."

I have always found it especially difficult in situations where men are speaking duplicitously to me; it is even more challenging when I am forced to play along, as I was at this moment. I was, and still am, sure that the only honest thing Atticus had said was he went snooping in town and somehow discovered the identity of our plutocrat. The idea that concern for my welfare played any part in his snooping was a total fiction, yet I felt compelled to play along, if only to buy myself some time.

"That's very…heartwarming to hear, sir," I was awash in conflicting emotions; proud that I was able to lie right back, and disgusted with myself for doing so. "I'm happy to hear you've taken such an interest in my welfare."

"Don't get a big head now, Pullus." He chuckled, and I could tell he was enjoying himself thoroughly, which only made me hate him more. "I'm no more concerned about you than any of the men in the Legion." His smile vanished as if it had never been there, and he stared at me coldly. "But that's in the past. What's at question now is how badly you want to be in the Sixth of the First."

"May I have some time to think it over, sir?" I asked him, but while I was not expecting him to agree, he surprised me considerably.

"Of course," he said genially. "This is a big decision! I completely understand! Take as much time as you need!" He paused, then added, "As long as it's not too long. Let's say...by tomorrow? At this time?"

Swallowing hard, I understood this was as much as I could expect from him, so I agreed, pretending I had a choice. I saluted him, then when he dismissed me, I turned and marched out of his office, trying very hard to walk steadily and not weave about as if I was drunk. At least, this was my intent, but just before I reached the door, Atticus called to me.

"Oh, and, Pullus?" I turned, knowing I was not going to like whatever came out of his mouth. "To this point, I haven't believed it necessary to report to the Princeps that I have a man in my Legion who seems to have more money than a man of his station has any right to, especially someone related to Titus Pullus." Something in my face must have prompted him to add, "Oh, I know all about your grandfather's elevation to the equestrian order. And I know that the Princeps confiscated most of the money that's required for elevation. And yet, you still seem to have money." The Primus Pilus raised his hands in what I suppose was a helpless gesture, as if he had no choice in the matter. "That seems to be something the Princeps should know, after all. You understand, surely."

I did not bother replying, suddenly beyond caring how he reacted. When I left the Legion office, I did not go directly back to my hut, choosing instead to take the long way around as I tried to think of a way out of this. The elation I should have been feeling at being promoted was completely gone, leaving only the bitter taste that comes from being used as a piece in the game, played by my Primus Pilus.

Perhaps it was the mention of my current Optio's name that prompted me to seek him out, although it took a bit of time. I finally found him out on the training ground, working the stakes on his own; the rest of the Century was scattered about the camp on a number of small working parties, from which I had been excused for my meeting with Atticus. Seeing me approach, he stopped what he was doing; the sweat that covered his upper body making him shine in the sunlight. We were in that time between spring and summer, where we could still expect a few more cold nights and perhaps a freak storm that brought snow, but this day was a warm one, which was why Asinius had stripped to the waist.

"When you're in third position, your arm is out too far, Optio," I told him by way of greeting, which prompted a scowl from him.

"According to you," he growled; it was a topic of much debate between the two of us in my role of weapons instructor, and it was one of the few areas where we were not of a like mind. "But it works fine for me."

"It's a bad habit because it isolates your sword hand out too far from your body," I retorted, then when he opened his mouth to argue the point, I hurried on, "but that's not why I'm here. I need to ask your advice on something."

"So the Primus Pilus has spoken to you," he replied, dropping the *rudis* on the ground and grabbing a cloth he used to towel off his upper body.

"He has," I confirmed. While I was not surprised Asinius knew, what I was unsure of was the depth of his knowledge, prompting me to ask, "Do you know what my two choices are?"

"No." He shook his head, then spat on the ground. "That's not something the Primus Pilus deemed to be something I should know. Which," he added in a careful tone, "is certainly within his rights."

Anyone who did not know Asinius was unlikely to determine the Optio's true feelings from his statement, but I had known the man for some time, and I knew him well, so I could tell there was an undercurrent of anger in his tone. I told him the choice the Primus Pilus had laid at my feet, as well as the price he was demanding, and despite everything, I felt at least a flicker of pleasure at the look of dismay that crossed my first Sergeant's features.

"That...*bastard*," he muttered, yet while his tone was soft, I still felt a stab of anxiety as I glanced over at the men nearest to us who were also working on their forms; fortunately, they were too absorbed in their exercises to pay us any attention. "I've known he was greedy ever since we had to pay him when he took over, but eight *thousand sesterces*?" Sighing, he shook his head again, then asked, "So what are you going to do?"

"That's why I'm standing here," I snapped, the stress of my looming decision fraying my already strained nerves. "I was hoping you could tell me!"

Asinius did not reply, at least immediately; he instead gazed at me steadily and I was regretting my outburst, aimed at a man whose help I was seeking.

"I wish I could," he finally broke the silence, "but I honestly don't know."

I was about to utter some sort of surly retort, then thought better of it, and we stood in silence for several heartbeats.

"If," he spoke first, "you buy the post in the Sixth, what do you think will happen?"

"You mean, other than my father skinning me alive?" I replied dryly, but I considered for a moment, actually thinking about it for the first time since I had stumbled out of Atticus' office. "Well," I concluded, "the good thing is that it'll keep Atticus from carrying out his threat to let the Princeps know about my family's...situation."

As I glanced over at Asinius to gauge his reaction, my stomach suddenly seemed to twist over on itself at his expression of doubt.

"That," he finally said, "might be true. But I don't know if I'd be so sure about that."

This surprised and disturbed me in equal measure, so I asked him to explain his thinking.

"What do you know about all that's been happening in Rome?" he asked me.

I told him what little bit I had heard in the inn during our return journey.

"That's true," he granted, but continued, "as far as it goes. But the possibility of Tiberius' return has apparently created quite a furor in Rome among the upper classes."

"Why?" I was genuinely mystified.

"Because there are some who believe that Tiberius' return is just the first step in his plan to force Augustus to name him as heir," he explained.

I considered this, yet while I could see the logic, and actually agreed with Asinius' assessment there would be some who would view Tiberius' actions in the most sinister light possible, I still did not see how this was connected to my dilemma, and I said as much.

"Let's say," Asinius replied, "that this is actually true, that Tiberius is determined to claim what he sees as his just reward for his service to the Princeps…"

"You mean to Rome," I cut in. "What Tiberius did was for Rome, not one man."

Asinius gazed levelly at me for a moment, then asked, "You don't think that Augustus believes that service to Rome and service to him are one and the same thing?"

Instantly, I understood his point, and I nodded at him to continue.

"What kind of leverage would Tiberius have that might prompt the Princeps to name him as heir?" he asked me.

He did not have to expand on this because I instantly understood, at least I thought I did.

"His hold over the army." I breathed the words even as my mind turned this over. "Particularly the Legions he's commanded, especially the Legions on the Rhenus."

"And here," Asinius pointed out. "Augustus is likely to consider us as part of Tiberius' support."

"But there's the Legions in Hispania. And Africa and Syria," I pointed out. "Tiberius has never commanded any of them, so they outnumber us."

"And how long would it take for Augustus to summon those Legions? And what kind of turmoil would there be in those spots if the army really disappeared from their posts to come to the aid of the

Princeps? Meanwhile, how long would it take the Legions on this side of Our Sea to march on Rome? If that's what Tiberius asked of us?"

"I don't think Tiberius would do that," I offered, but I admit Asinius had certainly planted the seed of doubt, and I was beginning to understand where he was taking this conversation. "But if he did," I went on, "Augustus would want to know how many Legions would stay loyal to him, and how many to Tiberius."

"And what better way for our beloved Primus Pilus to prove his loyalty…?" Asinius began, but I finished, "…than by throwing him the truth about me and my family." I closed my eyes and took a deep breath. "And the fact that we somehow managed to have more money than he thought would make it doubly sweet for him, to tie up this last untied knot that's my family and my Avus."

I understood it was not his intent to make me feel worse, yet I did nonetheless, and I suppose my expression was one of such misery, he put a hand on my shoulder to offer some comfort.

"Honestly," I mused, "I might be fucked either way I go, then."

It was a bitter, bitter draught to swallow, although it did provide me with a bit more clarity, and while it was not until later that I realized it, I made my decision right then, or at least the bare bones of how I would approach things. However, at this particular time, my mind was still racing as I returned to the section hut, which was deserted. Frankly, I welcomed the solitude, at least for the moment, and I sat at the long table to think. This was the first moment, of many to come, where I really missed the counsel of Diocles; I had actually found my feet initially taking me out of camp but in the direction of town, not the stakes, so accustomed to going to our Greek freedman as my first source of advice that my muscles seemed to guide me, much as they did at the stakes. But he was gone, and I admit my eyes filled with tears as the true scope of the loss of Diocles from my life demonstrated itself in a tangible way for what was the first but would not be the last time. Following closely on the heels of this sense of loss was another one, yet while it was in a more intangible manner, it was no less important, and that was the wisdom and knowledge contained in the dozen scrolls that contain the account of the life of Titus Pullus. I had often remembered bits and extracts from those scrolls that I used as a guide, but for some reason, at this moment, I truly missed the presence of the scrolls themselves, sure that if I could have just consulted them, the answer to my dilemma would be contained therein. After all the challenges and dangers my Avus faced, especially in this arena of Roman politics, I ardently believed that the best solution to my dilemma was probably located somewhere in those scrolls. Yet I did not have them, so instead, I tried to recall as much as I could from his account, desperately seeking guidance. Obviously, I sat there for some time, although it did not seem that way, because the door burst open, and my comrades from the section came filing in.

"Pullus, you lucky bastard," Metellus called out, "where were you when we were mucking out the stables?"

"Where do you think?" This came from Balbinus, whose thin, sallow face twisted into a sneer. "Right where you see him now, sitting on his ass."

Honestly, I cannot say I would have reacted much differently if I had been in a better frame of mind, but I would like to think so. My recollection is that I somehow went from sitting at my normal spot at the table to having a fistful of Balbinus' tunic, our faces separated by no more than a hand's breadth as I shook him so hard, I suspect his teeth rattled.

"I'm your fucking Sergeant, you ignorant, inbred *cunnus*," I snarled at him, and the look of stark terror in his eyes as I handled him as easily as a dog does a rat was deeply satisfying.

I felt a hand on my bicep, and I turned my head to see Domitius standing there, the only man unafraid of me when I was in this state.

"Sergeant Pullus," his use of my rank, I know now, was calculated, and it was a good maneuver, "Gregarius Balbinus meant no disrespect." He turned to look directly at the man whose feet were dangling an inch above the wooden floor. "Did you, Balbinus?"

"N-n-no," my nemesis stammered. "I didn't! I s-s-swear it, Sergeant! I didn't mean anything by it! I was just…"

"You were just," I supplied for him, although my sudden ire was cooling off, "talking when you shouldn't have been. Right, Balbinus?"

Even as I was speaking, I released my grasp of his tunic, dropping his feet back to the floor and he landed with a substantial thudding sound that, personally speaking, I found quite gratifying.

"Yes, Sergeant," he assured me, and while he opened his eyes as wide as he could to show his sincerity, it was the sheen of sweat on his upper lip that made me feel better. "I wasn't thinking. Just talking!"

"That's a bad habit of yours, isn't it, Balbinus?" I asked him; my tone was pleasant, yet neither he nor any of the others were fooled, and I felt Domitius' glare, although I ignored it.

"It is, Sergeant," he agreed fervently.

"Then at least we've identified something you need to work on," I told him genially. Turning to Domitius, I continued to ignore his look of displeasure. "I need to talk to you. In private."

Without waiting, I walked the length of the hut, not bothering to look back to see if he was following because I knew he was. Exiting the hut, I stood in the street as he followed a few paces behind me, but as he approached, I saw his mind was still on what had just taken place.

"Titus," he snapped at me, completely uncaring about our difference in rank, which was another reason I valued his friendship, "that was completely unnecessary! Balbinus wasn't doing anything different than he normally does! He was just running his mouth!"

"I wasn't in the mood today," was my only explanation, then before he could make an issue of it, I continued, "I've got a decision to make, and it impacts you as well, so I want to talk to you about it."

"About your promotion," he interrupted me. "I know about it."

There was no reason I should have been surprised, but at this point in my day, I did not need much excuse to be nettled, and I snapped, "Pluto's cock! Is there anyone who *doesn't* know?"

"No," he replied immediately, in such a way I could not stop myself from laughing, although I did give him a playful shove.

"And do you know *where* I'm supposed to be going?" I challenged him, and was somewhat mollified when he shook his head.

"That," he admitted, "I don't know. And from what I've been able to find out, nobody does but the Primus Pilus." Domitius looked up at me sharply, then added, "And you, obviously."

"I do," I replied, then told him essentially the same as I had told Asinius.

My close comrade and best friend's reaction was to whistle, his face grave as he said, "That's a tough choice."

"I know," I acknowledged, "but I've thought about it, and I think I've decided what I'm going to do. But," I made my tone hard because what I was about to say was important, "I want your promise that you'll go along with my decision."

"I can't do that," he protested. "At least, not without knowing what it is!"

"You can," I insisted, "and you will. So, promise me!"

"No!" Domitius shook his head stubbornly; at least, this was how I viewed it. "I'm not promising to something I don't know anything about."

"Fine," I sighed in exasperation. "I'll tell you."

And I did. The fact that he listened intently, without interrupting, was troubling to me because I suspected I knew the reason for it. Once I finished, he did not hesitate in confirming my suspicion.

"That," he said bluntly, "is one of the worst ideas I've ever heard."

Normally, anyone saying something this pointed to me would have been guaranteed a similar response in return, yet somehow, I managed to maintain control of my tongue; I suppose this was due in large part to the fact that I knew he was correct, and how much I respected him.

Therefore, instead of arguing, I simply asked him, "All right. What should I do?"

"Pay the money," he responded instantly, except when I explained the things Asinius and I had spoken about, his confident expression vanished.

"I hadn't looked at it that way," he admitted.

Rather than simply take credit for this line of thought, I told him, "Neither did I, Titus. It was Asinius who brought it up."

"That," he rubbed the back of his neck as he stared down at his feet, "makes sense. Asinius is a very clever man. So," he tilted his head to look back up at me, "I take back what I said." He paused for a moment, then grinned and added, "But only partially. Now it's just a bad idea, not the worst one."

As I am sure he intended, I had to laugh at that.

"It's a risk either way I go," I agreed, "but at least this way, I'm the one choosing my poison."

With nothing left to be said, we returned to the hut, where I spent a restless night tossing about in my bunk, making enough of a racket that Domitius grumbled at me to either stop or go sleep elsewhere. I managed to stop, but not sleep.

"I'm sorry, would you repeat that?" Primus Pilus Atticus' mouth was hanging open, and I felt at least a glimmer of satisfaction at his clear stupefaction.

"Of course, sir." I had to concentrate on keeping an even tone. "I said, I've chosen the First of the Ninth for my post."

"But…why?" It was a rare moment, seeing the normally implacable Primus Pilus so bewildered. "Why would you choose the Ninth over staying in the First Cohort?"

"Because I don't have the necessary funds to purchase the post in the Sixth," I answered.

For reasons I can only guess, this seemed to banish part of his confusion, but it was replaced by, at the very least, irritation.

"That's not true and we both know it," he growled at me. Pointing a finger, he accused me, "You're just doing this to spite me!"

"Sir?" Now I borrowed Atticus' expression of bewilderment, or at least attempted to as I protested, "Why would I do this just to spite you? Primus Pilus," I tried to be as earnest as I could without it ringing completely false to my own ears, "I don't know where you got your information from about how wealthy my family is, but it's not correct."

Atticus glared at me, saying nothing for several heartbeats, but when he was the one who broke the silence, I was completely unprepared for what came out of his mouth.

"Then how much can you afford to pay for the post?"

Suddenly I was not only confused, I was worried, because I thought he had suddenly decided that taking the worst posting in the Optionate of the 8th Legion was something for which he felt justified being paid.

This was what prompted me to ask him, "Which one?"

"The one in the First, of course," he snapped.

Shaking my head, I insisted, "Primus Pilus, it doesn't matter how much it costs. I simply don't have the money. Bear in mind," I decided on a half-truth, "that my brother and I just went halfway across the Republic and back, and that's expensive."

Atticus kept his eyes fixed on me, and there was nothing even remotely friendly in them.

"Very well," he finally sighed, disgustedly throwing the stylus he had been twisting about in his hand as we talked onto his desk. "You win. Or," he gave a harsh chuckle, "you lose, if I'm being honest. It's the First of the Ninth for you." His lips pulled back in a grimace when he uttered this, as if he was actually tasting the defeat; at least, so I thought, yet this was not the case, as he was about to reveal. "It's no secret that it's the worst Cohort in the Legion. I'd even wager it's the worst in the Army of Pannonia."

It was an astonishing admission for a Primus Pilus to make to anyone, let alone someone like me who was so far subordinate to him. I suppose it was what emboldened me, thinking that if we were pulling up our tunics, as we like to say, I might as well join in.

"Why can't you…fix it?" I asked.

For a bare instant, I was sure I had committed a terrible blunder, because the unfriendly demeanor returned and he fixed me with his cold stare, while I realized I was holding my breath.

Apparently, so was he, because he let out an explosive snort, then actually answered me, "Since you're heading there, you might as well know the truth. I can't fix it because your new Pilus Prior has…friends in high places. So," he shrugged, "I'm stuck with him." Atticus gave me an evil grin then. "But I'm not as stuck as you're going to be." The smile fled his face so quickly that it might have been my imagination it was there in the first place. "Now that you know there's no chance of things changing in the Ninth, are you *sure* you can't suddenly *find* some money somewhere?"

I admit I was tempted, but I had resolved to myself that I would not, could not waver in my choice, and I said as much, exposing me to another of my Primus Pilus' glares of anger before he dismissed me by way of a disgusted wave. Despite the lack of formality, I was determined not to give him anything else he could use to chew on me, executing a formal about turn, then marched across the room. I had already begun the mental process of resigning myself to a posting in what men liked to joke was in the vestibule of Hades, the First of the Ninth Cohort.

Then, just as I was about to pull the door open, Atticus called out, "Pullus!"

What now? I thought as I turned back about, sure he had just thought up something new and original about the Ninth with which to torment me. However, while Atticus was never the riddle that his predecessor had been, he was still capable of surprising at least me, which he proceeded to do now.

"You're not going to the First of the Ninth," he spoke just loudly enough for me to hear him. Closing his eyes for an instant, he sighed, "That would be a waste of your abilities, and while the Ninth may be hopeless, I want my other Cohorts to be better than any of the others in the army. You're going to the Sixth after all."

Now it was my turn to stand open-mouthed, my hand still on the latch of the door, and I actually felt physically dizzy at the sudden reversal in my fortunes.

"T-thank you, Primus Pilus," I began, but he cut me off with a short, chopping motion of his hand.

"I don't need your thanks," he snapped. Leaning forward on one elbow, he extended his other hand to point at me as he said harshly, "You better not fuck this up, Pullus. I will be *very* unhappy if you prove to be lacking in any way. So much so that I'll be more than happy to do whatever I need to in order to rectify my mistake. Are we clear?"

"Yes, sir." Just to be safe, I snapped to *intente* and assured him, "I won't let you down."

"You already have," he muttered sourly.

Then, he seemed to resign himself, because instead of his stylus, he actually took a quill and dipped it into the inkpot and scribbled what I felt sure was his signature on a vellum scroll, on which the most important documents are recorded, and that it was my promotion warrant he was signing.

As he finished, he looked up and said, "I'm sending Crito with your warrant to the *praetorium* and suggesting it take effect immediately. From what I've been told, you're acquainted with your Hastatus Posterior."

"Yes, sir," I replied, still trying to come to grips with my new reality. "Hastatus Posterior Galens was my..."

"Yes, yes, yes," he cut me off, irritated. "I'm well aware of how connected all of you veterans of Pannonia are, and you in particular. I don't have any desire to hear about how wonderful it will be to be reunited with him."

"No, sir." I was not sure what to say, so I decided to ask, "Am I dismissed?"

All I got was another wave; it did not seem Primus Pilus Atticus was in the mood for any other conversation. I had walked in a Sergeant in the First Cohort and I was leaving as an Optio, but what I had not anticipated in the slightest was that it would be in the Cohort of my dreams. As I either walked, or floated out of the Legion office, I remember thinking, now all I have to do is figure out a way to get Domitius out of the First Century and into the Sixth. It never occurred to me, at least in the moment, that Domitius might have wanted to stay put.

It was true Aulus Galens had been my Optio when I was in the First Century of the Fourth Cohort, but our former Primus Pilus had promoted him into the First Cohort as part of a deal forced on him by my former Pilus Prior Gnaeus Corvinus that also saw Appius Asinius become my Optio not long after my transfer into the First of the First. Galens' elevation from Optio all the way into the First Cohort had been unusual, yet he had clearly acquitted himself in such an exemplary manner that when Atticus took over the Legion, he had found no cause to replace him. My enthusiasm and joy at being reunited with my former Optio was tempered by the memory of my introduction to the First of the Fourth, when I arrived from Arelate as a fresh-faced youngster, eager to become a *Tirone*. In fact, it had been

Galens who was there waiting for me outside the *praetorium* once I had finished the process of signing the enlistment document, and it was remembering how he knocked me off my feet with a single punch that I am afraid was foremost in my mind as I approached the Sixth Century's office. While I did not think he would greet me in the same manner now that I was his Optio, it was still with some trepidation I entered the outer office of his quarters. Seated at the single desk was a clerk I knew by sight; he introduced himself as Pridaxes, and he was on the young side, at least to be a clerk of a Century of the First Cohort.

"We've been expecting you, Optio Pullus," Pridaxes stood up, a smile on his face that I barely noticed as my mind tried to adjust to what my ears had just heard.

Pridaxes was the first man to actually address me by my new rank, and it was a wonderfully confusing thing to hear, so it took me a moment to react.

"Is that my new Optio?" I instantly recognized Galens' voice, which sounded like a man constantly battling a sore throat. "Get in here, idiot! Let me see how the gods have fucked me this time!"

While I was somewhat certain he was jesting, I was unsure enough to march in, keeping my eyes above his head, then stopping in front of his desk to render as perfect a salute as I could manage. To this point, I had performed perfectly, which of course meant I was about to mangle the moment.

"Sergeant Titus…er…Optio Titus Pullus reporting as ordered, Hastatus Posterior Galens."

Making matters worse, I winced at my own mistake, and Galens pounced.

"First, you don't even know what fucking rank you are, then you make faces at me?" I saw his head shake back and forth, although I somehow managed to maintain my gaze at the wall behind my new Centurion. Leaning to look past me, he called to the clerk, "Are you sure this is the right man, Pridaxes?"

As I mentioned, I only knew Pridaxes by sight, but I did not need to know him well to hear that he was clearly enjoying a chance to jump in with his Centurion for some fun at my expense.

"I believe so, Centurion," he called out from behind me, "but perhaps there's a mistake? Should I run to the *praetorium* and check?"

"That might be a good idea." Galens rubbed his chin, having the kind of swarthy jaw that made him look as if he always needed a shave. Then, he waved a hand, I presumed at Pridaxes, who was somewhere behind me. "But we don't have time to fuck about. So," he heaved the kind of sigh I knew was meant to convey the weight of the world upon his shoulders, "I suppose we'll just see if we can make something of this big oaf."

Only then did he stand up and move from around his desk, giving me a smile that was missing his bottom teeth as he offered his arm.

"Welcome to the Sixth of the First, Pullus. I'm happy to have you here."

It is hard for me to recall the specific order of events over the next few days as I got settled into my new post and role of Optio in a Century of the First Cohort. Suddenly, I went from being responsible for sixteen men to a hundred-sixty of them, all of them hard-bitten veterans of the Legion. I was now in my seventh year under the standard, so I was confident in my knowledge of the rhythms and life of the Legion, at least as dictated by our Primus Pilus. If I had been transferred to the 13th, the 15th, or any other Legion, for that matter, I would have been forced to relearn how things were done in that Legion. Back when my father was under the standard, the only time men were moved from one Legion to another was either in the case where the receiving Legion had been subjected to higher casualties than the one sending men, or if a man was either suffering or creating a problem whereby the only solution was to move him elsewhere. This is no longer the case, and even during my time, the movement of men from one Legion to another has become more prevalent. Not in my particular case, however, at least for this, my first big promotion; this certainly helped in my transition, because even when it is within a Legion, there is an adjustment period for both the rankers and the newly promoted man like I was then. While it may sound odd, it was a relatively minor matter that kept catching me by surprise, which was the white stripe that is sewn onto the shoulder of all

Optios' tunics. At least in my case, I kept spying that stripe in the bottom corner of my vision, and for the first several weeks at least, it tended to catch me off guard. The one event I clearly remember is the night before my first official day with my new Century. Although I had already moved my belongings to the quarters the Optio shares with the *Signifer*, Gnaeus Horatius, and the *Tesseraurius*, who at this point, was a man named Spurius Stellatinus, I walked two streets over to my now former Century, seeking out Asinius. I found him in his private quarters, filling out a series of reports, but although I knocked, once he bade entry, I strolled in and pulled up one of the two extra stools squarely in front of his desk, then dropped onto it without waiting to be given permission as would have happened just a couple days before.

While I grinned at him, he regarded me with a raised eyebrow for a moment, then with a straight face, said, "And how long have you been waiting to be able to do that?"

"Oh, about a day after I showed up."

This did prompt a laugh, then he stood and came from around the desk to offer me his arm, which I took.

"Congratulations, Pullus." His tone was quiet, but Asinius had never been overly demonstrative, and perhaps this was why his words meant that much more to me. "And I'm glad to see you decided to pay the Primus Pilus the money."

"I didn't," I answered, except he obviously did not believe me because he simply gave me a wink as he tapped the side of his nose, which prompted me to say, with some heat, "I'm telling you the truth! I didn't pay him a *sestertius*."

My former Optio examined me closely, his expression changing as he moved back around the desk, dropping heavily into his chair, as if his legs had given out from under him.

"That," he finally responded, "is strange." Evidently, I made some sort of face, because he added hastily, "Don't mistake me, Pullus. I'm happy that you didn't have to come up with the money. But you're saying he still gave you the Sixth?"

"It wasn't quite that easy," I admitted, going on to explain what had happened.

Personally, I felt justified in my pride at forcing our Primus Pilus to back down in this matter, yet Asinius clearly did not agree, which instantly worried me.

"So you called his bluff," he mused, looking down at his desk, where one of the tablets was open in front of him, although I was sure he was not seeing it. "He can't have liked that very much."

"No," I agreed, albeit reluctantly; Asinius was taking my mind down a path I did not care to go, but even then, I knew it was out of concern for me. "He was...upset."

This elicited a bark of a laugh from Asinius, although it did not hold much humor.

"I can imagine," he said dryly, then fell silent for several heartbeats, still seeming intent on whatever the report was before him. Just as I was about to break the silence, Asinius beat me to it, looking up at me with a solemn gaze as he said, "Pullus, I'm not going to lie to you. I think that this may be a case where you won a battle, but run the risk of losing the war. Like Pyrrhus," he added helpfully.

"I know who Pyrrhus is," I snapped, although I could not have articulated why I was suddenly the one who was irritated; perhaps it was because Asinius had removed the blindfold from my eyes and forced me to confront the nagging doubt that only then did I understand had been lurking there ever since Atticus signed the warrant. "Do you think," I modified my tone since I was in essence asking him for help, "it's a trap? That he's putting me in some sort of position that he's sure I'll fail?"

"No," Asinius replied quickly enough, yet there was a catch to his voice that did not comfort me in the least. "I don't think so. But I do think that this is going to turn crossways in his gullet, and it's going to eat at him." Leaning back, he regarded me for a moment before continuing, "Pullus, I'm going to tell you something that can't leave this room. Do I have your word...as an Optio of Rome?" Despite the gravity of the subject, he grinned at me, and I realized he was saying it this way on purpose.

"Yes, Optio," I intoned. "I give you my word as a fellow Optio of Rome."

The levity of the moment evaporated instantly after I said that, except instead of just coming out with it, Asinius appeared to gather his thoughts. However, while I knew this was his way, I cannot say I bore it patiently as I squirmed on the stool.

At last, he began, "I've been Atticus' Optio for more than five years now, and I've come to know the Primus Pilus better."

"That makes sense," I replied, which seemed to irritate him.

"Thank you for confirming something I already know," he said acerbically, then, "May I continue?" Naturally, I nodded, and he went on, "And there's something you need to know about the man that I've observed, which is he holds a grudge."

Honestly, at this point, I was neither surprised nor unduly alarmed; in my experience, I had met more men who did hold a grudge rather than the opposite.

Asinius went on, "And while he's not as greedy as Urso was, he's close. That's bad enough, but he has a vindictive streak that I'm afraid may come into play with you because you thwarted him."

I confess this was when my discomfort began burgeoning into concern, although I was still not completely convinced.

"If he wanted to get even with me," I pointed out, "he would have put me in the Ninth and been done with it. That would have fucked me pretty well, don't you think?"

"Yes," Asinius agreed, then added, "and no. First, having you in the Ninth would be unlikely to help your career, and I wouldn't be surprised if you finished your first enlistment still as Optio in the same spot. But that's not only slow, it's something that's outside of his control, to a point." Heaving a sigh, he looked directly into my eyes. "But if you're still here in the Cohort, he's got a lot more control over what happens to you."

I considered this for several moments, turning it over in my mind as I tried to gather my thoughts.

"So what if I went ahead and paid him the money?"

I could hardly believe my own ears, but Asinius did not look surprised in the slightest; he had clearly gotten here ahead of me. And, as I was about to learn, had already thought it through.

"That," he said flatly, "would be about the worst thing you could do at this point." He must have seen my doubt, because he pressed, "Think about it, Pullus. You already have the post. The warrant's signed and I assume it was approved by the Legate?" I nodded, so he continued, "But now you're going to offer him the money? Why, exactly?"

"Because," I admit I could feel the mule in me starting to kick, "that's what it's about! The money!" I was returning his gaze as I said this, and his own expression caused me to falter. "Isn't it?"

"It was," Asinius agreed, "but it *was* about the money. Now it's about his pride and the fact that a man twenty years younger than he is got the better of him. Besides," he finished with ultimately the most compelling reason for me to accept his argument, "if he took the money, then decided to use what he knows, or thinks he knows about your family to curry favor with the Princeps, what would be the first thing you would do?"

"Make sure the Princeps knew I had paid off Atticus," I answered miserably, because I was now convinced.

We sat together in what I can only describe as a glum silence, then I suddenly thought to ask him, "So how do you know about this vindictive side to the Primus Pilus? Did he do something to you?"

"No." Asinius shook his head. "Not to me. But do you remember when he first arrived? From Rome?"

"Not just from Rome but from the fucking Praetorians," I pointed out. "But yes, I remember."

"And do you remember how there was this mysterious other candidate for my post? Someone he knew from the Praetorian Guard?"

I assured him I did, and I admit, for an instant, I was tempted to point out that not only was I aware of it, I had been the one who outbid Asinius' competitor to purchase the post for my former Sergeant; thankfully, I dismissed it as an unworthy thing to do. While it was true Asinius had not repaid the debt, it was because I refused to accept any of his money, which was one more thing my father had not been happy to hear. Instead, I held my tongue as he explained further.

"Well, you know how it turned out, at least on this end," Asinius went on, "but while I don't know any details, our Primus Pilus was furious with my competitor. Apparently, Atticus had arranged for this other man to hand over a thousand *sesterces* to the Primus Pilus as a sign of good faith. But for whatever reason, the money never showed up."

"But," I objected, "he told us that as long as we matched the bid, Optio was yours! So why would he want this other man to just hand over a thousand *sesterces*?"

"Obviously, the poor bastard in Rome didn't know about that part," Asinius explained patiently. "But the details don't really matter; here's what does." He leaned across the desk and lowered his voice. "One night, not that long after Atticus took command, he invited me out into town as a way to get to know each other. And, let's just say," I saw the glimmer of a sardonic smile on Asinius' features, "he hadn't heard about my capacity for wine."

For the barest instant, I felt a flicker of sympathy for Atticus because I myself had been subjected to Appius Asinius' prodigious ability to drink massive quantities of wine and not have it affect him as it did lesser mortals.

"Anyway, that's the drunkest I've ever seen him. Although," he held up a hand, "we haven't gone out many times after that. But that night, Bacchus got hold of him, and he talked." Now Asinius rolled his eyes and groaned, "And I mean a *lot*. Frankly, I thought he'd never shut up."

"What did he talk about?" I asked, suddenly curious about this insight into the man who commanded our Legion, and our destinies.

"Himself," Asinius replied immediately. "Or the Princeps, but always in some sort of association with Atticus. He has a very high opinion of himself, does our Primus Pilus." Even before he said it, I knew what was coming when he grinned and added, "Like someone else I know."

"Does this story have a point?" I asked sourly.

"Yes," he laughed, "it does. And here it is. It was near the end of the night, and he had suddenly gone quiet. And I was thinking, 'Thank the *gods*,' but he wasn't through. That's when he brought up the subject of that other Praetorian." Asinius stopped smiling then, his expression changing as he told me, "And how that man had tried to outsmart Atticus somehow; he didn't say any more than that, just that this man had tried to fool Atticus. Or at least, that's how he saw it. But Atticus was quite proud of the fact that, before he left for Rome, he had planted something among this man's possessions in the event that something like this happened." Now Asinius was scowling as he recounted the story. "So our Primus Pilus sent a message to some other friend of his, one that he did trust, telling him that Atticus had become concerned about this man's activities but hadn't had time to do anything about it before being called to Siscia. He told this friend to look for this item in the man's gear that Atticus said would prove the man's guilt." Asinius paused as he sighed deeply; only then did he look back into my eyes, and his own were grim as he finished, "And everything happened just as Atticus planned. The evidence was discovered, the man was arrested, and he was brought before a Tribunal."

"And?" I really did not want to know, yet for some reason, I also felt compelled to know. "What happened to him?"

"That," Asinius replied, "I don't know with any certainty because I've only heard Atticus' side of it. And he was quite drunk by that time, and he might have been lying to begin with."

"Then what," I pressed him, "did Atticus tell you happened to him?"

He did not reply, at least verbally, just made a simple, slashing gesture across his throat, yet while I had suspected this would be it, I still felt a jolt of shock strong enough to make me gasp aloud.

"What was this piece of evidence that was so damning it got a man executed?"

Asinius did not reply immediately, choosing instead to pretend to examine the tablet once more, although I managed to wait him out.

Seeing this, he relented, at least partly, asking me, "Do you know the duties of the Praetorians?"

"To keep order in Rome," I said after thinking about it, because frankly, I did not know that much about them, at least then. I had an afterthought and added, "And I suppose to make sure Augustus stays in one piece."

My companion nodded in confirmation, explaining, "Exactly that. But they don't just stand around guarding the Princeps, at least from what Atticus told me. They have a section of men who act as spies in Rome, and their job is specifically to watch a bunch of men from the upper classes who have drawn the suspicion of the Princeps for one reason or another. And part of their job is to intercept messages being sent from one suspected conspirator to another. From what Atticus told me, over the years, quite a pile of these messages have been collected, and he said that most of the time, nothing's done to the men who wrote them. But the various letters, dispatches, written instructions, and the like are never thrown away. They're kept," Asinius finished ominously, "just in case they're needed to build a case against one of these men in the event they go from words to deeds. So Atticus took one of those letters and placed it among this man's property."

"But you just said they don't act on them," I argued.

"They don't," Asinius seemingly agreed, then added, "with the men of the upper classes. But a man of the Praetorian Guard, in possession of something that indicates his loyalty may be in doubt?" This time when he looked at me, he pinned me with his gaze, clearly trying to drive the point home. "That's what Atticus did to a man over a thousand *sesterces*, Titus." That Asinius used my *praenomen* was more than enough to ensure I was taking every word seriously. "What do you think he might do in order to get even over eight thousand? But," he stood back up and walked around the desk to put a hand on my shoulder, "there's probably a lot more to whatever happened between Atticus and this man that ran back years. I just want you to keep it in mind and be careful."

Suddenly, my promotion did not seem quite so wonderful. It was not until after I left Asinius' quarters that I realized I had completely forgotten why I had come to see him in the first place, hoping to pick up some hints about how to be a good Optio. After all, I thought glumly, it might not matter how good a job I do.

Even with the threat posed by Atticus to which Asinius alerted me, I was soon so absorbed in all that comes with being an Optio of a Century of the First Cohort, while I cannot say I forgot, it certainly was pushed into the background of my worries. I suppose part of it was based in a certain amount of hubris on my part, thinking I would perform my duties in such an exemplary manner that the Primus Pilus would have no cause for complaint. All I needed was something happening that would end this stretch of peace and quiet in Pannonia; it had been more than three seasons since the last time there had been anything noteworthy happening that called for us to use our swords in anger, at least with the 8th. Meanwhile, I simply did my best to impress Galens and, by extension, Atticus, and I started the best way I knew how, by facing each of the men of the Sixth in a sparring session. One improvement over my introduction to the First Century was that when I was promoted to Optio, Galens also named me weapons instructor, just as I had been in the First, except unlike with Bestia, I did not have to humiliate the man I replaced to do so since the post had actually been vacant for a few months, when the former instructor had been moved up into another Century of the First. While I managed to go undefeated, it was not without considerable difficulty with no less than three of the men; one of them was more than likely a draw, although Galens declared me the winner. I did not care for him doing so, but I understood it; the first few weeks for a new Optio are the most crucial in asserting his authority over his new command, and by declaring me victor, Galens was announcing to the Century I had his full support. Actually, I was fortunate in other ways, where once again, my size and reputation discouraged the men from testing me in other ways that rankers favor when trying a new Optio to see how far they can go with him. Ultimately, my greatest challenge lay in my attempts to have Domitius transferred into the Sixth Century, which Atticus seemed bent on thwarting, which was easy enough to do with the stroke of his pen every time Galens put in the request. However, it was not at my behest; in fact, I had tried to stop Domitius from risking the ire of the Primus Pilus by continuing to insist on putting in his transfer request. Yet, this was an example where the reforms of Augustus actually served to protect Domitius, at least officially, because rules had been created and codified, and they said a man could request transfer without fear of retribution or punishment. Domitius actually went to the *praetorium* to consult the written regulations, a copy of which are kept there and made available for all men to consult. He had to have help; Domitius is literate, but only functionally so, and reading the dense verbiage that are regulations for the Legion of Rome was something he was not comfortable attempting on his own. Somewhat to my surprise, I learned it had been Crito who also risked the wrath of the Primus Pilus, accompanying Domitius to help him not only find the relevant passage, but to interpret it. Yet, as I learned later from Crito himself, it was actually Domitius who, after hearing Crito recite the regulation three separate times, spotted the flaw in the wording. Naturally, I was not present, but I heard about it from Metellus, Avitus, and a couple other former section comrades who were present when Domitius presented his request yet again. When Atticus erupted in a fit of temper, threatening Domitius with being put on the punishment list, my friend responded by reciting word for word the regulation, and pointing out that there was in effect nothing in writing limiting the number of times a ranker could request transfer. I am sure it was an oversight, nothing more; the flaw might have been exploited elsewhere in other Legions, but this was the first I had ever heard of it being tried, so as far as I am concerned, Titus Domitius was the first man to exploit this technicality. And in doing so, he became something of a hero to the men of his section, at least at first; however, there was no way word of this did not whip up and down the Legion streets, demonstrating an important point that served as a reminder to me, and should to all officers. While men love their Legion, and they may hold their Centurion and Optio in high regard; when it comes to the monolithic entity known as the "army," men of the ranks wage their own private battles against it on a daily basis. It was something my Avus pointed out in his account that I saw firsthand more times than I can count; when men of the Legions are not actually battling an enemy of Rome, and when they are not brawling with each other, they are engaged in a struggle against the army, who they view as a heartless foe whose primary goal is to find ways to take a man's money, strips of skin, or in extreme cases, his very life, just not by standing in the ranks against some howling barbarian. Domitius' exploitation of this flaw in the regulation was universally cheered by all men under the rank of Optio, while the officers saw it in much different terms. All Optios with one exception, of course, but I was not sanguine that Atticus would not find a way to exact a punishment of his own. And yet, days turned into weeks, but while Domitius remained in the First, neither did he get striped nor was he on the punishment list, at least any more than he had been before. Finally, one day in September, long after both Domitius and I had resigned ourselves that he would remain where he was, he came bursting into the Legion office, where Pridaxes and I were checking our figures and sums for the deductions the army had managed to exact from the men under my charge. If his broad grin was not enough, the scroll he was waving was eloquent in itself.

"He finally gave in!" he exclaimed, completely forgetting the normal behavior expected of a Gregarius presenting himself to an officer, but of course, so did I.

"What?" I was confused, to put it mildly. "What are you talking about?"

"I think he's saying he's now in our Century, Optio," Pridaxes informed me helpfully.

My distraction was such I did not even register that Pridaxes was lightly mocking me, and I had to shake my head in an attempt for it to sink in that my friend was actually standing in front of me, holding the order of transfer.

"But…why?" I finally asked him. "I mean, why now? After all the times he's said no."

Domitius' grin faded, and I was worried there was something he was about to tell me I would not like. While he did have news, however, it was not what I expected.

"I'm not exactly sure, but I think it has something to do with the messenger that came to the office while I was there," he told me. "I only heard a tiny bit of what was said because I was still outside with Crito, but it sounds like something's happening up north with the Taurisci." Shrugging, he handed over the scroll to Pridaxes as he added, "All I know is that when he saw it was me, he just cursed and asked me if he approved this, would I promise never to darken his door again. He said he's got enough to worry about now, whatever that means."

This prompted me to laugh, and I heard Pridaxes snicker as well.

"I suppose we'll find out quickly enough," I mused, while at the same time I was slapping him on the back. "You've always been a pesky little bastard," I joked, yet I was serious when I said, "but I'm glad you were. It's good to have you here."

And it was; this was especially true because before the day was out, we knew more about why our Primus Pilus was so distracted, when all Centurions and Optios were summoned to the forum, the only place that would fit all of us. After we assembled there, Atticus appeared a short while later, just not from the direction of our area, but the *praetorium*, accompanied by the broad stripe Tribune, a man named Quintus Cassius Scaevola, who was a bit long in the tooth for the post, which ironically enough, made him one of the better Tribunes we had. He was not much to look at; slightly built, especially when walking next to Atticus, who was fairly broad across the shoulders, and his hair was already thinning, although he did not try to hide it like Divus Julius supposedly had. Once in front of us, they had a brief discussion, and I saw Scaevola give the Primus Pilus a nod, which was explained when it was the latter who actually addressed us.

"The Taurisci tribe has apparently declared war," Atticus began, the ripple of movement and low hum of the officers of the Legion commenting to each other starting immediately, except he was not through. "Not on us, but on the Carni," he went on. "And the Carni have asked for our protection."

"Why us?" Galens muttered. "The 13th's closer…"

If he was going to say anything else, I could not tell, because Atticus was saying, "And the 13th is already busy at Lake Pelso, which means we're the closest."

"Does that answer your question?" I tried not to snicker, although I was not very successful.

"We'll be marching at first light, day after tomorrow," Atticus ordered, "but in light marching order, without heavy baggage. Our first order of business will be to march to Emona because the *duumviri* of the town have requested the presence of a Legion. They claim," I believe even those men farthest away could not have missed the curling of the Primus Pilus' upper lip, "that the auxiliaries are mostly drawn from the Taurisci and can't be trusted to maintain order. Apparently, many Roman settlers have fled to the town, and it's a huge mess." Scaevola leaned over and whispered something in his ear, and the Primus Pilus listened, then gave a quick nod. "Our orders are to march as quickly as possible because, according to the Carni emissary, they've had two villages already put to the torch and he claims that hundreds have been slaughtered. Centurions, attend to me! Optios, go get things started!"

With that, he spun about, rendered a salute to the Tribune, then began moving in more or less the same direction as the rest of us. I joined up with Asinius; during my brief time, I found I sought him out more than the other Optios, but if they were offended, they were not sufficiently so to bring it up.

"This is the first time we've ever been called out to keep people from killing each other, not kill them ourselves," Asinius commented, and I had to laugh, especially since I had not thought of it in this way.

"Maybe it'll be over before we get there," I suggested, but I did not fool Asinius in the slightest, and he shot me a look that seemed equal parts amusement and scorn.

"You don't wish that," he shot back, then punched me lightly on the arm. "Remember, I know you! This is going to be your first chance as an Optio to show the rest of us Optios how much better you are at it than we are."

"That won't be hard," I scoffed, then before he could do more than give me a shove, we had reached the spot where we split up to go to our areas.

"I bet my boys are ready before yours," he called over his shoulder.

"You're on," I replied instantly, then thought for a heartbeat. "But what are the stakes?"

He turned about, but kept walking backward as he challenged, "How about your sword against six months of standing watch for you?"

"You wish." I laughed. "That sword's worth an entire enlistment of standing watch!"

"If you're too afraid," he taunted, but he did manage to duck the dirt clod I picked up and hurled at him.

He turned his corner then, and I turned mine, my mind racing trying to think of all that needed to be done, just not as either a ranker or even a Sergeant. Looking back, I realize this was the first time where what it meant to be Optio really hit me, as I quickly understood I would not be getting any sleep this night. If I was lucky, perhaps I would get a watch the next night, but I could not dwell on it, and in a somewhat strange way, being overwhelmed actually served to my benefit; I was too busy to be tired.

The 8th was actually ready to march by a watch after noon the next day, except it was decided not to strike out, and as a reward for our preparation, the Primus Pilus gave the men the liberty of the town until midnight. Once Galens inspected the Century and indicated he was satisfied, I was released as well, but instead of Siscia, I headed over to the Seventh Cohort's area to find Sextus. When I determined he was not in his hut, I instantly knew why, which meant I was going into Siscia despite this not being my intention. Nor did I need to search, heading directly to Diocles' apartment, yet while I thought I was ready for what I would find, nothing could have been further from the truth. I can only plead ignorance because of my new duties, but I also know this is not much of an excuse. Whatever the cause, I was completely unprepared for what I found when I knocked on the door to the apartment, although I will say it was opened quickly enough. Except that it was Alex who answered the door, giving me my first shock; it also forced me to think back and recognize I had not been by to visit for more than two months. Even in that short period of time, he had visibly grown, not in his height as much as his facial features; at least this was my first impression. His sullen expression, on the other hand, was one with which I was familiar, because it had become more and more prevalent on the journey back to Siscia, and the weeks afterward when I was still a regular visitor.

"He's here," was the boy's only greeting, then he turned about and walked away.

The fact that he did not head to the room he had shared with his siblings but to the one I still thought of as belonging to Sextus and me on the rare occasions I spent the night took me a moment to comprehend as far as its meaning. Only then did I really become aware that my brother was seated at the table, except he was by himself. When I turned to look at him, the expression he had on his face was eloquent warning of trouble to come, between his bright pink ears and his jutting lower lip. Birgit was not to be seen, at least at first.

"I thought I'd find you here," I said, or at least I began before I was interrupted.

"*Meum mel*," Birgit called from the room she and Diocles had shared, "who's at the...?"

She stopped, both physically and verbally, standing in the doorway, her mouth open as she stood there, her face even paler than normal.

"Oh," I could tell she was trying to sound happy, as if my sudden appearance was a pleasant surprise, "Titus! It's so nice to see you! It's been..."

For some reason, she could not finish, although I suspect at least part of the reason was due to where I was pointing, down at her belly, with my mouth hanging open. Granted, I did not know much about childbirth, but I knew a pregnant woman when I saw her.

"Quite a while," I finally managed, "obviously." I could not seem to force myself to stop pointing down at her swelling abdomen, but it was my brother I turned to and added, "You certainly have been busy."

"Titus," Birgit interrupted, and I sensed her stepping fully back into the main room. "Please, Titus," she begged, "let us explain!"

"Explain what?" This was when I did look at her, and my own face felt like a mask as I stared at her with a fury that both surprised and disturbed me. "How babies are made? Because," I said scornfully, "I'm pretty sure I know."

"That's enough!" Sextus jumped from his chair; I blame the sudden movement occurring at the edge of my vision as being truly responsible for my next action, as I spun about on one foot while unleashing a right fist that caught him square on the chin.

I must admit it was a decidedly peculiar feeling, at least for me, because I felt extremely gratified to see the soles of my brother's *caligae* as he flew backward, yet horrible at the same time.

"Titus!" Birgit shrieked, except it was to Sextus she went, kneeling down at my brother's side. From what I could tell, he was unconscious before he hit the ground.

I stood there dumbly, staring down at the both of them, wondering why I was so angry. But, dear reader, although I realized why I felt as I did, it was not because of any jealousy on my part, and although it was envy at the thought that Sextus had won Birgit's heart, it was not based on my desire for Birgit. As I stared down at her, trying to revive my brother, knocked unconscious one more time by me, what came to me was the realization that I was still angry about all that had transpired with Giulia. It was true she had been dead for more than two years by this point, at least if the story Sextus had been told was to be believed, yet the loss I felt still ached in me; what surprised me was how deeply felt that hurt still was. Also, I admit I was angry at my brother because I felt he was betraying the memory of Diocles in some way, and I suppose, to some extent, I still feel this way. The traditional mourning period is one year, yet while the rational part of me recognized that matters were slightly different between Sextus and Birgit, I discovered in that moment I harbored real resentment towards my brother.

I suppose this was what prompted me to mumble, "Tell him he better be in formation in the morning," before wheeling about and leaving the apartment.

Descending the stairs, I got barely a half-dozen paces when I heard Birgit's voice call my name, but I ignored her. I walked back to camp, paying no attention to the men who were already well on their way to being drunk, lost in my own thoughts.

The 8th Legion marched out of the gates, exactly on schedule, and my brother was in his spot in the ranks – sporting a swollen jaw, but he was there. I know, because I slipped away to check on him before we actually officially answered the call to formation. He spotted me, glaring at me but making no attempt to call to me, nor I to him. Our private battle aside, the Legion was ready to march, although "resigned" would perhaps be a better way to describe it because none of us had ever experienced anything like this before. Galens and I had discussed it briefly; I took some comfort in the fact that my Centurion seemed as mystified as I felt about what was expected of us. Our other interaction concerned where to place Domitius, newly arrived to the Century, except on this, Galens proved inflexible.

"He's going into the Tenth Section," he declared firmly. "And I'm moving Flavius up into the Second Section. He's a good man and he deserves it, and Petrosidius is still in the hospital."

"But Domitius is better with a sword than Flavius," I argued vehemently. "Remember, I've faced both of them! Domitius is better! It's why he's in the First Section to begin with!"

Galens could simply have told me to shut my mouth; instead, he patiently explained, "I don't doubt that's true, Pullus. But you also know that it takes the men on either side and behind a man to adjust to the way a new man fights." Shaking his head, he said simply, "We don't have time for that. Right now, he's in the Tenth. Understood?"

When put that way, even if I had been disposed to argue, it would have been next to impossible. Besides, of the two of us, Domitius was unfazed by the news.

"It doesn't really matter where I am," he explained, "as long as I'm in the Sixth. That way," he grinned, "I can make sure you aren't using my will to wipe your ass or something like that."

"How do you know I already haven't?" I retorted.

It made no matter; when we marched out of the gates, Domitius was in the rear rank, which I actually found made it easier for us to talk, since the Optio marches on the opposite side of the Centurion, putting me a matter of four men between us since he was at the little end, nearest to me. It was a bit strange, being outside the formation, yet it served to remind me that there was now a separation between me and men who I had viewed as just like me not long before, and it was now a barrier both physical as well as mental. This was certainly an adjustment; what was even more of one was becoming reacquainted with the rhythm of campaign life again. While we went out into the countryside, there is a significant difference between going out for one or two days then returning and what we were doing now. The fact that we were heading off into the unknown actually worked to the advantage of the officers, because the men were so busy speculating about what we would be facing they did not have the time to moan about their plight. However, it was on the first night where I got the first true taste of what being an Optio was about when, once the assignments were given out, I was not bent over like those men who had been my comrades just a short time before, digging a ditch. Because we stopped later than normal, much of the work was done in semi-darkness, since the days were becoming shorter; personally, I was thankful for the gloom because it hid my beaming smile as I relished the feeling of not throwing dirt over my shoulder. It was actually quite a heady sensation, which made it difficult for me to contain myself from strutting around a bit, pointing to a man who I thought was doing too much leaning and not enough digging. I was sure the feeling would wear off, and it did, but I confess this first day on the march was quite wonderful. If the men of the Sixth noticed, they did not seem disposed to point it out, although I did hear a few muttered comments as I walked by, but honestly, they could have been doing nothing more than the normal complaining.

Once camp was made and the Primus Pilus announced the duty schedule and I heard that Sextus' Century was standing watch, I decided to approach him while he was at his post on the wall, which I learned from Tiburtinus, who, I must admit, did not look happy to see me.

"What did you do to your brother this time, Pullus?" he asked me, and even by torchlight, I saw the coldness in his gaze.

"Why do you think it's me?" I protested, yet instead of replying, he just continued with his stare, and as I often did when I had been the subject of this look when he was my Optio, I wilted under it. "All right," I admitted, "it was me."

This prompted a snort as the Centurion shook his head, saying scornfully, "Tell me something I don't know. Like," he stopped moving his head to resume his stare, "why."

"That's not really your business, Centurion." The words flew out of my mouth before I could consider a more tactful way of phrasing it. "It's a family matter!"

Tiburtinus stiffened, and I suddenly became aware of his *vitus* as it started moving about in small circles, which I knew from experience meant it was about to be used. Except that it was not; officers do not strike other officers, even if they are subordinate, and this was another moment when I realized being an Optio actually meant something.

Suddenly, the Centurion exhaled in an explosive gust, his lips thinned down into a bloodless line that I also recognized as the sign Tiburtinus was struggling to maintain his composure. However, I was certainly not prepared for what came out of his mouth.

"You're...right, Pullus," he finally managed. "The cause isn't my business. But what *is*," he did poke me in the chest then, except it was with his finger, "my business is the result. If your brother hadn't been able to march, I would have been required to determine the circumstances. Or," the scornful note returned to his voice, "don't they teach that to new Optios in the First Cohort?"

He was correct in every particular, and it served to remind me that things that had once been straightforward, like punching my brother in the jaw, were no longer quite so clear. While it is true that I had once punched my brother as a Sergeant, there is a fine but important distinction when it comes to the next ladder on the rung. And what I had done, if viewed in a strictly official manner, was actually not a minor violation of the regulations pertaining to officers' ability to impose discipline on a Gregarius not under his direct command. The only potentially mitigating circumstance was that our clash, such as it was, occurred out in town. All of this flashed through my mind, whereupon I was struck by a horrifying thought.

"You didn't report this to the Primus Pilus, did you?" I asked.

For once, the look of contempt he gave me caused a feeling of intense relief instead of the normal sense of guilt and shame I suffered whenever he had aimed this expression at me.

"Of course not," he snapped, clearly offended I had even suggested it, but this also served to send the finger back to jabbing my chest. "But that's not the point, Pullus!" For the first time, the tone of his voice softened, if just by a fraction. "You're an Optio now," he continued, "and that means something. Like the fact that you can't just solve a problem by knocking it out." He paused for a couple heartbeats as he glanced over his shoulder, as if to see if anyone was listening, which puzzled me, at least at first. "Is it true?" he asked me then. "That you knocked him out with one punch and he flew halfway across the room?"

I stared at him in disbelief.

"Who told you that?"

"Who do you think?" he snorted, then shook his head with what I suppose was disgust and amusement. "You two are unbelievable sometimes. You knock your brother out, and your brother brags about how hard you hit him." For the first time, he gave a real grin as he added, “At least, that’s what I think he was doing. He’s not easy to understand right now.”

“Oh gods,” it came out of me, “I hope I didn’t break his jaw!”

“Now you’re worried?” Tiburtinus mocked me, and I could not help laughing.

However, when I moved to head up the rampart to find Sextus, Tiburtinus’ good humor vanished, and he restrained me with a hand on my chest, shaking his head firmly.

“No.” He was using his command tone now. “I don’t give you permission to go up there. Besides,” he grabbed my arm and turned me about as he finished, “you’ve got your own men to worry about. I’ll take care of your brother.”

With that, he gave me a shove, and I had no choice but to obey. Although I had not spoken with Sextus, I did feel a bit better, and I could not fight a grin from creeping over my face as I thought about how strange it must seem to other men that one brother would actually be proud of being knocked out by the other.

One feature of autumn in Pannonia is that it rains and rains. While the Primus Pilus did not explain why we were marching in light order, without the wagons of the baggage train, there was no need. Even without the wagons, our progress was slower than it would have been just a month earlier, yet we still managed to cover more than twenty-five miles a day, arriving in Emona three days after leaving Siscia. What awaited us there was a scene every bit as chaotic as had been described, one of the relatively rare occasions this was the case. The town was bursting at the seams as terrified Roman settlers were joined by what appeared to be a fair number of Carni women and children, obviously sent there by their men. Seeing the chaos, the irony was not lost on me, or any other veteran of Pannonia, for that matter; most of the time, the native tribes hated us…until they needed us to save their skins. The Taurisci tribe is as large in number and power as the Breuci, while the Carni are one of the smaller. But the Carni have one ally; the terrain in which they live, at the northern border of Pannonia where it joins Noricum, which is extremely rugged, with real mountains whose steep slopes are covered in thick stands of pine and alder trees, and the valleys are usually narrow, cut by cascading rivers that carry the snow from the peaks. I will say it did not have the same horrible reputation of the ground to the south of Emona and north of Siscia, the place where rebelling tribes always tried to flee and where my father's career had been ended. However, this was due more to the fact that not even the 13th, in whose normal territory this area was, had had any reason to go there. When the Taurisci quarreled with another tribe, they tended to go north, into Boii lands, or sometimes northwest, into Noricum. Not this time, although we did not know why at that point; before we left Emona, we would learn more, or at least the Primus Pilus did. Regardless of the cause, the first order of business for the Legion was to restore a sense of order and security, which was why the Primus Pilus ordered a Cohort to stay behind. Considering the identity of the Cohort, I will say I was extremely thankful that Primus Pilus Atticus had placed me in the Sixth of the First because it was the Ninth left behind. What I am about to relate is not a slur against the men of the Ninth, who were no worse, or better, than any of the other junior Cohorts, but against their Pilus Prior and, to a lesser extent, their Centurions. Putting it simply, the Ninth was ecstatic they were being left behind, and while part of this attitude can be attributed to the presence of wine and women, most of their joy seemed to be based in the idea they would not be facing any danger. In fact, when we left Emona the second full day after we arrived, what appeared to be the entire Ninth Cohort lined the streets, seeing us off with cheers as lusty and full of good wishes as those of the settlers and Carni refugees. It left a sour taste in my mouth, and one glance over at Domitius, whose eyes were straight ahead, refusing to acknowledge our comrades, as the entire Century was doing, showed I was not alone in my disgust. Marching northwest, following the Savus upstream, two days outside of Emona, we reached the settlement of Carnium, a village perhaps half the size of Emona, whose population was almost equally split between Romans and Carni. It had sprung up because, like the Maezaei, the Carni's major export and source of wealth was iron, although they had never been accused of selling to tribes across the Danuvius hostile to Rome like the Maezaei. Being accurate, Carnium would have been half the size of Emona if there had been anyone there. It was from Carnium that those fleeing refugees had come, both Roman and Carni alike, and the Taurisci had clearly sacked the settlement. However, there was one oddity that I did not notice, at least until Domitius pointed it out.

"Optio," he called to me, always careful to address me by my rank in front of the others, "do you notice anything strange?"

"Other than it's deserted?" I shook my head. "Not really."

"This place has obviously been sacked," he said, but then pointed around to our surroundings, "but all the Roman buildings are still standing, while all those belonging to the Carni have been put to the torch."

He was right; apparently, the Taurisci wanted to send a clear message to Rome that their quarrel was not with us. And it had been fairly simple to do; like all such settlements, at least those I have seen, there are two distinctly different sections to any place shared by Romans and natives. As often happened, the river had provided a clear boundary, where the Carni portion of the settlement was on the opposite bank; or more accurately, the smoking ruins were. This also was an aid to the Taurisci in ensuring that no Roman property was damaged, not that it mattered. The Primus Pilus sent a Cohort across the wooden bridge, which was still standing, although its pilings were scorched and its decking was slightly charred, giving orders that they search the rubble for any survivors. To nobody's surprise, there were none, although I did hear an Optio from one of the Centuries call out to what I assumed was a friend of his in the Second standing next to us, that they had found a dozen corpses who had clearly died of their wounds after the attack.

"A couple of them look pretty fresh," I heard him say, "so they probably held on as long as they could and we just missed them being alive." He shrugged as his Century went filing past to resume their spot. "Not that we could have done anything for the poor bastards."

"No," Galens' voice made me jump; he had swung behind the formation to my side, "but we might have been able to learn something useful."

We did not tarry any longer in Carnium, the Primus Pilus pressing us on. We were still heading northwest and following the Savus, which is a big enough river so that this would turn out to be the widest valley in Carni territory. It also made it the most populated, with a string of small settlements, arranged like gems on a necklace, hung along the "neck" of the Savus. Most of them could barely be called a village; just a cluster of a few huts and outbuildings arranged along family and clan lines. There were a couple larger ones, although none even the size of Carnium, yet what they all had in common with Carnium is that they were empty of villagers, and the few buildings had been put to the torch. The only difference lay in how recent the sacking had been; it had become obvious that the Taurisci had marched up this valley, slaughtering any Carni they found and destroying their homes and barns, and winter was coming. Already in the mornings, we could see our breaths for the first full watch of the day, although the rain that had plagued us the first week had at least subsided. At every location, we did essentially the same thing we had at Carnium, the only difference being in the identity of the search party, and the amount of time it took. Then, after the fourth, or perhaps fifth such scene, we came upon what was clearly the farm of a Roman settler. It was distinguishable for a number of reasons, not least of which the stout wooden wall that surrounded the house, barn, and a couple of outbuildings. In addition, the house was a villa, built in almost an identical layout to our family's home in Arelate, albeit on a much smaller scale. What made it stand out even more was the fact that it was largely untouched, although one gate was hanging by a single hinge. But it was also deserted, and I know I was not alone in assuming that we had probably seen the occupants in Emona. For some reason, though, the sight of the undisturbed farm seemed to anger the Primus Pilus, and I watched him stalking about, Asinius with him, but he never got close enough for me to hear exactly why he was so upset. Because of the time of day, the order was given to make camp, and as soon as I could, I sought out Asinius.

"Why's the Primus Pilus acting like he could chew through nails?" I asked him.

"Because the fact that the Taurisci have specifically been avoiding killing Romans or even damaging their property is a problem," he explained, but I did not see his point, and said as much.

"If," he was using his patient tone that he sometimes used with me, which I hated, "they had done something like that, then our orders would be clear."

"Exact retribution," I answered grimly, beginning to get an idea of where he was heading.

That Roman Legions are used in such a manner is no secret, nor is it a new practice, but under the divine Augustus it has become a matter of policy, not just custom. Whenever anyone, native tribe, or confederation of tribes, or even a lone warband, takes a Roman life or damages Roman property, our response is usually swift and always sure, except it is not done in a commensurate fashion. If a Roman citizen is murdered and it is not considered an act of war or rebellion on the part of the perpetrator, the accused will have his day in court, and only he will be punished if found guilty. But if it is a situation such as the one we were facing then, matters are handled much differently. For example, if it had been just the Roman farmer who lived here, the Primus Pilus would probably have been content with the heads of five to ten rebellious tribesmen; the whole family, however, would see one of the small settlements we marched through put to the sword and the buildings torched. What made matters even more problematic for us was that we were not in Taurisci territory but Carni, so even if we wished to exact some sort of punishment, we would have to catch the marauding Taurisci themselves.

"Yes," Asinius agreed to my statement, "but now we don't have any real justification to do that because they've been very careful about not hurting Romans. So," he sighed, "the Primus Pilus is trying to figure out what we're supposed to do."

While I could understand this now that it was explained, there was still one major issue that I saw, and I pointed it out to Asinius.

"We have to catch them first."

"That we do," he agreed. He slapped me on the shoulder, then we returned to our respective Centuries.

By following the Savus, once we had gone perhaps fifteen miles from Carnium, we actually left the Roman road where it swings north through a low pass. Instead, we continued following the river, and in doing so, the terrain grew rougher, and our progress slower. Our mounted contingent of cavalry, acting as scouts and flank security had informed the Primus Pilus that the way we were going was still on the Taurisci trail; they, too, had foregone the Roman road. Except that their reason for doing so, at least the assumption on our part, was that they were heading into the heart of Carni territory, where their most productive mines are located. Although we reached the end of the valley, it was too early in the day to stop, but the scouts had reported the next good spot for a Legion camp was still more than ten miles away, which would have put us well after dark and making camp. Under normal circumstances, this would have been a hardship but nothing we could not overcome; without knowing the exact whereabouts of the Taurisci warband, however, which the scouts had estimated to be perhaps seven thousand strong, the Primus Pilus rightly decided not to run the risk. While it was true the Taurisci had been careful not to antagonize us, it did not take much imagination to think that some rash young warrior, or group of them, would strike from the darkness while we were occupied with constructing the camp. Therefore, we made our encampment along the river, at a point where the valley had narrowed considerably, and the track that led up into the hills ringing the northwest terminus of the valley plainly visible. One slight irregularity was the presence of yet another Roman farmhouse, larger than the previous one but identical in its abandonment, at least at first, and no signs of molestation. That the farm was untouched is something I can attest to from firsthand observation, because it was the Sixth that Atticus sent to search the buildings. As at the last farm, everything of any value that was portable had been taken; although we had no way of knowing with any certainty, I felt fairly sure the owners had taken their most prized and valuable belongings with them and they were not in the possession of any Taurisci warriors. In all honesty, it was quite eerie, poking about the villa and two barns that in all respects looked perfectly in order, except there were no people, or any large animals, for that matter. There were a dozen chickens or so, which I had to stop the men from snatching up and taking them back to camp for a nice change from pork. Unsurprisingly, this was not a popular order, but there was only some grumbling that I chose to ignore, as did Galens. He and our *Signifer,* Florens,, were talking quietly, and I felt Galens' amused gaze as he watched me chastise a man from the Third Section who tried to hide a chicken under his cloak. The ranker, a scoundrel of the first grade, named Tiberius Laetus, had put the chicken's head under its wing to put it to sleep, but even under a *sagum*, it is hard to hide a chicken. Not long after my promotion, I had copied my former Optio's example of using a shortened handle of a turf cutter, since Optios are no longer allowed the *vitus*, which I was using to good effect on the back of Laetus' legs as he yelped in pain, trying to hop away while denying the presence of the chicken. Naturally, his sudden movement roused the bird, who apparently did not care for being smothered under a *sagum*, so Laetus' cries were joined by the terrified squawking of the chicken who also was flapping its wings, causing Laetus' garment to jump about around him in such a way that made it almost impossible for me to keep a straight face. Otherwise, this was the only excitement we had searching the farm, and Galens set such a leisurely pace for both the search and our short march there and back that the camp was all but finished when we got back. Which, as Galens had informed me, was exactly what he was trying to accomplish. It was a minor action on his part, certainly, yet it served as an important lesson for me in the ways a good leader can show the men under his command he has not forgotten what it is like cutting turf, digging a ditch, or chopping trees.

By taking our time performing the task we had been assigned, the men of the Sixth were able to more or less march directly through the newly constructed gates and straight to where the Century slaves had already erected their tents. Of course, this was not done without a fair amount of gloating on the part of the Century, as they cheerily reminded their friends in other Centuries and Cohorts that they had been able to avoid any labor. Naturally, this engendered all manner of jeers and taunts from the men whose sweat and toil had created this camp in which we would all sleep, safe and secure. Still, as my Avus had commented, the gods smile on you one moment, then piss on you the next, which the Sixth discovered when Galens returned from the *praetorium* to inform us that we had guard duty that night. Not, however, the most favored shift, immediately after the camp is erected, or the second most after that, the last one before dawn. No, we had been chosen for the guard shift in the third watch of the night, right in the middle, which meant we would have enough time to prepare our meal or retire for the night, but not both. As always, the men opted for the meal; going on short sleep is a fact of life in the Legions. It also meant that what occurred on this night would take place while we were on watch, and I have often wondered if this was an accident, or was part of the plan. Before any of this could take place, however, what I only determined later was an unexpected wrinkle as far as the Primus Pilus was concerned came when a small group of civilians appeared from the trees that lined the steep slope of the ridge that served as the boundary of one side of the valley. As we discovered, the party consisted of the farmer, his family and slaves, or at least some of his slaves; the rest of them were still with his livestock, safely hidden in the forest on the side of the ridge. Meeting with the Primus Pilus, the farmer established his identity, and according to what was said around the fires, Atticus only grudgingly allowed the man, his family, and his property to reoccupy their home, and I often wondered during the events that transpired because of Atticus relenting and permitting this, how he felt about doing so, because I cannot imagine he recalled this with any pleasure.

Only in the time immediately afterward did I attach any significance to events that, when they occurred, seemed to be of no moment. The first event was the one I just described, and the second happened as we marched into camp. Because of our status as men of the First Cohort, we are nearest to the *praetorium*, and when it is in a camp for a single Legion, that means just a stone's throw away. In Siscia, where there are Tribunes, Legate's bodyguards, and the like, we are further removed, but not in a marching camp of a single Legion, with just the Primus Pilus in command. This is mentioned to explain why we were actually marching directly through the forum, because it was the most direct route to our waiting tents. We had yet to learn how Fortuna had chosen to piss on us because the duty roster had not been announced, and a part of me wonders if the gaiety and buoyant spirits of the men, having seemingly escaped from the onerous tasks that are part of our everyday life, played a role. Certainly, Primus Pilus Atticus gave us a sour look as he stood there, next to the erected *praetorium*, which was actually nothing more than his own tent. It was not the look I had cause to remember, but the fact that he was not alone, although this was not unusual in itself. What made it slightly odd was that it was not Asinius or the Pili Priores who clustered around him, but men of the First Century. Not all of them; there were no more than a dozen men standing there, all of them clearly listening intently to what the Primus Pilus was saying. Asinius' absence only became noteworthy after the fact, but what I can say is that even in the moment I noticed that Balbinus, the man who had once been the rock in my *caligae* when I had been his Sergeant, was one of the men, along with his close comrade Appuleius. Other than my passing glance, though, I gave them no mind. The second factor is that the First Century was our successor on the guard shift, which, again, was slightly unusual but hardly irregular enough that it alerted me, or anyone else, I assume, that something was afoot. Finally, it was the timing of the actual occurrence that caught our attention that, again, only later, did I find problematic. None of this was in my mind, however, other than my taking note of the seemingly motley collection of Gregarii surrounding Primus Pilus Atticus. As Optio, my first responsibility was to make sure my men were fed, as strange as that may sound. However, as I had learned long before, on my first campaign, there are men in every Century who would willingly trade their ration of food for the daily ration of wine. Since our ration is cut by water when on campaign, this becomes doubly important to those men who are firmly clutched in the grasp of Bacchus. Consequently, one of my unofficial but important duties, at least as deemed by Galens, was to make the rounds of those fires of men he knew were likely suspects, ensuring they had contributed their rations to the section pot, and not made the section go wanting. Before I was promoted, I confess watching Galens when he was my Optio, then Tiburtinus and Asinius was more for amusement than anything else, not thinking it very important. In fact, when I first observed this behavior, I was positive it was nothing more than a way for Centurions to keep their Optios busy; not until I assumed the position did I understand that it is, in fact, an essential task, because not only does it create a situation whereby the offending man does not take in enough food to perform his duties, by trading them, they are shorting their section comrades. Being so absorbed in this task, I quickly forgot what had only been a slightly unusual moment; frankly, I was just happy none of the men had shorted their section rations for wine, at least this night. Once the men were fed, only then did I stop to eat my meal, then we settled in for the short rest before our guard shift began. While I had not thought I would, I must have dozed off, because when I was roused by the slave assigned to keep track of time, I was jerked from an extremely pleasant dream. The interruption did not make my mood any better, which was already soured by standing watch in the middle of the night. Nevertheless, as is the duty of the Optio, I roused the Century and had them assemble in the Century street, waiting for Galens. When he arrived, we marched off and started at the Porta Praetoria where, as Optio, I was responsible for meeting with my counterpart in the relieved Century, whereupon we made the circuit of the camp. At each designated post, we exchanged our pairs of sentries, with the relieved Century growing larger, and the relieving Century growing smaller. Once the perimeter of the camp is relieved, only then do we change out the walking posts within the camp, finally ending at the *praetorium*, where the watch officially changes hands between the two Centurions. Normally, the Optio is not present for this because he has already begun his first circuit of the posts, checking on his men to ensure they are alert and actually doing their jobs. The Centurion goes to the Porta Praetoria; this is his spot for the entire guard shift, so that either the Optio, or *Tesseraurius*, who acts as the Optio's supernumerary, or assistant, while the *Signifer* and *Cornicen* stand with the Centurion, the former usually acting as the Centurion's runner, and the *Cornicen* is there to sound the alarm should the Centurion order it. Once everything is done, then the boredom of what is in almost every case a mundane and routine duty takes hold, but in my first shift as Optio back when we were still in Siscia, I discovered, to my surprise, there is a hidden benefit in being the second in command. The reason is based in the fact that, whereas the men on the walls are stationary, for those of us who are forced to walk around, either in my role or on the walking post, it is not only next to impossible to fall asleep, at least unless you stop and find a place to hide, which sometimes happens, it also helps pass the time.

For the first two parts of our watch, it was a completely normal shift, during which I made the circuit more than a dozen times, stopping only at the Porta Praetoria to report to Galens that, as usual, nothing exciting was happening. Aside from men falling asleep, the next biggest challenge for an Optio or Centurion is keeping the men from passing the time by talking to each other. While chatting with a comrade does help pass the time, and as men always try to argue, keeps them from falling asleep, it is still not allowed, because it not only distracts men from their true job, it also makes it harder for them to listen to the night sounds for any hint that trouble is approaching. Naturally, falling asleep is the most serious offense; on campaign, it usually draws a sentence of death, or at least a flogging with the scourge. Talking, on the other hand, is an offense that my turf cutter handle, or Galens' *vitus* was sufficient punishment, and this at least I did use on a couple occasions that night. Then, well into the final third of our watch, I had just left the Porta Praetoria, and was walking the rampart to the corner of the camp where the Praetorian gate side and the Porta Sinister walls meet, when I heard a shout, down the rampart in the direction I was already heading. Breaking into a run, I moved as quickly as I dared in the torchlight, but I cannot say with any certainty when I became aware that what light there was came from more than just the torches along the wall. Off to my right, out in the darkness, there was a sullen, orange glow that, even in between glances, was growing in strength. I reached the men who had raised the alarm, although I was sure I knew what they were sounding the alert for, especially since they were both looking at the fire.

Lifting his javelin and pointing it in the manner we are trained, the Gregarius, a man from the Seventh Section named Trebellius, said simply, "Looks like there's a fire out there, Optio."

Oh, really? I was about to say, but realized how petty that would look to him and his guard companion, also from the Seventh, named Visellio.

"So I see," I said instead, then we stood and watched for a moment as the glow turned into a fully defined fire, with tongues of flames suddenly leaping up into the air.

"Isn't that in the direction of that farm?" Visellio asked, and I instantly realized he was correct.

"Who'd do that now?" I wondered aloud, but it was clear they were as mystified as I was.

I sent Trebellius off to summon Galens, while Visellio and I stood watching as the buildings that had once been a prosperous farm burned to the ground. For a moment, I thought Galens might sound the alarm so another Century could be dispatched to do what they could to fight the blaze, but by the time he arrived, it was clear that every building was fully aflame, sending a tower of fire and smoke high in the air above itself.

"Why would the Taurisci come back and torch that place?" was Galens' comment, a variation of the same question I had been asking myself. "Especially when they've been so careful to avoid damaging anything Roman?"

"What about those people?" I believe this was Visellio who asked. "It's too far away to see if any of them made it out. Should we go look for them, Centurion?"

Galens did seem to consider it for a moment, then shook his head, replying, "If they made it out, they're headed this way. And if they didn't," he gestured at the fully involved fire, "it's too late to do anything for them now."

Honestly, while I found it puzzling, it was little more than a nagging thought I did not spend much time thinking about; at least, at that moment. Galens, deciding nothing could be done, did not bother sounding the alarm by the *cornu*, although he did send a runner to the *praetorium* to inform Primus Pilus Atticus.

"Pullus," Galens ordered after he sent the runner on his way, "get back to walking the rampart. I doubt anything's going to happen, but this might be a trick of the Taurisci to draw our attention away. In fact," he thought for a moment, "go over to the opposite side, now. Cut across camp. If they do try something, they're likely to do it over there. I'm going to stay here and wait to see if any of the poor bastards at that farm make it over here."

I did as he bid, but while he was correct about a trick, it was not by the Taurisci.

The next morning, before we broke camp, the Primus Pilus ordered the entire First Cohort out of the Porta Sinistra, marching us to the farm, which was still sending a column of smoke into the early morning sky. Galens had informed me at the end of our shift that nobody from the farm had appeared at our gates, and I assumed, as he did, they had all perished in the fire after they had returned from hiding. The irony was certainly not lost on me, although this was little more than a passing thought, that the farmer and his family had fled and survived the Taurisci, then apparently perished in the fire that, as hard as it may have been to admit, occurred under our collective noses. When we got to the farm, nothing was left standing, except for the wall, which was a bit scorched but otherwise intact, while all the buildings contained therein were completely destroyed. After performing a cursory search, the only oddity was the absence of corpses, but the place had been so thoroughly destroyed that we assumed there was nothing recognizable left of the family, since they had not reappeared. Once we were done with the search, we fell into formation, then stood watching Atticus walk around the ruins, with the other Centurions with him, but we could not hear anything other than the mumbling of their conversation. I did happen to be watching when I saw my Centurion, along with our erstwhile Primus Pilus Posterior Aulus Macerinus suddenly react sharply to something Atticus said, then exchange a look behind the back of the Primus Pilus. This is the moment I think of when I suddenly became, if not wary, then at least alert that there was something going on above and beyond what appeared before us. Whatever it was, when I saw the Pilus Posterior open his mouth and start speaking, he clearly did not finish before the Primus Pilus, whose back was to me, cut him off with a motion of his *vitus*, in a move we had learned was his way of ending any kind of discussion. This was prelude to the Centurions returning to us, whereupon we marched back to camp, where the breaking of it had already begun, forcing us to hurry to catch up. Even under the best of conditions, leaving a marching camp entails a fair amount of rushing about, but with a veteran Legion, even starting behind the others was no great challenge. And despite our late start, we were still in our spot in the forum ready to march well before all the other Cohorts were. As a result, as usually happens, while the men were waiting, they were allowed to ground their packs and move about, and as usually happened, rankers wandered over to talk to friends in other Centuries, their only restriction they stay within the

Cohort area. It was because of this I learned something troubling, when Domitius sought me out, after he returned from elsewhere.

Saluting, he said formally, "Optio, may I speak with you privately? It's a…personal matter."

Even before he had opened his mouth, I could tell something was troubling my friend, but I was certainly not prepared for what was to come.

Once we got far enough out of earshot, Domitius said quietly, "I think I know who started that fire last night." Hesitating for a moment, we both glanced around before he continued, "I just talked to Metellus. He told me there was a specific reason why the First Century relieved us."

Actually, he did not need to go any further, because just this piece was enough for all the things I had noticed the day before fall into place.

"Atticus," I breathed. "He sent some men out to start the fire. But," I was troubled by something, "how, exactly? I mean, I know how they could get back in, if Atticus was the commander of the guard. But when did they leave? Because it wasn't during our shift. It doesn't make any sense."

"Unless," my friend rejoined, "they were outside the camp immediately after we finished it." Seeing my expression, he obviously took it for doubt because he pressed, "Think about it, Titus! It would've been extremely easy to do! And it wouldn't take many men…"

"About ten," I interrupted, suddenly thinking about the small group surrounding Atticus in the forum the day before. Another thought struck me, and I added bitterly, "I should have known when I saw that bastard Balbinus standing there! That *cunnus* is just the kind of man someone like Atticus would use."

"You're saying that because you hate the man," Domitius argued.

This stung, but I also was sure it was not just my personal enmity, and I pointed out to him, "Have you forgotten that Balbinus was one of Urso's men first?"

My friend's expression changed, telling me this had indeed slipped his mind, and it was to his credit he admitted, "You're right.

I forgot about that." Heaving a sigh, he said, "So they went out, waited until dark, went to the farm, started the fire. Then waited again until the First relieved us to come back in?"

He phrased it as a question, but it had the ring of truth to it, so I agreed.

"But," I mused, "that still doesn't tell us why he'd do that."

"I'm not so sure," Domitius replied quietly.

Then, just as he was about to advance his theory, there was a shout from Galens telling us to hurry and form up, cutting it short. Not that it really mattered; we had barely gotten started on the day's march when Galens called me up to his spot. When I trotted up, he veered away from the men, drawing us away from the avidly prying ears of the rankers.

"The Primus Pilus is convinced that it was the Taurisci who fired that farm," he told me, his face expressionless, and he refused to meet my gaze as we walked. "He says that makes things simple. We're going to hunt down this warband and then we're going to…"

"I know what we're going to do," I interrupted him, forgetting for the moment he was my superior. "We're going to make life easier for the Primus Pilus and win him some accolades."

"It's not just his life that'll be easier," Galens replied. "It makes things less confusing for us." Glancing over at him, I saw him shrug, then he finally met my gaze, grinned, and said, "We just kill the problem."

"That's certainly easier," I agreed, but felt compelled to say, "to a point. Let's just hope we can do it without losing anyone."

The Hastatus Posterior, who had looked away, turned back to eye me carefully.

"So," he said softly, "now you're beginning to see one of the things nobody tells you about when you decide you want to get promoted, aren't you?"

He did not have to expand; I knew exactly what he meant.

"Yes," I finally replied, feeling the lump that suddenly appeared in my stomach turn over. "Yes, I do."

"No." He shook his head. "Right now, you *think* you know. But," his chuckle held no real humor in it, "you will, Pullus. You will."

Less than a watch into the march that day, a cry was raised from the lead Century that a rider was approaching. Very quickly, we saw it was one of the auxiliary cavalryman, part of the *ala* acting as scouts, the bearded rider, helmet pulled low over his eyes, trotting up to the Primus Pilus before sliding off his mount. When he handed Atticus a wax tablet, we actually continued marching while he stood off to the side, reading whatever was contained in the message.

My Century was just passing by when he snapped it shut, telling the rider, "Tell your Decurion to keep them in sight at all times! I don't want to lose them!" The man saluted, but before he could gallop away, Atticus added, "And I want updates every sixth part of a watch! Let me know if they suspect we're as close behind as we are!"

I could not help noticing how the cavalryman did not bother saluting, but the Primus Pilus was so excited, he made no issue of it. He was now a short distance behind us since we had marched past him, so he went trotting past us back to the front, and because he was on my side of the formation, I could not miss the grim smile on his face. Immediately after he returned to the head of the formation, the lead Century changed the direction of the march, turning slightly to begin ascending a ridge we had been paralleling as we traveled up the valley. A few miles before this, the ridge we were now ascending had essentially split the valley in two as the Savus neared its source and began branching off into two separate streams. We had been following the eastern branch, but now we were climbing directly up the slope that separated the two, and between the grade and the thickness of the trees, our normal cohesion fell apart as we were reduced to small groups of panting men struggling uphill. This was another moment that was my first time experiencing one of the benefits of my new rank, because unlike the men, I was unencumbered, my belongings packed on my very own mule. Truthfully, it was shared with our *Signifer*, Marcus Florens. Regardless of my lighter load, I was panting almost as much as the others, and at some point, I found myself next to Galens, whose face was streaming with sweat as well.

"What," I managed between gasps, "did the dispatch say that put the Primus Pilus into such a lather? We could have turned around and backtracked for no more than a couple miles and gone around this fucking thing."

"I'm not sure," Galens' voice was as strained as mine, "but whatever it was, he's got the bit between his teeth."

That he most certainly did; despite his age, he led the way, although he was still behind the lead Century, yet I was beginning to grow concerned because of his seemingly headlong pursuit. Still beside Galens, I glanced over at him and saw him staring fixedly at the Primus Pilus' back, and I knew the man well enough to see he shared my apprehension.

When Galens paused just long enough to wipe the sweat off his brow, I stopped as well, checking on the Century, somewhat dismayed to see how the normally straight ranks were now so shattered that we looked little better than a barbarian mob. First Section men were mixed among Fifth, Seventh with Tenth, all of them struggling because our Primus Pilus was not only setting a furious pace, but had chosen to charge straight up the hill instead of a more gradual course moving back and forth across the slope.

"I hope he knows what he's doing," I heard Galens mutter after he had squeezed out his felt liner which, despite the chill in the air, was full of his sweat.

Primus Pilus Atticus obviously did, or at least the dispatch had given him information about what lay atop the ridge, because once we crested, there was a clearing just large enough for the Legion to return to at least a semblance of formation, although some of the rear ranks were among the trees. Better still, the view from the ridge allowed us all to look down and see the westernmost branch of the valley as it continued for perhaps two more miles before ending with some low hills farther north. This branch of the Savus was a bit wider than the one we had been following, and from above, one could clearly see the trail along the river left by the Taurisci. While the leaves had changed color, they had not yet fallen, making it difficult to see much beyond that, although I was sure I caught a glimpse of flashing silver near the base of the hills that I was confident was a lake of some sort. Once the nine Cohorts had reached the summit and had been given time to move back into formation, then catch their breath, we went plunging down, naturally reaching the bottom more quickly than it had taken to get to the top. In some ways, descending is harder than ascending, if only because one has to use the muscles of the legs differently; then there is the hazard posed by rocks dislodged by comrades further upslope, although this was somewhat mitigated by the vegetation, so that between the underbrush and trees, only a couple of men were struck by a bounding rock. Every so often on that descent, I would hear a sudden yelp of pain, and once I heard the distinct hollow metallic ring as a bounding rock struck someone in the helmet, which caused me to stop and check, but it was not anyone in our Century. Later, we learned that despite most of the men who were hit by the debris only suffered bumps and bruises, one man had been knocked unconscious and had to be carried down the slope by his comrades. Otherwise, we reached the bottom safely, but once more, we had to pause to regroup. By the time this happened, however, our enemy was the time of day, as the sun was no more than a hand's breadth away from setting behind the series of mountains that lay directly in our path. Even as the rest of the Legion was finishing their descent, I saw another rider approaching from our direction of travel, quickly dismounting to hand the Primus Pilus another wax tablet, which he read rapidly. Subsequently, rather than continue the march, the Primus Pilus summoned the Pili Priores to him, leaving us standing in formation, catching our breath. I stood next to Florens, watching the conference, wondering aloud what awaited us.

"The way he's acting, I wouldn't be surprised if he keeps pressing on in the dark," Florens commented, and I glumly agreed.

This, however, turned out to be only partially true. When Galens returned, he informed us what was about to happen.

"We're settling down here, but not making camp," he told me, his face set in an expression that I knew was his attempt not to convey his feelings about our orders, which was eloquent in itself. "Then, once it's dark, we're leaving a couple Centuries behind to guard our gear, then moving forward."

He paused, which prompted me to ask, "Moving forward to where? And for what?"

"If you'd wait, I'd tell you, idiot," Galens retorted; I suppose he was either catching his breath, or more likely, marshaling his thoughts. "The last dispatch rider told the Primus Pilus that the Taurisci have reached the shores of a good-sized lake, and it looks like they've decided to bed down for the night instead of trying to find a way around it now." Galens paused again, except this time, I managed to keep my mouth shut, and I was rewarded when he continued, "Apparently, the way the lake's situated, there's a high bluff on one side overlooking it that the Decurion believes makes going around on that side next to impossible. And the opposite side doesn't look much better, and the Decurion thinks that's why they're stopping early."

This news answered one question about why the Taurisci had halted prematurely; my guess was their leader was as unfamiliar with this territory as we were, and worried about leading his men on a path around the lake that turned out to be a dead end, yet there was something that still nagged at me.

This time, when Galens stopped talking, he turned away from me and was about to issue orders; I put my hand on his arm to stop him so that I could ask, "Centurion, did the rider say anything about whether they know we're on their trail?"

A look of irritation flashed across Galens' face, but I saw my question had actually struck home because he said, somewhat grudgingly, "As far as I know, they don't, but the Primus Pilus didn't say one way or the other. Now," he asked sourly, "may I issue orders to our Century, Optio?"

My face suddenly became hot, and I mumbled something that he ignored. All up and down our column, arrayed along the narrow valley floor, the bellowing voices of Centurions issuing orders split the air, and now Galens' joined in. His orders were met with the reaction I expected, mainly because I shared their dismay; spending a night out in the open, without even the canvas of a tent between us and the elements, was not an appealing prospect. Nevertheless, we quickly got the men settled down, the slaves unburdening the mules, then leading them to the stream to water before hobbling them and strapping on their feedbags. Meanwhile, men got as settled as they could, quickly breaking out rations, yet as quickly as they did so, the Primus Pilus shouted the order there would be no fires, apparently worried that the rising smoke would alert the Taurisci, now supposedly about three miles away from us. While we were screened from view by the thick forest, it was true that the smoke from several hundred fires could hardly be missed, but this did not make the men any happier.

"Don't worry, boys." I walked among the Century, most of whom were now sprawled out, using their packs as bolsters to lean against. "I don't think you're going to have to worry about getting cold. We're only staying here a little while."

This did not seem to cheer any of them, and when I caught Domitius' eye, I saw he was as displeased as the rest of them. In spirit, I was with the men, but this was yet another example of how I had to separate myself from my comrades and friends. As the men chewed their cold rations – most of them, being veterans, had long since learned to squirrel away hunks of bread, bits of pork and cheese, for just such occasions – Atticus held another meeting, except this one included all Centurions and Optios.

The Primus Pilus had retreated to the banks of the stream, some two hundred paces away from where the men were gathered, and he wasted no time in telling us, "We move just before dark. We're going to use the last of the light to get to those trees." He pointed at the forest that ringed the far edge of the valley. "We're going to deploy on line in between the two ridges," he continued using his *vitus* to indicate the dispositions, "from that slope over to the opposite one." He turned back to us and gave us a grim smile. "Then we're going to advance through the trees until we're in position."

Atticus stopped speaking, although unlike Galens, he was not just catching his breath, and as he gazed back at us, I had the distinct impression he was expecting us to applaud or otherwise demonstrate our appreciation for his genius.

Instead, it was the Secundus Pilus Prior, Vibius Terentius, who asked, "In position for what, exactly?"

Honestly, I cannot say which was more unusual, that a subordinate would put the question in all of our minds so bluntly, or that Atticus looked surprised to be asked such an obvious question.

"What do you mean, Terentius?" Atticus scoffed. "We're going to teach these Taurisci bastards a lesson they're not going to forget, that's what!"

Galens and I exchanged glances, as did all the men around us, looking to their superior or subordinate, or to the men they naturally tend to stand with during such moments. Although this was still one of the few times I had attended such gatherings, it did not take an expert to see that the looks men were giving each other were for the purpose of seeing who would speak first, urging their counterparts to be the one to break the silence. Finally, as seemed to always happen, it was Aulus Macerinus, who had been our Primus Pilus for a short period of time after the death of Urso, before Atticus arrived in Rome, who served as our spokesman.

"Primus Pilus," Macerinus' tone was formal, "when you say we're going to teach them a lesson, what exactly does that mean? Are we going to…"

"We're going to give them a taste of Roman iron," Atticus interrupted impatiently.

"But they haven't actually attacked any Romans, or done any damage to Roman property," Macerinus protested.

Atticus gave his second in command a wave that clearly demonstrated his impatience. "What do you call what happened to that farm last night? That," he pointed back in the general direction of the farm, which was on the other side of the ridge, "was Roman property!"

Suddenly, the atmosphere changed more quickly than it takes to describe it, and once more, I saw men looking at each other, except this time, there was a low buzzing as the officers of the Legion mumbled to each other. And now Macerinus looked quite unhappy at being the one who had spoken up, because there seemed to be a silent agreement among the rest of us that he continue in his role as our spokesman.

"Primus Pilus," Macerinus finally replied, "while it certainly looks…suspicious," I admit I winced, because from my viewpoint, that suspicion was not aimed at the Taurisci, and I saw that Atticus took the word the same way, because he suddenly stiffened as the Pilus Prior plowed on, "I'd simply point out that not only do we not have actual proof it was the Taurisci, but that it was simply property that was destroyed. No Roman lives were lost. At least," he did think to amend, "from what we saw. There weren't any bodies in the ruins of that farm."

"And who would do that besides the Taurisci? And did anyone lay eyes on that farmer and his family when we went and searched the place? Or any of his slaves, for that matter?" Atticus asked, but while his tone was soft, I, for one, heard a distinct undercurrent of menace.

Obviously, so did Macerinus.

"I-I-I can't think of anyone else who'd have done such a thing," the Pilus Prior stammered, and despite the fact that a part of me recognized that I would in all likelihood have done the same thing, there was another part that caused my lip to curl in disdain as Macerinus rolled over and showed his belly to the Primus Pilus.

"Neither can I, Macerinus." Now that he had clearly won, Atticus' demeanor became almost genial. "Which is why we're going to punish them for their perfidy!"

"Isn't that a bit…drastic?"

Glancing over, I was merely confirming that the question did come from a voice I had recognized, the question coming from Numerius Plancus, the Quartus Pilus Prior now that Corvinus had retired. Something I had observed long before I enlisted was how Pili Priores who have been in that post for a period of time tend to have Centurions under their command who are similar, at least in outlook and approach to the job, and Plancus was a good example of this trait. Like Corvinus had been, he was known as a hard, tough leader who could engage in debauchery and revelry that any Gregarius would envy, and strive to emulate. And, as he was showing at this moment, like Corvinus had been, he was utterly fearless when it came to braving the ire of his superior. And he definitely managed to do that.

"Why, Plancus," Atticus sneered, "I wouldn't have picked you as one who'd be reluctant to get stuck in. That's something I'd expect from…" He named the Nones Pilus Prior, which as I am sure was his intent, elicited a collective gasp of shock from us at what can only be called a mortal insult.

Plancus' face went white, the contrast made even starker by his red soldier's tunic and transverse crest, but somehow, he managed to reply, "Nothing could be further from the truth, Primus Pilus. I assure you that you'll see my sword will be just as wet as any man's in the Legion!"

"Good." Atticus went right back to an almost bantering tone. "Now that that's settled, you're dismissed. The order to move will be coming shortly."

Leaving our gear behind, the Legion began the advance, with uncovered shields but still in column, at least until we reached a point just short of the edge of the forest. All the Primus Pilus' commands were done verbally and not by *cornu*, which meant there was a slight delay in our deployment. The width of the valley was such that all nine Cohorts would not fit, even when we were arrayed in our two-Century-deep formation, where three Centuries per Cohort were in the leading line. Ultimately, the Eighth and Tenth served as a *de facto* reserve, and by the time Atticus was satisfied with our dispositions, the last of the sun had just dipped behind the hills. Yet, even as I stood there wondering how in Hades we were going to manage to maneuver through the woods with our formation intact, let alone not stumble into the Taurisci, my question was answered. Somewhat to my chagrin, I had forgotten that it was a full moon, which was now rising to our right as the sun set to our left. As often happens during the autumn, it seemed to be much larger than normal as it rose just above the ridge we had crossed not long before, and I began to think my fears were unfounded. Then, Domitius said something, calling to me from his spot in the formation just as we were about to enter the trees that shattered my newfound confidence.

"Optio," he called out, and when I looked over at him in the last light of day, his face was grave, his lips in a tight, thin line, "does this remind you of another night?"

"Not until you brought it up," I snapped; I was truly upset with my friend because, honestly, I had been happily ignorant about the similarities to the night when the previous Primus Pilus had used a full moon in order to set a trap for rebelling Colapiani tribesmen.

It had been the most trying night of my life to that point, and I glared over at Domitius, yet even as I opened my mouth to hurl some sort of threat or imprecation at him for bringing it up, I also remembered that it had been Domitius who suffered a grievous wound that had almost taken his life. And that he had been my companion during that night, as we fled from one place to another, trying to avoid the horde of Colapiani warriors who had crept up in the darkness to descend on what they had been sure was a sleeping Legion, only to find that they, in fact, were the ones being fooled. Nevertheless, Domitius' mention of that night summoned a host of memories, few of them pleasant, making it hard to concentrate on my job as we entered the shelter of the trees. My composure was further threatened by the way the trees diffused the light of the steadily rising moon, bathing all of us in a silvery light. Actually, it was slightly different from that other night because like also often happened in autumn, there was a golden tinge to the moonlight, at least early on, that I know farmers called a harvest moon. Thankfully, my eyes quickly adjusted, and I took some comfort when I realized that not only was the vegetation not quite as thick as it had been the other time, the slope was much shallower than it had been as well. Actually, when we reached the edge of the forest, my eyes told me there was no hill at all, but fairly quickly, we found that this was not the case. However, the slope was not steep; my estimate was that this low hill rose no more than a hundred feet, which meant it was difficult to tell when we were at the top. As I mentioned, we were in a line of seven Cohorts, with a double line of Centuries, but in a change from our normal alignment, where the First would have anchored the right, Primus Pilus Atticus had put us squarely in the middle, with the Second Cohort to our right, and the Third Cohort to our left. As the Sixth Century, we were actually in the second line, immediately behind our Third Century and next to the Fourth Century of the Third. What this meant in a practical sense was it actually made my life slightly easier, because we had the Third Century directly to our front, and the light was still strong enough that I could align my side of the formation with them. Every so often, I would have to step over a fallen tree, or in the case of a deadfall, we would have to move one way or another so that our path was not always in a direct line straight ahead, but that was really the only challenge. Then, catching us by surprise, we heard the hissed warning of the Optio of the Third just ahead of us, telling us to come to a halt, which meant it was understandably ragged. Still, we came to a stop, then waited as our

Primus Pilus presumably sent a section ahead to scout. At least, this was what I assumed was happening, but honestly, I had no idea. Neither did anyone else, judging from the way the men were fidgeting about, although they managed to refrain from whispering their speculation to each other; at least, once I raised my turf cutter handle in a silent threat. In moments like this, time is impossible to judge, at least for me; my guess is that we stood there for at least a sixth part of a watch, before the Optio of the Third, Gnaeus Considius, came trotting back to where Galens was standing at the front of the Century. My Centurion beckoned to me, and I moved quickly to where he was standing, along with Florens and our *Cornicen,* Tiberius Velinus.

"We've located the Taurisci," Galens explained, waving the Third's Optio away now that the message was delivered. "They're camped along the shore of the lake, but there's a...complication." I certainly did not like the way my Centurion uttered the last word, but this time, I waited for him to continue, and I was glad I did. "But the Primus Pilus is going to turn it to our advantage." He went on to explain, "There's a high bluff overlooking the lake on the eastern side. According to the scouts, the part of the bluff directly above the lake is a sheer drop of more than a hundred feet." This prompted a whistle from me, but Galens ignored me, continuing, "The Taurisci aren't camped on the bluff, which the Primus Pilus thinks means that the part of the bluff the scouts can't see, as it curves around the shore of the lake is the same steepness, which is why they aren't up there, because it would trap them." He hesitated for a moment, then finished, "But just to be sure, he's sending the Eighth and Tenth around the long way. They're going to set themselves up on the bluff to either cut the Taurisci off in case they can get up there and there's a way down on the other side we can't see. And even if they don't, the Primus Pilus is sure that they'll at least be able to rain javelins down on them when we attack."

It took a moment for my mind to absorb what Galens had just told me, although it did not take nearly as long for the cascade of doubts to begin flooding through me.

"How long is it going to take for them to get in place?" I asked, just the first problem that popped into my head.

"He's giving them a watch," Galens' tone was flat, which was telling in itself, and I suppose he was thankful that the shadows cast by the moonlight hid his expression, at least for the most part.

"And how are we going to know they're in position?"

Now Galens took a deep breath, which gave me an instant to brace for his answer.

"They're going to wave torches once they're in position."

Frankly, I did not know what to say to this, particularly since we were not standing far away from the men, who I knew from firsthand experience, were avidly listening to our exchange.

Finally, I simply asked, "So what do we do in the meantime?"

"Sit down," Galens replied. "We're going to stay here for two parts of the watch, then start moving into the final position over the last part." Sensing he was done, at least for the moment, I saluted, which he returned, then just when I turned to relay the order, he grabbed my arm. "Tell them to keep their mouths shut, and no dicing or anything else that might make noise. I have to go talk to the Primus Pilus."

For a brief instant, I felt a flare of hope that Galens was about to at least try and talk Atticus out of this course; my Centurion must have somehow understood this, because I saw him shake his head.

"The Primus Pilus wants all of the Centurions from the Cohort with him to talk about the details. That's all," he emphasized, and I understood the implicit warning in his voice, which forced me to shut my mouth and stop my plea to Galens that he at least try and change the mind of our Primus Pilus.

Instead, I nodded and he turned away, leaving me to relay the orders. Not surprisingly, there was some muted grumbling, but after I poked a couple men with my handle, they settled down to wait. Since they could not talk, nor could they gamble, most of the men took advantage of our pause to try and catch some sleep, some using their packs as pillows, others leaning against trees. Meanwhile, I occupied myself by watching the moon slowly rise, the golden hue disappearing from the orb as it rose above the ridge, the normal silvery light returning. Without a pack of my own, I was forced to find a tree against which I could sit, trying to get as comfortable as I could, ruing the fact that my rations were back with the mules, under guard by the slaves and a single Century. It was not only that I was hungry, but having something to do, even as mundane as eating, would have kept my mind occupied and stopped it from going places I did not want it to go. Granted, my experience to this point was not as extensive as that of our Primus Pilus who, despite his time with the Praetorians, had served with the 2nd Legion in Cantabria, not to mention their time under Augustus during the civil war. Regardless of this disparity, I was not feeling much confidence in this plan, although I also admit my viewpoint is colored now by all that transpired. I did, however, take some odd comfort in the fact that I could tell just by Galens' reaction I was not alone in my concern. One thing I vividly remember from that night was the sudden stab of envy I felt as I watched the rankers of my Century who were happily oblivious to what their futures likely held. All they knew at this point was they were stopping for a period of time, the length of which they had no clue about, then they would receive another order. It is a simpler life, certainly, and one that holds its own rewards, in an odd way. Then, in the next moment, I realized that, when I had, in fact, been sitting there, among friends and comrades, I had been obsessed with knowing what awaited us, and how I always tried to listen in on the conversations between my Centurion and Optio, just like the one that had taken place between Galens and me shortly before. Despite myself, I felt a chuckle escape my lips, which caused some of the rankers' heads to turn, which served to make the moment even funnier to me because I knew exactly what they were thinking. Why's he laughing, they wondered? What does he know that we should? Somehow, I managed to stifle a full laugh, but to keep my mirth from spilling out, I reached down and pinched my arm, specifically on my old scar since it was still tender. It was drastic, but it worked, and I finally managed to resign myself to the moment and at least keep my thoughts from taking me places that would not hold any profit.

"Pullus!"

My name was accompanied by a hard kick to my foot, which prompted me to leap up, my heart suddenly racing, both from fear and shame that I had clearly fallen asleep.

"Sorry to rouse you from your peaceful slumber," Galens had obviously been the one who kicked me, "but it's time to move."

Shaking my head to clear the last tendrils of sleep, I was further ashamed to see the men of the Century had already been roused, although they were doing much the same as I had just done. Without any command I heard, the Third Century suddenly began moving forward, and while we quickly followed, it was ragged, without the precision we normally displayed. Because we had begun moving so swiftly after I was awakened, this is the first moment I remember looking up at the moon to judge how much time had passed. Again, my recollection is certainly influenced by what was about to happen, so I cannot say with any confidence that I really saw what seemed to be a slight shadow on the bottom edge of the full moon. If I did, I certainly did not give it more than a passing thought, my attention required on other matters that at least seemed to be more pressing in the moment. We certainly did not move as quickly as we had when moving into our first position, and this final advance was made in fits and starts, with frequent stops as the sections sent out in front of each Cohort called a halt for one reason or another. Because of our position behind the Third, and my spot at the rear of my Century formation, I was lucky to just get a glimpse of the front rank of the Third; seeing beyond that was an impossibility. Then, at some point, I realized I could not even see the front rank of the Third either, and this was when I can positively say I looked up and over my shoulder at the full moon. Except it was not full any longer.

"What the...?"

I believe this was all that came out, but I was moving more quickly than I had been as I said it, trotting up to the front before cutting across the front rank to reach Galens.

"What are you doing?" he snapped, but he did not bother looking over at me when I fell into step beside him. "You're out of your spot!"

Rather than reply, at least verbally, I simply pointed upward. Following my finger, my Centurion actually came to a sudden stop as he stared upward.

"What the fuck...?"

"That's what I said," I agreed, then added, "more or less."

Since I had stopped with Galens, the Century continued, although naturally, the men on the outer file immediately next to us, seeing us moon gazing, copied us and no amount of discipline could stop the sudden ripple of chatter, even if the men remembered to whisper.

"Shut your mouths," I snapped.

"Optio," a ranker used his spot in the middle of the formation to stay anonymous, although I felt sure I recognized the voice, "it's getting darker! Maybe this is a sign from the gods!"

I opened my mouth to argue, except nothing came out, and I confess I was not altogether certain this was not the case. Fortunately, before I could allow my mind to start running away with the idea this assault was doomed to fail, Galens grabbed me roughly by the shoulder plate of my armor.

"Go find the Primus Pilus, now! Make sure he's aware of what's happening!"

I did not hesitate, trotting ahead until I was at a spot where I could once more cut across the front of our second line and reach a point just behind the First, before changing direction to run forward. Honestly, I was not confident that Atticus would be in his spot, thinking it likely he would be moving along the front line of the other Cohorts, making sure our alignment was what he wanted. Fortunately, I found him exactly where he was supposed to be, next to Capulo, carrying the Legion eagle, Varus the *Cornicen* on the opposite side. Unsurprisingly, he could not hear my approach over the thudding footfalls of his Century, so when I called out, he whirled about in surprise.

"Optio Pullus," he returned the salute I offered once I slowed to match his pace, "I hope you have a good reason for being out of your place!"

Instead of answering immediately, I pointed up at the moon; even in the short amount of time that had elapsed, the shadow creeping across the face of the moon had grown.

"What…?" Atticus muttered and, like Galens, came to a complete stop, staring up at the silver-white orb with an open mouth.

"Hastatus Posterior Galens sent me," I told him, thinking that this would be self-explanatory.

I was wrong. Atticus shut his mouth abruptly, and while the brim of his helmet shadowed his eyes, I saw his jaw set and his lips seemed to disappear into a thin line.

"And?" he asked irritably. "Or is that it? He just…sent you? To do what, exactly?"

Suddenly, I realized I had no idea how to answer, although I finally managed, "What are we going to do? I mean, if we lose the rest of the moonlight?"

"Why, we're going to teach the Taurisci a lesson," he replied, and if he was pretending to be surprised, he did a good job of it. "What else would we do?"

"What if we lose the rest of the moonlight?"

"How do you know we will?" he challenged. "Are you suddenly an expert in the habits of the moon and stars?" Atticus' laugh was mocking, as I am sure he intended it to be. "Can you tell me with any certainty that," he pointed up at the moon, "it's going to get any darker than it is right now?"

"No, sir," I admitted.

"Then I suggest you get back to your spot and do your duty to make sure your Century is ready to do what needs to be done," I suppose he felt the need to emphasize his words by pointing his *vitus* back in the direction of the Sixth.

"Yes, sir." I turned and began trotting back in the opposite direction, but I was pulled up short.

"Pullus," he called out, "how about you do your job, and not worry about me doing mine, neh?"

There is no way to know what was in his mind, yet I felt certain his goal was to take me down a peg. However, instead of snickers or muttered agreement, my former comrades of the First Century remained stolidly silent, except for the stomping feet and creaking bits of gear. Even in the gloom, I could see Atticus' expression at this sign of silent support for me, which I admit made me feel a bit better, and I did not bother answering him. I also wonder if this played a role in later events.

"Well?" Galens asked when I got back.

I could only answer with a shrug, and he muttered a curse, then told me to return to my position, which I did. My heart was steadily pounding now, but it was not from the exertion alone. The 8th continued forward, and with every step, what light there was grew dimmer.

By the time we stopped, it was impossible for me to see past the front of my own Century, and the moon was obscured more than halfway. However, there were other sources of light, in the form of the fires of the Taurisci, which were arranged in a line across our front. Being veterans of the province, we knew it was common practice for whatever warriors were on sentry duty to keep the fires fed throughout their watch, although we had no way of knowing how many sentries there were. Nor could we know how experienced those guards might be; if we were lucky, they would be the greenest warriors in the bunch, the ones who found themselves staring into the fire and thinking of home, thereby ruining their night vision. There was just enough light left from the moon, now about three quarters obscured that through the last of the trees that ended perhaps two hundred paces away from the fires, I could see the lake beyond reflecting both the flames and what little moonlight was left. To our right, I saw the darker bulk of what I was certain was the bluff, and it, in fact, did thrust up into the sky, obscuring the stars, although I thought it was well more than a hundred feet. From what I could tell, the ring of fires were arranged in something resembling a scythe, with the open side facing toward the water, and I assumed this was because the Taurisci camp followed the shoreline. I will say that the Primus Pilus had managed to maneuver us so it looked as if our Cohort was aiming right for the middle of the camp, but we now crouched down, presumably waiting for the signal torch. I found myself staring up at the bluff, until it disappeared, merging into the blackness around it, which prompted me to look for the moon. It was gone, except before I could examine the sky more thoroughly, the air was suddenly split by the sound of a *cornu*, blatting out the notes that served to launch us in our assault on the Taurisci. Only later did we learn this premature signal was ordered by Atticus when one of the sentries sounded the alarm.

"All right, boys!" I heard Galens bellow. "Let's kill these bastards!"

If he said anything else, it was drowned out by the full-throated roar of not just our Century, but the entire Legion as we suddenly leapt up and went half-running, half-stumbling across the remaining space. I will say it was the slowest charge I had been part of since I was a *tiro* in the early days of training, when we walk through a maneuver before we try it at full speed. By the time the front ranks of the Centuries of the seven Cohorts reached the edge of the Taurisci camp, total chaos reigned, as I heard the thudding sound of men stumbling and losing their balance, whereupon the comrade immediately behind the unfortunate tripped over his body, eliciting curses and yelps of pain, well before first blood was drawn by an enemy. At least, I believed we were in total disarray, until someone in the enemy encampment had the presence of mind to kick the burning logs of the fire just to our right front, scattering the burning brands and immediately dispersing the light. The only light, as it turned out, because the moon had completely disappeared from view, despite there not being a cloud in the sky above us. Probably within no more than thirty heartbeats, the warriors in the immediate vicinity of the other fires had followed the example of the first man, or men, meaning what little illumination there was remaining was quickly extinguished. Then, we were fighting in a darkness so smothering and complete that instead of the normal sounds of metal clashing with metal, or the deeper thudding sound of shields smashing into something, there rose a clamorous sound I had never really heard before as men on the same side began colliding with each other in the gloom, judging from the surprised curses filling the air. It is difficult to describe at all, and impossible to do so with any real clarity, what it was like, because as we all quickly discovered, while our eyes had somewhat adjusted to the darker gloom caused by the vanished moon, the sudden disappearance of the scattered fires removed what residual light there had been just a couple of heartbeats before. As I instantly discovered, even when there is relatively little light available, our eyes somehow adjust, at least somewhat; removing even this small amount instantly renders Romans incapable of fighting in the manner in which we are trained. It also makes it impossible to know exactly what happened in any sense wider than the world around me within my physical reach. Consequently, even as the smaller sparks and embers were still floating in the air, some men in the first rank either slowed down significantly, or stopped completely, trying to regain their bearings and adjust to the new conditions. Which meant, not surprisingly, those of us in the second rank of Centuries could not see this; the only thing that saved me from a collision into the back of someone was because of my spot even with and slightly separated from the rear rank. Nevertheless, my ears plainly told the story, as a sound that was akin to when two forces rush at each other collide, except there were no shouts, cries, or shrieks in anything but Latin. And, because every man had discarded his javelin and drawn his sword, inevitably, an onrushing man of the second line would go careening into the backs of comrades who, if they were lucky, were struck by the shield of his unintentional attacker. Judging from the shrill screams in at least three or four spots within my earshot, some were not so lucky, taking an inadvertent sword thrust to the back. Immediately, the sheer, piercing sound of whistles began, as individual Centurions attempted to provide some sort of clue about their own positions, clearly counting on the combined experience of the men to be able to judge by sound where they were supposed to be. This was confusing enough, but then the shouting started.

"Sixth Century! On me!"

"Third Century! Rally on me!"

"First Century! Come to me, you bastards!"

In one sense, I was lucky, because Galens had been one of the first to begin yelling, and he was roughly in the spot I would have expected him to be, although I was one of the few. It is hard to lay blame at any individual Centurion's feet; I certainly could never remember a moment where the Centurion needed to supply the Cohort number as well as the Century, even during the night in the town when Urso died. Comparatively speaking, in truth, the light provided by the town burning down around us was as close to being in broad daylight as possible, especially when compared to this night. Despite the fact that I was sure I knew where Galens was, getting to him was another matter entirely, nor was I sure this was what he wanted. Nevertheless, I had gone perhaps two steps when I was struck a terrific blow from my right side that would have knocked me flat, and probably out, if I had been smaller.

"Optio," I heard a voice I thought belonged to a man in the Fifth Section gasp, "is that you?"

Honestly, I was not sure who I was, and it took a moment for my head to clear, yet even as it did, I was groping out for my unseen assailant, finally feeling a shoulder plate.

"Yes, it's me, you fucking idiot," I growled. "Where are you going?"

"I don't know." I did not need any light to hear the edge of hysteria in his voice. "I can't see a fucking thing! Where are the barbarians? Pluto's cock, where are *we*?"

Automatically, I opened my mouth to answer, except realized I had none to give; I was as confused as he was. Forcing myself to think, I decided the first step was to try and determine our position relative to the Taurisci. It is important to relate that, even as I was trying to do this, the roaring sounds of mayhem were all around us, as men were calling for each other, the Centurions kept blowing their whistles, and there were intermittent sounds that were more common to a fight, as a man's shield struck that of a foe, or a sword blade struck home. Standing there, I know now it was no more than a half-dozen heartbeats I was motionless, yet it felt like more than half the night passed as I tried to get my bearings. Finally, I decided the noise coming from one direction seemed to be more akin to a fight between foes instead of friends, and I physically turned the ranker, who was actually facing in a perpendicular direction to where I thought the fight was going on.

"Let's head this way," I finally said. "It can't be any worse than where we are."

When I began moving in that direction, I still had a grasp on the ranker's armor, but before we went three or four paces, he lurched away, and I lost my grip on him.

"Gebellius!" I bellowed; that was who I thought it had been, but honestly, I never found out if I was correct. "Where did you go?"

"Optio?" I heard him call, but he seemed to be several paces off to my right.

Had I been moving in a straight line or had I been veering off to the left? I wondered. Or did he swerve to the right? There was no way to tell, except when I decided to move towards him, I ran into someone else. This time, it was a happier surprise, at least for me, although this time, I knocked the man off his feet. I heard him gasp in surprise when we collided, then the sound of him crashing to the dirt, followed instantly by a round of cursing.

"Watch where you're going, you fucking idiot!" Domitius snapped, albeit from his spot on the ground.

"That's no way to talk to your Optio," I answered, laughing despite all that was happening.

"Titus?" He sounded both surprised and happy. "Help me up, you big bastard!"

He shouldn't be addressing me that way, I remember thinking, but frankly, I was so happy to hear a familiar voice, I did not really mind. However, when I automatically bent over and offered my hand, we both discovered the futility. I suppose we both looked rather silly, waving our hands about in a blind attempt to make contact.

Finally, he grumbled, "Never mind. I'll get up on my own." An instant later, the position of his voice changed, yet when he spoke again, once more, I found a laugh escaping from me.

"What's so funny?" he demanded.

"Since I'm going just by the sound of your voice, I realized there's not much difference between when you're sitting on your ass and when you're standing up," I told him. "I guess I never realized how short you are."

"Very fucking funny," he growled, except I used it as a guide, reaching out once more, touching his shield first, then using that to find his shoulder. "But what do we do?"

"Head towards the sound of the fighting, I suppose," I said.

So we did, except this time, I kept a firm grip on my friend's shoulder, and I was reminded of the saying about the blind leading the blind.

Piecing it together later, we determined that most of the Centurions, after their first attempts to restore some semblance of cohesion, quickly gave up the attempt, which explained why both their verbal cries and their use of their whistles stopped. Instead, without any directive from Atticus, the Centurions of the 8th, in the mark of a truly veteran Legion, simply began urging men to move to the sound of the fighting. This was not only understandable, it was really the only alternative, yet what it meant in a material sense was that the 8th was crippled in its ability to fight as a Legion this night. As all new *Tirones* are told, and any veteran who has faced barbarian tribes can attest, the Legions of Rome are not the most potent fighting force in the world because we field the best warriors. Indeed, if one were to bring an observer from a faraway land who has never been to Rome or knows anything about us other than our reputation for our military prowess, then ask them to pick out the Roman from an array of men who were not attired for battle, I do not believe any of them would be able to correctly identify the Roman Legionary, with the possible exception of me, or my Avus, perhaps. Otherwise, I am fairly certain they would be more likely to pick out a Suebi, or another German, even a Taurisci, whom it is said are distant relatives to the tribes of Germany. Whoever they picked, it is very likely they would not pick out the man who stood just a few inches above five feet tall, and who normally weighed perhaps a hundred twenty pounds, and that is at the beginning of the campaign season when we are all fat from the winter. I offer this as the reason why, in this fight, most of the men were at a disadvantage, at least during this period of absolute and total darkness. Oh, there were small, guttering flames scattered about, where the logs and branches that had been part of a fire were strewn, but the moon was still missing, and the only other light was from the stars. With Domitius more or less in my grasp, we inched our way forward, trying to determine how the fight was going just by the sounds. Finally, we reached a point where, directly in front of us, I could hear the grunting, cursing, and moaning of men locked in mortal combat, punctuated by the clanging of iron against iron.

"What do you want to do?" Domitius shouted at me.

In answer, at first, I shrugged, feeling a little foolish for doing so. Then, I had a thought.

"Grab on to the back of my harness," I told him. "I'm going to get stuck in, then you can help."

"Help how?" he asked me, and I heard the doubt in his voice. "I'm just as likely to stab you as one of those *cunni*."

A part of me understood he was speaking the truth, except now that I had heard the sounds of a fight, my blood had been stirred, and

I was determined to take part; it had been a long time since I had done anything but spar with the men of my Century.

"If you do," I told him, "I'll fucking kill you. So just make sure you don't."

He did not reply, but I felt his hand move around my own *segmentata*, then find my harness.

"Ready," he announced.

Without hesitating, I went forward as quickly as I dared, without a shield and only my sword out in front of me. Before I had gone more than three or four steps, something slammed into me with terrific force, this time, from my left side, staggering me so much that for a dreadful instant, I was sure I would lose my balance, and more importantly, my feet. My heart had already been hammering; now it felt like it would leap out of my chest as my arms swung around in a desperate attempt to regain my balance. Then I was saved by a strong hand clamping down onto my left forearm, the grip so strong that I yelped from surprise and pain, although I was relieved at the same time.

"Thanks, Titus," I gasped as I got my feet back under me.

Since I had been staggering to my right, my body was leaning at an angle; when I straightened up, it brought me closer to my unseen savior, who I still believe to this day it was natural to assume was Domitius.

"Thanks for what?" I heard, but from behind me in a spot where there was no way it could have been Domitius.

And, as I straightened up, it was not my eyes or my ears that gave me the bare instant of warning, but my nose, as the stench created by a combination of unwashed clothes and body, smoke, and all the other things that identify a barbarian reached my nostrils. In the same instant, just as my mind was coming to grips with the meaning of where Domitius' voice came from and the smell, there was a low, feral growl from my direct left, while the hand gripped my forearm even tighter. This marks the last clear memory I have of the next few heartbeats, as for the third time in a short period, I was assailed by a body hurling himself at me, except this time, the impact knocked me off my feet. I remember a very brief sensation of falling, made even more disorienting by virtue of the fact that my eyes could not see when I was about to hit the ground, immediately followed by an impact that, at least for perhaps an eyeblink of time, lit my world up, in the form of countless tiny stars bursting in front of my eyes. Hearing the whooshing sound of a man's breath being forcibly expelled from his lungs, I was only dimly aware that it came from me; I was acutely cognizant of the weight of another man on top of me, although he had lost his grip on my arm. I quickly discovered why, as what I assume was the same hand blindly flailed about in the vicinity of my neck. Thankfully, for me anyway, his hand landed several inches below my neck as his fingers scrabbled wildly for my throat, his miss giving me just enough time to tuck my chin tightly against my chest. My world had been reduced down to one where there were only two of us, and I was struggling to get my breath back, except it was impossible to do so with this barbarian's weight on me. Because of this, all thought of taking my own offensive action was banished, as the part of a man's mind whose only task is to keep him alive, at all costs, took control. Therefore, instead of bashing the man with my fists; my sword was somewhere around me, the one time the Vinician grip had failed me when it was knocked from my hand by the impact with the ground, I concentrated my rapidly waning strength on getting both my hands in position to shove my attacker off of me, at least enough to draw a breath.

"Titus! Titus! Where are you? I can't fucking see you!"

Despite the fact that my conscious mind knew Domitius was within one or two paces, he actually sounded as if he was at least a hundred away, and I could not spare the breath to give him a clue that I was at his feet. Even as Domitius was shouting for me, my foe, now that he had a better idea of our respective orientation, brought his other hand up, except instead of my throat, his fingers started jabbing down at my face, in a blind attempt to gouge out at least one of my eyes. His nails were long; at least, they seemed to be more like the claws of a wild cat, and there was a burning sensation as he raked his fingers down my cheek. His other hand had crawled up my chest and he was trying to force it under my chin to wedge my head up to expose my throat, and I will say he was extremely strong, the muscles of my neck screaming in protest at the strain. As active as he was in trying to kill me, I was no less so in my quest to stay alive, and I finally managed to bring both of my arms between our bodies, despite the scales of his armor gouging into the flesh of my forearms. The stars that had burst forth when I hit the ground had disappeared, but only briefly; now they returned as my lungs struggled to suck in enough air. Using every bit of my strength, or what was left of it, I pushed against the body of my enemy. Instantly understanding what I was trying to do, he changed his tactic of trying to gouge me, that hand now fumbling away from my face, and I felt him first find, then grab one of the shoulder plates of my *segmentata*, beginning to pull violently in an attempt to stop me from shoving him up and off of me. For the span of perhaps three or four heartbeats we both exerted all of our strength in a simple, brutal contest, as he attempted to smother me and I struggled to get breathing room. I distinctly remember thinking that this would have been a good time for Domitius to finally find me, but then I realized my arms were no longer at the same angle; I had managed to push him away enough, and without hesitation, my lungs suddenly filled with air of their own volition, the stars vanishing once more. Obviously realizing he was thwarted in his attempt to kill me by suffocating me, he suddenly released his grip on my shoulder plate, while I felt the easing of the resistance against me. By allowing me to immediately push his body farther away, his now-free hand returned to the vicinity of my face, except this time, his fingers thrust down in the vicinity of my mouth, giving me an opportunity I did not waste, despite somehow knowing that by opening my mouth, I could no longer keep my chin tucked in with the same level of strength. There was no real way I could have been able to comprehend this with any level of forethought, yet somehow, I knew I needed to take the gamble.

When I opened my mouth, two things happened simultaneously, as what I had determined was his left hand that he was still trying to jam under my chin was suddenly allowed to do so, and he did not hesitate, my throat suddenly feeling as if it was about to be crushed, cutting off the supply of air that I had just regained. However, I was counting on the second action to ensure his grasp of my throat was brief, as my teeth bit down on no less than three of his fingers, while I used every bit of the strength left in my jaw muscles. As I hoped, the hand around my throat immediately released its grasp, but while that was a relief, the shrill scream just a matter of inches from my ears was almost as painful as everything else that had happened. This was bad enough, but the sudden gush of bile rushing up from my stomach that filled my mouth to mingle with the taste of another man's blood as I continued to bite down against the bones of his fingers, feeling my teeth grating against them, was one of the most unpleasant sensations I had ever experienced. In retrospect, I should have let go, because there was no way I was biting through the bones of three fingers; I knew my Avus had bitten off the smallest finger of one his enemies, but I had all but this man's pointing finger in my mouth. Not surprisingly, when he jerked away, while he relinquished his grasp of my throat, he was more concerned with his right hand, and put more of his strength into that one. And despite relaxing my bite, I was not quick enough, so that when he yanked his hand back, I felt two of my bottom teeth on the left side snap off, sending a bolt of pain that, ironically, helped clear my head of the last of the stars and cobwebs. My own bellow of pain I barely heard, but when he jerked away, lifting his upper body away from mine, my own hands were moving, aiming for his throat. My mouth was full of blood and bile, so I turned my head and spat as much out as I could in order to resume breathing through my mouth at the same time. As I recall it now, this was the moment I became aware of another change. It was still dark, certainly, but a part of me realized I could just make out the outline of my foe's head, enabling my hands to aim for the right spot, more or less. I believe that when he sat up, his legs straddling my body at a point just above my waist, in an understandable but ultimately fatal reaction, he had temporarily forgotten he was supposed to kill me, and instead, was clutching his injured hand with his good one. And this was all the opening I needed, but despite having a better idea of where his head was, I still missed his throat, my right hand colliding with his lower face. Fortunately, for me anyway, the space between my thumb and fingers hit just below his nose to cover his mouth, and I managed to clamp my hand tightly enough around it that, despite his attempt to do so, he could not open his jaws. My sword might have been knocked from my grasp, but my hands are still extremely strong, and instantly adjusting my method of attack, instead of using my left hand to grab his throat, I slid it along his lower jaw to grasp the back of his neck. Clearly understanding what I was attempting to do, he began to try and pull his upper body away from mine, and in doing so, actually lifted my upper body off the ground, yet he could not wrench himself free from my grasp. I believe he realized the futility of this, so that when I started pushing up and away from me with my right hand while pulling the back of his head in the opposite direction, he tried to resist with the last of his strength. My grip on his lower jaw was aided by the thick beard, allowing me to entwine my fingers in it for extra purchase, wrenching what would have been a shriek of pain from my enemy if he could have opened his mouth. I felt the muscles of his jaws contracting in a manner that was similar but different to what I had done perhaps five heartbeats before, except that he was trying to open his mouth instead of clamp it shut. Even in the moment, I remember his lips, pressed against my palm, peeling apart so I suddenly felt the rough texture of his teeth, and I understood his intention was to sink them into my palm. At least, if he had been able to open his mouth, except he never did, and slowly but inexorably I was wrenching his chin towards his left shoulder. Now that I could breathe deeply, I felt my strength returning, but this man was fighting for his life, and was not willing to give in. Sucking in a breath, I summoned one, great effort, shoving my right hand up and away from my own body, as if I was reaching out to grasp his left shoulder, while I did the same thing in the opposite direction with my left hand. I was rewarded by a sudden, snapping sound that I felt more than I heard, vibrating up both arms, while underneath my left hand there was a sort of a ripple under the man's skin, which I am sure was his neck finally giving way. My enemy did not cry out, but I felt an explosive gust of breath escape out his nose as his last breath left his body, and I must say it was a profoundly disturbing experience, different from any other man I have killed, before or since. What was worse, at least in a practical sense, was that what had just an eyeblink before been a living, fighting foe instantly became dead weight. I am also afraid my own strength gave out, because when his body slumped forward towards me, my arms could not keep him from doing so, and he collapsed on top of me. For my part, I was so exhausted that I just lay there for the moment, my senses slowly widening back out so that I became aware that my fight was not the only one that existed. I will never know with any certainty, but I suspect that this entire event lasted no more than thirty or forty heartbeats.

"Optio Pullus! Titus!"

As he told me later, after he lost his grip on my harness, Domitius had been calling my name continuously, yet this was my first memory of hearing it after the time I described previously. Gasping, both from the exertion and the return of a dead weight on my chest, it took me a moment to regain enough breath to reply.

"Over here," I believe I said.

"Over where?" I heard him mutter, but then when I turned my head in the direction of the voice, this was the second instant where I realized I could make out the outline of my friend, just barely.

Understanding that, despite the returning light, it was easier for me to see him outlined against the sky than it was for him to find me against the ground, I repeated myself once, twice, then perhaps a third time before he shuffled over. When I bent down, I heard him gasp when his eyes managed to make out my situation.

"What are you doing with this fucker lying on top of you?"

"What do you think?" I snapped, then told him, "Drag him off me."

I sensed more than saw my friend bend down, then fumble around before he evidently found a spot he could get a good grasp of the corpse. The sense of relief when the weight shifted off me was intense, but even as I sat up, a stench assaulted my nostrils.

"Great," I heard Domitius groan, "this *cunnus* just *cac*ed himself."

"You think?" I muttered.

Before I got to my feet, I swept my hand around, searching for my sword. However, while I found my precious Gallic blade, it was because I caught the barest glint of the metal, so that even as I grasped the handle, I glanced up and was surprised, no, shocked to see that the moon had reappeared, or part of it at least. Only then did I belatedly start paying attention to anything beyond arm's reach, but thankfully, my previous inattention did not cost us our lives. Domitius was still next to me, except he seemed to be growing more visible with every heartbeat. From everywhere but directly behind us came the sounds of a fight; still, it was unlike anything either of us had really heard before. Perhaps the best way to describe it is that there was a somewhat muted quality to it; only as the moon reappeared did I understand why, because this battle with the Taurisci was more in the nature of a brawl that one would encounter in a *taverna* in Siscia. Except for the swords and shields, of course, and the fact that men were intent on killing their opponent instead of just beating them senseless. Shouts, cries, curses, screams, in both our tongue and that of the Taurisci, were now accompanied by the return of the bone whistle commands of Centurions who had obviously become aware of the return of the moonlight and realized what a disorganized mess of a battle was taking place. And, as my eyes drank in the growing light, I saw that at least within my limited range of vision, our boys were getting the worst of it, and the reason goes back to our inability to fight as a team. Instead, I could just make out easily a dozen darker shapes, except separated and spread around my front without any sense of order or a pattern I could discern. There were no ranks, no files; just men trying to kill each other in the dark.

"Come on," I told Domitius, yet when I forgot again and pointed with my sword, it was still too dark to see where I was indicating, which prompted me to just tell him to follow me.

There were already quite a few bodies underfoot, making the going treacherous, especially since some of them were moving. Normally, we would have either ended, or helped, those men, but it was still too dark to tell friend from foe. Using mostly my ears, I headed in the direction of where there seemed to be the most men. Of course, this also meant it was where the fighting was heaviest, causing me to risk a glance over my shoulder, relieved to see my friend was still behind me. By the time we were just a few paces away from the rear of the last ragged line of men between us and the fighting, the moon was fully visible again, and the light from it was enhanced by the moonbeams bouncing off the reflective surface of the lake, which was now in view less than two hundred paces ahead. In between the shoreline and me were the Taurisci, in their disorganized mass, then our comrades, who were only just beginning to get organized by their Centurions.

This included Galens, as I heard his distinctive voice calling out, "Pullus! Get over here!"

Making my way to him, I remember being struck by how, compared to the total darkness bare moments before, between the moonlight and its reflection off the lake's surface, it seemed almost like daylight in comparison. Which, of course it was not, meaning I stumbled over what was at least one of my wounded comrades, who yelped in pain, then cursed me roundly in our tongue as I mumbled an apology, although I kept going, intent on reaching Galens.

When I reached his side, he pointed with his *vitus* at a spot, telling me, "I want you over there. We need to get these bastards formed up so we can go help," he moved the *vitus* to a spot closer to the lake, and I saw the depth of our line facing the Taurisci was no more than three men deep, "the Second out." While I moved to the spot he indicated, he continued shouting, "Sixth of the First! On me! Hurry, you *cunni*! These fucking savages don't know they're beaten!"

Domitius was one of the first, but now that the visibility was as good as it was going to be, the rest of the Century found their way to our formation within perhaps thirty heartbeats after I took my spot. Even so, I took a quick count, and was disturbed to see we were missing more than twenty men, except Galens was not willing to wait, giving the command to march the moment he heard me shout our readiness. Being at something of an awkward angle – the Second was more to our left than directly in front of us – it meant a bit of maneuvering to get us aligned to match the Second, but Galens handed that responsibility to me as he moved forward to let the Centurion commanding them we were in position to relieve them. Honestly, I thought Galens' identification of the Century was a guess, but when the Centurion, responding to the tap on the hip that his *Signifer* gave him to alert him he was needed, backed away and turned around, I saw it was indeed Macerinus. There was too much noise to make out what was said, but then Macerinus blew his whistle in the series of long and short blasts that alerted the Second they were being relieved. One by one, the men of the leading rank engaged the Taurisci across from him, either trying to end his foe, or at least send him reeling backward, then quickly stepped a pace to the side before backing up. Except this time, instead of taking their normal spot behind the man that was a member of his particular file, each of them came streaming back through our formation. Consequently, it was not long before the First Section of the Sixth began battling what I could see was an ever-thinning mass of Taurisci, but after a moment's observation, something did not seem to make sense to me. By the time we joined the fight, I would estimate that the Taurisci were perhaps a dozen deep, although they had been compacted down to a smaller front than the Legion was using, and on both flanks, I could see some of our men who were actually standing at about mid-calf level into the water. This was not what disturbed me; what was puzzling was how quickly the mass of Taurisci seemed to be reduced, especially when compared to what I was seeing in front of us. The barbarians currently engaged with my men were steadily moving backward, except it was not because we were inflicting losses at a rate that would explain the speed of their backward movement. I got the answer by virtue of a sudden disturbance, out in the lake of all places. Whereas the moon's reflection was an oblong patch that was rippling in a rhythm that matched the time of the small waves caused by the gentle breeze, part of that patch was obscured by the bodies of the Taurisci. It was from this direction the gentle motion suddenly transformed, changing to what to my eye looked like small whitecaps, pulsating in a much more rapid fashion than just a moment before. Yet, even as I was taking this in, my mind trying to comprehend it, several dark shapes, looking like large, pointed knives, thrust into view.

"Boats! The bastards have boats!"

Almost as quickly as my mind matched the evidence to the shouted description, a question followed.

"Where are they going?"

Then I could not pay any more attention as a shout from the front alerted me that one of our own was down. From the sound of the voice, I determined it had happened to a man just one file from my side of the formation, so I did not hesitate, pushing past the first file into the space, moving rapidly forward, just in time to see the wounded man half-falling, half-staggering into the space, whereupon the second man reached down to grab his wounded comrade to drag him back to the rear. As helpful as it might have been, his aid elicited a cry of pain, followed by a string of oaths, then I was there, bending over and grabbing the man by the collar of his armor.

"Can you walk?" I shouted, but he shook his head, prompting me to modify my grip.

Grabbing one wrist, I squatted down and draped the arm it was attached to around my own shoulder, then stood. This wrenched a cry of pain from the man; I had recognized him as a man from the Fourth Section, Publius Vicarius, and my grimace joined his, mainly because I had no desire to cause the man more pain.

"Easy, Vicarius," I muttered as I sidestepped towards the rear, "I'm sorry I'm hurting you, but we need to get you to the *medici*."

"I know, Optio," it was easy to tell his teeth were clenched, "but it hurts like Dis!"

"How did it happen?"

I wanted to take his mind off the pain, although I felt sure I knew the cause.

"My shield was too far outside," he muttered, and even through the pain, I heard the rueful tone in his voice; this was, in fact, something I had constantly reminded him about, by way of my *rudis* leaving massive bruises on his inner thighs.

I was about to give him a tongue lashing of the first degree, then quickly changed my mind; if this did not cure his problem, nothing would.

Just before I was about to lay him down, he suddenly said, "Optio, I…I don't…feel…."

Whereas just an instant before I felt him at least trying to help me in my task; now, his body went completely limp. Cursing, I simply used my left hand to grab him around the waist and pick him up to carry him the last few paces to where I saw small knots of men who were not in uniform, each of them bent over a dark shape on the ground. When I did, this was when I became aware the entire left side of my lower body getting wet, but it was not water; the liquid feeling warm and quickly turning sticky. Rather than get him to the *medici*, as soon as I reached a pace beyond the back rank, I dropped him, while in the same motion, began removing his *baltea* and baldric. Vicarius had landed facedown, so I pushed him over with a foot, then knelt, wincing at the spray of blood that, as it always does in moonlight, looks as black as ink. The wound was just above his knee, on the inside of his thigh, a sure sign he was correct in his assessment about his shield being too far out. Well, I thought, even as I worked rapidly, if he lives, I can ask him. Wrapping the thinner baldric about three finger's width above the wound, I yanked it tight, eliciting a horrible moan of pain from him.

Although his eyes were closed, I still muttered, "Sorry about that. But, hopefully, you'll live."

Relieved the flow had come almost to a stop, I fastened the baldric so it would not loosen. Then, since he was unconscious, I am afraid I was not at my gentlest as I heaved him up and over my shoulder, striding the last few paces to the nearest *medicus* who, unfortunately for him, was already occupied with another man. Seeing that the wounded man was not only conscious, suffering a wound to the face of some sort that the *medicus* was just beginning to wrap in a bandage, and that he was not from my Century, I laid Vicarius down at the man's feet.

"You need to stop with him and take a look at this man," I ordered.

The *medicus* had obviously not heard me approach, because he jumped at the sound of my voice, giving out a yelp of fright. But then when he turned around, he glanced down at Vicarius for only a moment before shaking his head.

"I'm sorry, Optio." His accent placed him as a German, perhaps Marcomanni; the gods know we had captured a fair number of them. "But I'm not through with this man. Besides," he glanced back at Vicarius, then shook his head again and said flatly, "There's nothing that can be done for him. He's already lost too much blood."

Now, it was true Vicarius' face looked like bleached bone in the moonlight, and even I was forced to admit that he was much, much paler than even Titus Domitius had been when he had been seriously wounded during our night action against the Colapiani a few years before. And honestly, I cannot say whether it was the dismissive tone the *medicus* used, without even touching Vicarius, or his accent; whatever it was prompted me to fill my hand with my Gallic sword.

"Maybe," I spoke quietly, but I could see I had his undivided attention, although his eyes did seem to be focused more on the point of my sword, now about a hand's length away from his face, "you didn't hear me. You need to let that man hold his bandage." When he did not move, only then I roared, "*DO IT!*" Unfortunately, I made matters inadvertently worse, rattling the *medicus* so badly that he dropped the bandage in the dirt, exposing the other man's wound.

I had been wondering why this Gregarius had not protested, then I saw that in fact, he could not, because some sort of edged weapon had sliced the muscles connecting his lower jaw to the rest of his face, so that it hung down at an impossible width.

"I'm sorry, Gregarius," I said, "I didn't realize you were wounded as grievously as you are. But," I turned my attention back to the *medicus*, who had retrieved the bandage and was frantically wiping the dirt from it, "you're not going to die, and my man might. If this *cunnus* doesn't stop fucking about."

This prompted the *medicus* to simply hand over the bandage to the man to apply to his own face, and he did not need to be whole for me to see the look of disgust and apprehension at the idea of applying a bandage covered in bloody dirt to his face. This, however, was not my concern. Waving my sword in a silent gesture aimed at Vicarius, the *medicus* duck-walked over to him, peering down into his face, which was still, while his eyes were closed. But he was breathing; I could see the shallow rise and fall of his armor, so when the *medicus* still hesitated, I gave him a gentle poke in the back with the tip of the sword for extra incentive. In response, he leaned over to press his ear against Vicarius' chest, and I did not need more light to see his grim expression.

"Optio," he sat up, and while he was fearful, he still looked directly at me, which I respected, "yes, this man is alive. But barely. He has lost as much blood as his body can afford."

"Can't the butcher sew that back up?" I asked him.

The *medicus* bent down again, this time to peer more closely at Vicarius' leg. When he looked up at me, his grim expression had, if anything, become more pronounced.

"He could," he granted, except before I could get my hopes up, he added, "but to do that, he would have to loosen the tourniquet. By the time he got the vessel sewn up, I'm afraid your Gregarius will lose what little blood he has left." Shaking his head, he assured me, "Optio, I'd love to be able to tell you that this man can be saved, but…" He did not finish, just shrugging in a way that needed no further elaboration.

"Fine," I finally muttered, "then it's in the gods' hands."

"It's in the gods' hands," he agreed.

I admit, I felt a bit foolish at my display, so I quickly wheeled about and returned to the Century without another word. By the time I got back, I could now clearly see more than a half-dozen small boats, the oars roiling the silvery water around each one as the occupants rowed furiously away. My assumption was they would cross the lake, but instead, even as I was watching, it became clear they were heading for the small island in the middle of the lake. Stifling a curse, I turned my attention back to the fighting, just in time to hear Galens blow the whistle again, sounding the relief. Determined to get my sword wet, as we say – I do not really count breaking a man's neck – I strode back to the Century, except I did not stop at my normal spot, moving immediately to the front. Because of our missing men, the others in the Century, as we are trained to do, had adjusted accordingly, which actually put Domitius on the outside file, and two ranks farther up than his normal spot in the Tenth. Furthermore, this put him as the second man, at least until Galens' whistle blew again, just as I reached the front, prompting the man in front of my friend, who I recognized as a younger Gregarius, a relatively new addition to the Century named Carfulenus, to thrust out with his shield, catching the Taurisci in front of him with a solid blow. So solid was it that the man, wearing a conical helmet and a mail vest that was longer than normal, who either did not have or lost his shield, took a staggering step to his right, forced to use his long sword to remain standing. When a man is in a vulnerable position like this, it does not pay to hesitate, so I took advantage of my longer stride to take a giant step forward in order to put my sword within range. It would have been a relatively easy kill, except that Carfulenus, in his excitement, forgot to step to his right, using the safety provided by the shield of the man of the file next to him. Instead, he moved directly into my path, and I barely managed to stop my blade, which I had brought up into a high second position, with the intent to plunge it down into the face of the momentarily helpless foe, whose only defense was his left arm waving feebly in front of him.

Free of a shield myself, I reached out and grabbed Carfulenus by the back of his armor, roughly yanking him backward and to my left, snarling at him, "You went the wrong way, you fucking idiot! Now get to the rear! I'll sort you out later!"

Domitius, who had already stepped into Carfulenus' spot, did not hesitate, sizing up the situation in an eyeblink, and I do not believe even if it had been broad daylight that my eye would have been able to track it as the point of his blade shot forward. The Taurisci had managed to arrest his stumble, but was still in a position where his only defense, his sword, was oriented in such a way he could not bring it up and forward in a sweeping parry. Although I did not see the actual movement, since my eyes were fastened on the man I had been so sure I was going to kill, I could not miss the sight of Domitius' point plunge into the left eye of the Taurisci, who let out only a short, sharp scream as he immediately collapsed to the ground.

"Lucky bastard," I growled at my friend, who merely laughed at my ire, although his inability to make a retort was at least partially because a warrior leapt over the fresh corpse to thrust a spear at Domitius.

My original intent was to return the favor, so to speak, taking advantage of the momentary vulnerability of this new attacker, whose spear landed a solid blow that was blocked by Domitius' shield, the deep, thudding sound made louder because it was so close. Attacking from the man's right as I would have been, as the point of his spear was momentarily lodged in the wood of Domitius' shield, would have made up for what I viewed as his theft of my kill, but it was not to be. Indeed, I unwittingly put myself in jeopardy, because once more, I was already beginning my thrust when, out of the corner of my vision, I sensed a blur of movement coming from my left. Without any time to think, once more, the watches of training paid dividends as my body twisted from the waist, pulling my left shoulder backward, which my torso naturally followed. Despite moving in a direction that was essentially away from the thrust, when the point of the Taurisci's spear struck me in the side, even as it glanced off the curved plate of my *segmentata*, it hit me with sufficient force that it almost drove all the breath from my lungs, and I felt a jolt of pain. Naturally turning my attention to this new threat, in another of the odd memories, what

I recall now is how the most visible thing about the man who was trying to kill me was the gleaming teeth he displayed, his lips pulled back in either a snarl or a savage smile, framed by a drooping mustache favored by some barbarian warriors. Because of the way I moved, when I twisted away from his thrust, for a brief instant, as the momentum of his own weight behind his attack caused the spear to continue moving in my general direction, if the action were to freeze, it would appear to an observer that the Taurisci's spear had been laid more or less along my side, underneath my armpit, with my left arm partially extended above the shaft. So, before he could withdraw his spear, I dropped my left arm, trapping the shaft between my arm and torso, while I grasped the heavy ash with my left hand, perhaps halfway down its length. In what was essentially one motion, the moment I felt the shaft in my grasp, I gave a tremendous yank, pulling the shaft back towards me and, as if he had not been grasping it all, jerked it from his hand, then continuing the movement, discarded the spear behind me. Counting on this as a distraction, even as I was yanking backward with my left hand, my right hand was thrusting forward, and although it was without the normal amount of power behind it because of the competing directions my body was going, the point of my own blade struck with enough force that, while he blocked with his shield, it was wrenched from his grasp. While his situation was grim, if he had kept his head, he would have...kept his head, so to speak. Instead, deprived of both his offensive and defensive weapon, although it was understandable, his choice to make a desperate lunge for his shield, which had actually more or less slid down his leg, meant he was vulnerable for a span of perhaps a heartbeat, as he was forced to look down for the handle of it. And in battle, a heartbeat is an eternity of time, so this time, when I launched my thrust, my body was in perfect position, and my aim was true, plunging into the base of his neck, under the rim of his helmet and above the collar of his armor, his body toppling over to lie atop the man Domitius had dispatched. As I turned my attention back to the situation with my friend, I was in time to see him land a crippling blow, not with his sword but his shield, shattering the spearman's right arm after he overextended himself.

"Ha!" Domitius shouted as this last Taurisci went staggering away, clutching his now-crippled arm. "You're getting slow, Optio! Two to one!"

"You didn't kill both of yours," I argued, but before we could continue our mock quarrel, Galens blew his whistle for the relief.

Like the veteran he was, Domitius, who was unoccupied and had no need to shove anyone away, stepped to his right, while I stayed put, determined to at least draw even with my friend, as he moved backward, crowing all the way back to the rear how he had bested the Optio.

I never got my chance, because the fight did not last much longer after this moment, the remaining Taurisci, pushed back to the edge of the lake, suddenly throwing down their weapons, the sound of metal hitting rock different from the normal sounds of the fighting. Fortunately, at least for the Taurisci, this was not like the night in the Varciani town, when the fighting was so bitter and lasted so long that when the remaining tribesmen did surrender, it was too late. Of course, much of our bloodlust that night was because of Urso's slaying; this night, while the battle had been a confused affair, and was certainly hard-fought in the sense that it required the Legion to fight in a manner different from the style to which we were accustomed, this was not enough to ensure that the surrendering barbarians were put to the sword. Oh, I have no doubt that, in the span of time, some of their men did not fall immediately after whoever of the Taurisci first shouted the order to surrender; once a man's bloodlust is aroused, it is difficult to suddenly turn it off the same way a barkeeper turns the spigot on an amphora of wine. Still, it was not that long before the sounds of fighting had died out, replaced with the panting, cursing, and moaning coming from both sides. Still, no more than a dozen heartbeats passed before Centurions began bellowing orders to their respective Centuries, the *Corniceni* blew their signals for men to assemble, and more than anything, the cry for the *medici* rang through the night air.

"Pullus!" Galens' voice cut through it all. "I need the butcher's bill!"

As it turned out, this was easier said than done. Not long after the fighting stopped, most of the twenty previously missing rankers made their way back to the Century, but even after doing so, there were still five men missing. Along with the five missing men were a half-dozen who had fallen when we relieved the Second, including Vicarius who, at least at that moment, still lived. Therefore, I was forced to walk along the ground between the edge of the trees and the point near the shore of the lake, searching among the fallen, both wounded and dead. This is a grim business, which was why I called Domitius over to me.

"You're going to help me look for our missing," I told him, but thankfully, he agreed immediately, although I could see from his expression he found it as trying as I did.

Together, we walked slowly along, making our way from the shore, in the direction of the tree line, but we were far from the only ones. Essentially, every surviving Optio was doing the same, but in the area in which their respective Centuries had been, creating a line of us, stopping when there was a pile of bodies, under which one of our own might have been hidden. Fairly quickly, Domitius found one of ours, although he was dead.

However, Domitius felt sufficiently alarmed that he called to me, "Optio! You need to come see this!"

As I made my way to him, I stopped just long enough to dispatch two wounded Taurisci, then I reached Domitius, who was squatting down next to what I saw were two bodies. As bright as the moonlight was, it still was not until I was next to him before I could determine one of the bodies belonged to us.

"It's Vetruvius," he told me grimly, then pointed down, "but look how he died."

I mimicked him, squatting down as well, peering at where the ranker from the Fourth Section, a gnarled, older veteran, seemed to be clutched in a strange embrace with the Taurisci I assumed was his killer. The pair appeared to be holding onto each other, and I was suddenly struck by an odd thought, because I imagined this was how Sextus and I had appeared when we were young and a thunderstorm had come in the night and we sought comfort with each other. Except there was nothing tender or loving about what I was seeing; the

Taurisci, somewhat on his side, still had both hands around Vetruvius' neck, and the Gregarius' face had gone what I was sure was a dark purple but looked black in the moonlight. Protruding from just under the breastbone of the Taurisci was what I knew was Vetruvius' *pugio*, and this more than anything else told me how desperate the struggle had been.

"It looks like the Taurisci managed to get inside Vetruvius' shield," Domitius commented, then pointing to the way the bodies were entwined, said, "then they both lost their feet." His face looked white in the moonlight as he glanced over at me and finished grimly, "Titus, there's no way this barbarian should have gotten inside Vetruvius' shield."

"No," I agreed with a sigh, "you're right." I thought for a moment, then told him, "But remember how dark it was just a bit ago. I doubt poor Vetruvius could have even seen this *cunnus* before it was too late."

"True," Domitius granted, then stood up, which I did as well. "But at the same time, he shouldn't have been able to get that close."

I thought about what he said for a moment, then slowly, the realization of why this had happened came to me.

"It's because," I spoke slowly, letting the idea form more fully, "we don't train for this kind of a fight. We," I shook my head, "have to keep our enemy at sword's length."

Domitius considered this for a moment, then he seemed to accept my explanation.

In an offhanded manner, he said, "Too bad we don't know what to do when something like this happens."

He did not wait for an answer; I do not think he expected one, but as we continued on our search for the remaining missing, my mind was turning over what he had said. By the time we discovered the rest of our missing – Vetruvius turned out to be the only dead man, but one of our wounded, a ranker from the Eighth Section named Petrosidius, was in the almost identical position as Vetruvius had been, with the exception that it had been the Taurisci who had used his dagger to inflict a stab wound to Petrosidius' upper chest – I had formed an idea. It could wait, however, because we still had other matters with which to contend, mainly what to do about the Taurisci who had escaped. At least, this was the case as far as our Primus Pilus was concerned.

Primus Pilus Atticus summoned the Centurions and Optios of the First Cohort, but only after taking the reports of the Pili Priores, and since we got to his side quickly, I was able to hear each Cohort commander give his casualty report. At the same time, I heard more than one of them comment about how some of their casualties came about from circumstances they found unusual.

"Half of the men I lost just had the *cac* beaten out of them," was how Pilus Prior Plancus put it, but by his bitter tone, I could tell he was less than happy about not just the losses, but how they occurred.

Regardless of the circumstances, once the Primus Pilus took their reports, he turned to the officers of his Cohort.

"Those barbarian *cunni*," he turned and extended his *vitus* in the general direction of the island out in the lake, "have rowed out there to the island. They think they're safe." He turned back to us, but because of the shadow, I could only see his mouth, appearing as a bloodless slit and turned down at the corners. "But we need to find more boats, because we're going to row out there and finish them off."

Whenever I was in the presence of Primus Pilus Atticus, much like I had done when I had been a ranker in the First Century, I made sure to be at the rear of whatever crowd was gathered around. In this case, it gave me a vantage point that enabled me to see the other Centurions exchange uneasy glances, but Atticus either missed, or more likely, ignored the looks.

"What are you standing there for?" he snapped. "Go find some boats!"

Naturally, we all scattered, although as Galens and I walked away, he muttered, "And who're the lucky bastards going to be who get to paddle like fucking ducks across this fucking lake to face those fucking barbarians who'll see us coming? Even," he added, "with the dark."

I sensed this was actually not meant to be answered, so I kept my mouth shut, instead walking with him along the shoreline.

"How far are we supposed to go?" I finally decided this was actually a practical question, but Galens did not seem to agree.

"How the fuck should I know?" he growled at me. "He just said 'Go find some boats,' didn't he? He didn't say anything about how long we were supposed to look or how far we were supposed to go."

While this was certainly true, I felt somewhat confident the Primus Pilus did not expect us to circumnavigate the lake, although roughly half the Centurions and Optios had gone in the opposite direction, so we would presumably meet somewhere on the far shore. Not lost on me was the possibility that not all the Taurisci who fled did so by boat, yet it quickly became clear Galens was of a like mind, because our progress was steady, but slow. I believe we did not go more than a half mile along the western shore of the lake before Galens stopped us.

"Fuck this." He shook his head. "We're not going any farther. We're likely to run into some of those bastards who didn't get in a boat and there's only two of us."

Without waiting for me to reply, not that he needed my permission, Galens spun about and headed back to where the Legion was still consolidating itself. When we got back to the Primus Pilus, I admit I was somewhat surprised when the reports of all the First Cohort officers was the same, that they had not found any craft to use to cross the lake.

"Are you telling me that there were only six boats on this entire lake?" Atticus fumed, taking the time to look each and every one of us in the face, including me.

Very quickly, I determined the other Optios seemed to have the same thought, that we would let our superiors answer the Primus Pilus. All of whom, it seemed, were equally determined to let one of their counterparts speak up.

"Have you all suddenly turned into mutes?" he snapped, looking around the rough circle. "Or just forgotten how to speak?"

"No, sir. It's just that we didn't find any boats."

I was only slightly surprised that it was Tiberius Numerius Ovidius, the Primus Princeps Prior, who spoke up, although if going strictly by protocol, it should have been Macerinus. But I had known Ovidius for most of my life; he had been my father's Optio, and was one of the most respected men in the Legion. During off-duty hours, he and Galens were about as close as my father and Corvinus had been, which made sense on a number of levels. Ovidius was about five years older than Galens, but where my Centurion was stocky in build and of average height, Ovidius had a wiry build, and was at least two inches shorter. But he was as tough as old leather, about as brown, at least as wrinkled, and the moonlight made those wrinkles appear like black crevices of an unimaginable depth. Like the rest of the men around me, his eyes were hidden in the shadow cast by the brim of his helmet, only the lower half of his face giving any clue about his expression. His chin was set, his lips drawn into a tight line, and one did not need to know him as well as I to see how uncomfortable he was. Perhaps Atticus picked up on this, because he leaned forward slightly, holding his *vitus* with two hands behind his back as he peered at Ovidius.

"Oh, really?" The Primus Pilus' tone dripped with suppressed anger. "And how far along the lake did you go, Ovidius? Because you weren't gone very long."

This was certainly true; his half of the officers sent by Atticus to scour the eastern side of the lake had actually been standing there when we returned, telling me that even without communicating with each other, the Centurions were of a like mind about wandering around in the dark. Frankly, this was something Atticus should have recognized as well, but if he did, he certainly did not act like it. Rather than accepting or even deigning to ask his most senior officers what their reasons were for not going very far along the shore, instead, we had to endure a tongue-lashing from him about how lacking our obedience to his orders were.

Finally, it was Macerinus who clearly had endured enough of the tirade because he interrupted, "Primus Pilus, I believe we get your point. But it does lead me to ask a question."

Atticus looked surprised, which I suspect was why instead of excoriating Macerinus for stopping him from his tantrum, he said, "And what question is that, Macerinus?"

"Just this..." The Pilus Posterior's voice was calm, in stark contrast to how worked up the Primus Pilus had gotten. "What were we going to do if we found some boats?"

"Why, row across the lake to that fucking island and finish these bastards once and for all," Atticus declared, still seeming to be surprised at what I suppose he thought was a rather obvious and unnecessary question.

"Ah," Macerinus replied softly, nodding thoughtfully; at least, this was what I think he was trying to portray, but I also saw the rest of the small knot of men exchange glances. "I see. So, you'd have us row up to that island, without any way to conceal our movement, then hope the Taurisci allowed us to jump out of our boats and wade onto shore before attacking us?"

When put that way, I saw Atticus suddenly stiffen, and more importantly, his air of confidence seemed to wilt a bit. Nevertheless, he was not ready to signal his surrender.

"Surely we can handle a bunch of savages who've already been beaten," he argued, then shrugged. "I didn't say it wouldn't be a bit bloody, but that's what we get paid for, after all."

"Yes, that's what we get paid for," Macerinus agreed, except he was not through. "But while I'd agree they've been beaten here, I got a good look at the men who got away. I'm sure the commander of this bunch was in one of those boats, and if he's a member of the nobility of the Taurisci, it means the men that are with him are their best warriors." Now it was Atticus who was shifting about, turning his head to stare out at the island as Macerinus continued, "And considering they've got nowhere else to run to, especially when they see we have boats of our own and can just chase them down if they decided to keep going to the far side of the lake, I think it's safe to assume they're not going to be willing to surrender. After all," he finished, "if surrendering was something they were willing to do, they'd have stayed here with the rest of this bunch."

He waved a hand at the mass of men who had been forced to sit down while a Century guarded them. It was impossible to know with any certainty, but just from a glance, my guess was we had around two to three hundred prisoners. Not until daylight came would we be able to get an exact count of the dead and wounded; first, though, we had to finish this night, and I was afraid that Macerinus' plan had rebounded and Atticus would feel his authority was being threatened by this small insurrection among his Cohort. Consequently, my relief was secondary to my surprise when he finally gave a grunt.

"Very well," he said at last, heaving a sigh that I suppose was meant to communicate his overall displeasure. "If you and your men don't have the stomach for it, I don't suppose I can expect any of the other Pili Priores to feel any differently." He pointed away from the lake, back to where the rest of the Legion was busy cleaning up. "Go attend to your duties, and we'll let those *cunni* live to fight another day."

Walking back to our own Century, Galens waited until we were out of earshot before he said, "That's a relief. I was afraid Macerinus had pissed on his feet there for a moment."

"So did I," I replied honestly.

"Well, no matter." He yawned, reminding me I was tired as well. "Let's get the boys sorted out. Get me a butcher's bill. Then we'll find out what's next."

I did as he commanded, and before too long, we were ready for orders from the Primus Pilus, who seemed to have put our balking behind him, because he said no more about it, at least in my hearing. This was why, consequently, I find it difficult to admit that, even if it was for a completely different reason, the Primus Pilus was right; we should have finished those nobles on that island because they would come to cause us more trouble than I could have imagined.

By the time the sun rose, the battlefield by the lake was about as ordered as such a scene can be, with our wounded arrayed in neat rows, attended by *medici* and comrades, while our dead were arranged in a similar fashion, but separated by a couple dozen paces from the wounded. Unfortunately, the Gregarius Vicarius was one of those waiting for the ride in Charon's Boat; he had succumbed to the loss of blood shortly after the fighting stopped, never regaining consciousness. One of the duties of the Optio is to find a deceased man's close comrade and inform him of the loss of his best friend, because it is the surviving man's responsibility to come and place the coin in his friend's mouth, then cover the deceased's face with their *sagum*, or whatever serves as a shroud. The covering of the face serves a purpose both ceremonial and practical; it gives the man charged with the overall responsibility for supervising the dead a visual sign of which men have gone through their penultimate ritual, and which have not. Our losses were not especially heavy, especially considering the conditions, which, as one might expect, were the topic of much conversation and speculation by the men as to the cause and meaning of the moon disappearing. Judging just by the men of the Sixth Century, who represented a typical sample of opinion, it became apparent that judgment was evenly divided about what had occurred. Most importantly, at least from my perspective, it also revealed the deep level of ambivalence the men held about the justice of our actions against the Taurisci.

"The gods were letting us know they don't approve of us trying to slaughter those poor bastards," I heard Marcus Gabinius, a man from the Sixth Section, declare to the rest of his section as they sat in a small circle, gnawing on their rations, drawn from the mules that had been brought to our location shortly after first light. "That's why they made the moon disappear, to warn us away!"

"That's nonsense," scoffed Quintus Vatia, who was seated next to Gabinius and was, in fact, Gabinius' own close comrade. "If the gods wanted us to stop, they would have kept the moon covered!"

"Then why did they send the shadow to cover it up in the first place?"

This came from a third man, but despite his back being to me, I recognized him by his voice and the back of his head. His name was Vibius Scaurus, and I saw his question had not only made Gabinius uncomfortable, it scored points with the rest of the section who sat listening, their heads nodding as they turned their attention back to Gabinius.

Who, it must be said, suddenly did not look particularly comfortable, shifting his position on the ground, and I could almost see the wheels of his mind turning as quickly as they could. But as I knew from experience, those imaginary wheels in the mind of Marcus Gabinius were not only small, they did not turn particularly swiftly either; deep thinking was not one of his strengths.

Stubbornness, however, was, and finally, he admitted, "I don't know," but when his comrades jeered, he insisted, "and none of you bastards know, either! Who knows why the gods do what they do?" Shaking his head, he said, "But what I do know is that they weren't happy at what we did! Anyone with any sense can see that!"

I had been standing nearby, pretending not to be listening as I chewed on my own piece of day-old bread, yet while I briefly considered intervening and offering another explanation, as quickly as the thought came, I discarded it for a number of reasons, not least of which being that if I did as much, it would be for the purpose of showing off. I remember the feeling of surprise at myself, along with a fair amount of pride at this sign of a budding maturity, where I was able to think past the moment of gratification I would feel at being able to demonstrate my superiority in yet another way by recognizing that such a display would not go unnoticed by others who might not be as impressed. And, if I am being completely honest, the truth is that my knowledge about what had caused the phenomenon we had witnessed just a couple watches before was, while certainly deeper than that of Gabinius or his comrades, hardly profound. At the same time, I also somehow recognized my desire to spew my knowledge at these men was not based solely in my desire to impress, but as a way to honor the man who had been the one who taught me what admittedly little I do know of the moon and stars above. Therefore, while I managed to refrain from blurting out what had come to my mind as I listened to men debate about the deeper meaning of the disappearing moon, I went and sought out someone to whom I could divulge what I knew, someone I trusted. Obviously, I found Domitius who, like Gabinius and Scaurus had been, was seated with his section mates, but he jumped up readily enough when I gestured to him.

"So," I began, once he was next to me, making sure to walk away from the others, "what's the feeling of the Tenth Section?"

"About what?" he asked, although I was sure he knew what I was talking about.

"What do you think?" I retorted, then pointed up to the sky, despite the fact that it was now daytime.

"Ah," he laughed, "you mean the gods hiding the moon from us to give us a warning not to continue the attack?"

I admit I was a bit surprised, and I said, "Not you too! Is that what you think?"

He shrugged uncomfortably, looking away as he responded, "No." Then he shook his head and amended, "I don't know. Maybe."

"Well, I'm going to tell you something that should change your mind," I said firmly, then went on to explain what I had been taught by Diocles. "While I don't know what causes things like what happened last night, what I know is they're not random events. Diocles taught me these things happen in a regular pattern, and that there are learned men who would have known the moon disappearing last night would have happened, down to the watch it happened."

I was not surprised at the look he gave me expressing his doubt better than any words could have, yet neither did he dismiss what I said outright.

"So," he spoke slowly, "you're saying that there's someone who could have told us the moon was going to disappear before it happened?"

"Yes," I nodded firmly. "That's exactly what I'm saying. So it's not because of what we were doing. The gods didn't hide the moon as a warning to us."

He considered for a moment, then asked simply, "If it's not the gods who caused this, who is?"

"That," I admitted, "I don't know. But what I do know is that even if we hadn't attacked last night, it would have happened."

Domitius glanced around at our comrades seated nearby, then turned back to me and suggested, "Maybe you should tell everyone else about that. Because right now, most of them are sure it's a sign from the gods. And," he added ominously, "that it wasn't a good one."

Sighing, I shook my head, telling him, "I wish I could, but I don't think that's a good idea."

"Why not?"

"Because," I explained, "think about what would happen. I'd tell the men what I do know about what happened. Which," I pointed out, "isn't all that much if I'm being honest. Just that this wasn't an event prompted by our actions, and that it was going to happen no matter what. The first thing someone would ask is, 'How do you know that?' And how would I explain that?"

Domitius thought for a moment, then answered, "You could tell them the truth, that…"

"That I had a private tutor?" I interrupted. "How many rankers have a private tutor?"

"That's true," he granted, but I was not through.

"And then what happens?" I pressed. "How long before one of the men gossips to a friend in another Century about their Optio who knows things only rich men would know? Then, how long before their Centurion hears?" Shaking my head, I said, "If it was someone like Ovidius, I know he'd keep his mouth shut because of his loyalty to my father, and the same goes for our Centurion. But if it was someone like," I named the Nones Pilus Prior, "how long would it take him to go running to Atticus to tell him one of the Optios in the Legion was some uppity rich boy?"

"But *he's* an uppity rich boy," Domitius began, but before I could say anything, he suddenly nodded his head, giving me a grim smile, "which is why he'd want to run and tell, so he's not the only one who's viewed like that. How long would it take?" he repeated, then gave me a grin as he answered his own question. "How far is his place to the Primus Pilus'? Well, he's always been a fast runner, so...."

This did make me laugh, although it was from equal parts amusement and relief that he had clearly been convinced.

Then, his grin faded, and he gestured back to where our comrades were still discussing the previous night's event, and asked, "But what are you going to do about this? As it stands right now, I'd say more than half of the boys think this was a warning from the gods, and that the Primus Pilus is risking their wrath. And," he added superfluously, as far as I was concerned, "if they punish him, what's that mean for us?"

He was right, in every particular; nevertheless, I still had no intention of opening my mouth, and he never divulged any detail of our conversation that day. By the time we were ready to march away from the lake, it was an article of faith among the rankers that our Primus Pilus had ignored the warning sent by the gods, in the form of a disappearing moon. Consequently, when all the events that transpired after this battle involving the Primus Pilus occurred, the doomsayers among us practically strutted around the camp, declaring their interpretation of the signs given to us that night had been correct.

Under different circumstances, I would have rather enjoyed being a bystander for the Primus Pilus' coming misfortunes, but since I was directly involved and, in fact, in many ways was under a greater threat than even he was, it is hard for me to keep that in mind, even now.

I had gone to check on Sextus as soon as I was able, which was shortly after the sun came up the day after the battle, and I was relieved to see that he was unharmed, at least physically. However, the cause for his shaken state of mind was not from the same cause as the rest of the men; while Sextus had never been as dedicated or avid a student as I, he retained enough from Diocles to understand the same thing I did concerning the loss of the moon for a brief period. No, what had rattled him was the circumstances in which he found himself, like a number of men that night, rolling around on the ground, fighting for his life in utter darkness.

"I didn't even see him coming," he told me as we sat on the ground together. Shaking his head, he glanced over at me, and said, "One moment I'm fumbling along, trying to follow Pamphilius," I did not know the man personally, but I knew he was the Legionary immediately in front of Sextus in his file, "and I was trying to grab for his harness. Well," he gave a rueful laugh, "I grabbed something all right. It just wasn't Pamphilius."

"That's almost exactly what happened to me." I had to laugh as well, then went on to explain the specifics.

"So you were off your feet too?" he asked me, and I sensed a glimmer of, if not satisfaction, then relief that his big brother had been in similar straits.

I realized then that at least part of his apprehension in telling me was in the expectation of a lecture about how stupid and careless it is for a Legionary to lose his feet in a fight. His surprise when I suddenly draped an arm about his shoulders was actually a sweet moment.

"I not only lost my feet," I told him frankly, "the fucker landed on top of me and knocked the wind out of me."

"So, how did you…?"

I described the fight, at least as I remembered it; I had long since learned it is inevitable that what I recall from such moments are bits and pieces that only after the fact can I piece together, and even then, there are fractions of time missing. When I was finished, he whistled and shook his head.

"And here I thought I had it bad having to use my *pugio* to kill the fucker," he said, then shot me a sidelong grin, "but you've tried to break my neck a half dozen times and couldn't do it. So," he teased, "he couldn't have been *that* tough."

Laughing, I gave him a shove, then we sat in silence for a few moments, and my mind turned to other matters.

"Sextus," I began, "about Birgit..." I felt his body stiffen, and while I was not looking at him directly, I saw his mouth open to say something, but before he could, I held up a hand and said, "...I just want you to be happy. And," I took a deep breath, "I can see Birgit's happy as well. So I want you to know that while I can't say I'm thrilled at what's happened, I accept it. Besides," now I did turn to look at him, grinning as I added, "I need to be around to make sure your son can have a good example."

My brother's eyes had taken on a shine, although as I hoped, he laughed at my comment, then shoved me and retorted, "What are you talking about? I'm the best example of Roman manhood in the family! You," he pointed, "are just a big ox. Whereas I," he sat up straight, drawing his torso up erect while extending his hand in the same manner as the statues of the divine Augustus, "should be the model for all future monuments of Rome!"

"A big ox that can still stomp you into the mud," I pointed out pleasantly. Then, I turned serious, because while I was sincere about my acceptance of what had happened between Sextus and Diocles' widow, I still had serious reservations about the stability of this new relationship, just not because of Birgit. "Sextus," I warned him, "you know that your days of carousing and acting like you don't have a care in the world are over. Right?"

"I do," he nodded, his demeanor matching mine now. "I know that I can't come crawling home drunk, and I know that I've got responsibilities now."

"And not just to Birgit and the baby," I pointed out. "You're now the *paterfamilias* to the children of Diocles. And, baby brother," I warned him, "if you fail in those responsibilities, you and I are going to have..."

"I know," he protested. "No, Titus, I do! I understand, please believe me!" He stopped for a moment, then heaved a sigh, and added miserably, "Alex hates me, though. And he always will. And," he admitted, "I can't blame him."

"No, you can't," I replied honestly. "But he doesn't hate you." He was about to argue, except I held up a hand again and continued, "He hates what you did. But he doesn't hate you. He loves you. As do Gisela, and Titus, and Scribonia. It's just that he's the oldest son," I explained, "and he saw himself as the head of the family now. Then, you came along and…" I shrugged, but said nothing further.

"Well," he finally replied after a long silence as he absorbed this, "you'd know about how the oldest of four thinks."

"I do," I agreed firmly.

"So," Sextus looked over at me, his eyes beseeching help from his big brother, "what do I do?"

"You prove to him you're a worthy successor to Diocles," I answered. "As far as the other part? About how he views himself?" Shaking my head, I remembered back to the boy I had been, feeling the enormous weight of the responsibility I felt in the absence of our father, and his was only temporary. "That's something he's going to have to work out for himself. All you can do is support him. And," I thought to add, "you need to give him a bit more leeway than you might be inclined to do. He's going to challenge your authority…"

"Going to?" He cut me off with a laugh that had a bitter edge to it. "He's well past that point." Sighing, he said, "He fights me on everything, Titus!"

I nodded, although I admit I felt a bit guilty; I had been making myself scarce from the apartment as I tried to adjust to the idea of Sextus and Birgit as a couple.

"I know," I sighed, wishing I could offer my brother more encouragement than I was doing at the moment, yet I also felt compelled to keep the best interests of Alex in mind. "And all I can say is that, hopefully, it will pass."

"If it doesn't?" he asked me, so miserably that despite myself, I had to laugh.

"Then," I slapped him on the shoulder, "you count the days until you can send him to the Legion!"

The look Sextus gave me was equally amused and scornful.

"As if Birgit would allow that," he scoffed. "Or have you forgotten how she is, seeing how long it's been since you've come by?"

As much as I deserved that, I felt my face redden, but I managed to stifle the defensive retort, thinking it was my penance for my behavior.

"No, I remember," I sighed.

We sat there for another moment, then I stood up.

"I have to get back to my boys," I told him. "Just remember what I said, all right?"

"I will," he promised.

I know that he meant it when he said it, yet I also knew my brother well enough to understand that there was a good possibility a moment would come where his spirit, no matter how willing, would not be able to withstand the demands of his fleshly desires. Still, in that moment, I admit I was as optimistic as I had ever been that, at last, Sextus had become a man in every sense of the word.

Our return to Siscia took longer than normal because of our wounded, so the final two days of our return was in freezing temperatures, at least at night. As often happened in such conditions, some of our wounded succumbed to their injuries along the way, although it was only a half-dozen men. Marching with us were more than three hundred Taurisci prisoners, and of the wounded among them, probably about twenty altogether died as well. Entering the camp without any ceremony, the Primus Pilus dismissed us to attend to the myriad duties that are required to settle back into our camp routine, while he went to the *praetorium* to report our return. While I did not give it a great deal of consideration, I did wonder what, if anything, Atticus would tell the Legate about the night attack on the Taurisci, particularly as it pertained to his justification for doing so. In retrospect, I can see how the circumstances involving the disappearing moonlight took precedence over the concerns of some of the Centurions about the pretext for attacking the Taurisci, at least after that night. And, in all honesty, it would have been highly unlikely that anything would have been made of the events Atticus used as justification for our attack if we had rowed across the water and finished the rest of the Taurisci. This is said in hindsight, and we were still a couple months away from learning of the complications, so in the meantime, life in the Legion went on as before. It was only a few days after our return when I approached Galens with an idea that had formed in the aftermath of the fight.

"We need to train the men to fight dirty," was how I put it to Galens.

"Fight dirty?" he asked me with an upraised eyebrow, sitting back in his chair as he regarded me. "What the fuck does that mean?"

"Of the casualties we suffered," I asked him, "how many happened when it was dark and we got all mixed up with the Taurisci, and how many once we got organized?"

"We took more when it was dark," he agreed, but I could tell he was being cautious. "So what are you saying, exactly, Optio?"

"I'm saying that we need to learn some basic moves that gladiators use," I answered.

"Gladiators?" His faint interest turned to scorn, and he shook his head. "That's ridiculous! We're not fucking rabble!"

I realized I had committed a tactical blunder, so I amended my approach.

"Gladiators is the wrong way to describe it," I said. "But back when I was a boy in Arelate, I got some tutoring from the *lanista* there, and I used what I learned that night."

"That night?" He was clearly startled, and I realized I had not made any mention of my hand-to-hand struggle with the Taurisci in the dark. "You got into a scrap?"

"I did," I confirmed, "and I lost my feet. And," I added, "the bastard landed on top of me. And yet," I spread my arms out and grinned, "here I am. Untouched and still as handsome as ever."

Galens snorted in response, but I saw he was impressed.

"So," he finally asked, "how did you do it?"

By the time I finished describing my private battle, I could tell he was not only impressed, he was convinced.

"And you say you learned this from that *lanista*?" he asked me thoughtfully.

I only nodded.

"Well," he said at last, "that's something to think about. Let me take some time and I'll let you know when I've decided."

At our formation the next morning, just before we took our places, Galens came to me and said simply, "Figure something out and let me know when you're ready. We'll put it on the training schedule."

I must admit I felt quite proud of myself; this was my first major contribution to my Century. My one wish is that the feeling could have lasted longer.

Almost exactly three months after our return to Siscia from chastising the Taurisci, it was late December and we were in the grips of our winter routine, and there was a blanket of snow over everything except the Legion streets, which were churned and muddy from the constant traffic. Otherwise, snow clung to the roofs of the huts, and whenever we stood watch, we did so bundled up against the cold. Personally, I could not have been happier with my circumstances, at least in a professional sense. In my role as weapons instructor of the Century, my program of teaching the men some throws, blocks, and assorted other maneuvers I had learned as a boy from Vulso was not only popular with the men, it attracted the attention of the Primus Pilus, in a positive way. Not only did he have me teach the rest of the First Cohort, he ordered the Pili Priores to select men from their own Cohorts for me to train in the methods used by the men who fight to the death in the sand. Oh, make no mistake; I was physically sorer and more tired than I had been since I was a *tiro* and, as I discovered, there were men who either knew their own assortment of moves, or were quick studies, and at times, I found myself pushed to my limit. But not only did it hone my own skills, the daily activity kept me from accumulating the normal winter flab that usually plagues us and makes springs so difficult.

And, if the truth be known, I discovered to my intense surprise that I began looking forward to the birth of Sextus' child, although not as much as Sextus or Birgit. Unfortunately, while the younger children were also eager, the same could not be said for Alex, but I must give Sextus credit; he tried to spend more time with the boy than the other children. According to Birgit, she was less than four months away from the birth; naturally, both my brother and I accepted her word for it. I had resumed spending my off-duty time at the apartment, and it seemed to naturally work out that Alex sat next to me when we had our evening meals. However, I was not blind to the fact, nor was Sextus, that by choosing to sit with me at one end of the table, Alex was placing himself at the opposite end from Sextus, although nothing was said about it. Otherwise, at least the other children seemed to have adjusted to the change in their world, and Scribonia had begun calling Sextus Tata. Which, it must be said, did not sit well with Alex, and while he never openly corrected her or objected, there was no mistaking the fierce scowl on his face every time the girl did so. Birgit chose to ignore Alex's looks, as did the other children, particularly Scribonia, and I got the strong sense that at least part of her use of the familial word for the new *paterfamilias* was to torment her brother, something I could understand. Much the same had taken place in my own home, although in my case, it was not from our youngest sister Miriam, but from Valeria, who, in her own way, knew how to provoke me in ways that Sextus could not. And she was fleet of foot, meaning I was rarely able to catch her when she did something to anger me. The difference between my own childhood and what I was witnessing now was due to the temperament of Alex, who did not have the need to stamp his authority over his siblings in the same manner I did. I freely admit that, as a child, I was a bully, although my one and only defense is that I was as much of one with older boys who were my size and even larger. It is a thin gruel for an excuse, I know. Here in Siscia, we had just sat down to the evening meal, on an unremarkable evening, after a routine day, when my world was upended, in the form of a knock on the door.

"Are you expecting anyone?" I asked Sextus and Birgit, but they both shook their heads.

Since I was nearest to the door, I heaved a sigh in such a way that it drew a laugh from the children as I hoped it would, then rose from the table and walked to the door. Opening it, I needed a moment for my mind to catch up to my eyes; while I was not sure who to expect, the man standing there was the last on my list.

"Crito?" I frowned, my mind finally grasping the significance of the identity of the caller, and I made what I believe is a natural assumption. "What are you doing here? Are we being alerted?"

So sure was I that the only reason the chief clerk of the Legion would come to the apartment was because of some emergency that required the entire Legion to be summoned, I did not wait for him to answer. Instead, I turned to Sextus to tell him our dinner was over, but then the clerk interrupted.

"Optio Pullus." Something in Crito's voice caused me to turn back to face him, and this was the first I remember seeing something in his expression that sent a stab of alarm through me. "There's no emergency. At least," he amended, "for the whole Legion." I saw the bump in his throat bob, but it was his refusal to meet my gaze that gave me just an instant's warning, "The Primus Pilus sent me to find you, specifically. You're to attend to him in the Legion headquarters."

"Me?" I fought a sudden urge to vomit up what little I had eaten. "When does he want me there?"

"Immediately," Crito said, then shifted uneasily, "and I'm to bring you with me. Optio, please." There was no missing the begging quality to his tone, making me wonder what dire punishment Atticus had threatened Crito with as an incentive to find me. "Come with me. Now."

Naturally, I obeyed, taking only enough time to don my fur-lined *sagum* and bid a hasty farewell to Sextus, Birgit, and the children, although my brother had come to his feet as well.

"I'm coming with you," he announced, but I waved at him to sit back down.

"There's no need." I believe I was trying to assure myself as much as him. "I'm sure I'll be back before long. Although," I tried to grin at Birgit, "I'm afraid you might have to reheat my dinner."

Sextus just looked at me steadily for a moment, then gave a minute shake of his head.

"Titus," he said softly, "I'm coming with you."

Frankly, I did not argue with him. After a quick embrace and whispered goodbye, Sextus collected his own *sagum*, similarly lined with fur, and came to stand beside me at the door, facing Crito. Who,

I must say, looked thoroughly miserable, and I am sure it was not because of the cold weather. The three of us left the apartment, and while I was apprehensive, it did not occur to me I would not cross the threshold of this place for some time to come.

"I've been summoned to Rome," the Primus Pilus announced to the assembled officers of the First Cohort and the Pili Priores, all of us gathered in Atticus' private quarters.

Which meant it was extremely cramped; in fact, I was standing just outside the doorway, along with Asinius and the other Optios present; even in moments like this, rank has precedence. This declaration by the Primus Pilus was met with a ragged chorus of gasps of surprise and muttered words that I assumed were meant to be heard by Atticus and assure him of the support of his Centurions. Frankly, it was hard for me to pay attention, mainly because I was so relieved I actually became physically dizzy to the point I had to grab the frame of the door. Asinius caught this, as he always did, giving me a sharp glance, then Atticus resumed speaking, having paused after his first words, I supposed to give us time to absorb this news. Or, I remember thinking, he wanted to give us a chance to show our concern.

"The reason for my summons is to answer charges," to this point, his voice was flat and emotionless, but I detected the first quaver in his tone, which was understandable, "that I ordered an illegal and unprovoked attack on the Taurisci tribe."

He paused again, except this time, it was because he had to, as the room exploded with the sounds of the Centurions, either decrying the charge, or commiserating with the Primus Pilus about the injustice. Standing just outside his private quarters, we Optios were a bit more subdued, but Asinius and I exchanged a look that told me our thoughts were running along similar lines. The babble of Centurions trying to talk over each other was allowed to continue for a couple of long moments, and thanks to my height, I was able to keep my focus on Atticus; my suspicion was that he was gauging the reaction before he continued.

Finally, it was Macerinus whose voice prevailed over the others, and I heard him ask, "Who's accusing you of these things, Primus Pilus?"

For the first time, the Primus Pilus showed a glimmer of emotion, yet it was not exactly what I would have expected from a man who was facing what had to be the most serious challenge to not just his career, but his life.

"Apparently, the chieftain of the Taurisci and some of his nobility who escaped our fight by the lake." Atticus actually smiled as he said this, although it was without any humor.

Still, I instantly understood why he did so; we had refused to finish them off, and this was the result. At least, I am certain this was the implication, although he did not come out and say so outright.

Fortunately, Macerinus also recognized the undercurrent, and he was the one who expressed regret for the rest of us, saying, "Primus Pilus, we owe you an apology. We should have listened to you when you ordered us to find boats. Although," he added hastily, "if you recall, we didn't find any boats we could have used."

The instant Macerinus' last words came out of his mouth, the atmosphere in the room changed, and I heard Asinius suck in a breath; or perhaps it was me. Hopefully, I thought, Atticus is too distracted to notice. Except he was not, and while I was not happy, nor was I surprised that he immediately pounced.

"Pilus Posterior," he turned to stare, hard, at his second in command, "forgive me if I misheard you. As I remember it, you all told me there were no boats to be found, at all. Although," his mouth quirked as if he had just swallowed a turd, "I also distinctly recall that none of you seemed to make much of an effort. But now," his face hardened as he moved his gaze to the other Centurions of the First Cohort who, as one might expect, were closest to where he was sitting at his desk, "I'm hearing something different. So, I admit I'm confused," I am sure I was not the only one who could discern he was anything but, "that now I'm hearing you say you might have found boats, but you made the determination that they were not worthy for our use. Is that what I'm hearing you say?"

While I know the silence could not have lasted the full watch it felt like, the pause was still profound, and from my vantage point, I could see every other man in the room was now staring at Macerinus. For the second time since I had become familiar with the man, I found myself silently wishing he would do the smart thing and not the right thing, remembering how he had stood before our former Legate and refused to lay the responsibility for the slaughter of Varciani noncombatants at the feet of our newly deceased Primus Pilus, Urso, Atticus' predecessor. Once more, however, he disappointed me.

"Yes, sir," Macerinus replied, and while the Primus Pilus had allowed us to stand at ease immediately after he began this meeting, I could see the Pilus Posterior standing at *intente*. "While it's true that those of us you sent along the eastern side of the lake found some boats, their hulls had been holed, and they were sunk with rocks." He shook his head and finished, "We determined that they couldn't be salvaged."

Atticus considered for a moment, then without turning his gaze away from Macerinus, he raised his voice, calling out, "Optio? Is that true?"

My first thought was wondering which Optio he was asking, but I got my answer when Asinius suddenly stood up straight in what I imagine was an unconscious imitation of Macerinus.

"Yes, sir," he replied, without hesitation; at least, not much. "I saw the boats myself. It's true they were in shallow water, but…" His voice trailed off.

My attention had been on Atticus, yet when Asinius stopped in such a manner, it caused me to glance over at him, and I saw he was looking acutely uncomfortable, making me wonder why. I got my answer within the next couple of heartbeats.

"But you determined they weren't usable," Atticus concluded for him. Then, he shook his head, and said, "And yet, one thing I remember is that none of you were wet when you returned to me. But somehow, you were able to see these boats, lying on the bottom of the lake. Yes, yes, it was shallow," he raised a hand towards Macerinus, who had opened his mouth, I assumed to make that very point, "but it was also at night, with just the moonlight." Sitting back, he regarded Macerinus first, then turned to look at Ovidius, the other Centurion who had been on the eastern side of the lake, and there was nothing remotely comforting in the look he gave them. The silence drew out again before he finally said, "But I'm sure it's as you said. Those boats were probably worthless." Without any warning, this was when he leapt to his feet and bellowed, "*But that wasn't your fucking decision to make!! It was MINE!*"

Standing there, leaning on his fists, Atticus glared at Macerinus from behind his desk, his chest heaving, his face twisted into a mask of rage; and, I was positive I saw, more than a little fear. The recipient of his wrath continued standing at *intente*, but he did not make a sound in reply, instead continued to stare at the imaginary spot above Atticus' head. Meanwhile, the rest of the Centurions looked as if they had collectively been exposed to Medusa's gaze, turning to statues, and I felt fairly positive they were collectively holding their breath. Frankly, I was happy to be standing where I was; even that slight separation was a blessing, although I was as immobile as the rest of the assembly. Without moving my head, I glanced over at Asinius, and while he did not seem to glance my way, I saw him give an almost imperceptible shake of his head. Oddly enough, this slight movement set off a chain of thoughts in my mind that, to my horror, threatened to make me laugh, although I have no idea why.

Fortunately, I was saved when the Primus Pilus, heaving a sigh as he did so, dropped back down into his chair, saying tiredly, "But it's too late for that. So there's not much point in me worrying about it." He began glaring again, starting with Macerinus, then moved from him to Ovidius, then to the other First Centurions, ending with Galens.

It was the Secundus Pilus Prior who, clearing his throat, asked, "What can we do, Primus Pilus?"

Atticus laughed, but it was a bitter one, and he answered, "Oh, I suppose you could make some sacrifices to Fortuna, Mars, and Bellona. Otherwise," he shrugged and added, "this is something I have to face on my own. Although," for the first time, he turned his attention from just the Centurions, looking in the direction of the door, and somehow, I knew it was no accident that his eyes found mine as he finished, "I'm allowed to bring witnesses in my defense."

At least I can say I had some warning of what was to come, although it was not much.

It was not long after this statement that the Primus Pilus dismissed the meeting, but as the men were filing out, he called out, "Galens, Pullus. You stay."

My Centurion had almost made it to the door, so he was facing me and I did not miss the sudden stab of alarm that crossed his face. As for myself, I waited for the rest of the men to file out, trying not to read too much into the fact that none of them seemed to be interested in looking me in the eye, but just before I entered, I felt a hand grab my arm.

"Titus." Asinius had been the man to stop me, and he whispered, "Don't. Do. Anything. Stupid."

I only answered with a nod, partly because Atticus was looking at me, while Asinius was standing to the side of the doorway and was not visible, so I did not want to draw attention to my former Optio and friend. The main reason, however, was I did not have enough saliva in my mouth to utter more than a croak like a frog. Still, I entered the office, closing the door when Atticus ordered me to do so. But I, and I suspect Galens, was unprepared for Atticus' next action.

Gesturing to two of the chairs, which had been shoved against one wall, he said, "Please, both of you take a seat."

Frankly, I found this much more alarming than how he had behaved towards Macerinus, but I imagine that was his intent. What he did next was even more disconcerting, as he stood at the same time we were sitting down, moving to a low cabinet on which an amphora of wine sat. Grabbing it and three cups, he returned to his desk, sat down and, without asking us, started filling them.

"Primus Pilus," I spoke up, trying to keep my tone as respectful as possible, "I appreciate it, but I don't care for any wine."

He did not appear offended; instead, he gave a chuckle that, to my ears, sounded like the first genuine note of emotion he had sounded.

"Don't worry, Pullus," he assured me, "you will. But," he grinned at me as he set the cup on the edge of the desk nearest to me, "I won't let it be said I forced any man to drink. I'll just put it here, in case..."

Galens was not as shy, taking the offered cup, although he did wait until the Primus Pilus began quaffing his own.

Finished, Atticus smacked his lips and said, "Now, I know both of you are dying inside to know what's going on. I mean, what's *really* going on."

This was something neither of us could have denied, and we did not even try. Sitting back, he stared down into his cup, any good humor vanishing as quickly as it had come.

Finally, he said, "As far as the particulars of my recall to Rome, everything I told the others is the truth. While I don't know the full details yet, what I do know is that those Taurisci…bastards who we let live didn't go back to their own lands. Or," he allowed, "if they did, it was just long enough to pack up their things before they went straight to Rome. Once they got there, they managed to get an audience with the Princeps, where they accused us," he paused for a moment, then amended, "actually, me specifically, with an unprovoked attack on them."

Once more, he fell silent, although this was to take another drink of his wine; mine was still untouched, but I suppose this prompted Galens to ask, "But what about that farm they burned down? The night before we hit them by the lake?"

"They're denying having anything to do with that," Atticus replied, yet as he did so, he was looking directly at me. "In fact, they're claiming that I sent my own men to that farm and started the fire."

For the first time, I began to get a glimmer of an idea about why we were sitting there, although it was clear Galens did not yet see it.

"But that's just their word against yours!" he protested. "Surely the Princeps isn't going to take their story seriously! They're barbarians! You're a Primus Pilus!"

That, I had to admit, was certainly where my thoughts had gone, but the Primus Pilus frowned, and he actually looked a bit uncomfortable as he replied, "Supposedly, they have a witness who's willing to testify he saw Romans setting fire to the farm, not the Taurisci."

"Who?" I am afraid I blurted this out, despite my intention to remain silent and let Galens do the talking.

If Atticus was irritated, he did not seem so; I took this as a sign of how worried he was because he answered, "I don't know." Hissing in clear frustration, he continued, "I wish I did. But if they have witnesses, then I'm going to bring my own. Which," he looked at Galens, then me, "is why you're coming with me to Rome."

That was when I reached for the still-waiting cup of wine, draining it in one swallow.

The walk from the Primus Pilus' quarters was largely silent as Galens and I absorbed all that had happened to turn our respective worlds upside down in our own way. Reaching his quarters first, we stopped for a moment.

"I better get packed," he said, "because dawn will be here before you know it." He barked a humorless laugh. "I don't even have enough time to get drunk."

Saluting him, we parted, yet before I had any conscious thought of doing so, I was almost at the gate, heading into Siscia before I remembered two things. The first was that Sextus had come with me and was waiting in my quarters, yet that was not the real reason my body had automatically made its way towards the apartment. I came to a stop, fighting the sudden welling of tears as I realized that, once more, I had been heading for Diocles and his counsel. Sighing deeply, I forced my tears to remain behind my eyes, as much for the horrifying thought of the guards at the gate seeing an Optio weeping like a woman as anything else, then turned and headed to my quarters. Naturally, Sextus was waiting for me, seated with the other three occupants of the hut in their part of our shared quarters, but one look at my face got him to his feet, while I mumbled an apology to the others, staggering into my private room.

"Well?" he asked, but before I answered, I pointed to the half-empty amphora of wine.

Like Atticus, I filled more than just my cup, although when he demurred, I insisted, promising he would need it, whereupon I went on to explain everything as he sat silently, listening. Once I was finished, before he replied, he got up, walked to the amphora, and refilled his cup. Which, as I am sure he hoped, made me laugh; and, of course, hold out my own to refill it.

"So," he finally spoke, his voice husky, "what are you going to do?"

"What do you mean 'what am I going to do'?" I shot back. "I'm getting on a horse tomorrow, and I'm riding to Rome."

"I know that," he replied testily. "But I'm talking about once you get there."

I still did not really understand what he was saying, and I told him as much.

He seemed to consider something, before he said carefully, "Didn't you tell me once about some Tribune that was out here who promised to help you if you needed it? Someone that was connected to Avus as well?"

I had honestly forgotten completely about Tribune Claudius and his promise to me. It was true it had been a few years before, and in the aftermath of Urso's death and meeting Atticus for the first time, yet the instant Sextus said the name, I realized I should have thought about him.

"Thanks for reminding me," I told him, but he just raised his cup.

"Of course," he said simply, then moved on to another topic, one that I had actually thought about, if briefly, while I was walking to my quarters. "What about Tata? What should I tell him?"

"Nothing," I said instantly, but my brother shook his head adamantly.

"Titus," he said, using a tone of voice I had not heard from him before, and I was struck by the thought he sounded like me when I was lecturing him about something, "that's not going to happen. He needs to know. Everything," he added, except in a way that made me a bit uncomfortable.

"What do you mean, 'everything'?" I asked him.

"Like what's really going on," Sextus replied.

"I told you," I protested, "it's because Galens and I had the watch when that farm was burned! Atticus wants us to testify we didn't see anyone leave the camp!"

My brother regarded me for a long moment, and there was something in his expression I did not like.

"Titus," he sighed, "I hope you know what a load of *cac* that is." He took a swallow of wine before he continued, "I'm sure you remember Balbinus."

"Yes, I remember Balbinus," I snapped, but there was a sour taste forming in my mouth. "I haven't been away from the First that long."

"So you remember how much he likes to talk," Sextus replied, then said nothing else.

I cannot say why, yet somehow, I knew he expected me to understand, and accept his words without forcing him to say it aloud. Yet for some reason, I suppose I needed him to verbalize all of it.

"Yes, I remember. But what does that have to do with anything?"

The look my brother gave me was scathing, and I saw he was actually becoming angry as he retorted, "Please stop playing games, Titus! I know you know exactly what I'm telling you!" He took a deep breath and closed his eyes. "Balbinus was letting everyone know how smart the Primus Pilus was being in making sure we had created the evidence Atticus used to go after the Taurisci."

I considered this for a moment.

"The chances of word of a Gregarius running his mouth getting back to Rome are pretty slim…" He cut me off.

"That's not why I brought it up. The point is that the fact that the Primus Pilus used some of us to start that fire isn't the secret he might think it is. And if I know about it, then…" He did not finish, nor did he need to do so.

"Every man in the Legion knows," I sighed, yet as I sat thinking about it, I was moved to say, "But if that's the case, and the Princeps' *Inquisitores* question enough men, there's no way it'll stay secret. By the time we get to Rome, and this Tribunal starts, I'll know. Which means I'll be able to decide how I'm going to testify."

Once more, Sextus remained silent and only stared at me, but with an expression that made me even more uneasy and realize I had missed something, or at least he believed I had. Still, I could not see why he looked even more worried than I did; granted, testifying in a Tribunal was not something I was looking forward to, yet at this point in time, I was merely a witness, at least as far as I was concerned.

Seeing I was not going to say anything, Sextus said, "Titus, you need to consider the possibility that the reason Atticus is bringing you along for more than the purpose of being a witness."

"Like what?" I asked warily, hoping I was not thinking along the same lines now that he brought it up.

"Like to use you and what he knows about our family as a bargaining chip, in the event that something goes wrong," my brother replied quietly.

In fact, I had caught up with him, and for a moment, I was sure I would throw up the wine I had just ingested. Naturally, I had informed Sextus of Atticus' implied threat when he made it, since he was in essentially the same position; I did not believe then, nor do I now, that Augustus would have cared whether it was due to me or my brother who led to information that our Avus had managed to thwart him in at least one way. We sat there for several moments in miserable silence, sipping our wine.

"Well," I finally said, "I guess I'm definitely looking up Claudius when I'm in Rome."

This made Sextus laugh, and despite the reason for it, I could not stop myself from joining in. By the time he left my quarters, I was reeling, which made packing more difficult, but I still felt better about what was happening. This is not to imply I felt good about it, just not as bad as I did before talking with my brother. The next morning, however, was another story.

Chapter 5

Our entire party numbered ten; the Primus Pilus, both of his body slaves, Galens and his slave, and me. The other four men were troopers provided by the Legate, ostensibly as an escort, except these men were all German, whose command of Latin was limited to understanding and affirming orders. And, as Atticus quickly learned, they were not there to follow his commands; they were there to ensure we arrived at our destination. Their own instructions did not appear to include making sure we did not move out of earshot to talk, however, but early on, Atticus showed no interest in having Galens for company, and certainly not me, which I knew suited both of us. Consequently, Galens and I spent most of the first couple days discussing our dilemma, wondering what awaited us. It was sometime during those days that Galens mentioned something, as a joke, that we both laughed at in the moment.

"What if," he mused, "we manage to get that fucking Tribune who caused us all those problems on this Tribunal? What was his name?"

"Paullus," I answered, understanding immediately to whom he was referring, although the idea was so ludicrous that it made me laugh.

Which means I should have known better. Otherwise, because we were in the grips of winter, our progress was slower than normal, yet I did not mind all that much because not only had I brought all of my cold weather clothing, I had managed to procure the same chestnut stallion with the four white socks I had ridden to Arelate and back. Naturally, I was also reminded of how willingly he had charged at the young spear-wielding bandit outside of Luca, despite the fact that I felt confident he had not been trained for war. While he was not the equal of Ocelus, I also recognized that there would never be a horse who would measure up to the gray champion in my eyes. Still, this horse had his own personality, and although not his equal, I definitely saw some of the same characteristics in him that were shared with Ocelus. He was a high-spirited animal who, as I had discovered on the ride to Arelate, enjoyed being run, and was also fond of nipping at me when he thought I was hiding a treat from him, like an apple. Unfortunately, for both of us, apples are hard to come by in the dead of winter, meaning I had more than my share of bruises from where the chestnut grabbed at me, presumably searching for his daily treat. Nevertheless, once more, I enjoyed being on his back, and at least once or twice a day, we would go for a run. The first time, I must admit, was the most enjoyable, if only because our German escorts came galloping after me, clearly worried that I was trying to escape. I admit I led them a merry chase, but they were more than equal to the task; I consoled myself with the idea I was simply rusty in my skills.

Our route took us from Siscia to Salona, where we were to catch a boat to cross the Adriaticum to Aternum, prompting the first disagreement between Atticus and our German escort.

"I'm not crossing the fucking sea in the winter," the Primus Pilus had declared.

In this, he had both Galens and me as allies, but the Germans were obviously nonplussed by the Primus Pilus' obstinacy, and it fell to the commander of the contingent, named Amalric, a brute of a man whose beard was plaited, with hair as black as a crow's wing, to stand up to the Primus Pilus.

"My orders," was Amalric's only reply, and it became clear fairly quickly this was almost the total extent of his vocabulary in Latin, and he made it obvious what those orders were by pointing to the ship.

"Fuck your orders, you stinking barbarian," Atticus snarled, then used his *vitus* to point to the gray-blue waves, which were flecked with the foam from the steadily driving wind. "If you think I'm getting on a fucking boat to cross *that*, you're out of your fucking mind!"

"My orders," Amalric said stubbornly, crossing his arms across his chest, and for whatever reason, it was the first time I noticed the number of arm rings the cavalryman was wearing.

"Your orders *what*?" Atticus snapped. "What does that even mean?"

"My or..." Amalric only got part of the word out before Atticus waved him to silence.

"I know, I know," he grumbled. "Your fucking orders."

Sighing, for the first time, he glanced over at both Galens and me, but if our Primus Pilus could not budge Amalric, I was not sure why he was looking at us, although the thought crossed my mind that perhaps Atticus was considering telling me to thrash Amalric. Which, as hard as it is even now for me to admit, I was not sure I could do. He was shorter than I was, but that was the only difference in our comparative size, although more than his bulk, the sight of those arm rings told me he was not a man with whom I wanted to trifle. Even so, despite this thought, I could not help noticing Atticus was not just irritated at the thought of getting aboard a ship; he was truly frightened. The idea that this man, one whom I grudgingly respected, at least as far as his ability to lead a Legion performing its primary mission, was scared at the idea of crossing the water actually made me feel better.

Then Galens pointed out, "Primus Pilus, if we take the long way around, mightn't that get us in even deeper *cac* with the Princeps? I mean," he added earnestly, "he's expecting us to be in Rome in, what…?"

"Two weeks," Atticus replied shortly, but he still was clearly unhappy.

Fortunately, he did not put up any further argument about boarding the ship, and before the sun was fully up, we were boarded, both ourselves and our horses, pulling out of the protected harbor and into the rough seas. I do not believe a full watch had gone by before our entire party, Germans and slaves included, were clutching the rail, puking up the contents of our stomachs into the heaving, dark water. Fortunately, because our orders gave us not only priority, but the choice of the various craft scheduled to depart Salona when we arrived, we did not have to suffer that long, with the ship Amalric commandeered relying on both oar and sail. Naturally, there is rarely, if ever, something good without an aspect correspondingly bad, and for us it was that, despite the speed, the stench coming from below decks of the slaves chained to the oars guaranteed our stomachs would have been roiling even if we had been crossing a pond. I had been on a ship once before when my family, at least as my family had been constituted then, minus my father, traveled to Arelate the first time. That had been from Tergeste to Ariminum, yet I had been so excited at the novelty of being aboard a ship, I barely noticed the passage itself. The worst part of this particular voyage was the segment during the darkness of night as I found it impossible to get comfortable under the canvas shelter set up at the rear of the vessel, and judging by the way the others were rustling about, I was not alone. Subsequently, the three of us were in a terrible mood when the sun came up, although of course it was the Primus Pilus' outlook that had the most impact on our lives, and although I resolved to avoid him, this proved impossible onboard a ship. Consequently, shortly after dawn, we were both expelling the contents of the light meal we had listlessly consumed, and while I cannot speak for the others, I suspect their logic was the same as mine. Putting something in my stomach would either help it settle down, or it would at least give me something to puke back up; the previous two watches had seen me dry heaving, which as impossible as it may seem, is more unpleasant than actually vomiting food up. Apparently, the Primus Pilus had the same thought, because I found myself leaning on the railing next to him, and at least at first, we were both too occupied to speak. Unfortunately, this was not destined to last.

Once we had both stopped retching, Atticus turned his gaze towards the dark line of land off the bow of the ship. We had been informed we would be making landfall in Aternum by midday, not a moment too soon for any of the passengers, I had no doubt.

Suddenly, without turning his head, he asked me, "So, Pullus, have you ever been to Rome?"

"No, sir," I replied, which seemed to surprise him enough that he turned to look at me.

"Really? I'd have thought you'd been at least once. Given your grandfather."

"My grandfather didn't care for Rome all that much," I said, once more letting my mouth run free before my brain examined my words.

Now it was my turn to be surprised, because this clearly amused the Primus Pilus.

"I don't blame him." He chuckled, but there was a bitter edge to it. "Rome's a dangerous place. Oh," he waved a hand in the general direction of our ultimate destination, "don't get me wrong. There's a lot to see. And do." He added this with a leer. "Every shape, size, and color of woman is there, boy, willing to do whatever you want. Provided you can pay, of course."

"Of course," I agreed, smiling politely as I wondered where this was heading.

I found out, although the Primus Pilus was not quite through talking about Rome.

"But," the grin vanished from his face, replaced with a scowl that was in direct contradiction to his mirth just an instant before, "it's a city full of vipers! You can't trust anyone there! Least of all your...*comrades*." His face twisted into a bitter grimace. I saw him glancing over at me out of the corner of my eye; perhaps it was my own expression that caused him to relent, somewhat. "At least in the Praetorian Guard, it's like that. I will say that I'd forgotten how it is in the Legions." Sighing, he added with what sounded like a wistful tone, "In the *real* army."

I cannot say what moved me to do so, yet once more, I uttered the first thing that came to my mind.

"Why did you join the Praetorian Guard, then?" I asked, truly curious. "I mean," I added hastily, "since it's as bad as you say?"

Atticus regarded me for a moment, then shrugged.

"I don't really remember it being much of a choice, actually. The Princeps asked me to join, but I don't have to tell you that when the Princeps asks, it's really an order. Oh," he sighed, "I was happy about it. At least, at first. It was a step up the ladder, and I'd set my sights on being Primus Pilus. I saw this as a good way to help me get there."

"And," I swallowed hard before I decided to plunge ahead, "was it worth it?"

The look Atticus gave me was one that seemed to be equally composed of amusement, scorn, and if I am not mistaken, regret.

"Was it worth it?" he repeated, then appeared to consider it for a moment. Finally, he shrugged, and I cannot say I was expecting the answer that came. "Honestly, I haven't given it a lot of thought. I suppose it was, considering that I'm standing here now, as a Primus Pilus." Then, his tone changed, and there was no mistaking it, even over the moaning of the wind across the water. "*Your* Primus Pilus. Which," he turned slightly so that he was squarely facing me, and he crossed his arms as he said, "is what we need to talk about now."

"Sir?" I confess I was trying to forestall what I knew was coming. "I'm not sure I know what you mean."

"That's a load of *cac*," he replied calmly, yet he did not seem to be irritated; I learned why when he added, "Not that I blame you for trying to avoid the subject. If I were in your boots, I'd do the same. But," he pointed a thick, blunt finger at me, "I'm *not* in your boots. I'm in mine. And now I need to know I can count on you to support your Primus Pilus."

I suppose I should have been thankful that, by letting me know what he expected my testimony to be while we were still in transit, the Primus Pilus gave me time to think through my options. Not that I felt that way at the time, however, particularly given the warning Atticus had given me.

"Pullus, do I need to remind you of our little talk not that long ago?" was how he put it, once he had drilled me on the version of events he would be putting forth at the Tribunal. "Now," he held up an admonishing hand, and his tone became regretful; at least I believe this was what he was attempting, "I know we've had our differences in the past, but, Pullus, I consider you to be the best junior officer under my command." Even then, I understood he was not saying this to make me feel better, but to provide a warning about all I stood to lose. "And I have no desire to destroy a promising career. But, make no mistake," he leaned forward and poked me in the chest with that damned stubby little finger, "I'm willing to do whatever it takes to protect my own career. Even if it means destroying yours." Standing back up straight, he gave me a hearty smile I suspect was meant for Galens, who I had noticed was trying to surreptitiously observe our exchange. "Now, do we understand each other?"

I assured him we did, very well. Perhaps the only thing positive I can say about our talk was that I suddenly stopped noticing how sick I was, and the remainder of the voyage passed more swiftly than before. As the captain had promised, we arrived at the dock in Aternum at almost exactly midday, giving us a watch of travel time, and we did not waste it. In fact, we rode for perhaps a third of a watch past nightfall, although I do not think it was more than a passing thought by any of us that we were vulnerable to the bandits who typically prey on travelers who find themselves wandering about after dark. Additionally, the road from Aternum is on the right bank of the Aternus (Pescaro) River, making it next to impossible for any bandits to spring an ambush from that side. When we arrived at the small station of Interpromium, once more the advantage of being under orders from the Princeps demonstrated itself. Since we were latecomers, not only were all three rooms of the only inn occupied, the kitchen had been closed. At least, until the Primus Pilus waved the scroll bearing the seal of Augustus himself in front of the innkeeper, who was forced to rouse not only the kitchen slaves, but all the guests in one of the rooms, which we appropriated for ourselves. Not surprisingly, the guests whose slumber had been rudely interrupted were enraged at this interposition; at least, until Amalric drew his long cavalryman's blade, which had, if not a soothing effect, definitely calmed the ardor of the displaced guests. The innkeeper was less surly, but only marginally so, although before too much time had passed, bowls of stew and bread that was not quite stale were produced, along with a few small cheeses. I contented myself with the bread and cheese, not so much because my stomach was still in a delicate stage from the voyage, but I was not sanguine about the probability that the bowls of stew did not contain the expectoration of the slaves, or the innkeeper, for that matter. This did not seem to occur to my traveling companions, who spooned up their helpings with a gusto that comes from having a truly empty stomach. It did not take long for me to begin rethinking my position, although

I still refrained from partaking of the stew, and when I grabbed more than my share of the bread and cheese, none of the others objected. We retired immediately after our meal, settling into the confiscated room as comfortably as possible, except I quickly determined that while the two beds accommodated a pair of normal-sized men apiece, I would have taken up enough of one bed that Amalric and I would have been uncomfortably close. Rather than pull rank, I just rolled up in my *sagum* on the floor, quickly falling asleep despite the hard surface.

When morning came and the slave assigned to announce the time came to wake us, what I recall about this day was how stiff I was when I arose, something that had never been a problem before. When we descended for our meal before starting out, the previous occupants of the room we had occupied, or so I presumed, were already sitting at a table; I say they were the travelers we had ousted judging from the murderous looks they gave us over their cups of spiced wine, although this was all they did. We ate quickly, and once more were on our way, heading for Corfinium next, followed by Alba Fucens, on the shore of Lake Fucinus, where we stopped for the night, fortunately well in time to find proper lodgings, at least without having to shove anyone out of a room. One thing I noticed; the closer we got to Rome, the tenser the atmosphere among all of us, even the slaves belonging to Atticus and Galens. I must admit I felt a bit left out, not having a body slave of my own, but it was something my father had made abundantly clear, both before I left for the Legions, and reminding me when we came home with Diocles.

"Yes, I know there are some Optios who have a slave," he had granted, except his mouth was set in a way I knew very well, "but you're not going to be one of them."

Frankly, I did not argue the point; in the moment, I had thought to myself this suited me perfectly, yet now here I was ruing the fact that I had to fend for myself, rubbing down my horse myself, making sure he was fed and watered, and then attending to my own personal needs. Matters were made worse by virtue of our nearing Rome and whatever awaited us there, especially since we would be wearing our uniforms, and it would have been nice to have some help making mine presentable. Not surprisingly, it was Atticus who was the tensest, but I forced myself to not fall into a sense of security based on the idea I was just there to serve as a witness, constantly reminding myself that Atticus had made it clear I was there for his own purposes. Still, as much as I was sure I had not let my guard down, I was served a very much-needed reminder, and it is yet another time where I felt the *numen* of my Avus playing a role, reminding and informing me at the same time.

The actual moment did not happen for two more days, when we first saw the walls of the city, and despite the circumstances, it was hard for me to quell a sudden rush of excitement at the idea of finally laying eyes on the city for which we march, and in whose name we endure so much. Even Atticus' gloomy mood was abated, at least somewhat, as Galens and I rode the last couple of miles side by side, talking about what lay beyond those walls. I had learned early on that Galens had never been to Rome either, but like all men under the standard, including me, his head had been filled with the locations of so many different purveyors of every imaginable vice, supplied by our comrades who had been there, I seriously doubted either of us could remember one of them. It was as we chatted I began to get the first notion I was seeing something, if not familiar, with which I was at least acquainted in some way, despite the fact that I had never been here before. The cause of it was the line of other travelers stretching back from the gate we were entering, to perhaps four or even five hundred paces, where the tail of the line was located.

Because we were under orders, Amalric grunted something I assumed was a command to follow him as he steered his horse out of the line and began trotting past those waiting to gain entrance. Even if the motley collection of foot-borne, wagon-drawn, or mounted travelers were inclined to voice a protest, Atticus had ordered us to wear our uniforms, complete with decorations. The only thing we were not carrying, at least openly, were our swords, which were packed on one of the two baggage animals. All in all, it should have been a moment I remember with a great deal of pride and fondness, the day I came to Rome for the first time, wearing not only my tunic with the white shoulder stripes under my *segmentata*, but the golden arm rings I had taken from Vergorix after I slew him in battle, and awarded to me by Nero Claudius Drusus, along with the two golden finger rings from Draxo. The only things missing were the silver arm cuffs I had taken from Draxo and the torq that Urso had supposedly sold, although the last I saw of it was when I handed it to him. Any positive feelings, however, were wiped away as, without thinking, I gave an inadvertent gasp of shock as that tickling sensation in the back of my head finally came to full flower.

Unfortunately, Galens heard me, and he gave me a look that seemed to be one of wary curiosity as he asked me, "What is it, Pullus? Why did you jump like you'd seen a *numen?*" He made a point to peer around in front of us, as if searching for whatever it was that had startled me, laughing as he did so.

"No reason," I mumbled, but the truth was that, while I knew Galens was jesting, he had not been as far off the mark as he might have thought.

The cause of my reaction came from the realization that, while I had not personally been here in this spot before, I knew someone who had, and more importantly, I had read all about it. The final piece of what had puzzled me was in the form of the gate into the city we were entering, the Porta Tiburtina, so named because we were on the road that leads directly to Tibur. When we had gone by Tibur earlier in the day, I had been aware my Avus had done so as well, because I remember reading about how he and Diocles stopped to admire the many fine estates that dot the landscape. It was not until we were within a hundred paces of the gate itself that it hit me; the first Titus Pullus had used this exact same gate when he had returned to Rome to face Tribunal charges for his supposed role in the Marcus Primus affair. And now, I realized with a hard knot forming in my stomach, here I am, doing the exact same thing, entering through the exact same gate, with the same name, more or less. This realization was extremely disconcerting, I must say, although I did remember to take notice of the huge junction of no less than three aqueducts, started by Marcus Agrippa that had been nearing completion when my Avus came to Rome. He had commented on this convergence of these three aqueducts in his account, which now were not only finished, but had already begun showing signs of weathering, while thin lines of moss grew wherever two sections of the aqueduct were joined. The gate was massive, and at least clad completely in marble, although I was sure that the gateway itself was built of brick, with the two huge, wooden doors swung open, where men of the Urban Cohorts were inspecting all who passed through the gate. However, what was most striking was the sight of what was clearly a new inscription, in the white marble from the Carrarra region, of course, and while our Primus Pilus was producing the rolled scroll affixed with the seal of the divine Augustus, I took the time to read the inscription itself, which I thought was oddly appropriate considering the circumstances.

Imperator Caesar Augustus, son of the divine Julius, Pontifex Maximus, Consul for the twelfth time, Tribune of the Plebs for the nineteenth time, Imperator for the thirteenth time, restored the channels of all the aqueducts.

Even today, several years later, I can still recall that inscription word for word, as I have just written it. In fact, dear unborn reader, if you ever have the chance to visit Rome, as I did, by all means, go to the Porta Tiburtina and see for yourself if I have not transcribed it correctly. It took me some time to fully understand why this seemingly benign inscription, one of hundreds, if not thousands I have seen in my lifetime, on all the various monuments we Romans love so much, stuck with me, yet even now, I vividly remember the shiver that ran up my spine as I read the words. Perhaps it was the idea of the actual power that lay behind the words themselves, one infinitely more potent than the strength it took for the mason to actually chisel them out. Simply put, what was encapsulated in those lines was the announcement of the fact that they were describing the most powerful man in our world, and I would argue in both known and unknown regions. For it is unfathomable to me that there is another city, state, country or however one cares to style themselves, whose leader wields a commensurate level of power and influence over each and every human being who lives within the bounds of the lands claimed by Rome. Following hard on the heels of this realization was another one; it was this very man who had commanded our presence here, and who controlled our fate, one way or another.

As expected, we were immediately allowed into the city, although unlike the original Titus Pullus, I am afraid I barely noticed my first real glimpse of Rome, or at least I do not remember much from it; only a couple of moments stand out. Entering from the Porta Tiburtina, the Campus Martius is almost directly to the west, on the far side of the city. Since neither Galens nor I had more than a basic knowledge of Rome's layout, we merely gave our horses the lead to follow along behind Atticus who, now that he was back in Rome, was also back in complete command, although we still had our German complement until we entered the Campus. What we had no way of knowing at the time was that Atticus had two routes to choose from, yet for whatever reason, chose the one that led us directly into the Subura, coming down off the Esquiline Hill where the gate is located. Honestly, we smelled it before we saw it, although it was more a matter of degree than anything truly different from what had assaulted our noses when we first passed within the gates. The stench created by so many people crammed together is inescapable, but the Subura is a world unto itself, and even from horseback, there is a real feeling of entering a deep, dark, and extremely foul-smelling canyon. Galens and I were riding side by side, and as we descended the hill down into the depths, we exchanged a glance as the garb of the throng of people, all of whom seemed to be in a hurry, changed, both in quality and the care each had seen. The cleanliness, or lack thereof, of these inhabitants' clothing was matched by the amount of dirt and grime on the exposed parts of their bodies. Which, of course, did not do anything positive for the stench. Being brutally honest, the thought crossed my mind that the Primus Pilus' order to wear our uniforms was not just so we were properly attired when we arrived at the Campus Martius, but to dissuade the throng through which we were riding from pulling us off our horses, cutting our throats, and leaving our stripped bodies for the Urban Cohorts to pick up. At least, judging from the way the people being pushed aside by our horses were looking at us.

"It's hard to believe that Divus Julius lived here once," I commented to Galens, who stared at me in open disbelief.

"*Gerrae*!" he exclaimed, looking around us, then back at me as he shook his head. "Everyone knows that Caesar was a patrician! He'd never have lived somewhere like this!"

Oh, I felt quite smug, I must admit, knowing this to be just one of the facts gleaned from my Avus' writings.

"Just because a family is old and is of the patrician class, doesn't mean they have money," I explained. "And before Caesar's birth, all of the Julii had fallen on hard times."

Galens considered this, and for the briefest flash of time, I actually considered pointing out how appearances with our social superiors were not always what they seemed by using my family as an example of Head Counters who had the ability to elevate themselves, but for a variety of circumstances, could not do so. This urge only lasted as long as it took for the thought to run through my mind. Besides, I could see that Galens was convinced, and impressed at my knowledge, which did not hurt my feelings.

"It's just hard to imagine," Galens finally said. "Besides, his family isn't doing so badly now."

I laughed at his understatement, then we both lapsed into silence as we approached a series of multi-story buildings located on both sides of the street we were following, and I am afraid any attempt on my part to appear unimpressed was gone as we entered into what was essentially a canyon. We had certainly seen them coming, but I suppose I had not really been paying attention, and now I craned my neck upward, gaping at these buildings that were taller than any I had ever seen. In terms of their design and form, they were not that much different than the rows of *insulae* back in Siscia, except none back there were more than two stories, while I had to do a recount to make sure I had correctly seen that these buildings were composed of five levels. In itself, this was impressive, but clearly, whoever builds these structures is not too concerned with the quality of the construction, since by the time the building has thrust up above the third level, it starts to lean. I confess this was when I recalled more from my Avus' account, when he had much the same reaction seeing these tenement buildings leaning toward each other so that the width of the street was one dimension, while the space between the tops was much, much narrower. In fact, I was certain that, at a point roughly halfway through the Subura, the buildings started to actually touch, because despite it being broad daylight, at street level, there were guttering lamps hung from their brackets, usually outside what looked like some sort of shop, although I could not even tell what they were selling. Nevertheless, we emerged from the section known as the Subura intact, even if I had already begun to scratch from the fleas and vermin I was sure were crawling all over me. I chided myself for my overactive imagination, until I glanced over at Galens to see my Centurion scratching his free arm.

Catching me looking at him, he grinned and said, "By the gods! I can't wait to get to a bath and kill these fuckers that just hopped onboard."

"Good," I had to laugh at his change in expression at my approbation of his affliction, "because I thought it was just in my head!"

"No, it's not just in your head," he assured me. "I thought Augustus had created more baths than Rome has ever had! But I didn't see one of them back there," he jerked his thumb behind us at the receding Subura, "who look like they've taken a bath in the last month." He reflected for a moment, then amended, "If that."

"I'm sure he did," I agreed, "but that doesn't mean he can force them to go to them."

"That's a surprise," Galens muttered; least I believe this is what he said, but he was not only hard to hear over the chattering of the people around us, he was not disposed to repeat himself.

Reaching a spot where what Atticus identified was the Palatine Hill was located to our left, I was relieved to see we were not following the street that leads up the hill, heading directly to Augustus' mansion. I suppose to anyone outside the Roman army, it might seem strange that three rankers, even as highly placed as one of them was, would take themselves to the private residence of their leader, but as I learned very early in my life, the Princeps controlled our entire world from the comfort of his own home. Other than those times he absented himself from the city, of course; then the power traveled with him. I cannot count the number of times I had heard more experienced men, starting with Titus Pullus, and on through my father, talk about Augustus' almost inhuman ability to manage every facet of our incredibly complex government and military, down to the smallest detail. My most fervent desire, before I swung my leg over the horse in Siscia, was that I would never find myself required to be anywhere near the divine Augustus' presence and, frankly, I had been somewhat expecting Atticus to lead us up the hill first. Once it became clear we were continuing on, for the first time, I became aware I had been sweating profusely under my *segmentata*, and I must say I breathed easier once I was sure we were heading for the Campus. Helping take my mind off that worry was the view we had gained of the sacred precincts, and the Forum, which I have heard described as the beating heart of Rome. I remember being struck by the thought that this was appropriate; the heart is below the head, and if the Forum was truly it, its mind was located up on the Palatine Hill, now behind us as we rode. We skirted the edge of the Forum, swinging to the north around the Capitoline, and once more, I felt my jaw dropping as I gazed upward at the temple of Jupiter Optimus Maximus, which had been rebuilt at Augustus' direction, and while the angle was not the best, I caught a glimpse of the god's golden thunderbolt. When I looked over at Galens, I felt better because his mouth was hanging as wide open as mine was.

"Everything's so…white," he finally said, "If you put together every statue and inscription made of marble I've seen in my life, it wouldn't even come close to what's around us."

Until Galens uttered this, I had not given it any thought, but I quickly understood he was correct; even Arelate, with all its newly constructed temples and the completed theater, would have been swallowed by what we were seeing. Edging around the Capitoline, my mind was still reeling from the sights of the Forum, despite the fact that I have no real memory of what I saw that day, although I do remember fervently hoping I would have the opportunity to spend time seeing everything there was there to see. Then, we drew near yet one more wonder. There was actually a porticoed building between our party and the temple dedicated to all of the gods, but that only obstructed the bottom portion of the temple, leaving the soaring dome that would have dwarfed the *insulae* of the Subura by more than twenty more feet; at least, this was my first impression, although I quickly learned I was mistaken. Both Galens, and as I noticed, the slaves, abruptly stopped their mounts; I did as well, all of us staring in profound amazement at the sight of what, to my untutored eye, looked very much like a bowl set upside down. Except that unlike a bowl, the sides of this enormous object were not smooth, but arranged in a series of concentric and ever-shrinking circles. Our Primus Pilus, along with the Germans, had continued on for perhaps twenty or thirty paces before one of them noticed we were not still following behind. Although my gaze was fixed on the dome, trying to understand how something so huge could just seem to hover in the air, I noticed Atticus turn his horse out of the corner of my eye.

"What are you two gawking at?" he called out.

Galens pointed up at the top of the temple, but I suppose Atticus could not see, because he came trotting back to where we were, looking over his shoulder as he did so.

"What, that?" he scoffed. "That's the Saepta Julia! It's where the mob comes to vote!" He laughed and added, "You two *are* a couple of provincials, aren't you?"

My face suddenly became hot, and I could see a flush on Galens' face, before my Centurion's eyes narrowed suspiciously; then I turned my attention back to Atticus, and saw him grinning at us in a way that gave the lie to his words.

"We're not talking about *that*," Galens pointed at the long, narrow colonnaded building obscuring the lower part of the domed temple. "We're talking about that thing up there! But you knew that, didn't you?"

Atticus laughed and admitted, "Yes, I did. I just liked seeing both of your faces!" Turning his horse and maneuvering it so he was by our side, facing the same direction, while he tried to sound casual, I heard the pride in his voice as he said, "That, boys, is Agrippa's Pantheon."

Naturally, we had heard about this temple to all the gods, yet frankly, I had dismissed most of the descriptions as the kind of exaggeration men will make when they are trying to impress their friends about something they have witnessed or seen but the others have not. Now I realized that, if anything, their descriptions had fallen well short of the mark.

The Primus Pilus began reciting his knowledge about the construction and dimensions of the Pantheon, explaining, "The top of that dome is one hundred fifty feet high, and you can see how it's round." We both nodded, and he went on, "Well, imagine a big, round ball. What you're seeing is the top part of the ball, cut in half."

When he did not say anything else, it moved Galens to ask about the significance of what he had just said.

This is for you, Diocles, I thought, even as I interrupted, "It means that the temple is one hundred fifty feet across as well."

It was supremely satisfying to see the look of startled surprise on Galens, and even more, the similar expression on Atticus' face, although it was mixed with what seemed like equal parts irritation.

"Is that true, Primus Pilus?" Galens asked him.

"Yes," Atticus replied testily, "although there's nothing special about knowing. Everyone knows that!"

I know he aimed this at me, although I do not believe he intended to embarrass Galens as well, whose color had returned to normal, but the flush came back as he mumbled, "I didn't."

Atticus at least had the grace to look discomfited, although if Galens was expecting something even in the vicinity of an apology, for all I know, he is still waiting.

"Yes, well," Atticus went on awkwardly, "anyway. The entry doors are forty feet high, and the oculus is thirty feet across. The doors and the oculus," he explained, "are the only sources of light. Except, of course," he added offhandedly, "for the altar lamps and the like." Apparently, he believed he had served his purpose as a tour guide, because he kicked his horse, resuming his progress. "Now, if you two will hurry up, we don't have time for any more sightseeing." To emphasize his point, he put his mount into a trot, reaching Amalric and the three other cavalrymen, all of whom had been staring in open bemusement at our gawking.

"Hopefully, we'll have time to see it up close," Galens sighed, then we resumed our way as well, hurrying to catch up. "I really want to know what that thing's made of."

The Campus Martius as described by Titus Pullus had, if anything, become even more developed, with more buildings, although they were all constructed of brick. Nevertheless, the part of the Campus we were taken to by Amalric I am fairly sure was the same large building that housed my Avus, another parallel that I at least understood could be viewed in two ways. Reporting to the *praetorium* first, the Primus Pilus ordered us to wait outside while he presented our orders to the duty Tribune. Fortunately, we did not have that long to wait; a slave appeared who told us he was ordered to escort us to the quarters Galens and I would be sharing. Unloading our baggage, which in both our cases consisted of our packs, including our weapons, rolled in cloth bundles and tied, we followed the slave up to the second floor.

As we had walked down the hallway, open on one side, Galens noticed the majority of the rooms on the first floor seemed to be unoccupied, so that when the slave began ascending the stairs, he was prompted to ask, "Why are we up there and not in one of the rooms on the first floor?"

Judging from his reaction, this was not the first time the slave had been asked this question, because he did not hesitate answering, continuing his climb up the stairs, informing us, "The first floor is reserved for Primi Pili, Pili Priores, and Camp Prefects."

"That figures," Galens grumbled, but the slave's answer caused me to linger an extra moment, staring down the length of the hallway, wondering exactly which room had been occupied by my Avus, and if somehow I could manage to find out.

I was forced to hurry and catch up, reaching the other two just in time for the slave to open the door to where we would be staying until...when, I wondered? Ushering us in, Galens pushed past the slave to immediately claim the cot farthest from the door, while I dropped my pack on the other one. Looking about, I was surprised to see that, in fact, the quarters were relatively spacious, while there were niches directly above the heads of each bed for our respective household gods. Next to each cot was a cupboard, atop which sat a frame with several slots, presumably for the storing of reading material or small items. In the middle of the room, between the two beds, was a small table with two chairs, and along the far wall, a sideboard holding two basins and two pitchers of water.

I was unable to resist the urge for some fun, pointing to the frame, telling Galens, "I know you're not going to be using that. Do you mind if I use it?" Grinning at him, I produced the handful of scrolls I had brought with me. "There's not enough room in mine for all these."

Galens replied by grabbing his crotch and grumbling about Optios who did not know their place and thought they were Cicero; at least, I believe that was what he said. As we were settling in, the slave lit the lamps and opened the single, shuttered window on Galens' side of the room. Once he was done, the slave rattled off a number of pieces of information about where the officers' mess was located, the times it was open for the morning and evening meal, and where the latrine and baths could be found. He said it so rapidly that, when we compared what we each had heard, everything was hopelessly muddled. Unfortunately, he vanished so quickly we did not have the opportunity to clarify our misunderstanding. However, it was not long before we had another visitor; neither of us had finished unpacking when there was a sharp rap on the door, followed by it swinging open so rapidly I found myself unconsciously reaching down for the bundled sword still lying on my cot. Fortunately, it was the Primus Pilus, who wasted no time.

"We've reported in," he told us. "Now I'm going to the Princeps' residence to find out the exact date for the Tribunal. And which Tribune I'm going to be stuck with for my defense."

Suddenly, I was reminded of our purpose for being here in Rome, the growing excitement I was feeling at being able to wander the city washed away by the flooding tide of reality that this was not a leisure trip.

"When you get back, will you come and let us know what's expected of us?" Galens asked.

"Of course," Atticus replied, although he seemed uncomfortable as he said it; we learned why when he added in a manner I suppose he thought was offhanded, "first thing tomorrow." He paused again, then said, "I'm not staying here. I'm quartered…somewhere else," he finished lamely.

I did not take his meaning, and when I shot a glance at Galens, I saw he was no less mystified.

"If you're not quartered here," my Centurion asked Atticus, "where are you staying?"

Now there was no mistaking his discomfort, his face turning darker as he answered Galens, "I'm going to be staying at the Praetorian barracks. They found some room for me there." He shrugged but would not meet either Galens' gaze or mine.

"I'll bet they did," Galens muttered, but just so I could hear.

Promising he would return the next morning, Atticus left, leaving the two of us, if not bewildered, at the very least at a loss about what was expected of us.

"Once a Praetorian…" Galens looked for a moment if he was about to spit on the floor, then seemed to think better about it. Sighing, instead, he said, "Maybe he'll have more to say tomorrow," Galens suggested.

"Maybe," I agreed, but more for form than any real belief that this was likely. "Until then, what are we supposed to do?"

I suppose I should have known better, because Galens' face immediately lit with a smile.

"The Primus Pilus didn't say anything about being restricted to our quarters," he said. "And in case you didn't notice, we passed a half-dozen spots that looked like they'd provide a couple of country boys like us with some entertainment we're not likely to forget."

I should have argued the point, yet as I told myself then, he was my superior, after all, which meant I should obey his orders. First, however, we had to get a bath to not just wash away the grime of our journey, but to kill whatever vermin had managed to hop aboard during our trip through the Subura.

Facing the prospect of anything like a Tribunal, even when one is ostensibly just there as a witness, is a daunting prospect. When one is as hungover as Galens and I were the next morning, mere words cannot adequately describe the scope and scale of the challenge. Nevertheless when, as he had promised, our Primus Pilus returned to talk to us the next morning, both Galens and I did our best to appear as if our minds were firmly fixed on the upcoming proceedings. On that subject, it was hard to tell the exact state of mind our Primus Pilus was in, but I freely admit that my perception might have been altered by the amount of energy I was putting in to avoid throwing up all over his boots. And, as I discovered later, Galens was in a similar state. Still, from outward appearances, Atticus seemed to be in about as good a frame of mind as one can be under such circumstances.

"The Tribunal won't be for another week," he told us. "That gives me the time to prepare my defense. Which means," he glared at both of us, but I was sure his look in my direction lingered several heartbeats longer, "that you need to meet with my defense so he can prepare you for your testimony."

"Have you met him yet?" Galens asked.

Atticus shook his head, answering, "No, not until this afternoon. But I was told his name."

"And?" Galens asked once it became apparent that the Primus Pilus was not going to immediately volunteer the man's identity.

"His name is Lucius Arruntius," Atticus replied.

Galens did not immediately reply, but I could see he was wrestling with the name, knowing it from somewhere. When it was obvious he was not making the association that I had, I decided to speak up.

"Wasn't he one of the Princeps' admirals at Actium?" I asked, but Atticus shook his head.

"No," he told me, and did not seem disposed to add anything before he relented, "It's his son."

This should have been welcome news to our Primus Pilus. Keeping in mind there are no appointments or decisions made concerning the army, at any level, without the approval of the divine Augustus, from where I sat, this seemed to be about the best news for which he could have hoped. Appointing the son of a man who was known as a staunch and trusted supporter of the Princeps as his defense seemed, to me anyway, that this Tribunal would be nothing more than a formality. And yet, Atticus looked anything but happy about it.

Galens might not have read the situation the same way I did, but he could interpret our Primus Pilus' expression, which prompted him to ask, "Primus Pilus? What is it? What's wrong?"

Atticus took a deep breath, clearly considering how forthcoming to be, then finally he shrugged and said, "It's just that there's this supposed witness. I tried to find out who it was, but those *cunni* at Augustus' villa wouldn't even give me a hint. They said," his mouth twisted into a sneer, "that it would be improper for me to be informed until the Tribunal."

"I thought it was that Taurisci chieftain," I offered, but he shook his head.

"No, they've already left Rome," he replied disgustedly. "And besides, the word of a barbarian, even if he is some sort of headman or chief, wouldn't be enough to create all…this." He waved a hand in the air, pursing his lips as he did. "No, this has to be a Roman citizen. But…who?"

I was struck by a thought, except it was not one I had any intention of raising with Atticus, yet when I glanced over at Galens, judging from his expression, his mind was running along similar lines.

"Well," the Primus Pilus spoke suddenly, standing up from the small table in our quarters, "I suppose I'll find out next week. In the meantime, I'm having my meeting with this Arruntius fellow in about two parts of a watch, so I need to get going."

"Will we be needed today?" Galens asked, but Atticus shook his head.

"I doubt it," he replied, then gave the both of us a shrewd look. "Besides, if you two don't get the chance to see at least part of the city, I'll never hear the end of it. So you have the day off to go sightsee and fuck about."

I experienced a distinctly odd feeling at his words; this was an uncharacteristically kind thing for Atticus to do, let alone say it aloud, and it made me wonder if he was in more trouble than he had been letting on. And, I reflected, if my sudden hunch about, if not the exact identity, then at least the role of this mystery witness was correct, he could have good reason.

Naturally, our first stop was the Pantheon, and I, for one, quickly realized that as impressive as it had been at a distance, approaching it up close was simply staggering. The doors themselves are noteworthy; hearing they are forty feet high, then seeing them as one stands next to them is quite a different thing. The doors themselves are faced in bronze, divided into four panels apiece, each panel with a relief depicting a scene from the lives of what I assumed was each god with an altar inside. Like the doors, while the columns supporting the front porch were of granite, the capitals were made of bronze, and arranged along the roof of the porch were statues of the gods, all of them life-sized and painted. Frankly, I felt better knowing that Galens was staring open-mouthed just as I was doing, and together, we entered the temple, our eyes immediately drawn upward to the oculus. The day was sunny, so the beam of light appeared as if it was hurled down from the heavens by Apollo, forming a circle of light on the temple floor, and to my eye at least, the tiny motes of dust that seemed suspended in midair reflected the light just enough to be visible as they floated in front of us. For whatever reason, this only added to the air of awesome majesty. There were perhaps two dozen other people inside the temple, most of them either kneeling or laying their offerings to one of the gods. We were there long enough that I noticed the temple attendants wasting no time in hurrying over and scooping up whatever had been offered, although they seemed content to wait for the supplicants to at least exit the temple.

"Look how plump those fuckers are," Galens muttered. "You know that every offering that's edible goes straight down their gullet."

Despite the atmosphere, I found it hard to suppress a snicker at his observation, mainly because it was clearly true none of these attendants had ever missed a meal. From the Pantheon, we made our way south to climb the Capitoline, where once more, the both of us were struck dumb by the sheer size and opulence of the temple to Jupiter Optimus Maximus, although the temple is referred to as Jupiter Capitolinus. I knew that it had long been the largest and grandest of the temples to the gods, but it had recently been refurbished by the divine Augustus, so that the seated figure of Jupiter was rendered as close to lifelike as it is possible to be. The statue representing the god is massive, although as I am sure is the intent, both Galens' and my eyes were drawn to the gold thunderbolt, clutched in the right hand of the god, which was drawn back as if he was about to hurl it down on us puny mortals below.

"You know," Galens whispered, his eyes still pinned on the sight before us, "that Augustus ordered the thunderbolt to be made of pure gold and not just gilded."

I had heard that as well, but perhaps I am cynical, because I found it impossible to believe that this was true. Nevertheless, either the tarnish that makes gold's gleam dull over time had not yet set in, or more likely, in my mind, there were slaves assigned to the task of polishing it. No matter what reason, the gold gleamed like fire in the light. While we were there, I thought it might be politic of me to actually make a sacrifice. The problem, frankly, was Galens, because the offering I planned on paying for, while not the most expensive, would cost well beyond what might be the expected means of an Optio in Rome's Legions. It had taken quite a bit of doing, especially given the lack of time I had been given to prepare for such a long journey, but I had managed to scrape together more than two thousand *sesterces* in coin, which I had concealed inside the secret compartments I had sewn into all of my *sagum*. I made the silent decision to come back at the first opportunity as we exited the temple, walking the short distance to the Tabularium. We were not allowed entry, but since it overlooks the Forum, Galens and I contented ourselves with just standing outside, looking down on the bustle of activity.

"I've never seen so many people crammed into one spot before," Galens commented, and I agreed, then felt compelled to add, "And they're all in a hurry too."

"That they are." Galens laughed.

Before much time passed, we grew bored, although we did not give the other temple, dedicated to Juno Moneta and where the treasury is located, more than a passing glance before we descended the paved street that leads down into the heart of Rome. To our immediate left was the Forum of Divus Julius, its centerpiece the Temple of Venus Genetrix, and while Galens was only mildly interested, I insisted we go in; only now will I admit it was for the purpose of showing off, at least at first. Naturally, the temple is in the middle of the relatively small forum dedicated to Divus Julius, which is surrounded by covered porticoes, and I strode across the paved square to the temple entrance. This time, the temple attendant at the door took a look at us, seemed disposed to at least attempt to stop us, then clearly thought better of it. Unlike the temple of Jupiter, this one was almost deserted, but the supplicants who were there immediately caught my eye, and before I could stop myself, a hard lump suddenly came up in my throat.

"What's the matter with you?" Galens demanded as he stepped alongside me, where I had stopped several paces away from the statue of the goddess. "Why are you blinking so much?"

Waving a hand at the row of candles arrayed nearby, I lied, "The smoke from the candles." Before he could say anything, I pointed at the line of men kneeling and whispered, "Notice anything about them?"

Galens examined them, although it took a moment for him to recognize why I had pointed them out, then he quietly gasped, "They're veterans!"

"More than that," I replied, still in a whisper, "they look like they're the age of my Avus."

There were only four of them, and I had no idea if they had arrived together or come singly, drawn to the temple, but I was about to find out.

Originally, I was content to let the four men finish their prayers; they finished at roughly the same time, and I could not help noticing how difficult it seemed to be for them to climb to their feet. What struck me in the moment was the obvious physical toll their lives under the standard had taken on them, forcing me to recognize I was looking at my future, and that was if I was lucky. They had turned and were filing past us, when one of the men, the next to last, cast the kind of cursory glance one does at someone within their range of vision, not with any real intent to examine, but marking those around him as a possible obstacle or threat. At least, this appeared to be how he started, yet suddenly, when he looked in my direction, he stopped abruptly, his seamed, weathered face going as white as curdled milk. To my alarm, he actually staggered a step backward, colliding with the last man in their group, who had been examining the coins he had remaining after his offering, muttering to himself. The trailing man went stumbling sideways, unable to keep his balance, hitting the mosaic floor of the temple with a solid thud, accompanied by the whooshing sound of air leaving his lungs. Meanwhile, as both Galens and I stood there gaping, the two leading men spun about, presumably to see the cause of the commotion, and like the pair of us, their attention seemed to be caught by the man who had started it all, probably because, completely oblivious to sending a man I assumed was a friend to the floor, he was pointing directly at me.

"P-P-Pullus?" His voice was quavering, the kind of croak that seems to be possessed by the very old, and the finger he was pointing at me was shaking as much as his voice. "Titus Pullus?"

"Yes?" I replied cautiously; Galens was already moving to help the fallen man to his feet, and out of the corner of my eye, I saw the attendants scurrying over to see the cause of the disturbance. "I'm Titus Pullus."

The other two men turned their attention to me as well at that point, and their reaction matched their compatriot's, so before I could comprehend what was happening, I found myself surrounded by what became a quartet of old men. If this was not strange enough, the first man stopped pointing to reach out and gently touch my left arm, his finger lingering on the horrible scar, except he began frowning as he looked down at it, as if something was wrong.

"It's not him," one of the others said, the first of the others to speak, his voice a harsh, croaking one that bespoke of decades of bellowing orders, and it seemed to snap the first man out of his examination, as the old veteran added, "Besides, Albinus, this is hardly more than a boy!"

"I know that," the man who had been identified as Albinus growled, then lifted his hand to point again, "but look at him! Tell me you're not looking at the Primus Pilus!"

I am somewhat chagrined to say this was the first moment it all fell into place.

"I'm," I told them, "Titus Porcinianus Pullus," and suddenly, it was hard to swallow as I added, "Titus Pullus was my grandfather."

"Wait!" exclaimed the fourth veteran, who after being helped to his feet joined the other three clustered around me. "You're Gaius Porcinus' boy?"

"I am," I replied, and his face broke into a broad grin that only had three teeth that were visible, thrusting out his arm as he did so.

"By the gods," he exclaimed with a laugh, "I remember when he was a sprout even younger than you!" Then his smile faded; I immediately guessed why, and was proven right when he said awkwardly, "I heard about what happened to him. It saddened me. He was a good man, a good Legionary…" He shrugged, his eyes dropping.

"Well, hopefully, you'll be happy to know that he's adjusted to life away from the standard," I told him. "He and my mother are in Arelate now, with my youngest brothers."

"Ah, living the life of leisure." This came from the man who had been silent to this point. "But as much as I hate to interrupt this, let's go outside where we can talk more freely. The rabbits here," he indicated the attendants who were now glowering at us, albeit from a safe distance, "are getting nervous."

Seeing the sense in this, the six of us went back out into the forum, whereupon the man who had noticed me first thrust out his arm and introduced himself.

"I'm Quintus Albinus," he offered, and hearing his complete name served to drop the last piece into place in my mind.

"You served with my grandfather in the 10th as one of his Centurions," I said, and I could tell he was pleased; I also knew he was unaware that my Avus had recorded the events of his life.

Consequently, I knew much more about Quintus Albinus than I am sure he imagined.

"That I did," he confirmed; his voice still had the quaver but was stronger than before. "Although I didn't start out that way."

Before I could say anything else to Albinus, the man who had suggested we go outside, and who appeared to be about ten years younger than Albinus, was next to introduce himself.

"Servius Macrianus," he announced, and his grip was noticeably stronger than that of Albinus, and overall, he had a more vigorous air about him. "I was one of your grandfather's Centurions too." His eyes bored into mine as he said with a quiet intensity that, frankly, I found a bit unsettling, "He was the greatest Legionary Rome's ever produced, and he was the finest leader I ever served under."

Even with my unease, I felt my chest swell, and I was sure my heart would burst, except I could not resist glancing over at Galens, who had been silent this whole time, wondering how he was taking me getting all the attention; I need not have worried. By unspoken consent, it was clear the introductions would be made with all four men, and this time, it was the man who had taken the fall, and I saw with some concern he seemed to be favoring his leg, which he noticed.

Grinning, he shook his head, jerking his thumb back at the temple as he told me, "This? That's not from back there. That's from a fucking Parthian arrow. It pains me sometimes, but," his smile faded, and while his intensity did not match that of Macrianus, it was close as he finished emphatically, "I'm alive. And that's thanks to your grandfather." Offering his arm, he said with a laugh, "I'm the only one among us that never got higher than Gregarius. So this bunch," he indicated his companions, who were standing there, looking on amusedly, "are always squabbling with each other about who's going to tell me what to do next!" That made both Galens and me laugh, as did the other three men. "I'm Gnaeus Tullius, but of all of us, I'm the only one who can say he was in the same fucking Century as your grandfather! He wasn't just my Primus Pilus, he was my Centurion!"

"I'm honored to meet you, Tullius," and since he had been the one who mentioned my father, I added, "and I know my father will be happy to hear that you're still on this side with us."

"For now," he agreed, with a chuckle both rueful and, perhaps, bittersweet, and I suppose it was a natural reaction coming from a man who was nearing the end of the string given to him by the Fates.

The final man, who was of an age with Macrianus, at least from appearances, stepped forward to give me his own arm.

"I'm Tiberius Celadius," he said. "I was the Secundus Hastatus Posterior when I retired. After Actium."

I could not miss the bitter tone in his voice, although it did not surprise me much; I can still recall even now, more than twenty years later, hearing the same edge in my Avus' voice when he spoke of the disbanding of the 10th Equestris. And, while I know it was not Celadius' intent, my mind instantly traveled through the web of years and connections that ultimately led to the divine Augustus, and why I was in Rome in the first place. Nevertheless, I shoved this down into the recesses of my mind, determined to enjoy this moment.

In fact, learning Celadius' post prompted me to remark, "So you served under Sextus Scribonius."

"I did," he replied with a fond smile. "He was a good man as well."

"That he was," I agreed. "My father often told me he learned as much from Scribonius as he did from my grandfather." Only then did I think to add, "As did I. Just not on the training field."

Celadius looked surprised, and I explained, "Scribonius was actually the man who taught me my letters and how to read in Latin. Along with other subjects. Then Diocles took over."

This prompted another reaction, this time from all four, their craggy, beaten faces splitting into grins.

"Diocles!" Tullius chortled his name. "I'd forgotten about Diocles! He practically ran the Legion! How is that old Greek? Still buggering goats?"

I was saddened to be the bearer of the news of his passing, and although while this clearly saddened them, none of them looked surprised.

"I'll be following him shortly," Albinus put it, yet it was without any bitterness or rancor, something I did not understand at all then, and only partially comprehend now.

"You know," it was Macrianus who interjected, making a sweeping gesture back to the temple, "your grandfather and Scribonius are just as responsible for that temple there as Divus Julius. Them and all the men of the first *dilectus* of the 10th."

I will not deny the thought had already occurred to me, even as we were ascending the steps into the temple, yet I did not think it was proper to mar Macrianus' observation by saying as much. Instead, I agreed, then thought of something.

"I suppose," I began, "you've heard about Scribonius…?"

"That he's dead too?" Macrianus nodded, saying, "Yes, we heard the news." This seemed to prompt something in Macrianus, who added, "I doubt you know this, Pullus, but there was a period of time when I was a frequent guest of your grandfather's for dinners.

This was back when we were in Ephesus…" His voice trailed off, and he appeared to be thinking. "…or maybe it was Damascus." Shrugging, he said, "Anyway, it was one of those places. But it would just be your grandfather, Scribonius, Quintus Balbus, your father, me, Diocles. And," he paused for a moment, then added, "Miriam." Cocking his head, he examined me, and I sensed he was trying to calculate my age when he asked, "You never knew her, did you?"

"No." I shook my head. "She died before I was born. But," I could not suppress a sigh as I thought about the melancholy that even now still sometimes descends on my mother when she thinks of her, "I've heard a lot about her, and what a wonderful woman she was."

Surprising me, Macrianus shook his head vehemently, except it was to say, "She was more than wonderful, Pullus. She was one of the kindest, gentlest people I've ever met." Suddenly, his eyes began to gleam, and in that moment, I recall thinking that, perhaps, Macrianus had been in love with Miriam himself. "And," he continued, although he had turned to stare off somewhere else, probably back through the mists created by almost thirty years, "she was good for your grandfather." Returning his attention to me, he gave me a look that was difficult to interpret. "I'm sure you've heard stories, Pullus. About your grandfather." He leaned closer, then glanced over at his old comrades, who had remained silent, although it was not from disinterest. "Well, I'm here to tell you that most of them are probably true."

As I am sure he hoped, this prompted a laugh from all of us, and I tried to assure him that I had no doubt this was so. This prompted a lively discussion among the four of them, and for the next period of time that, only later, did I realize was at least a third of a watch, these four old men tried to outdo each other in retelling the exploits of my Avus. While I will say I had heard, or more accurately read, of some of them, there were new stories I heard this day. One particularly memorable moment came when Tullius was defending his status as the one who was most qualified to expound on the man Titus Pullus.

"None of you bastards were a ranker in his Century," he insisted, plowing through the good-natured jeering of the others, "and I've got the *vitus* marks to prove it!"

"So he used the *vitus* a lot?"

This came from Galens who, like me, had mostly been listening, and I wondered what prompted the question.

Tullius gave a snorting chuckle. "If we were lucky, he would. Because, strong as he was, you didn't want him coming after you with his hands!" This seemed to jar a memory from his mind, and he related, "I remember one time, back in the first civil war," his battered features were crossed by a shadow as he spoke, "we were marching from Massillia down to Brundisium to take ship to go gods know fucking where, and one of my friends, Figulus, thought he'd be sly. I was new meat then, and Figulus took me under his wing and showed me the tricks. Anyway, marching through Etruria, or maybe we were even down to Latium by then, the Primus Pilus had given orders that nobody could leave camp at night. He seemed to be under the impression that we were some thieving, whoring, drunken bastards that he didn't want to turn loose on the good citizens." He gave me a grin that was more leer than anything as he confirmed, "And he was right to think so! Oh, we were drooling whenever we marched through one of those soft, plump towns with the merchants' daughters, and all that...prosperity," this was the word he finally settled for, "just lying around, waiting to be taken. Anyway, old Figulus had figured out that he could hide in the wagon that made the daily run for supplies that we requisitioned on the march. It was a daily routine, that wagon coming and going, and I'll say he got away with it for a few days. He never missed formation, morning or evening, but after that, he'd be gone. So, one day, the Primus Pilus calls him over for a chat, and they talk nice as you please." Laughing at the memory, Tullius went on, "It was really a cruel thing your grandfather did, because once he was done chatting with Figulus, asking how he was holding up on the march, and that sort of thing, he dismissed him. I was standing there, along with all the other boys in the Century, and here comes Figulus, his back to the Primus Pilus, marching up to us with this big grin like the cat who got the cream. And we all knew he had gotten away with it. But," Tullius' smile turned to at least a partial grimace as he finished, "we were wrong. Just before he got back in formation, the Primus Pilus stopped him, then beat him bloody. And I mean *bloody*. I was still a young pup then, you know, while Figulus was one of the boys from Hispania from Pompey's 1st salted into our ranks when Divus Julius formed the Legion. I'd never seen anyone get whipped that badly. Or that quickly."

Now, I, in fact, had read my Avus' recounting of what he had done to Figulus, but I certainly was not going to interrupt or stop him, although I was moved to ask, "And?"

"And what?" Tullius looked at me, puzzled. Then, his face cleared, and he said, "Ah. And did Figulus ever try that again?" His answer came with a snort, as he simply finished, "What do you think?"

Even if I had not read about it, I would have known.

Finally, Galens began getting restless, and I made our excuses, but not until after the four men extracted a promise from me, although I was not sure I would be able to keep it.

"While you're here in Rome, you need to meet us at the *taverna* we like to go to," Albinus said, then went on to name the spot and give its location. However, when I asked which night, he just laughed and said, "Why, every night, of course!"

With that, we all clasped arms once more, then Galens and I made our way to the main Forum, but in a silence that lasted longer than made me comfortable. The one thing it did allow, for me anyway, was to turn over the meeting in my mind, and this was when I decided to tuck away this piece of information about where I could find these former comrades of my Avus, saving it for when I would need it.

"Your grandfather," Galens finally broke the silence, "scared the living *cac* out of me."

Sure that this was from a specific moment, I turned and asked, "Really? When?"

"When?" Galens chuckled. "Every time he got within arm's reach of me, that's when." Suddenly, he seemed to realize my meaning, and he added, "No, I'm not talking about anything like what they were talking about. I mean, just in general. He was Camp Prefect the first five years I was in the Legion, and just seeing him up close, with all those scars, and hearing all the things he'd done, I thought I'd drop a load whenever he looked in my direction."

This, I had to admit, was something to which I could relate, although in my case, it was more a matter of my own desire to never give my Avus reason for disappointment in my actions. Inevitably, however, as all children do at one time or another, my activities caused my Avus to give me a look that, while I am sure it was not the same as the one he cast towards men like Galens, was no less fear-inducing. The difference was that my fear was not based in the idea of physical punishment; as harsh a disciplinarian as Titus Pullus was, he never raised a hand to me or my siblings who were lucky enough to be alive when he still walked the earth.

This thought was what prompted me to say, "Trust me, I know how you feel. I loved him, but I feared him almost as much."

"That's as it should be," Galens countered, then made a slight shrugging motion as he added, "boys scared of their fathers. Or grandfathers. Otherwise, every man I've ever known would have ended up breaking his neck on his own doing something stupid."

I had to laughingly agree. By this point, we had descended the rest of the way down to the Forum, where we stopped at the Milliarium Aureum, from which all distances are measured throughout the world. We stood there for a bit, arguing with each other about whether it was just gilt or made of pure gold; I argued for the former, Galens insisting he had it on good authority that it was, in fact, made of pure gold, which had been melted down from the mounds of golden bricks that Augustus confiscated from Egypt's treasury after Actium. I must admit, when he brought up the possible source, I experienced a glimmer of doubt about my conviction that it was merely leafed in gold. Almost directly in front of us, as we continued on the Via Sacra, was the Rostra, except this day, there was nobody noteworthy orating, although that did not stop a knot of mostly men from standing at the foot of it. This is not to say nobody was speaking; there were perhaps a half-dozen men actually standing on the Rostra, all of whom were talking, all at once, but we quickly determined they were lawyers shouting their supposed accomplishments in the hopes of landing a client. Certainly, this was why we stopped, as Galens and I exchanged a sidelong glance.

"We might as well listen and see if any of these bastards are any good," was how he put it. "If anything, maybe we can pick up some hints on how to at least talk like a fucking lawyer."

At first, I thought he was joking, at least about the idea that one of the men above us might prove a worthy champion for whatever lay ahead of us, especially since we were there only as witnesses. However, one peek at his face gave the lie to the idea he was jesting, his face set in an intent expression, listening as, one after the other, each lawyer spoke about the cases he had won and the circumstances surrounding them. Judging from appearance of the small crowd craning their necks up at the men, I had the impression that their interest was more for entertainment purposes than anything else. When one man claimed to have won a case, at least one or more of his competitors would contest his boast, shouting that he had only been there as an assistant, or the jury had been bribed. In fact, as I stood there observing, this seemed to be the most common accusation and way to undermine another lawyer, by announcing to the crowd that it had not been rhetorical skill but gold that had been the key to victory. Finally, I had heard enough, and I tugged at Galens' tunic impatiently.

"Come on," I urged him, "surely you've heard enough by now."

"What about that one?" Galens pointed up at a thin, balding man of perhaps fifty years, his hair in between the stage of gray and white, and somewhat unusually, with a full beard that did not look as if it had been clipped or groomed in some time.

In fact, my first thought was that any barbarian would have been proud to have a beard of that magnitude, if not the coloring. However, it was his toga that told the tale as far as I was concerned.

"What about him?" I echoed Galens. Then, before he could reply, I also pointed, but at his attire, saying, "Last time I checked, those were supposed to be white, not gray because it hasn't been washed since the gods know when. Or frayed at the hem."

Galens turned and glared at me, clearly upset.

"That might not mean anything!" he insisted. "Besides, he sounds like he knows what he's talking about. At least," he amended, "more than the rest of that bunch."

"Why are you listening to them anyway?" I demanded. "We're not the ones in trouble. We're just here to swear before the gods and tell the Tribunal whatever it is Atticus wants us to say."

He gave me a long, searching look then, and my sense in the moment was he was trying to gauge my sincerity, and I clearly recall thinking about how dismaying it felt to be under suspicion.

But then he just shrugged and said, "That's true. Besides, I thought they were funny."

"I may not know much about the law," I told him, "but I do know that is *not* the first quality you want in a lawyer."

The rest of our time in the Forum we spent just wandering around, gawking like the provincials we were. While we drew some attention as we continued our tour, I came to the conclusion it was not from our behavior; both Galens and I spotted at least a dozen others looking as wide-eyed as I am sure we did.

"It's you, you big oaf." Galens elbowed me in the side as he responded to my open wondering as to why we seemed to be drawing attention when other provincials did not. "You always forget how big you fucking are, Pullus."

Which was, and is, certainly true, although I personally do not think it that unusual. When one lives in their body, I do not think they give much thought to their outward appearance and what reaction it might cause in others; unless one is a woman, of course. Speaking of women, while I never learned why, we were actually in time to see a procession of sorts, of the Vestal Virgins, as they walked in a single line from the temple of Vesta, back to their residence, which also serves as the home of the *Pontifex Maximus*. We only caught a glimpse, just the tail end of them as they seemed to float above the ground, this illusion made by their long, flowing gowns. It was Galens who pointed out to me there were only five of the priestesses.

"The other one's in the temple. There's always a Vestal there to make sure the goddess' fire doesn't go out," he said.

"I wonder why they were all out at once?" I wondered, but when we asked some of the citizens who had stopped to watch, none of them knew either.

All around us, the Forum was pulsing with life, and both Galens and I were content to just stand and watch, choosing a spot near the Temple of Divus Julius. Unlike the Temple of Venus Genetrix, this was one of the busiest spots, with a steady procession of people entering and exiting. At first, I thought this was nothing out of the ordinary. Until, that is, I actually began closely observing those who visited and I noticed that, not only were they uniformly male, they were clearly more prosperous than the average Roman. I did not see any man wearing an iron ring, or *togate,* for that matter, but more than one of them were undoubtedly from patrician, or perhaps old plebeian families. I say this because, no matter what their attire, their entire being practically screams out their status, starting with the tilt of the head, lifting the nose up to a level whereby I suppose they can somehow either avoid the stench or provide a visual indication of how much beneath those around them are in comparison. More than anything, it was the way they behaved as they pushed their way through the throng; Caesar's temple is located at the intersection of the Via Sacra and what I learned the locals call the Via Palatina, because it leads up to the hill overlooking the Forum. More than once while I was watching, a man would visibly recoil when he brushed up against someone of clearly inferior station, although to be fair, some of the people I saw wandering about were as filthy as any barbarians I had seen. Some of the upper classmen had bodyguards, mostly former gladiators, at least judging by the look of them, although I did see at least two men I was sure had been under the standard. Galens, meanwhile, had his attention on a construction project, which we learned was actually the rebuilding of the Basilica Julia, where the civil courts are normally held, and looked near completion. Elbowing him, I told him what I had seen, then he stood and watched for several moments as well.

"What's that all about?" I asked him, although honestly, I felt certain he would not have any more idea than I did; I was wrong.

"They're putting on a show." Galens' laugh held little humor. "Just like those bastards over at the Rostra."

"A show?" I was mystified. "A show for what?"

"Not for what," he replied. "For who."

This answer prompted me to turn about to stare at my Centurion, studying his face for a few heartbeats as the meaning came to me.

"Ah," I said at last, "they want to be seen sacrificing to Divus Julius."

"And who would it matter to that men are seen demonstrating their loyalty to Caesar?" Galens asked, although by this time, it was a rhetorical question, because I had caught on.

In fact, before we departed Rome, I would learn even more details about this seeming mystery, but that came later, although I was about to learn at least part of the cause fairly shortly.

By the time we returned to the Campus, all both of us wanted was nothing more than a hot bath, a good meal, and the chance to rest a bit. I find it odd, but while we were both fit men, our time on horseback had taken the sap out of our legs, as we like to say, because while neither of us would say so, at least aloud, I could see Galens was as tired as I was. Regardless of our needs, we had to console ourselves with the bath, and while the meal was not anything special, it sufficed. Otherwise, we were to be thwarted in our hopes, because while we had been touring the Forum, Atticus had been conferring with the Tribune assigned to his defense, whereupon our Primus Pilus reconsidered and decided we would be needed that day after all. Or, at least what was left of it. We had just returned from our meal, after enjoying the bath, followed by a good massage and scraping, of course, and I had seated myself at the table, resuming the reading of one of the scrolls I had brought, while Galens stretched out on his cot, when there was a sharp rapping at the door.

"Are we expecting anyone?" I asked Galens, but like me, he had no idea who it could be.

Which, in hindsight, seems somewhat silly; nevertheless, I was surprised when I opened the door to find Atticus standing there, only in tunic but like any good Centurion, holding his *vitus*. This was not all he brought with him, though, because standing next to him was a man who appeared to be just a couple years older than I, and I am afraid the first thought that came to my mind as my eyes rested on him was how much he reminded me of the stream of upper class men parading through the Forum, showing their devotion to Divus Julius.

Still, I snapped to *intente* after I drew the door fully open, saying loudly enough so Galens could hear, "Primus Pilus, sir! Good evening! We weren't expecting you."

He gave me a sour look as he said, "Oh, I'm sorry! Please forgive me, Pullus. I didn't mean to disrupt your plans." Entering into the room as he said this, he made for the table, taking the seat I had just vacated as he finished, "It's not like there's anything more important than whatever you two have cooked up for your debauchery tonight, like a Tribunal."

I could see he was not in a good frame of mind, and I hurried to apologize. Only then did Atticus seem to realize he had left the man I presumed was his defender standing just inside the doorway, unintroduced to either of us.

"Oh, yes," I suppose he was trying to sound contrite, "please forgive my rudeness, sir. This is Tribune Lucius Arruntius. He's been assigned to defend me against these charges."

Frankly, I was not sure what I was supposed to do, so I remained at *intente*. It turns out it was a good thing, because while Galens had swung to sitting position from his cot, he had not risen yet, something the Tribune clearly did not appreciate.

"Really, Atticus," his voice was a perfect complement to the show of disdain emanating from him, "is this how bad it's gotten in the Legions, that officers don't rise when their superiors enter the room?"

"No, sir." Galens was the one who answered, cutting off Atticus from whatever he was going to say, which clearly displeased the Primus Pilus even more. "I mean, I apologize, Tribune. It's just that we weren't expecting…"

"Yes, yes," Atticus interrupted, waving a hand towards Galens in the same way one swats at an annoying insect. "I know I told you that you'd have the day off. But the Tribune here insisted that we meet immediately. So," he gave us both a grim smile, "here we are."

Now it was Arruntius' turn to look irritated, although I do not know if it was because Atticus had answered for him, or what was more likely in my mind, the Primus Pilus had dropped Arruntius' fat in the fire by making it clear this was not Atticus' idea.

"Yes." The Tribune gave a thin smile, I supposed to try and appear as if he was not incredibly put out just by being here. "Well, let's get on with it, shall we?"

"Very good, sir," Galens had come to *intente* himself by this point. "Then allow me to introduce my Optio..."

"That won't be necessary." Arruntius had placed a number of wax tablets and a couple of scrolls on the table, and his attention was turned on them. "I know who he is." Then he turned about to look at me, and this time, the smile was missing as he said, "And I've already heard quite a bit about him."

At that particular moment, I was not surprised, assuming with what I believe is justification that my identity had come from Atticus' mouth, but as I was about to quickly discover, I was wrong.

My turn came second, after Arruntius spoke with Galens, although I was listening intently as well. Consequently, I knew what to expect, or at least hoped I did. It started with Arruntius asking Galens to describe the night we had the guard duty, in his own words, taking notes as he went. Since Galens and I had gone over what we would say during our journey, nothing he said was a surprise. However, despite my belief that Galens had acquitted himself perfectly, giving an account of what happened that night I was sure was satisfactory and, more importantly, aligned with what Atticus had expected from us, Arruntius obviously did not feel the same way. Instead, he made Galens go over it again, then again.

Even Atticus was prompted to ask, "Is this really necessary, Tribune? It's not like the prosecuting Tribune is going to ask the same questions over and over."

"Oh, really?" Arruntius twisted in his seat to stare at the Primus Pilus, the corner of his lip lifted in what can only be described as a sneer. "Are you sure of that, Primus Pilus? Can you guarantee that the prosecutor won't ask the same question, just a different way? Because I can assure that, not only can he do so, he almost certainly will."

Despite his tone, his actual words made sense, and I saw Atticus understood this as well; Galens just seemed resigned to going over and over things until he was told he was done.

Returning his attention to Galens, Arruntius resumed his examination of my Centurion, reminding me of the drilling all new *tiros* must undergo during training, hearing the command "*Repitate!*" over and over as we learn the basic movements. As I sat listening, I realized this was essentially the same thing happening here, that Arruntius was just ensuring that the answers Galens provided would come immediately, without him having to think about it. And I began to relax, thinking I understood what would be required of me. That belief lasted as long as it took me to take Galens' place in the seat across from Arruntius.

"Now," he heaved a sigh that I did not like the sound of at all, "we come to you."

This was bad enough, then when I glanced at Atticus and saw he was looking everywhere but in my direction, my gut started twisting into knots; it was the best I was going to feel for some time. Gesturing to me to begin, I did so, essentially repeating what Galens had said, except Arruntius made no move to stop me, and I began to think I was imagining that I was supposed to play a different role. Then, when I got to the part where I had been summoned by Trebellius at the sight of the fire, he raised a hand.

Arruntius was staring down at one of the tablets, which I could see was scribbled with notes, although I could not see what they said, when he said, "This is when you actually saw the Taurisci warband, isn't it?"

"It is?" was my immediate and instinctive response; this was the first moment when I discovered that my testimony was supposed to be different from Galens'.

"Yes, it is," Atticus snapped, seemingly jarred from his boredom at hearing us repeat ourselves over and over. "You don't remember? You told me you'd gotten a clear look at them because they were outlined against the fire!"

"Oh," I managed, and at least tried to look a bit crestfallen as I added, "that's right. I forgot."

Arruntius, however, was not fooled in the slightest, except that he turned to glare at Atticus, who once more was looking everywhere but back at the haughty Tribune.

"Atticus," Arruntius snapped, "what's going on here? You told me that your Optio here was the one who clearly saw the Taurisci! It certainly doesn't sound that way to me!"

Oh, I was in quite the quandary, sitting there right between the two, with Atticus to my left and Arruntius to my right, feeling about as panicked as if the crossfire were real missiles of some sort.

Before I could stop myself and think matters through, I interjected, "No, sir! I did see them! It just...slipped my mind."

Even as the words left my mouth, I inwardly winced; only an idiot could miss how weak this sounded, and while I suppose it was a good sign that Arruntius pounced on such a lapse so quickly, I certainly did not feel better about it in the moment.

"Slipped your mind?" He repeated himself incredulously, "Slipped your mind?"

Sighing, he shook his head and sat back, giving me a hard stare. I was certainly expecting some more excoriation from the Tribune, but I was completely unprepared for what was about to come.

Tossing his stylus down disgustedly, he muttered, "I can't say I wasn't warned about you, Optio."

My initial reaction was to stare at Atticus; I was completely unprepared for the look of confusion on my Primus Pilus' face, and the thought flashed across my mind that, if he was acting like he was surprised, he was doing a good job.

Seeing my gaze on him, Atticus then said something completely unexpected, both for the words and because he seemed equally upset, protesting, "Whatever he's talking about didn't come from me, Pullus!"

Tearing my eyes away, I returned my attention to the Tribune who, suddenly, seemed equally uncomfortable. It was not until I felt Galens' hand on my shoulder, firmly pressing me back into my seat did I realize I had started to rise, although I had been very aware I had clenched my right fist, which was still resting on the table.

"Would you care to explain that remark, Tribune?"

That this came from Atticus meant my attention was still on Arruntius, so I saw the flash of some emotion cross the Tribune's visage that could have been surprise, I supposed because the question came not from me but the Primus Pilus.

Arruntius did not reply, at least immediately, choosing instead to stare down at the tablet; I was beginning to think he was going to refuse to answer when he spoke in a way that suggested he was choosing his words carefully. "Let's just say that Optio Pullus'…reputation is something that's come to the attention of certain men in Rome."

Before, I had been apprehensive; now I experienced a sensation that I had heard other men speak of but had always thought was meant in a figurative sense, as it felt like the blood running through my veins suddenly went cold. It is a uniquely distinctive and unpleasant feeling, and I was only dimly aware that someone sucked in a breath; I still do not know whether it came from me or Atticus. Or Galens, for that matter.

"How so?" Atticus asked, then his tone turned a bit harder as he demanded, "And who are you talking about?"

I suppose I derived some solace from the fact that the question had come from Atticus, although I was aware his concern had nothing to do with my own well-being. Nevertheless, I was happy that someone other than me asked the two most pertinent questions. What I was not prepared for was the answers I was about to get, because as I was about to learn, I was completely mistaken in my assumption that this was in some way tied to my family, and Augustus, at least in a direct sense.

Unmindful that the topic of this exchange was sitting between them, Arruntius snapped back, "That's none of your concern, Primus Pilus!"

"I disagree." Atticus was no less vehement. Stabbing his finger in my direction, he insisted, "This is a junior officer in my Legion! Not just in my Legion, but in my Cohort! And I've been watching his development because he's on my list to be elevated to the Centurionate!"

Despite all that was happening, this caused me to gape at the Primus Pilus, who seemed to notice me again for the first time.

Sparing me little more than a glance, he did say with a shrug, "I was going to tell you when we got back to Siscia that I've decided to put you on the list for promotion."

The rush of emotions that came over me threatened to finish the job of roiling my stomach begun just a few heartbeats earlier, yet the flush of surprised happiness that I suppose was inevitable at Atticus' words lasted the amount of time it took for my heart to beat one time before flushing it away with the recognition of the significance of the timing. He said "when we get back to Siscia," I thought dismally, which is his way of reminding me not to lose my head and do anything stupid, like tell the truth at this Tribunal. This was the carrot he now dangled in front of me; before this point, all I had seen was the *vitus* that would be used to beat my dreams of advancement to death. There is no way for me to know with any certainty, even now, whether or not he had actually planned on this enticement before Arruntius made his unfortunate remark, or if he realized in the moment I would be worried enough about whatever this information Arruntius supposedly possessed to turn the table on Atticus by offering him up before he could do the same to me. The combination of the warnings I had received from Asinius and Sextus had alerted me to one likely reason the Primus Pilus was insisting I accompany him to Rome, and being fair, when I put myself in his *caligae*, I could easily see that Arruntius' words had changed the game. I cannot say all of this went through my mind in that handful of heartbeats, at least in any conscious sense, but this was the essence of my state of mind as I sat there, waiting for Arruntius' response to Atticus' challenge.

Finally, it was the Tribune who broke from the staring contest between the two of them first, making a gesture of disgusted surrender with one manicured hand as he sniffed, "Fine. Have it your way." Turning to look at me, he eyed me in much the same way I imagine he would if I was a two-headed calf, something worthy of attention only because of some extraneous factor; in the case of a calf, it would be the extra head. In mine, it turned out to be something completely unexpected, at least by me. "It turns out that you made such an impression on the departed Nero Claudius Drusus that he mentioned you to his brother, Tiberius."

That much I knew, because when Tiberius selected me to be one of his brother's bearers the final mile back into Mogontiacum, he had told me as much.

"I only met Tiberius once," I protested, "and then it was just as he assigned me as one of the men of the honor guard when we entered Mogontiacum."

Arruntius merely shrugged, and said in an offhanded manner, "I'm not saying there's any substance to the talk." His demeanor changed slightly, and he sat, examining me more closely before he asked abruptly, "How much do you know about what's going on in Rome? The political situation, I mean?"

My instant decision was to play the Stupid Legionary role to the hilt.

"That the Princeps is the First Man in Rome," I replied earnestly, "and that we're doing better than we've ever done in our history."

"Yes, yes," Arruntius was clearly irritated by my obtuseness, "and we all make daily sacrifices that he live many, many more years. But," he refused to be lured off the scent, "surely you have more of an idea than that."

Sensing he would not be swayed, I said cautiously, "The only other thing I've heard is just about who might succeed Augustus." Shrugging, I decided this was as far as I would go, trying to convey this by finishing flatly, "And that's all I know. Nothing more."

For the first time, I saw what seemed like the barest glimmer of a smile on the lips of the Tribune, which just deepened my confusion.

"That," he said softly, "is a very wise approach, Pullus. I have to say I'm impressed. Given what I've heard, I was expecting to meet a lumbering, giant oaf who's strong as Hercules but with little better than porridge for brains."

Even as he said this, I knew he was probing me, that this was a test; it did not make me want to grab him by his oily hair and slam his patrician head against the table until his brains came out any less, but I was justifiably proud of myself for my restraint, saying nothing in response. I expected Arruntius to be at least somewhat disappointed I had not taken his bait, yet if anything, he seemed more pleased than before.

Once he understood I was not saying any more, he continued, "Well, while I suspect you may know more than you're letting on, I don't blame you for your caution. And right now, matters are…delicate."

"How so?" Atticus broke in for the first time, which did not please Arruntius.

"If you didn't interrupt, you'd know by now," the Tribune replied tartly. "Now, where was I? Ah, yes, you see, the thing is there's some...concern about the Princeps' seeming hesitation in naming a successor for that regrettably inevitable day when he crosses in Charon's Boat. And there are...factions in the Senate who disagree about who it should be."

"So?" Atticus clearly was unwilling to let Arruntius go uninterrupted. "What else is new? The Senate's been squabbling since long before any of us were born."

"Yes, well." Arruntius' voice seemed to drip with acid as he gave the Primus Pilus a look of such disdain that I half-expected Atticus to do what I had dreamed of doing just a few moments before, although he restrained himself, albeit with much the same reluctance I had felt, judging from his expression. "Be that as it may, this is a dangerous situation, no matter how many times it's happened before. And now that Tiberius is rumored to be about to return to Rome, the atmosphere has become more...tense." He hesitated for a moment, then took a deep breath before plunging forward, saying, "There's some fear that on his return, he's going to take matters into his own hands, and force Augustus into naming him as heir and successor."

Frankly, my first thought was that anyone who tried to force the divine Augustus into doing anything was probably not long for this world, although I certainly did not voice that opinion.

Instead, I decided to get back to the subject nearest to my heart, asking, "So I don't see how that has anything to do with me. Why is anyone worried about me when it comes to Tiberius?"

"Because," Arruntius explained, "you're a symbol, of sorts."

It was at this point I decided to stop thinking I could not be more confused.

"A symbol for what?"

Arruntius regarded me for a long moment, then asked quietly, "Do you really not know why?"

"No," I almost shouted the word, so frustrated that I knew myself well enough to know that, despite my best attempt, I would be unable to restrain myself from physically lashing out much longer.

"Pullus," Arruntius explained patiently, "whether you know it or not, you're connected to Augustus, through your grandfather."

And, there it was, out in the open. Nevertheless, I refused to give this Arruntius character anything whatsoever he might use against me; worrying about Atticus was more than enough.

"What happened to my grandfather," I tried to keep my tone level, "is that he spent forty-two years under the standard and was one of the first Camp Prefects."

"He also faced a Tribunal because of the Marcus Primus affair," Arruntius answered quietly. "Or did you forget that part?"

"No, I haven't forgotten," was all I said.

"Well," Arruntius continued, "I suspect you know more than you're letting on, but since this is your first time to Rome...Atticus told me," he added when my eyes narrowed in suspicion. "Anyway, what you may not know is that your grandfather's exoneration of those charges didn't sit well with....certain parties."

While I and my entire family were aware of this, why this was the case was still a mystery. We could certainly make some assumptions, and, in fact, my Avus had done so, in the privacy of his account, which is just one reason our family guards those precious scrolls so carefully. However, in this moment, I sensed that if I was careful, I might learn more, and perhaps even learn if Titus Pullus had guessed correctly.

This was why I decided to be honest, at least to a point, telling him, "I knew that much."

"Do you know why?"

This I was not willing to divulge, so I shook my head.

"Well," Arruntius sighed again, "the fear was that there would be men who'd use your grandfather as a...symbol, of sorts."

"A symbol for what?"

"That the Princeps isn't infallible, that he can make mistakes." The Tribune paused so long I thought he had finished, but he began speaking again, saying, "And if he makes mistakes, there are still men in the Senate who would capitalize on that."

This was the moment I realized that, although my Avus had been correct about his status as a symbol being the cause of his problems with the upper classes, the reason for their enmity was not based in the supposed danger he posed as a man rising above the station the gods had chosen for him, at least entirely. Instead, it was about exploiting an opportunity to attack the Princeps, albeit indirectly.

"I still don't understand where Tiberius fits in this," I replied, and when I gave Atticus a quick glance, I saw he was listening intently, giving me the impression he was still in the dark as well.

"If the rumors are true," Arruntius asked, "and Tiberius is determined to claim what he sees as his rights, how do you think he'd go about it?"

"With the Legions on the Rhenus." Atticus was the one who answered, reminding me how politically attuned he was.

"And Pannonia," Arruntius said pointedly. "I recall he once commanded the Army of Pannonia, in his first campaign against Rhaetia."

"That was some time ago." Galens surprised the rest of us, causing us all to turn and look at him. His face turned red, and he mumbled, "But I see your point."

"Thank you so much," Arruntius sneered, yet seemed content to only lift his lip before returning to the subject. "If Tiberius were to raise the Legions to march on Rome, what better symbol to you men in the ranks than the namesake and grandson of Titus Pullus? The man who thwarted the designs of our beloved Princeps by being found not guilty at a Tribunal that was supposed to do the opposite?"

I stared at him, trying to determine if this was actually a jest on his part, except his face remained deadly serious, and even more unsettling, he was returning my gaze without flinching.

"I...I'd...never be part of that," I gasped. A new, even more horrible thought came to me. "Does Augustus think that's what's going to happen? Has he..." I had to swallow before I could get it out, "intercepted a letter or something like that?"

"No," Arruntius replied, and my body suddenly sagged, but then he added, "at least as far as I know." This certainly did not help my emotional state, although I felt a bit better when he said, "Honestly, I haven't heard anything to suggest that Tiberius has given the slightest indication that he's disposed to do so. This is just what some men are saying."

"But why would these…men," I had to bite off the word I wanted to use, "be engaging in groundless speculation if there's no evidence to support their belief?"

"Because," Atticus broke in, and there was no mistaking the bitter twist to his mouth as he said, "that's what the upper classes of Rome do, Pullus. Political games and all this kind of whispering is like their mother's milk. And to them, we're just pieces to be used and sacrificed."

Only then did he seem aware of his audience, and his face reddened as he muttered a half-hearted apology to Arruntius. Who, I noticed, did not seem offended in the slightest.

Instead, he inclined his head as if he was acknowledging a compliment, although his words did not match his manner, saying, "Be that as it may, Atticus, this is the world in which we live. And this is what men are saying. About Tiberius and," he gestured to me, "your Optio." Nothing more was said for several moments, then Arruntius cleared his throat and announced, "Now, we need to get back to why we're here."

It was somewhere around this point in time I decided to claim the marker given to me by one of my former Tribunes, the man Claudius whose father had played a role in all that occurred with my Avus. Now, I thought grimly, I find out if his offer to help whenever I needed it was just talk. The problem, I realized, was how to go about initiating contact, but while outwardly, I was answering Arruntius' questions in the manner he found suitable, my mind was hatching a plan on how to go about doing that very thing.

The watch was late by the time Atticus and Arruntius were satisfied that Galens and I were sufficiently prepared. We also were told why the seeming rush, when we were both under the impression the Tribunal was not scheduled to occur until a week after our arrival in Rome.

"The Tribunal's been moved up to the day after tomorrow," Atticus informed us, waiting until just before he and Arruntius were about to depart.

"What?" I was happy that it was Galens who was the first to express his surprise. "But why? I thought you'd have a week to prepare!"

"I don't need a week," Atticus replied shortly. "I'm the one who requested that it be moved up."

I am not sure why this disturbed either of us, yet it clearly did, as my Centurion and I exchanged a glance. Regardless of our feelings, I think we both understood that, in all reality, it was not our decision to make, although I recall feeling a bit unsettled. And it made it even more important I contact Claudius as quickly as I could. Therefore, as soon as they had departed, I sat down and withdrew the one clean sheet of vellum I had brought with me; this was not a task for a wax tablet. However, I did not use the entire thing, and despite the circumstances, I suppressed a grin at the sound of my father's voice inside my head complaining about the cost of such things and how there was no need to use an entire sheet. Although it must be said my decision to use just a small scrap of the precious material was due more to the idea that it could be easily hidden than the expense.

"I have to go out," I told Galens, once I had composed the message.

"Now?" he asked, and for a brief instant, I thought he would pull rank and forbid me. Instead, he shrugged and said, "You're a big boy." He gave me a long, searching look, then asked softly, "Do I want to know?"

"Probably not," I answered him honestly.

"I thought as much," he grumbled, then made a point to reach for the amphora of wine to pour himself a cup. "Don't expect me to wait up for you."

Despite my mood, this made me laugh, and I promised I did not expect him to do so. I made sure to change into one of my Optio's tunic, and I put on my *baltea* as well, hoping this would be sufficient to keep the Urban Cohort or the *vigiles* from stopping me for being out past the normal curfew. However, as I learned as soon as I left the boundary of the Campus, if there was a curfew at all, it was being ignored. The streets were certainly not as crowded as they were during the daylight hour, but it was far from deserted. My biggest problem was finding the spot Macrianus had told me about; all I can say in my own defense is that when he described the location, it did not seem as if it would be a challenge to find it. As I discovered, the streets of Rome, once beyond the sacred precinct and the Forum, are a maze, although in the direction I was heading, it was not as dangerous as the Subura. I was at the base of the Capitoline, but on the opposite side from the way Galens and I had ascended, and I think this increased my confusion. Finally, I was forced to stop and rack my brain, trying to remember everything Macrianus had told me. As acutely aware as I was that every moment I spent was one I could ill afford to waste, I started to become desperate as I realized I was lost. Then, somehow, one piece of seemingly extraneous information came back to me, when Macrianus had made what seemed to be an offhanded remark.

"When you're coming from the Campus, you'll pass by the theater that the Princeps built for his son-in-law." He paused an instant, then thought to add, "Well, his dead son-in-law anyway."

This memory prompted me to approach a woman who, judging from her appearances, was plying her trade, asking her for the whereabouts of Marcellus' Theater.

"Why?" She laughed, and honestly, at that moment, I was thinking she was somewhat attractive...until she opened her mouth to reveal a set of rotting, blackened teeth. "There's nothing happening there at this time of night! But," she actually lifted the hem of her filthy robe to reveal her nether parts, "if you're looking for something to do..."

Understanding I had to at least appear interested if I was to expect any kind of help, I answered in the same bantering tone she was using, "I might be. As soon as you tell me where the theater is from here."

Her professional smile vanished, and even in the guttering light of the lamp dangling from the bracket on the building behind her, there was no way I could miss the hardness there.

"Fucking soldiers," she spat. "You're all lousy fucks anyway!"

Sighing, I realized this was going nowhere, so I reached into my purse tucked under my *baltea*, fumbling for a silver *denarius* piece. The whore did not miss the move, and I saw her eyes drop down to my waist; I was sure I could hear the wheels in her grubby mind turning. Nevertheless, I finally felt the ridged edge of the denomination coin I wanted and, in one motion, withdrew it from my purse and flipped it to her. It did not surprise me in the least that, even in the dark, she was able to track the winking silver of the coin as it tumbled through the air, snatching it with an expertise I must admit impressed me. Her smile immediately returned; suddenly, I experienced a pang of regret I had made her do so, because I was now close enough to smell her breath, telling me she had already had a busy night, if one takes my meaning.

Still, she was cooperative, turning and pointing to the corner. "Take a right, then follow this street until you get to the Tiber, then take a left. The theater'll be to your left, because if you turn right, you'll drown."

She laughed at her own wit, yet despite not thinking her funny, I tried to chuckle, and I made sure I was polite and thanked her for her help, ignoring the fact that she had been paid. While she remained standing in the same spot, I was sure I could feel her eyes boring into my back, and when I got to the end of the street to turn in the direction she indicated, I risked a glance, but she was gone. Now that I had a general direction in which to travel, my frame of mind improved, and I chided myself for being so suspicious that the whore was up to something I would not like at all. And, in seeming support of my reproof of myself, just as she said, I reached the Tiber, turning left as she directed. I went no more than a quarter of a mile when I saw, looming up ahead to my left exactly as she said it would be, the theater building. Even in the dark, it was impressive; the side facing the river is flat, with a large, colonnaded porch, while the rest of the building is curved into a semicircle. Although not nearly as high as the Pantheon, even as preoccupied as I was, I took a moment to admire the three levels, each of them with a series of arches. The columns of the bottom level are Doric, the second level Ionian, and the third level are done in the style of Corinth; it is quite an impressive structure. Regardless of my appreciation, I did not tarry long, because with the theater as a landmark, I was able to find the place. In fact, it was little more than a block past the theater, located on a street running along the Tiber. Honestly, I heard it before I saw it, but as I was following the sounds of revelry, suddenly, a figure lurched out from a doorway, staggering a few steps before falling down into a puddle in the street. Drawing nearer, I saw it was a man, pushing himself up out of the puddle that I was fairly certain was composed of a fair amount of horse piss, yet as he did so, he was laughing uproariously, so I ignored him and entered the *taverna*. Standing just inside the door, waiting for my eyes to adjust, as I surveyed the crowded room, I had the distinct feeling I was back in Siscia, with one slight difference. While the men sitting in groups around tables were clearly men like me, under the standard, the one difference was their ages; they all looked to be more than forty years old. None of them paid me any attention, at least at first, which suited me since it gave me time to scan the crowd. My relief when I saw Macrianus, Albinus, and Tullius was so overwhelming that, for a moment, I thought my knees would give way, but I managed to stay upright and make my way to where they were seated, in the far corner. Once I was well into the room, this was when the other patrons noticed me, and even as I continued towards Macrianus' table, I tensed, waiting for someone to make some sort of remark or challenge, as often happened when I went out into Siscia. I should not have been worried; these were old veterans who no longer felt the need to prove themselves in a brawl. There was still a surprise in store for me, however.

"Pullus!" Macrianus shouted, standing up and gesturing with his wine cup. "Get your big ass over here so we can buy you a drink!"

As I walked over to where the trio were seated, I suppose I noticed that even more men were turning to look at me, but I was not really paying attention to them.

"Where's Celadius?" I asked Macrianus as we clasped arms.

"That *mentula*?" he scoffed as he offered me a chair. "He always goes home early."

"So what brings you out crawling in the gutter?" Tullius asked, once my cup was charged.

I explained what I needed, producing the scrap of parchment, which Macrianus took without hesitation.

"I'll make sure he gets the message," he told me, yet while he seemed certain, I was somewhat uneasy, not just about what I was asking him to do, but the possibility he might not know how to find Claudius.

He must have seen my expression and interpreted it correctly, because he assured me, "Pullus, I know what to do. I'll get him the message before midday tomorrow."

Before I could properly thank him and express my gratitude, I felt someone grab my shoulder, but with a grip that instantly made me tense. Thankfully, I only turned my head without coming to my feet to see a man, perhaps fifty, looking down at me with eyes blurred with drink, while the expression on his face instantly reminded me of Albinus' when we had run into them, so therefore I had a moment's worth of preparation.

"Did I hear right?" the man demanded. "Your name's Pullus?"

"It is," I answered, enduring his drunken examination of me as he looked at me from head to toe.

"You must be related to the Prefect." He said this as if he was passing judgment and had found me satisfactory in his inspection. "Because you're a big bastard, just like him!"

"My mother might not appreciate you saying that," I told him mildly, "or my father."

I had meant it as a jest; a barbed one to be sure, although in the manner of all drunken men, his reaction was delayed by a number of heartbeats, then a look of horror crossed his face.

"I-I'm sorry," he stammered. "Honestly, I meant no offense. I was just so surprised to see you..."

"None taken." I did stand up then, both to offer him my hand in the proper way, as equal to equal, but also to impress upon him that he was, in fact, talking to the grandson of the man who shared more than just the name. "I'm Titus Porcinianus Pullus. Who might you be?"

While he was visibly weaving, his grip was strong, and I pretended not to notice the sudden gleam in his eyes, having seen it before with Albinus, Macrianus, and Tullius, all of whom remained seated, grinning up at the pair of us standing there. The other man's mouth was open, then it shut, then it opened again, yet nothing came out; I assumed he was so overcome with the memories that must have been triggered by seeing someone who reminded him of his glory days, he could not think of what to say.

"This mute," Tullius finally broke the silence, "is Aulus Turbo, late of the 13th Legion."

"Ah," I smiled at him, "the 13th! They're part of the Army of Pannonia now. I'm an Optio in the 8th. The 13th's up in Poetovio most of the time nowadays."

Turbo returned my smile, yet seemed content to just stand there, swaying back and forth as if he was on a ship in rough seas, still regarding me as I started to grow uncomfortable.

Finally, I indicated that he was welcome to pull up a chair; I had conducted my business, after all, and I decided it would not hurt to linger a bit. Just to avoid giving offense, I told myself, I certainly did not intend to fall into the arms of Bacchus.

Once we were seated, I asked our new addition, "Were you in Gaul?"

A look of confusion crossed his face, along with what appeared to be worry, but before he answered me, he glanced over at Tullius who, although he was smiling, seemed to be slightly troubled by something over and above the acquaintance of two generations of Rome's Legionaries.

Finally, Turbo answered hesitantly, "I've been to Gaul, yes. To…" his face screwed up as he apparently tried to think of where, before he said, "…Lugdunensis, I think."

"That's not what he means, Turbo," Tullius interjected, yet as he did, he gave me a wink. "He means were you part of the first *dilectus*, under Divus Julius."

Turbo's face cleared, and he shook his head. "Ah. No, I wasn't. I joined after that."

I was about to probe further, then decided against it; the 13th's role in the civil war had been one that stained the honor of the Legion, so instead, I just asked him, "Were you with the Legion when it was sent to Pannonia?"

Turbo nodded, but then seemed content to sip from his cup without saying anything more. Macrianus suddenly spoke up, asking Turbo about something, which gave Tullius the opportunity to lean over to whisper to me.

"It's not the drink, Pullus," he explained. "Turbo hasn't been right in the head for a long time. Something happened to him in Parthia. As near as we can figure, when we were near starving, he ate some sort of root. Or," he shrugged, "maybe he was one of the men who drank from that poisoned river, although I doubt you've heard much about that."

I assured him I did indeed know something of Parthia, at least as much as one who was not there can; I had not been born yet, and it was my father's first campaign, but growing up under his roof meant I heard his cries in the night sometimes. When, as any child, I was curious as to the cause and asked my mother, all she would say is it had something to do with his time on that campaign. Not until Diocles died did I hear him speak of it. And, of course, my Avus wrote about what has become a legendary campaign to all men under the standard, if for the wrong reasons. Any man who can boast of being in Parthia will never buy a drink whenever he's in a gathering of Legionaries.

"The funny thing is," Tullius was going on, "he was right for a long time. But then, just a few years ago…" He said no more, gesturing with his head, and I glanced over to see that Macrianus had finished speaking to Turbo, who was now staring at a spot on the wall opposite him, in much the same manner as we do when at *intente.*

"What's he doing now?" I whispered, except when Macrianus answered, it was in a normal tone of voice.

"He just…goes away," Macrianus explained, or at least tried. "And there's no need to whisper. When he's like this, this place could burn down and he wouldn't notice."

"And how often does he get this way?"

Macrianus exchanged a glance with Tullius, who shrugged in response, and I suppose it prompted Macrianus to tell me quietly, "Almost every night."

"Then how does he get home?" I asked.

"One of us takes him with us." Tullius was the one who answered this time, in an offhanded, casual manner. "He sleeps at our places." His laugh was tinged with what sounded to me like equal parts of bitterness and melancholy as he finished, "I don't even know where his apartment is, or if he even has one."

"He's not the 10th," Albinus spoke for the first time, "but he's one of us."

This, unfortunately, was the last truly tangible and solid memory I have of that night, because Turbo was the first veteran who came to pay their respects to my Avus, through me, but he was not the last.

I was awakened the next morning by a punch on the shoulder, opening my eyes with a gasp because it had not been a light blow. Galens was standing above me, glaring down at me with a scowl.

"Wake up, you big oaf," he growled at me. "And," he pointed down to a spot I could not easily see, "clean this mess up."

I rolled over, or at least started to, but the sudden stab of pain in my head, which was accompanied by my stomach suddenly doing a flip, at least gave me a hint of what he had pointed out. My eyes could not seem to focus, although they did not need to be sharp to know that the slimy puddle on the brick floor of the room was what had caused Galens' ire, or at least was partly responsible. Unfortunately, the odor that hit my nostrils as I swung my feet onto the floor, careful not to step in it, caused another rebellion to flare in my stomach; somehow, I managed to keep whatever was left in me down. Not, it must be admitted, without wrenching a groan from my lips, but Galens was never the most sympathetic person to begin with, and this moment even more so because he was clearly irritated.

"Stop moaning like a fucking baby," he snapped. "You did it to yourself, so I don't want to hear any crying."

"I'm not crying," I protested, then allowed, "I might be moaning, but I'm not crying."

"Whatever you're doing, just shut up. And," he repeated his gesture, pointing down at the floor, "clean that up."

"I heard you the first time," I grumbled. "Just give me a moment, will you?"

"We don't have a moment," he shot back. "We're supposed to meet with the Primus Pilus and Arruntius again today."

This was news; at least, I believed it was, since I had no recollection of hearing anything like this the day before, even when I was still sober.

"When did you find this out?" I asked him.

"This morning," he admitted grudgingly, then felt compelled to fire another shot, "while you were snoring like Cerberus!"

"Is that why you hit me?" I asked, realizing as I did so that my shoulder was actually sore, and began moving my arm as I rubbed the joint.

"Which time?" This finally seemed to amuse Galens, causing him to grin at me.

"How many times did you hit me?"

"Oh," he sounded casual, "I lost count."

"No wonder my arm hurts," I muttered, but I was also looking for a rag or something to mop up the leavings from my stomach.

"Serves you right," he retorted, "between your snoring and that mess, it's the least you deserve."

I did not argue the point; by this time, I was too focused on keeping from adding to the mess as I began soaking it up.

Something occurred to me then, and I asked him, "When did I get in? And, more importantly, *how* did I get here?"

This prompted a laugh, and Galens told me, "Macrianus and Tullius came carrying you in." He thought for a moment, then shrugged. "About a watch ago, maybe a little more."

"What?" This caused me to stop what I was doing, standing up and staring at him, trying to determine if he was having some fun at my expense. "Are you serious?"

Holding his hand up, he intoned solemnly, "On Jupiter's Stone. But," the tone of his voice changed that informed me our banter was finished, "enough of that. Finish cleaning up, and get in uniform. We're supposed to meet them at the beginning of second watch." He leaned over to look past me, squinting out the opened window, and announced, "Which means you've got less than a sixth part to be ready."

I surveyed the progress I had made, and while the floor was now clean, the sour smell was still there, which prompted me to say, "I need to go find one of the slaves to bring a pail of water and a brush if we're going to get this stink out before they get here."

Galens shook his head, telling me, "They're not coming here this time. We're meeting them."

"Where?"

"At the *praetorium* here," he told me. "Apparently, the Tribune thinks it will do us both good and help us be prepared if he runs us through what's going to happen, in the room where it's going to happen."

"I wonder," I mused aloud, "whose idea that was? Arruntius' or Atticus'?"

"It doesn't really matter," Galens pointed out. "Does it?"

No, I realized, it did not, although I was happy I did not have to involve myself with the aftermath of my night of debauchery. Now, I thought dismally as I pulled on my last clean Optio's tunic, all I have to do is not throw up on either of their *caligae*. I washed my mouth out with vinegar, although it must be said the sour taste of it reminded me of the wine I had vomited up, but I did manage to eat a piece of bread that Galens had brought from his own breakfast, which made my stomach feel a bit better. Once I was dressed, he inspected me, as I did him, since there were no bronze mirrors. Satisfied, we exited the room, and walked over to the *Praetorium* as I tried to force my headache away.

"I hope you had fun at least," Galens commented as we strode along the walkway from our barracks to the main building.

"I wish I could remember," I told him honestly.

Frankly, all I could recall was the reason I had gone there, and this more than anything else helped drive the last cobwebs of drink from my brain as I worried about the success or failure of Macrianus' mission.

Both the Tribune and the Primus Pilus were waiting for us in the large room that serves a variety of functions, most commonly for meetings of senior officers who are summoned to Rome for one reason or another. Against the far wall was a long table, behind which were five chairs; between us and that were two more tables, slightly shorter, with two chairs behind each one.

"I see everything's ready," I muttered to Galens as we walked down the center aisle, between the chairs arranged on both sides, filling up the rest of the room.

"How do you know?" he asked, but before I blurted out where I had learned how to recognize a room configured for a Tribunal, I managed to stop myself.

"I don't remember," I lied. "I guess I heard someone talking about it before."

I felt his eyes on me, but there was no time for him to press further, as both of us stopped where the pair of our superiors were waiting for us, sitting on the edge of the long table.

Returning our salutes, Arruntius pointed to a chair and ordered, "Go get that chair and sit in front of where we're standing."

I did so, exacting a petty revenge by dragging the chair across the floor rather than carrying it, taking an inordinate amount of satisfaction at seeing both Atticus and Arruntius grimace at the noise of the legs scraping across the stones, although they did not make an issue of it.

"All right," Arruntius beckoned to Galens, yet surprising me and Galens, he did not indicate the chair I had just placed, but one behind the long table. "Centurion, sit there. Primus Pilus, if you would sit next to him. And Pullus," he was moving behind the long table as he pointed to the chair, "have a seat."

Arranged in this manner, with the three of them looking at me, Arruntius ran through the questions, both the ones he was going to ask, and those he deemed likely that the prosecution would ask. I freely admit that, once I understood what his objective was, I was skeptical that facing three men I knew, rather than five strangers, would have any impact on me at all, but I quickly learned differently. Indeed, it might have been the fact that I knew Galens and Atticus so well, and Arruntius at least a bit, that it actually made me uncomfortable to have them staring at me as Arruntius rattled off questions. Later, when I had a chance to talk to Galens about it, he said he felt the same way, and my respect for the Tribune went up a notch. We spent perhaps a third of a watch in this manner, then Arruntius announced he was satisfied that we were as prepared as we could be. From my perspective at least, I did not think the prosecution had a chance, yet there was something in the manner of both Atticus and Arruntius that made me rethink this.

Galens was clearly of a same mind, because when the Primus Pilus dismissed us, he blurted out, "What don't we know?"

"What do you mean?" Atticus asked, his tone cautious, but I just happened to be watching Arruntius, whose posture stiffened as well.

"What I mean is that neither you or the Tribune seem very happy, sir," Galens answered immediately. "And it makes me think you both know something we don't."

"That's not true," Atticus protested, then hesitated before adding, "at least, not exactly." He exchanged a glance with Arruntius, which the Tribune answered with a shrug as he said softly, "It's up to you."

Atticus turned back to the both of us and explained, "It's not that we know anything that you haven't been told. Do you remember when I said there's supposed to be a witness?"

We both indicated we did.

"We still don't know anything about who it is," Atticus admitted.

Before I could stop myself, I blurted out, "But wait! Isn't that against the regulations governing a Tribunal? I thought you were supposed to be informed about the identity of the witnesses against you!"

Once more, the Primus Pilus and Arruntius looked at each other, except this time, it was Arruntius who replied, "Once more, you impress me, Pullus. Of course, it makes sense anyone in your family would know about the rules of a Tribunal." His smile at his own jest was not matched by mine as I stared at him coldly, causing it to fade, and he hurried on, "Yes, well, be that as it may, you're essentially correct, Optio." He paused and took a deep breath before he plunged on, "But for whatever reason, it's been deemed by the Tribune who was appointed as the presiding officer that the identity of the witness be withheld from us until tomorrow. At the Tribunal itself."

"That's not just!" Galens broke in, and while I did not doubt his sincerity, I did wonder whether the actual cause of his indignation came from a sense of outrage at the injustice, or because he was letting Atticus know his feelings. "How can they do that?"

"No, it's not," Arruntius agreed, "but according to the Tribune, it has to do with matters of security."

"And who's the presiding Tribune?" I asked Arruntius, more out of curiosity than any thought the name would mean anything to me.

"That's not…important," Arruntius said, clearly evasive, yet it quickly became clear he would not provide a name, which made me wonder at the time if this was something else he did not know.

As we would find out the next day, he knew, very well; still, I do not fault him for keeping his identity from us, because there is no way to say what might have happened.

We arose even earlier than normal, although both Galens and I had spent the night before the Tribunal going over our uniforms, polishing our respective decorations, and in my case, scrubbing the plates of my *segmentata* over again when I was dissatisfied with the job one of the slaves assigned to the task had done.

"What about our weapons?" I asked Galens, but I was not surprised when he shook his head.

"They're not allowed," he told me.

I opened my mouth to argue the point, because I knew that this restriction is only for the Forum and Curia, not the Campus. After all, it does not make much sense to have the area where the men of Rome train for war forbidden to weapons, but I did not say anything. As always, we inspected each other, and were just finishing when the knock on the door came. Opening it, only Atticus was standing there, fully dressed as we were, with his *phalarae*, his torq, but only one arm ring, which made me feel a bit smug. Even then, I experienced a stab of regret that I did not have the torq I had taken from Vergorix, but there was nothing to be done about it. His crest, unlike Galens', was white, signifying his status as Primus Pilus, and standing there in his *hamata*, holding the *vitus*, I had to admit that he at least looked the part.

"Are you two ready?" he demanded. "Arruntius is going to meet us there." We assured him that we were, but he stopped us, pointing down to Galens' side, saying, "It doesn't look like you're ready to me! Where are your *gladii* and your *pugiones*?"

It did make me feel better knowing I had been right, but we hastened to go and attach our weapons, then subjected ourselves to his inspection. With me, he straightened my tunic so the seam down one side was straight; with Galens, he flicked away some lint I am sure is only visible to Primi Pili, then gave a grunt, which we knew was his signal that we met his expectations. He confirmed this by wheeling about to begin striding away, leaving us to chase after him. It is not a long walk from where we were quartered to the *praetorium*, and while I cannot say I felt like I was reliving a moment from my own past, as we ascended the stairs to the building proper, the idea that the first and greatest Titus Pullus had made the same walk was foremost in my mind. In some ways, this added to the case of nerves I was experiencing, and when I peeked at Galens walking beside me, I saw a trickle of sweat running down his temple from under his helmet, despite the fact that it was not only cool, but the sun was obscured by clouds. Otherwise, his face was expressionless, and I strove to adopt the same mien as we entered the building, the three of us doffing our helmets as we did so, holding them under our left arms. Somewhat to my surprise, I noticed that Atticus had shorn his hair, the style of which he had brought from Rome as a Praetorian, but had kept, at least up until this moment. I thought it odd, since the longer hairstyle that is even more popular now a decade after that day, had taken hold among a fair number of men in the Legions, which had all started because the divine Augustus wanted to hide his unfortunate ears sticking out like jug handles. Was this some sort of statement that Atticus was making? I wondered. For a non-Roman, such considerations must seem very strange, wondering about a haircut, yet considering that Marcus Tullius Cicero once excoriated, in writing, of course, and not to his face, the habit of Divus Julius of scratching his head in a certain manner that the former thought some sort of affront to tradition, perhaps this makes my observation more understandable.

Our hobnails crashed against the stones of the floor, the noise preceding us so that when Atticus came to the double doors leading into the main room we had been in the day before, although he paused for a moment, once he threw open the door, I could see past him and spot the row of faces arrayed at the table all looking expectantly in our direction. Up to this point, Atticus had naturally taken the lead, with Galens flanking him on one side and me on the other, both of us a bit behind him. And, as one might expect, we were matching our pace to his, but he had gone only a couple of steps into the room, just enough for us both to pass the threshold when he came to a sudden and unplanned halt. Even as he did so, despite being behind him, there was no mistaking the gasp of surprise I was sure could be heard by everyone in the room; because of the angle I was at, I did not yet have a clear view of all of the members of the Tribunal. Since he stopped so quickly, both Galens and I could not avoid drawing even with him; when we did, I instantly understood why Atticus was so shaken.

"What's *he* doing here?" Galens' voice was as much of a whisper as he could make it, yet I suspected he could be heard on the far side of the room, even if none of the waiting men gave any sign.

Atticus did not reply immediately, nor did he move for what was probably three or maybe four heartbeats, but it was long enough for my own mind to process, if not the meaning, at least the identity of the man I was sure was sitting in the spot reserved for the ranking Tribune. Arruntius had risen from his chair at the table to our left, and was looking at the three of us just standing there as if we had just gazed on Medusa's face. So many different things went through my mind in this moment, it is hard to pick them out, but one distinct recollection is the expression on Arruntius' face, which was grim and unsmiling. And, if he had been surprised at the composition of the Tribunal, he had had enough time to recover before our arrival.

"Primus Pilus Atticus," the Tribune who addressed him rose from his spot in the center of the table, and while he was smiling, there was nothing pleasant in it as he said, "so nice to see you again! Although," he tried to change his expression to reflect the gravity of the moment, but did a poor job of it as he added, "I wish it could be under more....pleasant circumstances."

Naturally, I was not about to utter a squeak; this was something for Atticus to handle, except that for a moment, I was afraid he had been struck mute. Finally, in a voice sounding like he was being strangled as he spoke, he answered, "Thank you, Tribune Paullus. It has indeed been a fair amount of time."

The circumstances involving the placement of a man as the presiding Tribune in Atticus' proceeding, who the three of us had last seen more than five years before, in Pannonia, we did not learn about until after the fact. When, it must be said, it was too late to do anything about it, although it is hard to say what Atticus could have done even if he had been forewarned. Yet the fact that somehow Lucius Aemilius Paullus had managed to get involved in this matter was something I did not believe boded well for the Primus Pilus, and one glance over at Atticus' face told me his thoughts were similar.

It was Arruntius who broke the spell by clearing his throat, indicating the seat next to him, saying, "Primus Pilus Atticus, if you'd sit here next to me, please."

Then, gesturing to Galens and me, he pointed to two of the chairs in the row behind the table, although he did not say anything. As we sat down, I took a quick look around, noticing, among other things, that the Tribune who was supposed to present the case for the prosecution was not yet present. For the briefest instant, the thought crossed my mind that perhaps he would not show up, or would but announce the matter had been dismissed for consideration. Returning my attention to the five Tribunes in general, and Paullus in particular, I knew nothing of the sort would happen. In the intervening time since I had last seen Paullus, he had put on quite a bit of weight, but his sparkling white *toga*, with the folds draped very crisply, bore the purple stripe that marked him as a member of the Senate. Which, as I sat there thinking about it, made his presence even more confusing; and, I thought glumly, more dangerous for Atticus. Putting it in its simplest terms, Paullus' status was much loftier than was called for in a Tribunal like this. For his part, after his initial greeting, Paullus had pointedly turned his attention away from us, and was conferring in whispers to two of the other Tribunes, who were not only his junior in rank, but in years. As I examined the five men, I guessed that Paullus, who looked to be in his early to mid-thirties, was at least five years older than the next oldest Tribune. Only after he was finished with whatever he had been saying to the others did Paullus return his attention in our direction, and even from where I was sitting, I could see the gleam in his hair from the undoubtedly expensive pomade a slave applied, while there was a sheen to his skin that spoke of a recent oiling down. I also noticed his nose was tilted at the degree I remembered, although to be fair, he was no less haughty than Arruntius. Who, at that moment, was arranging a stack of wax tablets on the table, along with some scrolls, all while whispering to Atticus, who was understandably intent as he listened. Because my eye had been drawn to Arruntius and Atticus, I cannot say how long he had been doing so, yet I became aware, by way of that feeling I believe every person has, the one that informs you that you are being watched, that Paullus had turned his examination onto me. When I turned my head, my eyes met those of the senior Tribune, who had been staring at me, apparently fixedly, but I could tell he was having trouble placing me. It would have been fine with me if he never did, yet even as I turned my gaze away, not wanting to allow him more time to look at my face, I saw the dawn of recognition.

"You." He pointed directly at me. "Optio, is it? What's your name, boy? I know you, don't I?"

Oh, how I wished he had not called me a "boy," but I managed to keep my tone level as I replied, "We've met before, sir. When you were with the Army of Pannonia, I was in the ranks then."

I decided on the spot not to give any more information, with the hope that he would not press, but it proved a vain one.

"Yes," Paullus replied, drawing at the end of the word and making it sound like the hissing of a serpent, which I thought oddly appropriate. "I remember now. You were in the…8th, weren't you?"

"Yes, sir," I affirmed, then said no more.

Which, I imagine, had something to do with the sudden look of irritation as he noticed my position for the first time.

"Why are you sitting down when you're talking to me, Optio?" he suddenly snapped. "I believe it's customary for a man from the ranks to maintain the position of *intente* when addressing his superior!"

I managed to stifle my groan, but just barely, coming to my feet, knowing what was coming next.

"By the gods, you're huge!" he exclaimed, then started nodding his head as he said, "Oh, yes! Now, I remember you! You were in the ranks, all right. But you were in the First Cohort! And," his eyes narrowed, "in the First Century as well! That means your Centurion was that…" He was getting worked up now, his mouth twisting and while I did not know what epithet he would use, I knew it would be one that Urso would have slit him open for uttering. However, he surprised me somewhat by modifying his words, if not his tone. "…man, Publius Canidius, wasn't that his name? Although," he smiled, but it was a mean one, "as I recall, he had a nickname that you rankers loved. What was it?"

"Urso," I managed, although my teeth were clenched, and I only remembered at the last instant to add, "sir."

"Yes, that's right." Paullus laughed now. "The Bear. But things didn't turn out so well for him now, did they? So I suppose perhaps he wasn't quite as ferocious of a bear as he thought."

I understood by the glittering malice in his eyes he was baiting me in much the same way actual bears are, practically daring me to take umbrage at his words. However, like with everything else Lucius Paullus did, aside from being a dangerous nuisance, he was not even competent at insults, because he was aiming his invective at the wrong man. This is not to say I did not care for his words, but my relationship with my first Primus Pilus was so tangled and complicated that it was, and still is, impossible for me to summon up any clear feelings about the man. Galens, on the other hand, admired and respected the Primus Pilus a great deal, even given that he had been essentially foisted on Urso by Pilus Prior Corvinus as part of a bargain aimed at keeping a promise Corvinus made to my father. Shortly after my promotion, I had actually broached this subject with Galens, and I admit I was surprised to learn that, despite the circumstances, Urso had treated Galens fairly, and given him an opportunity to prove himself worthy of leading a Century of the first Cohort. Consequently, as surreptitiously as I could, I reached out and pushed Galens back down in his chair, while still remaining at *intente* myself.

"Sit. Down." I hissed at him; unfortunately, Paullus did not miss this.

"Was there something you wanted to say, Optio?" he asked me pleasantly, at least on the surface.

"No, sir," I assured him, but then he turned his attention on Galens.

"What about you, Centurion…?" The way he let the question linger told us he was expecting a name.

Galens did not commit the same error I had, popping up as if he had a ballista under him, saying crisply, "Primus Hastatus Posterior Aulus Galens, Tribune."

"Galens," Paullus repeated the name, then said, "You seemed as if you wanted to say something a moment ago, Centurion Galens. What was it?"

"Er," Galens fumbled. "No, sir. Nothing at all."

Paullus actually looked disappointed, then he waved a weary hand, ordering us, "Very well. Take your seats, Galens, and…" He cocked his head. "…I just realized I didn't get your name, Optio. You might as well give it now since you'll have to do so when it's your turn to bear witness."

Taking a deep breath, I answered him, "My name is Titus Porcinianus Pullus, Optio of the Sixth Century, First Cohort."

Paullus had already begun looking down at a scroll in front of him, and as I feared, hearing my name caused his head to shoot back up.

"Well, well," he said softly. "I take it you're related to *the* Camp Prefect Pullus?"

"Yes, sir," I did not hesitate, "he was my grandfather."

For the span of a couple heartbeats, he stared at me, yet he revealed none of his thoughts before he finally gave a nod and said, "Very well, Pullus. Now we know you and Galens here are the witnesses whose names were submitted. Sit down."

I was more than happy to comply, but frankly, I was puzzled, and I turned to whisper to Galens, "Does it seem like Paullus doesn't know much about this case at all?"

My Centurion looked surprised, and he asked me what I meant.

"If he had read our statements that were taken and sent ahead of us to Rome," I pointed out, "he'd already know our names."

He considered for a moment, then nodded and whispered back, "That's true."

Then, he leaned forward, I presumed to ask Arruntius about this, except before he could, there was another crashing sound of footsteps, and from the sound of it, there were more than three men. We all turned just in time to see the door open, then a man wearing a *toga* entered the room. Obviously the prosecutor, we barely noticed him at all, because trailing behind him there were indeed more than three men, accounting for the excess noise. However, there was an added element, an almost musical, tinkling sound, which we heard approaching before we saw what caused it.

"Chains?" I heard Galens mutter in puzzlement, yet before I could respond, the second door was swung open to allow three men to enter abreast, whereupon we saw the source of the sound.

Two armed Legionaries wearing the blue of the Praetorians were clearly escorting the man in the middle; keeping him upright would be more accurate, although it was not as much the sight of the man whose battered face was almost unrecognizable, but the fact that he was whole enough we could identify him that caused such a stir.

"Balbinus??"

It must be said that Arruntius had warned Atticus of another witness besides the Taurisci, but I, and more importantly, Atticus had assumed it was the Roman citizen whose farm had been burned. Who, it turned out, was present as well; he came in behind Balbinus and his escort, even though we barely noticed him. At least, Atticus, Arruntius, and Galens were unaware of his entrance, but I just happened to tear my gaze away from my former comrade, who was being dragged to one of the several chairs behind the prosecuting Tribune, to see another pair of men entering. One was wearing a *toga*, yet it was easy to see it was one that had either been borrowed or rented because of the ill-fitting way it draped the man's body and the fraying hem dragging the floor. He was in his forties, with a similar weather-beaten look to him as a Legionary, just without the hardness that comes from a life under the standard, leading me to guess this was the farmer. However, it was not him who riveted my attention, but the other man. I did not know him, really, yet I did in a way, because I knew I had seen him before. It took me the amount of time for them to reach the prosecution table, and honestly, if this second man had not turned to glance in my direction, no doubt drawn by the same instinct that had prompted me to notice Paullus' eyes on me, I am not sure how long it would have taken me to place him. However, when he did so, I saw the one crossed eye that marred an otherwise handsome countenance, although while he smiled as he had at the inn on the road back to Siscia, it was not the same friendly smile he had given me then. Or, perhaps it was, except the circumstances were such I was sure the grin he gave me now was sly, as if he had pulled a prank on me and his identity as the prankster had just been revealed.

"Did you know about this?"

While the question was not aimed at me, I was sufficiently interested that I turned my attention to Arruntius, waiting to see how he answered Atticus' question; although the Primus Pilus was whispering, one did not have to know him at all to hear the fury there.

"No," Arruntius shot back, matching the volume of Atticus' query, and the tone. "I told you, they wouldn't tell me the identity of the witness."

"You mean witnesses," Atticus muttered, "as in there are two, not one."

"Yes, I can count as well as you," Arruntius parried, while Galens and I looked at each other; I believe he was thinking the same thing, that this was not the time to argue about the counting abilities of the man defending you. "But I can guess who that one is," Arruntius did not point, but gestured with his head to where the civilian had taken a seat, behind Balbinus and his guards. "The question is, who's the one in chains?"

"One of my men," was all Atticus offered, and I confess I had to smother my own irritation at his clear evasiveness; Arruntius was no less put out.

"So I gathered," he whispered harshly, "but there's more to it than that, isn't there?"

Now Atticus looked distinctly uncomfortable, shifting in his seat as he tried to avoid Arruntius' glare, hard to do since their faces were just inches away.

"He's in my Century," Atticus finally allowed, then closed his eyes as he continued, "and he does...jobs for me." Pausing, he finished, "Off-the-books types of jobs."

This caused Arruntius to sit bolt upright from his previous posture, leaning with elbows on knees as he conferred with his client, letting out a hiss of what I suppose was frustration as he did so. Meanwhile, as this exchange was taking place, the prosecuting

Tribune had just finished arranging the tablets containing his notes and whatever other evidence he planned to present.

"The prosecution is ready to proceed, Senior Tribune," the sound of the prosecuting Tribune's voice yanked all of our attention away from the small crisis at our table, and I turned my examination to the man who had just spoken.

He was a thin, reedy-looking thing, and being honest, while I was sure his *toga* was his own, it did not fit much better than the one worn by the farmer. His hair was, like everyone else's in the room with the exception of the three of us, long, except in his case, it was long in the back only, because the hair on top was thinning to the point I could see the gleam of his scalp. Most tellingly, at least as far as I was concerned, he had a weak chin, a characteristic I had first heard mentioned as an indicator of softness by my Avus, but which I have since seen borne out with my own eyes. I suppose this was what gave me a glimmer of hope, thinking that perhaps, just as had happened with my Avus, there had been an arrangement made to have an incompetent Tribune at the helm of the prosecution. The only problem with that, I reflected, was I already knew the level of Paullus' own ineptitude, although his was caused more from an excess of arrogance and belief his bloodlines alone bestowed competence, making me wonder if my suspicion was accurate, how much worse this man could be.

Whose name I was about to learn when he announced, "My name is Quintus Caecilius Metellus Creticus Silanus," I had to suppress a snicker at his insistence on using every one of his names, "and I have been charged by the Princeps, our beloved Augustus, with presenting the case against Gaius Sempronius Atticus, Primus Pilus of the 8th Legion, for his use of unauthorized force against a resident tribe of the province of Pannonia who was not in open rebellion against Rome."

He stopped then, and I wondered why until Arruntius stood up and made his own statement, "I am Lucius Arruntius, and I have been charged by the Princeps with the defense of Primus Pilus Atticus against these charges." He paused for a moment, making me think he was finished, then he pointed at Balbinus, who was slumped over and refusing to look in our direction, as Arruntius continued in a forceful manner, "And I would like to go on record that I strenuously protest the inclusion of a witness about whom the defense was not informed, nor have we had time to examine on our own."

This certainly caused a stir, not least by Atticus, who suddenly turned to stare up at his counsel, with what to my eyes looked like an almost pathetic hope; he should have known better, considering who would be making the decision.

"Lucius Arruntius," Paullus snapped, "this isn't the time to make such an objection! Or perhaps," he glared at the Tribune, "you didn't bother to read the regulations concerning a Tribunal!"

Oh, I had seen Paullus give this kind of look before, to Urso, to his fellow Tribune Claudius, even to the Legate who was technically his senior, but my respect for Arruntius went up a notch because he neither flinched, nor did he back down a bit.

"I can assure you, *Senior* Tribune," the way he emphasized the word, and more importantly the way Paullus reddened informed me that Arruntius had not rendered this as a compliment, nor had Paullus missed his intent, "I am very familiar with the regulations. And one of them concerns the availability of witnesses for *both* sides to be presented to the defense, before the Tribunal, for examination."

"As you were told, that wasn't possible," Paullus snapped, "because of this witness' late arrival to Rome. And," he added as he pointed directly at Atticus, "it was the Primus Pilus who requested that the Tribunal be moved up!"

"But I didn't know that this...witness was going to be here!" Atticus spoke up, and despite my ambivalence towards the man, I could not suppress a wince, sure I knew what was coming.

I was correct, because Paullus slapped a hand on the table, making a cracking sound that was the loudest noise to this point as he raised his own voice to warn Atticus, "Primus Pilus, you were advised before this proceeding was convened about the rules covering it! Do I need to remind you that you're not to speak *one word* unless directed to by this Tribunal?"

If it had been me, I would have been hard pressed to refrain from leaping the table to shove that waggling finger Paullus was pointing right up his ass, and I could see the Primus Pilus was no less outraged. Regardless, he had not gotten to his post by indulging in fits of temper, but I could clearly see the tension in his shoulders and back as he restrained himself.

"Yes, Senior Tribune," just the monotone he was using told me how tightly he was holding onto himself, "please forgive my outburst. It won't happen again."

"See that it doesn't," Paullus shot back, "or there will be consequences!"

Turning his attention back to Arruntius, he resumed his harangue, saying, "You'll have the chance to examine this witness when it is your turn, which is more than sufficient."

"I disagree," Arruntius did not give an inch, which only enraged Paullus more.

"I don't care if you disagree," the presiding Tribune snapped. "That's my ruling!" He actually paused, but Arruntius did not say anything else, which caused Paullus to give him a mean little smile. Then, he returned his attention back to Silanus, who, it must be said, did not look all that happy to be there, making me wonder if this task had been forced on him. "Now, Silanus, you may proceed."

Except Silanus just stood there, also not saying anything, which judging from the reaction of not just Paullus but Arruntius, was completely unexpected. Paullus opened his mouth, yet before anything came out, the Tribune to his left, a fit-looking man perhaps my age or a little older, but with an air about him that reminded me somewhat of Claudius, leaned over and whispered something in the senior Tribune's ear. Even more interesting was Paullus' reaction, as his face turned a deep red, except he did not seem angry, which puzzled me, at least until he finally spoke.

"Yes, well," suddenly, he did not seem so assured as he fumbled for the words, "it's been brought to my attention that we're *not* ready to proceed, because we haven't heard the auspices from the *haruspex* assigned to make the traditional sacrifice before any proceedings of this nature." Turning to the Tribune who had alerted him, he continued in a slightly louder voice, "My apologies, Lucius Nonius Asprenas, since that was your responsibility. Would you care to tell the court whether or not it is correct to proceed, according to the *haruspex*?"

Rising to his feet, the now-identified Asprenas intoned that, in fact, all the prescribed rites had been performed, in the proper manner, and that the omens and auspices as read in the liver and entrails of the sacrificed animal by the *haruspex* were good; the Tribunal could now officially commence. Nobody, not even Atticus, appeared surprised by this pronouncement; frankly, I would have been shocked if the *haruspex* had stopped the proceeding on religious grounds, and he would have been a very brave, or very foolish man to do so. I suppose that once, long ago in our history, such things did happen, but I have certainly never heard of any official meeting or ceremony being postponed because there was a spot on a pigeon's liver, at least when it was a matter involving a member of the lower classes. Still, I did believe I caught a flicker of disappointment on Atticus' face, although I suspected it was more for the hope of a postponement in order to prepare for whatever Balbinus had to say than anything else.

"Very good. Thank you, Asprenas." Paullus' voice matched the tone Asprenas had used, which I imagine was their idea of sounding official and possessing *gravitas*.

More interestingly, though, I also took note that Paullus seemed respectful of Asprenas, making me wonder more about the Tribune, and honestly, raised him in my eyes for this reason alone. Asprenas only nodded his head in answer, sitting back down in his own seat.

"Now," Paullus sighed, "we may begin. Tribune Silanus."

And so, the Tribunal of my Primus Pilus began.

In order to present their case, Silanus, acting as prosecutor, felt compelled to begin with a rather long-winded explanation of the current political situation in Pannonia. At least, the political situation as viewed in Rome; on more than one occasion, Galens and I exchanged glances at Silanus' characterization of the civil climate in the province, which he made sound positively settled and as peaceful as Latium itself. Finally, Arruntius stood to object, but Paullus snapped at him to sit down and remain silent, waving at Silanus to continue. I cannot say the prosecuting Tribune was the worst public speaker I had heard to that point, but he was definitely near the bottom of the list, and he plodded through his opening statement with the same flair and emotional display as a plow horse in the traces. Oh, he covered the major points, and setting aside my utter boredom, there was a part of my mind that winced at how thoroughly, if unimaginatively, Silanus built his case. To hear him tell it, the Taurisci and the Carni were not actually in a dispute, at least one of any consequence, and certainly not one that called for such a heavy-handed response by Rome, in the form of us, the 8th Legion marching out to kill some of them. Where he got his information, I have no idea, but in essence, his assertion was that the Taurisci's foray into the lands of the Carni was more in the nature of a friendly visit, although he did grant there was undoubtedly some sort of friction, also agreeing how it was likely that perhaps a Carni hut or two might have been burned down. He even allowed that it was probable there was some blood shed between the two native parties, except he characterized these as isolated incidents, more likely the result of drunken brawls between high-spirited warriors, and nothing so widespread or of a scale that required the Taurisci to be chastised in such a bloody manner. As I stated earlier, the least I can say is he was thorough, and I observed how almost every member of the Tribunal was as bored as Galens and I were, sitting there listening, our collective asses and minds growing more numb with every passing moment. However, only Paullus seemed to be paying close attention, which in turn got me to do the same, except I suddenly started watching Paullus, not Silanus. As I listened, my suspicions started to grow, then I saw something I would have thought impossible, at least if I had not seen it for myself. With Silanus droning on, I realized that Paullus' lips were moving, yet not just in a random fashion; his mouth was silently mimicking the words that were actually being spoken by Silanus! It reminded me of the one time I had attended not a play, but a rehearsal, where the director was doing the same thing as the actor recited his lines, waiting to jump in with a prompt in the event the actor forgot. Shooting a glance at Galens, I immediately saw how his eyes had glazed over, so as casually as I could, I leaned forward and reached out to touch Arruntius on the elbow. Although I did not have a good look at his face, from the way he jumped, I suspected he was in much the same state as Galens, but he turned to face me readily enough.

"What is it?" Despite his whisper, I heard the irritation.

"Watch Paullus," was all I told him.

He looked confused, glancing once over at the senior Tribune, then back at me, asking, "Why? What are you talking about? I don't see anything."

"Look again, and look…"

I got no farther.

"*Silete*!" Paullus shouted. "Or I'll have you up on a charge for disrupting this proceeding!"

I did not reply, but I did sit back, keeping my eyes on the floor as I did, while Arruntius shot me a look that was half-puzzled and half-angry. When I did not say anything, Paullus contented himself with glaring at me for a long moment before turning his attention back to Silanus.

"You may resume, Tribune. You were speaking of the delegation from the Taurisci who came to Rome."

There is no way to tell what is in another man's mind, so I cannot say whether or not this was a mistake on Paullus' part, where he jumped ahead of what I was now sure was a statement that, if he had not written himself, he had definitely had a hand in creating, or if it was his way of prompting Silanus to move ahead and skip over some parts. What I could see was that Arruntius noticed it as well, because he suddenly sat up straight and resumed paying close attention. While I do not blame Arruntius, I do believe that by doing so, he alerted Paullus that Arruntius had noticed something, because once Silanus resumed, while Paullus' own attention remained on the prosecuting Tribune, his lips did not move once. I will say the disruption did serve to jolt the other Tribunes sitting in judgment to sit up straight and try to refocus their minds on what was taking place.

Fortunately, for all of us, Silanus did not take much longer with his opening statement, finishing by suddenly pivoting and pointing in such a dramatic fashion I was tempted to see if more of an audience had crept into the room, as he declared, "As I have just shown, the situation in Pannonia was as tranquil as any province in the Republic, until Primus Pilus Atticus disrupted that peace by his untoward and unwarranted actions against the Taurisci!"

By the time Silanus was through, Paullus was positively beaming, reminding me of Diocles when one of his charges had excelled at solving a problem or given a clever answer to a question. Fortunately, at least for Atticus, Paullus was the only one of the five Tribunes who looked impressed; I could not begin to count the number of stifled yawns and the amount of fidgeting I saw during that interminable address.

Paullus, glancing up at the large window behind him, announced, "It's almost midday. We will recess for two parts of a watch, then meet back here, where the prosecution will present their witnesses."

He did not wait for any response, standing up suddenly and stepping sidelong behind the table, heading to the door on the far end of the room, causing me to remember reading about this side room in my Avus' account. The rest of the Tribunes filed out behind him, while Silanus turned and said something to the Praetorians. Throughout the entire first part of the morning, Balbinus had not once looked up from where he was staring at the floor, and when one of his guards grabbed him roughly by the chains binding his wrists to jerk him to his feet, as much as I disliked the man, I felt a pang of sympathy at his hiss of pain. Apparently, I was the only one so disposed, because Atticus had twisted about in his chair to glare at his former man, who I immediately noticed was removed from the room by way of the same door that Paullus and the others had used, Silanus following along behind them, with the farmer next to him. Then, just that quickly, it was only the four of us sitting alone, and my impression was that Atticus was still slightly stunned. Finally, it was Arruntius who broke the silence.

"This," he said quietly, "is going to be more difficult than I thought."

"What were you trying to tell me earlier?" Arruntius asked me as we sat outside, having finished eating a light lunch.

I was surprised, and somewhat touched that one of Arruntius' slaves had been waiting outside for us to emerge, carrying a basket of food and two skins of wine, one of which Atticus immediately grabbed and started guzzling down, not that I could blame him much.

Even better, there was enough food for all of us; apparently, Arruntius had instructed his slave to pack extra because there were portions for each of us, in the normal amount to which we were accustomed, meaning I ate more than everyone else. The Tribune had made us walk a short distance away, and we were sitting on some benches set under a tree but far away from the *praetorium*, or any other building, for that matter, so that nobody could overhear us talking. I told him what I had seen, which caused his eyebrows to suddenly plunge down towards each other in a look of concern.

"Are you sure of that?" he pressed, and I assured him I had watched long enough to know it was no coincidence or that Paullus was not just mouthing words to a favorite ditty.

Despite the fact that this involved Atticus, of all of us, he seemed the most disinterested; truly, if I did not know better, I would have said he was suddenly unconcerned, as if he already knew the outcome.

Considering for a moment, Arruntius finally said, "I can't say it surprises me all that much. Paullus is…" He caught himself, aware, I am sure, that Paullus was a member of his own class, and he apparently settled on, "…persistent when he thinks he's been wronged."

This prompted Galens to speak up in protest. "But the Primus Pilus never wronged him! At least," he amended, indicating Atticus, who was still sucking on the wine skin and looking up at the clouds, "not this one. Now, if it had been Urso," he gave a grim smile and finished, "that would be another story."

For whatever reason, Arruntius looked at me as if for verification.

"It's true," I agreed. "Primus Pilus Canidius was the one who brought Paullus to grief, not Primus Pilus Atticus." I must say it felt strange talking about the man as if he was not sitting right next to me. "He had just taken over, then Paullus was gone, back to Rome."

Arruntius considered for a moment, then finally shook his head.

"Then we can't really worry about that. No," now he turned to look squarely at Atticus, "we need to talk about this witness, Balbinus. What don't I know about this?"

"Nothing." For the first time, Atticus seemed to pay attention, yet despite the fact that he addressed Arruntius, he would not look at him. "There's nothing to tell, really."

"Then why did you look as if you'd seen a *numen* suddenly rise up from the ground to take you to Hades?" Arruntius scoffed, clearly not buying what the Primus Pilus was selling. Now it was my turn not to look in the Tribune's direction, fearing what came next. Which, of course, meant this is precisely what happened as he swiveled his gaze and fixed it on me. "Pullus, what is he not telling me?"

"Nothing," I echoed Atticus, although I, for one, could clearly hear the falseness in my voice; I just hoped I was the only one who did. "Besides, how should I know what he's not telling you?"

Clearly frustrated, Arruntius jumped from the bench and began pacing, his head down as he pressed his lips tightly together, I assumed to keep from exploding in anger. Wheeling, he pointed down at Atticus.

"Atticus, I don't think you realize what you're up against here." He spoke severely, and it was easy to see Arruntius had grabbed Atticus' attention, except the Primus Pilus was getting angry, not more worried. "But if what Pullus says is true," he cut me off as I was about to protest at what I took as his doubt, mollifying me by saying, "and I think it is, then for whatever reason, you have at least one Tribune on that panel set against you already. The only way I can be effective and make sure that you don't lose the other four is if I know everything. And," he had moved so he was standing directly in front of Atticus, whereupon he leaned down to look the Primus Pilus directly in the eye to say emphatically, "I mean everything about this Balbinus and why he's a witness against you."

"Because they tortured him," Atticus replied bitterly. "You saw the bastard! They beat him until he said whatever they wanted him to say!"

"That," Arruntius granted, "is one possibility. Or," his tone grew harder, "they got the truth from him."

"The truth?" Atticus scoffed. "What truth is that?"

"That he was the one you sent to set fire to that farm," Arruntius replied quietly, and I could feel Atticus' body tense through the wood of the bench. "Actually," he amended, "he didn't go alone, I'm sure. But he was one of them. *That* is another possibility…isn't it?"

Only when I began to grow dizzy did I realize I was holding my breath, and one look over at Galens told me he was no less tense.

"That," Atticus finally broke the silence, "is…possible."

Only Arruntius maintained his composure; Galens and I both took the moment to suddenly exhale, while Atticus looked, if anything, slightly relieved.

"As I thought," Arruntius said quietly, then seemed to consider something before he muttered, "Yes, I can work with that."

While I knew Atticus was trying to at least seem detached and unworried, there was no mistaking the flash of relief on his face at Arruntius' words.

"What are you going to do?" Galens asked, but Arruntius shook his head.

"You let me worry about that," was all he said, then he caught us all by surprise. "But there's something else I need to talk about, and we don't have much time left."

I could not blame Atticus for looking wary, but the Tribune waved a hand dismissively.

"It's not anything more about Balbinus. And," he turned to address Galens and me, "this concerns the two of you as well. What I need to know is," he paused for a moment, before asking, "how much of what Silanus said about Pannonia and its current state is true?"

"Almost nothing," Atticus just beat the pair of us, although our wording was different.

"'All's quiet in Pannonia,'" was how Galens put it, making no attempt to hide the bitterness in his voice.

"'All's quiet in Pannonia,'" I agreed, and despite the circumstances, we both had to laugh at what had become a grim joke.

"So I take it, all's *not* that quiet in Pannonia," Arruntius observed, yet he bore a troubled expression, which prompted me to ask him, "Why's this so important? I mean, for the Primus Pilus' case?"

To his credit, Arruntius did not hesitate. "Because it tells me this is much more than what it seems." Shaking his head, he explained, "I don't have time to give you a full explanation, but suffice it to say this. Do you remember our conversation the first time we met, Pullus?"

I did, very well; in fact, it was my fervent hope that when I got back to our room on the Campus, I would have a message waiting for me from Claudius, such was my concern stemming from that talk.

Seeing me nod, Arruntius went on, "There have been…accusations." He held up a hand to signal a change. "No, accusation is too strong a word. There have been…suggestions that the reports the citizens of Rome are receiving about Pannonia are not exactly accurate. The same men I mentioned during our first conversation are putting it about that the Princeps is trying to hide the truth about Pannonia, that conditions are deteriorating there, and that it needs a firmer hand on it than has been applied previously."

The three of us looked from one to another, but I was of a mind to defer to Atticus to respond to this, except he remained silent.

Consequently, it was left to Galens to voice the problem with this assessment, "Going harder on them than we already are is likely to make things worse. Sir," he thought to add. "These barbarians in Pannonia are wild, and the truth is they love to fight, just for the sake of it." Shaking his head, Galens concluded, "Don't mistake me, Tribune. We can march through the province and slaughter every one of them, if those are the orders we're given. And we can burn everything to the ground too. But what then? Because, please believe me, Tribune, as wild as these Pannonians are, there are even wilder tribes on the other side of the Danuvius. If we removed the tribes that inhabit the province now, you might as well send a written invitation to those Scythian tribes like the Iazyges to come swimming across the river and settle down."

When Galens finished, I looked at him, impressed with his evaluation of the situation, mainly because we had never really talked about the larger problems in Pannonia. There is a simple reason for this; ultimately, it does not matter what we think. We have a job to do, and when we are given orders, we carry them out. While I never once heard Atticus give his real reason for inventing the pretext for an attack on the Taurisci, which had led us to this moment, I still do not believe his actions did any more damage to our relationship with the tribes of Pannonia than had already been done, just by virtue of our presence alone. Pannonia had been a province of Rome for more than two decades by this point, and there had been many, many improvements; I am not just saying that as a Roman, but as someone who has spent a significant portion of his life there. The roads were better, allowing for faster travel, and more importantly, they were safer than they had been. Even between the time of my childhood and now, a fair amount of time after the Tribunal, the improvement has been dramatic. While it is true we brought the sword, we also brought our more advanced techniques for farming, for mining, for just about every industry, enabling the people who live there to enjoy a level of prosperity they had never experienced before. And yet, as any veteran of the province could tell you, while all of the tribes tolerated our presence by this point, at least most of the time, the majority of them still hated us, and never wasted an opportunity to vent their hatred in some form, usually violent and bloody. Consequently, in my opinion, the only thing Atticus was truly guilty of is perhaps accelerating a violent confrontation that was going to happen, regardless of whether or not he sent some men out to burn a farm.

Unaware of my internal musing, Arruntius still stood, considering what Galens had told him, until he finally said, "I understand what you're saying, and I'm not saying I disagree, Galens. But the reality is that if the Princeps wants it to be known by the citizens of Rome that 'all is quiet in Pannonia,' as you like to say, then that's ultimately for the good of all of us."

Certainly, at least on the surface, and as far as the majority of the citizens of the Republic are concerned, what Arruntius said was true. However, I could not stop myself from thinking that those citizens who, believing the province was, in fact, settled, then decided to relocate to Pannonia, only to find the reality was far different, especially if it was by way of a raid on their farm or inn by a marauding tribe, might not see things the same way. Nevertheless, this was a sentiment I was not eager to share.

Ignorant of my personal misgivings, Arruntius continued speaking. "That's why I believe this is about more than just Atticus." Turning to the Primus Pilus, he explained his thinking, "What you did with your actions was bring attention to the province, at a time when the Princeps doesn't want that attention on it. And," he took a deep breath, "as you just confirmed, the truth is you *did* invent a pretext for attacking the Taurisci." I saw Atticus' mouth open to say something, except Arruntius cut him off by saying, "But luckily for you, that's not the actual charge. It's for responding excessively, and as Silanus more or less admitted in his statement, the fact is that the Taurisci were outside the boundaries of their territory." Shaking his head, the Tribune finished by saying, "Balbinus is actually not as pertinent to the issue as the prosecution thinks."

Then it was time for us to return to the *Praetorium*, and I observed Atticus was walking with more of a spring in his step than he had when we exited; I just wondered if his newfound optimism was justified. Never far from the front of my mind was the only other Tribunal with which I was familiar, and how the decision rendered by the Tribunal had obviously not gone the way Augustus wanted. And that, I reminded myself, had been almost twenty years before, when the Princeps was still in the process of solidifying his hold over Rome. By this time, it was hard for me to imagine this Tribunal would render a verdict that ran counter to his wishes, no matter how compelling an argument Arruntius made. Frankly, I was just happy I was still only peripherally involved; my most fervent hope was that this remained the case.

As soon as we reconvened, Silanus called as his first witness not Balbinus but the older man who, indeed, turned out to be the farmer I thought him to be. Clearly uneasy, he nevertheless swore his oath before the gods to tell the truth, then sat in the chair placed in front of the Tribunal, between them and the two sides presenting the case. However, unlike what had happened during Titus Pullus' Tribunal, the man's chair was situated so that while he was not directly facing us, neither was he facing the Tribunal, away from us. Instead, he was seated so we were to his left, and Paullus and the others to his right.

"Would you give your name for the record?" Silanus began.

"My name is Manius Fusus." His voice had a tiny quaver in it, but otherwise, he did not hesitate.

"And what is your role in this proceeding?" Silanus was looking down at a tablet, on which I was sure the questions were written, presumably in order.

"I owned the villa and farm that was destroyed that night," Fusus replied, yet as he did so, he shot a bitter glance over at Atticus.

"And what night was that?"

The way Fusus replied, without any hesitation or thought, told me that Silanus had been at least as thorough in rehearsing with this witness as Arruntius had been with us.

"September 14th of last year," he answered immediately.

"And what do you remember of that day?" Silanus' tone was almost gentle, and I felt a glimmer of disquiet, because to this point, he had not seemed to be bright enough to possess any subtlety.

"Everything." Fusus almost spat the word, and now there was no disguising the impotent fury as he continued to glare over at Atticus. "It was an eventful day."

"How so?" Silanus prompted.

Fusus proceeded to describe how he had awakened early that morning, arming his slaves and making preparations for the arrival of the Taurisci. Like any man who brought his family to Pannonia, Fusus paid close attention to all of the internecine dynamics and feuds between tribes, and the Taurisci had been marauding for almost two weeks by that point. But when the Taurisci arrived, shortly before midday, despite the size of the warband, they approached Fusus' villa under a flag of truce, their purpose apparently only to verify that Fusus was, in fact, a Roman citizen. Once this was established, Fusus described, to a level of detail I thought interesting, how he stood on the low wooden wall that enclosed their villa, their barn, their slave quarters, and the other storage buildings, as the Taurisci went moving by, his family having gone up into the relative safety of the wooded slopes as a precaution. The way he made it sound, I could easily envision the Taurisci appearing like a rolling wave, except that the blue was interspersed with mottled greens, browns, and yellows, which were part of the Taurisci colors. And just like a wave, they went surging past the villa, on both sides, and while Fusus readily admitted there was nothing friendly about the warband, and that those who could speak camp Latin hurled curses, and worse, at the farmer, their assault was only verbal. Once past, only then did he allow his family, slaves, and their livestock to return to the villa.

"So when I went to bed that night," was how he concluded his testimony, "I was sure the worst had happened, and that there was nothing more to worry about. Their chieftain had assured me they had no quarrel with Rome, just the Carni, and we would be unmolested. He," Fusus turned to glower at Atticus, "kept his word." It had been clear that as the farmer got deeper into his testimony, his agitation caused by the memory grew, until this point, when he suddenly, without being prompted by Silanus, rose from his chair to point. "A barbarian kept his word, but not this man, this *Roman*."

Despite my interest in Fusus' testimony, I could not avoid glancing over at Atticus to see how he was reacting, and I saw his face had flushed a deep red, there being a set to his jaw I had long before learned was a sign of an impending outburst of rage. Arruntius clearly saw it as well, yet all he did was place a hand on the forearm of the Primus Pilus, who reacted in a startled manner, glancing down at the hand. Then, I saw his body visibly relax as he gave an almost imperceptible nod.

"What do you mean by that, Manius Fusus?" Silanus asked him.

"When he and his Legion showed up," Fusus suddenly looked uncomfortable, and for a reason I only deduced immediately afterward, he actually shot an uneasy glance at me, "I was...concerned."

This appeared to take Silanus by surprise, making me wonder if Fusus was wandering a bit, but he asked Fusus to explain.

Now Fusus actually started squirming in his chair, except he continued looking at least in my direction as he answered, "Let's just say that everyone knows that when the Legions march by, you may suddenly...misplace some of your property."

This was when I understood why he was so uneasy, and why he was looking in my direction, because I felt the uncoiling in my stomach that signaled the beast of my anger had been wakened. Luckily, I was not alone; Galens muttered an oath, but the only reason he was not chastised for it was that the noise of some of the Tribunes snickering at Fusus' calling us thieves covered it up. Strengthening my suspicion this had not been part of the plan, Silanus suddenly rocked from one foot to another as he shot an uneasy glance over his shoulder in our direction.

"Yes, well," Silanus fumbled, "be that as it may, do you recall your conversation with Primus Pilus Atticus?"

"You can be sure I do," Fusus answered immediately, his face grim, and suddenly, he did not seem so eager to glare at Atticus, or any of us. "When they showed up, I came out to meet them, as a good Roman should. That was when I met with Primus Pilus Atticus."

"And what was this conversation about?"

"He asked me how long before his arrival the Taurisci had come by, and I told him that it was less than a full watch."

For whatever reason, Fusus stopped speaking then, and for the first time, Silanus seemed caught off guard, although he recovered fairly quickly, asking, "What else did he say?"

"That we could sleep well that night, knowing we were safe now that his Legion was there." While I expected him to be angry, I was not prepared to see the sudden rush of tears that made the farmer's eyes gleam. Then he thought to add, "And that he was going to make sure that we stayed safe because of what he had planned for these barbarians."

When I glanced over at Atticus, just his appearance caused me to close my eyes and stifle a curse; that this was true was clearly written on his face. I suppose it should have made me feel a bit better that he did look somewhat ashamed, but I also understood how this sounded. Fusus' last statement caused a reaction among the Tribunal as well, as the Tribune Asprenas leaned over to whisper something, not to Paullus, but to the Tribune to his left. The flanking pair on the opposite side of Paullus reacted in a similar way; only Paullus did not do anything, other than give a malicious smile.

"That's not how things turned out, did it, Manius Fusus?" Silanus asked.

"No, it's not," Fusus shook his head, and now the tears started to flow as he recounted the night. "It was somewhere around the beginning of the third watch when Monases, that's one of my slaves, sounded the alarm there was a fire."

"And how did this Monases know that?"

Silanus seemed to be back on firm footing again.

"Because he was awakened by someone pounding on the door to the slave quarters, shouting at them to wake up," Fusus explained, then paused for a moment before adding, "and they were shouting in Latin."

This, I thought dismally, was getting worse by the moment, and I could see Galens felt the same way, as did Atticus, who had stopped even looking in the farmer's direction.

"What happened then?"

"As I said, Monases immediately came to the villa and woke me up. When I got up, I made sure my wife went and got our children, while I hurried outside to get everyone organized to fight the fire. But," when he shook his head, I actually saw one of the tears get flung away from his cheeks, "it was too late to do anything. The fire was already out of control. The barn was fully aflame, and the slave quarters had already started burning as well. It was obvious that whoever," I suppose he could not avoid glowering over in our direction, "started the fire did it in more than one spot."

"What happened to the animals in the barn?" Silanus asked.

"We lost most of them," Fusus answered. "Just one of our two plow oxen, a milk cow, and a couple of goats was all we could save."

"What about your family?"

"They were all fine," Fusus admitted, but this prompted him to return his gaze back to Atticus specifically, as he added bitterly, "although my youngest girl's dog was burned alive inside the villa, which was totally destroyed."

Silanus actually paused then, I suppose to allow the scope of Fusus' loss to settle in, and I must admit that when hearing it put in such terms, I felt a stirring of shame that overwhelmed my earlier ire at his words about the Legion. Having the loss described in this manner made it seem more real, and even in the moment, I realized that the most upsetting part was hearing about his daughter's pet, even if I cannot really say why this bothered me so much; judging just by the facial expressions of most of the Tribunal, they were of a like mind.

"So, Manius Fusus," Silanus resumed, "you've told us all about the scope of your loss, and the circumstances in which this loss occurred. But," he raised his hands in an exaggerated gesture as he shrugged his shoulders, "how do you know these men were not simply Taurisci who could speak our language? After all, wouldn't it make sense that the barbarians would attempt to turn the suspicion onto someone else, and who better than the very Legion who had been pursuing them?"

"Because I saw them with my own eyes," Fusus replied instantly, then amended slightly, "at least, I saw three of them." Suddenly, he swiveled in his seat so his body was facing in the right direction for him to point directly at Balbinus. "And he was one of them! I saw him that night, within the walls of my own property!"

During this entire exchange, Arruntius had been scribbling away in his wax tablet, since he was forbidden to interrupt the testimony, but this brought his head up as he stared intently, first at Fusus, then at Balbinus, who still had not given any indication he was paying attention at all. For the first time, I was sure I saw a glimmer of, if not happiness, a grim sort of pleasure on the face of the Tribune; unfortunately, it did not last long, in fact, vanishing with Silanus' next question.

"But, Manius Fusus," Silanus did his best to appear puzzled, "it was the middle of the night! How can you be so sure you saw this man you indicated, this" he had to walk to the table to consult a tablet to provide Balbinus' full name and rank, "Miles Gregarius Tiberius Balbinus?"

"When your barn is on fire, it provides a lot of light." Fusus actually laughed at his own grim joke. "I saw him as clearly as if it was noon."

Arruntius visibly reacted, exhaling and muttering something under his breath as he dropped his stylus, which I saw Paullus noticed and clearly relished the sight.

"Thank you, Manius Fusus," Silanus concluded, then the Tribune turned and addressed the Tribunal, announcing, "I have no further questions for this witness."

Paullus did not answer, at least verbally, simply waving a hand in dismissal, while Fusus stood up and walked back to his chair, but he did take the longer way around on the far side of the prosecution table, for which I could not blame him much. Meanwhile, Silanus had returned to his table, and was now shuffling among the tablets, presumably looking for the list of questions for Balbinus. As I sat there, I realized there was something gnawing at me, and I took the opportunity to lean forward to ask Arruntius a question.

"How come Silanus didn't ask Fusus how much money everything he lost was worth?"

Arruntius did not answer immediately, considering for a moment before shrugging and telling me, "I'm not sure it matters. This isn't a civil trial for damages, so the cost of the loss isn't important; it's the loss itself that is at issue here, because it happened to a Roman citizen." He did glance over at the Tribunal before he added, in an even softer whisper, "At Roman hands."

Atticus was ignoring this exchange, choosing instead to glare at Balbinus, who was being helped to his feet in the same manner as the Praetorians had used at the recess, once more causing his face to twist in pain. When he shuffled to the chair, the chains around his ankles made that same, almost musical tinkling sound we had heard when he first was brought into the Tribunal. One of the Praetorians shoved Balbinus down into the chair, none too gently, which puzzled me because he had not been required to take the oath he would tell the truth; I quickly learned why.

"Need I remind you, Gregarius Balbinus, that the oath you gave at your confession is still binding?" Paullus demanded.

"No, sir," Balbinus mumbled, barely audible, which did not please the senior Tribune in the least.

"Speak up, man," Paullus snapped. "I can barely hear you!"

However, rather than answer, Balbinus instead looked over at Silanus beseechingly, and I noticed that the prosecutor looked uncomfortable.

"Senior Tribune," he said awkwardly, "while I understand what you're saying, and I agree he needs to be audible, there are…complications that make that difficult."

"Complications?" Paullus echoed, clearly uncomprehending, then pointed down at Balbinus. "What's so difficult about speaking up?"

"Er," Silanus stumbled, "it's difficult for him to do so because during his…interrogation, he sustained an injury."

Paullus immediately went from his state of irritation to one that I would liken to a spectator at the games who is about to see blood in the sand, avidly interested.

"What kind of injury?" he asked eagerly.

"A broken jaw," Silanus answered.

"Ah." Paullus actually sounded disappointed, I suppose because it was so mundane an injury. "Then continue. And try to speak up, Balbinus. You don't want to have to repeat yourself, neh?" He actually sounded jovial.

"Yes, sir," Balbinus managed; he was steadfastly keeping his eyes from roaming anywhere near where we were seated.

"Now, Balbinus, you've heard the testimony of Manius Fusus that he saw you, and positively identified you as one of the men who set fire to his farm. What do you say to that?"

Despite the gravity of the moment, I found it difficult to suppress a chuckle at the look of confusion that crossed Balbinus' face, and even with the distortion from his bruises, it was easy to read his expression. What the fuck do you expect him to say? I wondered.

Finally, Balbinus managed a cautious, "That I feel bad about it?" Then, he hastened to add, "Sir?"

Now Balbinus was not alone in his confusion, as Silanus looked as bemused and completely at a loss about how to proceed.

"Tribune Silanus." For the first time, a Tribune other than Paullus or Asprenas spoke up, the one at the far end of the table, directly across from us, prompting the prosecutor. "Perhaps you could phrase your question a bit differently?"

"Is he allowed to do that?" Galens whispered; Arruntius did not turn around; he did shake his head, prompting my Centurion to make a snorting sound that caused Paullus to look sharply over at him, although he did not say anything.

"Yes, er, thank you, Tribune Secundus," Silanus replied, then spun about to face Balbinus again, demanding, "Were you a party to setting fire to that farm, Balbinus?"

"Party?" Balbinus, if anything, looked more confused. "N-no sir." He shook his head, wincing as he did. "It weren't no party. Or a festival either."

It was everything I could do to keep from bursting out into laughter; I could have told Silanus putting a word like that into the question would have confused the ranker, because this was the kind of term that only had one meaning in Balbinus' world.

"What I mean," Silanus was clearly struggling to control himself, "is, did you take part in the burning of the farm of Manius Fusus?"

"Oh," Balbinus began blinking rapidly, "that's what you meant. Then, yes, sir." Whatever composure Balbinus had managed to hang onto began evaporating, yet when he finally looked in a direction other than straight ahead of him, it was to his direct left, where the cross-eyed man was still seated, observing everything taking place, whereupon Balbinus began physically shaking. "I-I-I already told that to Dolabella! Please, please, sir! I told you everything already! I confessed everything, so please…" His voice trailed off in what to my ears sounded close to an almost feral moan, the man clearly out of his mind with fear.

Naturally, this prompted me, and the others I was sure, although they were somewhat behind me, to look over at the now-named Dolabella. Who, I instantly saw, was the only man who seemed to have maintained all of his composure, because out of the corner of my eye, I sensed the Tribunes all shifting uncomfortably in their own seats. Whether or not it was in disgust at Balbinus' naked fear, the acknowledgement of how his confession was obtained, or the cold smile that Dolabella was casting on Balbinus, I do not know. Whatever the cause, my suspicion and hostility to this man who had been so friendly when we met on the road increased dramatically.

"Balbinus," I turned away from Dolabella because it was neither the voice of Silanus nor Paullus who I heard, but Asprenas, and his tone was gentle as he assured the man, "you have nothing to fear anymore. It's true that this Dolabella had to be…harsh during his interrogation of you, but have you confessed everything? Have you answered every question?"

"Yes!" Balbinus cried, literally, and he seemed to be thrilled to have an excuse to look away from Dolabella and turn his back to the man so he could face Asprenas, practically shouting, "Yes, Tribune!

I swear it! I swear on Jupiter's stone! I answered all of his questions! I did! And I told him everything he wanted to know!"

"Then you have no reason to fear, Balbinus," Asprenas replied soothingly, yet while I was suspicious, I must say his sympathy and compassion seemed sincere. "This is the final part, then you'll be done. You just need to answer Silanus' questions."

"What about him?" Balbinus' voice suddenly changed to one that sounded both petulant and fearful as he lifted both hands so he could jerk one thumb over in the direction where we were sitting. "Do I have to answer his questions too?"

"Do you mean Tribune Arruntius?" Asprenas asked him, and when Balbinus nodded, he nodded his own head regretfully, yet his voice was firm as he answered, "I'm afraid so, Balbinus. But, not until tomorrow, neh? So, answer Silanus today, then you can rest and get your strength to answer Tribune Arruntius tomorrow."

The knob of Balbinus' throat bobbed up and down, then he nodded and returned his attention back to Silanus. Now that he was ostensibly back in control, Silanus continued with his questioning.

"Balbinus, we've established that you were there to set fire to the farm of Manius Fusus." He paused for an instant, perhaps to build the suspense, before asking, "Who gave you the orders to set fire to the farm?"

If Balbinus had been swallowing hard before, now I watched as the knot seemed to be bouncing like a pig bladder pumped with air, as he struggled to find the words that would betray Atticus.

Finally, he managed to croak, "The Primus Pilus did."

Then he stopped, prompting Paullus to hiss in frustration, yet before he could say anything, Silanus told Balbinus, "Gregarius, while I know who you mean, for the purposes of this Tribunal, I am going to need you to say his full name and title. And," he thought to add, "the Legion number. For the record, you understand."

No, Balbinus did not understand in the slightest; I could tell by the way his eyes started darting wildly about as he tried to think of a way where he would not have to utter our Primus Pilus' name. While I never learned with any certainty, my guess at the time was that, in Balbinus' mind, if he could somehow avoid uttering Atticus' name, the Primus Pilus would find it in his heart to forgive him. Or at least, not flay him at the first opportunity. The silence stretched out, but there was no help coming for Balbinus from any quarter.

At last, he exhaled a breath with such force it sounded like he moaned, and he closed his eyes as he said, "Primus Pilus Atticus of the 8th Legion gave the orders to set fire to the farm of…" His face screwed up as he tried to recall the name of the farmer, who was sitting not more than five feet away from him and whose name had been mentioned at least a dozen times.

"Manius Fusus," Silanus supplied, prompting Balbinus to nod his head.

"Yes, him," he answered.

"And do you know why your Primus Pilus gave you these orders?"

As soon as Silanus asked the question, I had to bite the inside of my cheek, knowing what was coming, which was Balbinus replying simply, "Yes."

Then saying no more than that. At last, Silanus' patience ran out, so he lifted his arm to point in the direction of Dolabella, and while he did not shout like I am sure Paullus would have in his place, there was no need; just the gesture was enough to add the required menace to his words.

"Do we need to have Dolabella here remind you of the meaning of cooperation?" was all he said, but Balbinus shook his head so violently, and was so gone with fear, I clearly saw silver strands of his saliva being flung all about.

Apparently, Silanus was splattered in the process because he suddenly took a hopping step away from Balbinus, issuing a croaking sound that I suppose was a mark of his disgust.

His witness was oblivious to this as he started babbling, "No! No, sir! No! No, you don't need to have Dolabella remind me of anything! I remember, I swear it!" Pausing only long enough to swallow, Balbinus practically shouted, "The Primus Pilus ordered us to set fire to the farm because he needed a reason to attack those savages we'd been chasing for a week! He was tired of following behind them and seeing what they'd been doing to the other barbarians, the…the Carni," he remembered, "yes, them! We'd come across a half-dozen villages that had been burned to the ground by then, and the number of bodies we found I can't even count that high! He said the only way we could stop them was by giving them a taste of Roman iron! And to do that, he needed us to burn down that farm because it belonged to a citizen! I swear that's why!"

It became clear that once Balbinus got started, getting him to shut up was another matter entirely, because he continued this prattling, while Silanus tried unsuccessfully to calm him down, mainly by making a soothing gesture with both hands as he tried to shush Balbinus. His actions reminded me of a man trying to calm a panicked horse, which I suppose is not that far off the mark, but when Silanus was unsuccessful, it took Paullus intervening with a roared order to my former comrade to shut up or he would, in fact, be turned over to the untender mercy of the man Dolabella before Balbinus stopped. Fairly quickly, it became obvious that Paullus had gotten through to Balbinus; in truth, this was the most effective thing I saw the senior Tribune do any of the times I was around him, because now Balbinus was hunched over in the chair, trying to pull his knees to his chest, yet being prevented by the chains, while he moaned softly, although at least he wasn't ranting any longer. Eyeing Balbinus with open disgust, Paullus directed a question to Silanus, asking him if he had any further evidence he wished to present. The prosecuting Tribune said no, then reserved the right to call more witnesses after the defense presented its case. Since I knew about this practice from my Avus' Tribunal, I was watching Atticus, but Arruntius had obviously informed him about this part and that it was standard; only Galens looked alarmed, so I whispered it was normal and I would explain later.

Paullus then declared, "This Tribunal is adjourned for the day. Tomorrow, the defense will present its case. In the meantime, Primus Pilus Atticus, you are restricted to your quarters on the Campus Martius, with the exceptions of the baths and to take your meal in the officers' mess there on Campus."

I was not surprised to see that neither Atticus nor Arruntius felt the need to point out to Paullus that Atticus was staying somewhere off the Campus, although I was somewhat curious what his reaction would have been if he had known. There was no chance of this happening, however, because the words were barely out of Paullus' mouth before he was on his feet and scurrying for the side door again, followed by the other Tribunes as before. It was almost a repeat of the earlier procession, except that Silanus conferred with the Praetorians who had been sitting there this whole time, looking about as bored as it is possible to be while remaining conscious. Despite the fact that I could not hear what he said, it did not take much to determine what his instructions were, because the two men immediately stood and walked over to where Balbinus was cowering in his witness chair. Roughly grabbing him by the chains binding his wrists, the larger Praetorian abruptly yanked them upward, jerking Balbinus out of his chair, causing him to yelp in pain. And before I had any conscious thought, I found myself suddenly standing, just a pace away from the two Praetorians, both of whom were clearly surprised.

"There's no need for you to treat him so roughly." When I heard the anger in my voice, I was surprised it was actually real and not contrived. "He's been cooperative, and he's a man under the standard. You need to treat him with some respect."

"He's a prisoner, Optio." The older of the two was the one who spoke. "And he's our responsibility, not yours. We'll treat him as we see fit."

"What's your name, Gregarius?" My voice was quiet, but I did not have to yell for this to be insulting, and I knew it.

"I'm a Praetorian, Optio," the man shot back, "not some fucking Gregarius in one of your Legions."

"One of my Legions?" I affected surprise, turning to look at someone else, not my Primus Pilus, but at Dolabella, who had stood and was watching us; at least so I thought since I found it hard to tell because of his eyes. "I thought they belonged to Rome. And I thought that you're supposed to be Romans in the Praetorians. But maybe I was wrong."

As I hoped it would, this clearly enraged the Praetorian, who took a step closer at me, except the effect of menace he was trying to project was ruined because of the way he was craning his neck. He was of medium height, and had what most would say was a muscular build, but the gods know I speak the truth when I say when he was next to me, he looked like a stripling youth. I believe he realized this, even as I stared down at him coldly, while he suddenly did not appear quite as certain, or as menacing as I am sure he intended.

"You will treat this prisoner in a gentler manner," I said slowly. "Or you and I are going to have a problem. Is that clear?"

"I'd listen to the Optio if I were you, Rufio," a new voice interjected.

I did not take my eyes off the man whose name I now knew was Rufio, so I could not see who had spoken, yet since it was not any of the men on my side of the room whose voice I recognized, I knew it was Dolabella, recalling the sound of his voice from the inn. Regardless of the warning, or perhaps because of it, Rufio did not seem disposed to listen, at least at first.

"You don't give us orders either, Dolabella," Rufio said this with an assurance I was certain was forced, and the thought came to mind this probably would have gone more smoothly if the other Praetorian was not present, so this one did not need to preserve some form of his *dignitas*. "And neither does an Optio from the Legions."

"Actually, that's not true." Arruntius added his voice, except he spoke with the inborn authority that comes not just from a man's rank, but from his birth. "If you could read, you'd know that an Optio in the Legions' rank is exactly the same as an Optio in your precious Praetorians. And if I'm not mistaken, you're not an Optio. Are you?" By this time, Arruntius had moved to my side, his *toga* draped over his left arm, and while he and Rufio were of a height, the latter seemed to shrink before my eyes.

"No, Tribune," he finally relented.

"Then that means Optio Pullus here gave you a legal order, did he not?"

The muscles of Rufio's jaws bunched so tightly I thought they would spasm, yet he managed to get out, "Yes, Tribune, he did." When he turned back to me, it was hard for me to remain angry because the sight of Rufio trying to avoid looking me in the eyes by choosing that point above a superior's head all rankers use to stare at that meant his eyes were almost rolling back in his head, making him look as if he was about to faint. Who knows? Perhaps he was.

"Now, do you remember what I said?" I asked him, deciding on the spot not to prolong this confrontation for the pure purpose of ensuring this man understood he had been conquered.

"Yes, Optio," Rufio answered tonelessly, "the prisoner is to be treated gently."

Realizing I had actually used that word, I felt the need to amend myself a bit. "That doesn't mean you need to tuck him in. But," my voice turned hard again, "he's not a dog to be yanked around like I just saw you do. Is that clear?"

"Yes, Optio," I had to admit Rufio was doing a very good version of The Stupid Legionary, but then he hesitated for a moment before he finally got out, "I understand. And I will obey."

Satisfied with this victory, I did not bother saying anything else, stepping around the Praetorian as if he no longer held my interest, which I also knew would infuriate him. Instead, I went to Balbinus' side, where he was standing, quivering with what I was sure was a combination of exhaustion, pain, and fear, and in this moment, I could not really remember why I had despised the man so much. Seeing him in this pathetic state, and viewing the damage that had been done, it was impossible for me not to feel sympathy for him.

"Balbinus," I spoke quietly; having observed his behavior, I understood more yelling or even speaking in a loud voice would have the opposite effect I intended. "I'll see you tomorrow. And I want you to tell me if these…" I just jerked my thumb over at the two Praetorians, both of whom were visibly fuming. "…treat you poorly. All right?"

"Yes, sir," he mumbled, and it was something of a surprise that he actually sounded respectful, given all that had passed between us when I was his Sergeant. "I will." Then he looked up at me through the one eye that was not completely swollen shut and asked, "Once this is done, can I go home, Optio Pullus? I told them everything! I cooperated with them!" He began crying, making me think this had not been a good idea. "I know I've done the Primus Pilus wrong, I do! But I couldn't take it anymore…" His body started to shake as he became racked with great, heaving sobs, which he tried to cover up with his hands, except the chains were not long enough. "I just want to go back to the Legion, sir! That's all! I just want to go home!"

Not knowing what else to do, I gave the poor man an awkward pat on the shoulder, saying only, "I'll see what I can do, Balbinus."

Then I motioned to Rufio, who obeyed readily enough, despite being openly sullen about it, but they did not drag Balbinus away, instead matching their pace to his as he shuffled out of the room. Only then did I glance over my shoulder and see both Atticus and Galens were no longer there; I turned and just caught Arruntius' back as he exited, slightly ahead of Balbinus and his escorts. The only people left were me and Dolabella, who had moved to a spot so he could sit on the prosecution's table, presumably to watch the show.

When I turned to face him, he smiled at me again. And yet, while it was the identical smile he had given me at that roadside inn some time before, it was different at the same time, with the same sly quality I had ascribed to him earlier that day, although now the added awareness he had a hand in what happened to Balbinus certainly did not help. Not lost on me was the knowledge that Balbinus was a man who, as much as I loathed him, was a comrade. Now, as Dolabella regarded me with that smile, there was an added smug quality to it that I did not care for at all.

"Was that your handiwork?" I asked him coldly.

"Some of it," he admitted with a cheerfulness I found obscene, "but not all of it. I prefer more...subtle methods."

"Who are you?" I asked him, to which he just shrugged.

"I'm just like you, Pullus," was his answer. "A loyal servant to Rome."

"To Rome?" I echoed, not bothering to hide my skepticism. "Or to one man in Rome?"

"They're one and the same thing, if it's the right man we're talking about." And while he replied easily enough, I detected a sudden shift in the man.

For some reason, I was reminded of what I have come to think of as the great serpent that lies coiled inside me, waiting to be unleashed. Perhaps it was the way he seemed to unfold himself from his seated position on the table, with a slow, lethal grace that gave the lie to the cheery smile he presented to the world, standing erect so he could take a step closer to me. Perhaps he thought this might intimidate me, but I doubt it; what little I knew about this man, I could see he was intelligent and unlikely to think that someone of my size and experience would be cowed.

"And which man is that?" I challenged him, realizing even as I did so I was on the precipice of a crumbling cliff that could collapse from under me at any moment, yet I still felt the need to press forward.

"Perhaps," Dolabella answered softly, moving closer to me as he did so, "you should be the one answering that question, Pullus. To which man are *you* referring?"

"Nobody," I replied flatly, refusing to be intimidated, despite the fact I probably should have been, considering Arruntius' warning about my perceived connection to Tiberius. "Because I serve Rome. All of Rome," I emphasized, "and not just one man." I should have stopped there, yet unlike all the other times where my mouth got me in trouble, where I only became aware of my error after the fact, in this moment, standing there facing Dolabella, I knew I had said enough and that there was no need to add anything. So, of course, I did the exact opposite thing I knew to be the right, and smart thing to do, by finishing, "No matter who it is."

This clearly caught Dolabella by surprise, but he recovered quickly.

"That's...interesting, Pullus," was his only reply.

"Pullus! Hurry up!"

Galens' gravelly bellow was about as welcome a sound as I could have heard, and I wasted no time in turning to leave.

"I'm sure we'll talk again," Dolabella called out, but since it was to my back, I did not bother to reply.

"I'm fucked," Atticus put it glumly as we sat in our quarters, which somehow had become the meeting place for the four of us. "Balbinus just fucked me up the ass."

"Not necessarily," Arruntius replied, which surprised me, as it obviously did the other two.

The more time I spent around Arruntius, the more I had begun to like him, even though I would never trust him. Still, while he was a haughty bastard, he also seemed to genuinely care about Atticus and his future, while his clear contempt for Paullus was a huge endorsement, and I knew I was not alone in my thinking.

"How so?" Atticus challenged, clearly unconvinced. "He came out and said I ordered him and the others to torch that farm."

"He did," Arruntius agreed, "but he said more than that as well." He looked at the small pile of wax tablets that had been delivered shortly after our evening meal, which he said contained the transcript of the testimony of the witnesses. After sorting through them, he found the one for which he was looking, saying, "Here it is. Do you remember when Balbinus was talking about when you gave him the order? I mean, the reasons you gave him?"

"Somewhat," Atticus said warily, and I was sure he was trying to keep his hopes tamped down.

"Well, let me refresh your memory," Arruntius replied, then spun the tablet around so that Atticus could read it, which caused me to wince, inwardly of course.

As I had learned by my proximity to the Primus Pilus, although he was literate, he was not a keen reader, and I assumed this was because it was clearly a struggle for him. Now, Galens and I sat in embarrassed silence, since we both knew this, while Arruntius, seeing our reaction, gave us a puzzled glance. But then, seeing Atticus' lips moving as he painfully worked out the words, a slight flush crept up the Tribune's neck as he realized why we were behaving this way.

Clearing his throat, Arruntius said, "Actually, Primus Pilus, would you mind if I summarized, for the benefit of Galens and Pullus here? I should have thought of that before."

There was no missing the look of relief on Atticus' face, and he assured the Tribune this was a splendid idea.

"What I'm going to capitalize on tomorrow when I begin our case will be based on what Balbinus said about how the Primus Pilus was worried because of damage the Taurisci were doing as they raided through Carni lands. If you remember, he specifically mentioned that the Primus Pilus here gave Balbinus, and whoever was with him, his reasons for ordering the burning of the farm, and that they were based on his concern for the lives being lost."

Oh, I thought, this is about as thin a porridge as I've seen, but rather than point out how ludicrous it was to think that a Primus Pilus of a Legion had the welfare of a barbarian tribe in mind, I went to what I saw as the other flaw, objecting, "But remember that Silanus spent almost a third of a watch on how 'all's quiet in Pannonia.' According to him, this was nothing worthy of calling out a Century of auxiliaries, let alone a full Legion."

"That's true," Arruntius granted, "except that's where Silanus made his mistake."

"How so?" Galens asked, and honestly, I still did not see it either.

"Because his own witness contradicted the earlier testimony Silanus gave when he painted that beautiful picture of a peaceful province." He paused for an instant, then grinned as he said, "And Silanus didn't correct Balbinus, as he should have. Instead, we now have two different accounts of what conditions in Pannonia were like."

"Which opens the door for us," Atticus mused, and I could see the struggle taking place as he tried to keep from letting his hopes run free.

"Which opens the door for us," Arruntius repeated, nodding as he did so, "and I plan on walking through that door."

I thought of something potentially troubling. "But that was also at the end of Balbinus' testimony, when he was ranting and raving because he was out of his mind with fear."

"About that," Atticus interjected, and his voice was not warm, nor was the look he gave me when he said, "you and I are going to have a talk about why you seem so concerned with the welfare of a man who's trying to ruin my career!"

"That," Arruntius spoke up, "isn't exactly the truth, Atticus. And I suspect you know it." Seeing the Primus Pilus begin to react badly, he hurried on, "I'm not saying what he did should be forgiven, necessarily, but you saw what they did to him."

For a moment, Atticus glared, first at me, then Arruntius, before a huge sigh escaped him, which seemed to contain much of his ire with it.

"I know," he said wearily. "I know he held out as long as he could. But," he snorted with a fair amount of what sounded like disgust, "he was always a weak fucker. Being honest, if I had to pick one man out of that bunch who would fold up his tent, it would have been Balbinus."

A nasty thought occurred to me, which I debated about bringing up, but then decided it was something Atticus deserved to hear.

"Do you have any idea how Dolabella found out that Balbinus was the weak elk in your herd?"

When I asked this, I felt sure it was something that Atticus had not considered before; after all, he had just seen Dolabella in the room that morning, nor had I been afforded the time to inform him I had seen the man before. Except that not only was he unsurprised, he seemed to have a ready answer.

"While I don't know for sure, I can guess," he admitted, then gave me an odd look, one I could not readily interpret, and my confusion only deepened when he added, "And you should be able to guess too, Pullus. You were his Sergeant. And you know there are no secrets in a section."

While I certainly knew his last statement was true, I did not see to what he could be referring; at least, at first. Then, as I sat there thinking about it, feeling acutely conscious that Atticus was studying me as I pondered, it slowly came to me.

"Oh, *cac*," I muttered, then looked Atticus in the eyes as I said, "It's because of the boys, isn't it? I was just thinking it was because he had a big mouth and liked to talk big in the *tavernae* out in town."

Atticus gave an almost imperceptible nod, causing me to sit back and take a deep breath, as I tried to stop the sudden spinning in my mind, wondering what this loose thread, pulled by Dolabella, might manage to unravel. The thought crossed my mind; would we have another situation where our Primus Pilus' illicit activities threatened the Legion, even if it was in a different way?

"Would you two please inform me what's going on?" Arruntius demanded.

Neither of us replied at first, and I did wonder if Galens had been aware of this aspect of Balbinus' character, despite the fact that he was in another Century. Normally, this would mean he did not, but Balbinus' pursuit of buggering boys, the younger the better, and in conjunction with the man's propensity to brag about it, was hard to keep secret.

Finally, I relented and explained, "Balbinus' tastes when it comes to matters of the flesh are…particular." Instantly understanding playing such semantic games was not in anyone's interest, I hurried on, "He likes boys, around ten or eleven years old."

Atticus seemed to take this as a signal to take up the explanation, "My guess is that this Dolabella character found out somehow, or maybe some ranker he's paying off within our Century or Cohort told him. It's not something Balbinus would want known, at least in a wider sense."

"You mean outside his Century or Cohort?" Arruntius interjected. "Because if he's as talkative as it seems Pullus is indicating, it would be hard to keep it a secret."

"Yes," Atticus nodded, "that's what I mean. It's almost as likely that Dolabella heard about Balbinus' pastime from someone other than Balbinus himself, from someone inside the First. So I think that's how Dolabella first made contact with Balbinus, probably setting him up to catch him."

"Then why torture him?" Arruntius asked pointedly. "If that's, in fact, how Dolabella snared your rabbit, just the threat of exposure would be enough to make most men talk."

This was true enough, but it prompted me to say, "Maybe that's how Dolabella started, using exposing that to the Legate as a threat, but Balbinus still wouldn't talk. That's when he went to more…vigorous," was the word I used, "methods."

Even as I said this, my recollection of Dolabella telling me he preferred tactics other than outright torture was still fresh in my mind. Arruntius considered this for a moment, while Atticus' head was already slowly nodding, and the Tribune quickly joined with his own agreement.

"That," he admitted, "is a good likelihood. But honestly, ultimately, it doesn't matter. He gave us this opportunity, and I don't plan on wasting it."

This brought the other thing nagging at me, and I brought it up, saying, "But remember, Balbinus was barely making sense by that point."

"It doesn't matter," Arruntius pointed down to the tablet, "because it was entered into the official record. Once it's written down, and then it's accepted by the Senior Tribune, it's official and part of the record."

"How do we know Paullus accepted this?" Galens asked.

"Because these," now Arruntius picked up a tablet and waved it, "aren't made until after the Senior Tribune allows them to be copied. These aren't the originals; they're copies. But since they're part of the official record, they are word for word the same. They have to be."

"Paullus isn't going to like that much," I mused.

This made Arruntius laugh as he agreed, "No, he's not! Especially since it's because of Silanus allowing Balbinus to give his testimony that ran counter to what Silanus described earlier without correcting him, and because of Paullus missing it."

This was actually a cheerful thought; not quite as happy, at least as far as I was concerned, was that there was no answer from Claudius waiting for me when we returned. Regardless, I was feeling a bit more optimistic I would not need his help, particularly if Arruntius had any success the next day.

Frankly, I was more nervous the next morning as we entered the *Praetorium* than I had been the day before, and I sensed Galens was of a similar outlook. However, our Primus Pilus, while he did not have a spring in his step, seemed to be in a better frame of mind. Perhaps he was feeding off the aura of quiet confidence emanating from Arruntius, and out of all of us, the Tribune seemed to be the most eager to resume the battle. It made me wonder if his ardor for conflict extended to the real battlefield. Not that this mattered, and I dismissed the thought as we prepared ourselves. The room was undisturbed, with Galens and I resuming our same seats, except this time, we were the first to arrive, except this day we did not have to wait long for Silanus to arrive, followed by Balbinus and his escort, which I immediately noticed was composed of different Praetorians than before. I briefly considered trying to find out if this was a routine matter of a different shift, or if Rufio's absence was due to our confrontation the day before, then quickly dismissed it as irrelevant. Besides which, the side door was opened and Paullus emerged, followed by Asprenas, the Tribune I recalled was named Secundus, and the other two members of the Tribunal. Not surprisingly, the proceedings were ready to begin more quickly than the day before, with Paullus reminding those who had sworn oaths before they were still binding. Somewhat troublingly, the one man who did not seem ready was Arruntius, who continually glanced over his shoulder at the door, as if expecting someone.

He was, actually, and we quickly learned who it was when, as soon as Paullus indicated to him in a signal to begin, he stood and said, "Senior Tribune, where is the man Dolabella? He's not here today."

"How should I know?" Paullus replied irritably. "And why do you want to know? He wasn't on the list of witnesses!"

"No, he wasn't," Arruntius agreed, except he was not through, "but that's because the defense was unaware of his existence, or his role in these proceedings before yesterday. I plan on calling him to testify. Therefore, I request he be sent for immediately."

Paullus did not even seem angry at this potential disruption; if anything, his expression announced that he was completely flummoxed, his mouth opening and closing a couple times before he managed, "You can't do that! If he's not on the list, he can't be added!" Then he turned to Asprenas, who had resumed his seat to Paullus' left, and while he tried to speak softly, he was clearly audible when he asked, "Can he?"

Asprenas whispered something to Paullus, but I did not need to hear what he said to know that Paullus did not like it.

Obviously reluctant, Paullus returned his attention to Arruntius to inform him, "As Tribune Asprenas has reminded me, I'd forgotten about that provision in the regulations. Therefore, I withdraw my objection, and it is noted in the record that Tribune Arruntius is within his rights." Turning his attention to one of the slaves who, frankly, were normally part of the furniture, always there but waiting to do someone's bidding, Paullus commanded, "Send someone to fetch Dolabella immediately. Silanus," Paullus pointed to the prosecutor, demonstrating the normal arrogance of a member of the upper classes, assuming that these men had not heard the man's name dozens of times already, "can give you his whereabouts." Suddenly, in an afterthought, he asked, "Can't you, Silanus?"

Fortunately, the Tribune indicated he could, and the slave designated for the task listened as Silanus gave him directions to find Dolabella, even as he was scribbling what I assumed was his summons to appear, to be given to the agent.

Seeing his request fulfilled, Arruntius continued, "While we wait for Dolabella, I'd like to question my first witness." He paused for an instant, although my only question was whether it would be Galens going first, or me, but we were both in for a surprise when he said, "I call on Tribune Silanus."

If Paullus had been upset by Arruntius' demand for Dolabella's presence, this sent him to completely different level of anger, and his face turned almost as purple as the stripe on his *toga*.

"What?" The single-word question came out sounding as if he was being strangled. "Arruntius, have you lost your mind? You can't question the prosecuting Tribune!"

"I can when the Tribune makes statements as part of his case that I wish to refute." As I sat there observing, I became sure that Arruntius was being as calm as he could manage, precisely because it served to make Paullus even angrier. "And in his opening statement, there are errors there that have a direct impact on this matter."

This time, Paullus did not bother with consulting Asprenas, but what he did surprised me considerably. Rising quickly, he gestured to the other Tribunes, and they made their way to the side door, disappearing behind it, presumably to confer on this question.

"That," Arruntius remarked, "should be an interesting conversation."

The subject of this debate remained seated, glaring over at Arruntius, who airily ignored him as he grabbed a seat on the edge of the table, folding his arms as we waited.

"Tribune," Galens' tone was cautious, "forgive me for asking, since you clearly know the regulations. But…" He hesitated. "…can you do that?"

"Centurion, are you asking me if there's a regulation that gives me the ability to examine the prosecuting Tribune?" When Galens only nodded in reply, Arruntius shrugged and said simply, "I have no idea. But if I didn't try, we'd never know."

I glanced over at Silanus, but while he was still staring at Arruntius, if not with hostility then at least a fair amount of ire, I deduced he had not overheard Arruntius, who had spoken barely above a whisper. It is impossible for me to say with any certainty, yet my guess is that it was at least a sixth part of a watch we waited before the door opened, and the Tribunes came trooping out, with Paullus in the lead, of course. He did wait to let the others take their seats before he spoke, and just from his expression, I was confident I knew the answer.

"After conferring with my fellow Tribunes," I am not sure how he did so, but Paullus managed to convey his disapproval of the decision he was rendering, "it's been decided that, due to the detailed nature of Tribune Silanus' opening statement," he paused to take a breath, as if by delaying he could somehow change the word he was about to utter, announced, "your request to examine Tribune Silanus as a witness is…accepted."

Both Galens and I demonstrated our happiness; I clenched a fist and shook it in front of my chest, while Galens let out a breath that sounded very close to a cheer, which prompted a glare from the senior Tribune. Honestly, immediately after I did it, I felt sheepish, wondering why I was so happy, since I had no real idea what Arruntius was planning; I found out soon enough.

Silanus was required to sit in the witness chair and take the oath to speak only the truth; once that was done, Arruntius wasted no time, asking his first question, "Where did you get your information about conditions in Pannonia?"

Silanus actually looked startled, which made me wonder what he thought Arruntius was going to ask about.

Nevertheless, he answered cautiously, "From a number of different sources."

"Ah." Arruntius acted as if this was unexpected, nodding his head while he began pacing back and forth in front of Silanus, who was watching his examiner as if Arruntius was a wolf and Silanus was a sheep. "That's interesting," Arruntius said, "but could you be more specific?"

"Specific how?" Silanus asked plaintively. "I'm not sure what you mean."

"What I mean," Arruntius replied immediately, but patiently, "is whether or not any of your sources included anyone attached to the Army of Pannonia."

The change in Silanus' posture and demeanor was something I found interesting, and he turned cautious, saying only, "It depends."

"Depends on what?"

Silanus grimaced, but answered, "It depends on your definition."

Arruntius made a show of appearing puzzled, except that I, for one, certainly could tell he was not, "Definition of what exactly, Silanus? It's very straightforward. Concerning these sources you used to determine what kind of conditions existed in the province, did any of them hold a posting with the army?"

As subtle as it was, I could see that, like I had, Silanus determined very quickly this seemingly innocuous question had pinned him neatly.

Still, he hesitated for a moment, but finally allowed, "Not officially, no."

"Really?" Arruntius raised one eyebrow in an exaggerated fashion. "Well then, at least these sources actually went out into the province and determined the nature of conditions personally. Didn't they?"

"I don't know," Silanus admitted, shifting in the chair. "I'd assume they did."

"You'd assume?" Arruntius pounced immediately. "That sounds like you didn't actually ask if their observations came from firsthand experience."

"I didn't ask." Silanus was beginning to get rattled, and because of the sunlight coming through the high windows, the light was such that it caught the beads of sweat on his brow, reflecting each one with a golden hue.

"So for all you know, these...sources you used could have sat in a *tavernae*, drinking wine and listening to gossip about what was happening! Isn't that true?"

Now that Arruntius had his quarry by the throat, he was not about to let up, and his entire being related his implacability as he moved closer to Silanus, glaring down at the man. Who, I thought with grim humor, was acting as if some sort of insect had crawled up his leg the way he was squirming.

"I'm sure that's not the case." Silanus was openly desperate for succor and looking to the Tribunal for aid.

Following his glance, I immediately saw that Paullus was clearly disposed to intervene and had even opened his mouth when something I thought was very interesting happened. Reaching out, Asprenas put a hand on Paullus' arm, which elicited two reactions at the same time, one of them my involuntary wince because I knew how Paullus was likely to react at being touched, having witnessed it before. And he fulfilled my expectations, at least at first, his head swiveling from Silanus, first to the hand on his arm, then up at Asprenas, his brows knit tightly together and his mouth curling into what I was sure would be some sort of snarled reprimand at being touched by one of his inferiors. Then, while I was not in a position to tell for sure, a look passed between the two that, if not completely stopping Paullus' outburst, subdued it sufficiently that nothing actually came out of the senior Tribune's mouth. What surprised me even more was that when Paullus returned his attention back to the exchange between Silanus and Arruntius, nothing issued forth from him that would rescue Silanus either.

Arruntius also saw this and pressed, "How can you be so sure, Tribune?" Before Silanus could answer, Arruntius continued, "Isn't it true that your description of the province of Pannonia is based completely on second hand reports, from men you know, here in Rome? That you have nothing substantive to support your position? Isn't it true, Tribune, that this…" I do not know if his sneer was a contrived piece of theater, or if he had just worked himself up to it, but either way, I thought it a nice touch. "…so-called report on Pannonia is nothing more substantial than smoke, blown away by a strong breeze?"

The questions came so rapidly that Silanus kept opening his mouth, but was continually cut off by our Tribune; then, finally, Arruntius ran out of breath.

"I-I…" was all Silanus could get out before Arruntius held up a hand, and did something that mystified me at the time.

Announcing to both Silanus and the Tribunal, he accompanied his words with a dismissive wave. "I have no further use or questions for the Tribune." When Silanus remained seated in the witness chair, gaping in dumbfounded confusion, Arruntius added, "You may resume your place at the prosecution table, Tribune."

Personally, I did not blame Silanus for looking to Paullus, or any of the other Tribunes for that matter, for some sort of guidance, except they appeared just as bemused as he obviously was. After a few heartbeats' of time, Paullus made a grunting sound, nodding his head to indicate he gave Silanus his leave to move.

Before he reached his old spot at the table, however, Arruntius then said, "I now recall Manius Fusus so that I may examine him."

The farmer was sitting in the spot he had occupied the day before, and like Silanus before him, he was clearly startled, except this time, neither Paullus nor any of the other Tribunes behaved as if this was unusual. As he took Silanus' place, I had to suppress a grin at the way Fusus approached the chair, circling around it, keeping it between him and Arruntius, who waited patiently. When he sat down, his expression made me wonder if he expected some sort of hidden spikes to suddenly protrude from the wood, although he kept his eyes on Arruntius.

"Citizen Fusus," Paullus informed the farmer, "the oath you gave before the gods is still binding on this day, just as it was yesterday. Do you understand?"

Fusus merely nodded his head, never tearing his gaze away from Arruntius, who was favoring him with a smile, I supposed to put the older man at ease, even though it clearly was not working. Only pausing for an extra moment, as if to gather his thoughts, Arruntius began his questioning of Fusus, and over the next sixth part of a watch, perhaps a bit more, the Tribune used Fusus to completely dismantle Silanus' assertion about the peaceful nature of the province in which the farmer had lived for more than fifteen years. As I sat there listening, it was easy to see the growing consternation on Paullus' face, along with the one named Secundus, yet what I found interesting was that the other three, including Asprenas, gave nothing away with their expressions. Their demeanor made it impossible to determine their feelings about seeing not only the prosecution's foundation being eroded, but the casting of Silanus in, at the very least, an unflattering light. Yet, none of them objected, nor tried to stop Arruntius' relentless and methodical questions, and I finally realized why. It was bad enough that the farmer was an unwitting, and from the way he squirmed uncomfortably while answering Arruntius' question, unwilling participant to the dismantling taking place, but if either Silanus or the Tribunal, in the form of Paullus, were to try and cast doubt on what Fusus was describing, then it called into question his testimony from the day before. While I did not hold a very high opinion of Silanus' ability, it was easy to see he understood this as well as I did. And, being fair to the farmer, he answered the questions honestly, describing the true state of affairs that had come about from the conflict between Taurisci and Carni. Arruntius did not stop there, however, or at least he tried not to, asking Fusus to recount how this upheaval and instability was nothing new, but he did not get very far before I saw Asprenas nudge Paullus, who put a stop to matters.

"Very well, Tribune Arruntius," Paullus grumbled, "you've made your point." He actually closed his eyes, as if he could not bear to look at Arruntius as he allowed, "Perhaps matters in Pannonia weren't quite as…peaceful as Tribune Silanus described. But," for this, he did open his eyes, glowering not at Arruntius but at the Primus Pilus, "that doesn't mean what the Primus Pilus did is justified!"

"No," Arruntius agreed, which clearly surprised the senior Tribune, "that's what's being decided here, over the course of these past two days."

"That is indeed true." This actually came from Asprenas, and again, I saw Paullus display the same attitude with this Tribune I had seen with everyone else, shooting the man a poisonous glance, except once more, he did not say anything.

Before anything else could be made of this, the door behind us opened, and we all turned to see the slave Paullus had dispatched, followed by Dolabella. Who, I immediately noticed, was not wearing his usual sly smile; in fact, he looked very unhappy. The only man who looked unhappier than Dolabella was Balbinus, who had spent the day slumped in his chair in between the guards, and when he saw his tormentor, he gave a low moan of fear that was clearly audible to me. Regardless of Dolabella's reluctant attitude, he approached when Paullus beckoned, standing uneasily in front of the Tribunal table.

"Tribune Arruntius has demanded your presence for questioning," Paullus' tone was abrupt, "and since you weren't required to testify yesterday, you must swear an oath before the gods, administered by me."

Dolabella was rocking uneasily, and while I could not see all of his face, the expression on what I could made me think he was about to refuse before he finally gave an unenthusiastic nod. Paullus either did not notice or did not care about the quality of his agreement because he made no comment other than to intone the words for the sacred vow that Dolabella was to repeat. Which he did, except now I detected none of the cool confidence he had displayed during our exchange the day before. In many ways, his demeanor was a close match to that of Fusus as he took the seat occupied by the previous witnesses.

"Citizen Dolabella," Arruntius began, "since you're clearly involved in this matter, in what capacity do you serve our Republic?"

Now that he was seated, he was at the proper angle where I could see his crossed eyes, so he might have been looking at Arruntius, but like his predecessors, he began shifting in the seat, making me wonder if there was indeed something wrong with it.

Despite his obvious discomfort, Dolabella answered, "I'm afraid that my status is...complicated, Tribune."

"Complicated?" Arruntius theatrically arched an eyebrow, and actually turned to look at first the Tribunal, then those of us on his opposite side as he said with a clearly counterfeit geniality, "Well, I know that the members of the Tribunal and the rest of us gathered here are intelligent enough that I have every confidence we'll understand when you explain how...complicated your status is!" Arruntius paused in his speaking as he moved so he was towering over Dolabella, then spoke in a cold, commanding tone, "Now, please explain. What's your role in all of this?"

There is no way to know exactly how long the silence dragged on, as Arruntius glared down at Dolabella, while he stared straight ahead, not meeting the Tribune's eyes, although it certainly seemed as if it took the better part of the day.

The only thing I am certain about is that none of us were prepared for the moment when Dolabella broke his silence by saying, "I request a private audience with the members of the Tribunal. And," this was when he did look at Arruntius; at least I believe so, since one eye was staring directly at me, "with both the defending and prosecuting Tribunes."

This, understandably, clearly took Arruntius by surprise, as he actually seemed to stagger back a step, but his shock was no less than that of Paullus or any of the other Tribunes.

"That's not proper!" Arruntius finally managed. "Senior Tribune, I strongly protest at this obvious attempt by Citizen Dolabella to delay answering my questions! And," every word seemed to be restoring his equilibrium, causing him to speak more forcefully, "his attempt to intimidate this Tribunal!" He turned to Paullus, finishing, "I'm sure that the Senior Tribune sees through this attempt as easily as I do!"

That, I thought to myself, is one of the smartest things he's done. This belief was based on my knowledge of Paullus and his vanity. And it appeared, at first, as if it was about to work, because Paullus began glaring, not at Arruntius, but at Dolabella, although none of us would ever learn what he was going to say. Once more, it was Asprenas who reached over, although while it began with a seemingly gentle touch, when Paullus reacted again in what I thought of as his normal manner, his counterpart's own countenance hardened as he gave Paullus a cold stare. Paullus jerked his arm away; at least, he tried to, except Asprenas obviously tightened his grip because the senior Tribune could not extricate his arm from his grasp. Not a word was uttered between them as each man glared at the other, but after my observations of the two over the previous two days, I cannot say I was altogether surprised when it was Paullus whose body suddenly sagged, then turned his attention back to Arruntius and Dolabella. Both of whom, like the rest of us, were transfixed by the silent struggle for power between the supposed presiding Tribune and one of his nominal subordinates.

When Paullus did speak, his voice was curiously subdued, but he was audible when he said, "Very well, Citizen Dolabella. We'll hear you in private."

"Senior Tribune!" Arruntius exclaimed; even through the fold of his *toga,* I could see his body go rigid with what seemed to be unfeigned anger and dismay. "This is most improper! Again, I must protest!"

"I don't care…" Paullus began, but before he got any further, it was Asprenas who interjected, his tone calm, and reasoned, "Tribune Arruntius, perhaps you could cite the regulations that would prohibit this request being granted?"

All eyes turned to Arruntius, yet even before the words came out of his mouth, I was sure the others knew the answer as well as I did, because his posture had instantly changed, the rigid spine seeming to evaporate, causing his shoulders to slump as he dropped his head, shaking it and saying in a dull voice, "No, Tribune Asprenas, I can't."

"Because," Asprenas actually sounded gentle, "there is no such regulation, is there? Do you acknowledge this, Tribune?"

Arruntius hesitated for a moment, then nodded his head and said simply, "I do."

Only then did Asprenas, whose hand had never left Paullus' arm, relax its grip, giving me the strong impression that much in the same way the upper classes set great store in the ivory baton of *imperium* that bestows power, Asprenas was relinquishing that imaginary symbol back to Paullus. It was in this moment my suspicions were confirmed, at least in my mind; Asprenas was the true power on this Tribunal, not Paullus. It did make me wonder how someone as prideful as Paullus could handle this reality, but while he was clearly unhappy, he did as Asprenas had silently commanded.

"This Tribunal will convene, in private, immediately. Those not involved in this discussion will remain here." He seemed to consider for a moment, then said grudgingly, "Although I suppose it's permissible for you to go outside. As long as you stay in the immediate area in front of the building. Just be prepared to be summoned again when we're done with our meeting." He stood, as did the other Tribunes, then a look of malicious humor crossed his face, and he addressed Balbinus, "Except for you, of course, Gregarius. We wouldn't want to give you any ideas about scurrying off like some rat, would we?"

Under such circumstances, I believe Balbinus retaliated in the best, and only, way that he could, not even bothering to look up from the floor. Frankly, I do not think the man heard Paullus' jibe, although the Praetorians on either side did give the Tribune a smirk, but I saw this was more from formality because it was expected of them than from any real humor. For his part, Paullus' own grin faded quickly, and he turned to stomp off, which did cause me, and I noticed Galens as well, to smile at his retreating back.

"That was about as good an 'eat *cac*' as Balbinus could have given," he muttered.

Dolabella had risen from his chair, moving so he could fall in behind the Tribunes, and as he did so, Arruntius beckoned Atticus to his feet.

"You're coming too," Arruntius whispered.

Only in retrospect was it possible to see this was a tactical error on the part of Arruntius, although I certainly find it hard to fault him. Nevertheless, having Atticus stand with an obvious intention of joining this meeting caught the eye of Secundus, who called out to Paullus, who had just reached the side door.

Turning, Paullus' eyes narrowed as he took in the sight, then he quickly shook his head and said sternly, "Tribune Arruntius! The Primus Pilus is not part of this meeting!"

"But this concerns him more than any of us!" Arruntius argued. "He has every right to hear what this…citizen has to say!"

"Not if I say he doesn't," Paullus shot back. "And he's not attending this meeting. That's my decision, and it's final!"

Without waiting for Arruntius to respond, he opened the door and disappeared, while Arruntius gave Atticus a helpless shrug and whispered something to him. Then, he gave the Primus Pilus an awkward pat on the shoulder and turned to follow the others into the far room, leaving the rest of us to sit there. Atticus, his earlier air of confidence suddenly evaporating, stood there watching with a troubled gaze, for which I did not blame him. To that point, it had seemed to be a good day for him; now, everything was changed, and just like every member of our class, the Primus Pilus was undoubtedly right to be worried that his social betters were now secreted away, discussing matters that had a direct impact on his future, yet without his presence. I do not think it is untoward for me to say that, better than anyone else left in that room, I had more reason to understand the cause for his concern, knowing from bitter experience, albeit more indirectly, how rare it was for anything good to come from such a meeting of upper class men as far as Head Counters are concerned.

Galens rose, and walking over to Atticus, reached out to touch him on the shoulder, saying, "Primus Pilus, let's go outside and get some air."

At first, Atticus seemed disposed to argue, then I saw his glance go over to the two Praetorians, instead giving an abrupt nod, although he did not say anything. Following the pair outside, nothing was said until we were more or less in the same spot we had been the day before, where it was next to impossible for anyone to come close enough to listen in.

"What the *fuck* is that about?" Atticus finally burst out, his expression one of bitter confusion, and I felt an unexpected stab of not just sympathy, but chagrin that I could not offer anything remotely comforting.

Neither, it became apparent, could Galens, who only offered a shrug.

Our lack of response seemed to irritate the Primus Pilus even more, and he said sourly, "I wasn't just asking to hear my own voice."

"Sorry, Primus Pilus," Galens offered, while I mumbled my own apology.

"This," even as I heard my own voice, a part of me was screaming an order to stop; of course, I did not, "has to have something to do with the Princeps."

"You think?" Atticus retorted scornfully, clearly unimpressed with my grasp of the obvious. "Tell me something useful!"

Sighing inwardly, I debated how far down this road I was willing to go, except at that moment, I looked to Galens. Unfortunately, I could tell by his expression he did not intend to utter a word, forcing me to make my decision.

"Primus Pilus," I began carefully, "have you done anything that might give the Princeps offense?"

He shot me an angry glare, growling, "You mean, besides this?" Then, his expression softened, and he seemed to consider the question more seriously. Because my attention was on him, I was sure I saw a sudden shadow cross his face, except he just shrugged and said, "Nothing I can think of. At least…" The way his voice trailed off caught Galens' attention as well, and we exchanged a concerned glance.

However, when Atticus did not finish, it was Galens who prompted him, asking gently, "'At least' what, Primus Pilus?"

This seemed to yank Atticus away from his thoughts, and he looked startled for an instant, but he did finally say, "The only thing I can think of is that I haven't been as…diligent in keeping up my," he seemed to search for the right word, settling on, "correspondence with him."

Something stirred deep in my gut, and I could easily see Galens was no less disturbed. It was clear to see he was interpreting Atticus' term in the same manner I was; Atticus had been remiss in submitting his reports as a spy for Augustus.

"So," I tried to keep my tone from betraying my emotion, but I could still clearly hear the coolness in my tone, "the Princeps is upset because you don't write him letters as often as you used to?"

Atticus confirmed my suspicion by the way his face darkened; more tellingly, he did not even seem angry at my tone.

"Something like that," he admitted.

"Primus Pilus," Galens' voice was strained, and I understood he was trying to keep from making the same error I had just committed, "may I ask you, why did you stop this correspondence?"

"I didn't stop," Atticus protested, then looked away as he amended, "exactly." Shrugging, he continued, "I just haven't been doing it as often as I'm sure he'd like."

"Or," again, I could not stop myself, "is it that you're not telling him the things he wants to know about?"

Atticus gave me an angry look, except it did not last very long before he relented, sighing, "Yes. That's probably the reason."

"Why did you stop?" Galens asked.

This seemed to make Atticus uncomfortable, and he fumbled for an answer before finally saying, "Because I'm out there," he waved in a generally eastern direction, "and he's here. Because I'd forgotten what it's like to be in the Legions. The *real* Legions. Not," his mouth twisted in a grimace of disgust, "those *cunni* in the Praetorians."

As I stood there listening, I experienced a moment of confusion as I studied Atticus' face as he talked, trying to identify the emotion I saw there. Finally, it came to me; was it an expression of guilt? I wondered. I had certainly never seen anything like it before on his face, yet as I stood there, I became more certain. Even so, I experienced a deep unease because he was looking everywhere but in my direction.

"Was there something specific that you didn't relay to the Princeps? About anyone in particular?"

In the eyeblink after the words left my mouth, I was certain I got my answer; if he had been slightly red before, now his face turned an even darker hue. It was the way his entire body jerked, as if my words had been a bolt from a scorpion, and there was a moment I was sure I was about to vomit on my Primus Pilus.

Instead of answering me, he actually turned to Galens instead, and asked, "Do you remember the conversation Arruntius had with him?"

I cannot say I cared for the way he jerked his thumb in my direction, nor did I like that he was addressing Galens, yet in the moment, I suppose this was the easiest way for him to deal with this unpleasant topic.

"Yes, Primus Pilus," Galens replied cautiously, "but I'm not sure…"

"I bring it up because what Arruntius said is related to what *might* be troubling the Princeps, at least as far as I'm concerned." Galens did not reply, verbally at least, yet his look of confusion I believe prompted Atticus to heave a sigh as he understood that he would have to articulate his meaning. Only then did he glance at me as he continued to explain, "The Princeps is worried about Tiberius, and as Arruntius pointed out, apparently, some men in Rome have been putting it about that your Optio here," he stopped suddenly to correct himself, "actually, his name, is something Tiberius plans to capitalize on in his effort to rally the Legions to his cause." Sighing, while there is no way to be sure, when he finally looked directly at me, his expression was as close to apologetic as I had ever seen it as he finished, "The Princeps wrote me, wanting to know what I had heard in this regard, and if Pullus was acting in a…suspicious manner."

He stopped then, making me feel as if I had somehow careened down a slope to the edge of a cliff and was actually tottering on the precipice, trapped in that moment when one either recovers themselves, or goes hurtling off into the void.

Finally, I could take it no longer, and I blurted out in a tone that under any other circumstance would have seen me flogged, "And? What did you tell him??"

As unusual as my outburst was, his response was no less so, and in a recess of my mind, there was that detached observer who pointed out that, if one were to judge just by our respective demeanors in this instant, I am sure most men would judge me to be the Primus Pilus and Atticus the Optio.

"Nothing!" Atticus protested. "I never responded to him! At least," he admitted, "about you."

Perhaps I should have been grateful, but I was not; if anything, I was even angrier, and I could not seem to stop myself from demanding, "Why didn't you tell him the truth? Why didn't you write back to him and tell him I'm not part of anything?"

Atticus did not respond, at least verbally; instead, he only gave a shrug. Which, as much as I am ashamed to say, was the final blow, and before I could do anything to stop it other than turn my head, I vomited the contents of my morning meal. The only consolation was I somehow managed to avoid fainting as well, although I did stagger a bit, while both Galens and Atticus looked on with what I perceived to be an embarrassed horror. Before either of them could make a comment, however, a voice called out from the porch of the *praetorium*, summoning us back inside.

One did not need to know Arruntius to interpret his demeanor, if only because his complexion was an almost perfect match for his *toga*. He was standing at the table when we entered the room where the Tribunal was being held, and as we drew close enough to see his eyes, I saw an expression there that, even in the short association with the man, I felt sure was a reflection of a state that was new to him, a sort of helplessness that is an integral part of every Head Counter's life.

"What is it?" Atticus demanded, clearly interpreting Arruntius' manner in the same way I had. "What's wrong?"

Arruntius did not reply verbally at first, instead shaking his head, to which the Primus Pilus understandably reacted, reaching out and grabbing the folds of Arruntius' *toga* draping one arm.

"By the gods, man," Atticus' voice was clearly pleading, and it made me uncomfortable to hear my Primus Pilus act in this way, "this is my career! This is my life! What is going on?"

The Tribune opened his mouth, but then the door on the far side opened, and Paullus emerged, followed by the rest of the Tribunes. This seemed to goad Arruntius to speak, yet when he turned to address Atticus, I certainly did not expect what he would say, and I am sure Atticus did not either.

"Primus Pilus," Arruntius spoke in a whisper, yet with an urgent tone as he glanced over his shoulder at the Tribunal members walking to their spots at the table, "I don't have time to explain right now, but you need to trust me. I swear to you that everything will turn out well for you. Just let me do what I have to do right now!"

He did not wait for Atticus to reply, turning about to face the Tribunal, who had just settled back into their respective seats, leaving the Primus Pilus to stare at his defender open-mouthed, although he did remain silent. While the Tribunes were getting settled, I looked over to watch Dolabella walk back to his seat, and of everything going on that was disturbing me, seeing how his confidence seemed to be restored, the evidence of which was the smirk reappearing on his face, was the worst part of it. You're still a cross-eyed monkey; this was the thought running through my mind as I glared at him, and I cannot express how pleasing it was to see him meet my eyes, then quickly look away as the smile vanished.

"This Tribunal is now resuming." Paullus' announcement jerked my attention away from Dolabella, but as I turned back to face the front, I glanced at Silanus, and if I had hoped to get an idea of what was about to happen, he was no help. If anything, I thought, he looks as upset as Arruntius, which made no sense to me whatsoever; however, I could not give this any more thought, because Paullus continued, "We will resume where we left off." Turning his attention to Arruntius, Paullus said to him, "You may continue presenting the defense of the Primus Pilus, Tribune."

Whereupon Arruntius took a deep breath, holding it for a moment before letting it go in a long exhalation, then closed his eyes and said so quietly I was sure I misheard him, "The defense has nothing more to present at this time, Senior Tribune."

Atticus, being closer, clearly heard Arruntius and his reaction told me I had understood correctly when he turned to stare at Arruntius as if the man had transformed himself into some sort of animal in front of his very eyes.

"*What*?" Atticus' voice sounded like he was being strangled, his shock so profound that he actually staggered back a step. "Are you mad? What are you doing? What are you doing to *me*?"

Galens instinctively took a step closer to the Primus Pilus, my Centurion's shock clearly matching mine, while naturally, Atticus was the most affected. And it came as no surprise that Atticus' shock instantly transformed into rage, something that Galens had obviously anticipated, because when Atticus suddenly lunged at the Tribune, he was there to restrain him. However, somehow, Arruntius did not seem either afraid or angry at Atticus' sudden hostility, offering a helpless shrug as his only defense. Galens held Atticus in a firm grip; I saw his fingers pressing into the meat of Atticus' bicep, but while the Primus Pilus turned his angry glare to his subordinate, after a heartbeat's worth of time, he suddenly slumped and gave a slight nod to Galens, letting him know it was safe to release him.

"Primus Pilus!" Paullus emphasized his shouted warning by slamming his hand on the table. "There will be no further outbursts tolerated of any kind! Is that clear?"

Atticus did not answer, at least immediately, instead choosing to glare back at Paullus, and it struck me that, as a Primus Pilus, Atticus was not often talked to in such a manner, nor was he thwarted, which seemed to be at least part of the cause for his struggle to retain some composure.

Finally, he muttered, "Yes, Senior Tribune, I understand."

Instead of being satisfied, Paullus chose to continue glaring at Atticus for another several heartbeats, as if he wanted not only to subdue the Primus Pilus, but to vanquish whatever spark of defiance remained in the man.

Abruptly, he broke his stare, glancing over at, of all people, Asprenas, who gave a very faint but visible nod, which prompted the senior Tribune to turn back to us and announce, "Very well. Thank you, Tribune Arruntius. Tribune Silanus," he turned to the hapless prosecuting Tribune, and just by his tone, I knew Paullus was merely going through the formalities when he asked, "Tribune, do you have any other evidence you wish to offer?"

"No, Senior Tribune," Silanus replied, and as I studied him, I was struck how his demeanor seemed much like a man who had been sentenced to death coming to grips with the announcement he had been reprieved, only to be sentenced to a life of slavery.

"Considering that both sides have presented their respective arguments," Paullus announced, "we will now end the trial portion of the Tribunal. My fellow Tribunes and I will now meet in private session to deliberate. Primus Pilus," he returned his attention to Atticus, who now seemed to be in more of a daze than angry, "once more, you are confined to your quarters until we have reached a decision. We will meet here, tomorrow, at the beginning of second watch, where you will be informed of our decision."

Without waiting for a response, Paullus suddenly stood up, as did the other Tribunes; only Arruntius seemed to keep his head, and he called out, "Senior Tribune!"

At first, I thought Paullus would ignore him, but after a couple more steps, he turned, his annoyance clearly conveyed as he snapped, "What is it, Arruntius?"

Ignoring what I assumed was Paullus' deliberate omission of Arruntius' rank, the Tribune calmly pointed out, "You said that the Primus Pilus was confined to his quarters. Surely you mean the same restriction as yesterday, that he can still avail himself of the baths and the officers' mess?"

As we all quickly learned, this was not an oversight on the part of the senior Tribune.

"No," Paullus replied immediately, and emphatically, "he cannot! My order is that he is restricted to his quarters! I'm sorry, Primus Pilus," his tone suggested he was anything but, "you'll have to endure a night without bathing. But don't worry," he smiled malevolently, "we'll endure your stench. For a day," he added, and I saw I was not the only one who took this ominously.

Without waiting for Arruntius to argue, the Tribune spun about and walked the rest of the way to the exit, disappearing along with the other four Tribunes, of whom only Secundus ventured a look over his shoulder. We were left, still standing there, open-mouthed and trying to grasp what had just taken place.

"What did you do to me?"

Returning my attention back to where Atticus and Arruntius were standing, side by side, I saw the Primus Pilus was less angry than bewildered, staring at the Tribune, who was still looking as pale as he had when we first entered the room. What, I wondered, a hundred heartbeats ago? It could have been a hundred years considering all that had transpired.

Turning to look Atticus in the eyes, all Arruntius said was, "You have to trust me." Shaking his head, he added only, "That's all I can say. You'll understand tomorrow."

"But what happens if it takes longer than the rest of today to come to a decision?" Galens asked.

Arruntius continued to shake his head, saying only, "It won't."

Then, despite my additional voice demanding more than this, the Tribune refused to say anything else. Turning abruptly, Arruntius gathered the scrolls scattered on the table, thrusting them into the hands of his slave, who had appeared from seemingly nowhere, then once relieved of that burden, turned and began walking towards the door at the back of the room that led to the exit from the *Praetorium*.

"Come on, Primus Pilus," Galens said gently, "let's get away from this place."

Guiding our commander by the elbow, Galens indicated with a motion of his head that I should follow, which I did, except I stopped when I got to Dolabella. He was still seated, watching all that had taken place with a look that, to me at least, communicated his great amusement at what just transpired here. Only later, once I had the opportunity to think about it, I realized that what I was about to do was not based on my love or devotion to my Primus Pilus; only now will I say with utmost honesty that my major concern throughout this whole Tribunal was that I escape with my career, and my life, intact and undamaged. Yet, somehow, in the moment when I looked down at the cross-eyed little man and his smug expression, in much the same way I had felt about Urso in the last moments of his life, when I had tried desperately to save him from Draxo's axe, despite the fact that my former Primus Pilus' death made my life much less complicated, I just could not stand by and let Atticus fall. Consequently, I caught the other man by complete surprise when I reached out and grabbed a fistful of his tunic with my left hand, and despite it taking a bit of an effort, I lifted him up bodily, not only from his chair but from the ground, so that his feet dangled just inches off it. In retrospect, what I did to Dolabella was markedly similar to the way I had once treated Balbinus, who, for the first time, showed some animation as he watched what was taking place.

Pulling his face close to mine, I cannot say I was not grimly satisfied at the sudden look of terror in the man's eyes, or eye, and despite the fact that I was not yelling, I believe this made me even more menacing as I said quietly, "I don't know what you said in there, you cross-eyed cocksucker, but know this. If you said anything that damages the Primus Pilus, I am going to kill you, slowly." I believe the effect was heightened by the fact that, with every word, I was shaking him back and forth in much the same way a dog does with a rat, which I thought, and still think, was an appropriate comparison. "Are you hearing me?" I asked him.

"Y-y-you're making a huge mistake," he finally managed as he used his right hand to try and wrest my grip from his tunic, to no avail. "Do you know who I am?" To my ears, this sounded like the last squeak of a desperate mouse.

"I do," I replied flatly. "A dead man."

Only then did I release my grasp, dropping him to the floor as he gasped for breath; I suppose my grip on his tunic had been such that it was a bit suffocating. As he caught his breath, I turned away from him and walked to Balbinus.

"Balbinus." In contrast to how I addressed Dolabella, my tone was gentle, and I even crouched down so our eyes were on more of a level, asking him, "How are you doing?"

"Optio Pullus," he mumbled, "I'm doing fine. They," his eyes darted to one of the Praetorians, who was openly glaring at me, which I ignored, "have left me alone. And," his battered features lit up, slightly, "they let me have some wine last night!"

"That's good," I enthused, patting him on the shoulder, then stood to leave him.

"Optio," he squinted up at me, making me wonder if his eyes had been permanently damaged by the beatings he had endured, "does this mean I can come back now? To the Legion?"

A lump appeared in my throat, surprising me considerably, yet the best I could manage was, "It's still too early to know, exactly, Balbinus. But," I promised, "as soon as I know, I'll make sure you hear about it."

I did not wait for him to reply, turning about to follow the others, stopping only long enough to glare down at Dolabella, who I caught throwing poison at me with his eyes, at least until I turned about and we were face to face. Choosing to ignore this challenge, I hurried outside, and I did not arrive a moment too soon.

As I learned afterward, my initial impression was correct; Galens was doing his best to keep Primus Pilus Atticus from attacking the Tribune who, up until just moments before, had seemed intent on providing the staunchest defense that Atticus could have expected. What I saw in that instant was Galens grasping Atticus by the waist from behind him, as Arruntius seemed to, if not accept the beating in his future, was at least apathetic to the idea Atticus was intent on beating him bloody. Before I reached them, Atticus broke free of Galens' grasp, leaping at Arruntius, whose actions matched his demeanor, making no attempt whatsoever to evade Atticus' lunge. This was when I intervened, breaking into a sprint to tackle my Primus Pilus in the instant before he himself was about to slam into the Tribune. My momentum drove both of us to the ground, and even as I landed on top of him, forcing the air from my superior's lungs, I was cringing, not from the impact but at the likely punishment that awaited me. The fact that we were both wearing our armor was a mixed blessing; it protected us while adding to the force of the collision with the ground at the same time.

Lying atop the Primus Pilus, I could hear him struggling for breath, then he finally managed to gasp, "Get off me, Pullus! That's an order!"

I obeyed, reluctantly, then when I offered my hand, he only glared up at me and slapped it away, pulling himself to his feet.

"You," he half-growled, half-gasped, "I'll deal with you later."

"Primus Pilus," Galens appeared so suddenly it surprised me, "he just kept you from being executed! It doesn't matter you're a Primus Pilus! You were about to attack a superior!" My Centurion dropped his voice to a whisper, glancing over at Arruntius, who was standing there in a seeming daze, and I at least appreciated how difficult it was for Galens to lower his voice. "Not to mention he's a patrician!"

Only then did Atticus react, Galen' words causing him to jerk his glaring attention away from the Tribune, and while I would not say he was sheepish, he did look somewhat embarrassed. Not until I reached the Centurionate myself did I understand how it must have felt to have not just one but two subordinates essentially save him from himself. Being completely frank, the position Atticus was in is one with which I have too much experience, where my own actions threaten not just my life but all that I hold dear.

"Fine," Atticus finally grumbled, then turned to address Arruntius. "I won't kill you, Tribune. But you owe me an explanation!"

When we were in the *praetorium*, I did think Arruntius' reluctance to explain was due to our surroundings and the proximity of probably hostile ears; he disproved this belief by shaking his head and saying only, "Believe me, Primus Pilus, I wish I could. But I can't. Not yet."

Instantly, I looked at Atticus, expecting him to spring at the Tribune again, yet while his jaw was jutting out and he was clearly fuming, he made no move.

"All right," he answered abruptly. "So when can you tell me?"

"Not until tomorrow," Arruntius replied, prompting a snort of disgust from the Primus Pilus, although this was all he did.

Instead, he spun about on his heel and began stalking away, leaving Galens and me standing there with Arruntius.

Once Atticus was out of earshot, I turned to the Tribune and asked, "So what *is* going on?"

Arruntius laughed, without much humor, I will admit, saying only, "If I can't tell him, I certainly can't tell you."

Sighing, I looked at Galens, who shrugged and said only, "I don't know about you, but I plan on getting drunk tonight."

Without waiting for an answer, he followed after Atticus. Giving Arruntius a shrug, I hurried after my Centurion; while I did not intend to lose my senses, I confess that a few cups of wine seemed to be as good an idea as any other.

All I can say is that if I did not sleep that night, I was sure that the Primus Pilus was in no better condition. Nevertheless, at the appointed time we agreed to meet, he was standing there, once more in full uniform, and the thought crossed my mind as I wondered if Paullus would think to order us to surrender our weapons before we entered. The circles under Atticus' eyes were so dark he looked as if he had been in a fight, yet otherwise, his face reflected none of the turmoil he must have been feeling. Still, I could not help feeling a stab of shame at my intense relief that neither Galens nor I had to face any questioning, even if it was from someone like Silanus. Now all that remained was to find out if Galens and I would be returning to Siscia alone, although I did not dare say this aloud, even to my Centurion. Arruntius was waiting for us outside the *praetorium*, but although Atticus refused to say a word to the Tribune, Arruntius' demeanor personally puzzled me, which was not nearly as grim as one might have thought. When we entered the room, Silanus was already there waiting, but neither Balbinus and his escorts, or the cross-eyed Dolabella were present, nor did they ever show up. During the time we waited for the arrival of Paullus and the other Tribunes, nobody spoke a word, the silence quickly becoming oppressive as Atticus sat, stiff-backed and staring straight ahead. His body slave had obviously worked through the night, because I had never seen his decorations gleaming the way they did, catching the rays of light from both the windows and from the lamps that were lit to add illumination. Frankly, it made me feel a bit shabby in comparison, but I consoled myself that it was not my fate being decided this day.

Because of the quiet, we were able to hear the Tribunes rustling about in the far room before the door opened, and, in truth, I was sure I heard at least one raised voice. Clearly, so did Atticus, who turned to stare at the closed door, undoubtedly straining to listen as much as I was, and I am sure everyone else present. The muffled voices never rose to a level where we could hear anything intelligible; however, it became apparent that there was some sort of fairly spirited disagreement taking place.

"What in Hades is that about?" Galens muttered to me.

"I don't have any idea," I whispered, "but I can bet it involves Paullus in some way."

Apparently I said this more loudly than I intended, because I heard a snorting sound that I recognized as what passed for a laugh from the Primus Pilus, and I glanced at him to see something like a smile, albeit sour and twisted, on his face.

"That's one bet you'd be sure to win," he commented, which in turn elicited a chuckle from both Galens and me; Arruntius seemed oblivious, keeping his attention on the far door.

Suddenly, there came a noise much louder than the bickering voices, which to my ears sounded like a piece of furniture being upended, yet before any of us could speculate, the door was jerked open, whereupon Paullus emerged. Instantly, I was sure we were seeing the cause of whatever had been upended, because rather than his normal sneer, the senior Tribune wore a mask of true rage, his mouth twisted into a grimace, while his hands were clenched into fists as he stomped to his spot. Savagely yanking the chair from its spot under the table, Paullus literally threw himself into the chair, causing the folds of his *toga* to flap about his body in a most unflattering way. Following him was one of the Tribunes whose name I never learned, then Secundus, who gave the appearance of a man wishing he were anywhere else. Only afterward did the fact that Asprenas was the last man to enter gain significance, and of all the Tribunes, his face was the hardest to read. He was also the last to settle into his spot, but if we were expecting Paullus to begin the proceedings, it quickly became clear he had no intention of doing anything other than sit there, arms crossed and obviously sulking. Finally, Asprenas made a sound, clearing his throat, causing Paullus to turn and glare at the other Tribune, who was ostensibly junior to him in rank, and there was no mistaking the look of poisonous hatred Paullus gave the other man. Who, I noticed, did not seem in any way affected by this open display of hostility, which I was sure made Paullus even angrier; nothing is worse to a man like Paullus than to be considered so insignificant that even his hatred is of no consequence. Even worse, at least as far as Paullus was concerned, was that despite nothing being said, we witnessed Paullus bending to Asprenas' will, because the senior Tribune finally broke his gaze away to turn and, clearly reluctant, face the table where Atticus and Arruntius were standing.

"After careful deliberation," Paullus spoke abruptly, but he was difficult to hear because he was hoarse almost to the point he had no voice left, "it is the decision of this Tribunal that, while Primus Pilus Atticus may have acted in a more...aggressive manner than was prudent," he paused and closed his eyes before continuing, "his actions do not reach the level where he should be found guilty of the charges laid before him."

Atticus suddenly collapsed, and it was only luck that his chair was right behind him to catch his weight. Naturally, Paullus, needing something to vent his frustrated anger on, pounced on this.

"Nobody gave you leave to sit, Primus Pilus," he snarled. "This Tribunal hasn't finished announcing its decision!"

Somehow, Atticus found the energy to stand back up, although inwardly, I had to grin at how he did so without any haste, exacting his own revenge on the senior Tribune.

Once Atticus was back on his feet, Paullus continued, "However, while his actions do not rise to the level where he is worthy of being punished, this Tribunal does find there is sufficient cause to determine that the Primus Pilus was responsible for ordering the farm of Manius Fusus to be put to the torch. Therefore, this Tribunal is ordering Primus Pilus Atticus to compensate Citizen Fusus for his loss, in the amount of…." Paullus paused, and to this day, I am sure he did so only to prolong Atticus' torment, especially given the malicious smile on the Tribune's face, "….fifty thousand *sesterces*."

An explosive gasp escaped from Atticus' lips, and for an instant, I thought he might collapse again, then I saw him surreptitiously grab the edge of the table with one hand to remain standing.

The Primus Pilus' reaction seemed to please Paullus, who went on, "This amount is to be paid to Citizen Fusus immediately, in cash."

"*What*??" This was the first thing Atticus said, spluttering, "I can't come up with that much money right now! Not here in Rome at least!"

"That," Paullus shot back, "is not the concern of this Tribunal. What is," he pointed a finger at the Primus Pilus, "our concern is that Citizen Fusus is compensated for his loss."

"But his farm isn't worth anywhere near that!" Atticus protested, which had no impact on Paullus, who shrugged and said simply, "That's your opinion, which doesn't mean anything. It's what this Tribunal thinks that matters, and we are all agreed," he actually paused and looked to either side of him, glaring in what I took as a warning, "this is the value of his farm. And, Primus Pilus, know this," Paullus warned, "until you produce the amount, and present it to Citizen Fusus in front of witnesses, *in the Forum*, you will remain in Rome until such time that you fulfill the terms of our decision!"

I found it somewhat interesting, in a morbid way, to observe the range of the Primus Pilus' emotions, judging them simply from the array of colors his face turned. When he was informed of the amount he was expected to pay, he went white, reminding me of the coloring of Arruntius' face the day before, yet when Paullus relayed the conditions, as quickly as the blood fled, it came rushing back into his face, suffusing it a deep, almost purple color as his features contorted into a mask of enraged but impotent fury.

"This," he hissed, then got no farther because for the first time, Arruntius spoke, cutting him off with a whispered, harsh warning.

"Don't say a word." Even whispering, the command in the Tribune's voice was clear to hear.

Personally, I thought this was a mistake and would serve only to goad Atticus into an outburst that would end up costing him dearly, at least if my instincts were correct, and mine were clearly aligned with those of Arruntius. However, I was surprised, verging on shocked that Atticus did not object, let alone punch Arruntius in the mouth. Somehow, he seemed to sense that Arruntius was actually trying to help him, although it clearly took an effort for him to subside, but he finally did, turning back to face the Tribunal.

"Primus Pilus," Asprenas was the one who spoke next, which caused Paullus' own face to twist into an expression very close to the one worn by Atticus, and my suspicion was that Asprenas was doing this precisely because he knew Paullus would react in this way. "You've heard the decision of the Tribunal. However, I want the record to reflect that, should you abide by the terms of this decision, there will be no adverse entry made in your record, and you will resume your post as Primus Pilus of the 8th Legion. Now," his tone was almost gentle, "do you understand the decision of the Tribunal?"

For a matter of a couple heartbeats, it appeared likely that Atticus was going to say "No," but he did not, except instead of answering verbally, he just nodded his head.

Which Paullus clearly was not going to accept, opening his mouth to say something, then Asprenas cut him off before he could, saying, "Let the record reflect that the Primus Pilus has indicated he understands the decision." He paused for a moment, and I understood why when he added, "Do you accept the decision of the Tribunal?"

This was something new, I was sure; or more likely, I thought, this was something Asprenas was doing strictly for Atticus' benefit. As I sat there trying to think through the reason he would do so, a possibility came to me, that this was less of an offer of an avenue for Atticus to appeal than it was a warning; after all, I realized, who would he appeal to if not Augustus? And, given what Atticus had said about a possible reason for the Princeps' displeasure with one of his Primi Pili, it was highly unlikely Atticus would avail himself of this seeming offer.

I had just reached this conclusion when Atticus replied; consequently, I was not surprised when he said, through gritted teeth, "Yes, Tribune. I accept the decision."

"Good." For the first time, Asprenas showed some sort of emotion, and while I had only known him for two days, I was sure there was a fair amount of relief in his expression.

Turning to Paullus, Asprenas inclined his head, reminding me of my earlier thought about the passing of the baton.

Paullus did not seem to appreciate the gesture, however, but he still turned to Atticus and, with a wave of his hand and a simple, "This Tribunal is concluded," it was over.

Before anything else could be said, the senior Tribune leapt to his feet and, in one motion, turned to make a hasty exit, not looking back once, which I supposed was understandable; if I had been soundly defeated in such a thorough manner, I would not cast a last look at the field on which it happened. Secundus lived up to his name by being the next man to follow until only Asprenas was left, giving me the sense he was waiting. Which he was, because once the last of the other Tribunes were out of the room, only Silanus was left, but when Asprenas gave him a look, he leapt to his feet and scurried out the same exit used by the Tribunes. Finally, it was just Atticus, Arruntius, Galens, and me left, the three of us standing as the Primus Pilus sat back down on his chair, trying to absorb all that had taken place.

Asprenas got our attention by clearing his throat again, and again, while his demeanor and tone were nothing like that of Paullus, it nonetheless was as clear a command as if it had come from the Primus Pilus himself when he said, "Would you gentlemen please allow me a private word with your Primus Pilus?"

Nevertheless, both Galens and I looked to Atticus, despite the command from Asprenas, but he waved a hand, saying, "Go back to your quarters. I'll meet you there."

We naturally obeyed, except when Arruntius turned to leave as well, Asprenas stopped him with a word, so it was just Galens and I who exited the room. Unsurprisingly, neither of us were willing to speak until we were a good distance away from the building, then we both began talking at the same time, arguing over what just happened, and more importantly, what it meant.

Finally, Galens concluded, "We're not going to know until the Primus Pilus gets back."

I understood this to be the truth, so when we got to our quarters, we wasted no time in filling cups for ourselves and settling down to wait.

"It was a warning," Atticus' tone was suitably grim, "from the Princeps."

"And a reminder," interjected Arruntius, "about who truly wields the power in Rome."

It was perhaps a third of a watch later when the Primus Pilus showed up at our quarters along with Arruntius. In what was probably the best indication of the ordeal both of them had just undergone, the instant they were inside our room, Atticus, with our help, shrugged out of his *hamata*, and the way he carelessly threw it on my bed, seemingly oblivious to the marring of his decorations, was most telling. Arruntius did the same with his *toga*, except he was careful about how he draped it over the back of his chair as he settled down at the table, grabbing for the amphora, just beating Atticus to it. But when he poured the first cup, he wordlessly handed it to the Primus Pilus, who accepted it gratefully and gulped it down so quickly Arruntius was not finished pouring his own before Atticus thrust his back out for a refill. Once both of them had fortified themselves, they informed us about what they had learned from Asprenas.

"But why?" Galens asked Atticus, except he did not elaborate, shooting a glance at Arruntius.

"He knows the same things you do." Atticus waved a hand in dismissal of Galens' concern. "I've told him everything I can think of, including that business I told you about."

Knowing he was referring to his stoppage of his messages to the Princeps, there was no need for any more explanation. Meanwhile, Arruntius answered Galens' query with one word, or more accurately, one name.

"Tiberius," Arruntius replied.

"Is the Princeps really that concerned that Tiberius might try and force him to name him as heir?" I asked, and I admit I was skeptical, although I realize now that I based my assumption on what little I had gathered from my limited time in the presence of Augustus' stepson.

"Apparently so," Arruntius answered. "Now," he shrugged, "is Augustus right to be worried? I don't know. But based on what I've heard, I'd say he is."

"So I still don't understand," Galens admitted, looking somewhat embarrassed. "What does any of this have to do with you, Primus Pilus?"

"Honestly, I don't know," Atticus replied, yet as I sat there, I could not help noticing something in the manner of our Primus Pilus that made me believe he was not being forthcoming. Either oblivious to or ignoring my examination, Atticus continued, "But my guess is that he's just being prudent."

"If I'm being honest," Arruntius spoke next, "I've never heard any man who's been whispering about Tiberius claim they heard anything from Tiberius' own lips, treasonous or otherwise. As far as I'm concerned, I think what's happened is that some men began speculating about what *might* happen, and that speculation took on a life of its own. Now," he sighed, "things are so convoluted about who said what and when they said it that it's impossible for the Princeps to know whether they have any substance. So," Arruntius glanced over at Atticus, "as the Primus Pilus says, he's just being cautious."

As I chewed on what was being said, I realized it made sense, as far as it went. Still, there was a part of it that did not add up to me.

"So," I spoke up, "let's say that this is true, that by yanking on the chain of…." I was about to use a term I knew would enrage Atticus, choosing instead to say. "…someone he's trusted in the past, he's sending a warning that he's still the man in power." Turning to Atticus, I asked bluntly, "How does the money come into play?"

While I expected Atticus to react strongly, I anticipated it would be aimed at Augustus; I was wrong.

"That fucking...*cunnus*, that minion, that…" Atticus was so enraged, he actually seemed to lose the capacity for coherent speech, which prompted Arruntius to break in, saying dryly, "The Primus Pilus is referring to our esteemed Senior Tribune." Since the Primus Pilus was still struggling to regain his composure, Galens and I looked to Arruntius for an explanation.

"I suppose," he began, "that you both noticed something…odd, is perhaps the best word, about the Tribunal."

"You mean that it was Asprenas who was really running the Tribunal," Galens beat me to it.

"Exactly." Arruntius nodded, yet before he could say more, I felt compelled to stop him.

"Before you go any further, Tribune," I began, "could you explain something?"

He answered, "If I can."

"If Paullus was only a figurehead to begin with, how the fuck did he get on the Tribunal?"

I saw just by Atticus' reaction he was extremely interested as well, staring at Arruntius intently, and I assumed Galens was of a similar mind, meaning we were all looking at the Tribune, who did look somewhat uncomfortable under the scrutiny of these three men of the lower classes.

However, to his credit, Arruntius did not hesitate in answering, "Because of his name. Or," he amended, "because of his father's name, to be more accurate."

While this made a certain amount of sense, there was another aspect that did not, but before I could bring it up, Atticus beat me to it, asking, "That explains why he was on the Tribunal, but why in Hades was he the Senior Tribune?"

This time, Arruntius did hesitate, and, in fact, looked a bit ashamed as he admitted, "Money."

"Money?" Atticus echoed, looking confused.

While my initial reaction was similar, a sudden thought came to me, and I was sure I had the answer when I ventured, "Let me guess. This was about his *dignitas*, wasn't it? He couldn't stand the thought of not being in charge? So he, what, offered the Princeps a bribe?"

As soon as it left my mouth, I cursed myself, and Arruntius' wince reinforced that I had made a foolish error, while I felt Atticus' eyes turn towards me, although he did not speak.

"Pullus," Arruntius warned with a shake of his head, "that's a very unfortunate choice of words. And I hope you know better than to utter them aloud again. Ever," he spoke emphatically.

"I'm not stupid," I protested, which prompted a snort from Galens, causing me to amend slightly, "At least, I'm not stupid enough to say it again."

"Good," Arruntius replied, then nodded as he confirmed my suspicion. "But essentially, you're correct, despite the unfortunate choice of words. It was about his pride, nothing else. And yes, he offered the Princeps a…" He searched for a word that would not get him in trouble, settling on, "…a fee for the prestige of being Senior Tribune. Although," he thought to add, "he was informed from the very beginning that all decisions regarding the Tribunal were not his to make."

"Asprenas," Galens breathed, but Arruntius only partially agreed.

"About some of the details regarding how the Tribunal was conducted," he said, "but ultimately, the verdict was decided before the Tribunal ever started."

"So you were always going to be found innocent," Galens mused.

This drew a bitter laugh from the Primus Pilus, who shot back, "If you think being beggared in the process is being found innocent, then yes, I suppose so."

Since he brought up the subject of the money, I was moved to ask him, "Speaking of, what are you going to do, Primus Pilus?"

He shot me a bitter, angry look, then seemed to understand it was a natural question, because he shrugged and said, "The only thing I can do. Pay it."

I sensed Galens looking at me, and when I returned it, we communicated silently, because he made a coughing sound before he asked, his tone tentative, "Primus Pilus, does that mean we're going to have to wait here in Rome with you?"

The Primus Pilus stared at Galens, but I thought there was something odd about his expression, as if he was trying to understand what, at least to me, was a simple question. Then, his face cleared, and he nodded, saying softly, "Ah. I understand. You mean, are you going to have to wait for a messenger to go to Siscia, get a draft from my plutocrat, and get back here?"

Galens did not reply verbally, just nodded his head, which prompted Atticus to look, if not uncomfortable, then somewhat cautious as he answered, "Actually, there's some good news on that front. I have funds deposited here that I can use. So," he looked down into his cup as he finished with a forced casual air, "we won't be here for more than two or three more days."

This was certainly good news, yet I could see from Galens' reaction he had barely heard this, his mind still trying to grapple with the seemingly casual way Atticus mentioned producing a sum that was a staggering amount for a man like the Centurion. While it was true that as a Centurion of the First Cohort, Galens made a fair amount of money, not only did this represent five years' worth of wages, as I was learning as Optio, there is a fair amount of an officer's pay that goes back into his Century or Cohort. The idea that the Primus Pilus did not have to scrape together every *sestertius*, take out a loan, or in some other way beggar himself was something I could see troubled my Centurion. Personally, I found it grimly amusing, happy I did not have to go to my father to release that sum of money, because while we had it, there would be no way to do so without it coming to the attention of, if not Augustus, then someone who would waste no time in informing him. The truth was that, unlike Galens, I was not surprised in the least Atticus had access to this level of wealth, reminding me that, as much as most Head Counters loathe the upper classes, for most of them, their fondest dream is to become one of them.

"But tonight," Atticus suddenly slammed a hand down onto the table, "we're going to celebrate!" Turning to Galens and me, for the first time in days, his smile was genuine as he told us, "I'm going to take you country boys out into Rome and show you how a Praetorian debauches!" Only then did he seem to realize the Tribune's presence, and he turned and offered politely, "Of course, you're invited as well, Tribune. Although," he grinned, "I'm afraid that your reputation might suffer irreparable damage."

Rather than be offended, Arruntius laughed, and I saw it was not forced, waving a hand as he said, "I'm sorry, Primus Pilus, I'm afraid I have to decline. But not because of my reputation. I'm just afraid I couldn't keep up!"

For the first time since our arrival, the atmosphere in our quarters was not strained, so that before more than a dozen heartbeats had passed, we were all laughing uproariously, and I am sure it was as much from relief as it was anything humorous.

As it turned out, we did not go out carousing that night; despite the early end to the day, the toll of the previous days had exhausted the Primus Pilus. Being honest, I did not mind, and I knew Galens did not either. However, it also enabled me to be present when there was a knock on the door shortly after dark, which I answered. Standing there was a slave, but even before I read the bronze placard around his neck, I recognized him, having seen him many times in Siscia.

"Master Titus Pullus," the slave, a scrawny specimen with an accent that might have been from somewhere around Syria, and he did not pose my name as a question, "I bring you greetings from…"

"I know who," I interrupted abruptly, feeling Galens' eyes on my back, knowing he would be curious, and I whispered, "No names."

The slave did not reply, verbally at least, just nodding, then produced a small scroll, handing it to me as I moved my body in such a way that it blocked Galens' view of me taking it from the slave, who whispered, "I'm to wait for your reply, and if you accept, the time you will be there."

Unrolling the scroll, I cursed because there was no way I could make out the words in the dim light of the doorway. Sensing my dilemma, the slave whispered the contents of the message which, frankly, did not make me feel much better. The idea that someone who is liable to be tortured was privy to information like this did not make me sanguine that any contact I made with Claudius would be secure. And, in the moment, I felt a bit sheepish I had been so quick to send him a message, especially considering I had never been called before the Tribunal. Even so, at the same time, I did not want to give offense to a man who, if I did not need his help then, might be my only hope in the future. This is my defense for what was about to happen, and it is hard for me to think about doing things differently. Provided, of course, I did not know what was awaiting me. Since I did not, I simply whispered back to the slave I would be arriving at Claudius' villa shortly. Nodding his understanding, the slave simply vanished into the night, leaving me to turn around and come up with an excuse to give Galens about why, not long after we had agreed it was a night for rest, that I was going out.

To his eternal credit, he asked simply, "Is this part of something I don't need to know?"

Despite myself, I had to grin, replying, "Yes, you don't need to know."

He waved one hand at me while grabbing for the amphora with the other, saying only, "Good. I didn't want to share this with you anyway."

Over the years, I have often had cause to wonder how differently things might have turned out if I had not answered the summons from Claudius and agreed to meet with him. Particularly so because my intent was only to thank him for answering my plea for help, and inform him circumstances had changed, so his assistance was no longer needed. Despite my no longer needing his help, neither did I want to burn a possible bridge; honestly, I was quite proud of myself for thinking along these more strategic lines, and I distinctly remember having the fleeting thought that my Avus would have been proud of me for thinking this way. Perhaps it was remembering the first Titus Pullus that occupied not only my thoughts as I made my way from the Campus, but my attention as well, thereby allowing me to be followed, although I would not learn of it this night at least. While it was dark, it was not yet late enough for curfew, making the streets crowded as people either made their way home, or to their favorite *tavernae* or brothel. Of course, this meant that those citizens of Rome who viewed all their fellows as either prey or prospective customers were also out, so I did have the presence of mind to keep one thumb hooked under my Legionary's belt, between my coin purse and the *pugio* we are allowed to wear out and about. Nevertheless, while I retained my sense of awareness for anyone who came within close proximity to me as I walked, it still shames me that it never occurred to me to turn around and at least attempt to determine if I was being followed. I suppose this is just proof that, at heart, I was still a provincial, wandering around Rome without giving any thought to the possibility there were eyes watching me, and these eyes were anything but friendly. Claudius had a villa on the Palatine, and I admit just the idea I would be anywhere near the residence of the Princeps made me nervous. Fortunately, when I followed the directions on the message, I actually only climbed partway up before turning onto a street that followed the contour of the hill, on the southern side. When I reached the villa, the slave who had summoned me was waiting outside to lead me into the courtyard area, the centerpiece of which was a fountain, the water burbling out of the mouth of a fish, while what I assumed were nymphs, satyrs, and the like lounged underneath the waterfall created by nothing more than the pressure of the water arriving from the faraway mountains. If I am being completely forthcoming, I remember more about that fountain than anything else, because I was not there very long. As I was ushered into the *triclinium*, Claudius was there waiting for me, a little older and, frankly, a bit heavier than when he had been one of the Tribunes assigned to the Army of Pannonia. Still, his manner was warm, and he greeted me effusively, offering me wine, which I accepted more out of politeness than any desire.

"Tribune," I began, using his old rank, but he waved me off with a laugh before I got any further.

"Pullus, I'm not a Tribune any longer. Claudius is perfectly acceptable."

"All right, Claudius." I admit the name sounded strange in my mouth without his rank in front of it, or adding some sort of sign of respect for, if not his rank, then his status as man of the patrician class. "I just came to personally thank you for answering my…" I fumbled for the right term, then decided to call it what it was. "…plea for help." I was happy to see him smile at my characterization. "But earlier today, the Tribunal rendered their decision."

"And?"

I believe it was in the way he asked the single-word question that first gave me pause, although I answered readily enough. "The Primus Pilus was found innocent of misusing the Legion and the use of excessive force against the Taurisci." Then I thought to add, "But he does have to pay the man whose farm was destroyed for the damages."

I had no expectation that Claudius would react one way or another, but while his face was impassive, I clearly saw his body stiffen, but all he said was, "Ah. Really? That's…interesting."

Suddenly, I did not want to be there any longer than politeness allowed; there was something in the other man's manner that made me extremely uncomfortable.

This was what prompted me to hurry on. "Yes, it is, I suppose. Anyway, I was never required to testify, and we're leaving Rome the day after tomorrow."

"Back to Siscia, eh?" Claudius' tone and demeanor was hearty, yet there was something that rang false with it to my ears. "I can imagine you'll be happier back there."

"You have no idea," I answered instantly, and with such fervor, I suppose it caused Claudius to forget, at least temporarily, whatever was bothering him enough that he laughed heartily at my eagerness to be shut of Rome.

"Pullus," he was still laughing, "I don't blame you a bit. In fact, there's a part of me that wants nothing more than the simple life with the Legions."

If I had to do it over again, I would have refrained from asking the question that popped out of my mouth. "Then why don't you? We need good Tribunes and Legates with the army."

"Would that I could," Claudius answered without hesitation, "but that's just not possible." Judging by his demeanor, I was not inclined to ask why, yet I seemed to have roused something in him, because he suddenly started pacing about so vigorously that the wine in his cup, which I had instantly noticed was made, at least partially, of gold, sloshed over the rim and splashed onto his expensive tunic, which he did not even seem to notice. "Don't mistake me," he muttered, "I'd be more than happy to do that very thing. But there are…forces," the look he gave me when he uttered the word made me extremely uneasy, "that are keeping me here in Rome. Forces," his otherwise handsome face twisted into an ugly grimace, "that are too powerful to fight. Even," his laugh was bitter, "for men of my status."

Rather than answer or say anything he might construe as either support or interest in what he had to say, I offered, albeit awkwardly, "Yes, well…I just wanted to come and thank you personally for honoring your promise." Then, before he could reply, I stepped closer to him and thrust out my hand, lying, "I'd love to stay longer, but the Primus Pilus and my Centurion are waiting for me." I did manage a grin, along with a wink. "They're waiting for me to start the celebration for the Primus Pilus' exoneration."

If Claudius was offended, he hid it well, accepting my hand and laughing. "I'd love to be a mouse in wherever you're going to be. That would be something to see!"

"I just hope I survive!" I told him, thinking that just because it was not happening tonight, this did not make my sentiment a lie, exactly.

With that, I departed Claudius' villa, although I did tarry for an extra moment to admire his fountain, wondering if I would ever be able to be in a position to have something this exquisite without worrying about the ramifications.

Galens was clearly surprised when I entered our quarters, and I instantly saw he was well on his way to being drunk, causing me to walk over and check the amphora, picking it up and moving it in a circular motion so I could judge by the sloshing sound how much was left of what had been an almost full amphora; it was down to the dregs.

"You've been busy," was my only comment.

Galens glared at me, reminding me that he was a belligerent drunk, reinforced by his almost bellowing, in a voice much louder than was needed to address someone standing a couple paces away, "What do you care? You left me here! What did you expect me to do?"

"Nothing," I assured him, not wanting to inflame him any further; fortunately, he subsided and, in fact, was snoring loudly before I could disrobe and lie down on my own cot.

However, try as I might, I did not follow him; my mind was still going over my conversation with Claudius, except that I cannot say with any real certainty whether my unease stemmed from his words or his manner. While he had certainly not said anything objectionable, I could not shake the feeling that it was more his manner that was untoward than anything he actually said, yet I could no more take a firm grasp in my mind of why I felt this way than I could tackle a column of smoke. Nonetheless, despite my inner turmoil, I obviously fell asleep, because when the time slave came and rapped on the door as the signal to rouse us, I jerked awake so violently that I fell out of my cot. Which, as one might expect, Galens thought was quite funny, although his good humor did not last long as he winced at the stab of pain in his head.

"That's what you get for laughing," I mumbled as I sheepishly pulled myself off the floor.

"Shut up," he growled, massaging both temples with his fingertips as he glared at me. It was easy to see he was considering whether or not to bring up the night before, and I was hoping he would decide not to do so; it was a forlorn one, as he demanded, "So. Where did you go last night?"

I considered for a moment as I made my cot, trying to determine the best course of action, then finally turned and asked him bluntly, "Are you sure you want to know?"

"I might as well," he replied instantly, which told me he had actually been thinking about this. "Since there's no telling how and when it might bite you in your ass."

This, I had to admit, was a likely outcome; if only I had known how soon that very thing would happen, and how much trouble it would cause me, I might have made a different decision, both in telling Galens and visiting Claudius in the first place.

"Right after we met with Arruntius the first time," I began at last, "I went and met with Macrianus and the others we met that day at the Temple of Venus Genetrix. "That," I could not help grinning at my Centurion as I added, "was the *first* time you asked me if you wanted to know what I was up to."

When I paused to frame my thoughts, Galens interjected, "Is that who you went to see last night?"

Shaking my head, I answered, "No. That first night it was to give Macrianus a message to deliver to someone else. It was that man I met with last night."

"And?" he pressed. "Who was this man it was so important to see?"

"Do you remember the other Tribune who was with us?" I answered indirectly. "I mean, back with Urso and all that mess?"

He nodded, but then he had to think for a moment before he answered, "You mean…Claudius? Wasn't that his name? I mean," he added hastily, "I assume you mean one of the Tribunes who actually did something worth a brass *obol*."

This prompted a laugh from me, and I confirmed, "Yes, that's the one. The man who knocked Paullus out."

"Every once in a while, we get a Tribune who's actually not as useless as tits on a man," Galens agreed, albeit in a roundabout way, then shook his head. "But why would you need to meet with him?"

Taking a deep breath on the fly, I decided to be fully forthcoming with Galens, going on to explain the connection between the Claudius family and my own, and how the former Tribune had approached me in Siscia with his offer of assistance whenever I should need it.

Shrugging, I finished by simply saying, "And I thought I'd need his help after what Arruntius told me about being a symbol."

Galens' retort was one I would have cause to remember, and think about, at length when he grumbled, "I wish I had someone like that to watch my back."

As I was about to learn, Galens was actually the lucky one between the two of us, because my association with Claudius did not turn out to be beneficial for me at all.

The first hint of what was about to befall me came not long after we were roused by the slave, whereupon we quickly completed our daily routine of preparing for the coming day. What was on our schedule was to accompany Atticus to the Forum, where he would hand over the marker to the farmer Manius Fusus to fulfill the judgment of the Tribunal that he compensate the man for his loss. Not lost on either Galens or me was how it took our Primus Pilus all of one day to gather what was a huge sum, by anyone's standard. I vividly recall the thought that made me shudder, how my own father would have reacted at the news that, out of our fortune, which even now is somewhere in the neighborhood of a million *sesterces*, he would have to produce such a sum. And yet, the fact that Atticus did not have to send to Siscia for the funds was telling; he obviously had left a substantial sum behind here in Rome, which made me wonder about how much Praetorians got paid. It is certainly the case they are well compensated, and he was a Centurion of Praetorians when he was selected for the office of Primus Pilus; still, I was sure he was using more than just his salary that he had managed to save up. Atticus had informed us we would not need to be in uniform nor be armed since he was not actually handing over the bullion but the marker Fusus would take to whatever plutocrat the Primus Pilus used here in Rome, so honestly, there was not much for us to do to get ready. In fact, we were sitting at the table when there was another knock on the door, except this time, it was louder than normal, making both of us jump up from our respective chairs.

"This," Galens opined, "is getting old." Being the junior man, he naturally expected me to go to the door, and as I did, he asked, "I don't suppose you're expecting anyone?"

I only shook my head in answer, walking across the room to open the door, but while the fact that it was the Primus Pilus was not altogether surprising, nor was the fact that Arruntius was standing beside him, seeing the two other men clad in full uniform, wearing the blue tunic and matching crest of the Praetorians, rocked me to my core.

"Primus Pilus?" I asked, and I heard the uncertainty I was feeling in my voice, yet I pulled the door open nonetheless. "Is there something wrong?"

"We're about to find out," he said grimly as he stepped past me to enter the room.

Arruntius followed, except when the Praetorians made to enter, it was Atticus who spun about and snapped an order to wait outside. For a long moment, it appeared as if they did not intend to obey, but when he stood there, glaring at them, they remained outside, and I closed the door.

Without engaging in any pleasantries, or even acknowledging the sudden entrance, Atticus spun about and pointed a finger directly at me, demanding, "Pullus, where did you go last night?"

If his goal was to catch me off-balance, he did a wonderful job of it, my body reacting before my mind with a sudden gush of sweat I could feel, cool and clammy on my brow. My first instinct was to lie and say I had gone to see Macrianus, or even that I had gone to a whorehouse, but between Galens' warning glare from his spot, behind both Atticus and Arruntius, and my realization how unlikely it was he was asking without already knowing the answer, I decided on the truth. At least, a version of it.

"I went to see one of our old Tribunes; you probably remember him." I tried to sound casual. "Claudius?" I at least attempted to make my shrug not too elaborate. "He heard I was here in Rome, and I just went to pay my respects."

Deciding this was as far as I would go, I shut my mouth, while Atticus considered what I said. Not, I saw with some alarm, that he seemed disposed to accept my seemingly nonchalant explanation.

However, he surprised me considerably when he did not respond, at least to me; instead, he turned to Arruntius, giving what seemed to be a grim nod, as if my words confirmed his fears, saying, "You were right."

"Right about what?" I blurted out the question, looking over at the Tribune, who was regarding me impassively. "What's wrong with going to see someone I know?"

"Nothing," Arruntius was the one who said this, but my relief was short-lived as he added, with what sounded like a tinge of bitterness to my ears, "and everything."

"Fuck." That it was the Primus Pilus who muttered this did not help my frame of mind, although when he turned and without another word pointed to one of the chairs at the table, naturally, I obeyed and took the one to which he had pointed.

Once I was seated, he wasted no time, telling me, "Pullus, I won't lie. This isn't good news we're bringing. Your…visit," I cannot say I cared for the way he inflected what was an otherwise innocent word, "to this man Claudius was noticed."

"By who?" I demanded, then somehow sensing he was not the right man to ask, I turned and confronted Arruntius, "And why? What does it matter who I see?"

Perhaps it was in the way the Tribune, who I had come to at least respect, did not meet my gaze when he muttered, "It depends on who it is. And," this was when he did meet my gaze, "what it's for."

Before I could make any comment, Atticus broke in, "Pullus, you were followed last night."

"By who?" I repeated as they looked at each other.

Finally, Arruntius asked with a sigh, "Does it matter, Pullus? Do you deny meeting with Claudius?"

"No," I answered cautiously, "but I think it matters a great deal who reported my visit to someone."

"Who do you think it was? It had to be that cross-eyed *cunnus* Dolabella!"

Not only did this outburst from Galens clearly shock both the Primus Pilus and the Tribune, it also gave me the answer, because there was no mistaking the sudden look of, if not guilt, then at least shock on the faces of both men that my Centurion had clearly guessed correctly.

"Is that true?" I addressed Atticus, believing I had a better chance of getting the truth from him than from the Tribune.

"Yes."

At least Atticus did not disappoint my belief, although the fact that it came from him made it no less disturbing.

"And what the fuck was he doing following me?" I asked bitterly.

"Why do you think, you fucking idiot?" Again, it was Galens who interjected, going on, "You basically made him eat *cac* because he's such a fucking coward." Pointing an accusing finger at me for emphasis, he went on, "You had to make sure he knew that, and now he got his revenge!"

As much as it angered me, I also was honest enough with myself to recognize this as nothing more than the truth, however bitter it may have been. Still, it did not explain one thing.

"All right," I admitted, "so I rubbed his nose in it. And I did visit Claudius. What does that matter? Why is meeting with him such a bad thing that it brings both of you here?"

They exchanged a glance, then I saw Atticus dip his head, which Arruntius seemed to take as a signal that he be the one to explain.

"Do you remember our conversation?" was how he began, "about you being a symbol to certain men in Rome?"

"Yes, I remember," I assured him, trying to stem the sudden rush of panic that felt like a black, surging flood akin to the one that almost overwhelmed me the night Domitius and I had been isolated from the rest of our comrades.

"Well," Arruntius explained, "Claudius, or more accurately, his father, is one of those 'certain men.' In fact, he's suspected of being one of the prime conspirators in trying to convince Tiberius to march on Rome."

I cannot say how, yet somehow, I managed from either fainting, vomiting or, worst of all, both.

"I didn't know any of that!" I gasped, taking bare comfort in the fact that I was seated. "How could I have been aware of any of this?"

"That," Arruntius replied grimly, "is what the Princeps wants to know."

Honestly, it took at least a dozen normal heartbeats before his words sank in; I was still trying to cope with what I had been told before this. Then, his last words seemed to penetrate, making me realize that, if I had been concerned before, it was a pale shadow to the terror I felt now; except as I was about to discover, this was just the surface of my fear.

"Which is why we've been ordered to bring you to him," Atticus' tone was a match for that of the Tribune, and I took some comfort in the fact that he looked distraught, although I was sure it was nowhere near my current state. "He wants to ask you some questions."

I do not know how and, honestly, I do not remember saying anything at all, but Galens told me later that I somehow managed, "At least that explains why the Praetorians came with you."

Chapter 6

I wish I could say I remember much of the walk from the Campus, past the Septa Julia and Pantheon, although what I do remember is that we did not go the most direct route, which would have taken us through the heart of the Forum. Instead, we circled around the other side of Capitoline, which took us through the Porticus of Octavia, dedicated to the sister of the Princeps, where there are small temples to Jupiter Stator and Juno Regina. Walking through the heart of the Velabrum, what I do remember is the stench of the Forum Boarium, and of course, the bustle of all the people moving about their business. Otherwise, my mind was occupied with my immediate future, and I wondered if I was taking my last breaths as a free man; or my last breaths at all. Surely, I thought to myself, just the fact that I met with a man who might have been under suspicion was not enough reason to punish me, yet regardless of my insistence, another part of my mind kept reminding me of who I was, and more importantly, whose name I bore. Therefore, perhaps I can be forgiven for the morbid turn my thoughts took, as I wondered if, at long last, Augustus would be able to even an old score. Of course, that depended on how much he knew about my family's true circumstances, although I felt certain that, by this time, he knew everything. How many times had I heard the old saw about when a sparrow fell in the Forum, Augustus knew of its death before it hit the paving stones? I wondered bitterly.

To take my mind off my predicament, I turned to Galens, who had insisted he accompany us despite Atticus' growled warning not to do so, thanking him for his support.

"Support?" He grinned at me. "I'm not here to support you! I just want the chance to see the old boy's house!"

As I know he intended, this made me laugh, temporarily forgetting my troubles, yet I could not resist the urge to get a measure of revenge, and I told him, "Oh, I'll make sure you do! I plan on telling him how you were the one who led me astray in the first place!"

I felt a stab of guilt at the way the color fled from his face as he looked at me, wide-eyed, trying to determine if I was serious, but it was more of a pinprick than a real stab, and I could not refrain from laughing.

"You bastard," he grumbled. "That wasn't funny."

"Yes, it was," I countered, then before I could say another word, a strong hand grabbed my arm on the opposite side of Galens, and I turned to see Atticus glaring at me.

"Pullus, this is fucking serious," he said, but it was the intensity of his tone more than the words that wiped the smile from my face as if it had never been there. "I don't know exactly what Dolabella told the Princeps, but from the way it sounds, you need to gather your wits before you stand tall in front of Augustus."

Realizing he was right, I thought to ask him, "You know him, Primus Pilus. You've been around him. Tell me how I should handle this."

"First, don't think you're more clever than he is," he answered instantly, "because you're not. Nobody is." Pausing to think, he added, "And always keep in mind one thing. When he asks you a question, you can be sure he already knows the answer beforehand. He's just testing you to see if you can be trusted." He turned to look up into my eyes, and for the first time, I was sure I saw a true sense of sympathy and concern for me in the expression of my Primus Pilus and, frankly, this scared me more than anything. Atticus finished just as we began the ascent of the Palatine with, "And be sure and tell him the truth. Even if you think it's going to anger him."

Swallowing hard, I countered, "And what if I do that, and he does get angry? What then?"

"Then," he snorted, although I could not tell if it was a laugh, "you're fucked." He must have realized how this sounded, or perhaps he saw something in my face, because he reached up and patted me on the shoulder and said quietly, "I'll be there with you, Pullus."

This surprised me; before this, he had not mentioned he would be there as well, but when I looked down at him, he refused to meet my gaze. Then, we reached the sprawling house on the Palatine, where there were two men who could have been the twins of the pair of Praetorians who had escorted us, shoving the civilians who moved too slowly out of our path. One of our escorts broke away and trotted ahead to where the pair were standing, exchanging a few words with them, jerking his thumb at us as we approached. Reaching the entrance, both Galens and Arruntius were stopped by the guards, so I turned to offer Galens my hand, trying to think of something witty to say, except my mouth was too dry. Instead, I contented myself with a nod, which he returned as we clasped arms.

"Pullus," he said quietly, "don't do…"

"I know," I finally managed to croak. "I won't do anything stupid."

Turning away, I was in for one more surprise, albeit a bit more pleasant, considering the moment, when Arruntius actually offered his own hand.

"Optio, I'm sure everything will be all right. The Princeps is a wise man, and he knows Rome needs men like you under the standard."

Honestly, I was so surprised that I just managed to mumble something completely unmemorable, feeling a sudden rush of heat to my face. Then, Atticus and I entered what is ostensibly a private residence, but is in fact, the true seat of government for the most powerful nation on this earth. Acutely cognizant of this, I made an effort to quell the growing sense of panic, choosing to do so by studying the villa itself as we entered. There is a quite long hallway leading to the entrance vestibule, the walls painted in gold and bordered in a long rectangular shape with red. Atticus and I marched behind the Praetorian, the same man who had escorted us and was now our guide, and the echo of our hobnails on the floor, which in this entrance is still made of close fitting paving stone, was quite loud. The better to hear someone coming, I remember thinking, wondering if this was indeed the purpose. Then we reached the vestibule, whereupon the Praetorian took first a left turn, past an intersecting hallway, down which I could see several doors on each side, before making a right. Directly ahead of us was a single door, although it looked wider and taller than normal, for which I was thankful since it meant I did not have to duck my head as I normally did.

"Wait here," the Praetorian directed, pointing to the floor.

Then, without waiting to see if we obeyed, he continued to the door, knocking softly in what, to my ears at least, sounded like a prearranged signal of two knocks, followed by a brief pause, then another three.

"That lets the Princeps know who it is," Atticus muttered under his breath, confirming my suspicion.

There was a muffled response, then the Praetorian opened the door, but only just enough for him to slip through, without allowing either of us to see into the office.

"That's another trick of his," Atticus whispered, then with an urgency brought on by the lack of time, he continued, "Now, remember. I'll start the talking, but once it's your turn, just be honest. Understood?"

I could only nod, which was good because the door opened abruptly, and the Praetorian beckoned.

"The Princeps will see you now," he informed us, then stepped aside just enough to let us pass through, and I wondered where the Praetorian would be while we had our audience.

Probably outside, waiting for Augustus to call him and drag me off under arrest, I thought dismally. Thankfully, before my mind could dwell on this delightful prospect, my body reacted from the years of habit, and I believe there was no outward hesitation as I smartly marched in behind my Primus Pilus, who crossed the length of the room to snap to *intente* in front of it. Actually, things were happening so quickly at this point, I did not have time to do anything other than what my body knew how to do as I followed Atticus, then stepped to his left, precisely aligned with him, locking myself at *intente,* and staring at the wall behind the desk.

"Primus Pilus Gaius Sempronius Atticus and Optio of the Sixth Century, First Cohort, Titus Porcinianus Pullus, reporting as directed by the Princeps," Atticus rapped out.

And there I was, within arm's reach of the man who not only controlled the destiny of my Avus and his family, but of every soul throughout what is just now being called the Empire of Rome, both citizen and subject. There was a sudden roaring sound in my ears that made it difficult to hear, and it took all of my willpower to keep my gaze on the wall, which I noticed was predominantly red instead of gold, although the red was a deeper, richer tone than the hallway. And painted in the direct middle of the wall, immediately behind Augustus' back, was a picture of a window, with the outdoor scene depicting a lush garden landscape in the middle of it, giving the impression that one was looking outside and not at a wall. It was stunningly lifelike, and I experienced the absurd desire to reach out and actually touch the wall, just to make sure it was, in fact, a painting. Fortunately, I was saved from myself by the Princeps.

"Primus Pilus Atticus," Augustus began, but he only returned our salute with a nod and not with one of his own, while I used the corner of my vision to see when Atticus brought his arm down in acknowledgment, so I did as well. "Considering that we talked just yesterday, I hope you'll forgive me when I spend most of my time talking to your Optio."

Describing this moment is somewhat difficult, because honestly, I was still staring so hard at the spot on the wall, I just barely could see the Princeps. In fact, the only thing I could make out at this point was that his blonde hair was now almost completely silver, although he was not balding like Divus Julius had been. The only other thing I could tell was that he had turned his face to study me, which in turn caused my heart to start fluttering so violently I was sure he could see my tunic jumping about, and I really wished we had worn our armor, except not just to hide my beating heart, but protect it as well.

"Titus Pullus." His voice concealed his age more than revealed it; at least, to my ears, he sounded like a much younger man than someone in his sixties. What confused me more than anything, though, was the way he said my name, with a kind of melancholy, bittersweet note, which was when it came to me; he was not uttering my name, but that of the man to whom it first belonged. "Looking at you, it's as if I was suddenly your age, or even younger, and it's your grandfather standing there."

Before I could stop myself, I felt my head drop slightly, as did my eyes, and there are no words to convey how powerful the feeling of shock was that coursed through my body at what I saw. He was an old man! Here was the man, under whose statue I once stood as a ten-year-old boy, swearing I would have vengeance on him for the injustice he had perpetrated against my Avus, and now that he was within arm's reach, I saw Augustus, the man. Not the Princeps, the Imperator, the Caesar who is always depicted as eternally youthful, never aging, but a man with a wrinkled, seamed face and bad teeth. That, however, was not the most shocking aspect to what I saw in my first glance; his eyes, which had supposedly been a vivid blue that men like my Avus swore were twins to those of Divus Julius, were now rheumy, with the yellowish cast that many old people have, but more than that, they were glistening with tears! Augustus was on the verge of crying, just because of my resemblance to my Avus, I thought with such a muddle of emotions, I still cannot say which one predominated.

Still, he must have seen something in my face, because he chuckled softly and waved a hand as he said, "And here you are, seeing an old man in front of you, wondering where the real Augustus is, neh? He must be using me as a substitute for such mundane matters. That's what you're probably thinking, neh?"

He stopped then, and it took a couple heartbeats for me to realize he was expecting me to answer.

"N-no, sir," I finally managed, inwardly wincing at how awkward I sounded. "I mean, that's not it, sir." Except when I tried to frame exactly what I *had* been thinking, I realized he was, in fact, correct, and I suppose Atticus' admonition was still fresh enough that I corrected myself and said, "Actually, that is it, sir. It's just that I've seen your statues, and, well…"

"I never get old, do I?" he finished for me, his tone wry and amused.

"No, sir," I agreed.

"Well, if I didn't know better myself, I'd swear that I was looking at Camp Prefect Titus Pullus," he said genially, still seated, although he had leaned back to examine me better. "Although you're him as a young man, before he became Camp Prefect. How old are you, Pullus?" he asked abruptly.

"Twenty-five, sir," I answered, while I thought to myself and prayed to the gods that I made it to twenty-six.

"Ah." He nodded his head. "Well I hadn't met your grandfather when he was that age. He was already the Primus Pilus of the 10th." The way he clipped the name of the Legion made me think he caught himself and omitted the Equestris nickname, but I could have been imagining it. Going on, he mused, "It was after…Munda, I believe. Yes." He nodded. "That's right. He'd been wounded, quite badly. Did you know that?"

"Yes, sir," I answered, then before he could delve into how I had known this, I made up a lie, saying, "His best friend Sextus Scribonius was my tutor as a child, and he told me about it."

Augustus did not react in a way that indicated he suspected anything, simply nodding and saying, "Yes, I remember Scribonius. Not quite as tall as your grandfather, but very lean. And a good Centurion. But your grandfather," he shook his head, "would have died if it hadn't been for my father. Did you know that, Pullus?"

I admit that, for an instant, he had thrown me, which was doubly inexcusable, since I claimed my status as grandson in the same way Augustus claimed his own status as son of Divus Julius.

Fortunately, I managed to recover quickly enough and reply, "Yes, sir. I mean," I added hastily, "I don't know the details, but I know that Divus Julius was involved."

"Oh, he was more than involved." The older man's tone turned severe, as if he was scolding me like a child, which made me uneasy. "He sent his personal physician to minister to your grandfather. The man never left your grandfather's bedside! It was quite a close-run thing. But your grandfather was nothing if he wasn't strong."

Pursing his lips, he shook his head, and the way he did so deepened my concern, while at the same time, the thought flashed through my mind of how differently the upper classes thought, where just making sure my Avus was attended by a competent physician was enough, at least to Augustus, to give his adopted father the actual credit for saving my Avus' life, not the physician who did the actual work. Thankfully, this example of upper class thinking also put me on my guard.

"In fact," now the smile was gone as if it had never been, and there was a sudden coolness in the rheumy blue eyes that reminded me of the way my Avus had described the Princeps once, as reptilian, "he wasn't just physically strong. He was quite headstrong and prone to doing things his own way." Reaching out, he picked up a scroll, just one of many on his desk, and unrolled it, while I immediately noticed he did so in such a way there was no way I could see it. He examined it, or pretended to for a moment, before lifting his eyes and asking me, "Do you know about our...history? Between your grandfather and me?"

Just that quickly, in the amount of time it took for him to utter these words, I was suddenly standing on the edge of a precipice, one that was crumbling underneath me so rapidly I barely had time to think about the best way to save myself, which I am sure was his intention.

"I know that he served Rome, faithfully and well," I cannot say how I managed to sound as cool as I did, "and that his name is revered throughout the Legions. Not a day goes by where I'm not told by some veteran that my grandfather was the greatest Legionary they ever saw."

More than Augustus' reaction, I was informed by how Atticus stiffened, despite the fact that he was still at *intente*, that I would be in for a tongue-lashing from him after this, provided of course that I survived. The Princeps, however, simply sat back, regarding me for a long moment without saying anything, but when he did speak, what he said was completely unexpected.

"Primus Pilus," he still spoke quietly, without a trace of emotion, "would you please wait outside? I wish to speak to Optio Pullus alone for a bit."

As surprising as this was, Atticus' reaction shocked me to my core, because he did not move, at least at first.

"Princeps," he began, speaking carefully, as he should have, "I just want to say that although Optio Pullus may let his mouth run too much sometimes, he is a good man..."

"Have I suggested that I believe otherwise?" Augustus interrupted, but while the volume of his voice was the same level, one would had to have been deaf to miss the warning in it. Before Atticus could reply, he continued, "While I appreciate your display of loyalty to one of your subordinates, Atticus, given your recent…difficulties, do you really think refusing my request is wise?"

I heard the Primus Pilus expel a breath that sounded as if he had been punched in the stomach, which, in the moment, I believed was an apt comparison. Regardless, let me be clear; I did not then, nor do I now fault my Primus Pilus for withdrawing from what ultimately was my battle, not his. Particularly given, as the Princeps had pointed out, he had so recently extricated himself from his own difficulties. Saluting again, Atticus executed an about-turn, and I heard his heavy footsteps cross the part of the floor covered with a carpet, then reach the portion next to the door that was bare mosaic. As one might expect, the hinges of the door were well oiled, so there was no real sound as he opened it, then exited the room. The Princeps did not speak as Atticus left, choosing instead to regard me with his gaze, and since I did not hear the door close, I cannot say how long this silence lasted, but finally, he resumed speaking.

"You know," his tone was conversational, yet his eyes never left me as he said, "I actually think about your grandfather quite often now." Since it was not clear to me whether or not he was expecting some sort of comment, I remained silent, and what might have been an expression of irritation flashed across his wrinkled face, although he continued, "He was a remarkable man, Pullus, and the gods know that he was loyal to my father." After he said this, he paused as he pierced me with his gaze, and I understood why when he said, "Unfortunately, I never felt that same sense of loyalty your grandfather showed to Divus Julius, and I admit, during those years, I wasn't as…secure in my position as I am today. And, over the last few years, I've come to realize that I perhaps …overreacted with your grandfather."

He stopped then, except his eyes stayed on me, giving me the strong feeling he was gauging the impact his words were having on me, but honestly, at that moment, I was more concerned with remaining vertical, the sensation caused by his words being so strong I actually felt dizzy. Am I hearing this right? I wondered. Is Augustus apologizing for how he treated the first Titus Pullus? In some ways, I was fortunate because it would not take much longer for me to understand that, like so many men have learned over the years, Augustus' purposes are clear only to him, and are always with a goal that is obscured to everyone else, and this conversation was no exception.

Whether he saw my confused state and this was the sign he was looking for, or he was going to go ahead no matter what my demeanor, I have no idea; all I do know with any certainty is that he said, "That's why I've allowed your family to retain the wealth that your grandfather accumulated. Which," he acknowledged with a smile that struck me as more embarrassed than humorous, "I freely admit did escape my attention for some time. Much of the credit for that goes to your freedman." He thought for a moment, then came up with, "Diocles, was it?" I nodded, and he went on, "Yes, he was very shrewd with his investments. And," his wrinkled mouth quirked in what I suppose was a small smile at his own wit, "I did have other matters on my mind that were a bit...weightier. However, by the time I learned this, despite my confiscation of what I had been informed was the bulk of Titus Pullus' wealth, much had changed, for both of us, I suppose. As I said, it's been many years now since I've had to worry about men trying to bring me down to advance their own ends, ignoring what's best for Rome." His entire face twisted then, the vertical lines of his face deepening as he grimaced, presumably at the thought of those he saw as rank opportunists, worried more about their personal ambitions than the good of Rome. Apparently, it took some effort on his part to regain control of himself, yet soon enough, his demeanor had returned to the same flat and seemingly uninvolved visage, as if he was discussing the number of chickpeas contained in a barrel. "Nevertheless," he continued, "while I'm not inclined to do anything about your family and their situation, much depends upon you, Optio."

Of course, I almost said this aloud, and it took a huge effort for me to keep my face from reflecting the bitterness I felt as I realized that, naturally, this largesse from the Princeps was not going to be free. Still, I suppose I managed to exact a tiny revenge, because I steadfastly refused to say a word, forcing him to continue talking, which he seemed to realize as he heaved a sigh, then asked patiently, "Would you like to know what it is I require of you, Pullus?"

"Not particularly," I blurted out; apparently, the look of horror that must have crossed my face at my intemperate honesty, rather than angering the Princeps, seemed to amuse him a great deal, as for the first time, he actually laughed aloud.

In fact, he obviously considered my reaction so humorous that he seemed consumed with mirth, his whole body shaking with the rumbling sound that, frankly, started to alarm me, because to my ears, he sounded as if he was wheezing, reminding me that when he was younger, he had been afflicted with breathing problems. And, just for a moment, I was accosted by the peculiar feeling that came from the thought he might actually keel over, dead, except the happy relief at this idea was instantly swept away by the knowledge that, if that happened, nothing would save me. However, he managed to regain control of himself and remain in the land of the living, wiping away the tears from his wrinkled face.

"You," he finally managed, "are definitely the grandson of Titus Pullus." Shaking his head, the smile remained, but I once more had the feeling that his mind had gone back to wherever it had been earlier, as he continued, "He had a habit of saying the first thing that popped into his mind as well. Actually," Augustus looked back up at me, "that honesty is refreshing, Pullus, at least now. I can't say I found it amusing back in your grandfather's day, but now, I'm surrounded by sycophants, flatterers, all manner of men whose only goal is to tell me what they think will work to their advantage. So I have to admit that it's nice to have someone who doesn't guard their tongue very well and is honest." Then, as quickly as it came, the good humor vanished, while the look he gave me was once more tinged with ice. "However, that kind of honesty can be dangerous as well, and not just to you, but to Rome." He picked the scroll back up from where he had dropped it; at least, I assumed it was the same one, except there were so many on his desk, it was hard to be sure. Abruptly changing the subject, again, which I was determining was a tactic he favored, and I drew some comfort from my recognition, he at least seemed to read from the scroll. "Last night, you made a visit to a man here in Rome, someone whose...activities are of interest to me." He looked up to pin me with his stare, and when he did, I would swear on the black stone the rheum was no longer visible, that all I saw was the icy blue gaze that seemed to transfix me as surely as if I had been pierced with a javelin. "You know to whom I'm referring, I'm sure."

Of course I did, but I suppose it was a reflex action that caused me to ask, "Do you mean Claudius?"

"Yes, Pullus, I mean Claudius," the Princeps replied patiently. Leaning back in his chair, he continued staring at me as he asked, "What did you two talk about?"

"I was just renewing our acquaintance," I answered, but it was more to stall for time than any real hope he would be satisfied with this half-truth.

Or half-lie, the thought flashed through my mind, and naturally, he was not so easily put off.

"Really?" Tilting his head as he said this, I was reminded of reading in my Avus' account how, when he was still known more commonly as Gaius Octavius, in the aftermath of the murder of Divus Julius, he had perfected some of his adoptive father's mannerisms, and this was one of them. "That's all? Because," once more, he consulted the scroll, "according to the report I have here," he shook the scroll, "the amount of time you spent there at his villa would suggest that you did more than just drop by to say hello."

Making an instant decision not to try and prolong what I was, and still am sure was the inevitable, I told Augustus, "I'd sent him a message, asking for his help when I thought I might need it. So, when it turned out I wouldn't need his help, I decided I still needed to meet with him personally to thank him."

Although I had no real expectation it would happen, I still felt a pang of disappointment and concern when the Princeps asked, "Help for what, exactly, Pullus?" I did not answer immediately, trying to come up with an explanation that would not put me into even more difficulty, yet before I could, he held up a hand, "Wait. I can see you're hesitating, but rather than protract your discomfort, allow me to guess." Naturally, I was not going to object either way; I also had a morbid curiosity about how accurate his "guess" would be. As I was about to learn, I should not have been, as he said, "I can imagine that your concern was whether or not you were somehow a target of this Tribunal. Given your relationship to Prefect Pullus, and our…history." He allowed a small smile, but when he went on to say in such an offhanded manner, it was impossible to miss how contrived it was. "And, of course, that there are men who view you, through your status as the heir of Titus Pullus, as a symbol of sorts. A symbol," suddenly, the coolness in his eyes spread to the rest of his face, and I was sure there was more than a hint of anger in his voice as he continued, "that would be used by unscrupulous men to convince my stepson that he would have the support of the Legions, thereby inducing him to act in an…intemperate manner." Suddenly, a subtle but unmistakable change came over his features, which seemed to me to contain a vestige of sadness, mixed in with his anger. "And there's the other matter between us. As I'm sure you know, Tiberius is not only my stepson, he's my son-in-law, although that's about to change."

Whatever I had seen an instant before was washed away by the clearly visible anger that returned, and I noticed in the moment he had actually picked up yet another scroll, which he was twisting in his hand while his mind went wherever it was. He paused then and returned his attention back to me, I suppose studying me to see how I was absorbing this lesson in how, when all is said and done, Augustus does know everything that happens in Rome. Obviously, he was referring to the matter with his daughter Julia and her infidelity with the son of Marcus Antonius, which I have deliberately not mentioned, nor do I intend to, and I concentrated on keeping any hint of my knowledge of the gossip from my face. Meanwhile, his voice lost some of its edge, and I would like to think he felt some sort of pity for me as, in a lapse that was as horrifying as it was unavoidable, I reached out to grab the edge of his desk to avoid toppling over, not from the impending divorce of a member of the upper class, but from what had preceded it.

"Ah," he nodded as his eyes went to my white-knuckled grasp, "I see that I've made a good…guess." The Princeps again smiled at his own jest, although it did not last long as he confirmed what I realized was, ultimately, the truth of the matter of my visit to Claudius. "And the man you visited last night is one of the conspirators in this…misguided attempt to convince a good man to go astray. Now," he folded his hands, and asked me, "did Claudius mention any of this to you? Or did he give you the impression that there was more he wished to discuss with you, other than the Tribunal?"

In retrospect, I am glad I had not relinquished my grasp of his desk, as the import of his last question hit me with all the force of a punch square to my gut. How had he known this was the very thing we had talked about? Was it just an educated guess? After all, I reasoned in the fraction of a heartbeat before I knew an answer was expected, this was certainly a reasonable assumption, and did not necessarily mean Claudius was being spied on in his very own *triclinium*. In that instant, a fragment of memory flashed through my mind's eye; had the slave who poured the wine lingered longer than one might expect? In fact, had he left the room at all?

"Not really," I replied slowly, still trying to think through the details of my conversation with my former Tribune.

I wish I could say my decision to essentially betray a man who had only offered to help me was either difficult, or that it took me longer than the amount of time it takes to draw a couple of breaths, but it did not. And perhaps it is a rationalization, yet I did not see where I had much choice, particularly now that the Princeps had demonstrated how much he already knew.

This was what prompted me to add, "But he did act…surprised, I suppose, when I informed him that the Primus Pilus had been exonerated."

"That's no wonder," Augustus smiled grimly, "since that wasn't how it was supposed to go." Obviously seeing my expression, he held up a hand. "It's not how it sounds, Pullus. I never had any intention of allowing the Primus Pilus to be found guilty. However, Claudius, and others," his mouth twisted, "thought they would be clever, and mark the dice by putting one of their own as Senior Tribune. They were sure the man would be able to force the others to go his way."

"Paullus?" I gasped, completely forgetting myself. "But Claudius and Paullus hate each other!" Shaking my head, I insisted, "I'm sorry, Princeps, but I've seen the two of them together, when they were in Pannonia."

"I didn't say they cared for each other, Pullus," the Princeps replied dryly, then shrugged and added, "but this is politics. Not friendship. And," he said casually, "my information is that your friend Claudius was opposed to Paullus' inclusion and argued that it should be someone else."

"But…why?" I felt as if I had been thrown overboard into stormy waters and was doing my best to just stay afloat. "How does a vote of *Condemno* for the Primus Pilus help their cause?"

"Because I'd be blamed," Augustus replied frankly. "And they'd use it as proof that I no longer had the best interests of the Legions in mind. And," he pointed at me, "there's you and what you represent. They were counting on two things, Pullus. The first was a guilty verdict for your Primus Pilus. The second," now he began wagging that finger at me, and despite the fact that it was Augustus doing so, I felt the stirring of the same anger I always experience when this gesture is aimed in my direction, although the irritation did not last long when he said, "is that they were counting on you, Pullus. They were counting on you living up to the reputation of not just your grandfather, but *you*, to do or say something…rash. You do know," Augustus added, "that despite your youth, you've already garnered a reputation as a hothead, don't you? Just like the man for whom you're named?"

How does one respond to that? I wondered. It would have been a lie if I said I was not, but the fact that my impulsive nature had reached the attention of the Princeps was an acutely uncomfortable sensation.

That was what prompted me to admit, "I do know that, sir." I could not help a sheepish grin as I said, "And yes, I know that it comes from my grandfather. My parents always reminded me about it."

"As they should have," he replied severely, and honestly, I could not argue that, even if it had not been Augustus who said it. Continuing, he said, "They were counting on you saying or doing something that, when combined with your bloodline, they could use to rally support among your comrades in the Legions. Naturally, if you did so, I would have been forced to respond by ordering your arrest, which would be yet another example that would be used by those men to show your fellow men of the Legions I no longer appreciated or respected them. And then…" He did not finish, but there was no need.

Then, they hoped it would convince Tiberius that, given the admiration and respect in which he is held by men like me, he had, if not the right, then at least the muscle to convince the Princeps to do what so many of us believed he should and name Tiberius as heir to Rome. Thankfully, Augustus seemed content to allow me to work through the vast amount of information he had just dumped on me, and as I did so, I realized that everything the Princeps had told me made sense. In fact, I can still recall the sinking feeling in my gut, the kind that comes when a man recognizes something he hears and then understands is a truth, no matter how awful.

"What do you want me to do, Princeps?"

The fact that he did not seem a bit surprised at this sign of my acquiescence did not sit well with me, but I swallowed down my irritation as I waited to hear my sentence. For, dear reader, make no mistake, this was exactly what it was, a form of penance I had to perform in order to allow my family to continue their collective lives undisturbed. At least, if I was reading the signs correctly, and I was sure that I was, and still am today.

What Augustus said next confirmed beyond all doubt that Claudius did, indeed, have a spy in his household; more importantly, I instantly knew his identity, when the Princeps said, "When Claudius asked to correspond with you after you returned to Siscia, you declined. Before you leave Rome, you're either going to go to Claudius yourself, or send a message to him that you've reconsidered, and you agree to write to him about the situation in Pannonia."

The request from Claudius that Augustus was referring to had happened at the very last moment, as he walked me out of the villa to the courtyard. It was when we were clasping arms that he made this request, to which I had demurred as politely as I could, on the pretext I was not much of a writer. Which, in my defense, at that point, I was not; this is certainly not an excuse I can use any longer! More importantly, at least for Claudius, there was only one other person present, the slave who had brought me to my former Tribune, and whom I was now convinced had never left the *triclinium* after bringing the refreshments. And, I remembered grimly, he was certainly there when Claudius had made his request for me to keep him informed. Honestly, while I thought his entreaty to me was a bit unusual, given he was no longer attached to the army, I simply put it down to the normal behavior of a man of the upper classes, for whom all matters political are almost an obsession, their need to stay abreast of developments one of their primary objectives in life. While it was true that prior to our meeting, Claudius had not struck me as such a man, I also reminded myself, as any ranker can tell you, the way men of the upper classes behave when they are out on the frontiers of the Empire, than when they are back in their natural environment of Rome, is often quite different. I suppose I should give myself some credit for the fact that it did not take me more than a heartbeat or two to recognize that, if the Princeps wanted me to communicate with Claudius, Augustus would be providing the words I was to use.

"And what do you want me to say?" I asked, then thought to add, "And how am I going to know what to say when I'm back in Siscia?"

Even as the question left my lips, I experienced an awful premonition that I already knew the answer, which was confirmed when he answered, "You'll receive instructions and the information I want you to include in your correspondence from one of my agents who's in Pannonia. You've already met."

"Dolabella," I only breathed the name, partially because of my loathing for the man, but also to avoid making Augustus aware of my feelings.

Which, as I quickly learned, was no secret.

"Yes." Augustus nodded, then his expression hardened, and he actually leaned forward as he pointed at me again. "And while I can understand how a man like you would hold Dolabella in contempt, you will never, ever threaten him again. Is that understood?"

Frankly, I blame the finger, because forgetting who I was addressing, I shot right back, "Then you need to tell that…man not to threaten me. Or my friends!"

I probably should have felt some satisfaction that my words clearly surprised the Princeps, although in the moment, I was sure it was my tone.

However, he seemed genuinely nonplussed, asking, "What do you mean, Pullus? Are you saying that Dolabella threatened you?"

I went on to relate the exchange between the man I now knew without a doubt was an agent of the Princeps and me, while Augustus just sat, listening.

Once I was finished, he considered for a moment, then admitted, "He shouldn't have done that. And I'll let him know in the future that if he acts in this manner, I'll be most...displeased. But," his tone, while not resuming its harshness, was still stern as he warned me, "I'm going to tell him what I'm telling you now. Whatever problems you have between the two of you will not have any impact on what I'm asking you to do. I expect the both of you to behave in a manner befitting those in whom I've placed a great deal of trust." He paused for a moment, then said, "I won't insult your intelligence by reminding you that you're not to breathe a single word about this. To anyone," he emphasized. "Not your brother Sextus," I do not know why I was surprised, but I was to hear my brother's name come from Augustus' mouth, and I had to fight the absurd impulse to grin at the idea of his reaction if I told him about this conversation. Which, of course I could not, as the Princeps continued, "your parents, or your Centurion. Not even your friend Domitius. Do I make myself clear?"

I assured him he did, indeed, and I was sure I had not missed the other message there in his warning. As he said, there was no need for him to remind me I was not to divulge the details of this conversation, and I only do so now because the Princeps will undoubtedly have left this mortal plane of existence by the time this account is read, but more than anything, I am certain he brought it up for the purpose of demonstrating just how much he knew about one man, out of the many thousands who march for Rome and out of the millions of citizens of this Empire. Perhaps this is, after all is said and done, one of the parts of the legacy passed down to me by the original Titus Pullus, of which I had no idea even existed back when I first decided I wanted to follow in his footsteps. As much as my size, it is this part of the legend of Titus Pullus that means nothing I did, or will do, can remain truly anonymous. And, as much as it pains me to admit it, when I was beginning my career, this was certainly a state of, if not fame, then at least some renown, that I longed to achieve. Now, however, there are times when I wish I could say what I want, do what I want, and just...*be,* without the constant measure and comparison with my beloved Avus. But, regardless of my desires, this meeting with Augustus still serves as a powerful reminder that this is the fate the gods have handed me.

I must say I was touched when I saw that Primus Pilus Atticus was standing in the hallway, just a couple paces from the Praetorian who, when we entered, I was aware might serve as my escort off to the Tullianum, or wherever men deemed dangerous by the Princeps were sent. Yet, here I was, and if not truly free, I at least had the ability to walk out of the residence, although I did so on perilously shaky legs. The Praetorian guard, who had not uttered more words than was absolutely necessary, escorted us back to the entrance, except once we walked outside, he turned back, beckoning to the other Praetorian who had been our escort, whereupon they both returned inside the residence. Galens was still there, although Arruntius was not, which did not surprise me all that much.

"Well?" my Centurion demanded, actually examining me from head to foot as if he expected the Princeps to have inflicted some physical damage. "You're walking out under your own power, so I suppose that's a good sign."

"It is," I agreed, glancing over at Atticus, who shook his head.

Motioning then with a nod, he reminded me we were still standing within earshot of the two Praetorians who had been posted outside when we arrived, although by their demeanor, it was impossible to say they were paying any attention to us. It would not serve to find out, I understood, so I followed the Primus Pilus as he walked away from the residence. He did not say a word, even when we were halfway down the hill, not stopping until we were in the middle of the Forum, which I immediately saw was by design; it is usually the case that the safest place to hold a conversation is in the middle of a crowd.

Leading us to a spot between the Temple of Saturn and the Milliarium Aureum, which as I had seen on our prior visit, is one of the busier spots, with people either hurrying about, or men standing in small groups like ours, which meant we did not stick out, only then did the Primus Pilus speak, asking bluntly, "So? What did he want?"

It probably is not surprising I had been dreading this question, almost from the moment I exited the office of the Princeps.

Clearly hesitating – I hoped by doing so, he would understand the position he was putting me in – I was at least partially rewarded when he relented somewhat, saying, "All right, tell me what you can say." He gave a sour smile. "At least that won't cost you fifty thousand *sesterces*. Or more."

During our short walk, I had been thinking furiously about exactly what I could say without betraying anything the Princeps would consider a violation of his orders.

What I settled for was not an outright lie, just one more of omission, telling Atticus and Galens, "He wanted to make sure I'm aware of how much he knows about me. And," I added meaningfully, "my family." Pausing, I went a bit further by saying, "And how he can take it all away if he chooses."

This prompted a bitter, barking laugh from Atticus, who agreed, "I know that feeling!"

Despite the topic, this made both Galens and me join in, but while the Primus Pilus looked irritated for an instant, he finally relented, and if not laughing outright, at least smiled in recognition of the moment, however ironic.

Then, it faded. "And? Anything else?"

"Not that I can talk about," I admitted, and I cannot express how relieved I was when Atticus accepted this with a nod.

"Trust me, boy," he told me with a heavy humor, "I've been in your boots before. I don't envy you a bit." Suddenly, what I took to be a look of anxiety flashed across his face as he asked cautiously, "Whatever it is you can't tell us isn't about me, is it? I mean, Pullus, I don't want to put you in a difficult spot, but..."

His voice trailed off, and I was happy I could assure him that the subject of our talk did not involve Atticus in any way, although my feeling was nothing compared to the obvious expression of relief that flashed across his weathered features.

"What about me?" Galens interrupted, trying to sound plaintive at being left out, which as I am sure he hoped also helped lighten the mood, if only for a moment.

While I am sure part of Atticus' motivation in bringing us to the Forum was to allow us to talk without fear of being overheard, I saw him glance up at the sun, grimacing in a way that suggested it was not because of the glare, instantly reminding me of what was supposed to take place this day.

"Now," Atticus' tone was understandably bitter, "let's go get this other fucking business over with. They should be here any moment."

"Where are you supposed to meet him?" I asked, having forgotten in all the excitement and fear of my meeting with the Princeps.

"At the new Rostra," Atticus told us, then with the air of a man resigned to a fate that holds no prospect of pleasure no matter how it plays out, he gestured to the spot two dozen paces away, "so we can stay here."

As one might expect, the farmer Manius Fusus arrived promptly, yet also not unexpected was the fact that he was not alone. Still, it was not the presence of the prosecuting Tribune Silanus, who had been appointed to oversee the transfer who caught my attention, but the half-dozen other men who were with the pair, five of whom were arrayed in a rough semicircle behind them, while the sixth man walked ahead, clearing a path. And he was doing it none too gently, I thought grimly, watching him shove a woman carrying a wicker basket so hard it caused her to stumble and lose her grasp of it. Loaves of bread went tumbling to the paving stones, while she cried out in a combination of anger and despair as, before she could recover, the urchins and other assorted scum who loiter in the Forum, just for moments of opportunity such as this, leapt to scoop up at least a loaf.

"That bastard," Galens growled, except when he moved to intervene, Atticus grabbed his arm, shaking his head. "Leave it be, Galens. We don't need trouble with a bunch of gladiators. Besides," he pointed out, literally, "it's too late."

Which it was, yet I did not have to know my Centurion well to understand our Primus Pilus' admonition to stay our hand did not sit well, even if what he said was true. For, as we had seen at their appearance, the farmer was taking no chances, having hired a complement of men who had once spent time in the sand. Or, I thought with some amusement, so they claim; among the other things I share with the first Titus Pullus, my regard, or lack thereof, for gladiators is akin to his, although I had not gotten my finger bitten off by one. At least, so far, I suppose I should add. Even as this thought crossed my mind, my tongue moved unconsciously to the two shattered stubs that were the remnants of teeth I had lost the one time I had tried something similar to what the gladiator Prixus had done to my Avus. It had taken weeks before those teeth lost their sensitivity, yet even now, if I drink something colder than normal, like from a rushing stream, or melted snow, I still feel a stab of agony. My one consolation is that the man whose fingers I had tried to bite off was dead, and I was not, but as I think about it, perhaps the fact that the missing teeth are on the side of my mouth and are not readily visible is another one.

"Come on," Atticus muttered, and we followed him as he crossed the short distance from our spot, meeting the oncoming party a few paces from the Rostra.

"You hang back a bit," Galens instructed me, using his head to indicate where he wanted me to stand. "I don't trust these fuckers."

Honestly, I was not sure what threat they posed, and I was not of this mind simply because I am Titus Pullus, and both Galens and Atticus were hard men in their own right. From the way I saw it, not only was Fusus about to become richer, meaning he had no cause to start trouble, it was the Forum of Rome at midday. There were a few men of the Urban Cohort about, but it was the presence of the crowd, and the number of witnesses there would be that convinced me the likelihood of any kind of mischief was minimal. Nevertheless, I stopped at roughly the spot Galens had indicated, which meant, because of the low-pitched buzzing sound coming from the talking of all those nearby, I could not hear what was said. Not that I needed to; just watching the two parties come together provided eloquent proof of the identities and respective roles in this exchange. Only a blind man could have missed who was the aggrieved party, and I had to suppress a wince when Atticus, after he had only reluctantly accepted the offered arm of Silanus, made it clear he had no intention of engaging in this rite with the farmer. Who, I noticed, looked more relieved than offended; the thought flashed through my mind that perhaps this was the moment he had worried about, and why there were these tough men standing at his back. But Primus Pilus Atticus did not achieve his post just to throw it away on what would ultimately have proven to be a futile act of revenge on Fusus, and I reminded myself that, being truthful, this was happening because of Atticus' own actions. I also freely admit that, by this point, our penultimate day in Rome, I found it harder to keep the idea we were there because of Atticus' decision foremost in my mind, which was threatened with being shoved out of my consciousness by the sympathy I felt for the Primus Pilus for what he had been forced to endure. All, I reminded myself, to prove a point and give him his own reminder, a bitter one at that, about who Atticus ultimately served. Despite the fact that I had deduced that, while it would hurt, fifty thousand *sesterces* would not ruin my Primus Pilus, it was hard to imagine any way in which he could put this setback in a positive light. Consequently, his surly demeanor was, at least in my mind, completely understandable, if not justified. There was a brief exchange of words after the formal introductions, then Atticus produced a scroll, tightly wrapped, and I could see there was a seal affixed to it. Handing it over with what I could see, even from my vantage point, was a visible effort, instead of directly to the farmer, Atticus handed it to Silanus, who did not seem surprised, and as I learned later, this is actually how such things are transacted. It was Silanus who broke the seal, opened the scroll, and examined it carefully, then nodded in what I suppose was his sign of approval that all was correct. Then, with what I thought was a ridiculous amount of ceremony, the Tribune, whose *toga* was certainly a sparkling white and draped perfectly, announcing his presence there was a formal matter, turned and handed the scroll to Fusus. Even from my vantage point, I saw the tremor of the farmer's hand as he reached for it, his eyes fixed on the scroll as if he feared it would take wings and fly away. It is hard for me to say how I felt about this man who, when all was said and done, was simply a victim of happenstance, yet who was also about to reap what, to the vast majority of not just Romans, but anyone, is a fortune. While certainly no expert in such matters, I am confident that the entire value of that farm was worth no more than ten thousand *sesterces*, and while I know that at least part of the rationale for awarding Fusus such a large sum was in recognition of the cost of starting over, and how he had lost a chance at future profit for some time to come, I knew this was a secondary consideration. No, I was and am sure, this was about punishing the Primus Pilus in a way that, while it did not damage his career, sent a message he was unlikely to forget for the rest of his days. With his future now seemingly secured, it appeared that Fusus thought it appropriate to say something because he opened his mouth, except that before anything could come out, Atticus spun about and stalked back away in my direction.

"Let's," he gave one of the most welcome orders I had received under his command, "get the fuck out of Rome before something else happens."

My last thought as I gave barely a glance over my shoulder at Manius Fusus was that, if he was a wise man, he would choose somewhere else to relocate his family, because I could not fathom my Primus Pilus enduring the presence of a man who he viewed as stealing a vast amount of money from him, even if it was in the northern reaches of Pannonia. And, it must be said, I never saw or heard of Manius Fusus again after this day in Rome.

There is not much to relate about our return to Siscia, other than to say the first few days were quite miserable, particularly for Galens, since neither the Primus Pilus nor I were in what could have even charitably been called talkative moods. Atticus' state of mind, however, was one composed of simmering anger, whereas I was in a more contemplative frame of mind as I tried to think of the shape my future would take now that I was spying for Augustus, but my thoughts certainly had a bitter edge to them as well. Not lost on me for one moment was the irony; speaking honestly, I think it was this aspect of my situation that occupied my thoughts more than the actual details of what I was supposed to do for the Princeps and how I was supposed to go about it. In retrospect, I suppose I should have taken some comfort in the sense of symmetry that came about as the result of my meeting with Augustus. After all, my Avus had done his best to avoid being embroiled in the machinations and maneuvers of the man he knew as Octavian, and had been unsuccessful. Why should I have been more fortunate? While I did arrive at this conclusion, I did not get there in the immediate aftermath; instead, I was more absorbed with the practical impact of my new circumstances. I had done as Augustus directed me, except I did not do it myself, paying one of the slaves on the Campus to relay the message, which I did write. In the message, I told Claudius I had reconsidered, and I explained my apparent change of heart as a way to show my appreciation for his offer of help, stating that in retrospect, I realized how ungracious my refusal must have seemed to him. In short, I lied much more easily on a tablet than I could have to his face, because while my feelings had changed somewhat, I still did respect the man. That, as I would come to learn more about him and all in which he was involved, is a viewpoint I no longer hold, and I can say this change started during our return. The more I thought about, I suddenly began wondering if, indeed, Claudius did care about me because of his stated reason, the honoring of an old debt of honor incurred by his father, or if like every other man of the upper classes, he viewed me as nothing more than an expendable piece in the vast game of tables played by Claudius and men like him. Between my quandary and Atticus' silent seething, poor Galens found us extremely bad company, at least for the first three or four days. Then, when we reached Aternum, essentially reversing the route we had taken to get to Rome, we found ourselves stuck there for four days, which proved to be too long a period to remain mired in misery, for either Atticus or me. And, if I am being forthcoming, our return to a semblance of a normal state, at least as much as our respective ranks allowed, was partially aided by Bacchus. It was on our second night in Aternum, when we had been informed there were no ships sailing the next day, and probably the day after, that found the three of us getting roaring, brawling drunk. Subsequently, it was just a matter of ill fortune for the sailors who frequented the *tavernae* along the waterfront in which we found ourselves, where Atticus and I, with Galens' help, took out all our pent-up rage and frustration on them. I say we did; honestly, I do not remember much, except for some fragmentary memories of throwing a man out of the *tavernae*. That there was a door that was closed apparently did not hinder me from ejecting him all that much nor did it stop him from sailing a fair distance, but what I do recall is waking the next morning sure that every inch of my body was hurting, including my hair, although since it is attached to my head, this may have actually been the source. More importantly, I do recall that two days later, when we finally managed to take ship from Aternum, I found myself with Atticus, once more leaning on the rail as we emptied our stomachs. Personally, I consoled myself with the idea I was still experiencing the aftermath of the massive hangover, here on the second morning after our debauchery; I did not ask the Primus Pilus for his excuse.

"You know, Pullus," he said suddenly, without any preamble or warning, "I just wanted to thank you."

This surprised me considerably, prompting me to ask, "For what, Primus Pilus?"

He was leaning on the railing, staring at the coastline of Umbria slowly slipping away in much the same way he had when we were heading in the opposite direction, and he did not turn to look at me as he answered, "For being willing to lie for me at the Tribunal."

My shock was profound, yet somehow, I managed to save me from myself, because instead of pointing out that he had ordered me to, and threatened me if I did not, I merely answered, "I wouldn't have let them convict you for doing something that needed to happen, Primus Pilus."

I cannot say who was more surprised, me or Atticus, as he turned to look at me, his mouth hanging open slightly, while I tried to deal with the shock that came when I realized I was speaking honestly. Whatever my feelings towards Atticus might have been, I realized I not only did not fault him for his actions against the Taurisci, deep down, I believed some sort of action against them was inevitable, and he had recognized this fact.

"Yes, well," he replied awkwardly, breaking his gaze away when I returned the look, "still, I do appreciate it. I just wanted you to know that I won't forget."

All I could think to say was to reply with a "Thank you."

He shrugged, seemingly absorbed in studying the land, but then he blurted out, "Sometimes, I wish I'd never become a fucking Praetorian and just stayed in the Legions." This surprised me, and I saw the flush creep up his face as he continued, "It's not just that life is simpler in the Legions, Pullus. The truth is that the men are better."

I confess this surprised me a great deal, since it is an article of faith that only the best of the best are considered for the Praetorians, however, I suppose it is a sign of how much a mark my Avus made on me, because it was something I never considered; his contempt for what had been called the Brundisium Cohorts during his time under the standard obviously rubbing off on me. Nevertheless, despite my personal feelings, I was honest enough with myself in recognizing this was not the case with the bulk of the men under the standard, or the average Roman citizen, for that matter.

"Really?" I asked, curious. "How so?"

"Oh," he waved a hand, "don't get me wrong. In terms of the ability to hold a shield and use a sword, the Praetorians are good. Very good." His tone was grudging, which, frankly, I found odd, considering this was where he had come from, yet I quickly learned why, as he continued, "but there's a lot more to being a Legionary than just that. Every one of those *cunni* in the Praetorians are..." He searched for the right words before settling on, "...politically oriented. They're all there because they're ambitious. Or greedy." This was when he gave me a sidelong glance as he admitted, "I should know because I was as ambitious as they come. But," he sighed, "I've figured out that it's not worth it. Men like us will never be the masters of our own fate." Atticus' mouth twisted from the bitterness of this truth, one I tasted no less, and still do to this day. "There'll always be a man higher up the ladder who makes us dance to the tune of his own flute. And as bad as it may be in the Legions," he sighed, "it's even worse in the Praetorians." Then, without any warning, which I am sure was his intent, Atticus spoke conversationally, "I suppose that Augustus wants you to spy for him." Not only his words but the way he said them caused my blood to freeze, and I suppose this feeling was betrayed by my body suddenly stiffening, because he stood erect and held out a placating hand. "I'm sorry, Pullus," he offered, "I shouldn't put you in that position. Believe me, I know what it's like." The chuckle that came from him was laced with so many different emotions, I could not determine which was predominant. "When I came to Siscia," he explained, "that was actually my first priority."

This was unexpected, and I stared at him for a moment, then asked, "On who?"

I suppose this could be considered a mark of my hubris, that my first suspicion was that Augustus had appointed Atticus as Primus Pilus of the 8th Legion with the goal of spying on a man who, back then, was a new Sergeant of a tent section.

"The Legate," Atticus replied promptly, naming the man who, even now, I do not care to identify.

"Well," I said carefully, "he must have passed, because his career certainly didn't suffer."

"He's an idiot," Atticus replied bluntly and immediately, then relented somewhat by saying, "but he's a loyal idiot. And for the Princeps, that's more important than competence."

This elicited a chuckle from me, although it was somewhat nervous.

"Still," Atticus went on, "it took coming back to the Legions for me to realize how much of my life I wasted."

How should I respond to this? I asked myself. Should I agree with him, that he's wasted a good chunk of his life?

"But I've learned my lesson," the Primus Pilus stood up, at least as much as one can on a rolling deck, "and I'm where I belong, with a Legion. And," he added with such bitterness it made me wince, "if I never see Rome again, I'll die a happy man! I piss on Rome and all that she's supposed to be!" Turning to me, his gaze was intense as he warned me, "Remember that, Pullus! Rome is a whore! And just like a whore, she can never be trusted!" He had certainly worked himself up; even so, I was still surprised to see the sudden glitter of unshed tears in his eyes as he finished, "And just like any whore, she'll break your heart. If you let her."

Now that sufficient time has passed to give me some dispassion about all that transpired over this two-month period, perhaps the best thing that came of everything when all was said and done was my rediscovery of the love of riding a horse, although in a practical sense and what had more of an impact on my career is gaining the trust, and to a certain extent, regard of my Primus Pilus. And, I suppose it is fair to say, I had developed a bond with the stallion who had been my mount for both legs of the trip, to the point where I began thinking about doing something that was not only impractical, but akin to the gloves, was almost guaranteed to raise even more suspicions about my circumstances. Yet, as I thought about it, I realized that, despite the fact that I was now in some form of servitude to Augustus, at the same time, I, and most importantly, my family had been freed from the concerns of maintaining a level of discretion. My reasoning was fairly straightforward and, I was sure, sound; the reason for our reticence about the fact that the Pullus family had much more money than people of our circumstances should have was based in the belief that Augustus did not know. A belief he himself had disabused when he informed me he was aware of our accumulated wealth, and had been for some time. Consequently, if the Princeps knew the thing my family had striven for years to keep concealed, yet had done nothing about it, what did it matter who else knew? Not lost on me at all was the recognition of the probable true purpose of Augustus informing me of his knowledge; that at any point in time, he could take the rest of the money, especially if I did not perform the task he had set for me. Nevertheless, even with this understanding, our circumstances had improved a bit, since I had no intention of doing anything that might displease the Princeps. Obviously, just by my father's nature, we would do nothing ostentatious, like build a new villa out in the countryside around Arelate in the fashion of many ambitious equestrian families, in emulation of their social betters, so they could boast of having a house in the city and the country. But what harm would come if I bought this horse? I wondered. On our first day out of Salona, our mood seeming to grow lighter with every mile we drew farther from Rome and closer to Siscia, I approached Galens, asking him for his thoughts on the matter.

"What the fuck do you need a horse for?" was his first question, followed with what was the obvious problem, "Especially since we walk everywhere we go."

"Because I'd forgotten how much I love to ride," I told him. When he gave me an amused look, my only defense was to shrug. "So I'd just like to ride in my spare time."

"Then do what everyone else does," he countered, amending, "at least every man like us. Rent the damn thing!" Pointing down to my chestnut, he reasoned, "I'm sure that old Tarentinus would be more than happy to rent you this nag anytime you want."

"Don't listen to him." I patted the horse on the neck. "He doesn't know horses. He's an infantryman, and they don't know anything about horses."

"And what exactly are you?" he hooted. "Last time we were on a march, whenever I checked, you were walking behind me!"

"I," I replied loftily, "am different. Remember, I have the blood of a man of the 10th Equestris."

"I won't argue that you're different, all right," he snorted. "Although I wouldn't put it exactly that way." Then he shrugged and said, "But I know you well enough to see you've made your mind up already. In fact," he finished with a grumble, "I'm not sure why you asked me in the first place."

"To pass the time," I answered immediately, which, as I had hoped, elicited a chuckle.

While it was true I had basically made my decision, I did respect Galens' opinion, and wanted to make sure he did not bring up some potential issue that had not occurred to me. The fact he mentioned, even if in a somewhat cryptic manner, the perception of men that an Optio in a Legion could afford to own a horse, and all the costs attendant to that ownership, was not surprising. Since Galens had not brought up anything unexpected, my mind immediately moved on to the idea of naming my new horse; it never occurred to me I might be thwarted in my desire by the current owner. Naturally, there was no way I would name him Ocelus; there is only one champion bearing that name. Nevertheless, I did want my future acquisition to bear an appellation that carried with it the same spirit as the gray stallion, yet while I started by asking Galens, we were quickly joined by Atticus, who trotted up alongside us. Whereupon Galens wasted no time in informing Atticus that he had an Optio, not just in his Legion but his own Cohort, who seemed to think he was too good to walk like real men.

Atticus' reply was non-verbal in nature; instead, he merely glanced down at his own mount, then regarded Galens with a raised eyebrow, who turned red and spluttered, "You know what I mean,

Primus Pilus! This one," he gave a disgusted wave, "wants to ride a horse for *fun*! That's just not right!"

The Primus Pilus was clearly enjoying Galens' discomfiture, but he showed my Centurion mercy by turning to me, asking, "Did I hear you right? You're thinking about a name?" When I nodded, this puzzled him. "How can you pick a name when you haven't even seen the beast?"

When I explained by pointing down to the chestnut, whose ears were once more turned slightly backward as if trying to hear his fate, this prompted a genuine chortle from Atticus, which was explained when he said, "What's that old man's name? Tarentinus? He's going to skin you alive!"

I started to argue, then thought better of it; he was in all likelihood correct, and in the back of my mind was the knowledge of a lecture in my future when my father learned I inevitably overpaid for what was, in essence, a luxury item.

"So?" I asked, more to change the subject. "Any suggestions?"

I was about to turn and admonish Galens not to do what he was about to, except he beat me to it, instantly offering, "Bucephalus!"

Groaning, I rolled my eyes, but when I assured him I would not make this poor animal suffer carrying the name of a horse who has its own statue, he protested, "Well, you can't name him Toes, can you? And you aren't going to name him just anything!"

"No, I want a good name," I agreed, and I admit a sudden lump formed in my throat as I explained, "I want something along the lines of Ocelus. You remember him, don't you, Galens?"

"That horse," he muttered, "scared me almost as much as your grandfather."

It took some time for me to regain my breath from laughing at the sudden visual image my Centurion's words had prompted, although once I did, I decided to defer to rank, asking Atticus for a suggestion.

Somewhat to my surprise, he did not offer something either flippant or vulgar, and seemed to seriously think about it before offering, "What about one of the horses that pulls Mars' chariot?" He paused, then his face cleared and he snapped his fingers triumphantly, offering up, "Konabos, isn't it? One of them?"

Honestly, I was not sure, and I admit I felt a bit of chagrin because Diocles had been nothing if not thorough in drilling the children Pullus on the gods and all the facts attendant to them, both in their Grecian and Roman forms.

"Phobos is another," Galens supplied, and I glanced over in some surprise, but he just grinned, saying, "I'm not a complete uneducated idiot, boy."

While I allowed these were fine names, they were still not exactly right, so I tried to explain, "I'm looking for something that's used by the barbarians too. One of their gods. That's where Ocelus' name came from. He's the name the tribes of Britannia use for Mars. That's where my grandfather got it from." While I cannot say this moment, one where I am sure the *numen* of my Avus would intervene and stop me from doing or saying something that would put me in peril, I will still cross the river and join him certain it was no less a case where he gently but insistently corrected my mistake, because before I had any conscious thought to do so, I blurted, "Actually, that's not true. It was Quintus Balbus, one of his best friends, who came up with the name."

I do not know why I said this, but it was worth it just because of the way Galens reacted.

"By the gods," he groaned, "now you bring up *him*? I've had nightmares about him! He got an ear sliced off during the Equestris' time in Gaul, along with half his face! Did you know that his favorite thing to do to prisoners was cut off their balls so he could use the sac for a coin purse?"

The gods know I am not exaggerating when I say it took quite an effort to remain mounted; certainly this is the hardest I laughed during this entire trip, and still ranks as one of the most humorous moments of my life. I suppose it was from a combination of things; the look of horror on the face of my Primus Pilus, the absolute sincerity of Galens, which combined with my knowledge of the fact that, as tragic as the death of Quintus Balbus was in the life of Titus Pullus and Sextus Scribonius, his two closest friends, I knew that this...unusual fixation of his died with him unrequited. Balbus died before I was born, although the gods know that between my Avus' account, Scribonius, Diocles, and a host of others, I heard much about this man whose own reputation for ferocity and devotion to his friends was eclipsed only by the first Titus Pullus. Still, I did not want this conversation to deviate from its original goal.

"So," I pointedly ignored Galens' comment, "do either of you know a name that's used by the barbarians in Pannonia?"

"No," Atticus admitted, "but I recall the tribes around the Dubis worship Taranis. He's their thunder god, as I recall."

This seemed to prompt Galens, who interjected, "Wait! What about that god who's like Mars and Jupiter combined that they worship up in Noricum?" He thought for a moment, then supplied, not without a triumphant grin, "Latobius! That's it!"

Which was how my horse got his name. Who, I must say, did not seem altogether impressed with this notable event at the time.

Fortunately for me, if not for my purse, Tarentinus was amenable to selling the horse who, even now, is stabled not far from where I am writing this, here in my quarters. Not that his acquisition came cheaply; about this, the Primus Pilus was right, and I suppose it is fair to say that Tarentinus read me correctly, that I was willing to pay more than the horse was probably worth. Still, I do not regret the choice I made, and he would prove to be a valuable way for me to divert myself from my duties, both official and secret. Our return to Siscia occurred the day before the Kalends of March, arriving around midday after being forced to spend the night out in the cold, although it was the only one the whole trip. Not that it stopped us from complaining, yet it was not due to the conditions as much as it was the anticipation of our arrival the next day. Word had been sent ahead of us about the Primus Pilus' exoneration, yet I was not surprised when he made no mention of his monetary loss, because ultimately, it did not matter as far as his running the Legion was concerned. Galens and I spent the last watch of our trip discussing our expectations for the condition of the Century, which had been left under the temporary command of Tesseraurius Stellatinus, while Atticus remained mostly silent, reminding me he had far more to worry about than a single Century. I recall this moment because it served as another example where I thought, be careful what you wish for, Titus. While the Primus Pilus had seemed more unburdened with every passing day, once we crossed back across the sea and arrived in Dalmatia, the nearer we drew to our home camp, the more distracted he became. Still, there was something subtly different in his demeanor, which I put down to the fact that he was simply shifting one set of worries for another, and the ones that occupied his thoughts now were more welcome than those that had rightfully consumed him prior to the ordeal of his Tribunal. Over the course of the first few days of our trip back, it seemed to be by unspoken but common consent that none of the three of us mentioned the proceedings; however, we are Romans, and even among the lower classes, trying to stop Romans from talking politics is akin to trying to reverse the tides. Between the three of us, we argued, posited, speculated, and virtually dissected each and every aspect of the Tribunal, yet even as we were doing so, in the back of my mind was the recognition that, just as I was doing, I had to assume the Primus Pilus was likely withholding certain bits of information for his own purposes. Somehow, though, there were a few salient points upon which we could agree, the first and foremost being our conviction that the situation with Tiberius was not one of his making. Nothing in our collective experience with the man, nor anything we had heard from other men of our station, led us to believe he was anything but what he appeared to be to us in the ranks, a dutiful Roman noble, doing his utmost to perform his duties in a manner befitting his status and the expectations created by that standing in our society. I will only go slightly further to say that, while neither Galens, Atticus, nor I uttered words to this effect, I believe we were also of a like mind that Tiberius had been given short shrift by the Princeps.

The closest any of us came was when Galens pointed out, "How many men has the Princeps tried to elevate over Tiberius? First," he held out a finger, "was Marcellus, but then he died. Now it's the grandsons..."

"Who are too young," Atticus interjected, but this did not dissuade Galens in the slightest.

"Today," he agreed, "they're too young. But while I didn't lay eyes on him myself, both of you," he indicated Atticus and me, "saw him up close. Does the old boy look near death to you?"

"Actually," I had to admit, "I thought he looked terrible."

"He's always looked like that," Atticus countered. "Remember when he was young and he had all that business with his wheezing." Shaking his head, he said firmly, "He's not going anywhere, at least anytime soon."

"May the gods make it so," I intoned, prompting both of my superiors to give me scornfully amused glances.

"I'm sure you're being sincere," Atticus' tone was dry; I did not reply.

"So," Galens continued doggedly, "while I'm not saying Tiberius has anything to do with all that talk, you have to admit he's been treated pretty poorly by the Princeps."

This was something I certainly did not argue, and neither did Atticus, but that was the extent of the talk about Tiberius and his rights. I suppose it would be fair to say that I was of two minds, although one state was certainly stronger than the other. One part of me believed that, as much as Romans of the upper classes like to talk about a man doing his duty to Rome, it was hard to be sympathetic when one of those men was forced to match his actions with those sentiments. Regardless of this side of the question, however, I could not help feeling, if not outright sympathy, at least empathy for Tiberius, experiencing a sense of kinship with the man because of a common thread that ran through both of our existences, and that was the Princeps. Like Tiberius, ultimately, our respective fates were controlled by one man, and I forced myself to be honest enough to admit that, not only were the stakes much higher for Augustus' stepson, he did not have the buffer of a go-between like I did. Not that I felt particularly grateful at having to deal with Dolabella, my only consolation being that he was still back in Rome and would not be coming back to Siscia immediately, so at least I would have at least a bit of time without the worry of being under the thumb of the cross-eyed *cunnus*. And on the subject of Dolabella, there was also the topic of Balbinus, who would be returning to the Legion once he was well enough to travel. Honestly, I do not know who was more surprised between the Primus Pilus and me when I approached him.

"I thought you hated the bastard." Atticus' tone expressed at least his doubt about my motives, for which I could not blame him.

"I do," I admitted, then changed the tense, saying, "at least I did. Now?" Despite my best attempt to come up with a reason that was somewhat plausible, instead, I could only shrug and conclude, "I think he's been punished enough. Don't you, Primus Pilus?"

For a moment, I thought he would assure me that he, in fact, did not agree, his expression hardening, yet when I did not flinch from his gaze, he finally relented, giving a disgusted grunt and dismissive wave as he looked away and said, "Fine, I suppose he has."

Aware that I was taking a risk, I still felt compelled to press him, asking, "Does this mean he can return to the Legion?"

"He can come back, but," he glowered at me, "he's not coming back to my Cohort! And definitely not my Century!"

As so often was the case, I had to bite my tongue to keep from pointing out that if Balbinus was not going to be welcome back in the First Cohort, it went without saying that he would not be marching in the First Century. Thankfully, I managed to refrain, and instead simply thanked him for his decision. Now all I have to do is find a Pilus Prior who's willing to have a man they can't trust in their Cohort, I thought, but that was a bridge that did not have to be crossed at this moment.

Since this was our official return, we reported to the *praetorium* first, although for Galens and me, it was more of a formality, while the Legate immediately summoned Atticus to a private meeting. Despite not being present, I did not have to be to know that, more than any real interest in hearing about the Primus Pilus' ordeal, Atticus was about to be pumped for information about the state of affairs in Rome, and ultimately, the most important matter, the subject of the Princeps himself. Given this virtual certainty, perhaps my feeling of relief was augmented by the thought that, of the two of us, the Legate would probably have been more interested in the results of my interview with the Princeps if he had known about it. Not that I would have been forthcoming, but I suppose the thought amused me that I am positive it never occurred to the Legate that a lowly Optio would be in possession of more relevant information than a Primus Pilus. Because my superior was with me, Galens laughingly assured me he knew I had arrived and would be ready for duty the next day, releasing me to take care of my immediate needs. The first of which, and the most urgent, was to take Latobius, who even over the previous couple of days had begun to respond to his new name, to the stables where Tarentinus ran his business. And, as I already mentioned, for the rest of his life, the old man probably celebrated the anniversary of the day he skinned some overgrown youngster alive, who paid twice as much for the chestnut stallion as he was probably worth. Still, he must have felt some pity for me, because the rate he charged for boarding my new possession was substantially less than normal.

"If truth be known," said the grizzled old man, clearly a former cavalryman by virtue of his bowed legs and features that were weathered even more than normal for a man his age, "I'm kind of fond of this big bastard myself." This was clearly demonstrated as Latobius nuzzled the man, shoving his nose into the folds of the old trooper's tunic, probably looking for a treat. "So I don't mind having him around."

Thanking him, trying not to wince as I presented him with the marker he would take to the man who handled my financial matters, I decided to not postpone the next task on my list, heading for the apartment that I still thought of as Diocles', wondering as I did if I would ever think of it as belonging to even Birgit, let alone Sextus. It is somewhat difficult to describe my state of mind as I walked the few blocks from the stable, barely noticing the sight of a couple men from my Century who, under normal circumstances, I would have stopped immediately, demanding to know why they were out in town during the duty hour. Not that I completely ignored them, instead just tucking away the memory as something to deal with later. Ascending the stairs, I tried to add up the number of weeks I had been gone with the supposed stage of Birgit's pregnancy, but the best I could do was with the realization that it would be close. I was about halfway up when a shrill, sharp scream, barely muffled by the outer walls of the apartment sounded, causing me to freeze, one foot hovering above the next step. In the immediate aftermath of what I knew was a feminine cry of pain, I was in a turmoil of indecision, as a part of my mind commanded me to turn around and return to camp. It's obviously not a good time, I reasoned to myself, thinking absurdly that Birgit would probably be upset that she could not properly greet me. Somehow, I managed to avoid flight, although I had to take a deep breath before planting my foot on the next step, continuing my ascent. Under normal conditions, the children had learned to identify both me and Sextus by our footfalls, and were almost always waiting with the door flung open. Not this time, however, another sign that perhaps there was some sort of distraction taking place. Still, I managed to knock, except I had to do it again before I heard stirring within the apartment. Then, just as the door was yanked open, there was another wail, except my ears instantly informed me this was not Birgit, but more of a mewling, quavering, and thin cry. Before I could take this in and allow it to register in my mind, the door was open, and Alex was standing there, looking up at me wide-eyed, yet almost eerily calm; I put it down to the circumstances that he did not greet me in his normal exuberant fashion after I returned from a long absence.

"*Salve*, Uncle Titus." He seemed intent on speaking formerly, as the *paterfamilias*, which in hindsight should have given me the hint Sextus was not present. "Mama's having the baby."

Without waiting for a response from me, he stepped aside, and I entered, saying, "So I hear."

The actual birth of my nephew, whose name I did not yet know, had seemingly occurred as I was climbing the stairs, meaning the children were sitting together at the table, and the image of them leaning against each other brought back memories of similar moments from my own childhood, as those of us who had come before waited to welcome a new addition to the family. Honestly, at this moment, not only was I ignorant of the child's name, but whether it was a boy or girl. Yet, before I could do anything other than set down the leather bag carrying the gifts I had brought, the children were up and running towards me.

Naturally, they did not do so quietly, prompting an irritated voice to call from the birthing room, "You children be quiet out there! Your mother doesn't need to hear a racket!"

"That's Antonia," Alex informed me at my inquiring glance, explaining, "she's the..." His face screwed up into a look of concentration as he tried to remember the correct term.

"Midwife?" I supplied, to which he nodded.

"I don't like her," the now supplanted baby of the family, Scribonia, pronounced. "She smells...old."

This made me laugh, but then the door to the other room was yanked open, and I experienced a moment where I forgot I was actually an adult, and a large one at that, the humor suddenly smothered by the scowling visage of the old crone, who glared at us with a disapproval that barely wavered at the sight of me.

"Are you the father?" she croaked; all I could muster was a shake of my head.

For whatever reason, this seemed to amuse her, at least so I believe, because while it was hard to identify as such, the strangled hacking sound that came from her was clearly not her last breath, so I assume it was a laugh.

"Praise the gods," she muttered, examining me from head to toe, "because a man your size isn't likely to be the father of that wee babe."

I do not know why, but this triggered a thrill of alarm; I saw I was not alone, the children suddenly stiffening, yet it was me who asked, "What do you mean? Is the babe all right?"

The crone waved a hand in a gesture that could have meant anything, then evidently seeing our alarm, assured us, "No, no. The babe's fine."

This was when I realized she had not actually spoken of the infant in a way that would indicate its sex, so I asked her.

This seemed to amuse her even more, although the look she gave me was as scornful as anything else, answering, "That's all you men want to know! Not 'how's the babe?'." She had altered her voice in what I suppose she thought was a reasonable imitation of a man's voice. "Or, gods forbid, 'how's the mother doing?'"

The glare she gave me was, quite frankly, unsettling, which prompted me to protest, "Why are you shaking your finger at me? I'm not the father!"

"No, you're not," she agreed, then in an exaggerated manner, she opened her eyes, the folds of them so pronounced I was sure she could barely see, then craned her neck around the confines of the apartment, the scorn still there as she asked what I understood was a rhetorical question, "But where *is* the Tata, eh?" She made that strangled sound again, and the gods know I am not exaggerating when I say she spat or at least drooled as she continued, "Nowhere to be found, that's where! Just like every man! Useless at moments like this!" Pointing a gnarled finger at me again, she began scolding, "Oh, you're wonderful at killing both man and beast! But how does that compare to a moment like this? Eh?"

If it had not been for the sudden gleam of tears I saw in the crone's eyes, making me realize she was truly upset at my brother's absence, the fact that she waggled that damned finger at me might have meant a much different conclusion than what actually took place. Crossing the couple paces to her, the way she suddenly shrank back as our relative sizes came into sharper relief ignited in me a stab of, if not shame, then some embarrassment that I had just been thinking of snapping the old woman's finger off like a twig.

"Antonia, is it?" I asked her, using the same tone I thought of as my soothing one that I had become reacquainted with during my time with Latobius, except she only nodded. "I apologize on the behalf of my brother."

I turned to Alex, knowing that he tried to keep his face impassive, but he was still young, although he answered readily enough, "We sent Theroios to fetch him."

"How long ago?" I asked, not understanding how it was possible that a messenger had not found my brother and brought him back in the length of time it took to have a baby.

This was when I was informed how limited my experience was, because it was the old woman Antonia who answered, "Oh, it wasn't long before you arrived, large Master." I had to suppress a grin at her characterization of me, as she went on, "This is her seventh child. By that time," she gave a coarse chuckle and I felt my face redden, although it was more because of the children as she said, "things aren't quite as…tight as they used to be." She gave me what can only be called a leer, and she actually nudged me in the rib with that bony finger, finishing with, “If one takes my meaning.”

I assured her I did, indeed, yet I did so facing away from the children.

Then, from the room, I heard Birgit call in an understandably tired voice, “Sextus?”

“It’s Uncle Titus,” Alex called out, and while I could not swear to it, I thought I heard Birgit take a sharp inward breath.

“Titus,” she called at last, “I’m so happy you made it back! Forgive me, I…” Her voice trailed off.

“Don’t worry,” I assured her, still speaking through the partially opened door, which the old woman had pulled back shut just enough to block the view into the room. “I know you’re busy.”

This made the children giggle at my awkward understatement, and I heard Birgit give an exhausted chuckle herself, then she called Antonia to her side. The woman obeyed immediately, grumbling under her breath that, of course Birgit was busy, she was having a baby, something that men knew nothing about; this was the last I heard as I turned and went back to the children.

While they were understandably distracted, they plied me with questions about Rome as I handed out their gifts, but it was young Titus who blurted out, “Did you kill any bandits this time, Uncle Titus?”

This made me laugh, but I assured him that, no, I, in fact, had not had to dispatch any criminals to Hades, which clearly disappointed him. Alex, on the other hand, kept his face very still, yet I saw he was disturbed by his younger brother’s question.

Then, before anything else could be said, Antonia reappeared to announce, “Mistress is ready to receive you now so that you can meet your new brother.” However, when the children all scrambled to their feet, as Gisela and Scribonia clapped in delight, Antonia held up a withered hand, and I suppose her look of embarrassment was because she had committed a blunder.

“Actually, children,” she told them, “the Mistress would like to see the large Master before you. But,” she hurried on, no doubt prompted by the complaints of at least three of the children, “then you’ll be next, I promise!”

Unsure why Birgit wanted to speak with me privately, I nonetheless did not hesitate, at least much, walking past Antonia into the room, where Birgit was now propped up with pillows, cradling the newborn in her arms. Without any warning, I was almost struck to my knees by such a powerful emotion, a mixed sense of loss and regret as it occurred to me that, if the gods had allowed it, I would already have experienced this moment, except with Giulia and my own child. Who, I was sure, would have been a son, yet what followed immediately after this thought was the realization that it probably had indeed been a son, given that his entry to the world had killed both Giulia and him. The suddenness and potency of this recognition forced me to stop in the doorway, grabbing onto the frame to remain erect.

Something Birgit did not miss, and I saw the flash of understanding in her eyes as she said softly, "Titus, I'm so sorry! Please, forgive me! I should have realized this would be painful for you! It's just that," she hesitated, looking down at what, from my vantage point at least, appeared to be a bundle of rags, "I wanted you to meet your new nephew."

Shaking my head, as much to clear it as to assure her, I managed, "Don't be silly, Birgit! I'm very happy to meet the little man!" Forcing a smile on my face, I pretended not to notice her studying me as I blinked away the tears, crossing to her bedside, whereupon I stood there like a big lump of meat.

"I-I'm not sure what to do," I admitted. "I was going to sit down so I could see him better, but I don't want to…hurt you."

This prompted a laugh, albeit a tired one from Birgit, who took her turn to set my mind at ease, telling me, "Titus, don't worry, I won't break! The hard part's over." Before I could say or do anything, she amended with a wry expression, "Well, mostly over. The gods know I won't be getting much sleep for the next few months."

This, I freely admit, had more of a profound impact on me than anything else she could have said; even today, I treasure my sleep a great deal, and of all the aspects of life in the Legions, it is the lack of sleep I despise the most. Hearing her openly acknowledge this was the fate she had chosen for herself, especially considering how her experience was such she knew what to expect, was a meaningful lesson on the power of motherhood. Despite her assurance, I settled on the edge of the bed gingerly, trying to ignore the pile of sodden, stained sheets just a couple of feet away as she proudly showed me what I could now see was something more than a bundle of cloth. Granted, there was more swaddling than baby; still, there was a tiny, pinkish-red face, with large, dark eyes that gave the lie to the impression there was nothing substantial contained in this bundle. It was, and is true that this tiny life was not one I had created, yet I still think back to this moment with a great deal of sentiment that is composed of almost equal parts sweetness and regret, joy, and pain.

"Have you picked a name?"

I barely recognized my own voice, so husky and choked was it, but she surprised me when she shook her head.

"My gods forbid naming a child before it's born," she informed me.

When I glanced up at her, I was struck by the radiant beauty she seemed to possess in this moment, although I am sure if I had said this, she would have protested, talking about the disheveled state of her hair, how pallid her complexion, and the circles under her eyes. Still, while I had always appreciated her beauty, and understood Sextus' fascination and desire for her, I believe this was the moment where I truly understood his feelings. And, I will not deny feeling a sharp stab of envy for my brother.

Oblivious to my internal observation of her glow, she went on, "Actually, we're not supposed to name a baby until its second name day, but Sextus says this is silly. So," for the first time, her face clouded a bit, "did Diocles." Before I could say anything, an expression of such intensity came over her features I experienced a deep unease, but the change was explained when she asked me, "Titus, do you think Diocles would approve?"

"I think," I told her with absolute sincerity, "he'd want you to be happy, and to move on with your life with someone who will protect you and his children."

Even with the guttering lamps, her look of relief was obvious, and she sank back against the pillows as she let out a deep exhalation. When she did so, she also, at least to my eyes, suddenly thrust the bundle at me, and without thinking, I reached out to take hold, not wanting to fumble what I was still trying to comprehend was a new human being just introduced to the world. In retrospect, I feel confident her action was not by accident, understanding that if I had been given time to think about it, I would have made excuses and fled the room with what would likely have been an indecent haste. Instead, I was presented with my nephew, so new to the world that he still had a slight gleam from the waters in which he had been swimming for nine months. Then his head moved, slightly, as he peered up at me, and I did not need a bronze mirror to know I had a smile that felt as if it would split my face. Perhaps it was prodded from the back of my mind to the front because of my thought about the length of time, and I started thinking, had it really been nine months?

"Why's he so…scrawny?" was what came out of my mouth, yet immediately after it left my mouth, I winced.

I should not have worried, because Birgit's response was to give a tired chuckle, as she assured me, "Titus, he's not scrawny! It's just that he's not as big a baby as you must have been."

This actually came as a relief, for two reasons; first and foremost, this boded well for the child's future. As oblivious as I was to such matters normally, one does not need to pay attention to know that a relatively large portion of newborn babes do not survive their first year. It was the second reason that was, if not as rational was at least as powerful. If the babe had been born my size, I could easily envision Sextus becoming suspicious. Apparently, I had lost myself, because when Birgit's hands suddenly thrust into view, interrupting my examination of my nephew, it startled me, which prompted another laugh.

"Give him here," she commanded, and of course I did, but if she was going to say anything else, she was unable to do so because of an eruption of noise from the other room.

"Where is she?" I heard Sextus' voice, but I had not yet gotten to my feet from the bed when he burst through the door, panting and with his tunic stained with sweat.

Actually, it was somewhat amusing to watch my brother's face as he tried to take in the scene, and he looked like a fish out of water, his mouth kept opening and closing so much.

"Titus?" He shook his head in the way one does when trying to drive sleep from mind. "What…"

"I'm glad you remembered my name," I said with a laugh, then I stepped aside and made a sweeping gesture towards Birgit, who if anything, was even more radiant, reminding me how much they truly loved each other. "Now go meet your new son."

"We were out on the stakes," he explained once we had retired from the bedroom to allow Birgit and the baby to rest from what is always a momentous day. "That's why it took so long. But you…" He shook his head again, looking across the table at me. "I certainly wasn't expecting to see you! At least not today!"

I shrugged and offered, "We made good time."

"And?" he demanded, yet despite my natural urge to torment my younger brother, he was in such a state, I took pity on him, telling him briefly of all that had transpired.

At least, the part I was willing to divulge, and I cannot explain with any clarity why I did not tell Sextus about my meeting with Augustus, but I never did. I suppose I can say with some truth that I did not want to ensnare him in my own trap, yet even as I write this, I know it is not the entire reason. While I cannot say he was suspicious, he was my brother, after all, and I could see the troubled expression cross his face, convincing me I was sure I knew what he was thinking; what is Titus not telling me? Regardless of the twinge of regret I felt, it did not persuade me to change my mind, and thankfully, he did not press the issue, for which I thanked the other event taking place in our collective lives at the moment. It was dark by this time, meaning the children, despite their protests had been bundled off to bed by Theroios, the freedman who had been hired by Diocles when he was still alive; like my mother, Diocles was naturally resistant to the idea of owning slaves, but whereas my father did not have the same ambivalence, in Birgit, the Greek had someone of a like mind. And, while the Greek's estate was not in the same league as the family he had served so well, it was substantial enough that Birgit could easily afford more than just Theroios. Again, like my mother, she was loath to allow another woman to perform any of the duties that comprise running a household, and I assumed her reluctance stemmed from the same place as what motivated my mother, the discomfort at the idea of being the master, not the slave. Whatever the cause, this meant it was just Sextus and me in the main room, while Antonia was dozing in the corner of what was currently the birthing room.

"This," Sextus mumbled as he stared down into his cup, "changes things."

I had to laugh as I teased him, "You mean you didn't know this was coming?" Shaking my head in mock sorrow, I sighed, "Apparently, Tata didn't do a very good job of teaching you where babies come from. You had nine months!"

"I know," he protested, "but there's a difference in knowing and…*knowing*." Sextus looked at me earnestly. "Do you know what I mean?"

Biting back my normal impulse, instead, I reached out and grabbed his shoulder, agreeing, "Yes, Sextus. I do know what you mean." Thinking for a moment, I am not sure what it says about me that the only analogy I could think of was, "It's like your first battle. The veterans tell you all about it, and you hear all the stories. But then," I shook my head, "it happens, and suddenly, you realize that you might have thought you knew what to expect."

"But you don't," Sextus finished, and it was a relief to see him nod his head in acceptance. "Yes," he said slowly, "I think that's a good way to put it. Although," he flashed a grin at me, "if it's all right with you, I don't think that's how I'm going to put it to Birgit."

This made me laugh, and I teased, "You mean you're afraid your woman won't like hearing the day your son is born compared to the first time you gutted someone?"

"That's exactly it," Sextus agreed, also with a laugh.

"You mean you're scared of your woman?"

The look he gave me was one of wry contempt as he shot back, "And you say you're not? You remember the day you tried to teach Alex his forms?"

Grinning, I only said, "I'm not sure what you're talking about, little brother." I made an exaggerated effort to sit up straight and throw my chest out as I boasted, "I'm Titus Porcinianus Pullus, Optio of the Legions and the man who…"

"Who slew Vergorix and Draxo," he cut me off wearily. "Yes, I know. But I was there that day!" He pointed at me, and the thought flashed through my mind that Sextus was one of the few men who could do this without it irritating me. At least, most of the time. "I saw the look on your face!"

"But I didn't run!" I argued, realizing how much I enjoyed these exchanges with my brother.

"Only because there was nowhere to run to," he retorted.

"It wasn't just that." I had to suppress my grin as I admitted, "I'd just never seen anyone move that fast before. Especially Birgit."

We laughed together about this, to the point where Antonia came shuffling out, giving us both such a severe tongue lashing that it still ranks as one of the most excoriating of my life. Sextus and I sat there, listening quietly, then swearing on the black stone we would make no more racket that night. Only then was she satisfied, doddering back to the other room, once more mumbling all manner of things that were not complimentary about men in general and the Pullus brothers in particular.

"Can I tell you something?" Sextus waited until she was in the other room, and his voice was pitched to a whisper. "That crone scares the *cac* out of me!"

"Me too." I do not who was more surprised, not just that I admitted this, but how quickly I blurted it out.

Which, as might be expected, forced us to try and smother our laughter as we both kept eyeing the door, waiting for the reappearance of Antonia. Thinking about that night even now brings a smile to my face, as the mighty Pullus brothers huddled in fear of an old woman with only a couple of teeth.

Whenever I, or even someone I was close to, experienced a moment like the birth of a child, or anything a man considers momentous, I do not think it is unusual when I say that I instantly thought back to the life account of the original Titus Pullus. I suppose it makes sense that, when one deliberately sets himself on a path to at least emulate a great man, one looks for parallels in the life of the man who serves as the example. This is not to say it is easy to do so, at least it was and is not for me, because inevitably, when I compare my experiences to those of my Avus, I always find myself lacking in some way. The birth of the boy who would be named Gaius Gallienus Pullus is an example, because he is my nephew, not my son. Still, I suppose it was inevitable that the occasion of the birth of Gaius brought back the pain of four years before, because it reminded me that while both the first Titus Pullus and I lost our firstborn sons, the circumstances were different. Honestly, I do not know which was the worst fate between us; is losing a child before one ever knows it better or worse than losing a son when he has only been on the earth a few years, as was the case with young Vibius Pullus who, along with my Avus' first woman Gisela and their daughter Livia, died of the plague in Brundisium? What I will freely admit is that it never occurred to me then that young Gaius was in any more danger than any other newborn babe simply because of his carrying the Pullus name, and I suppose this is a good example of my hubris. All I can say in my own defense is that Sextus never carried the burden of living up to the example set by our Avus to the extent that I did, and still do, and we have had multiple conversations where he has expressed his fervent thanks this was the case. And that infant is now a sturdy, active boy who is the youngest of the family started by Diocles, well on his way to adulthood.

On the subject of my nephew's slightly unusual name, this was the source of the first serious falling out between Sextus and Birgit, and as I learned, it was a continuation of a debate that had apparently first begun, not between my brother and Birgit, but with Diocles.

"She's dead set that my son have a name that reflects the other part of his blood," Sextus grumbled to me about a week after the boy's birth. "But I keep telling her that it will mark him as a provincial for the rest of his days!"

This, I had to admit, was certainly a concern, yet I understood two things; the first was that, despite her seemingly meek exterior, Birgit was every bit as determined and strong as our mother, but it was the second reason that forced me to stifle a smile.

"So," I asked instead, "what's the boy's name going to be?"

My brother shot me an irritated look, then gave a sheepish grin and mumbled, "Gaius Gallienus Pullus. It could have been worse," he protested over my laughter. "She wanted to name him after her tribe!"

It took me a moment to even recall which tribe Birgit and her mother were from, then even longer to wonder how on Gaia's earth Anatilli could be Romanized.

Once I thought about it, I admitted, "I think that's actually not a bad compromise."

"Compromise?" Sextus scoffed. "It's my son! I'm the…"

"No, you're not the *paterfamilias*," I cut him off, more amused than anything at his indignation. "Tata is the *paterfamilias* of the Pullus family. And what do you think he'd say?"

Sighing, my brother admitted ruefully, "That the key to a man being happy is by making his woman happy."

This was indeed a common refrain heard in the Pullus household, and the memory made us laugh together. I am sure part of our amusement came from the fact that at least a partial reason for our father's attitude was based as much in a healthy fear of our mother, which we not only understood, we shared. Iras Pullus is a small woman, but only in stature; not lost on either Sextus or me was, now that we both had read our Avus' story, was how she came into the lives of the Pullus family. Anyone, no matter their status, who survived in the house of the Ptolemies, especially one who was related by blood to Cleopatra, even if she was a slave, is someone worthy of respect, and at least part of that respect was based in fear. Perhaps I can be forgiven, then, at my amusement of seeing Sextus in much the same position as our father had been, and we toasted each other on Sextus' wisdom in realizing there are some battles a man is not destined to win.

Dolabella did not return to Siscia until early April, yet even while I knew it would have merely been postponing the inevitable, I was still bitterly disappointed that he arrived two days before the 8th was scheduled to go on a march out into the countryside. That we were about to depart was somewhat unusual, because we had not been scheduled to do so, but I suppose it was inevitable that the Primus Pilus was extremely unhappy with the state of the Legion on our return. Given our improved relationship, and my regard for Atticus had grown, I certainly saw signs of a certain laxness that had been missing when we left Siscia. Nevertheless, to this day, I believe his ire was based more on his lingering frustration and anger at all he had been through than from any real problems with the Legion. Our Century, on the other hand, was a different story, as both Galens and I learned very quickly that my sighting of a couple men out in the town when they should not have been there was the least of our worries. As we both learned, much to our dismay, Spurius Stellatinus was an utter disaster as a man in command. Perhaps the only good thing that could be said is that it was not because Stellatinus was crooked and took the opportunity provided by our absence to scrape up some extra cash by abusing his temporary authority. And he was not incompetent, at least when it came to his intelligence and knowledge of the proper way to run a Century; speaking plainly, Stellatinus was more worried about being liked than being a leader. The consequences of this certainly came as no surprise to either Galens or me, knowing full well that all but the most diligent men would not hesitate to take advantage of what is, in essence, a character flaw when it comes to leading men of the Legions. Also, speaking as a man who would be counted as one who was intent on doing his duty whether there was a *vitus* hovering above me or not, I will be the first to admit that even we find it hard to resist the urge to take advantage of a relaxing of the normally harsh discipline found under the standard. Almost every night of the week after our return to Siscia found both Galens and me dispensing bathhouse justice, although instead of my cut-down handle, Galens made me use a *vitus* because a solid ash stick in my hands had proven to cause a bit more damage than the grape vine. Even so, a good fifty of the one hundred forty-seven effectives on the roster appeared at a morning formation with a series of bruises that they did not seem to think warranted a visit to the *medici*. Despite this unforeseen development, it did not take long to put affairs back into order, but the Primus Pilus was still not satisfied and, frankly, he had been a terror in the days before we were to depart.

It should have been the turn of the 15th Legion to perform the spring parade of the province, except Atticus had convinced both their Primus Pilus and the Legate to give the 8th the dubious honor of reminding the natives that Rome had not gone anywhere over the winter. This was bad enough, and made it difficult for both the father and uncle of a newborn babe to spend much time with him before they left, but then Dolabella showed up. Of course, I did not see him arrive, nor was I aware of it until the night two days before our scheduled departure, when I was in my quarters, occupied with my own preparations for the march. So engrossed in what I was doing, I did not hear the rap on the outer door, and was only vaguely aware of the muffled talk, meaning I stabbed myself with the needle I was using to repair a tunic when Florens knocked on my door.

"Optio, there's a man to see you," he announced, which was unusual enough to get me paying attention, although I was cursing as I looked up, the drop of blood on my finger growing.

What had alerted me was the way Florens described this visitor; if it had been a Gregarius, the *Signifer* would have said as much, and if it had been a clerk from the *praetorium,* Florens would have known the man's name.

"Who is it?" I asked irritably, prepared to send whatever civilian it was on his way.

"Tiberius Dolabella." The combination of the name, and that the announcement came from the man himself made my heart leap in my chest, but I tried to keep my face impassive.

I was actually about to tell Florens I was busy, but before I could, the cross-eyed spy shouldered the man aside, although it was done gently, entering my quarters with a smile that from my perspective was composed of equal parts insolence and malice.

"I don't think I gave you permission to enter," I snapped, and it pleased me to see his face darken, while the smile faltered.

He recovered quickly, though, I had to admit, offering an elaborate shrug and saying, "I can always come back later. I have some dispatches to send off, after all."

Stifling the surge of anger, acutely aware it could only lead to bad things happening, I tried to sound offhand, replying, "That's fine. You're here now." Looking back over his shoulder at Florens, I gave him a nod, yet while he naturally obeyed, I saw the reluctance and was thankful for it. At least this was my initial reaction, then I understood how likely it was that my *Signifer* would be spending his time with his ear at the door, which would not be good for him or me, so instead, I made up a task on the spot, telling him, "Florens, I need you to go check with the Hastatus Posterior and find out when he wants to meet with me in the morning."

To his credit, his hesitation was barely perceptible; like everything in the Legions, the meeting times for officers of a Century occur at the same intervals, twice a day, yet while he quickly turned to go, pulling the door behind him, Dolabella was not fooled.

Waiting long enough to hear the outer door open, then close, he said, "That was wise, Optio."

"I don't care whether you think it is or not," I replied coldly, and when I shifted on my stool so I was facing him directly, I saw a flicker of nervousness at the movement that I found gratifying. "Now, what do you want?"

He was wearing a leather pouch slung over his shoulder, and he looked into it, then retrieved a scroll, which he held out.

"Put it on the desk there," I told him, and his mouth thinned down, clearly angry. "I may have to deal with you, but I don't have to soil my hands."

"You should be careful, Optio," I sensed he was trying to regain some semblance of control, while I was just as determined he did not do so.

Which was what prompted me to counter, "So should you." I stood up, only for the small victory of watching him physically flinch; I suppose the memory of being suspended inches off the floor was still relatively fresh. "Because you're out here on the frontier, Dolabella. Men disappear around here all the time. You should keep that in mind."

I suppose when he saw his usual attempt to intimidate was not working, he decided it wise to switch tactics because he held up a placating hand, changing his tone as he tried to reason with me, "Pullus, I…"

"That's Optio Pullus to you," I cut him off, yet while he flushed even darker, I was somewhat disappointed when he apologized, "Please forgive me, Optio. It's just that there's no need for this hostility! I understand your personal feelings, but that doesn't mean we can't have a mutually beneficial relationship nonetheless, does it?

It's the Roman way, after all! Men who may not care for each other on a personal level still may work together and cooperate for a common goal!"

"And what goal is that?" I asked out of curiosity, not because I was even mildly entertaining the idea of cooperation above the bare minimum.

"The good of the Empire, of course!" he exclaimed.

"The good of the Empire," I echoed, pretending to think about it, then asked pointedly, "as defined by who?"

"I think you know who," Dolabella replied quietly, yet despite the fact that I knew he was trying to give me an intent stare, that one eye was just so damned distracting I could not have remained focused on his words no matter what he said.

"Well," I answered finally, "as tempting as that may be, I'm afraid that if I spent more than the bare minimum amount of time with you, it wouldn't be good for either of us. Because," I finished pleasantly, "I'd just end up beating you to death and breaking every bone in your body."

I cannot say I knew Dolabella well, but no man readily accepts the prospect that he can be defeated so effortlessly that the man threatening him could be asking him to hand him a tool while they are working together.

Therefore, I was not surprised when his attempt at good humor vanished as rapidly as it appeared, but I could also see that he was, if not outright worried, cautious as he admitted, "Optio, I have no doubt you could do what you say you can to me, but at what cost then? You," I had to acknowledge the fact that he did not yell this actually made his words more menacing, "aren't the only man with friends, ones who'd be…displeased at my demise. And," he added, "there's more than just your own pride to think about, isn't there? I seem to have heard you celebrated a recent addition to your family. A new…nephew? Isn't it?"

If Florens had not thrown open the door to my quarters, I have no doubt whatsoever I would not be here to write these words. And he showed up not a moment too soon; Dolabella's face was a deep purple, his eyes had already rolled back into his head. In fact, one of the scraps I can recall is the interesting observation that for the first time, his eyes seemed to act in concert, since I could not see the darkened part in either eye.

"Optio! Optio! Pullus! Pluto's cock! Let go! You're killing the man!"

Luckily for Dolabella, not so much for Florens, my *Signifer* realized I was too far gone for verbal commands, so consequently, he jumped on my back, which did cause me to let go of Augustus' agent, except it was only to react unthinkingly by throwing Florens violently off my back, flinging him across my room. He landed against the corner walls with a deep, thudding sound that was accompanied by the rush of air from his lungs. It was not until I had already crossed the room and was reaching down for him that the look of terror on his face somehow penetrated the fog of my rage.

"Optio! No, please! I was just trying to stop you!"

This was when I became aware of not just the rest of my surroundings, but was conscious of how my lips were pulled back from my teeth in a snarl, and my vision had narrowed down to a point where all that existed was my intended prey. The only thing missing was the slowing of time, yet in every other respect, somehow, the beast that is always coiled there deep inside me had slipped the normally tight lead I kept on it, and for the first time in years, it had done so without my bidding. In its simplest terms, I had clearly been fooling myself in believing I had somehow found the method to control this violent monster of my rage, that it was at my discretion when it was unleashed. Even more than the obvious implications of almost strangling Dolabella, this realization shook me to the point I seemed unable to move, while Florens, seeing I was not about to pummel him, lowered his hands, then slowly climbed to his feet.

"Optio," his manner was understandably cautious, and he pointed over past me, "can I go check on him?"

I did not reply verbally, just nodding my head as he slipped past me while I remained standing facing the corner, my back to the both of them as I tried to grapple with what I had just done. Behind me, when I became aware of the sounds of two men breathing, one panting and one wheezing, only then did I turn around. Florens was crouched next to Dolabella, who he had helped to a sitting position, the latter holding his throat with one hand as his lungs struggled to draw in enough breath. I expected that when he did look in my direction, it would be with a stare that communicated his hatred and carried the silent promise he would be avenged. However, when he did finally meet my gaze, all I saw was fear, and for the first time, I felt a glimmer of what I suppose was hope that this was not another moment where the consequences of my intemperate action haunted me or my family. Finally, when it appeared he was sufficiently recovered, Florens helped Dolabella to his feet, and I wordlessly pointed him to the stool I had vacated.

Once Dolabella was settled down, I told Florens he was dismissed, and I admit I felt a glimmer of amusement when he did not obey immediately.

"I'm fine now, Florens," I assured him. "Citizen Dolabella is perfectly safe with me."

Florens was clearly unconvinced, but with a shrug, he exited the room as I made a mental note to thank him for staying put, since there was no way he could have found Galens and returned that quickly. First, however, I had to deal with Dolabella, who was still massaging his throat, although he kept his eyes on the floor and refused to meet my gaze.

I was not sure what I would say, but what came out was, "You shouldn't have threatened my nephew like that, Dolabella." He made no reply, continuing his study of my floor, while I relented, reluctantly, "But I shouldn't have reacted so…strongly."

Somewhat to my surprise, I saw the shadow of a smile cross his face at my characterization, but he still said nothing.

"Still," I continued with a sigh, "you're right in the sense we do have to work together for…however long. So I'll make a deal with you." This did prompt him to look up at me, and I admit I felt quietly relieved that his color seemed to be returning to normal. "If you don't make any more threats that concern me or my family, I'll be civil to you, and give you what you ask for." For the first time, I actually turned my attention to the neglected scroll, asking, "Does that have whatever information I'm supposed to put in my letter to Claudius?" Again, he only nodded, and I swallowed my irritation, thinking that he was being mulishly obstinate. With a sigh, I guessed, "And I suppose you want me to write to Claudius before we leave?" One more nod, and I just barely stifled a curse, yet I learned why he was so reticent when, once I dismissed him with a wave and he had gotten to the door, something occurred to me I had forgotten. "Did you bring Balbinus with you?"

He did not turn to face me, but shook his head, and when I demanded why he had not done so, I learned why he had been so reluctant to talk; his voice was barely audible and was harsh and raspy as he croaked, "Ask your Primus Pilus."

Before I could say anything, he was gone, and I did not pursue him. Instead, I turned to the scroll with a sigh, opened it up, then sat down at my desk to read it. Which, I must say, did not improve my state of mind, especially since it took me half the night to compose the message I was going to send to Claudius, incorporating the information the Princeps wanted him to have. As I did so, I pushed the feeling of guilt about what I was doing, harshly telling myself that, as brutal as it was, the matter was still simple. If I did not do this in a manner the Princeps found acceptable, I risked the future of not just my career, but the fortunes of my family. I believe it was only then the full import of the true brilliance and genius of the divine Augustus hit me; if he had confiscated the rest of our wealth, his leverage over us would be gone. And when compared to the fathomless wealth that is at the fingertips of the Princeps, even a million *sesterces* is a pittance. As I wrote the betraying words to a Roman nobleman who had offered me help, I had to offer a silent salute to the man at whose behest and for whose purposes I was working, even if it was a bitter one.

Since the day before a march is so hectic, I did not have the time to ask Atticus, nor did I particularly worry about the fate of Balbinus. It was not until we were actually formed up at the forum of the camp, in the short period of time where we stand about waiting for the command, I trotted over to the Primus Pilus.

"Did Dolabella find you?" he asked abruptly, but it did not surprise me that much he was aware the man was in Siscia.

"He did," I told him, then before he could ask anything potentially awkward, I beat him to it by asking, "I asked him if he brought Balbinus, but he said no. When I asked him why, he told me to ask you."

Atticus did not answer me, at least at first, except I got a hint when he suddenly turned and seemed to inspect the men of the First; over his shoulder, I saw Asinius fussing with the pack of what looked like Sido.

Keeping his gaze away from me, he told me flatly, "Balbinus is dead."

"What?" The surprise hit me hard, and I felt my jaw drop. "But how? I saw him before we left. He was healing fine!"

Only when I had a moment to think about it did I realize afterward I got my answer in the way he still refused to look in my direction as he gave a shrug and said only, "Apparently, his injuries were worse than they looked." When I tried to press him for more details, only then did he turn around and snap, "I told you all I know! Now get to your fucking Century and prepare for the march, Optio! Your Century has enough to worry about without bothering me about that bastard!"

Naturally, I obeyed, but when I approached Galens and informed him, he was anything but sympathetic.

"What did you expect?" he scoffed. "He betrayed the Primus Pilus! I don't want him back in this Legion any more than Atticus does!" He waved a disgusted hand, dismissing the matter with, "Now get to your spot! We're about to march."

Marching out of the gate, I do not believe we were more than a third of a watch into the day when I was struck, hard, by what I am still sure is the truth of the Balbinus affair. While it seemed to be the case where Atticus had no more regard for the Praetorians, I still thought it unlikely he had severed all his friendships formed over the years he had served in Rome. And Balbinus was guarded by the Praetorians. It also seems unlikely to me that Dolabella would have had a hand in it, because why would he do so? Simply because he did not want the inconvenience of being responsible for the man on the trip from Rome? With every passing mile, I became more certain that not only was Atticus aware of Balbinus' fate before Dolabella supposedly would have informed him, he was the one who orchestrated it. And yet, what did that matter? Perhaps Galens' attitude was the right one; if you cannot trust a man to be loyal no matter what he faces, do you really want to stand next to him when the barbarians are screaming down on you, ready and intent on parting your head from your shoulders? However, there was another possibility that, with every step we took, gradually went from another likelihood to a virtual certainty, and that was the idea that Atticus had not prevailed on an old Praetorian friend at all. When a man is on the march, he always tries to occupy himself with anything other than the mind-numbing routine of a march, at least when no contact is expected, which certainly was the case the first day out of Siscia. Unfortunately, in my case anyway, it was probably not a good thing I had something to think about, because my newfound regard and respect for my Primus Pilus underwent yet another assault. As I thought about it, I began connecting Atticus and Dolabella, and how mutually beneficial it would be for both of them if it had, in fact, been the cross-eyed agent who had disposed of Balbinus. Looking at it from his perspective, it was easy to see why he would be eager to do the bidding of the Primus Pilus and remove a man who Atticus no longer considered worthy of marching in the Legion. By doing so, he would indebt the Primus Pilus, and for a man like Dolabella, having a Primus Pilus in one's coin purse, as we like to say, is always a valuable thing to have. However, where I had trouble was in seeing why Atticus would avail himself of the mortality skill of a man working for the Princeps, especially considering how Atticus had just recently extracted himself from his own difficulties. While, at least after hearing both Atticus and Galens opine on the subject of Balbinus, I could understand why Atticus had no desire to see Balbinus' return, in any capacity and in any Cohort, to then extend this to his approaching Dolabella to have the man killed seemed to stretch the logic. And yet, the idea still nagged at me as the miles passed beneath our feet as we covered ground that was as familiar to me by this time as any spot I have ever been. Shortly after our first rest break, I was struck by the thought that perhaps Dolabella had acted on his own, knowing that Atticus had no desire for Balbinus' return, taking the gamble that by removing the man, he would be in the good graces of the Primus Pilus at the very least. By the time of our midday break, I realized I had to put this situation to bed in my own mind; I could not afford to let my attention wander any more than it already had, and I also was forced to accept that the only way I would find out would be to force the subject on either Atticus or Dolabella. And this, dear reader, was something I was unwilling to do, particularly since, as I was forced to acknowledge if only to myself, part of my pique stemmed from the fact that I had gone to some length to secure a spot for Balbinus in another Cohort. Probably not surprisingly, I had approached the Centurion who had not only been my Optio in the First of the First, but who had been Balbinus' as well. It had taken some convincing before he finally, and grudgingly, agreed a spot could be found for him.

Despite Tiburtinus' reputation for sternness, he also had a streak of humor in his makeup, which I was reminded of when he told me with a straight face, "I think I'm going to put him next to your brother. Too bad Balbinus isn't tall enough to go on your brother's sword side. But," he shrugged, and only then did I see a quirk of his mouth that indicated he was tormenting me, "at some point, your brother will probably have to rely on Balbinus to save his bacon."

Thankfully, he did not allow me to remain in tortured suspense, his own composure shattered by the clearly humorous expression on my face as I thought, what have I done? Sextus will never forgive me!

Speaking of my brother, somewhat to my surprise, he had not gone scurrying back to camp life as so many new fathers did, using the army as an excuse to get out of the bulk of the chores that are inevitable with a newborn babe. This is not to say he was actively involved in cleaning up the boy's *cac*, which he had been quick to inform me was in an amount that he swore on the black stone was the equivalent of a man my size. Still, he did relieve Birgit whenever he could to allow her to get some sleep, while the children pitched in to help. Frankly, I had been a bit worried about Alex and how he would react to baby Gaius, although I should not have been; very quickly, the boy took on the role of protector of his infant brother, a role he was fulfilling until the day the two were parted. Probably the biggest surprise was in the change to my brother as far as his seeming need to carouse and debauch himself, because it was this aspect of his life that he curtailed in order to fulfill his duties as the de facto *paterfamilias* of the Diocles branch of the Pullus family. Like most freedmen, Diocles had adopted the last name of his former master and friend, and I do not exaggerate when I say it was a source of enormous pride to his children. This was especially true with Alex as he grew older, although I will confess that inwardly I heaved a sigh of relief when I saw his interest in enlisting in the Legions wane. In fact, it was not long before we left, when I paid what turned out to be the last visit to the apartment, that Birgit asked me to attend to her in the bedroom that was now the nursery. Of course, I thought it was to show off Gaius and fill me in on his latest achievement, which seemed to consist of what Birgit assured me were momentous events like smiling for the first time, or how he seemed to be able to avoid smacking himself in the face with his own tiny fist. I was interested, do not mistake me, but I decided it was best to remain silent about my observation.

I was in for a surprise, because it was not the babe Birgit had on her mind, and she wasted no time, saying calmly, "I want you to make Alex your servant."

"My…servant?" I was more baffled than anything. "Why would you want him to do that? Besides," I pointed out, "you of all people should know just because he's not a combatant, he'd still be in danger."

"I know that," she snapped, and while her color had returned to normal, the two red spots on her cheeks never boded well for anyone, "but I also don't think he's going to get the dream of the Legions completely out of his head until he has a taste of what life is like."

I did not answer, instead chewing on what she said, and I realized she was just being shrewd, because my first thought was to remember how my friend Vibius Pacuvius had gone on campaign once, attending to his father, who was one of my father's Centurions, and learned the grim business of the Legions was not to his liking. Obviously, this was what Birgit had in mind, and the more I thought about it, I had to silently salute her foresight, and her knowledge of her son.

Finally, while I did not agree, neither did I rule it out, saying only, "Well, it can't be immediately, because we're leaving in just a few days."

"I know." She nodded, although her attention seemed to be on Gaius, cradled in her arms, who she gently rocked as we spoke. "It will give me time to bring it up with him, and make him think it was his idea."

"You mean he didn't bring this up?" I asked, startled, and she gave me a smile that was half-amused and half-scornful.

"You men." She laughed. "You think you're the ones who rule everything. Who do you think puts all those wonderful ideas in your head before they ever occur to you?"

Agreeing to think about it, I left the apartment both bemused and feeling a bit rueful, recognizing that Birgit was saying nothing more than the truth. Thinking back to my childhood, there were times when I would see my mother subtly manipulate my father into doing something, or taking a position on a subject that was, in fact, her own and not his. I suppose, being the oldest son, she made me something of a conspirator in her schemes, and I recall with great fondness how I would be forced to suppress a grin as I sat at the family table, watching my father suddenly make an announcement about some family matter, and knowing exactly from where it originated. My mother would catch my eye when she was up, bringing more food to the table or doing some chore, winking at me over my father's shoulder, and I admit a part of me felt sympathy for Alex, who was blissfully unaware that the idea he thought he had, in fact, did not belong to him. For a brief period of time, I did consider changing my mind and allowing him to come along on this foray into Pannonia. It was going to be a routine march; despite our absence, we were quickly reacquainted with the climate in the province, and there had not been anything more than the usual incidents over the winter. All in all, it was going to be a routine sweep through the province, starting with our old friends the Maezaei, who had been quiet ever since the incident a handful of years before.

And as my comrades and I, and the entire Pullus family would learn, there is no such thing as a routine march through a province like Pannonia. However, I cannot write of this, not yet. Not only has the winter ended and we are about to march again, even now, this is an episode of my life that is particularly painful, teaching me that as much as I mourned the loss of Giulia and our unborn child, the gods had yet to mete out even more pain and punishment. What makes it worse is that this agony was not confined to just me, but to my entire family. That, however, is for later.

Historical Note

Keen-eyed readers with a fluency with Early Imperial Rome might notice that there's a small discrepancy in the timeframe, at least as it pertains to the return of Tiberius from his self-imposed exile in Rome. However, careful readers will also note that *Fraternitas* is more about the political climate during the period before his return, which doesn't require his presence.

As far as exactly what was taking place behind the scenes during that period, there is a paucity of source material, so I acknowledge that what takes place in Rome during the period of Primus Pilus Gaius Atticus' Tribunal is my own speculation. However, as I've attempted to do in the previous installments of Marching With Caesar®, my intent is to do so within the bounds of credulity, and it's no secret that the upper classes of Rome, while acknowledging Augustus' complete control and ultimate authority, participated in jockeying for the spot on the ladder one or two rungs beneath him. Consequently, to me at least, it's certainly within the bounds of possibility that there were men who hoped to manipulate Augustus' stepson, capitalizing on the ambivalence between the Princeps and Tiberius. Hopefully, readers will agree.

On the various locations used in *Fraternitas*, again as I have always attempted, and in the spirit of the first author who I can point to as an influence on my own writing, Louis L'Amour, to be as precise as I can be in placing the action, either where the historical event occurred, or where it might have taken place, in those scenes that are a figment of my imagination.

The ancient town of Splonum, is an example: it is a real place, to the northeast of the town of Sanski Most, which is in the Republic of Bosnia and Herzegovina, located at Latitude 44.762854N and Longitude 16.685936E. The small fort that protects the town is where modern day Usorci is located at Latitude 44.838726N and Longitude 16.685792E, while the ruins of Splonum itself are located east of that, up the narrow valley. If, that is, the Barrington Atlas is to be believed.

The Gaius Calvinus Sabinus to whom I am referring is also a real person who held the post of Consul in 4 B.C.E., but while there is not any record that he was the Legate in Pannonia, there's no evidence that I was able to find that he wasn't. Which is one of the joys of writing historical fiction, where I don't have to adhere to the rigid standards of historical scholars.

When the 8th marches out during their winter progress through Pannonia, the village Titus speaks of, east of Siscia, is modern-day Kutina, in Croatia, located at Latitude 45.481212N and Longitude 16.774996E. It was later named Varianis, later in Roman history.

The area where Titus and his comrades have so much difficulty locating the Andizetes is largely unchanged in terms of the terrain. In fact, the ground over which Titus must traverse is within the confines of Gornje Podunavlje Nature Reserve, while the village of Kopacevo is the location of the village itself. Kopacevo is at Latitude 45.605102N and Longitude 18.787224E, while the preserve is directly east, with the river serving as the eastern boundary.

Colonia Aelia Mursa is now the modern town of Osijek, but while the ancient town was important strategically because there was actually a bridge across the Drava river, there is nothing I could find that would indicate this bridge was already in place when Rome conquered the region. However, while the tribes of Pannonia were certainly not endowed with the same engineering expertise as Rome, I also don't believe it was out of the realm of possibility that the bridge existed beforehand. Osijek is immediately east, along the Drava River, from Kopacevo.

Both the location of the pivotal battle, and the event that causes Titus and the 8th such problems are authentic, and I have actually walked the ground myself. The lake is Lake Bled, which is now in the Republic of Slovenia, located at 46.365736N and 14.093183E, and the terrain is exactly as I describe it. Approaching from the east, there are two large hills flanking the lake, and it's on the northern side of the lake where the high bluff is located, although now the Blejski Grad, or Bled Castle sits atop it. The hill on the southern side, while not appearing as steep when looking at it from the eastern shore, follows the contour of the lake, and there is a point where a tunnel has been bored through the rock to allow modern traffic to circumnavigate the lake. Also, there is in fact an island, on which there is now a monastery and small church. (If you go, try ringing the bell, and….good luck!)

It doesn't hurt that it's a stunningly beautiful place, and was in fact the vacation home of Josip Broz, more commonly known as Marshal Tito, the former dictator of Yugoslavia, and I thoroughly enjoyed seeing it, although I was there in October, not September as Titus and his comrades were.

Speaking of September, and why I chose this month, for that, my readers can thank "Starry Night," the astronomy program, which I have been using for research in conjunction with another project. From any point in the world, going back ten thousand years, one can "look" up at the night sky and see what it looked like from this vantage point. While I was playing with it, I stumbled on the list of lunar eclipses, going back several centuries, and because I had recently stayed up for a total lunar eclipse up here in Washington State, I got the idea, "What would it have been like to fight during a total eclipse?"

Therefore, while the battle with the Taurisci on Lake Bled is an invention, what's not is that on September 15, there was a total eclipse. And, as you have presumably read, it made matters even more chaotic than normal.

Finally, about the Pantheon and Titus' quoting of the dimensions. Even as I was writing this, I could hear voices in my head who will point out that the Pantheon we see today isn't the Pantheon that Titus would see. However, while I understand that, neither does anyone know with any certainty whether or not the remodeling done by Hadrian, or Trajan, or in fact exactly what the configuration of the temple was originally. From what I can determine, after reading the various scholarly arguments (which being honest seem mostly composed of multi-syllabic variations of "Is too!" "Is not!"), the only thing that can be said with any certainty is, we don't have any certainty. So, to those purists who will take exception to the presence of the dome that was the wonder of the ancient world and (even for a boy from Houston who was alive when the Astrodome was built and been inside more times than can be counted) is even now an impressive sight, I hope you at least take some comfort in the idea that this is an intentional act, not one where I simply didn't do my homework.

Printed in Great Britain
by Amazon

10386561R00363